HELEN CAREY

The Other Side of the Street

First published in Great Britain in 2017 by Headline Publishing Group
This edition published in 2018 by Cambria Publishing

ISBN 978-1-9164532-3-4

For my lovely mother-in-law, June, who sang Burlington Bertie at concert parties during the war, wearing a top hat.

Prologue

'Louise, what on earth are you doing up there?' Celia Rutherford called up the stairs. 'Daddy's waiting for his breakfast.'

Sitting at her dressing table, one hand behind her head holding a curl, the other poised in the delicate action of opening a tortoiseshell hairclip, Louise Rutherford rolled her eyes at herself in the mirror. But valiantly she held back the words that sprang to her lips in response to her mother's impatient enquiry. Because one of Louise's New Year's resolutions had been to try and be a nicer person, and that, she had quickly discovered, involved biting her tongue when people got on her nerves.

But maintaining her resolve to be nice in the face of her parents' apparent determination to treat her like a recalcitrant child wasn't easy. Louise felt she deserved better. OK, she might have made a couple of bad mistakes in the past, but it certainly wasn't her fault that Jack Delmaine, her lovely young husband of less than one year, had been killed during the assault on Italy last summer. Nor that his death had left her unable to support herself financially. It was hardly any wonder that she had been a bit cross and ratty. But now the moment had come when she needed to pull herself together or she was going to run the risk of losing all her friends.

'I'll be down in a minute,' she called down to her mother. 'I'm just doing my hair.'

Last night, on the advice of an article in *Vogue*, Louise had set her shoulder-length dark hair onto twists of cotton wool. Now she was attempting to pin it up into a style called 'pompadour and curls'. It was a ridiculously fiddly process, but she had mastered the technique now, and was hoping it would be worth the effort, even though the effect would be spoilt as soon as she put her mob cap over it at the factory.

Hearing a step on the staircase, she hastily fixed the final hairclip just as her mother appeared in the doorway of her room.

Her mother was wearing an uncompromisingly staid winter coat with a Women's Voluntary Service armband, a shapeless WVS beret, and thick-soled sensible shoes. Her eyes widened when she saw the array of discarded pins and twists of cotton wool on Louise's dressing table.

1

'For goodness' sake,' she said, striding across the room to turn off the electric light and open the blackout curtains. 'I told you I had to leave early this morning. Why are you wasting time with that now?'

Louise shrugged. 'Daddy told me off when I got home from the pub last night,' she said. 'He said I looked unkempt and I'd never find another husband if I didn't take more pride in my appearance.'

Her mother made an exasperated gesture. 'Well you're hardly likely to find a husband in an armament factory, are you? Anyway, it's too soon to be thinking like that,' she added more gently as she left the room. 'It's not six months yet since poor Jack died.'

Louise almost laughed. Because that was another of her New Year's resolutions. Much as she missed Jack, she was determined to find another husband as quickly as possible. In the absence of the ability to fund her own accommodation, a husband was her route to freedom, a route out of her parents' house.

And you never knew who you might meet on the way to work these days. After four interminable years of war, it now seemed as though an invasion of France might be edging onto the War Office agenda, and as a result there were lots of soldiers, and more importantly, officers, milling about all over London. Louise wasn't particularly knowledgeable about the progress of the war, but she knew an officer when she saw one, and she didn't want to miss her chance if one of them happened to be on the lookout for a wife.

To that end she had decided not only to be nicer but to revert to her maiden name. Men weren't interested in grumpy widows, or if they were, as an unlucky relationship with a sweet-talking cad last year had taught her, it was only for one thing.

'Don't forget to let the chickens out,' her mother called from the landing. 'And do hurry up, Louise. Daddy is getting impatient. He needs to get off to work.'

Louise delicately applied a frugal smear of Pond's cream to her face.

'So do I,' she said. She glanced at the clock on her bedside table. She had got into trouble earlier in the week for cutting it too fine. Being late was a dismissible offence. Mr Gregg had let her off that time with a warning. He knew she was one of his best machine-tool operatives. But she couldn't afford another misdemeanour.

Why can't stupid Daddy get his own breakfast? she thought crossly. But her father, Greville Rutherford, wasn't that kind of man. As well as being the owner of the local brewery, he was also the commander of the Clapham Home Guard battalion, and a churchwarden. All in all, he was a pillar of the community. And pillars of the community apparently saw it as their God-given right to be served and obeyed by their womenfolk.

Giving her face a quick dusting of Max Factor face powder, also recommended by *Vogue* for a 'healthy, finished look', Louise stood up and surveyed herself in the long mirror on the wardrobe door. She smiled and preened slightly, pleased with her new hairstyle. The demure curls complemented her pale clear skin and her nicely proportioned features. She looked gratifyingly pretty and fashionable in a discreet, patriotic way, although she suspected that her new slimline slacks would not go down well with her father. Even now, at this stage of the war, he disapproved of women wearing trousers. But it was icy cold outside and Louise was conserving her last two pairs of nylons for a special occasion. She was damned if she was going to walk all the way down to Gregg Brothers with bare legs.

Chapter One

Louise knew her father well. His eyes did indeed bulge alarmingly when she came into the breakfast room wearing her new figure-hugging corduroys. He himself was looking very correct in his well-pressed Home Guard uniform, his carefully polished major's crowns gleaming on his epaulettes.

'Goodness me, Louise,' he expostulated. 'What do you think you look like?'

'Oh Daddy, really,' Louise said. 'Lots of girls wear trousers nowadays.'

'Not girls of our class.'

'It's nothing to do with class,' Louise insisted. 'It's to do with warmth and practicality. There is a war on, you know.'

'Don't be facetious,' he said, taking his place at the head of the table.

Louise quailed. Her father might be out-of-date, but it was dangerous to annoy him. 'I'm not being facetious,' she said. 'Those frumpy Auxiliary Territorial Service girls who manage the barrage balloons up on the common all wear trousers. And some of them are perfectly posh.'

He snorted and Louise realised her mistake. Her father didn't approve of women in the armed forces, posh or not. According to him, they caused discipline problems. And to be fair, some of the current jokes bore him out. 'Up with the lark, to bed with a Wren' was one that was doing the rounds at the moment. But knowing that wasn't the kind of thing her father would find at all funny, Louise refrained from mentioning it, and instead withdrew to the kitchen to dish up his porridge.

There was no sign of any eggs, and she certainly didn't have time to go grubbing around in her mother's henhouse looking for some. Instead she cut two meagre slices of bread and laid them under the grill, then carried the porridge bowls through to the breakfast room.

In the good old pre-war days the Rutherfords had had a cook and a maid. But such luxuries were hard to come by nowadays, and when Jack had died and Louise had been forced to move back in, her mother had made it very clear that she expected her to do her fair share of the household tasks. Considerably more than her fair share as it turned out, since her mother spent all her time at the café that she ran with Mrs Carter down at the other end of Lavender Road, or endlessly beavering about with the stupid old WVS.

It didn't seem to occur to her parents that Louise might be too exhausted

4

after working long shifts at the factory to do chores. But then they didn't approve of her working at the factory in the first place. They didn't like her consorting with what her father called 'the hoi polloi'. Nor, for the same reason, had they approved of her helping out at the local pub this week while her friend Katy Frazer, the landlady, was in hospital giving birth to her second baby. But it had been an opportunity to practise being nice and obliging, and in fact Louise had rather enjoyed it, especially the way Katy's inadequate bar staff had jumped about to her command.

Aware that her father was watching her beadily, Louise sprinkled a fastidiously small teaspoon of sugar onto her porridge. He, of course, ate his with salt.

'I don't suppose those girls chose to be in the ATS,' she remarked as she began to eat. 'But they've been called up for war work. Just like me at Gregg Brothers.'

But her father wasn't impressed by her stoic patriotism. 'Well, you girls had better enjoy tinkering about with your little jobs while you can,' he said. 'Because once the war is won and the men come back, you'll be expected to resume your domestic duties at home where you belong.' He glanced over towards the kitchen door. 'Talking of which, is that burning toast I can smell?'

He was clearly pleased with his little joke, but as she rushed back to the kitchen, Louise didn't find it funny. She liked her job; it might be boring and repetitive, but she got a surprising amount of satisfaction from doing it well.

'It's not fair to say I'm just tinkering about,' she said as she set the toast rack down with a slight thump in front of him a minute later. 'Or to call it a *little* job. I'm doing exactly the same work as a man.'

'Then let me ask you this,' he said. 'Are you being paid the same as a man?'

'Well, no,' Louise admitted. She took a slice of toast and spread it with a thin smear of her mother's home-made raspberry jam. 'But that's not fair either.'

Her father had been making an ostentatious show of scraping the burnt bits off his own slice of toast, but now his knife stopped in mid-air. 'Fair? Don't talk to me about fair. We're at war, young lady, and the only reason you have a job at all is in order to free up fit young men to fight.'

Louise felt her resentment rising. Despite her best intentions, she couldn't resist the opportunity to goad him. 'Yes,' she said. 'And that's exactly the same as what the Home Guard does, isn't it? Freeing up fitter men to fight.'

It was a mistake.

His knife slammed back onto the table. 'Exactly the same …? I'll have you know, Louise, that all the men of my acquaintance are ready and willing to sacrifice themselves for their country. Look at your husband. Look at your

5

brothers. Bertram gave his life for his country at El Alamein. And now Douglas is in North Africa waiting to be posted to the front line in Italy. Is that something you would be prepared to do?'

He fixed her with an angry stare and nodded with satisfaction as her own heated gaze wavered and fell back to her plate. 'No, I thought not. And do you hear Douglas saying it's not fair? You certainly don't. He can't wait to go and do his duty.' Louise could hear the pride in his voice, and scowled resentfully. Her army-mad younger brother had always been the apple of her father's eye.

Greville paused to take a mouthful of toast. 'So that's the last I want to hear of this subversive nonsense,' he said. 'Discipline, honour, duty, self-sacrifice, courage. These are things you girls don't understand. The truth is that women are intrinsically unsuited to danger.'

'Do you really believe that?' Louise wasn't very keen on danger herself, but she knew women who had found themselves in very dangerous situations and coped perfectly well.

Her father finished his toast and put down his knife. 'It's not a question of believing it or not believing it,' he said. 'It's a fact of life.' He gave a short laugh. 'Can you imagine the panic that would ensue if women were posted to the front line? There's no time to powder your nose when you're under fire, you know. There's a natural order, Louise. Obviously in wartime we have to adapt to different situations, but when it comes down to it, you have to accept that we all have our place.' He patted his mouth with his napkin. 'And just now yours is in the kitchen. I don't want your mother to come home and find you have left everything in a mess as usual.'

With that he stood up, scattering toast crumbs all over the floor. 'You may have time to sit around arguing about things you don't understand, but I have a business to run, and a war to fight.'

Lying in bed in her mother's house in Lavender Road listening to her sixteen-year-old sister Angie's pitifully inadequate attempts to be quiet as she lumbered about in the dark bedroom getting ready to go to work, Jen Carter was wishing the last six months could be erased from her memory.

Jen was an up-and-coming actress, and last summer she had set off in high excitement for an ENSA tour of North Africa. But her ship had been torpedoed in the Mediterranean and she had ended up in a prisoner-of-war camp in Italy. The conditions had been horrible and the treatment they had received from their Nazi guards even worse. In the end, in desperation, she and Molly Coogan, a fellow survivor from the shipwreck, had managed to escape, eventually making their way to France, and then to newly liberated Corsica.

It hadn't been easy, but they had been resourceful, intrepid and incredibly lucky. And for a few days when she got home Jen had felt like a bit of a celebrity.

But that had quickly worn off, and somewhat to her surprise, Jen had found that the last thing in the world she wanted to do was talk about her ordeal. She didn't even want to think about it. All she wanted to do was hide away and recover her equilibrium. And ideally to sleep.

But even that was proving impossible.

Last night Angie had come crashing in at midnight and insisted on regaling her with an account of some dance hall she and Gino had been to, and how quickly the wonderful Gino had picked up the steps to the jitterbug. For Jen, already dangerously close to the end of her tether, it had been almost more than she could bear. An hour later, as Angie snored away contentedly and Jen lay awake tossing and turning, she had been hard pressed not to smother her sister with a pillow.

'Oh for goodness' sake, Angie, put the light on,' she said now as Angie tripped over something and bumped into her bed.

Angie giggled and flicked on the light switch. 'I was trying not to wake you,' she said.

Shielding her eyes from the sudden glare, Jen braced herself for an onslaught of her sister's relentless good humour. But thankfully she was saved by a shout from her mother downstairs.

'Are you ready, Angie?'

'Nearly,' Angie called back. 'I'll catch you up. I'm just going to say goodbye to Gino.'

There was a slight pause, then their mother's voice again, this time distinctly unenthusiastic. 'Well don't take too long about it,' she said. 'We're going to be short-handed in the café today, don't forget, because Mrs Rutherford is going to one of her WVS meetings.'

Angie waited until the front door slammed, then gave a gleeful little chuckle and switched off the light. 'You can go back to sleep now,' she said.

A moment later, Jen heard her scratch on Gino's door. And then that door opened and closed and Jen heard no more. She hesitated for a second, then resolutely pulled the bedclothes up over her head.

Angie had met Gino on the farm in Devon where she and their younger brother Paul had been billeted as evacuees at the beginning of the war. Paul was still there, but Angie had been sent back in disgrace for consorting with the Italian prisoners of war who were working on the farm. And now this blasted Gino had turned up here in London with the intention of marrying her.

Since Italy had changed sides, technically Gino was no longer the enemy, but what Angie saw in him was anybody's guess. A more unprepossessing young man was hard to imagine. He had a mournful expression, greasy hair and sallow skin. He was also plump almost to the point of corpulence, although why that was Jen couldn't imagine, because he turned his nose up at every dish her mother presented him with. 'What is this, please?' he would enquire. Then, when he was told it was mashed turnip or pilchard pie, he would push it sadly to the side of his plate with his fork.

For a few minutes Jen did indeed try to go back to sleep, but as the silence continued, she knew she was going to have to intervene. She couldn't just close her eyes and let her younger sister do something she might later regret.

Irritably she got out of bed, wrapping her eiderdown round her shoulders. 'Angie?' she called, shivering. 'You're going to be late for work.'

There was no response. Jen banged on the door. 'What's going on in there?' There was still no answer, so reluctantly she went in.

In any other circumstances, and if she hadn't already felt so grumpy, the scene that greeted her would have caused her to laugh out loud. Plump little Gino, dressed in one of her brothers' striped pyjamas, was lying flat on his back with Angie spread-eagled on top of him. In order to get his hand up Angie's skirt, he had twisted round so far that his head and right shoulder had slipped off the side of the narrow bed.

Angie, whose wake-up kiss apparently had the same kind of suction as a drain plunger, had been dragged down with him, which had seriously unbalanced the whole proceedings. They were both now in imminent danger of falling off the side of the bed. So much so that Gino's spare hand was already flailing frantically, trying to get purchase on the bedclothes. But he was impeded by the over-long arms of the pyjamas, and sure enough, even as Jen uttered a shocked 'Angie!', they both fell gracelessly to the floor in a tangle of limbs and bedding.

Angie, inevitably, thought the whole thing was hilarious.

'Don't be so prudish, Jen,' she said as she followed her sister downstairs a few minutes later. 'We were only having a quick kiss and a cuddle. We're not going to go the whole way, not until we're married.'

'Judging from what I saw, there didn't seem all that much further you could go,' Jen said sourly.

For a moment it looked as though Angie was going to take issue with this, but luckily she caught sight of the clock.

'Blimey,' she said. 'I'd better get going or Mum will kill me.'

And with that, having bellowed a few final endearments up the stairs to Gino, who was still recovering from Jen's untimely interruption, she finally took herself off to work.

Shutting the door firmly behind her, Jen padded down the narrow passage to the kitchen to make herself a cup of tea. It was so cold she could see her own breath. By the time the kettle boiled, despite the eiderdown round her shoulders, she was freezing. And not only freezing, but feeling even more out of sorts than she had before.

And this time she knew why. Angie's mad unthinking passion for Gino could hardly help but draw attention to her own very mixed feelings about Henry Keller.

Henry Keller epitomised everything any right-minded girl would want. Not only was he a successful theatre producer, he was also charming, handsome and thoroughly well-to-do. He had his own flat in Knightsbridge, one of the most fashionable parts of London, for goodness' sake. He was generous, funny, and keen to help her with her career. What more could she possibly want?

What indeed? If everyone thought she was clever to have escaped from the Nazis, they thought she was an utter fool not to jump at the opportunity of marrying Henry Keller.

Henry had proposed to her almost the instant she had arrived back in London, and it had taken her completely by surprise. Yes, he had flirted with her a bit during the previous year, when she was performing in one of his ENSA productions, and she had been flattered by his interest in her, but he had never given her any indication then that he actually wanted to *marry* her. Even now Jen wasn't really sure that he did. She suspected his proposal had been a spur-of-the-moment thing, born out of his relief at seeing her back in England safe and (apparently) sound. It was certainly at odds with his normal measured behaviour.

But unfortunately, arriving back in England after her ordeal in Italy, she hadn't been in a fit state to make such a life-changing decision. So she had prevaricated and that had made it all much worse.

All she really wanted to do was to step off the world for a while and wait for everything to be over. Not just the current awkwardness with Henry. The war too. The danger. The disruption. The trauma.

She blamed the stupid warmongering leaders, Hitler, Mussolini, Roosevelt and Churchill, and all the brutal, bloodthirsty men who followed their orders.

Not that Henry was brutal or bloodthirsty. As one of the key figures in ENSA, he was in fact in a so-called reserved occupation. But that didn't help Jen. It might have been easier if he'd been away fighting the Germans somewhere abroad. At least she would have had time to think. But no, the blasted man was right here in London, waiting for her to make up her mind.

And in the meantime, she had nothing to do except kick around her mother's house trying to avoid Gino.

Even now, she could hear him trundling downstairs and knew that she would be obliged to make him some breakfast. Over the last week he had followed her round the house like a puppy. Despite having been in England for well over a year, pretty much ever since his platoon had surrendered to General Montgomery's forces in North Africa in fact, Gino could barely string two words of English together. So Jen was compelled to talk to him in the really quite competent Italian she had picked up in the five months she had been in Italy.

He came shuffling nervously into the kitchen now, wearing an overcoat over the pyjamas, a muffler round his neck and Angie's bedroom slippers on his feet.

'Good God,' Jen said with a choke of laughter. 'You look like Charlie Chaplin.'

Gino's sheepish expression turned to one of dismay. '*Non capisco*,' he said. 'I don't know who is this persons.'

'Oh, forget it,' Jen said irritably, pushing a cup towards him. 'Just drink your tea. And don't you dare complain there's no sugar, because thanks to you being here, we've run out. *Non c'è zucchero. A causa tuo è finito.*'

She knew she was taking out her own frustration on him. But Gino seemed impervious. All he wanted to do was talk about Italy, his *mamma*, his village in Lazio, his vast numbers of relatives, and the beautiful food they all apparently used to eat together in the sunshine. The London winter didn't suit him at all. But Jen's mother, Joyce, had forbidden them to light the fire until she came home from work. Coal was both rationed and expensive. And Jen certainly wasn't going to waste her money on keeping Gino warm. Especially as there was no sign of him making an effort to earn any of his own. Instead he shivered around the house like some unhappy tropical animal stuck in London Zoo. The only time his eyes lit up was when Angie came home from waitressing at her mother's café, and then their gooey-eyed hand-holding and surreptitious fondling made Jen feel quite sick.

'It makes so cold,' Gino moaned now as he sipped his unsweetened tea with distaste. 'Why is this England always so cold?'

'If you hate it so much, why don't you go back to Italy and fight for your country?' Jen snapped at him suddenly.

But he just shook his head sadly. 'I no soldier. *Mia mamma* no want me to die.' As he smiled pitifully, Jen suddenly wanted to punch him. Or better still, stab him through the heart with the bread knife.

She realised she couldn't bear it another moment. Flinging the dregs of her tea in the sink, she turned back to the stairs.

'You'll have to sort out your own breakfast today. I don't feel very well. I'm going back to bed.'

*

10

Louise did her best to tidy up the kitchen. It wasn't part of her plan to deliberately annoy her parents. But sometimes they tried her patience to the absolute limit. She was still seething at her father's chauvinistic attitude as she hurried down the drive. Ahead of her the wide expanse of Clapham Common looked cold and grim in the early-morning light, matching her mood.

As she rounded the corner onto Lavender Road, she was almost knocked for six by a boy on a go-cart. As she leapt hastily to one side with a shocked scream, he screeched to a stop, and she recognised him as George Nelson, the adopted son of Pam and Alan Nelson, who lived in Lavender Road.

He was looking at her in some concern. As well he should, Louise thought angrily, as she clamped a hand to her hip. She had fractured her pelvis when a bomb exploded on Balham Underground station in 1940, and even though the doctors said her bones had mended satisfactorily, she was still left with a slight limp.

As the pain receded, she turned back crossly to George Nelson.

'Why aren't you at school?'

'I'm on my way to school.'

'Your school is in the opposite direction.'

'I'm going the long way round.'

Louise regarded him suspiciously. She wouldn't put it past him to have deliberately given her a scare. With his wide innocent eyes, soft blond curls and angelic features, he looked as though butter wouldn't melt in his mouth, but she knew from previous experience that he was a slippery little blighter.

Only last week she had caught him climbing over the wall that separated her parents' substantial garden from the back yards of the much smaller houses of Lavender Road. He had claimed that he was retrieving a ball, but there had been no sign of any ball, and Louise had suspected him of having some other nefarious purpose for the trespass: stealing eggs from her mother's henhouse, perhaps.

Even as she had the thought, her hand flew to her mouth. Damn. In her aggravation with her father, she had completely forgotten to let the chickens out.

'What's the matter?' George asked. 'You look as though you've seen a ghost.'

'I'll be seeing your ghost if you're not careful,' Louise said grimly. 'Now buzz off or you'll be late for school.'

She glanced at her watch and groaned. She hadn't time to go back. Nor had she time to call at the pub to check that everything was ready for Katy and the new baby's return. In fact she was barely going to have time to get to work. That was all she needed, she thought as she limped on down the road: another disciplinary encounter with Mr Gregg. If she lost her job, she really would be sunk.

Katy Frazer couldn't wait to get out of hospital. There had been a slight complication as she gave birth, and even though baby Caroline, named after her husband Ward's mother in Canada, was bonny and healthy, Katy still felt as though her nether regions were occupied by a large hedgehog. But that was the least of her troubles. Despite Ward's efforts to reassure her that everything was well at the pub, she had begun to suspect from remarks let slip by some of her other visitors that things weren't running quite as smoothly as he made out.

Ward might be a wonderful, if often absent, husband, but he was not a natural landlord.

But it wasn't Ward's easy-going nature that caused her visitors to squirm and change the subject. Nor was it the unruliness of Lucky, the ridiculously large dog he had brought back with him from Corsica as a Christmas present for two-year-old Malcolm. Nor the inadequacies of Katy's nervous, flustered mother, who was meant to be helping out while she was in hospital. No, what everyone was trying tactfully to conceal from her was the intrusive bossiness of her friend Louise Rutherford, who had for some reason taken it upon herself to oversee Katy's small, invaluable and, up until now, loyal staff.

Jen was the only person who had actually spoken out. But then Jen was never one to pull her punches. 'I don't know how Elsa has put up with Louise,' she had said. 'She's run the poor girl ragged with all her commands.'

'Oh dear,' Katy said. 'I'm sure she's only trying to be helpful.'

'Helpful? Jen had snorted. 'If you put a little black moustache on her, you'd be forgiven for thinking that Adolf bloody Hitler was running the pub.'

'But Ward said—'

Jen gave a sour laugh. 'She doesn't do it when Ward's there. Oh no, then she's all sweetness and light.' She put on an exaggerated lisping version of Louise's posh finishing-school voice. 'Yes, Ward, no, Ward, three bags full, Ward.'

Katy had been forced to laugh, but she could well believe it. Louise had always had a bit of a thing for Ward. 'I don't want her terrorising Elsa,' she said. 'Can't you say something to her?'

But Jen had raised her hands defensively. 'Oh no,' she said. 'I'm not getting involved. It's nothing to do with me.'

And that had surprised Katy. It wasn't like Jen to back off from a wrangle. But since she had come back from Italy, she had been different somehow. Certainly not her usual feisty self. Ward had noticed it too, but he felt she just needed time to adjust to normal life again.

Time, Katy thought now as she gathered her things together ready for

Ward to come and collect her. Time was the one commodity lacking in her own life. But maybe Jen just did need time to get over her ordeal. And Ward should know. As someone who spent most of his time working undercover in enemy territory, he more than anyone must understand what it was like to be living in fear of your life one minute, and rejoining the real world the next.

Katy was checking for the hundredth time that baby Caroline was snugly asleep in the wicker carrying basket when she heard his voice outside her door, and her heart lurched. Even now, after nearly three years, albeit intermittent ones, of marriage, Ward's Canadian accent still had the power to make her pulse accelerate.

Straightening up painfully, she swung round as the door opened. And there he was. Her husband. Her gorgeous husband, his thick dark hair slightly frosted from the cold, his grey eyes seeking hers, and his faintly apologetic smile already curling round her heart and squeezing it tight.

'What is it?' she said, alarmed. 'What's happened?'

'Nothing,' he said. 'Nothing at all. It's just that, well, I guess there was a bit of wild dancing in the bar the other night and one or two chairs got broken. And I'm afraid Malcolm has figured out how the soda siphons work and keeps trying to squirt your mother. Oh, and Lucky has eaten the lamb chops I got to celebrate your homecoming.'

Chapter Two

'You don't look quite yourself, Mrs Carter. Is there anything I can do to help?'

Startled by the courteous question, Joyce Carter looked up from sorting the café cutlery to find her friend Mr Lorenz watching her in some concern from the other side of the counter.

She hadn't noticed him come in, and was conscious she had been swearing under her breath as she disentangled the forks and spoons from the jumble Angie had left yesterday afternoon in her unseemly haste to get home to Gino.

'I wish there was,' she said. She raised her voice and called through the hatch. 'A round of toast for Mr Lorenz, Angie, and quick about it.' Then she lowered her voice again. 'I'm trying to think of a way to get rid of Gino.'

Mr Lorenz looked at her keenly, and Joyce was aware of a slight feeling of breathlessness. Because Mr Lorenz was, in fact, more than just a friend. Not in any physical way. Goodness, no. Nobody could be more correct in that department than Albert Lorenz. But out of the blue, just before Christmas, he had asked her to marry him. And since then, Joyce had felt self-conscious around him. Not that she didn't like him, because she did. She liked him rather a lot, even if he was the local pawnbroker, and Jewish. She wasn't bothered about that. No, it was the thought of getting married that terrified her.

She had been married before, of course. And the less said about that the better. Her husband, Stanley, had been a violent drunkard, and it had been a distinct relief when he had died. Albert Lorenz, on the other hand, had never been married at all.

Aware of her fears, he had suggested that they go on a little holiday to give them a chance to spend some time together, away from the curious eyes of their friends and family. To a hotel or a guest house. Perhaps by the sea. With separate rooms, of course, he had assured her hastily.

And Joyce had come round to thinking that that sounded rather nice. But then this damn Italian boy, Gino, had turned up and thrown everything into disarray.

'You don't approve of him?' Mr Lorenz said now.

Joyce stared at him. 'Of course I don't approve of him. He's an awful fellow. He's completely clueless, and lazy, and Italian.'

She couldn't quite bring herself to admit it to Mr Lorenz, but one of the things that annoyed her most about the ill-favoured Gino was that he turned his nose up at her cooking.

Of course Gino had failed to bring a ration book with him from his POW camp in Devon, so she had been forced to scrimp on the family meals. But she had done her best. Although frankly she would have preferred to let him starve, which, to be honest, if he stayed much longer, he was in danger of doing.

As Gino spoke so little English, it was hard to find out why he wouldn't eat, but when she had got Jen to ask him in Italian the other night, he had replied with a mournful shrug, 'This food, it has no flavour.' And that had annoyed her even more.

'He can't help being Italian,' Mr Lorenz remarked mildly. 'And he and Angie seem very fond of each other.'

Joyce snorted. 'They can't keep their hands off each other, if that's what you mean.'

He smiled at her over his wire-rimmed spectacles. 'Young love, Mrs Carter.' He raised his eyebrows a fraction. 'Does it not make you feel a little compassionate?'

Joyce suddenly felt unaccountably flustered. 'No, it doesn't,' she said. 'Angie is far too young, and—'

'What am I too young for?' Angie asked, coming through with Mr Lorenz's toast. She stared at Joyce anxiously. 'I hope you aren't going to stop me going to the dance competition at the Streatham Locarno tonight? I know the minimum age is seventeen, but they'll never know. Especially not when they see me dance with Gino.' She turned eagerly to Mr Lorenz. 'We make such a good couple, Mr Lorenz. Luckily Gino lets me lead because I know the steps better than him.'

'Ah,' Mr Lorenz said gravely. 'Yes, I imagine that must be a great help.'

Joyce eyed him suspiciously and caught a fleeting look of amusement on his face. That annoyed her too. Albert should be on her side, not Angie's. It was all very well for him to find it funny. It wouldn't be so funny if Gino got Angie pregnant and then scarpered back to Italy as soon as the war was over. Who would be left holding the baby then? It was hardly going to be Albert Lorenz, was it?

Joyce glanced around at her loyal customers enjoying their breakfasts. The café was her pride and joy. She and Mrs Rutherford had worked hard to make it the success it was. She hoped Angie's idiotic teenage crush wasn't going to spoil it all for her. 'Angie, you haven't got time to stand around gossiping,' she said sharply. 'Mr and Mrs Wilkes are still waiting for their omelettes.'

'Lawks, I'd forgotten all about them.' Angie giggled apologetically and

15

winked at Mr Lorenz. 'Now Gino's here, my head's all up in the clouds.'

As her daughter bumbled back into the kitchen, Joyce buttered Mr Lorenz's toast angrily. 'He's got to go. I've made up my mind.' And what was more, she was going to make his lack of food coupons her excuse. She could hardly tell Angie that she thought her boyfriend was a waste of space. She would just tell her she couldn't afford to keep him. If he wasn't prepared to join up and fight, then he would have to go back to Devon and work on the land, like the rest of the POWs. After all, why should he get off scot free when her three eldest sons were doing their bit for the war? Not that poor Bob was doing much, admittedly, stuck in a POW camp in Germany, but before that he had been fighting with the best of them in North Africa.

Joyce sighed. What a time they lived in when boys had to put their lives on the line just because some raving madman in Germany wanted to rule the world. Thank goodness at least her youngest son, Paul, was safe on Mrs Baxter's farm in Devon. And if the invasion of France came this year, as everyone expected, then surely the war would be over before he was old enough to be called up.

'And what about Jen?' Mr Lorenz enquired. 'Has she made up her mind about Mr Keller?'

'I don't know,' Joyce said. She cut the toast into squares and glared at it. What was the matter with her two daughters? They'd got it the wrong way around. At exactly the same time that Angie was encouraging this dismal Italian, Jen was spurning Henry Keller, one of the nicest, most eligible men you could hope to find.

She turned to the tea urn and placed a teapot under the spout. 'All I know is, if she's not quick about it, she's likely to miss the boat,' she said. 'A man like that isn't going to be kept dangling for ever.'

'Oh, I don't know,' Mr Lorenz murmured as he took his teacup and plate. 'I would wait until the earth froze over for you, Mrs Carter.'

By dint of half walking, half running the whole way to the factory, Louise had made it just in time.

'You've cut it fine,' remarked Mr Pitt, the kindly old door clerk, as he punched her card on the time clock.

Louise was still out of breath, so she didn't respond, but when one of her co-workers suggested that she had probably been out on the razzle the night before, she swung round crossly.

'As it happens, I was helping out at the Flag and Garter on Lavender Road,' she retorted stiffly.

'Oh, I say,' the man lisped sarcastically. 'I suppose that's one of the pubs Daddy owns?'

It was, of course. Her father's brewery owned most of the local pubs. But as Louise racked her brains for a suitably cutting retort, her bench-mate, a large, kind-hearted woman called Doris Smith, poked her hard in the ribs. 'Don't rise to his bait,' she said.

Louise made a face. 'I wish he'd leave me alone.' She raised her voice provocatively. 'Of course I'm much better at cutting bolts than he is, and he knows it. Maybe that's his problem.'

Perhaps luckily, the bell went then and the first drills began to shriek. Once all the machinery got going, the noise in the factory was deafening, but Louise had got used to it. She had got used to the dirt, too. The tips of her fingers were permanently stained these days from the sulphur grease they used to lubricate the machines, but she didn't care. She liked working at Gregg Bros. She liked the power of the lathe, the precision of the parting tool. She liked the crunchy feel of the tiny spirals of metal offcuts, the swarf, under her feet. Most of all she liked being good at the job. It was intricate work requiring intense concentration. The danger of making a mistake was high. One slip of the blade and you could easily lose a finger. But in terms of output, she was second only to Doris Smith.

And up until now she had liked the anonymity of the factory. She had forged a strange kind of friendship with Doris, and she had a pretty good relationship with Larry Gregg, the factory owner. The rest of the workforce, which mostly comprised men who hadn't been called up due to age or infirmity, had accepted her as a quick, dextrous worker, and that was that.

But then this wretched new man, Don Wellington, had arrived and spoiled the easy camaraderie of the place. For her, at least. Other people seemed to find him amusing, and egged him on by laughing at his pitiful jibes and jokes. One or two of the women even flirted with him, apparently attracted by his spivvy clothes and risqué conversation. But Louise couldn't bear him. In an attempt to put him in his place, she had once mentioned that her father owned the Rutherford & Berry brewery. He had never let her forget it.

'Watch out,' Doris muttered. 'You'd better get your skates on. Here comes Mr Gregg.'

But instead of harrying them to work harder as he normally did, this morning Larry Gregg called for them to down tools.

'Right,' he announced, as the machines quietened. 'There's a nice little War Office contract in the offing and I want to secure it. So by the end of this week I want everything looking spick and span.'

'What's the contract for?' Don Wellington asked.

Larry Gregg tapped the side of his nose. 'I can't tell you that,' he said. 'It's hush-hush. But what I can tell you is that for some of you it might mean a few more bob in your pay packet.'

There was a murmur of interest at that. 'About time too,' someone murmured.

One of the older women called out, 'What? For us girls too? I'll believe that when I see it.'

'Well you won't see it if you don't keep your mouth shut, Mrs Gibbons,' Mr Gregg retorted. 'And don't think just because I want you to tidy up that I'm not looking at productivity, because I am. Only the best of you will get the new work.'

'Mrs Gibbons is right,' Louise muttered to Doris as they turned back to their bench. 'He always favours the men.'

'Don't you start,' Doris said. 'My advice is to keep your head down and get on with it. And—'

'You're a woman after my own heart, Doris,' Don Wellington interrupted. He gave a crude laugh. 'That's generally my advice to pretty girls too.'

For a moment Louise didn't understand the joke, then she quickly averted her gaze. But unfortunately Don Wellington had noticed the sudden colour in her cheeks. 'Well, well,' he smirked. 'So we aren't quite as innocent as we make out, then? Goodness me, I hope Daddy doesn't know that.'

Forgetting all about her resolution to be nice, Louise was just about to snap out an angry retort when Doris started up her lathe, drowning out any possibility of further conversation. Louise glared at her, but Doris just shrugged her fat shoulders.

'Actions speak louder than words,' she yelled over the racket. 'And I want that pay rise.'

Having seen her husband off to work and George off to school, Pam Nelson turned her attention to baby Nellie. At thirteen months, Nellie wasn't quite walking yet, but she was a placid, smiley child and Pam's task for the morning was to take her down to the Welfare Centre to collect the allocation of orange juice, milk and cod liver oil that the Ministry of Food provided for the under fives.

Pam loved her little daughter with all her heart. And so she should, because Nellie represented the miraculous outcome of a longing so intense and so debilitating that it had almost caused the end of Pam's relationship with Alan. But as she set about wrapping the little girl up nice and warm, Pam was aware of a sense of guilt. Because dealing with Nellie was so much easier than dealing with George.

George's own mother had been killed when her house, the one right opposite Pam and Alan's on the other side of Lavender Road, collapsed on top of her during the Blitz. George had been left an orphan, and unable to conceive a child of their own, Pam and Alan had decided to adopt him.

18

Pam loved George too, of course. But he wasn't an easy child, and just recently he had developed a worrying predilection for violence. But when she expressed her concerns to her friends, they invariably responded with reassuring phrases like 'he'll grow out of it', or 'boys will be boys'.

That was all very well, Pam thought as she lifted Nellie into the pram, but boys didn't generally kill people.

Just before Christmas, George had been responsible for the death of a man called Barry Fish. Nobody knew precisely what had happened. George had gleefully admitted to firing a stone at him from his catapult, but whether it was the stone that had actually killed the unfortunate Mr Fish, or whether it had merely caused him to fall over and smash his head on the ground, wasn't clear.

And in the event, nobody much cared, not even the police, because Mr Fish had turned out to be a nasty piece of work with a history of molesting schoolgirls.

To George's dismay, his involvement had been carefully hushed up. 'But he was a bad man,' he had protested indignantly. 'He deserved to die.'

Pam hadn't known what to say. How could you convince a ten-year-old that killing was wrong, when you were stuck in the middle of a war in which hundreds of thousands of people had already died violent deaths? How could you even teach right and wrong? Hitler was evil. There was no doubt about that. But it was harder to feel that German civilians, for example, deserved to die in such numbers from the relentless RAF bombing raids. It had been given out on the wireless that two thousand tons of bombs had been dropped on Berlin only yesterday.

Pam hated those smug War Office statistics. Some of the Germans who'd died were probably as innocent as she was; they just happened to be living in the wrong place at the wrong time. Not that she would ever dream of saying such a thing out loud, of course. The only person who had ever dared to express anything like that had been a lodger they'd had at the very beginning of the war. A young Irishman, Sean Byrne. 'There's going to be bloodshed like never before,' he had said. 'And what I'm asking, Mrs Nelson, is will it be worth it?'

And now, suddenly, Pam remembered that that wasn't the only thing Sean Byrne had been asking. The truth was that she had been tempted. She and Alan had been having a difficult patch at that time. Due to some trivial medical condition, Alan had been turned down for the forces just when everyone else was joining up, wanting to be heroes. And it had demoralised him.

But then, mercifully, Sean had gone back to Ireland. And at Dunkirk, quiet, unobtrusive Alan had turned out to be a hero after all. Soon after that they had adopted George, and then Nellie had miraculously come along, and they had been happy ever since. Until now.

George had always been wilful – it was perfectly understandable after all he had been through – but this was more serious. This wasn't just stealing Katy Frazer's pram wheels to fit to his go-cart, or climbing over the back wall to scrump the odd apple from Mrs Rutherford's orchard. When Pam had tried to scrub the dirt out of his hair in the bath yesterday, in the regulation four inches of water, she had noticed a huge bruise on his back. He had winced when she had touched it, but he refused to tell her how he had come by it. He just put on his mulish face and wouldn't let her wash him any more. And now she was worried that he had got into some sort of trouble that she didn't know about.

What she needed was for Alan to be firm. But Alan wasn't good at being firm. One winsome glance from George's innocent eyes, and any hope of discipline flew straight out of the window. What was more, with his job at the brewery and his new responsibilities as a corporal in the Home Guard, Alan was rarely at home anyway.

Maybe she could bribe the information out of George. Perhaps that would be easier. She checked she still had a sweet coupon in her ration book, then squeezed the pram out of the front door and set off determinedly towards Clapham Junction and Mallow's, the only shop she knew of that still sold gobstoppers.

When Katy arrived back at the pub with Ward and the new baby, she immediately realised that things were worse than she had feared. Her mother was lying upstairs on her bed with a flannel over her eyes, and instead of getting ready for lunchtime opening, Elsa was on her knees in the cellar, trying desperately to scrub a floor that hadn't been cleaned in five years.

Katy didn't know where to begin. Her mother was fragile at the best of times. For the last couple of years, frightened of the bombing in London, she had lived with Ward's aunts in the country, but having bravely come up to town for Christmas, she had manfully stayed on to help out while Katy was in hospital. It clearly hadn't been a success.

Katy groaned, but a moment later all thoughts of her mother and Elsa were driven out of her mind. The back door opened and, with a hair-raising howl, Lucky bounded up the passage into the bar, followed by Malcolm.

As Lucky thrust his huge nose into the wicker carrycot, Katy felt a moment of panic. 'Stop him, Ward,' she shrieked. 'He's going to eat her.'

Ward laughed and patted the dog's head. 'Of course he won't,' he said. 'He's gentle as a lamb.' But Katy couldn't help noticing that he strategically placed the wicker basket on one of the bar tables, well out of Lucky's reach.

Although she felt ashamed of her outburst, Katy continued to eye the animal warily. Malcolm, though, seemed to have no qualms. 'Mummy! Mummy! Lucky does like baby,' he squealed in delight, scrambling onto a chair so that he could see his new sister.

Katy sighed. She had been away for two weeks and had fondly hoped that Malcolm might have missed her just a tiny bit. At two years old, most children were clingy and mummyish, but Malcolm was the complete opposite. He had clearly been having a whale of a time without her, terrorising his grandmother and becoming even more noisy and agile.

When everything had calmed down a little and Ward had taken baby Caroline upstairs to try and placate his mother-in-law, Katy went down into the cellar to remonstrate with Elsa.

'Miss Louise said I must do it,' Elsa said, looking up from her drudgery. 'She said all the floors must be spotless clean when you came home.'

Katy looked at her in exasperation. Life had not been easy for Elsa Distel. She and her family had escaped from France just ahead of the order to round up Jews. Until Katy had hired her to help in the pub, the family had been virtually destitute. 'But you were in charge, not Louise,' she said. 'You should have said no.'

Elsa hung her head. 'I was afraid. Miss Louise, she is sometimes very strong …' She tailed off, apparently unwilling to cast aspersions on Katy's friend.

It wasn't just Elsa who had been upset by Louise. Bella James, a fourteen-year-old schoolgirl who had been helping out in Katy's absence, seemed equally thrown off balance.

'She told me off for being too slow washing the glasses,' she said.

Even in her drab school uniform, Bella was one of the prettiest girls Katy had ever seen. With her youthful slenderness, dark hair, perfect features and flawless skin, she made even Jen, normally so lively and attractive, look colourless and weary.

It was unfortunate that Bella was the daughter of the local lady of the night. That and her youth made Katy uneasy about employing her in the public bar, but beggars couldn't be choosers, and she had needed to provide Elsa with some extra help while she was out of action. She hadn't known Louise was going to muscle in too.

Bella fingered a small wound on the ball of her thumb and glanced at Katy nervously through her long lashes. 'I tried to be quicker, and then I dropped one and broke it, and she told me I was careless.'

Katy winced. Glasses were in short supply these days, and she hated the thought of them getting broken.

'So what *are* you going to do about Louise?' Jen said when Bella had gone

21

off upstairs to see the baby. Jen had come over for a cup of tea and had been listening to Bella's excuses with obvious amusement. 'You could always set Lucky on her.'

Katy gave an obliging laugh, but inwardly she was groaning. All she wanted to do was settle down with her new daughter. She didn't need all these problems.

Ward had done his best, but the person who should have been in charge, of course, was her mother. But her mother's health was not good, although it wasn't clear what exactly was wrong with her, apart from a nervous disposition and a reluctance to do anything she didn't want to do. Her air of faded fragility and martyred sighs often had the effect of making Katy feel like throttling her. But despite her afflictions, Mary Parsons clearly felt she had to do her duty, and was unaware that her decision to stay on in London after Christmas had been met with less than enthusiasm by her daughter and son-in-law.

Jen put down her cup and stood up. 'Talking of which, I've left that idiot Gino alone in the house. I'd better go back before he attempts to light the fire and burns the whole place down.'

But when Jen let herself into her mother's house on the opposite side of the road, there was no sign of Gino. Nor was the fire lit. He had probably gone down to the café, even though her mother had forbidden him to set foot in there because of the distracting effect his presence had on Angie.

Relieved, Jen walked through to the kitchen. The surfaces were surprisingly neat and tidy, but there was a strange scattering of powder on the concrete floor by the sink. It took a while for her to work out what it was, but eventually she identified it as a mixture of salt and egg powder. Her mother would have a fit. Salt wasn't particularly scarce, but egg powder was on the ration. Both of them cost money, and money had always been tight in the Carter household.

Even though the café was always busy, her mother still had to scrimp and save at home. Of course it was actually Mrs Rutherford's café, and even though her mother did the lion's share of the work, Jen was sure Mrs Rutherford took more than her fair share of the profits. Those posh types always knew which side their bread was buttered.

Thinking of bread, Jen turned towards the cupboard to make a sandwich. It was then that she noticed the letter propped up against an empty milk bottle on the sideboard. It was addressed to her in strong, confident handwriting.

After a brief moment's hesitation, she tore it open.

22

My dear Jen,

I know I promised to wait for you to contact me, but something has come up, and I felt, in the circumstances, that you would want me to get in touch.

I ought to say straight away that I have no intention of using this missive to press you for a decision. As I hope you realise, I have no desire to force you into a relationship that you may later regret, although I do assure you that my feelings for you are unchanged.

My reason for writing is that I have just bumped into Larry Olivier. He has recently finished filming Henry V in Ireland and it seems that he and Ralph Richardson are now intending to re-establish the Old Vic company back in London after its Blitz exile to the north. They are therefore on the lookout for some suitable cast, which isn't easy with so many performers either serving in the forces or involved with ENSA.

As yet their programme is not fully decided, but one of the plays he mentioned is Peer Gynt, in which, as you may know, there are a number of female roles. When I said I knew a promising young actress who might fit the bill, he seemed quite interested.

If the idea appeals to you, you should go on Friday lunchtime to the New Theatre in St Martin's Lane, where they are holding some informal discussions. I recall that you know Juliet's final soliloquy from R&J. I suggest you prepare something like that just in case they want to see you perform.

Yours, in haste (but with undimmed affection),
Henry

Before she had even finished reading the letter, Jen could feel her heart thumping uncomfortably. The Old Vic? Laurence Olivier? A chance to rub shoulders with the big names? A chance to prove that she had real talent? Even a walk-on part would be something amazing. Was Henry mad? *Of course* it appealed to her.

But even as she pulled out a chair and sat down at the kitchen table, she felt goose bumps breaking out on her skin. Damn Henry, the thought suddenly. Why did he have to bring this up now? When she felt so brought down, so out of practice and so unattractively thin.

In the past, it would have been her dearest dream to perform with that calibre of actor. But now the very thought of walking into a theatre made her feel nauseous. Let alone delivering Juliet's dying speech.

She was surprised that Henry had remembered that. It had been such a long time ago, the first time she had ever met him, in fact, in a cinema during the Blitz. There had been a massive air raid and the manager had invited people to do turns on stage to while away the time once the main feature had ended. Henry had been in the audience with Ward Frazer.

Despite the sub-zero temperature in the kitchen, Jen could feel sweat in her armpits. Maybe she could pretend the letter got lost in the post. Or she could say she had something else on that day. But what? There was nothing more important than a chance to audition for the Old Vic company.

Even as half her brain frantically tried to think up excuses, a way out, the other half knew she was going to be at the New Theatre at St Martin's Lane at lunchtime on Friday. She felt her stomach heave, and with a convulsive movement, she leapt to her feet and was sick into her mother's sink.

Chapter Three

Celia Rutherford was indeed cross with Louise for failing to let the chickens out that morning. 'Really Louise,' she said at supper. 'It wasn't much to ask. They'd gone to roost by the time I got in, so they'd had no exercise or food all day.'

Louise pressed her nails into her knees under the table, trying to keep her temper. Honestly, she thought, you would be forgiven for thinking she had slaughtered the chickens and eaten the damn things for lunch, the way her mother went on. 'I'm really sorry, Mummy,' she said. 'But I was in a hurry to get to work and I just forgot.'

Her mother pursed her lips. 'And now I suppose you're going to say that you are in a hurry to get to the pub, just when I could do with some help clearing up the supper.'

Louise was opening her mouth to say exactly that when her father interrupted. 'Of course you'll help your mother, Louise. You have let her down once today as it is. If you wish to live here, you will have to learn to pull your weight with the domestic chores.'

But I don't want to live here, Louise wanted to scream. I'd rather live almost anywhere else on earth. I'd rather live in Adolf Hitler's bunker than here.

'What's more,' her father continued, 'I don't like you spending so much time at the Flag and Garter. It's not a suitable place for a girl like you.'

'Oh Daddy, really.' Louise could feel her hackles rising again. 'Katy Frazer runs a perfectly respectable pub, as you well know. After all, you own it.'

Her father's colour heightened alarmingly but luckily her mother hastily intervened. 'What's happened to all your finishing-school friends?' she asked. 'Why don't you look some of them up?'

Louise poked resentfully at her meagre portion of shepherd's pie. Most of her Lucie Clayton friends had got married, or moved away. Even her best friend from those days, Helen de Burrel, who Ward Frazer had recruited into the SOE, the top secret Special Operations Executive, had somehow become much more friendly with Katy and Molly than she was with her. And in any case Helen was now working in Tunisia.

There were a few girls left in London, of course, but the unpalatable truth was that they rarely invited her to anything any more. Louise had assumed that was because she was stuck all the way down here in Clapham, while they lived in smart little flats in the West End, provided by their parents. But now she wondered if it was because they had got fed up with her. She probably had gloated a bit too much about Jack in the early days. And none of them had approved of her unfortunate fling with Charlie Hawkridge. And yes, that had been a mistake, because, for all his smooth talk and sympathy, Charlie had turned out to be a compete cad. But how was she meant to have known that? It was all very well for her friends to act all superior about it, but they didn't know what it was like having your husband away all the time. She had been so lonely, and when Jack died, so bereft.

She pushed back her chair and stood up. 'Well I'm sorry to be such a disappointment to you,' she said. 'But at least I feel welcome at the pub. At least people are nice to me there.'

Pam's attempt to bribe George into telling her how he had come by the bruise on his back had failed miserably.

He just shrugged his shoulders. 'I don't know,' he had said. 'I can't remember.'

But she didn't believe him. There was something furtive in his demeanour. And now, as she came downstairs from settling Nellie in her cot, she had caught him in the hallway, scurrying through from the kitchen. As she rumpled his curly blond hair, it felt distinctly cold.

'Where have you been?' she asked.

He ducked away from her. 'Just in the back yard.'

'But it's pitch dark,' she said. 'What were you doing out there?'

'Nothing.'

She looked at him. 'George, what's the matter? Why won't you talk to me?'

For a second, as he met her eyes, she thought she saw a guilty look cross his face, but then he squared his shoulders defiantly. 'I am talking to you.'

'Yes,' she said. 'But not properly. I'm worried about you. Are you in some sort of trouble?'

'No,' he said. But it was too fast, too glib.

'You can have that gobstopper if you tell me what's going on.'

'There's nothing going on,' he said.

Pam sighed and was relieved when the front door opened behind her and Alan came in.

'Hello, my lovelies,' he said easily. He caught her rather desperate gaze and smiled reassuringly before leaning down to hug George.

But George apparently didn't want to be hugged. As he squirmed hastily away, he bumped into the hall table, and they all heard the crunch of

26

something breaking in his pocket.

'What was that?' Pam asked in alarm.

'Nothing,' George said. But as he stuck his hand in his pocket, an expression of horror formed on his face.

Pam glanced at Alan, but he was clearly as much at sea as she was.

For a moment the three of them stood in silence, then Pam pulled herself together. 'Show me your hand,' she said sternly.

Reluctantly George withdrew his hand from this pocket. It was covered in yellowish slime.

Pam recoiled in horror. 'George, is that egg?'

He nodded dully, and Pam felt her heart sinking. So that was where he'd been. In Mrs Rutherford's henhouse. She glanced helplessly at Alan and was horrified to see that he was struggling not to laugh.

But this was no laughing matter. 'That's stealing,' she said sternly to George. 'You know it's wrong to steal.'

He shrugged and kicked the floor. 'I only did it for a dare.'

'Who dared you?'

He hesitated. 'Someone at school.'

'Who?'

But despite her best efforts, it was obvious that he wasn't going to tell her. He just stood there tense and stiff, refusing to meet her eye, his mouth closed in a hard line. In the end, she sent him to bed. There didn't seem to be anything else she could do.

'Why didn't you say something?' she hissed at Alan as the bedroom door slammed above their heads. 'Why didn't you do something?'

'What could I do?' Alan asked. 'Make an omelette?'

'It's not funny,' Pam said crossly. 'It's always me that has to tell him off. And he's just getting worse and worse.'

'Hey, sweetheart, it's not that bad.'

'Not that bad?' she said incredulously. 'Greville Rutherford is your boss. What is he going to say when he finds out George has been helping himself to his eggs?'

'Hopefully he won't find out. And he only took one, after all.'

'So you're encouraging him into a life of crime?'

Alan laughed and shook his head. 'I'm doing no such thing. Give the boy a break, Pam. He said it was a dare. Forgive the pun, but his friends have clearly been egging him on. It was naughty, but frankly, I'm glad he had the guts to do it. I don't think I'd have dared at his age.'

Pam looked at him blankly. But perhaps he was right. Perhaps she had overreacted. Perhaps boys were different, just like men were clearly so different from women. She turned back to the kitchen. 'I'll get the supper,'

27

she said.

As Louise pushed through the blackout curtain of the Flag and Garter, the heat and noise hit her like a blast.

Katy was standing behind the bar, looking hot and unusually flustered. Louise caught her eye and waved, and saw Katy glance over at Ward, who was chatting to Jen Carter by the fireplace. Louise groaned. Some people thought that with her unruly auburn hair and flashing tawny eyes Jen looked a bit like Vivien Leigh, and Louise had to admit there was a faint similarity, although she very much doubted that Jen had anything close to Vivien Leigh's talent.

In Louise's opinion, Jen Carter had always been far too full of herself, and was probably even worse now that she had apparently received a proposal of marriage from the celebrated theatre producer Henry Keller. Nevertheless, she was determined to try and be nice.

'Welcome home,' she shouted to Katy as she approached the bar. 'It's busy tonight. What do you want me to do?'

Katy seemed to hesitate, or maybe she didn't hear. In any case, she didn't immediately respond. Instead she came out from behind the bar and beckoned towards the stairs. 'Come and see the baby.'

Louise hadn't seen Caroline yet. The strict visiting hours at the Wilhelmina Hospital had always coincided with her shifts at the factory. 'OK,' she said. But then she noticed that Katy was looking uneasy. 'Though wouldn't you rather I helped down here until things quieten down a bit?'

'It's all right,' Katy said. 'Ward will hold the fort.'

And indeed Ward was already easing himself through the crowd. Louise saw him smile reassuringly at Katy and felt a jolt of envy. With his athletic figure, regular features, thick dark hair and lovely grey eyes, Ward Frazer was an extremely attractive man. 'Hi, Louise,' he said. 'How are things?' He raised his eyebrows. 'I like the new hairdo.'

Louise touched her hair self-consciously. He was the first person who had remarked on her new style. 'Thanks,' she said.

'Are you coming, Louise?' Katy called rather impatiently. And reluctantly Louise turned away from Ward and followed her up the stairs.

In the shabby little sitting room above the bar, they found Katy's mother cradling the new baby in her arms. 'Malcolm's gone to sleep,' she said as soon as she saw Katy. 'But I'm worried this one's got gripe. She cries when I try to put her down.'

Katy took the baby, resting her on her shoulder. 'It's probably only wind,' she said.

'Isn't she lovely, Louise?' Mrs Parsons said. 'She looks just like Katy, don't

28

you think?'

Louise nodded obligingly, but what she actually thought was that Mrs Parsons needed her eyes examining. Under her tiny knitted bonnet, baby Caroline seemed to have the face of a small, wizened ape. No one could claim that Katy was a beauty, of course, but she didn't look like a monkey. And how anyone as gorgeous as Ward Frazer could father such an unattractive little creature, Louise couldn't imagine.

'I hope everything was OK when you got back,' she said when the baby had been put back in the cot by the window. 'I told Elsa and Bella to make sure the place was spick and span.'

Katy nodded. 'Oh yes, it was all fine.'

She didn't sound very enthusiastic, and Louise felt aggrieved. She had put a lot of effort into marshalling those two hopeless girls into some kind of useful action. 'I hope they told you about my idea for reorganising the scullery,' she continued. 'We agreed it would be so much more logical to wash the glasses from right to left, instead of left to right.'

Katy looked blank.

'Come downstairs and I'll show you what I mean,' Louise urged her. 'We could change it round tonight.'

'No, no, it's OK,' Katy said. 'We're so busy, and—'

'Honestly,' Louise persevered, 'it would make things much more efficient.' She eyed Katy expectantly, but her friend seemed more interested in fiddling with a blanket in the baby's cot. 'Katy? What's the matter?'

'Nothing's the matter,' Katy said. 'But I don't think I really need you to help any more now that I'm back.'

Louise couldn't believe her ears. After all she had done, slogging away every blasted evening while Katy was in hospital. She had a sudden horrific vision of endless empty evenings stretching out before her. Or worse, having to spend them listening to the wireless with her parents. But before she could say anything else, Jen suddenly appeared at the top of the stairs.

'I hope you've told her,' she said.

Louise looked from Jen to Katy, hating that they had obviously been discussing her behind her back.

Katy was looking equally cross at the interruption. 'You've been really brilliant,' she said. 'But with all of us here, it might be a case of too many cooks spoiling the broth.'

Louise felt bitterly aggrieved. If it wasn't enough that her parents were constantly telling her off, now Katy was giving her the cold shoulder too. After all her efforts to be nice and helpful. But maybe there was some other reason for her friend's unreasonable behaviour.

'Is this because of the broken chairs?' she asked. 'That wasn't my fault.

That was Jen's stupid sister and her wild dancing.'

Katy put a hand on her arm. 'No, it's not about that …'

'Why then?' Louise asked, pulling away. 'Why are you being so mean?'

Katy floundered. But of course Jen didn't hold back. 'Oh for goodness' sake, Louise,' she snapped. 'Can't you take a hint? It's because you're so bossy and annoying.'

'Jen!' Katy hissed.

But Louise had heard enough. 'I can take a hint as well as the next person,' she said. And grabbing her coat, she turned on her heel and ran down the stairs and out of the pub, vowing never to set foot in the beastly place again.

On Thursday evening, Joyce gave Gino his marching orders. When it came to it, it wasn't an easy thing to do, but although Angie tried to dispute her decision, Gino put up little resistance.

The following morning, Joyce handed him his train fare and a corned beef sandwich for the journey. She also gave him a sausage and mushroom pie for her long-absent youngest son Paul. And five pounds for Mrs Baxter, the woman who had taken him in at the beginning of the war. It didn't seem much considering the poor woman had housed and fed him at her farm for over four years, but at least it was something.

Joyce had expected Angie to be thrown into gloom, but she had misjudged her daughter's irrepressible good spirits. Within hours of seeing Gino off at Clapham Junction station, Angie had discovered that an American regiment was about to take up residence in a nearby barracks. American soldiers meant nylons, Hershey bars, chewing gum and Lucky Strike cigarettes, and Angie immediately started to make plans to winkle her way into their favour before they found recipients for their largesse elsewhere.

'So you aren't missing Gino too much?' Mrs Rutherford remarked drily.

Angie looked shocked. 'Oh, I am,' she said, clutching a hand to her chest. 'I miss him terribly.' She smiled winningly at her employer. 'But it's always best to make hay while the sun shines, so could you ask Mr Rutherford if he knows which day they are due to arrive?'

'I didn't want to mention it to Angie,' Celia Rutherford confided in Joyce later as she totted up the cash in the till, 'but the advance party has already arrived. When Greville called to introduce himself and to suggest some joint training exercises, the American captain in charge was very offhand, saying that their job was to prepare for the invasion of France, not train the Home Guard. Greville was most annoyed.'

Joyce was amused. She knew Greville Rutherford of old, and he wouldn't have liked that one bit.

But despite her husband's antipathy, Celia seemed to feel it was their duty to welcome the Americans. 'Lady Reading told us at the WVS conference that in the run-up to the invasion, Great Britain will be host to a huge number of soldiers of all nationalities,' she explained to Joyce. 'She said it's our duty to make them at home and keep up their morale in the face of what lies ahead.'

Joyce would never dare say so, but privately she was getting a bit fed up with Lady Reading, the founder of the WVS. Thanks to her motivating speeches, Mrs Rutherford was spending far more time on WVS business than in the café. Which meant that Joyce was run off her feet trying to manage everything on her own.

And it was all very well for Lady Reading to advocate a warm welcome to foreign soldiers, Joyce thought sourly, but not when you had a teenage daughter like Angie on your hands. Angie's welcome was likely to be considerably too warm. She picked up a carrot and chopped it irritably, wondering which was worse, the hapless Gino, or some tall, sweet-talking Yankee with more money than sense.

Angie wasn't the only person looking forward to the arrival of the Americans. Katy was mulling over ways to attract them to the pub. Americans were good for business, and with the brewery constantly squeezing her on the price of beer and spirits, she was always on the lookout for ways to boost her takings. The young wheeler-dealer Aaref Hoch had proved himself a dab hand at sourcing illicit American beer and boxes of ice for the previous batch of GIs, and Katy had made a nice return on being the only pub in the area able to provide the thin chilled lager that for some unaccountable reason they loved so much.

Formerly an admirer of Louise's, Aaref Hoch was now in a steady relationship with Katy's barmaid, Elsa. Aaref and his younger brothers had fled from Austria at the beginning of the war and, like Elsa and her family, had been taken in by Mrs d'Arcy Billière who lived in one of the large houses at the top of the road. As a Jewish refugee Aaref was exempt from military service. But all those other fresh-faced young GIs had since disappeared off to North Africa. By now they were probably fighting in Italy. Katy hoped they were OK. For weeks on end, the advancing Allied troops had been stuck at a place called Monte Cassino, having come up against fierce resistance from Nazi snipers holed up in an impregnable monastery overlooking the pass.

Thinking of Louise made Katy realise that she hadn't seen her since she had stormed out of the pub the other night.

She closed her eyes. She was exhausted. What with her mother fussing

31

endlessly about the baby, the dog growling at every stranger who came into the bar, and her friends all out of sorts, it hadn't been a restful homecoming at all.

What was worse, she knew that soon Ward would be summoned away again, back to his secret war. And she was dreading that moment.

Last time she had made a terrible fuss, and then had worried every minute he was away that she had disgusted him with her unpatriotic distress. This time she had resolved to be braver.

But her good intentions didn't prevent her expressing her dismay when he told her the following day that he would indeed be leaving in a couple of weeks.

'Where have you got to go?' she asked.

He smiled. 'You know I can't tell you that. But it's nothing dangerous.'

Katy tried to feel relieved, but she had learnt over the years she'd known him that his idea of danger didn't quite coincide with hers.

'Don't cry,' he said.

'I'm not,' she said, sniffing. 'I promise I'll be brave. If you promise you'll be careful.'

He chuckled at that. 'I'm always careful,' he said. 'And I'll come back just as soon as I can.'

She tried to return his smile. But it wasn't very successful.

Later, as she was feeding the baby in the privacy of her bedroom, Katy wondered if she would be able to bear the moment of departure. Or indeed the subsequent long days and nights without the comfort of Ward's reassuring presence. She pushed the thought away hastily and hugged her tiny daughter to her breast. She had coped before. She supposed she would cope again.

But what if this time he didn't come back?

At quarter to one on Friday, Jen found herself standing in St Martin's Passage, just round the corner from the entrance to the New Theatre, with its huge square columns and imposing, smog-blackened facade. She was reciting Juliet's speech silently to herself. But despite the fact that she had been practising it endlessly, she kept going wrong.

When she had learnt it at school, she had been word perfect, but now Juliet's convoluted phrases kept slithering around in her mind like eels. Jen suddenly wished she had a handy vial of poison she could take to put her out of her misery. Stupid old Juliet only had a 'faint cold fear thrilling through her veins'; Jen had complete and utter terror thrilling through hers.

But she knew that if she left it any longer, she was going to be too late. And if she had any hope of success, she needed to make a good first impression.

It didn't help that she had had very little sleep the night before. Thankfully, on Gino's departure, Angie had decamped into the other room, so there was no snoring for Jen to contend with, but instead she had been plagued with dreams. One had been particularly disturbing. She had been trapped behind a high wire fence, and a crowd of people, one of whom was Henry Keller, were standing on the other side, laughing at her. The more they laughed, the more she scrabbled at the fence, trying to get out. So much so that when she finally woke up, she had to turn on the light to check that her fingers weren't bleeding.

She shook her head. She didn't want to think about that now. Or ever again, come to that. She took a determined breath, checked that her hair hadn't escaped from its French roll as it had a habit of doing, and turned the corner.

But before she reached the theatre, two other girls came swinging down St Martin's Lane from opposite directions. They were both done up to the nines in fashionable little suits and stylish, jaunty little hats.

Catching sight of each other as they approached the theatre steps, they paused and did a dramatic double-take.

'I know you,' one of them screamed delightedly at the other, pointing a hand encased in a pale blue leather glove. 'I saw you do a marvellous Dido at RADA.'

The other girl put a hand to her chest. '*Speaks not Æneas like a conqueror? O blessed tempests that did drive him in!*' She laughed and opened her eyes wide. 'Talking of which, didn't *I* see *you* in *The Tempest* with John Gielgud just before the Blitz? You were wonderful. I ...'

Jen couldn't bear to listen to any more of their gushing mutual adulation. Walking straight past the theatre and on up St Martin's Lane, she felt a yawning gulf open up in front of her. Dido, RADA, *The Tempest*, John Gielgud. Those young actresses might almost have been talking a foreign language. Henry talked that language too. But to Jen it was like a secret code for a privileged little club, one that she wasn't a member of.

She was tempted to keep walking. But she also knew that she would never forgive herself if she did. So she gave the girls a few minutes to get their effusions out of the way, then retraced her steps.

The only person in the lobby of the theatre was a rather fussily dressed man in pointed shoes and a yellow bow tie. He was leaning back against the shuttered box office, smoking a cigarette in a long holder.

He raised his eyebrows when he saw Jen, but didn't straighten up or indeed make any comment.

Jen attempted a confident smile. 'Is this the right place for the Old Vic audition?'

He waved his cigarette negligently. 'And you are?'

With some difficulty, Jen kept the smile fixed on her lips. 'My name is Jen Carter,' she said.

He looked at her blankly.

'Henry Keller suggested that I came today,' she added stiffly.

Light seemed to dawn, in that the man eyed her with a fraction more interest. 'Ah, so you're one of Henry Keller's protégées, are you?' he drawled. 'Jane Carter, you said? I've not heard of you before. Where did you train?'

'It's Jen,' Jen said icily. 'Not Jane. And I didn't train. At least not formally. The drama schools all closed at the beginning of the war, just when I was starting out. So I've had to learn on the job.'

'I'm sure you have,' he said drily, stretching his arm to tap the cigarette into a large ashtray resting on the box office counter.

Jen suddenly wanted to punch the cigarette down his prissy little throat. She knew what he was implying. But never once in her entire career had she exchanged sexual favours for a job. Not even with Henry. And if that was what this man thought, just because she hadn't been to RADA and didn't have a fake gushing laugh or a cut-glass accent, then he could stuff his oh-so-wonderful Old Vic and all its poncey actors and actresses with it.

'I've changed my mind,' she said as a red mist began to blur her vision. 'I've decided that I'd rather go and work down a coal mine.'

And with that she turned on her heel and left the theatre.

Louise's Friday wasn't going well either. All week she had been smarting about that scene in the pub.

What business was it of a jumped-up little madam like Jen Carter anyway? Maybe her mother was right; maybe she ought to be socialising with girls of her own class, girls who knew how to behave. Maybe next weekend she would ring her Lucie Clayton friend Lucinda Veale and arrange to meet up in town some time.

In the meantime she had thrown her anger into her job. For the last two days her output had been better than ever, almost as high as Doris Smith's. She had knocked Don Wellington and the other men on the line into a cocked hat. If anyone was going to get picked out for a new project and a pay rise, it should certainly be her and Doris. And a bit more in her wage packet would mean that she might be able to afford to rent a flat of her own, and finally get away from boring old Lavender Road and its aggravating residents.

That morning Mr Gregg had insisted that everyone replace the metal safety guards on their machines. Nobody wanted to, because having the guards in place impeded their productivity. It was safer, of course, because the guards shielded their faces from the tiny sharp metal spirals that sheared off the bolts under pressure from the parting tool. But nobody much cared about safety. Not if it was going to affect output. And it had become a kind of badge of honour among the operators not to use them.

But now that he needed to impress an important prospective client, Larry Gregg was determined that everything on the factory floor should be tickety-boo. During their lunch break, he was going to inspect their individual workstations, and anyone who had failed to tidy up to the standard he required would have their wages docked.

In order to make her output tally as high as she could, Louise had decided to leave her tidying up as late as possible. So it was in some haste, when the lunch whistle sounded, that she swept the swarf off the floor, scrabbled round the back of her machine to reattach the guard, and grabbed an old cloth to rub the grime off the pulleys that controlled the drive belt.

In the process she got a smear of grease on her face, and it took her some time in the inadequate female washroom to clean up. By the time she joined her workmates in the canteen, the lunch break was nearly over and most people were smoking their last cigarette before resuming work. Don Wellington was one of the few still eating, and terrified that everyone would get up and go and leave her alone with him, Louise found herself gobbling down her tasteless corned beef pie and lumpy mashed potatoes.

But before she could start on her jelly and custard, the works foreman came hurrying into the canteen. 'Back to work!' he shouted. 'The buggers have arrived early. Get to it, everyone. We don't want them to catch us slacking.'

'We aren't slacking,' Mrs Gibbons remarked sourly. 'We're entitled to half an hour's break at dinnertime.'

'You'll be entitled to a kick up the backside if you aren't careful,' the foreman retorted.

And in fact the factory whistle had barely sounded when Larry Gregg emerged from his office with his precious visitors.

Before starting up her machine, Louise took a surreptitious peek at them to see what the fuss was all about. At first glance, they didn't look anything much. Three men, two tall, one shorter, all dressed in suits with overcoats over the top. The only one who looked remotely military was one of the taller men, who had a bristly moustache and a stiff, upright bearing rather like her father's. The shorter man looked distinctly scruffy; the knot of his tie was loose and he was wearing a cardigan under his jacket.

Louise only caught a glimpse of the third man because Larry Gregg was already ushering them fawningly along the production line, and she had to turn quickly back to her post. Next to her, Doris had already engaged her lathe to their shared drive belt, and the shrill whine of it whirring into action drowned out Larry Gregg's voice as he stopped just behind them.

As she set her own machine in motion, Louise strained to hear what he was saying, but before she could catch a single word, she felt an unusual vibration run through her fingers.

At first she thought it was due to the unfamiliar safety guard, but then her eyes flew to the drive belt and she saw the telltale glint of something caught in the pulley. Jerking back from the controls, she swung round to Doris. 'Disengage!' she screamed. 'For God's sake, Doris, disengage!'

But she was too late. At that precise moment the pulley jammed, and the sudden jolt on the lathe caused the blade to sever off Doris's parting tool.

Fully occupied with avoiding damage to her own machine, Louise missed the moment when the razor-sharp shard, having ricocheted off the inner rim of the safety guard, flew out straight into her friend's face.

As a terrible silence fell, she swung back and saw that the left side of Doris's face was already completely covered in blood. 'Oh my God,' she whispered.

Doris tried to speak, and one of her hands moved instinctively to the wound, but before it got there, she wobbled slightly, then her legs gave way and she collapsed, not very gracefully, to the floor.

Louise tried to catch her, to soften her fall, but Doris was a large woman, and in the end all she could do was stop her head bumping onto the concrete floor.

Nobody moved for a moment, then Louise looked up at Larry Gregg. 'For God's sake do something,' she shouted at him. 'Don't just stand there like a lemon. Get an ambulance.'

It wasn't the most respectful thing she had ever said to her boss, but it did at least spur him into action. Muttering an apology to his visitors, he shouted to the foreman to telephone the hospital and to summon Mrs Gibbons, who was trained in first aid.

Behind him Louise could see some of her co-workers, including Don Wellington, white-faced with shock, craning forward to see what had happened. But it was one of the visitors, the one she previously hadn't been able to see, who stepped forward and crouched down beside her.

'We should turn her onto her side,' he said. He spoke briskly, but with calm authority. 'We don't want her choking on her own blood.'

Numbly conscious that he had an American accent, Louise helped him manoeuvre the unconscious Doris into a better position. 'Is it her eye?' she whispered. 'Did it get her in the eye?' There was so much blood pouring down Doris's face, it was impossible to see where it was coming from.

'I don't know,' he said. 'I guess we have to hope not.' He glanced up as Mrs Gibbons arrived with the first aid box. 'Do you have something sterile in there?' He pronounced it *steril*, and Mrs Gibbons looked blank. 'A pad or a bandage?' he prompted. 'Something we can use to stem the bleeding.'

For once Mrs Gibbons seemed lost for words. But then she nodded obediently and clicked open the box.

Realising she was going to be in the way, Louise drew back, and stood up shakily, only to find herself face to face with Larry Gregg.

'How the hell did this happen?' he snapped.

'I don't know,' Louise stammered. 'Something got caught in the pulley. I saw it just in time ...' She stopped, mortified, because of course she hadn't been in time. Not for Doris.

But Larry Gregg was already leaning over the machine. 'Who cleaned this belt drive?' he grunted.

'I did,' Louise said. 'Just before lunch.'

'Then it's your fault,' he said.

'No, I ...' She stopped as he straightened up and held out a tiny silver coil on the palm of his hand.

Louise stared at it. A piece of swarf. She took it and fingered it incredulously. That was all it had taken to jam the pulley? But how on earth had it got up onto the drive belt in the first place?

'No, I swear, I—'

'I don't want any swearing,' Larry Gregg said. 'I just hope for your sake that Mrs Smith doesn't lose her eye. You can get your things and go home. I can't overlook this kind of carelessness. We will discuss it again on Monday.'

Louise gaped at him, aghast. 'But that's not fair. It wasn't me ...'

He ignored her and turned to the two men standing behind him. 'I do apologise,' he said obsequiously. 'But in view of this unfortunate accident, I wonder if we could postpone the rest of the visit until next week.'

The men looked at each other and then at the third of their number, who was still crouching on the ground by Doris's prostrate body. Perhaps sensing their eyes on him, he stood up and flexed his shoulders. 'I don't think there's much more we can do until the ambulance arrives,' he said. 'I can't say for sure, but I hope it may not be quite as bad as it looks.'

Larry Gregg immediately started gushing out his thanks. But the American ignored him. 'I'd kind of like to take a quick wash before we go,' he said.

The sight of his blood-splattered hands quelled Larry Gregg's sycophantic mumblings. 'Of course, of course,' he muttered. 'If you would like to follow me, I'll show you ...'

'I don't think you should be too hard on that girl,' the man said as they walked away. 'Even if it was her fault, she reacted real quick. She saved your machinery. Another moment and you'd have lost the lathe. I guess it's a shame the other woman didn't react as fast.'

'It's more than a shame,' Larry Gregg replied grimly. 'That other woman, Mrs Smith, is far and away my best operative.'

Five minutes later, Louise was standing outside the factory gates, having been escorted off the premises by the foreman. Even as she stood there, dazed and shaking, she heard the siren of the approaching ambulance and felt a sense of relief. If nothing else, at least Doris would now get some proper treatment.

Slowly she began to walk up the hill. She was just catching her breath on the corner of St John's Road when the visitors' military staff car came up behind her.

As the driver paused at the junction, Louise could see the other three men inside. The small, scruffy man was in one of the back seats, leaning forward, talking. The man with the moustache was sitting next to him, interjecting the odd comment. The third man, the American, was in the front passenger seat, looking out of the window.

Louise could see him clearly, although she tried not to stare. He was younger than she had thought. Surely not more than thirty. A strong face, with narrow, deep-set eyes. It was hard to read his expression. But he looked serious, thoughtful, possibly even annoyed.

Louise wondered if she dared try and catch his attention. She would have liked to thank him for standing up for her with Larry Gregg. He hadn't had to do that. She shivered convulsively. In all the time she had been working at the factory, she had never seen Mr Gregg so angry.

But then the car eased forward and swung away on the main road. The man hadn't seen her. Or if he had, he hadn't recognised her. And suddenly she felt very forlorn.

Chapter Four

It was Saturday morning, and Jen was sitting at the kitchen table with her head in her hands when she heard someone knock at the front door. She froze.

There was silence and then the knock came again, followed by Henry Keller's cool, cultured voice, always so out of place somehow in Lavender Road.

'Jen, are you there? I called at the café and your mother said you'd be in.'

Oh no, Jen thought. She closed her eyes. Then she opened them again and stood up quickly to check her reflection in the small spotted mirror that hung on the kitchen wall. Why couldn't he have called when she was upstairs, and could at least have put on a bit of face powder to hide the dark shadows under her eyes?

But she knew she was going to have to answer the door. She would look an idiot if she didn't and he found out she had been there all along.

So when he knocked again, she moistened her lips, patted some colour into her cheeks, ran her fingers through her unruly, sleep-rumpled hair, squared her shoulders and went to open the door.

Henry was standing on the step, bare-headed, in a smart navy overcoat turned up at the collar against the icy wind. His thick, well-cut hair was slightly frosted, and his attractive, strong-featured face looked unusually tense and chilled. Jen realised he must have walked all the way up from Clapham Junction, which would have gone against the grain with him because he normally used taxis if he could find them. When he tried to smile, his lips seemed too cold to obey.

'Goodness,' she said, affecting surprise, and trying to ignore her suddenly hammering heart. 'I hope you haven't been standing here for ages. I was out in the back yard so I didn't hear you knock. You look frozen to death. You'd better come in.'

'Thank you,' he said, and stepped gratefully into the narrow hall, closing the door behind him. Without waiting for his normal greeting kiss, Jen led the way back to the kitchen. It wasn't much warmer in there, but at least there was no wind.

'It's nice to see you,' she said nervously, as he drew off his gloves. 'But ... I thought we'd agreed that you'd give me time to ...'

'I did,' he agreed. He laid the gloves carefully on the table, one on top of the other. 'But that was before you stormed out of the New Theatre.'

Jen flinched. 'I didn't storm …'

'No?' His cool, assessing eyes rested briefly on her face. 'I heard that you're intending to enlist as a Bevin boy and go to work down a coal mine. That's very patriotic of you. But I'm not sure they take girls.'

Jen felt her temper rise. So that nasty little snitch had gone running to Henry, had he? She wasn't surprised. He had looked just the type who would enjoy causing trouble.

'I might have known that you'd come and tell me off,' she said bitterly.

Henry's brows drew together in sharp surprise. 'When have I ever told you off?'

She glared at him. 'Often,' she said. 'When we were rehearsing your ENSA show, you were always telling me I could do better.'

He inclined his head, his expression relaxing again. 'OK. Professionally, maybe, but not personally.'

Jen blinked. Was that true? She tried to think back, but her mind was a blur. She felt helpless in his presence. She couldn't concentrate. There had always been something about Henry Keller that flustered her. Certainly whenever she had worked for him, he had been a stickler for perfection. He had a critical eye, and she knew to her cost that he could see straight through any attempt to get by on second best.

When she didn't respond, he gave a slight sigh. 'I'm not an ogre, Jen. Yes, I may have pulled you up in rehearsals once or twice, but only because I wanted to get the best out of you. You have enormous potential and I wanted to help you develop it.' He shook his head with a slightly bitter smile. 'I almost wish you hadn't. It would certainly make my life a lot easier.'

'Well, I'm sorry if I embarrassed you with your Old Vic friends,' she responded huffily.

'You didn't embarrass me,' he said. But the emphasis was on the 'me'. The clear implication was that she had embarrassed herself, and that made Jen mad. Because she knew he was right.

'I don't care,' she said.

'Well you should care,' he said drily. 'Jason Cavell may be a bit of an arse, but he's very influential. He's a useful person to know.'

She heard exasperation in his tone and she didn't like it. 'I don't want to know him,' she said stiffly. 'I don't want to be helped by people like him. Or by anybody else come to that. I'd much rather make my own way like I always have. Professionally and personally.'

She saw him flinch, and cringed, mortified. She hadn't meant to say that. It had just slipped out. But it was too late to take it back now.

'OK,' he said quietly. 'If that really is your decision, then so be it.'

After a moment's hesitation, he extended his hands to her. She put hers into them reluctantly. His skin was still cold but she could feel the strength of his fingers. He drew her to him, held her against him briefly.

'I wish you well, Jennifer Carter,' he murmured into her hair. 'Always.'

Then he released her, picked up his gloves, walked back along the passage and let himself out of the front door.

Louise hated hospitals. The weeks she had endured at the Wilhelmina Hospital at Clapham Junction after the Balham bomb had left her with a desire never to set foot in one again.

But now she had to face up to visiting Doris, and she was nervous. What if Doris blamed her for the accident? What if she had lost her eye? And what if she didn't believe her when she told her what she thought had really happened?

In normal circumstances on an unexpected day off Louise might have gone shopping in the West End, but all she had felt capable of doing that Saturday morning was worry. She hadn't slept well. Her dreams had been haunted by Doris's bleeding face. Waking at four, she had lain for hours in the pitch darkness, thinking.

On her way to the hospital, she had called in at her mother's café to buy a bun or a slice of cake to smuggle into the Wilhelmina for Doris. Apart from the agony, the surly nurses and the boredom, Louise's one abiding memory of being in hospital was the ghastly food. Whatever state Doris turned out to be in, she was sure she would appreciate something tasty to eat.

The café was busy, the windows running with condensation. There was no sign of her mother or Mrs Carter, but Angie Carter, flushed in the fuggy heat, was doing something to the tea urn at the counter. 'Hi, Louise,' she said. 'Where've you been hiding? I haven't seen you in the pub for days. I hope you aren't avoiding us.'

Louise stared at her suspiciously. Was the blasted girl trying to discomfit her? Had Katy told everyone what had happened? But no, there was no guile in Angie. Not like her spiteful sister.

'No,' she said. 'Of course not. It's just that I've been busy with other things.' Like sitting at home listening to the wireless with her parents for nights on end, she thought resentfully.

'That's a shame.' Angie gave a conspiratorial giggle. 'Don't tell Katy, but there was much quicker service at the bar when you were working there.'

Somewhat mollified by the comment, Louise bought a slice of Mrs Carter's Victoria sponge and asked Angie to wrap it up in a piece of newspaper so she could conceal it from the eagle-eyed nurses at the

41

Wilhelmina.

Then, taking a deep breath, she walked up the road to the hospital.

Doris was sitting up in bed with a thick bandage dressing over her eye. As Louise hurried up the ward towards her, her shoes squeaking nervously on the well-scrubbed linoleum, she suddenly felt rather faint. Had Doris lost her eye?

But no, in the scheme of things, Doris had been lucky. The piece of swarf had missed her eye by a fraction of an inch. The eyeball was undamaged, but the lid had needed four stitches.

'I'm going to end up with a bit of a scar,' Doris said, peering unnervingly at Louise with her one good eye. 'But that's not too serious. I don't think it will mar my beauty, do you?'

Louise knew she was meant to laugh. For all her good points, Doris was certainly no beauty. But the last thing she felt like doing was laughing. Instead, with a furtive glance around the ward, she handed over the cake.

'Coo, you're an angel,' Doris whispered, and tucked in with alacrity.

'Mr Gregg doesn't think so,' Louise said. 'You know he's blaming me for what happened. He accused me of leaving a bit of swarf on the belt. I know I didn't. But he wouldn't listen to me. He sent me straight home. I'm sure he's going to sack me.'

Doris paused in mid-bite. 'He can't sack you if it wasn't your fault.'

'I think he will. He was absolutely furious. Mind you. I was terribly rude to him. I called him a stupid lemon. But he was just standing there not doing anything and you were bleeding to death on the floor.'

Doris gave a snort of laughter. 'He probably only sent you home because he thought you'd start spouting off about not normally using the protective guards. He had to do something in front of his important visitors. Make it look as if he was in charge.'

'He *is* in charge.'

'Well, yes.' Doris waved her hand dismissively. 'But even so. It was just one of those freak accidents. The irony is that if he hadn't made us put those damn guards back up, it would never have happened.'

Louise hesitated, then lowered her voice. 'I don't think it was an accident,' she said. 'I think someone put a piece of swarf on our belt deliberately.' She saw Doris's good eye widen and drew her chair closer to the bed. 'I think it was sabotage.'

Doris gave an incredulous gasp and began to choke on a crumb.

Louise waited impatiently for the spasm to pass. 'I've thought about it endlessly,' she said. 'There's no other explanation.'

Doris was staring at her through a watering eye. 'So who do you think it was?' she asked reluctantly.

This was the moment Louise had been working up to all day. 'I think it was Don Wellington.'

'Oh come on, Louise.' Doris groaned and lay back on her pillows. 'Just because you don't like him …'

Louise leaned forward urgently. She was convinced she was right. 'But don't you remember, he was late coming into lunch? I think he wanted our machine to go wrong to make us look bad, so he'd get the new work. I'm not saying he expected anyone to get injured, but—'

Doris held up her hand. 'Do you have any real proof?'

'Well, no,' Louise admitted. 'But—'

'Then don't point the finger,' Doris said. 'Everyone knows you don't like him. They'll think you're trying to shunt the blame. And that won't do you any good at all.'

Louise's shoulders slumped. 'But it's not fair. He—'

'Nothing in life is fair,' Doris interrupted sharply. 'Especially not for women. The sooner you learn that the better.' She brushed some crumbs off the stiffly starched sheet. 'Just take the rap with good grace, Louise. I'm sure Mr Gregg isn't going to sack you. But he will if you give him any lip.'

'What if I could prove it?'

'You can't prove it.' Doris said. 'So keep your mouth shut. Especially if, or more likely *when*, Don Wellington tries to rile you. Just for once, do yourself a favour, and don't rise to his bait.'

Katy was feeding Caroline in her bedroom when she heard her mother's panicked voice from the bar downstairs. 'Katy! Quick, come down! Oh my goodness, Malcolm, stop it!'

Hastily disengaging the baby's greedy little mouth, Katy struggled to refasten her bra. As well as her mother's frantic cries, she could now hear an ominous growling noise. Straightening her clothes with one hand, holding the baby against her shoulder with the other, she stumbled downstairs.

The scene that greeted her made the hair prickle at the back of her neck. The growling noise was emanating from Lucky. And to be honest, even though she was still nervous of the animal, Katy didn't entirely blame him, because Malcolm was straddling him, clinging to the thick fur on his neck like a little monkey while the dog desperately tried to shake him off. More than anything it looked like a bucking bronco scene from an American Western.

'Malcolm climbed onto him when he was asleep,' her mother shrieked in horror. 'And when Lucky stood up, he didn't let go. I'm sure he's going to get bitten. Stop it, Lucky, stop!' But the dog didn't stop, and as Katy took a step forward, her mother grabbed a soda siphon and began spraying wildly in the general direction of the dog.

Unfortunately it was Malcolm who got the full blast of the water, straight in his little face, and at once he did let go, flying off the dog's back and skidding away on the wet floor, behind one of the old leather chairs by the fireplace.

Momentarily there was silence, then Lucky bounded back towards the prostrate child. At once Malcolm started screaming.

'Oh my God,' Katy whispered. All she could see was Lucky's sturdy rear end, his tail quivering aggressively, and Malcolm's little legs thrashing about under him.

Almost throwing the baby into her mother's arms, Katy ran round to the other side of the chair, fully expecting to have to prise the dog's fangs from Malcolm's throat. 'Get off him!' she shouted.

But as she leaned down to try and drag Malcolm away from under the slavering animal, she realised that the little boy wasn't screaming in pain or fear; he was screaming with hysterical delight, trying to stop Lucky licking his face.

'Again, again,' he shouted, scrambling to his feet and making a grab for Lucky's collar.

The relief was so intense that for a horrible second, Katy thought she was going to black out.

'No,' she said, catching his arm. 'No, Malcolm. It's dangerous. You must be more careful with him. He didn't like it.'

'He did like it,' Malcolm insisted, trying to wriggle out of her grasp. 'He want to do it again.'

'No he doesn't,' Katy said. She glanced at the dog and was unnerved to find him watching her beadily, his head slightly on one side, ears pricked, panting. She took one look at his huge teeth and lolling tongue and shuddered. 'He was growling,' she said.

'He was playing,' Malcolm insisted.

'That animal ought to be kept outside,' Mary Parsons said. 'Tied up.'

'No.' Malcolm turned on her angrily, stamping his foot. 'Lucky stay here. Lucky good dog.'

Katy groaned. Secretly she agreed with her mother. But Ward had other ideas. Part of his reason for bringing Lucky back from Corsica had been to provide Katy with a guard dog. 'There's no point shutting him in the yard,' he'd said. 'I want him around so people know he's here.' If only Molly would come home, Katy thought now, as her hammering heart finally began to subside. Her friend Molly Coogan had been in the same prisoner-of-war camp in Italy as Jen. But instead of coming straight back to England, Molly had diverted to Tunisia to visit another mutual friend, Helen de Burrel.

By training Molly was a nurse, but she much preferred working at the pub, and she was going to be a godsend when Ward went away. Molly was calm and practical. She would know how to steady Katy's mother. She would help keep Malcolm out of trouble. She might even know how to deal with Lucky. Katy could hardly wait for her to get back.

She had barely had the thought when Lucky pricked up his ears and started barking. A moment later there was a tap at the door.

Dropping Malcolm's arm, Katy stepped forward, but Lucky got there first, his hackles rising.

Katy backed away nervously. 'Mummy, can you hold him back while I open the door?'

'I'm not touching him,' Mary Parsons said.

But Malcolm of course had no such qualms. Flinging his arms round Lucky's neck, he pushed the dog out of Katy's way.

The post girl was standing outside. 'Blimey,' she said, flinching back as she caught sight of the animal. 'What have you got there? A wolf?'

'It's our new dog,' Katy said. 'He's not as fierce as he looks.'

The girl seemed unconvinced. 'Here,' she said, delving in her leather sack. 'This is for you. From Tunisia.'

She eyed Katy expectantly, but Katy had become uneasily aware that milk had begun to seep through her jersey, so she took the flimsy airmail lettercard and retreated indoors.

Dear Katy,

I'm sorry I haven't written before, but so much has happened since I got here, far too much to put in a letter, and I thought I'd be home before a letter arrived anyway. But now something else has unexpectedly cropped up. Helen told me that your mother is staying with you, and that you have new staff, so maybe you no longer need me at the Flag and Garter? The thing is that I've been offered a job at one of the military hospitals here. They are starting some penicillin trials and (can you believe it?) they want my 'expertise'!!

But I don't want to let you down. So you MUST say if you need me. If you do, then send me a telegram c/o Helen and I'll take the first ship.

With all my love to you and to everyone, especially Jen, Ward, Malcolm, the Nelsons, and the new baby. I miss you all.

Molly

Katy leaned weakly forward on the table. She had never imagined that Molly, who had always hated nursing, could sound so excited about a hospital job.

If only Ward wasn't going away. If only her mother was stronger. If only Malcolm was less boisterous. If only she could afford more staff. If only…

But she knew she couldn't possibly ask Molly to come back, not when she was clearly enjoying Tunisia so much.

She heard a gasp of dismay and lifted her head just in time to see Malcolm reaching up to pull the soda siphon off the table where her mother had left it.

'No,' she said. 'Malcolm, NO!'

But she was too late. His little fingers were already pressing down on the lever.

His aim was good. He had clearly inherited that from his father as well. Katy could only watch in horror as the powerful squirt of water hit her mother right in the face.

As Mary stumbled back in shock, Katy ran over and grabbed the baby out of her arms.

'I'm so sorry,' she said. 'I don't know why he's being so naughty.'

But her mother was already weeping. 'I can't take much more,' she said. 'Sometimes I think that child really hates me.'

It went sorely against the grain, but Louise took Doris's advice, and when she meekly presented herself at Mr Gregg's office on Monday morning, she made no mention of her suspicions of sabotage.

To her relief, it was clear that Larry Gregg wasn't going to sack her. But nor was he going to let her off lightly. 'You knew we were trying to make a good impression,' he said. 'And not only did you cause a rumpus to end all rumpuses, you didn't show the proper respect.'

'I'm sorry,' Louise said humbly. 'I promise it won't happen again.'

But he didn't seem mollified. 'I can assure you that if you ever speak to me like that again, you will be out on your ear, young lady, make no mistake about it.'

And of course he took the opportunity to dock her pay.

Back on the line, the reaction of her co-workers was mixed. Some felt she had been unfairly treated; others seemed astonished that she still had a job.

Louise kept a close eye on Don Wellington. She had hoped he would look guilty or penitent, but he seemed exactly the same as always, with his smarmy, self-satisfied expression, his slightly too natty clothes and his over-oiled hair.

Inevitably it was Mrs Gibbons who was the most outspoken about the incident.

'Larry Gregg had to blame you,' she murmured, sitting down next to Louise during the lunch break. 'Because if it was a genuine accident, he'd have to pay compensation. What's more, when there's been an injury in the workplace, there's meant to be an investigation. He'd never have got away with docking a union man's pay without a proper investigation.'

46

Louise was shocked. 'Is that true?'

'Of course it's true,' Mrs Gibbons said. 'And you just wait and see what happens next week if Larry Gregg wins his precious new military contract. It'll be the men who get offered those better-paid jobs. Us girls will be told we don't have the appropriate skills.'

Louise jumped as someone chuckled, and swinging round, she discovered that Don Wellington was standing right behind them, blatantly listening to their conversation.

'What are you on about now, Mrs Gibbons?' he asked. 'Equal rights for women, is it?' He patted Louise on the shoulder in what she considered to be an overfamiliar way. 'You better watch out, darling. She'll be signing you up for the Communist Party if you're not careful. And I don't think Daddy would approve of that.'

Louise gritted her teeth. 'No, he wouldn't,' she said. 'But then I don't think he'd approve of someone signing up for factory work when he could be fighting for his country either.' And was pleased to see a spot of colour flare in his cheeks.

Mrs Gibbons gave a chortle of malicious laughter. 'Yes, why haven't you been called up, Don?' she asked. 'You look perfectly fit to me.'

'I've got flat feet,' he said.

That made Mrs Gibbons laugh even more. 'Well surely they could equip you with some flat boots?'

'You three will all get a boot up the backside if you don't get back to work,' the foreman shouted suddenly from the doorway. 'Didn't you hear the whistle?'

It didn't take long for Jen to start regretting what she'd said to Henry on Saturday. Even if she was too scared to marry him, the truth was that without his professional help, she was completely adrift. One way or another he had provided her with all her theatrical work for the last couple of years.

On Monday morning she'd gone to the library to look at the casting ads in *The Stage* magazine. All she could find was a part in a play she had never heard of in Bristol, and a repertory job in Edinburgh. She'd dutifully sent off letters, but neither of them had so far elicited any response.

The next step would be to start calling at production offices and theatres. It had been a long time since she had had to knock on doors looking for work, and the thought filled her with dread. But she had made her bed, she told herself, and now she had to lie on it.

But before she could do that, she received a nasty shock. Returning home from another abortive visit to the library late on Friday afternoon, she found a buff-coloured OHMS envelope lying on the doormat. Inside was an official notice from the Ministry of Labour and National Service.

To Miss Jennifer Carter

It has come to our attention that, despite being between the ages of 19 and 43, you are not currently registered for National Service. Unless you are already serving in the armed forces, or engaged in other bona fide defence activity, you are required to present yourself for interview at the York Road labour exchange on Wednesday 26 January at 9 a.m. You should be aware that failure to comply with this instruction is a punishable offence under The Emergency Powers (Defence) Act 1939.

As she stared in horror at the flimsy piece of paper, she heard an eerie wail start up somewhere in the distance. She felt her blood run cold. It was a noise she hadn't heard for a long time.

An air-raid siren. She had thought those were a thing of the past, in Clapham at least. In Berlin they probably sounded all the time.

Numbly she glanced at the peg behind the door where they used to keep their gas masks during the Blitz. There were two boxes hanging there. Presumably her mother's and Angie's. Her own gas mask had been lost with all her other possessions when the MS *Marigold* went down in the Mediterranean. Since Hitler and the Luftwaffe had turned their attentions to Russia, nobody seemed to bother with gas masks in London any more, so Jen hadn't made any effort to get it replaced.

She dithered for a long moment, heart hammering, wondering what to do, then made her decision. She certainly didn't want to sit in the perishing cold Anderson shelter in the garden with just her mother's hibernating tortoise for company. Nor did she want to go to the ghastly public air-raid shelter up on Clapham Common.

Grabbing one of the gas masks, she turned off the light in the hall and let herself back out of the front door. It was dark outside in the street and she could see the beams of light from the ack-ack searchlights up on the common criss-crossing the sky. Down the street in the other direction she could hear running feet, and someone shouting that planes were approaching. Dimly she recognised the voice of Mr Broome, the local air-raid warden.

And sure enough, even as she sprinted across the road, she began to hear the distant throb of aircraft engines.

The door of the pub was shut and locked and she banged on it frantically. 'Katy,' she shouted. 'Ward? Elsa? Can you hear me? It's me, Jen. For God's sake, let me in. I want to come and shelter with you in the cellar.'

Chapter Five

That night, two hundred and sixty-eight tons of bombs were dropped on London. The next few nights were equally bad. Nobody knew whether Hitler had finally decided to retaliate for the devastation the RAF was wreaking on Berlin and other German industrial cities, or if he was trying to disrupt plans for an early invasion of France. Whatever his motivation, he was clearly determined to give it his all.

By the end of January, the papers were calling it the mini Blitz. But there didn't seem anything very mini about it in south London. Where the bombs landed, the damage was extensive.

Amazingly, in those first few days, the only fatality in Clapham was an unfortunate man who was killed when the nose cap fell off an anti-aircraft shell fired from the gun emplacement on the common, the fuse exploding right on top of the Anderson shelter in his back garden. Elsewhere someone on fire watch had his arm severed by a segment of burning shell casing.

The following day, the local Home Guard company was tasked with taking over the manning of the anti-aircraft guns on Clapham Common from the Royal Artillery, releasing the regular soldiers for service overseas. Greville Rutherford was cock-a-hoop. At last the Home Guard ack-ack training would come into its own.

'Now we'll see what's what,' he said at supper that night. 'This will sort the men from the boys.'

'What about the girls?' Louise asked. 'Won't the ATS still be dealing with the searchlights and barrage balloons?'

He gave a sharp laugh. 'Not if I have anything to do with it. No, if we're going to do the job, we are going to do it properly.'

'I wonder how many bombers you'll bring down,' Louise said.

Her father looked irritated. 'I'm afraid you are betraying your ignorance, young lady. Do you realise how difficult it is to bring down a moving target with a heavy gun?'

'Well, no,' Louise said. 'But surely—'

'Well until you do understand what you're talking about, I suggest you don't pass comment,' he snapped. 'Our role is not to shoot them down but to put up sufficient flak to prevent them finding their targets.'

'So they drop their bombs any old where instead?' Louise suggested.

He was not amused. 'So they turn tail and flee.' He pierced a piece of sausage out of his toad in the hole and eyed it with relish. 'And I can assure you that with the Home Guard manning those guns, Jerry will soon notice the difference.'

But whether Jerry noticed the difference or not, over the next few nights the sirens kept on sounding and the bombs kept on falling. There certainly didn't seem to be much fleeing going on.

Even the excitement of the news that British and American troops had made a successful landing at Anzio in Italy was overshadowed by the relentless Luftwaffe assault on London. Italy didn't seem very important when you were spending every night huddled in a damp Anderson shelter or, in Louise's case, on an old mattress in the cellar of her parents' house, knowing that the moment she closed her eyes, the gun barrage would inevitably start again.

And on top of the possibility of being bombed at home, there was also the worry that the factory would get hit, which would put the kibosh on being selected to work on the new contract Mr Gregg was so eagerly anticipating.

So far the factory had survived intact, but every morning as she turned the corner on St John's Road and looked down the hill, she fully expected to see it in ruins.

Jen, on the other hand, had been hoping that a bomb would fall on the Battersea labour exchange.

She had barely had a wink of sleep since that first air raid. She had thought that sheltering with Katy and Ward in the pub cellar would be better than shivering in her mother's Anderson shelter in the back yard. But she hadn't taken into account Malcolm, who refused to go to sleep, Katy's mother, who wept and wailed every time they heard the guns, or Lucky, who prowled round the cellar like a caged tiger.

On balance she decided that the Anderson shelter was the lesser of two evils, but then she had to put up with Angie's incessant speculation about when Gino might be able to come back.

'I thought you had your heart set on an American?' Jen remarked at one point during a lull.

Angie's giggle was so loud that Jen worried the Luftwaffe pilots might hear it. 'Well, I do want to find a nice American,' she admitted. 'But only for stockings, and candy, and maybe a bit of dancing. My heart will always be Gino's.'

All in all, on the morning of her interview Jen was barely in a fit state to walk down to York Road, let alone fight her corner with the tough old biddy of an employment officer, who seemed entirely unimpressed by the fact that she had been languishing in an Italian prisoner-of-war camp for much of the previous year.

'Even if that's true,' the woman said, 'I am afraid it's irrelevant. You're not in a prison camp now, are you? You are therefore eligible for immediate conscription.'

Jen had a vision of some ghastly sergeant major marching in and bundling her off to the nearest military barracks. 'But surely I get a bit of grace,' she said desperately. 'I've only been home a few weeks.'

The woman raised her thin eyebrows. 'A few weeks?' she said. 'A few weeks off is a lot more than our gallant soldiers get.' She put on a pair of glasses and thumbed through some documents. 'There's a vacancy for a machine tool operator at Gregg Brothers,' she said.

Gregg's? Jen recoiled in alarm. That was where Louise worked. 'Oh no,' she said hastily. 'I don't want to go there.' She couldn't think of anything worse. Not only did factory work sound awful, but Louise would make her life a misery. Especially after their spat in the pub. It had been typical of Louise to get so hoity-toity about it.

Katy, of course, had tried to make amends, but then Katy had always been too soft on Louise. As far as Jen was concerned, Louise needed to be taught a lesson. Just because she lived in a big house and her father owned the brewery, she thought she was Lady Muck. And Jen was damned if she was going to give her a chance to lord it over her in the factory.

The woman pursed her lips. 'You will go where I send you,' she said. 'That is what conscription means.'

'But I'd much rather do something in Civil Defence,' Jen pleaded desperately.

The woman eyed her narrowly, then stood up and handed her a small docket. 'In that case,' she said. 'You will report to the WVS office on Lavender Hill at two p.m. on Friday. Ask for a Mrs Rutherford.'

Joyce was clearing up in the café when Mr Lorenz touched her on the elbow. She hadn't noticed him come in, and jumped, nearly spilling the contents of the tray she was carrying.

'Blimey,' she said. 'You gave me a turn.' She felt a stab of anxiety. 'You don't normally come in at this time of day. Has something happened?'

'No, no,' he reassured her hastily. 'Nothing's happened. Nothing bad, at least.' A tinge of colour stained his cheeks. 'I was just wondering if you might be able to join me at the Flag and Garter this evening for a little celebration?'

'Goodness,' Joyce said. 'What are you celebrating?' There wasn't much to celebrate at the moment as far as she was concerned. Not with this renewed night-time bombing. There wasn't much to celebrate in the wider war either, as far as she could see. Half the Allied forces were still stuck at Monte Cassino, and the other half were battling away to hold their position at Anzio, which had turned out not to be such an immediate success after all.

And goodness alone knew what horrors were going on in the Far East, with those nasty slitty-eyed Japanese. Admittedly there was news that the Russians had finally managed to break the siege at Leningrad, but not before well over a million people had either been killed or had died of starvation. There had been one report the previous winter that the inhabitants had even started eating each other.

Unaware of her melancholy thoughts, Mr Lorenz leaned forward and rested his hands on the counter. 'I have received word that a young cousin of mine is alive and well,' he said. 'I hadn't heard anything of him since he was captured in Poland by the Russians at the beginning of the war. Of course I had feared the worst. The Russians are not very much more sympathetic towards Jews than the Germans. But now it seems that a few months ago a number of the surviving Polish prisoners were deported to North Africa.'

'Blimey,' Joyce said. 'So where is he now?'

'In Scotland,' Mr Lorenz said. 'He's been sent to join one of the free Polish regiments, which are preparing for the invasion of France.' He shrugged self-deprecatingly. 'It perhaps doesn't seem much, but so many of my relatives have perished, it is worthy of a small celebration to hear of one who has survived.'

Joyce felt torn. 'The thing is, I really need to do some cooking for tomorrow,' she said. 'There's quite a few locally without electric after the raid last night, and they came piling in here for lunch and cleaned us out. I was hoping to do it this afternoon, but Mrs Rutherford has been off on WVS business and Angie and I have been run off our feet all day.'

'Of course, of course,' Mr Lorenz said at once. 'I understand. I don't want to take up your precious time.' But he couldn't hide his disappointment, and Joyce felt guilty.

'I tell you what,' she said. 'Why don't you fetch a glass of something from the pub and we'll have a little private celebration here while I'm cooking?'

At once his kindly face lit up. 'Well, if you are sure? That would indeed be delightful.'

Gratified, Joyce gave him a sly wink. 'And as Mrs Rutherford's not here to notice, I don't see why we shouldn't have a little bit of supper while we're at it. Just you and me. Do you like pilchard pie?'

When Pam Nelson opened the door to find Mrs Rutherford standing on her front step, she was certain that she had come to complain about George. She

52

knew he had been over the wall again, because she had found brick-coloured scuff marks on his trousers, and she prayed that Mrs Rutherford hadn't caught him raiding her apple store, or worse, stealing her precious eggs.

But no, Mrs Rutherford had called with her WVS hat on, and she wanted to enlist Pam's support.

'There are so many things we need to do,' she said gaily. 'We need people to man the emergency canteen, to find temporary accommodation for those whose houses have been damaged. We need help with sorting out donated clothes, with our laundry service, with encouraging people to donate blood, and if this beastly bombing goes on much longer, we may need to start evacuating the children all over again.'

'But …' Pam began, gaping at her in amazement.

'No buts, Mrs Nelson. We all have to do our bit. And the WVS needs all the help it can get.'

Catching sight of George lurking behind Pam in the doorway, Mrs Rutherford leaned forward. 'And what about you, young man?' she asked with a patronising smile. 'Are you doing your bit? We call children our little salvage cogs. We ask them to collect old pieces of metal, material, even unwanted books. The WVS is like a great big machine, you see, designed to help the war effort, and the things you collect will go into making new weapons for our brave soldiers overseas.'

'How do you make a weapon out of a book?' George asked.

Mrs Rutherford drew herself up to her full height. 'It's not your job to ask questions,' she said repressively. 'It's your job to collect as much salvage as you can. We are going to give prizes to whoever collects the most.'

'What are the prizes?'

'George!' Pam admonished.

He looked up at her, surprised. 'Well I don't want to do it if the prize isn't any good. If it was something like a go at firing a gun, or a ride on a tank, then it might be worth it.'

'It would be worth it whatever the prize,' Pam said firmly. 'It's not the prize that matters; it's the contribution you are making to the war effort.'

'That's the spirit,' Mrs Rutherford said. She cast an admonitory glance at George and then turned back to Pam. 'So, Mrs Nelson? What can I put you down for?'

'Well the thing is, I've got the baby, and—'

But Mrs Rutherford wasn't having any of that. 'There are plenty of things one can do even with a baby.'

So it was that when Alan came home from work in the gathering dusk, he found Pam painting their house number on the pavement outside the front gate.

'What on earth are you doing?'

Pam sat back on her haunches, surveying her handiwork. 'Mrs Rutherford asked me to do it. It's a WVS task. In case we get bombed. She brought me the paint and everything. Apparently some streets have been so heavily hit that the wardens can't work out which house is which, so they don't know who to search for.' She grimaced. 'I've got to do the whole street. But it's back-breaking work.'

Alan smiled sympathetically and helped her to her feet. 'Well, I've got something to cheer you up.' He delved in his pocket. 'Three tickets for *Dick Whittington* at the Grand, Clapham Junction. Someone at work had them going spare. I thought it would be a nice treat for George.'

'But what about Nellie?' Pam asked.

Carefully stepping over the paint on the pavement, Alan steered her into the house. 'Katy's offered to have her at the pub. Apparently Mrs Parsons spends every evening in the cellar with Malcolm and the baby. So Nellie can stay down there with them.'

Pam didn't like it. Mrs Parsons was such a hopeless, panicky woman. But Katy would be there too. And Ward Frazer, with any luck. Surely Nellie would be safe there for a couple of hours?

'I just can't believe it,' Jen wailed, leaning over the bar while Katy reluctantly poured her a stiff whisky. 'How can I be so unlucky? A choice between being at the beck and call of Mrs Rutherford and her frumpy old WVS biddies, or working in the same factory as Louise. And if I don't take one or other option, I'll get thrown into jail for contravening the National Service Act.'

'I must admit, I can't see you enjoying Louise's factory,' Katy said. 'If nothing else, you'd get oil under your fingernails. But you never know, Mrs Rutherford might give you something to do that you'd enjoy.'

'Like what?' Jen took a glug of the whisky. 'Painting house numbers on the pavement like Pam Nelson? Or sorting through filthy old clothes for bomb victims?' She shuddered. 'I can't think of anything worse.'

Katy smiled. 'You could always join the forces. The WAAF uniform looks very smart on the posters. Much nicer than the ATS one.'

Jen stared at her. Surely she wasn't being serious? 'Can you imagine me square-bashing and saluting and doing physical jerks?'

'Well, no,' Katy admitted. She had picked up a cloth, but now she hesitated. Instead of wiping the counter, she lifted her eyes to Jen's.

'What?' Jen asked suspiciously. 'What are you thinking?'

'Well, there is one other option.' Katy said. 'ENSA counts as National Service.'

Jen held her gaze for a long moment, then looked away. She had been trying not to think about that other option all day. 'I can't,' she said. 'I just can't. I can't go crawling back to him and ask him for a job. How would it look?'

'It's not ideal,' Katy admitted. 'But I honestly think Henry is the only person who can get you out of this fix. If you explained to the labour exchange woman that you were rejoining ENSA, you'd be off the hook.'

'But I'd be back on Henry's hook instead.'

'I can think of worse hooks to be on,' Katy said drily.

Jen threw her a hostile look. 'That's easy for you to say when you've already got such a lovely husband.' Then she saw Katy's face. 'I'm sorry,' she said contritely. 'I'd forgotten he was about to go away.' Katy always got in a state when Ward left on one of his secret missions. 'Obviously that is a drawback. But you have to admit it adds to his glamour. And let's face it. It's scary times for all of us at the moment. One shell landing in the wrong place and that could be the end of any of us. Or all of us, come to that.'

Katy frowned and looked over her shoulder nervously. 'Don't say that in my mother's hearing,' she said. 'I've been trying to convince her that the cellar is completely bombproof and that we can all feel more confident now that Mr Rutherford is in charge of the anti-aircraft guns on the common.'

Jen rolled her eyes. 'That doesn't fill me with confidence at all,' she said 'It would have been better if they'd sent the pompous old fool over to Germany to fire one of his guns right up Hitler's—' She heard a gurgle of laughter and swung round to find George Nelson standing behind her.

He gave her a naughty grin. 'I know what you were going to say,' he said. 'And it's rude.'

'You have no idea what I was going to say,' Jen said.

'I do so. You said you wanted Mr Rutherford to go and fire a gun up Mr Hitler's—'

'What are you doing here anyway?' Jen interrupted hastily. 'You are far too young to be in a pub.'

'We're going to the theatre to see *Dick Whittington*,' he said.

'Shame you aren't going to see *Puss in Boots*,' she said. 'Because you are definitely getting too big for yours.'

George bridled. 'At least I don't say rude words, like pompous and …'

But to Jen's relief, Pam and Alan arrived then with a sleeping baby Nellie, and the chance for any further pleasantries was lost in the bustle of getting the pram down the cellar steps. It took some time for Pam to brief Katy on every last detail of Nellie's care, but eventually she was satisfied and they re-emerged up the stairs.

'She'll be safe down there,' Katy said reassuringly as she ushered them all towards the door.

'Oh yes, the cellar is completely bombproof,' George said, materialising suspiciously from the back yard with an innocent smile on his face.

'That child is a precocious brat,' Jen said when they'd finally gone.

'I think he's cute,' Katy said. 'And Malcolm adores him.'

She had barely uttered the words when they caught sight of Malcolm coming through the back door, dragging Lucky behind him. The unfortunate dog was wearing one of Katy's mother's old-fashioned felt hats.

Jen couldn't help but laugh. Lucky looked just like the wolfy grandmother in 'Little Red Riding Hood'. But the neat bow under his jaw certainly hadn't been tied by two-year-old Malcolm's chubby little fingers.

Jen turned to Katy. 'And how cute do you think George is now?' she asked. 'Your mother is going to have a fit.'

Mr Lorenz didn't go to the pub to get drinks. Instead he brought a bottle of red wine someone had left in hock at his shop and never redeemed. Or so he said. It seemed an unlikely story, but Joyce wasn't going to complain. She hadn't seen a bottle of wine since the beginning of the war. The only problem was that she didn't have any wine glasses.

But Albert seemed to think water glasses would do just as well, and once they had toasted the safe arrival in Scotland of his oddly named relative, Leszek Zemniak, Joyce settled him down at one of the tables with the racing pages of the evening paper while she prepared her ingredients.

'I'm worried about these Yanks,' she called through as she carefully sieved the flour through an old pair of Jen's nylons to extract the bran. You couldn't get refined white flour for love or money these days, so she was stuck with using National Flour, but her cakes rose much better without the bran, and it came in handy as extra feed for Mrs Rutherford's chickens. 'Some of their soldiers are black, apparently,' she added. 'And can you believe it? The council has sent us a leaflet on how to deal with them.'

Leaving her mixture to settle, she pulled the offending leaflet out from behind the till.

'*You may be aware that segregation is a fact of life in America,*' she read out. '*Their attitude to coloured people is different from our own. Therefore if white Americans are present in a canteen or bar, you should make it your business to discourage Negro Americans from coming in at the same time.*' She looked up. 'What do you think about that? I think it's a cheek. Just because some of the Yanks are prejudiced against blackies, there's no reason why we should be.'

Albert nodded. 'Quite right, Mrs Carter,' he said. 'I admire your egalitarian spirit.'

'And listen to this.' Joyce continued reading. '*For example, for a white English girl to go about in the company of a Negro would be likely to lead to controversy. And might be misconstrued by the Negro himself.'*

She paused, remembering that last night in the pub she had overheard some self-appointed wit holding forth about the inadequacy of Utility knickers. 'Haven't you heard?' he'd said. 'One Yank and they're off.'

'Oh dear,' she said now. 'I hope Angie doesn't try to persuade some poor unsuspecting Negro to give her nylons or Hershey chocolate bars. Goodness knows what he might construe from that.'

But Albert just smiled reassuringly. 'I am sure he would construe exactly the same as a white man,' he said. 'That she is a lively young lady currently deprived of some of life's little pleasures.'

Joyce eyed him dubiously. 'As long as it's only little pleasures she's after,' she said darkly. 'Although on balance I think I'd rather she fell in love with a Negro than that miserable little specimen Gino.'

He laughed. 'Come, come, Mrs Carter, who's being prejudiced now?'

Joyce folded the offending leaflet and tucked it back behind the till. 'I suppose we're all prejudiced against someone or other,' she admitted, heading back into the kitchen to get the cakes in the oven. 'If it's not the Italians, it's the Irish, or blacks, or women.'

'Or Jews,' Albert murmured drily. And he was right, Joyce thought grimly as she fetched her next batch of ingredients from the pantry. After all, as far as she knew, even Hitler wasn't deliberately killing women just because they were women.

By the time she had prepared her pie fillings, her thoughts had moved on to Jen. 'She's mad to have turned that Henry Keller down,' she said. 'I don't know where she thinks she's going to get another man as nice as that.'

But Albert seemed inclined to be sympathetic. 'Perhaps she just needs a little time to get herself back on her feet after her experiences in Italy,' he said mildly. 'It can't have been easy for her.'

'Life isn't easy,' Joyce said sourly. 'Not for people like us, at least. What she needs is to pull herself together and realise that life isn't always a bed of roses.'

'She is only young,' he said. 'We all have dreams.'

Joyce started rubbing lard into the flour. 'What more can she possibly want than a nice, kind man who is in love with her?'

'What indeed?'

The dry question caused Joyce's hands to freeze in the bowl. Oh no, she thought. He had led her straight into a trap. Or maybe she had fallen into a trap of her own making.

She lifted her hands out of the bowl and felt the cool lumps drop off her floury fingers. Nervously she glanced over towards the door and saw that Albert was watching her with his glass in his hand and a fond smile on his face.

She felt her heart give a little kick. Maybe he was right. Maybe it was time to let their relationship move forward. Maybe now she had managed to get rid of Gino, they might even be able to take that holiday together.

She saw his colour rise slightly and realised that she was smiling back at him.

And then, unexpectedly, he stood up.

Apprehensively Joyce took a quick glug of her wine. What was he doing? Surely he wasn't about to try and embrace her? Not with her hands all covered with flour.

But he wasn't coming into the kitchen; he was looking away towards the front door of the café.

And now, over the hum of the oven, she too heard someone knocking.

There was a moment's pause, then Albert glanced back at her. 'Should I open it?'

Joyce nodded. 'But turn out the light first,' she said. 'The ARP post is on the other side of the road, and there's nothing Mr Broome would like more than to fine me for showing a light.'

He did as instructed, and a moment later two young men stepped into the café.

As Albert closed the door behind them and switched the light back on, Joyce was appalled to see that one of them was Gino. The other was a big, strapping lad dressed in rough country clothes. He was so big and strapping, in fact, that it took her a moment to recognise him. Surely it couldn't be …?

But yes, now that she looked at him more closely, this hulking great boy had the unmistakable unruly hair and freckly features of her youngest son, Paul. But what on earth was he doing here? He was meant to be in Devon, on Mrs Baxter's farm, well out of harm's way.

The boy glanced uncertainly from her to Mr Lorenz. 'There was no one at home, so Gino said why didn't we try here.' To her surprise he spoke in a strong West Country accent. When Joyce didn't immediately respond, he gave a nervous smile. 'Well,' he said. 'What do you think? Here I am. Back in London at last.'

Inadvertently Joyce's eyes flicked to Mr Lorenz, who was still standing by the door. He met her look of consternation with a twinkle of humorous resignation.

Dumbly Joyce turned back to the newcomer. 'Paul?'

'Yeah,' he said. 'It's me.' He stepped over and gave her a brief, rather awkward hug. 'I thought you weren't going to recognise me.'

'Of course I recognised you,' Joyce said. 'But what on earth are you doing here?'

Paul flexed his shoulders. 'Oh that's easy,' he said. 'When Gino said he was coming back to marry Angie, I thought I might as well come with him. I've decided to join up, you see. I know I'm only fifteen, but I'm quite big, so I reckon as I'll get away with it.' He grinned eagerly, his eyes shining. 'And if I leave it much longer, I might miss the invasion.'

Chapter Six

Louise was glad that she had obeyed *Vogue*'s exhortation not to yield to carelessness by throwing away an almost empty lipstick, because in preparation for her second encounter with Mr Gregg's important visitors, she was able to paint her lips with her last scraping of Tangee's patriotic 'Lips in Uniform'.

She had also redone her fashionable pompadour and curls hairdo. And her best overalls, the ones that had got covered in blood from Doris's eye injury, had come back from the Clapham laundry just in time for her to take them to work that morning.

But when she put them on in the ladies' washroom, she caught her finger on something sharp in the pocket. Disentangling it with some difficulty from the lining, she realised it was the piece of metal that Larry Gregg had picked out of the pulley and brandished with accusatory fury after Doris's accident.

Somehow it had survived the washing and pressing process at the laundry, and now here it was, a disagreeable reminder of how one's best intentions could so easily go wrong.

As Louise glared at it balefully, a thought occurred to her.

Hurrying to her bench, she crouched down to pick up another couple of pieces of swarf off the floor and examined them closely.

The tiny metal spirals were absolutely identical to each other, but not to the piece she had found in her pocket. Reaching across, she teased a couple of old pieces out from under Doris's empty bench. They were also exactly the same as each other, but slightly different from hers, and from the piece that had caught in the pulley.

Louise frowned. It hadn't previously occurred to her that each machine operator's offcuts would be different. She stood up and studied the pieces again. It was very marginal. Just the tiniest difference in the indentation, presumably caused by a slight variation in the angle of the parting tool. Someone with less accurate eyesight would hardly be able to see it.

'What's that? What are you doing?' Don Wellington's voice cut into her thoughts.

Closing her fingers over the pieces of swarf, Louise blandly turned to face him. 'Nothing,' she said. 'I just wanted to make sure everything was spick and span for the visitors.'

He lifted his eyebrows. 'I would have thought it was a bit late for that.'

Louise frowned. 'What do you mean?'

'Didn't you know? Mr Gregg has put up a list of the people he's recommending. And your name isn't on it.'

'What?' Louise stared at him aghast. 'Why not?'

He gave a complacent laugh. 'Presumably because of what happened last time they were here.'

But when Louise cornered Larry Gregg in his office a few minutes later, it turned out that wasn't the reason. The reason he hadn't put her forward was because she was a girl.

Louise couldn't believe her ears. It was just as Mrs Gibbons had predicted.

'Well what did you expect?' he said. 'It's a military contract. They're not going to want girls, are they? In any case, you're too late. I've already briefed the candidates.'

But Louise was fed up with his thoughtless chauvinism. 'Have they actually told you they don't want girls?' she asked grittily.

Larry Gregg looked peeved. 'Not in so many words,' he said. 'But surely you wouldn't want to—'

'You have no idea what I would or wouldn't want,' Louise interrupted. 'But I'm pretty sure *you* wouldn't want a visit from the Ministry of Labour. For example, I'm sure they'd be interested to learn that we don't normally use the safety guards.'

She was gratified to see him blanch. 'Oh come on,' he said. 'Nobody would take any notice of you.'

Louise pressed home her advantage. 'No, perhaps not. Because I'm just a girl. But I'm quite sure my father would know who to contact.'

Larry Gregg knew who Louise's father was. And he knew that as the owner of the Rutherford & Berry brewery, Greville Rutherford would certainly have contacts at the Ministry of Labour.

'That's blackmail,' he spluttered.

'No it's not,' Louise said. 'It's justice.'

There was a long pause, during which they both heard a vehicle drawing up outside. 'All right,' he said. 'I'll add your name to the list. If they are prepared to see you, well, that's up to them.'

Louise felt triumphant. It was nice to know that her father had his uses after all. She went to move away, but stopped and turned back to face Larry Gregg. 'And it's up to you to make sure that Doris gets some decent compensation,' she said. 'Or I will report you.'

Jen knew her way to Henry's office at the Theatre Royal, but she didn't like to go marching through without permission. Even ENSA was tight on

61

security these days. So, taking a deep breath, she poked her head into the nearest section of the partitioned lobby and asked one of the typists if she knew if Mr Keller was in.

The girl looked up. 'Do you have an appointment?'

Jen shook her head. 'No, but I'm sure he'll see me.' Or she certainly hoped he would. It hadn't taken her long to realise that rejoining ENSA was indeed her best chance of avoiding being enlisted in the WVS or some other equally unbearable National Service organisation. But now that she was here, it occurred to her that Henry could easily refuse to help her. She wouldn't blame him if he refused even to see her. After all, she had pretty much kicked him in the teeth last time they'd met.

The secretary looked somewhat doubtful too, but she obligingly took Jen's name and withdrew to another office, reappearing after a moment to say that Mr Keller was indeed prepared to see her.

Realising she had been holding her breath, Jen gave a sigh of relief. But as she made her way backstage to his office, she was conscious of feeling ridiculously nervous, and had to wait a minute or two to allow her pulse time to settle before tapping at the door.

Prior to ENSA's occupation of the theatre, Henry's office had been a dressing room. Now it was furnished with a couple of upright chairs, a clock and a large leather-topped desk covered in piles of scripts and other papers. A thin plume of blue smoke rose from a cigarette stub in the ashtray.

As soon she opened the door, Henry stood up and came round the desk to greet her. As always, he looked smooth and well groomed, and as always, his air of easy sophistication made her feel slightly cheap and tawdry. Today he was wearing a smart grey suit that had clearly been tailored to fit his well-proportioned physique. But unusually, as she had entered the room, Jen had detected weariness in his face. Or perhaps it was wariness. Either way it was quickly concealed behind his urbane good manners.

'Well,' he said, as he shut the door behind her. 'This is a surprise. A delightful surprise. But unexpected nevertheless.'

He spoke lightly, but she could hear the irony in his voice. He clearly wasn't going to make it easy for her.

'Have a seat.' He drew up a chair and held it courteously while she sat down. He stood for a moment looking down at her before returning to his own seat behind the desk.

Jen swallowed. 'This is really awkward after what I said the other day,' she began. She glanced at his face, realised she had no idea what he was thinking, and pressed on anyway. 'But I've come to ask you a favour.'

He sat back in his chair, but his eyes flicked briefly to a brass carriage clock on the windowsill. 'I see,' he said.

Jen fiddled with a loose thread from her coat. 'The thing is, I need a job.' She glanced up at him cautiously, and when he didn't respond, she tried to explain her predicament.

He heard her out in what seemed like stony silence, then stood up and went over to the window, looking out at the street below, his hands in his pockets.

'So you see,' she added lamely, 'I need to rejoin ENSA, otherwise I'm going to end up washing dirty laundry for the WVS.'

After what seemed like an eternity but was perhaps only a few seconds, he turned round. 'You don't look very well, Jen. Are you sure you're OK?'

Jen blinked. What had that got to do with anything? 'I'm fine,' she said.

He inclined his head. 'It's just that you haven't seemed quite yourself since you got back from Italy.'

To her horror, Jen felt the telltale prickle of tears. Turning her face away from him, she took a steadying breath and angrily blinked them away. She never cried. It was only because he was being nice. Well, nice-ish. Concerned at least. Which was more than most people had been. Certainly more than her mother had been.

'I'm just tired,' she said. 'I had a bad night. There was a raid.' She had, in fact, had to spend half the night crammed into the Anderson shelter with her mother, Angie and Gino, and her newly arrived younger brother. Despite the pleasure of reacquainting herself with Paul, it hadn't been an enjoyable experience. But she had told herself that if she could survive a night with Angie and Gino in an air-raid shelter, she could surely survive an interview with Henry Keller.

Now she wasn't so certain. There was something in Henry's meditative gaze that suddenly made her want to throw herself into his arms.

'Are you sure there's else nothing you'd rather do?' he asked. 'For the war effort, I mean? Something more useful?'

Jen felt a stab of panic. He didn't want her. He was going to turn her away.

Or was he just testing her? Testing her commitment?

'But ENSA *is* useful,' she said. 'It boosts the troops' morale.'

He gave a short laugh. 'You obviously haven't seen some of our recent shows.'

Jen smiled uncertainly. She knew how people sometimes interpreted the ENSA acronym. 'Every Night Something Awful?' she murmured.

'Exactly,' he said. He was silent a moment. Once again he glanced at the clock, and this time when he spoke there was a finality in his tone.

'Well I'll certainly see what I can do for you,' he said. 'But—'

'No.' Jen jumped to her feet and took an impulsive step towards him. 'The thing is …' She had been about to put a hand on his arm, but faltered, cringing inwardly at his slight, almost imperceptible recoil. He might as well have slapped her in the face. 'The thing is … I need it now, today, this morning. Otherwise I'll probably get sent to jail.'

Henry's brows rose, but otherwise he didn't move. She saw a muscle tense in his cheek. 'OK,' he said at last. 'But I want something in return.'

'What?' she asked nervously. And was surprised when he gave a faint sound of exasperation.

'I know you don't want to marry me,' he said. 'You've made that perfectly clear. But I do wish you wouldn't look at me like that.'

'Like what?'

'As though I'm going to jump on you the moment you lower your guard.' He waved his hand irritably. 'If you really want to work for me again, I want you to forget I ever mentioned the word marriage. Otherwise it's going to be a bloody nightmare for both of us.'

Jen blinked. It was unusual to hear Henry swear, but before she could respond, he had abruptly pushed back his chair and stood up. 'Wait here,' he said. 'I'll be back in a moment.'

Louise had barely got back to her workbench before the visitors were being ushered in by the foreman. It was the same three men as before. The small one looked just as shabby, but this time the older man, the one with the bristly moustache, was wearing uniform. The three pips on his shoulder and the field gun insignia on his cap badge told Louise that he was a captain in the Royal Artillery. The third man, the American who had helped her with Doris, was wearing a beige trench coat mackintosh over a smart double-breasted dark suit that made him look not altogether unlike Humphrey Bogart as Rick in *Casablanca*, one of her all-time favourite films. But before she had a chance to study him more closely, the foreman was already calling the candidates into the canteen.

Louise stepped forward eagerly, but had to wait while Larry Gregg consulted with the small scruffy man and the American. She couldn't hear exactly what they were saying, but she saw the small man glance somewhat doubtfully in her direction. In the end it was the American who made the decision, interrupting Mr Gregg with an impatient gesture of acquiescence. A minute later she too was summoned to the canteen.

There she found a dozen of her male colleagues already sitting in two neat, well-spaced lines at the trestle tables. The moustachioed artillery captain was standing up at the front by the serving counter. He had clearly been giving some kind of introductory speech, but he paused long enough to allow Louise a chance to find somewhere to sit.

After a moment's hesitation, she took the spare place next to Don

Wellington and was pleased to see him frown.

'What are you doing here?' he muttered.

She smiled. 'Mr Gregg had a change of heart.' He looked at her suspiciously, but she ignored him, although she hadn't expected Larry Gregg to capitulate so easily either. Nevertheless, she was still glowing from her success. She couldn't wait till her next visit to the Wilhelmina to tell Doris what had happened.

Belatedly she became aware that the captain had finished his introduction, and was now placing a small box in front of each candidate.

'In the box you will find the components of a small piece of equipment,' he said. 'And a diagram of the finished article. I want you to assemble it as quickly as you can. As I have already explained, we have designed a number of short exercises to ensure that we select the right people. Anyone failing to complete any of the tasks in the allotted time will be eliminated from the process.' He glanced at his watch. 'You may open the boxes now.'

Louise gazed at him in shock. Nobody had mentioned anything about tests. But obediently she lifted the lid of her box and inspected the contents. There were several short lengths of coloured wire, a silver coil, a number of metal pieces, all different shapes, a tiny glass vial, not dissimilar to the kind of thing nurses used to administer eyedrops, several microscopic nuts and bolts and a conical casing somewhat like the bottom of an ice cream cone. Her heart was already sinking like a stone as she unfolded the diagram. She had absolutely no idea what it was.

But determined not to be defeated, she laid out the pieces on the table in front of her and studied them carefully. It was relatively easy to see how certain bits fitted together, but actually fitting them was more difficult. Everything was so ridiculously small. To make things worse, the American had come into the canteen and was now patrolling around, watching what everyone was doing.

At one point he stopped on the other side of Louise's table. 'Kind of fiddly, huh?' he said when she looked up at him in despair. 'That's why we're looking for people with nimble fingers.'

'From what I've heard, she has very nimble fingers,' Don Wellington murmured from his spot further along the table. 'Isn't that right, darling?'

Louise felt sudden heat surge into her cheeks. How dare he malign her like that? He didn't know anything about her. And even if he had somehow got wind of the fact that she had had a couple of unfortunate affairs, she was hardly in the same league as Gillian James in Lavender Road, who entertained men for a living.

Her hands were shaking with fury, and a second later the fragile little glass ampoule slipped out of her grasp. Thankfully it didn't break, but she could feel the American's keen, unsmiling gaze on her and wished she could use her nimble fingers to throttle the life out of Don Wellington. But he was studiously getting on with the task, and judging from the smug smile on his lips, it looked as though he was much further ahead than her. She longed for a chance to spike his guns. If only she'd had time to discover if that piece of rogue swarf matched the offcuts from his parting tool …

Abruptly she paused in her work and looked up at the American with an ingratiating smile. 'I wonder, would I be allowed to use tweezers? I've got a pair in my handbag in the cloakroom. It would make it an awful lot easier to hold the wires steady.'

He looked at her thoughtfully but didn't respond to her smile, and she thought he was going to refuse the request, but then he lifted his shoulders slightly. 'Sure, why not? But don't forget the clock is ticking.'

Despite her bad hip, it only took her a minute to scurry to the locker room, another minute to scrabble through her handbag, and a third minute to sprint back to the canteen, including a short pause at Don Wellington's workspace.

And the tweezers made all the difference. By dint of clamping the tiny red wire, she was finally able to thread it through the narrow bolt. And that made it easier to screw the coil onto the mouth of the glass vial. It was terribly fiddly, and as she neared the end, her fingers were sweating, which made it even harder to keep her grip on the tiny components. But finally she managed it and sat back in her chair in satisfaction.

'I've finished,' she called out self-consciously. A couple of the other men groaned, but the captain made a note on his pad and came over. He glanced at her finished article, then handed it to the American, who inspected it closely, turning it almost caressingly in his long fingers. Finally, when Louise could hardly bear the tension another second, he looked up with a faint smile that momentarily lit up his rather severe features. 'Congratulations,' he said. 'That's a neat job.' And she felt as though he had given her a gold star.

Only seven of the men managed to complete the assembly test, none of them as quickly as her. The rest were sent back to the factory floor.

The next test was completely different. They were given a series of facts about a small group of islands somewhere in a nameless ocean. There was a piece of life-saving equipment that had to be transported from one island to another, but there were no aeroplanes and they had to work out the quickest way of getting it there by using post boats, which all had very complicated timetables. Louise hadn't done anything like that since she was at school, but she prided herself on her efficiency, and it didn't take her long to work out that much of the information they'd been given was redundant, and the best method would be for the package to be simply trans-shipped mid-ocean at a spot where the routes of two of the ships intersected.

Once again she was the first to finish. Two of the other men failed to work it out at all. Now they were down to six, and Louise began to feel excited. She had no idea how many people the American and his two colleagues were looking for, but the odds on getting selected were improving by the moment.

Katy had been on tenterhooks for the last two weeks, but when on Friday, having set off for work as normal, Ward reappeared back in the pub at lunchtime, she knew that the moment of his departure had come. Her heart trembled, and she took a shaky breath. 'When?'

'This evening,' he said. 'There's a flight tomorrow they want me to catch.'

'To where?'

He put on a severe face. 'You know I'd have to kill you if I told you.' He held out a hand and drew her to him. 'Corsica,' he whispered. 'Via Portugal.'

It sounded innocuous enough. But Katy was not reassured. 'Corsica means France, doesn't it?' she whispered back, and she felt his low laugh against her chest. Already she could feel her blood running cold at the thought of him once again in enemy-held territory.

'Maybe,' he said. 'But not straight away.' He drew back slightly and looked deeply into her eyes. 'I'm going to have to get packed up, but before I go, in case I don't get another chance, I just want you to know that—'

He stopped abruptly as Elsa came running up the cellar steps. 'Oh, I'm sorry,' she said. 'I didn't realise you were …' She stopped in confusion. 'But your mother is very upset.'

Even as Katy groaned, she saw the spark of amusement flame in Ward's grey eyes. They had been plagued by interruptions recently. If it wasn't an air-raid siren, it was her mother fretting about something, or the baby crying, or Malcolm asking a question, or the dog whining to go out.

But this interruption was the last thing Katy needed. As soon as Elsa had discreetly withdrawn, she looked up at Ward. 'What?' she said. 'What is it you want to tell me?'

But he was already disengaging from the embrace. He shook his head with a wry smile and touched her cheek with his fingers. 'Go help your mother,' he said. 'It'll keep till later.'

Louise was horrified to discover that the final test was a mathematical one. It involved working out the co-ordinates necessary to make a missile travelling at a particular velocity hit an incoming aeroplane. She stared at it in despair. She had loathed maths at school and had only just scraped through her School Certificate by the skin of her teeth. She could barely remember what velocity was, let alone how to work it out. Helplessly she glanced round the room, but all the remaining candidates seemed to be happily jotting down calculations. Don Wellington was even humming slightly under his breath, clearly well at ease.

Louise could have cried in frustration. If only she had known there was a maths test, she would have brushed up on her equations. But then she felt her heart accelerate. Suddenly she knew what she was going to do, and it terrified her. But it was her only chance.

Checking that nobody was looking in her direction, she felt in her pocket and brought out the piece of swarf that had got stuck in the pulley. As soon as Don Wellington put down his pencil, she surreptitiously slid it along the table towards him.

He turned his head suspiciously. 'What's that?' he muttered.

'Proof,' she said.

'Proof of what?'

'Proof that it was you who caused Doris's accident by deliberately sabotaging the drive belt.'

His eyes flickered and she knew at once that she was right. 'That's the piece of swarf that Mr Gregg took out of the pulley. Everyone's offcuts are slightly different.' Aware of the sudden tightening of his mouth, she quickly pulled the swarf back towards her. 'But this piece exactly matches yours.'

There was a pause during which she could almost hear him grinding his teeth. Then he looked at her long and hard. 'What do you want?'

She had to hand it to him, he was certainly quick on the uptake.

She nodded at the paper in front of her. 'The answer.'

He was silent again.

'I haven't shown it to Larry Gregg yet,' she murmured.

'You wouldn't dare.'

Louise looked at him incredulously. 'Of course I'd dare. I think he'd be interested to see it, don't you?'

'You're a bitch. And a cheat.'

Louise raised her eyebrows. 'Am I? Well I wonder what that makes you. At least what I'm doing hasn't caused someone to nearly lose their sight.'

Once again he didn't respond. Out of the corner of her eye she could see the American approaching.

'It's now or never,' she hissed.

'It's two hundred and thirty yards,' Don Wellington muttered through clenched teeth. 'And the angle is eighteen degrees.'

Jen was still waiting patiently in Henry's office. Or as patiently as she could manage in the circumstances. He seemed to have been gone for ages. She eyed the brass clock uneasily. She had already missed the appointment with Mrs Rutherford, and had just started wondering how long it would be before the labour exchange officer decided to set the police on her when someone knocked lightly on the door.

Before she could respond, it swung open and a young woman stepped into the room. She was wearing a chic figure-hugging pink jersey two-piece, a jaunty little beret, white kidskin gloves and a white mackintosh draped casually over her shoulders.

She stopped when she saw Jen sitting awkwardly on the upright chair, and let the door swing to behind her. 'Oh, hello,' she said. Her voice was light, almost musical. 'I was hoping to catch Henry.' She drew back her cuff and consulted a delicate gold watch on her wrist. 'Perhaps I am a fraction early, but nevertheless ...' She stopped as they both heard steps in the corridor outside.

A moment later Henry came into the room. He smiled when he saw the newcomer. 'Janette,' he said. He stepped forward and kissed her lightly on the cheek. 'I'm sorry, I've got a bit delayed.' He turned to Jen and held out an envelope. 'There you are,' he said. 'I hope that will do the trick for now. I'll be in touch next week with more specific arrangements.'

Jen stood up. It was clear she was being dismissed, and also clear why. She knew this girl. Not in the flesh, perhaps, but from the posters. This was Janette Pymm, an established stage and screen star, who last year had become one of the most popular forces pin-up girls. No wonder Henry was smiling. Their names had been romantically linked before.

Belatedly Jen realised that Henry was halfway through the process of introducing them. 'And this is Jennifer Carter,' he was saying. 'She's a talented actress too, although she has been out of action for a while.'

It was a generous intro and Jen was grateful. But she wasn't so grateful when Janette Pymm courteously held out her tiny gloved hand and asked: 'Oh really? No, I don't think we've met. Where did you train?'

As Jen floundered, Henry intervened. 'Come, come, Janette. Not everyone has the privilege of going to RADA.' He glanced encouragingly at Jen. 'She's home-grown talent. But none the worse for that.'

Janette Pymm gave a sudden tinkling laugh. 'You must be good,' she said to Jen. 'Dear Henry is usually rather snobby about that kind of thing.'

'Not at all,' Henry said.

Dear Henry indeed, Jen thought sourly. They were clearly on very intimate terms.

Suddenly she felt gauche and very much in the way. She took a hesitant step towards the door. 'It's been lovely to meet you,' she said to the actress. 'But I'd better go. I'm running rather late.' She glanced tentatively at Henry, wondering if he was going to kiss her goodbye. But he didn't show any sign of it, so she gave him an awkward smile instead. 'Thank you,' she mumbled. 'I'm very grateful.'

He inclined his head. 'I'm always happy to help.' He opened the door courteously. As she went past him, he looked at her through slightly narrowed eyes. He let the door close slightly behind him and lowered his voice. 'Jen, are you sure you're OK? You look very pale.'

Jen felt herself colouring. 'I'm fine.'

He smiled then, a strange, slightly conspiratorial smile that for some reason slithered into her chest and curled tightly round her heart. 'Then I'll be in touch next week,' he murmured. 'Until then, stay safe. Let's hope the bombers keep away for once.'

'I can't go on,' Mary Parsons said, dabbing her eyes. 'I'm sorry, Katy, but I just can't go on. My nerves can't take any more.'

Katy had found her mother sitting on one of the camp beds in the cellar, crying her eyes out. Malcolm, meanwhile, apparently oblivious to his grandmother's distress, was playing happily in the corner with two fire buckets full of sand.

It had taken Katy a few minutes to calm her mother sufficiently for her to get any words out. But now she wouldn't stop.

'It's the constant fear, the worry, the children. Malcolm is so naughty. I can't control him. He doesn't take any notice of me at all, and when we're out at the shops I'm terrified he'll run off and I won't be able to find him. And then there'll be a raid and—'

'But Mummy, listen ...' A couple of times Katy tried to interrupt, but it was hopeless. The litany went on and on. The worst thing was that all the fears her mother was expressing were Katy's fears too. Katy knew exactly what it was like to live in constant dread. She just suppressed it better than her mother did.

Even now she was worrying about Ward's departure. About where he was going. And what he might end up doing. Sooner or later she was certain he would be sent into France. He probably had a series of agents and saboteurs already there, primed and ready, just waiting for his command to begin a rearguard action against the Germans. And she knew how the Germans would respond. The way they always did. With vicious brutality.

Malcolm's voice suddenly broke into her thoughts. 'Why's Granny sad?' he asked. Lifting one of his buckets, he carefully tipped all the sand out onto the floor. 'Is it 'cos Lucky ate her slipper?'

And now Katy noticed that her mother was indeed clutching a mangled bedroom slipper. Lucky himself, of course, was nowhere to be seen, but as far as her mother was concerned, this latest canine outrage had probably been the last straw. The one that broke the camel's back.

Perhaps fortuitously, Malcolm's intervention had finally brought her mother's weeping to a halt. Katy extracted the ill-fated slipper from her limp grasp and patted her hand encouragingly. 'I understand your concerns, Mummy,' she said. 'I really do. But Ward is leaving us this afternoon, and I'm going to need you to help me with the children.'

There was a long pause, and then her mother shook her head. 'I can't. I just can't. It's too much for me.' She looked up at Katy with mutinously. 'I want to go back to the country. And I want to go today, before you persuade me to change my mind.'

Katy dug her nails into her palms. It was either that or scream. It's all too much for me too, she wanted to yell. What with the bombing, and the lack of staff, and Ward going away. It's been too much for me for years. And now I've got both a toddler and a new baby to deal with. And an uncontrollable dog.

But she didn't say any of it. She knew there was no point. Her mother might be weak and fragile about most things, but when her own well-being was at stake, she was as tough as old boots.

'All right,' Katy said resignedly. 'In that case, I suggest you go and pack. I'll go and find out about trains, and I'll send a telegram to Ward's aunts telling them to expect you later on this afternoon.'

The final stage of the selection process for the new jobs was an interview. One by one the four remaining candidates were taken in to Larry Gregg's office. Mr Gregg wasn't there. His place at the desk had been taken by the small, scruffy man. The artillery captain sat to one side on another chair. The tall American was standing by the window.

'Please take a seat,' the small man said when Louise came in. Unexpectedly, he spoke in a slightly drawling upper-class accent.

She sat down with her hands folded demurely in her lap, mainly to stop them shaking.

The man waited for her to settle, then nodded towards the silent American. 'Lieutenant Colonel Westwood here has been tasked with putting together a small, specialist Anglo-American team to develop an innovative piece of military equipment. He is looking for a couple of people to act as liaison personnel between the factory and the trialling unit. It would be a responsible position. You have completed our tests successfully, but now we want to know if you have what it takes to be one of those people.'

Louise blinked and glanced cautiously across at the American. 'I hope I do,' she said. He seemed awfully young to be a lieutenant colonel. But no less

71

attractive for that, in that stern, rather brooding sort of way.

Suddenly she realised he was looking at her too, and hoped he hadn't read her thoughts. 'But what is it you're developing?' she asked rather breathlessly. 'A new weapon or something?'

The small man shook his head. 'I'm afraid we can't tell you that,' he said. 'Certainly not until you have been fully trained and have signed the Official Secrets Act.' He paused, waiting for her reaction. 'How do you feel about that?'

Louise could hardly speak. How did she feel about it? She felt as though her heart was about to jump out of her chest in excitement. She could almost feel her eyes sparkling with glee. The Official Secrets Act? How glamorous was that! That would be one in the eye for her parents. But then she suddenly remembered about Helen de Burrel and Ward Frazer working as secret agents, and the horrendous times they had had in France. 'It wouldn't be dangerous, would it? I wouldn't have to grapple with Germans or anything?'

The scruffy man gave a short laugh. 'No, no, not at all. Rather the opposite, in fact. One of our primary aims is to prevent any hint of this new technology falling into enemy hands. That's why we are operating within such tight security.' He picked up a pen. 'We'll have to check your past history and so on. But in the meantime, you need to give us the names of a couple of people who would be prepared to vouch for you.'

'Vouch for me?'

'Yes, for your honesty, reliability, lack of radical political affiliation and so on.'

Louise stared at him blankly.

'I assume you don't have any radical affiliations?' he prompted her with a slight smile. 'Or any dark secrets in your past that might make you subject to blackmail?'

Louise wondered rather wildly if Mrs Gibbons would count as a radical affiliation. But much more worrying was who she could think of to vouch for her. Why had she chosen this moment to fall out with all her friends? She groaned inwardly. She could see she was going to have to eat humble pie with Katy. Katy was still her closest friend, even if she had been so ungrateful for her help in the pub.

'You could ask my friends Katy and Ward Frazer,' she said. 'Katy runs the Flag and Garter pub in Lavender Road. I've known her for ages.' She could surely rely on Katy not to say anything detrimental. But who else? Most of her finishing school friends would be bound to spill the beans not only about her ill-considered relationship with the silver-tongued cad Charlie Hawkridge, but also about the brief premarital affair she had had with the glamorous but perfidious Polish count Stefan Pininski. She had a nasty feeling both might count as dark secrets, even though neither of them could possibly make her susceptible to blackmail. Seeing, the small man's pen poised over his pad expectantly, she began to panic.

And then she suddenly thought again of Helen de Burrel. 'I have another good friend. But she's working in Tunisia at the moment.' She was on the verge of mentioning that Helen worked for the ultra-secret SOE, but stopped herself just in time. She didn't want them to think she was a blabbermouth. 'And there's my family, of course. My father is a major in the Home Guard. And my brother is an officer in the Coldstream Guards. He's also in Tunisia.'

The man duly noted it down. Then he gave an apologetic cough. 'I couldn't help noticing that you walk with a slight limp.'

Louise nodded. 'I was caught up in a bomb accident. I fractured my pelvis. But it was ages ago, right back in the Blitz.' She crossed her fingers behind her back and met his eyes bravely. 'It doesn't hurt any more.' At any rate, she consoled herself, surely not enough to preclude her from joining the Colonel's secret specialist team.

'So you reckon you'd pass a basic fitness test?'

Louise was startled. 'A fitness test?'

'Yes, everyone has to do that.' He gave a faint smile. 'Even girls. Although I believe the requirements are rather less stringent now than they were at the beginning of the war.' He glanced at the artillery captain as though for confirmation. 'You'd also have to undergo a medical examination before you join up, but—'

Louise gave a gasp of astonishment. 'Join up?'

He seemed momentarily perplexed. 'Yes, of course. Weren't you at the briefing? No, I suppose you came in late. But surely Mr Gregg made it clear to you that one of our stipulations was that those selected as liaison personnel will be required to join the army?'

'*The army?*' She gaped at him. She could almost feel the ground shifting beneath her feet. She thought she was going to fall off her chair. It took all her willpower not to put out a hand to steady herself.

'Yes. I thought I'd made it clear that this project is operating under the auspices of the military.' He gave another smile. 'Except in your case it will have to be the women's army. The Auxiliary Territorial Service.' His smile faded rapidly as he took in her expression. 'Is that going to be a problem for you?'

Louise knew her mouth had fallen open, but she seemed unable to close it. A problem? It wasn't a problem; it was a complete nightmare. The ATS? Like those awful hearty girls at the gun emplacement up on the common, doing endless square-bashing and physical jerks? All her friends would die laughing.

'Couldn't I join the WRENS or the WAAF instead?' she asked rather desperately. She would almost rather join the Hitler Youth than the frumpy old ATS.

But the man shook his head. 'No, I'm afraid it would have to be the ATS,' he said. 'But you wouldn't have to be with them all that long. Only for the period of basic training.' He threw a quick corroborative glance at Colonel Westwood. 'Our current intention is that after that you would mainly be based in the factory. But with occasional visits to the test site.'

That didn't sound quite so bad. But even so. She had had such high hopes for this new job, and now she felt as though a rug had been pulled out from under her feet. The last thing in the world she wanted to do was join the army. But even as she hesitated, she saw the men glance at each other. And now there was a change of atmosphere in the room. A frisson of doubt. They were losing faith in her. She knew that if she wasn't careful, she was going to blow her chance. Think of the money, she told herself. Just think of the extra money.

She could feel the dark, watchful eyes of the American on her.

'You seem kind of reluctant,' he said in his low, accented voice. And suddenly she did want to do it. She certainly didn't want him to turn her down.

She lowered her lashes and gave a comical grimace. 'It's only that I don't like the ATS uniform,' she said. 'It's so unflattering. But I daresay I could bear it for a week or two.'

They laughed then, as she had hoped they would. At least the small man and the artillery captain did. The American just narrowed his eyes slightly. 'If you have doubts, I'd prefer for you to express them now,' he said. 'We can't afford to make mistakes. This project is way too important for that.'

She shook her head frantically, willing herself not to colour up under his steady, steely regard. 'No,' she stammered. 'I have no doubts. I'd really like to do it.'

He held her eyes. 'OK,' he said. 'In that case we'll be in touch again next week.'

Chapter Seven

Clapham Junction was unusually busy. It was the beginning of the rush hour, and everyone was trying to get home before it got dark. Nobody wanted to linger too long in case the sirens started up. It wasn't much fun getting stuck on a train during an air raid.

Katy didn't blame them, but she wished they hadn't all decided to converge on the station at the same time. Saying goodbye to Ward and her mother was going to be hard enough without being buffeted by hurrying commuters and noisy groups of soldiers all fighting to get a space on departing trains. Ward was going to escort her mother as far as Victoria, but after that they would be going their separate ways.

In the pram, baby Caroline was almost invisible under her grandmother's suitcases, which were balanced across the top, and Ward had Malcolm clasped to one shoulder and his kitbag over the other. Malcolm had insisted on bringing Lucky, but that had delayed them, because the dog had been determined to investigate the smells on every corner on the way.

And now, before they had time to catch their breath, the Victoria train was pulling in, smothering everyone in a great cloud of smoke and steam, and causing Malcolm to scream with excitement. 'Want to go on train,' he yelled.

'No, you've got to stay and look after Mummy,' Ward was saying, battling to hold on to Lucky as he tried to chase the engine down the platform. Unfortunately, in so doing he bumped into the pram, and one of the suitcases fell down on top of Caroline, who immediately set up a screeching wail.

'I'm sorry,' Mary Parsons whimpered. 'This is all my fault.'

And then the train doors were opening and everyone was barging forward. Putting Malcolm down on the ground, Ward thrust Lucky's leash into Katy's hands while he heaved the bags up onto the train.

As she clung to the dog with one hand and Malcolm with the other, Katy caught his eye and realised that he was laughing. 'I'm sorry too,' he said. 'I didn't know it would be like this. I guess we should have left Lucky and the kids at home.'

And then Katy was laughing too. It was so ridiculous. This morning they had all been peacefully carrying on with their lives. Now everything was in turmoil, her mother was crying again, and Ward was trying to persuade

Malcolm to kiss her goodbye, which of course he refused to do. And then the whistle was blowing, doors further up the train were slamming, and without any further ado, Ward bundled her mother onto the train.

He quickly climbed down again to kiss the wailing baby, to hug Malcolm and to pat Lucky. 'You be good,' he muttered to the dog. 'I'm relying on you to keep them all safe.'

And then he was pulling Katy into his arms, which wasn't easy with Malcolm tugging at her hand, still insisting that he wanted to go on the train.

'Goodbye, sweetheart,' he murmured into her hair. Suddenly his voice sounded choked. 'I hate to leave you. You know that, don't you? But be strong. And be safe.'

Katy could hardly speak. She felt the strength of his arms round her, the hard wall of his chest against hers. The graze of his cheek against her skin. 'You be safe too,' she whispered.

He put a hand behind her head, looked into her welling eyes, and kissed her hard on the lips.

Then he let her go and stepped up onto the train. The door slammed. A moment later he had pulled down the window and was leaning out. Katy let go of Malcolm so she could reach up and touch his hand.

'What was it you wanted me to know?' she called up to him suddenly as the train juddered and started to move. Ward looked blank, and she stumbled along beside the window, dragging Lucky with her. But she couldn't keep pace with the train. 'In the pub earlier,' she called up desperately. 'You said there was something you needed to tell me before you left.'

Ward touched his fingers to his lips and then to his heart. 'I wanted to tell you how much I love you,' he shouted.

And then the train was picking up speed, and Katy could no longer see him through the billowing smoke.

She stopped and felt a terrible sense of loss wash over her. She was certain she would never see him again.

By the time the smoke had cleared, the train had gone.

And so had Malcolm.

Dropping Lucky's leash, Katy ran back down the empty platform towards the pram. Having apparently got over her shock at being almost squashed to death by her grandmother's suitcase, baby Caroline was waving her arms about, gurgling happily. But there was absolutely no sign of Malcolm.

Surely to God he hadn't somehow climbed onto the train? Or worse, fallen down onto the track? Katy could hardly bear to think of such an eventuality, let alone to look over the edge of the platform. She stared wildly around for a railway official to help her, but there was no one in sight. Clinging to the handle of the pram, she tried to steady herself, but her panic was such that she could hardly breathe, let alone think.

And then she heard Lucky barking. Swinging round, she saw him pawing at the door of the stationmaster's office. She caught her breath. Could it be? Almost spilling Caroline out of the pram in her haste to run back down the platform, she shoved the dog out of the way and pushed open the door. And there was Malcolm, perched unconcernedly on a chair, carefully inspecting the stationmaster's whistle.

'Here's your mum now,' the stationmaster said comfortably, then blanched as Katy slumped weakly against the wall. He came round his desk and patted her arm awkwardly. 'He's all right, love,' he said. 'I only brought him in here to keep him safe. I didn't want him climbing down onto the track. Because he's a plucky little feller, isn't he? You can see that just by looking at him.'

Valiantly Katy tried to pull herself together, but her answer was drowned out by two sudden piercing shrills on the whistle, and a new cacophony of barking from outside the door.

Louise was in a quandary. On the one hand she had been given a chance to get away, albeit briefly, from her parents. On the other, joining the ATS was the last thing in the world she would have chosen to do. She hated the thought of being bossed around by officious army women, although she was perfectly used to it, of course. Her parents spent all their time telling her what to do, and complaining when she didn't do it in the way they wanted. Just this morning her mother had accused her of losing the old saucepan she used to feed the chickens, even though Louise knew perfectly well that she had left it on the roof of the henhouse as usual.

Her father was equally annoying. He had been tasked with organising a parade in Clapham, and was relishing the chance of using the opportunity to settle a few scores with other local defence organisations, not least the newly arrived Americans, whom he still hadn't forgiven for snubbing him earlier in the month. 'I'll obviously have to offer them a spot in the parade,' he had said at supper last night. 'But I can assure you it won't be at the front.'

Louise had suddenly longed for the good old days when just by lifting a finger she was able to summon Aaref Hoch to take her out to the pictures, or for a jolly evening at the pub. But now that Aaref was stepping out with Elsa, it wasn't quite so easy. In any case, the pub no longer seemed convivial. That jumped-up little madam Jen Carter had seen to that.

No, in comparison to spending the evenings stuck at home with her parents, a couple of weeks in the ATS sounded almost like fun.

She decided to tell them about it as they sat down to supper that evening, but just as she was steeling herself, a letter from her brother in Tunisia arrived in the late post, saying he he had been wounded and was in hospital.

The war in North Africa had been over for months, the Germans and the Italians both defeated by the Allied forces. But it seemed there were still some pockets of local resistance, because according to Douglas's letter, his injuries had been incurred during 'a fracas with some natives'. The full extent of the damage wasn't quite clear – he only mentioned a broken nose and a fractured jaw – but it had apparently been serious enough to prevent him setting off to fight in Italy with the rest of his regiment.

'Damn bad luck,' her father said. 'But just like Douglas to make light of it. I expect we will hear in due course that he covered himself in glory. You see, Louise. That's the kind of grit and stoicism we look for in our young soldiers.'

Louise rolled her eyes. She obviously felt sorry for Douglas, but she was fed up with her father always going about how marvellous he was. In any case, it didn't sound at all like Douglas to her. In her experience, Douglas was usually far too ready to blow his own trumpet.

'Well I've got some news too,' she said, deciding that the time had come to blow a small trumpet of her own. 'I've been selected to join a special unit at work.' She unfolded her napkin and waited while her mother put the food on the table. 'But it's a military project, and in order to take part, I have to join the ATS.'

'What!' Her father had been bowing his head ready to say grace, but his chin jerked up so fast Louise thought he might break his neck.

'It will only be for a week or two,' Louise said hastily. 'Just for basic training. After that, I'll be working back in the factory.'

But her father was already wagging his finger at her. 'Oh no,' he said. 'I'm not letting you run wild in some military camp.'

'Oh for goodness' sake, Daddy,' Louise fired back. 'I'm not a child.'

Her mother leaned forward and put a pacifying hand on her arm. 'But what about your bad hip, darling? I hope you've told them about that?'

Louise felt like screaming. Whatever the ATS was like, it was surely the lesser of two evils. After all, plenty of girls joined up. How bad could it be? Nothing could be worse than having to put up with constantly being treated like some slightly gormless child.

'Yes,' she said, managing to hang on to her patience by a thread. 'I did.' She glanced down at the congealing food on her plate and took a calming breath. Then she lifted her head and turned to her father. 'It's all rather hush-hush, so I can't tell you what it's about, but they are going to want to ask you some questions about me. I think it's called positive vetting.'

Her father looked momentarily taken aback. 'My word,' he said. 'Although I don't suppose it will stay hush-hush for long if they've got girls involved.'

He gave a sudden chuckle. 'Nevertheless, I suppose it might do you good to have a bit of discipline drummed into you. Not that you'll last more than about five minutes if I know you.' He picked up his knife and fork. He had apparently forgotten all about grace. 'But if you do, perhaps I'll invite you to join my Salute the Soldier parade. The women's services will be marching at the back with the Girl Guides.'

'Mum?' Angie poked her head round the door of the front room, where Joyce was listening to Gert and Daisy on the wireless.

'What?' Joyce asked irritably. It was a funny show and she didn't want to be interrupted. She had only just got in from the café a few minutes before, and had been looking forward to a sit-down. It had been a busy day. Mrs Rutherford had been absent on WVS business, and she and Angie had been run off their feet.

Angie sidled into the room. 'Will you lend me some money? There's a swing ball in Battersea Town Hall tonight. It's Jimmy Andrews and it's bound to be good.'

Joyce frowned. 'What have you done with your wages?'

Angie looked sheepish. 'I've spent them. It was so exciting having Gino back, I treated everyone in the pub last night.'

'Well that's your lookout then,' Joyce said severely. 'Anyway, I don't like you being out and about so late. Not now we're getting all these raids again.' What she really didn't like was the thought of what Angie and Gino might get up to if they had to spend an unsupervised night together in a public shelter. It was bad enough having the blasted boy back in her house at all. But this time, as well as a ration book, he had brought a note from the Home Office authorising him to live in London. Joyce had no idea how he had wangled such a thing, but it made it very difficult to turn him away.

'But Battersea Town Hall's not far,' Angie said. 'Gino and me could run home from there if the sirens sound. Well before any bombers turned up.'

She was right, of course, but even so Joyce really didn't see why she should put her hand in her own pocket to sub a jolly evening for Gino. She would much rather buy him a uniform and send him back to Italy to fight.

But Angie seemed oblivious to her bad temper. 'Oh come on, Mum.' She gave an endearing pout. 'Pretty please. We'll pay you back next week.'

'We?' Joyce felt her eyebrows shoot up. But she knew Angie would give her no peace if she didn't stump up. So, grudgingly, she got up to find her purse. Behind her she dimly heard Daisy telling Gert that men were all the same. All mouth and trousers. Joyce gave a snort of derision. Gino didn't seem to have much of either. Even now he was standing behind Angie in the doorway like a wet fish.

'That's all you're getting,' she said firmly as she handed over four shillings. 'I'm not lending you any more. If you want Gino to stay here, he'll have to get a job and pay his own way.'

'Oh, he will,' Angie said as she pushed the silent Gino out of the house in front of her. 'I'll make sure of it. Otherwise we'll never be able to afford to get married. I know it's hard these days, but I'm going to want a nice dress and all the trimmings.'

Joyce was still standing in the hallway with her mouth open when Paul came clumping down the stairs.

'Hello, Mum,' he said. 'Are you all right? You look like you've seen a ghost.'

'No,' Joyce said faintly. 'Not a ghost, more of a nightmare.' She shook her head, trying to clear the awful vision of Angie and Gino walking hand in hand down the aisle of St Aldate's Church on Clapham Common.

Paul looked at her uneasily, then shifted his feet and gave her a wide, slightly guilty grin. 'That was a nice pie you left out. I ate Gino's portion and all, because he didn't like it, but I still feel a bit peckish and I wondered if I could have another slice.'

Joyce eyed him with affection. There could hardly be a greater contrast between Paul and that unresponsive goop Gino. Paul was such a kind, sensitive boy. She was pleased he had come home. Even though it meant another mouth to feed, and a very hungry one at that, although thank goodness he too had brought a ration book with him. She didn't mind the extra expense for him. She hadn't been able to give him much over the last few years, so she didn't grudge him a bit of food. But she wasn't going to let him join up. Not at fifteen. He might be big, but he was hardly more than a child. Far too young and innocent to go and fight. Certainly too young to die.

'They're taking boys your age into the Home Guard now,' she remarked as she followed him into the kitchen. 'I heard it on the wireless. You'd get paid and everything.'

She took out the pie, cut him a generous slice and watched him smack his lips as she put the plate in front of him. She was proud of his patriotism. Proud that he wanted to do his bit. But the regular army was no place for a big soft lad like him. He was barely out of short trousers.

'I'll ask Mrs Rutherford to talk to her husband,' she said. 'See if he might take you on.'

But Paul was shaking his head. 'I don't want to join the Home Guard,' he mumbled through a mouthful of rabbit pie. 'I don't want to miss all the fun. I want to join the infantry. I want to be right there on the front line. I want to kill Germans. And I want to see the buggers die.'

*

80

Louise was on her way to work on Saturday morning when she once again bumped into George Nelson on the corner. He was carrying a large sack over one shoulder and his gas mask box over the other. She wouldn't have thought anything of it if he hadn't ducked his head and tried to sidle past without talking to her.

'Where are you going?' she asked.

'To school,' he said shortly. He scuffed at a patch of dirt on the pavement. 'They're making us come in on Saturday mornings to make up for the time we've lost in bomb scares.'

'And you're taking the long way round again?'

He nodded.

'No go-cart today?'

'No,' he said. 'Mum confiscated it.' He cast her a baleful glance. 'Because someone complained that I was going too fast.'

'Well it wasn't me,' Louise said. But she could tell that the little brat didn't believe her, and that annoyed her. 'So what have you got in that sack?' she asked.

'Nothing.'

'It doesn't look like nothing,' she said.

'It's salvage,' he said grudgingly. 'Bits of metal and that. Your mother is giving a prize for whoever collects the most.'

'Oh yes,' Louise said. She'd heard about that. She had in fact overheard her mother trying to persuade her father to give the winner a guided tour of the gun emplacement. A suggestion he had adamantly refused. 'Good God, Celia,' he had said. 'Certainly not. The last thing I need is for some light-fingered child to start poking grubby fingers into our shell charges, or twiddling dials on the gun sights. These are highly valuable and very dangerous pieces of equipment, my dear.'

'But,' her mother had persevered, 'surely under supervision …?' She might as well have saved her breath.

'Under no circumstances,' he said. 'I'm afraid you'll have to find some other prize. Something less prejudicial to the war effort.'

'So what is the prize?' Louise asked George now.

'It's a white rabbit.'

Louise had to bite her lip to stop herself laughing. She wondered where on earth her mother had found a white rabbit. She could hardly have hit on anything less like a tour round the gun emplacement.

But George was looking surprisingly eager. 'I like rabbits,' he said. 'And I could use it for magic tricks.' Then his face darkened. 'But most probably Greg Garrow will win it.'

'Who's Greg Garrow?' Louise asked.

He dropped his gaze. 'Someone at school.'

'And why do you think he's going to win?'

George shrugged. 'Because he brings in more salvage than anyone else.' He kicked the ground irritably. 'And he doesn't even want a rabbit. He'll probably kill it as soon as he gets it.'

Louise was shocked. 'Good God,' she said. 'I'll have to tell my mother.'

'No!' George looked up sharply. 'No, you mustn't. Everyone will say I'm a telltale. Promise me you won't.'

Louise eyed him beadily. 'Then show me what you've got in that sack.'

He scowled at her. But it had been obvious from the start that he was trying to keep the sack out of her line of sight, so Louise wasn't altogether surprised that when he reluctantly lowered it to the ground and loosened the string round the top, the first thing she saw was the old saucepan that her mother used for feeding the chickens.

She lifted it out and held it up quizzically.

George had the grace to blush. 'It's so old,' he said. 'I didn't think she'd need it any more.'

Louise checked the rest of the sack's contents, but there was nothing else she recognised.

'OK,' she said slowly. 'I won't say anything. But if you steal from our garden again, I'll tell my father, and then you'll be in real trouble.' She glared at him. 'Now buzz off and go to school.'

Blasted child, she thought irritably, as he ran off with the clanking sack and the gas mask bumping on his thin shoulders. She had been intending to go and make her peace with Katy and Ward, but now that she was going to have to take the wretched saucepan back, she didn't have time. She would have to drop into the pub on her way home instead, and run the risk of Jen Carter being there.

But luckily when she called at the Flag and Garter that evening, Jen wasn't there. But nor, of course, was Ward, and Louise felt aggrieved that he had gone away without bothering to say goodbye. Now she would have to rely on Katy to help with the positive vetting business.

Unfortunately, the pub was very busy. As well as the usual Saturday crowd, there were several American soldiers, presumably the new arrivals at the local barracks. They had unusually loud, drawling accents. Elsa was fumbling about behind the bar trying to get caps off beer bottles for them. Behind her, Aaref's brother Jacob was clumsily hauling a barrel up from the cellar. Katy, busy loading a tray with empties, was unusually preoccupied.

And when Louise eventually waylaid her in the scullery, she seemed appalled by the idea of having to vouch for her. 'Blimey,' she said. 'What on earth will I say?'

'I want you to give me a good report,' Louise said. 'Just tell them that I'm a nice, reliable, honest person. And try not to mention Stefan Pininski or Charlie Hawkridge.'

Katy looked shocked. 'But I can't lie,' she said. 'Not to the security services.' As she put the tray down on the draining board and started unloading the glasses into the sink, Louise couldn't help noticing, with a flash of irritation, that they were still washing the glasses left to right, instead of the much more logical right-to-left method she had suggested.

'You don't have to lie,' she said tetchily. 'You just have to be a bit sparing with the truth.' She saw a flicker of unease on Katy's face and knew she was going to have to grovel. 'Oh come on, Katy,' she pleaded. 'I know I've behaved badly in the past. But I was young and lonely and … Look, I really want this. And I'm trying to turn over a new leaf. I'm trying to be a better person. Honestly I am.'

But now Katy was looking at her suspiciously. 'There's a man in this somewhere, isn't there?

Louise felt heat in her cheeks as a rather appealing mental picture of Colonel Westwood crept into her thoughts. 'No,' she said indignantly. 'It's just that living with my parents is driving me nuts. And if I can secure this new job, I might just about be able to afford a place of my own.'

Katy wiped a sudsy hand over her face. 'Well, OK,' she said reluctantly. 'I'll do my best.' She hesitated, and a tiny flicker of amusement crossed her face. 'But seriously, Louise, the ATS? With that awful uniform and everything? Are you sure it's what you really want?'

Louise was so relieved that Katy was going to co-operate that she was hardly listening. 'I'll be fine,' she said airily. 'The ATS business is only a formality. I'll be back at the factory after a couple of weeks.'

As soon as Jen set foot in the pub on Sunday morning, she could see that Katy was in a bad way. She was polishing glasses, but it was clear that her heart wasn't in it. There was a slumped look about her and her eyes were bloodshot.

Jen suddenly felt very cross with Molly. Even though Katy had told her to stay in Tunisia, she ought to have come back. She must have known how much Katy had been relying on her to help out at the pub. As for Katy's drippy mother, abandoning ship just as Ward was going away, well, that really took the biscuit. But then Jen felt cross with Ward too. It was all very well for him to go waltzing off on his derring-do adventures, but he always left Katy holding the baby, literally.

As Katy resumed her polishing of the glasses, Jen noticed that over in the corner, Lucky was gnawing at something that looked suspiciously like a shoe, while Malcolm meanwhile was busily smearing coal on the wall by the fireplace. When he saw Jen looking at him he smiled winsomely. 'I'm making picture of Daddy,' he said.

What?' Katy looked up in horror. 'No, Malcolm, stop it, that's naughty.' As she swept him off to the scullery to wipe his hands, she caught sight of what Lucky was up to. 'Oh no,' she said. 'That was one of my last decent pair of shoes.'

And hearing the weary despair in her voice, Jen felt her own heart sink, because she knew what she was going to have to do. She thought of Malcolm's shrill little voice, of the awful noise of the baby crying, and of the hare-brained Lucky's incessant whining during the air raids, and tried to hide the shudder that coursed through her.

'Look,' she said, when Katy had sat down again with a chastened Malcolm on her lap. 'I'm not doing anything at the moment, so why don't I come and stay over here for a few days to give you a hand?'

'Oh Jen,' Katy breathed. 'Would you? It would be such a help.'

Jen gave a slight grimace. 'As long as I don't have to change any nappies,' she said. 'I'm not very keen on poo.'

Malcolm's ears pricked up. 'Lucky sometimes does poo in the bar,' he said.

Jen caught Katy's eye. 'How delightful,' she said.

But Katy was looking troubled. 'What will your mother say? Aren't you helping her to chaperone Angie and Gino? And what about ENSA? What if Henry suddenly gives you a job in a completely different part of the country? Or even abroad?'

Jen flinched. It had given her considerable pleasure to hand over Henry's letter of employment to that horrid National Service officer. But the last thing she felt like doing was going away on tour. Bracing her shoulders, she smiled bravely. 'Well, I haven't heard from Henry yet, so I have no idea what he has in mind for me. As for Angie and Gino, as far as I'm concerned, they can go and jump in a lake.'

Chapter Eight

In the event, Jen had to wait over a week before she heard from Henry. And by then she was well ensconced in the pub. She had stayed over there once or twice before, but the addition of a lively toddler, a new baby and a badly behaved dog hardly made it a rest cure, and if that wasn't enough, there were the continuing air raids to contend with. It wasn't as bad as the Blitz, but it was bad enough.

Rather than carrying the children up and down like yo-yos every time the sirens went off, she and Katy decided to move all their bedding down into the cellar and sleep there. Or try to sleep. As well as the ack-ack guns, they sometimes heard the thumping vibration of an explosion. And when the all-clear sounded, they emerged in trepidation, having no idea what damage they would find in the outside world.

So far Lavender Road had been spared, but numerous incendiaries and HE bombs had landed in nearby streets, wrecking houses and killing at least a dozen people. The Plough pub in Clapham had a lucky escape when an incendiary fell down the chimney of a back room and landed in the fireplace, and a few days later, at the beginning of February, a shell landed on Clapham Junction station and wrecked not only a waiting room but also the very platform from which Katy had waved goodbye to Ward only a week before. The following week a lance corporal in the Home Guard was killed when a bomb fell right outside their HQ.

'It's getting too close for comfort,' Katy said grimly as she opened the front door to let Lucky out. It was as he came in again, having done his business, that she noticed an airmail lettercard lying on the mat.

'It's from Molly,' she said. She slit it open eagerly. 'Perhaps she's decided to come home after all.'

As soon as she started reading, though, her face fell. Molly wasn't coming home. On the contrary, she was loving her new job and wished that Katy could see her lording it about over the toffee-nosed Queen Alexandra nurses.

But then as Katy reached the end of the letter, to Jen's surprise she suddenly gave a choke of amusement.

'Listen to this,' she said, glancing up with an evil grin. '*I can't remember if I told you that Douglas Rutherford is stationed near here. Well, you may have heard that he's been injured. Apparently he's trying to make out that it happened during a scrap with some local insurgents, but I found out from somebody who was there at the time that what really happened is that he was taunting some poor inoffensive camel and it took umbrage and kicked him in the face!!'*

Jen burst out laughing. That was even funnier than the idea of Louise joining the ATS. She had never been a fan of the Rutherfords, and Douglas had always been a shifty, smug little git. It didn't sound as though the army had improved him one iota.

Her laughter quickly faded a few minutes later when Angie popped in to drop off a letter that had arrived for her at the house. She recognised the writing at once.

Dear Jen, it read. *I'll be passing Clapham on Friday evening, so I suggest we meet at the pub at seven-ish for a quick chat about your future. Henry.*

Jen sat back in her chair, grimacing as her sleeve stuck to something on the table. She yanked it off irritably. The public bar seemed very bleak in the mornings. It was icy cold and stank of cigarette smoke and old beer. Their earlier hilarity felt a long way away.

Your future. A few short weeks ago, it might have been *our future.* Unexpectedly, she felt a sense of despair wash over her. But it would never have worked out between her and Henry. He was too posh for her. Too well connected. Too everything. He was friendly with Laurence Olivier and Vivien Leigh, for goodness' sake. And Janette Pymm.

She screwed the letter up into a ball and threw it into the fireplace. Ridiculously, she felt close to tears.

Avoiding Katy's concerned glance, she put down her cup and stood up. 'I need some fresh air,' she said. 'I'm going to go and get dressed, then I'll take Malcolm and Lucky up to the common for half an hour.'

Katy was worried about Jen, and wished she could do something to help her. But Jen wasn't an easy person to help. She was proud and stubborn, and it was rare that she let down her guard. Even the news that everyone was soon to receive twenty-four extra clothing coupons hadn't lifted her spirits, because as she wasn't earning, she had no money to spend on new clothes anyway. Perhaps on Friday evening Henry would offer her a nice part in one of his ENSA shows and that would cheer her up. Katy certainly hoped so, although privately she doubted that Jen was really in a fit state to take on a new challenge. She had never known her friend so crabby and out of sorts, except perhaps at the beginning of the war when her Irish boyfriend, Sean Byrne, had scarpered off back to Ireland with barely a backward glance.

There was another aspect to Jen's low mood that was causing Katy some concern. On Friday morning a man called Mr Jones was coming to talk to her about Louise, and she wanted to make sure Jen was well out of the way.

Despite her occasional missishness, Katy was fond of Louise, and she didn't want some acerbic comment from Jen to spoil her chances of getting this new job.

Louise had had a bad time over the last few years, and even if she had made some unwise decisions on the man front, in Katy's opinion she deserved a lucky break. As for her desire to escape her familial home, Katy certainly sympathised with that. Having her own mother to stay had hardly been a bed of roses, but she would rather jump off a cliff than live in the same house as Greville Rutherford.

Mr Jones turned out to be a nondescript but surprisingly pleasant man, although Katy suspected that Jones wasn't his real name. She didn't find it too difficult to convince him of Louise's patriotism. Having deviously asked Jen if she'd mind taking the children and the dog down to Northcote Road to see if she could charm a couple of bones out of the butcher for Lucky, Katy was also able to assure her visitor that Louise was not only the soul of discretion, but also a loyal and helpful friend. She told him what a fine, upstanding young man Louise's husband Jack had been, and carefully refrained from mentioning either the infamous Polish count with whom Louise had had an unfortunate affair at the beginning of the war, or the ghastly Charlie Hawkridge, who had taken advantage of her loneliness while Jack was away at sea.

It was unfortunate that Jen and the children arrived back just as Mr So-called Jones was leaving, and Lucky wasn't the only one dismayed to find a strange man talking to his mistress.

'Who on earth was that?' Jen asked, when the security officer had hastily gathered up his notes, picked up his briefcase and, giving Lucky a wide berth, disappeared silently through the blackout curtain.

Katy wondered briefly about dissembling, but even though she had managed to pull the wool over Mr Jones's eyes, she knew she would never get away with it with sharp-eyed Jen.

'He came to ask me a few questions about Louise,' she said.

'Louise?' Jen paused in her efforts to help Malcolm take off his coat. 'What about her? What's she done now?'

'She hasn't done anything,' Katy said. 'But the reason she has to join the ATS is because she's been offered some better-paid work with the military. And she needed someone to vouch for her reliability and so on.'

Ignoring Malcolm's increasingly frantic wriggles, Jen raised her eyebrows incredulously. 'And you were prepared to vouch for her?'

'Well, I know she's not perfect,' Katy said, crouching down to extricate Malcolm from the coat. It was already too small for him, and he'd only had it a few months. God knew when she was going to have the time to go looking for another. 'But you must admit she's quite reliable.'

'Not perfect?' Jen looked at her in amazement. 'She's an absolute menace.' She gave a sour laugh. 'But it's typical, isn't it? Those kind of rich posh girls get all the lucky breaks.'

'I don't think it's because she's posh,' Katy objected, stepping back and almost tripping over Lucky, who was now lying in his favourite, inconvenient position at the bottom of the stairs. 'It's because she's good at her job. You must admit she's slogged away at that factory for ages. Anyway, I'm not sure it is such a lucky break,' she added. 'I can't imagine her enjoying the ATS, can you?'

But Jen didn't take the bait. 'Oh, she'll wheedle her way through somehow,' she said. '*Daddy* will pull some strings for her, and before we know it, she'll have ended up as an officer, like her ghastly camel-baiting brother.'

Katy groaned. Once Jen got on her high horse, there was no stopping her. So even though it meant she would have to get the children into bed on her own, she was glad when Jen announced that she had agreed to accompany Paul to the matinee showing of *Here Comes Kelly* at the Grand at Clapham Junction.

'The poor boy is bored to death kicking about at home,' she said. 'I can't think why he doesn't go back to Devon to work on the farm. He's never going to persuade Mum to let him join the army.'

'Well, don't forget that Henry's coming this evening,' Katy reminded her.

'That's why I'm going to the pictures,' Jen said. 'I want to take my mind off it. Don't worry, I'll be back well before seven.'

Louise's medical examination took place one lunchtime at an army recruitment depot in Battersea. It was a surprisingly cursory affair. The doctor weighed her and measured her, listened to her heart and chest and took her blood pressure. He noted her limp, but accepted her assurance that it caused her very little pain.

'If you were a man, I would have to turn you down,' he said. 'But I don't suppose it will cause you much trouble in the ATS. I expect most of your time will be spent arranging flowers in the officers' mess.' He gave a hearty laugh, signed a chit, and that was that.

Despite his self-confessed flat feet, it appeared that Don Wellington had passed his medical too, because a couple of days later he announced that he had received his call-up papers and would be starting training the following week.

Although it would be a relief to see the back of him, Louise was peeved that his call-up process and security checks had clearly been expedited more quickly than hers. She knew that Katy's interview with the security vetting officer had passed off well, but her father had been less reassuring. 'I told him that you were a perfectly well-brought-up girl, with a good education, but that you had recently picked up a lot of silly ideas about equality,' he said.

Now she was worried that his stupid pomposity might have spiked her guns. It would be extremely galling if in due course she had to witness Don Wellington lording it about at the factory with higher wages and new secret work while she continued labouring away on the boring old production line.

When she got home on Friday evening, she eagerly scanned the hall table, but there was no letter for her. What there was, however, was a huge pile of old books, which her mother was sorting through rather irritably.

'Somebody left these in the driveway,' she said. 'It's most inconvenient. Everyone knows the salvage is meant to be delivered to the school.'

Remembering George Nelson and the saucepan incident, Louise asked how the children's collection was coming on. Her mother seemed surprised at the question. Almost as surprised, in fact, as she had been to find the saucepan reinstated on top of the henhouse the previous weekend.

'Oh, my little salvage cogs are doing awfully well,' she said, straightening up. 'We'll be announcing the winner at the beginning of March.'

'Have you by any chance heard of a boy called Garrow?' Louise asked. 'I believe he is doing particularly well.'

But her mother shook her head. 'I don't know the individual children,' she said. 'I have arranged for a teacher in each school to log the amount that comes in. We'll tot it all up at the end.'

'And I gather the prize is a white rabbit?'

Again her mother looked surprised. She wasn't used to Louise taking an interest in her WVS work.

'Well, yes,' she admitted. 'We'll be giving one to the winner in each school. I had hoped to persuade Daddy to arrange something with the Home Guard, but he's too busy on the ack-ack guns. Mrs Trewgarth suggested the rabbits. Her granddaughter keeps two as pets, and unfortunately one night they got in with each other. So now she has several baby bunnies to find homes for.' She chuckled, and it was Louise's turn to be surprised. Her mother wasn't normally one to talk about anything remotely sexual in nature. Let alone laugh about it. And indeed, perhaps remembering who she was talking to, Celia was already sobering up and glancing at the grandfather clock in the corner. She took her coat off the peg.

'I've left supper in the oven,' she said. 'But you'll have to serve it up for Daddy, because I've got to chair a WVS meeting about blood donation this evening.'

Louise's heart sank. The last thing she wanted to do was spend the

89

evening with her father. In addition to his griping about the newly arrived Americans, he had now also got a bee in his bonnet about the potential threat of the as yet unseen black GIs.

'At the moment they are confined to barracks,' he had told her last night. 'But when they do let them out, it's bound to cause trouble. They aren't used to fraternising with white women, and goodness knows what liberties they might take, given the chance. So I want you to promise to keep well clear of them.'

But it was him Louise wanted to keep clear of, not the black GIs.

'Oh, and have you heard, darling?' her mother said suddenly as she put on her hat. 'Aaref Hoch has proposed to the little Jewish girl who works at the pub. Elsa, isn't it? I had no idea there was a romance brewing there, did you?'

Louise felt the blood drain from her face. Before Elsa's arrival on the scene, Aaref had been one of her most ardent admirers, and somehow, deep down, she had always assumed she could get him back if she wanted to.

And now it was too late. But even as she hated him for choosing someone else, she knew it served her right. It was entirely her own fault. If she had treated Aaref better, she could have married him. Her father would probably have had a fit at the idea of a Jewish refugee for a son-in-law, but it would have been better than nothing. And now she was left with nobody.

Aware of her mother's eyes on her, she forced a smile on to her lips. 'Of course I did,' she said. But the words stuck in her throat. She didn't need to ask her mother if Elsa had accepted Aaref's proposal.

What was more, everyone in Lavender Road knew that she had a history with Aaref. And she hadn't made any secret of her dislike of Elsa. If she wasn't careful, as soon as the news got out, they would all be laughing at her up their sleeves. Especially Jen Carter.

I'll have to go to the Flag and Garter, she thought. I'll have to go and prove that I don't care.

But first she had to get changed. She couldn't go in her drab old work clothes. And she had to do her hair. She wanted to look her absolute carefree best, even if it meant using the very last smear of her precious Tangee lipstick.

Her mother picked up her handbag. 'Well, I'd better be off,' she said. 'And don't forget to keep an eye on the toad in the hole. Daddy won't be pleased if it's burnt.'

It was as the front door closed behind Celia that Louise noticed a buff envelope caught in the hinge of the letter box. Yanking it out, she saw it was addressed to her.

It was her call-up papers and a travel warrant. She was to report on 6 March to an ATS training facility in Bracknell in Berkshire.

*

It was dark by the time Jen and Paul came out of the Grand. The film had run late, because after the Pathé News there'd been a short called *Soldiers on the Screen*, which was designed to show loved ones back home what their menfolk were up to in the service of their country. It mainly consisted of pictures of jolly young soldiers enjoying themselves in NAAFI canteens, riding about in canvas-sided trucks or marching in long columns on foreign roads, waving cheerily at the camera. It finished with some rather hazy shots of the war in Burma, and the ongoing battle for Monte Cassino in Italy.

'Cor, I don't half wish I could be there,' Paul said, craning forward for a better view.

Jen turned to stare at him, and saw that his eyes were shining in the darkness. 'Don't be daft,' she said. 'You're far too young.' Someone behind shushed her, but she didn't take any notice. 'Anyway,' she added, 'it's Gino who should be there. It's his blasted country after all.'

Thankfully the main feature, *Here Comes Kelly*, proved as good as they had hoped, even though the central character, the cocksure young Irishman Jimmy Kelly, played by Eddie Quillan, reminded Jen unnervingly of another young Irishman, one she had known at the beginning of the war. Sean Byrne too had had the gift of the gab, a seductive smile and come-to-bed eyes. For an instant Jen felt again the pain of that first love, that first betrayal. It was as if an old wound had been torn open, and it took quite an effort to disassociate Jimmy Kelly from her memories of Sean. But at least it took her mind off the war and her imminent interview with Henry.

Nervous about the time, she made Paul leave the cinema the instant the film finished. But as they hurried back down St John's Hill, they became aware of some kind of commotion outside the Granada Theatre on the other side of the road. It was pitch dark, so they couldn't see exactly what was going on, but they could hear dogs barking, irritable voices and lots of scuffling of feet.

'Let's go and see what's happening,' Paul said.

'No, we can't,' Jen said. She shone her torch on her watch and saw that it was quarter to seven. 'I haven't got time.' But then she heard one particularly distinctive bark, followed by a curse, a squeal and a pitiful whine. 'Oh no,' she said. 'That sounds like Lucky.'

It was indeed Lucky. At first it seemed he was trying to gain access to the theatre, and being chased off by two angry men. But as she and Paul drew nearer, it became clear that the object of Lucky's attention was a small, beautifully coiffured white poodle that was being clutched to the chest of a third man, who was wearing an extraordinary shiny lime-green suit.

Jen toyed with leaving Lucky to take his chances. But she owed it to Katy to bring him home if she could. Even though Katy didn't much like him, Jen knew she would be mortified if anything happened to him.

'Lucky,' she called sternly. 'Come here.'

Lucky, inevitably, took absolutely no notice at all. But the man in green swung round at once. 'Is that your dog?' he asked in a high-pitched, querulous voice.

'No,' Jen said. 'It belongs to a friend.'

'Well I wish you would catch him or shoot him or something,' he said. 'My poor little Pookie is completely traumatised.'

Sensing that Paul's sudden guffaw of laughter wasn't going to help the situation, Jen told him to run home and fetch some tasty morsel that might lure Lucky away from his inamorata. She knew from bitter experience that there was no hope of catching him any other way.

Paul seemed disinclined to leave the excitement, but eventually he went off, and in his absence Jen was able to discover what had happened. The man in green and his four performing poodles, the Canine Comics, were part of that night's variety show line-up at the theatre. Having arrived early, he had decided to take the animals up to Clapham Common for a run before the show, and had misguidedly chosen to return via Lavender Road. Lucky had somehow got wind of the poodles as they trotted past the pub, and had followed them back to the theatre, determined to press his suit on the unsuspecting Pookie.

In his attempts to rescue Pookie from Lucky's advances, the man in green had inadvertently let his other three poodles go, and they were now eagerly joining in the fray.

'I reckon your Pookie must be coming into heat,' one of the other men remarked as Lucky suddenly launched himself towards the poodle, nearly knocking the man in green off balance.

'Good God,' Jen said. 'I don't know anything about dogs, but even I had worked that out.' The man was obviously a complete idiot. What was more, the yapping of the other poodles was beginning to get on her nerves. 'Why don't you take Pookie into the theatre?' she suggested. 'Then we might be able to catch the others.'

The man in green was outraged. 'I'm not leaving my precious poodles out here all alone to be ravaged by that … that creature. They aren't used to that kind of thing at all.'

By the time Paul had come lumbering back down the hill with a slice of bread and butter, and they had finally captured Lucky, Jen was panicking about the time. She had wanted to freshen up and make sure she was looking her best for Henry. He had said seven-ish. Now, thanks to Katy's blasted dog, all she could do was hope it would be more 'ish' than seven.

Chapter Nine

Katy's afternoon had been going well. She had been thrilled by the news of Aaref and Elsa's engagement. She couldn't think of a more perfect match. After the traumas they had suffered fleeing from Nazi oppression in Europe, it was like a dream come true.

Then Bella James had popped in after school to play with the children, and in Jen's absence, Katy had asked her to stay on to put Malcolm to bed.

Bella was pleased. She was clearly missing helping out at the pub, and not for the first time Katy wished that the girl was either older, or less pretty, either of which would have made her a useful addition to her staff.

And then, at about half past six, just as Katy had served Mr Lorenz with a half-pint of Rutherford & Berry special, and he had settled down by the fire with the local paper, Angie Carter had come bouncing into the bar, followed by the lugubrious Gino.

'I've had a brilliant idea,' Angie said. 'I know you're always short-staffed. So why don't you hire Gino to help you?'

Katy was aware of a faint sinking feeling in her stomach. 'I'm not sure his English is quite good enough,' she said.

'Well, no,' Angie admitted. 'But he is learning. Aren't you, my darling?' She swung round as she spoke, but it was clear that Gino wasn't paying attention. On the contrary, he was looking rather longingly at the blazing fire.

Realising that something was expected of him, he blinked owlishly. '*Che?*'

Angie giggled, poked him with affectionate violence in the ribs, then turned back to Katy. 'Well, even if he can't serve at the bar, surely he could move barrels and wash glasses and sweep out the sawdust and that?'

Katy glanced at Gino dubiously. Young Jacob Hoch, Aaref's brother, usually did the heavy work for her, but he had recently joined the Boys' Brigade, which quite often now meant he wasn't available when she needed him.

But Gino?

'Couldn't your mother give him a job at the café?' Katy asked weakly.

Angie shook her head. 'I did ask her, but she said not in a million years.' She gave another of her irrepressible giggles. 'I think she thought we would spend all our time canoodling. And she's probably right.'

Katy bit her lip, but was saved from answering, because at that moment the door opened and a gaggle of American GIs came in. They weren't a group she knew, and by the look of them, they had already had quite a bit to drink elsewhere.

Her previous American customers had always been very courteous and polite, but these men seemed unusually boorish and brash. One bull-headed corporal in particular was rude to Elsa when she failed to understand his Southern drawl. Katy didn't like his ill-mannered arrogance, and in other circumstances she would have been tempted to boot him out. But a couple of his friends seemed to recognise Angie, and as she greeted them with a friendly smile, Katy felt powerless to turn them away.

'So what do you think?' Angie turned back to Katy eagerly. The GIs had moved off towards the fireplace, where Gino was now warming his hands. 'You could at least give him a try-out for a few days.'

'All right,' Katy said reluctantly. 'I've got a delivery tomorrow morning. Maybe he could come in and help unload the barrels.'

She watched Angie dance off to impart the good news to Gino, and knew that Jen would have a fit. And speaking of Jen, where on earth was she?

Katy glanced over her shoulder at the grandfather clock behind her, a nostalgic relic of her father's tenancy of the pub. It was seven o'clock, she realised in sudden panic, and that was when Henry had said he would—

'Good evening, Katy, how are you?'

She swung round, and there, standing on the other side of the counter in an expensive-looking navy overcoat and leather gloves, was Henry Keller.

It didn't take Louise long to get ready to go to the pub. Quickly she slipped on her favourite Jaeger black and white plaid skirt, which she had bought from Harrods last winter, a white shirt and a navy cardigan. It took longer to rescue her hair from a day under her mob cap, but by dint of splashing water on it and neatly curling a few strands into a hairclip, she eventually got it looking satisfactorily casual but stylish. There was nothing she could do about her hands; her fingers were permanently stained from the grease at the factory, but that didn't matter these days. She was doing her bit, after all.

To her dismay, at that moment she heard the crunch of a step on the driveway gravel outside.

Her father was just opening the front door as she ran down the stairs. 'Hello, Daddy,' she said brightly as she shrugged on her coat.

'And where do you think you are off to in such a hurry?' he asked.

'I'm going to the Flag and Garter,' Louise said. 'My call-up papers have come and I want to celebrate.'

'It's a bit soon for that,' he said, unbuttoning his greatcoat. 'Better to wait until you've completed your training, don't you think?' He gave one of his patronising laughs. '*If* you complete it.'

'Of course I'll complete it,' Louise said crossly. 'Why shouldn't I? There are millions of people in the army. They must all have done basic training. Why am I so different?'

His brows drew together sharply. 'You won't complete anything if you can't keep a civil tongue in your head, young lady,' he snapped. 'What's more, I hardly think being called up as a private soldier is much to celebrate. Look at your brother. He went straight into the Coldstream Guards on an officer's commission and …'

Louise couldn't bear it any more. Closing her ears, she draped her silk scarf carefully over her hair. As soon as he paused for breath, she picked up her gas mask box and smiled sweetly. 'Sorry, Daddy, I've got to go, but I promise to come straight back if there's an air raid. Oh, and Mummy told me to tell you that there's a toad in the hole in the oven.'

It was very cold outside, and she wished she had worn a warmer scarf, but it wasn't far to the pub, and she walked as quickly as she could, shining the dimmed light of her torch on the pavement in front of her.

She was so lost in resentful thoughts about her father that she nearly bumped straight into two soldiers standing at the corner. She jumped in alarm, and got even more of a shock when she played the torch over their faces and realised they were black. Black American GIs. For a second she was alarmed, all her father's dire warnings coming back to haunt her, but before she could move, or scream, one of them spoke.

'Excuse me, ma'am,' he said, blinking against the light. He had a normal American accent, but with a kind of strange, sing-song tone. 'Is this Lavender Road?'

He didn't sound as though he was about to take any liberties with her. On the contrary, he sounded deferential, almost nervous, as though he was fully expecting a rebuff. And she rather liked the sound of that subservient 'ma'am'.

'Yes,' she said. 'It is. Are you lost?'

'I'm not sure,' he said, and she could hear a tentative smile in his voice. 'We're tryin' to find the Flag and Garter public house.'

'That's where I'm headed, too,' Louise said. She pointed across the street. 'It's just up there on the other side of the road, where that taxi is parked.'

But the soldiers seemed oddly reluctant to move away. 'I guess we need to ask if it's OK for us to go in there,' the other man said. His voice was different, higher-pitched, but it had the same rather attractive musical drawl. 'Would we be welcome? What with us being black and all.'

He sounded awkward and Louise felt embarrassed for him. 'Of course you'd be welcome,' she said. 'This is England. We don't have a colour bar here.'

But the first man still seemed doubtful. 'The thing is, we were invited a couple days ago by this real nice girl called Angie, but she was kind of young, and well, maybe just a little bit ...'

'Drunk?' Louise suggested. She might have known Angie Carter would be involved somewhere along the line. 'Nevertheless,' she said. 'I'm sure she will be delighted to see you.' She urged the two men across the road. She was getting cold and she didn't want to arrive at the pub with a red nose.

Katy stared at Henry Keller in considerable dismay. She liked him, but she knew what Jen meant about him. Even though he had perfect manners and an easy charm, he made her feel tongue-tied and gauche, and she always felt she was about to say the wrong thing. And she felt it even more when he pulled off his gloves and asked if Jen had mentioned that he was coming in.

Idiotically, Katy looked at the clock again, but it was still seven o'clock. As she turned back, Henry gave her a dry smile. 'Do you think she's forgotten? Maybe I should go and find her at her mother's house?'

'No, no,' Katy said hastily. 'She's not at her mother's house. She's staying here in the pub with me at the moment. She's gone to the pictures with her brother. But she knew you were coming in and she promised to be back well in time.'

Henry inclined his head and pulled up a bar stool. He took out a silver cigarette case and tapped out a cigarette. 'In that case,' he said, 'perhaps you could give me a small whisky and soda.'

Oh God, thought Katy as she took one of her best glasses and held it up to the optic. The last thing she wanted to do was play piggy in the middle between Henry and Jen. And to think the evening had started off so well.

A sudden draught on her neck told her that the door had opened again, and she looked round quickly, hoping that it would be Jen.

But it wasn't.

It was Louise, dressed up to the nines. And bizarrely, she was accompanied by two black GIs.

'Look who I found lurking around outside,' she called across brightly. 'This is Ben, and this is Moses.'

Katy saw one or two of her regulars glance over with vague smiles of welcome, but the announcement had completely the opposite effect on the white American soldiers by the fireplace. One of them muttered an expletive, and as the rest swung round to face the newcomers, an ominous silence fell.

Henry Keller paused in the act of lighting his cigarette. 'Oh dear,' he murmured to Katy. 'I think we might have a problem.'

Even Angie was affected by the sudden change of mood in the bar. She had been on the brink of running across to greet the newcomers, but now she stopped and looked at the white GIs. 'What is it?' she asked, clearly perplexed. 'What's the matter?'

The corporal who had been rude to Elsa shoved her aside. He was a burly, thickset man with fists the size of hams. Advancing a couple of paces, he addressed the two black men. 'You aren't welcome here. Leave now and there won't be no trouble.'

He had reckoned without Louise. 'But they are welcome,' she said. She turned to Katy. 'Aren't they?'

Before Katy could answer, the corporal had taken another deliberate step forward. 'Get out,' he hissed. 'It's whites only in here.'

'Katy?' Louise cried. 'Do something.'

But Katy didn't know what to do. She had read the leaflets and knew that the official advice was to try to keep the white and black soldiers apart. It was clearly too late for that. She didn't see why she should turn the two black men away, but nor did she want an ugly brawl. One or two of her regulars were already casting hostile glances towards the bull-headed corporal and his cronies. Even Mr Lorenz had put down his newspaper and stood up, although it seemed unlikely that a bespectacled middle-aged Jewish man would have much impact on a troop of tough, bigoted GIs.

Beside her, she was aware of the tension in Elsa's nervous, shallow breathing. Upstairs she could hear Malcolm resisting Bella's efforts to put him to bed. She prayed he wouldn't choose this moment to come back down.

Suddenly she thought of Lucky. This was exactly the kind of eventuality Ward had been thinking of when he had brought the dog back from Corsica. But of course, now that he was finally needed, the blasted animal was nowhere in sight. But Katy knew that if she didn't do something soon, it would be too late. 'I'm the landlady of this pub,' she said loudly. 'And everyone is welcome here. Whatever colour they are.'

The corporal took no notice. He was still advancing slowly on the two black soldiers, who were looking increasingly uncomfortable. As a couple of the other GIs moved up behind the bull-headed American, Louise tried to block his way. 'Stop it,' she snapped. 'Leave them alone.'

The man barely glanced at her. 'Get out of my way, little missy,' he said. 'Or you might get hurt.'

Katy saw Louise's eyes flash with anger, but she stood her ground. 'It's nothing to do with you,' she said bravely. 'I told them they could come in.'

Katy was aware of her knees shaking. She recognised the aggressive look in the corporal's eyes. You couldn't run a pub in south London without knowing the warning signs of a potential fight. And she had a sudden appalling vision of what was about to happen. Violence. Injuries. Her precious bar being destroyed. A bloodbath. Newspaper reports. A terrible rift in the all-important Anglo–US relations.

Helplessly she grasped the counter for support.

And then to her surprise, Henry stepped forward.

He had taken off his overcoat, and his sleek double-breasted suit, club tie and leather brogues made an odd contrast with the burly corporal's rumpled battledress and heavy combat boots. Henry was slightly taller than the corporal, but leaner. If it came to blows, he would undoubtedly be at a disadvantage. But he seemed unconcerned about that. On the contrary, he appeared unduly calm, almost indifferent.

'What's your name, Corporal?' he asked. His voice was quiet, but it held a note of authority that Katy had never heard before.

Clearly the corporal recognised it too. His head swung round sharply. 'Crowe, sir,' he said. 'But—'

'And you are serving with the Eighth Infantry Division?'

The man straightened up involuntarily. 'Yes, sir. I am.'

Henry drew on his cigarette, tapping it thoughtfully into a nearby ashtray. Then he looked up and fixed the corporal with a steady gaze. 'Commanded by General McMahon?'

'Well, yes, sir,' the man stammered. 'But—'

Henry raised his eyebrows in cool interrogation. 'In that case, you presumably know that General McMahon is a stickler for discipline and restraint?'

For a long, tense moment the man held his gaze, but then at last he lowered his eyes. A second later, he took an involuntary step back, almost colliding with the two GIs behind him.

At once Katy knew that the immediate danger was over. If she could just get everyone to stop looking at them, it might be all right. She realised she had been holding her breath. Now she let it out and glanced rather desperately round the bar.

Mr Lorenz caught her eye and seemed to understand what she wanted. Picking up his empty glass, he came over to the counter. 'I'll have another half, when you've got a moment,' he said, for all the world as though nothing had happened.

Katy smiled at him gratefully. 'Of course,' she said.

As she busied herself with the beer lever, she saw Henry turn to Louise. 'I'm wondering if your friends might be more comfortable in the other bar,' he murmured. He smiled easily at the two black men. 'Just for now.'

Louise was looking rather shaken. 'They aren't really my friends,' she said. 'I'd never met them before tonight.' She nodded crossly towards Angie, who for once was standing still and silent, clinging to Gino's arm by the fireplace.

'It was Angie Carter who invited them.'

Henry looked amused. 'Then why don't we get Angie Carter to take them into the other bar,' he said. He smiled at Louise through the smoke from his cigarette. 'While I buy you a drink.'

Katy caught Louise's sudden flush of pleasure. And once again she felt her heart sink. Oh no, she thought. Oh no!

Until Katy rather reluctantly introduced them, Louise hadn't realised that her saviour was Henry Keller. But she had been impressed by his cool command of the situation, and she was more than happy to join him for a drink.

There was no doubt he had defused a potentially ugly scene. But as Angie Carter dragged the two black GIs off into the saloon bar, he made very little of it, shrugging off Katy's heartfelt thanks with graceful unconcern. Louise did notice, however, that he kept a casual eye on the group of white GIs and only relaxed fully when they left the pub a few minutes later.

'I think it was your mention of General McMahon that did the trick,' Louise said as she and Henry settled themselves on bar stools with a gin and tonic each. 'It was a bit of luck that you know him.'

Henry laughed. 'Good God,' he said, 'I've never met the man in my life. But I know he's in charge of the Eighth Division.'

Louise looked at him in wonder. 'Then how on earth did you know he's such a stickler for discipline and restraint?'

'I didn't. I made it up.' He smiled at her startled expression and waved his cigarette in a mollifying gesture. 'But I'm sure he is. In my experience, most generals are. Anyway, I didn't think Corporal Crowe would be any the wiser.'

'I don't know how you managed to stay so calm,' Louise said, remembering the aggression in the corporal's horrid piggy eyes. 'What if he had punched you?'

Henry drew on his cigarette unconcernedly. 'I wasn't going to let that happen,' he said. As he exhaled, he turned his head quizzically. 'But I quite thought *you* were going to punch *him*, especially when he called you little missy.'

It was as she burst into laughter and nearly choked on her drink that Louise heard a scuffle at the door. Swivelling round on her stool, she saw Jen Carter dragging Katy's dog through the blackout curtain.

Jen was clearly not in a good mood. As she released the dog, she looked distinctly narked. But that was nothing compared to the anger that crossed her face when she saw who Henry was talking to. Henry didn't make any comment, but Louise noticed his fingers tightening slightly on his glass, and thought how typical it was of Jen to come and spoil everything.

But as well as Jen glaring daggers at her, now Louise could see Katy trying desperately to catch her eye. Reluctantly taking the hint, she turned back to Henry. 'Thank you for coming to my rescue,' she said as she levered herself off her bar stool. 'And for the drink. But I'd better leave you to it. It looks like *I* might get punched if I stay here talking to you much longer.'

Henry's eyes glinted appreciatively as he politely stood up too. 'It's been a pleasure meeting you, little missy,' he responded promptly. 'I hope I can come to your rescue again some other time.'

So do I, Louise thought. Suddenly her knees felt rather wobbly. It was as much as she could do to move away without falling over. *So do I.*

Jen couldn't believe it. After dragging the love-crazed Lucky all the way back to the pub, to be greeted by the sight of Louise flirting her pants off with Henry Keller was about as much as she could take. And by the look of Louise's smug little smile as she flounced off to the saloon bar, Henry had not been averse to her attentions. It was only by dint of gritting her teeth so hard that they almost broke that Jen was able to cross the bar and greet him with any semblance of civility.

'Hello, Henry,' she said.

'Hello, Jen.'

There was a short pause, during which Jen remembered that she was now extremely late for this meeting. And if it was his taxi that she had seen waiting outside the pub, she had probably run him up quite a considerable bill.

'What would you like to drink?' Henry asked. 'I'm afraid I'm already on my third.'

Jen glared at him. 'I know I'm late,' she said. 'But I didn't mean to be.' She cast a baleful glance at Lucky, who was now reclining comfortably in front of the fire. 'Paul and I were on our way back from the pictures when we came across that asinine dog trying to ravish some idiotic performing poodle. I could hardly leave him there, not with Pookie in such a state ...' Aware that Henry had made a slight noise in his throat, she stopped and looked at him suspiciously.

'Pookie?' he enquired.

'That was the poodle's name,' Jen said crossly. And was taken aback when Henry gave a sudden choke of amusement.

She stared at him in surprise. But his laughter was infectious, and suddenly she realised that it had actually been quite funny. She also realised that Henry might have had a tad too much to drink. She waited while Elsa served them with a fresh round, and then described Pookie's owner and his lime-green suit. 'I think he was worried Lucky might ravish him as well,' she said drily, and was gratified when Henry's renewed mirth almost caused him to spill his gin and tonic.

Taking advantage of his good humour, Jen took the plunge and asked if he had found her a job.

He had been in the process of lifting his drink to his lips, but now he put it down again. 'Yes,' he said. 'I have.' He took out his cigarette case and offered her one, which she declined.

'Tell me,' he said as he lit up. 'How would you feel about helping us out with some admin in the ENSA offices?'

Jen was dumbfounded. In the offices? She didn't want to work in an office. She had never worked in an office. She wanted to sing. To act. She was a performer, for goodness' sake. What was he saying? That he had finally decided she wasn't good enough? Or was he punishing her for spurning his offer of marriage.

'But you must have millions of ENSA shows on the go,' she said. 'Why on earth can't I be in one of those?'

Henry was watching her through slightly narrowed eyes.

'What state is your voice in?' he asked.

Taken aback, Jen stopped and blinked. 'What do you mean?'

He waved his cigarette casually. 'How confident are you feeling? Really. About performing again. About singing. If I asked you to set off on a long concert tour of Scotland, for example?'

Jen quailed. She suddenly realised that the thought of standing up in front of an audience filled her with dread. The idea of going on tour was even worse. ENSA tours inevitably involved late nights and early mornings, and the endless travelling was exhausting. She remembered all too well the interminable army camps and armaments factories, smoke-filled canteens, draughty tents, and horrid lodgings with damp sheets and no hot water.

'I'm afraid your silence speaks for itself,' Henry said. 'In the past you would have jumped at the opportunity.' He held up his hand as she started to speak. 'No, Jen, listen to me. I know you don't want to admit it, but you've had a bad time of it recently, and you aren't over it yet. I can see it in your eyes. And I simply can't afford to send people out on tour if I'm not certain of their ability to cope.'

To her horror, Jen felt her eyes watering at the blunt words. Quickly she turned her face away. The thought of blubbing in the middle of the public bar was unthinkable. But if nothing else, her ridiculous, unwarranted emotion proved that maybe he was right. She never cried. Throughout her entire time in Italy she had only ever cried once.

'I could give you a chorus role in one of the London shows,' Henry was saying. 'But that would be a step back for you, and I don't want to do that. So this is what I am offering.' He drew on his cigarette and exhaled slowly. 'You can come and work in the offices at Drury Lane. As you say, we have a million shows going on all the time. It's very busy and we always need extra help. And then when you think you are ready, I'll find you a more suitable role on stage.'

He glanced at her questioningly, but Jen still couldn't trust herself to speak. She was mortified by his assessment of her state of mind, but she knew it was a kind offer. He didn't have to help her. He didn't have to do anything for her. Most men in his position would have told her to bugger off, or at the very least pull herself together.

She wondered suddenly if he was finding this as awkward as she was. If he was, he didn't show it. In fact he wasn't even looking at her now. He seemed much more interested in two black GIs who had just come through from the saloon bar with Angie and Gino. Angie was urging one of them to play the piano, and after a small show of reluctance, the man sat down on the stool and ran his fingers experimentally over the keys.

It quickly became obvious that the GI was an accomplished musician. After a rendition of 'Ain't Misbehavin'' that would have done credit to Fats Waller, he segued effortlessly into a quick-fingered swing number that made Angie scream with delight and grab the hand of the other black soldier. Within seconds there were two or three couples jiving energetically on the floor, and Katy was hurrying across to move her precious tables and chairs out of their way.

'That's what I call a performer,' Henry murmured. 'Shame I can't snaffle *him* for ENSA.' Reluctantly he stubbed out his cigarette and stood up. 'I must go,' he said. 'I have a taxi waiting outside. The driver has probably frozen to death by now.'

He shrugged on the navy overcoat that he had slung over the back of his chair and picked up his gloves. Then he glanced down at Jen with a frown. 'I know you think I'm being unduly harsh,' he said softly. 'But I'm not. You will be a star one day. This is only a slight delay. Just to give you time to get back on your feet.' He leaned over and kissed her coolly on the cheek. 'I'm away all next week, so come in a week on Monday, and we'll take it from there.'

Numbly Jen watched him move off across the room. She saw Katy shake his hand and Angie blow him a kiss. Mr Lorenz lifted his glass in a kind of toast, and one or two other regulars nodded approvingly. Even the black man at the piano paused a moment to raise a hand.

'What's Henry done to make himself so popular?' she asked Elsa, who was standing nearby, also watching him go.

'Did he not tell you?' Elsa said. 'He stop a dangerous fight between the soldiers. I think he is a very brave man, no?'

*

102

'George has got another bruise,' Pam said to Alan on Friday night as they got ready for bed. 'It's a fresh one, quite nasty, on his shoulder. But he wouldn't tell me how he got it.' She paused. 'Or rather, he did. He said he'd bumped it on the playground gate, but I didn't believe him.'

Alan was sitting on the bed, taking off his socks. 'Why not?'

'Because I can tell when he's lying,' Pam said. 'He tries to look extra innocent, but his eyes flicker away from mine.' She sighed. If only George was more forthcoming, it would be so much easier to deal with him. 'I'm sure it's something to do with this damn salvage competition,' she added as she slipped on her longest, thickest nightie. She had learned from bitter experience that when the sirens sounded, warmth and comfort were everything.

She was glad Alan was at home tonight. She hated being stuck in the Anderson shelter on her own with the children. Invariably they refused to sleep, and keeping them both amused for hours on end in an ice-cold corrugated burrow the size of a small pig sty was not an easy task.

'I thought at first it might keep him out of trouble,' she said as she slid under the covers. 'But now he's so keen to win this damn rabbit, and I'm beginning to wonder if he's bruising himself climbing into bombed buildings to find suitable bits and pieces. But he denies that too.'

Alan got into bed. 'Perhaps I should go and talk to his teacher,' he said. 'See if he's noticed anything untoward in George's behaviour at school.'

Pam was stunned. It was the first time Alan had taken her concerns seriously. She had thought of approaching the teacher herself, but mothers were discouraged from entering the school buildings. In any case, on the rare occasions she had met him, she had found Mr Grandison unpleasantly dismissive. 'Oh, Alan,' she said eagerly. 'Would you really?'

'I would,' he said. He reached over to turn out the light, then, pulling her to him, ran a hand down her back. 'And I have another good idea,' he added a few seconds later. 'How about you take off this extraordinarily voluminous nightgown?'

A few doors along Lavender Road, Joyce was also lying in bed, but she was trying to make out what was going on downstairs. She had been on the brink of sleep when she'd heard Angie and Gino come in from the pub. For a while she had listened to them chatting in the sitting room situated immediately below her bedroom. Then they'd been fiddling with the wireless, unsuccessfully trying to find the American station that played swing music. But after that it had all gone ominously quiet. And now her imagination was running riot.

She knew she was going to have to go down, but she was getting increasingly weary of policing Angie's activities. If only Jen hadn't decamped to the pub, it wouldn't all have fallen on her. And soon she would have to start policing her store cupboard, too. A couple of days ago she had pulled out her packet of powdered egg and found it half empty. At first she'd thought she was confusing it with the packet at the café. But this evening she had discovered that the flour jar was almost empty too. There didn't seem to be anything else missing apart from a sliver of the precious lump of cheddar she'd been saving for some potato and cheese dumplings. Albert was very partial to those and she had been thinking of inviting him over for a bit of Sunday lunch.

It was a mystery. But it was a mystery that would have to wait until she found out what was going on downstairs. The thought of Angie getting pregnant and bringing an illegitimate baby into the mix was sufficiently alarming to drag her from her warm, comfortable bed.

But when she slipped on her threadbare dressing gown and bedroom slippers and padded downstairs, she found that the sitting room was empty. The lights were on, of course, the fire had been rekindled, and the wireless was still chirping away in the background, as though fuel and electricity were free, unrestricted commodities, generously provided by the government.

Grimly she picked out the smouldering coals with the tongs and put them back in the fire bucket. Then she spread out the embers, and turned off the lights and the radio. She paused. Surely she would have heard them if they had come upstairs. Angie didn't know the meaning of tiptoe. Her attempts at creeping into the house silently normally consisted of a gurgle of hushed laughter and a crash as she overbalanced and knocked into the hall table.

Puzzled, Joyce glanced down the corridor. Oddly, the kitchen door was shut. But then she heard a telltale giggle. Surely they weren't at it on the kitchen table? Even Angie … No, the very thought was …

Joyce flung open the kitchen door and recoiled in shock.

The air was thick with white dust. On the other side of the room, a ghostly apparition was leaning over the sink apparently trying to disentangle her hands from some thick white glutinous substance, while Gino, looking like a plump little snowman, was standing on a chair lowering a long strand of something that looked horribly like part of an animal's entrails into a bubbling saucepan on the stove.

'What on earth?' Joyce said aghast. For a mad second she thought they were indulging in some extraordinary occult ceremony. But then she realised that the strange whitish powder that hung in the air was in fact flour. And the hideous entrail was actually a length of elongated dough. There were several more strips lying on the kitchen table next to her rolling pin, which itself looked as though it was covered in porridge.

Angie had the grace to look somewhat shamefaced. 'Gino wanted to try to cook something called tally telly,' she said.

'*Tagliatelle*,' Gino murmured helpfully from his perch on the chair. 'Is a type of Italian pasta. Is very nice.'

Joyce stared speechlessly at the glutinous mess on her table. It didn't look very nice. In fact it looked absolutely revolting. Damp, sticky and flaccid.

The only pasta Joyce knew was dried macaroni, which was on the ration, two boxes for one stamp. Before the war there had also been tinned spaghetti in tomato sauce, which was made by Heinz as one of their 57 Varieties, but she hadn't seen a tin of that for years. It had never occurred to her that it was possible to make your own pasta.

But although her professional curiosity was aroused, she was not at all impressed by the mess they were making in her kitchen, not to mention the unwarranted and unauthorised use of her flour. No wonder her supply had been dwindling if this was what Gino was up to when her back was turned.

'Gino misses his mother's cooking,' Angie explained from the sink. She was still trying to clean her hands, but the gelatinous mixture was sticking to her like glue.

'Does he?' Joyce said grimly. 'And does his mother make this kind of mess when she is cooking?'

Angie giggled. 'I tipped over the flour jar by mistake,' she admitted. 'But I promise we'll clear up afterwards. And if you like, we'll bring you a plate of tally telly to try in bed.'

'No, I wouldn't like,' Joyce said. 'I can't think of anything I'd like less.' She drew a breath and tried to reassert her authority. 'I'm very cross with you, Angie. It's very naughty of you to use my flour without asking.'

'But we thought you were asleep,' Angie said. 'And we'll get you some more tomorrow.'

'You can't just buy it, you need coupons,' Joyce said, annoyed. If only it was that easy.

But to her surprise, Angie shook her head. 'Oh, we won't need coupons,' she said. 'One of the GIs is a cook at the American barracks. It was him who gave us the recipe. His grandmother is Italian. He said he can smuggle us out a bag of flour any time we want.'

'Pity he can't smuggle you out some electricity as well,' Joyce said sourly. But of course Angie had an answer for that too.

'Don't worry about that,' she said airily. 'Gino will pay you back from his wages.' She saw Joyce's eyes widen and gave another giggle. 'He's got a job now. He's starting work for Katy at the pub tomorrow.'

Good God, Joyce thought. But she refused to back down. 'In that case, he had better get to bed,' she snapped. 'We all know he's not good at getting up in the morning.' She cast a disparaging glance at Gino, who had climbed down from the chair and was peering morosely into his saucepan. The pasta entrail had completely disintegrated in the water. Joyce sniffed as she turned away. 'And you can tell him his mixture is far too wet; that's why it's falling apart. He needs to use more flour when he rolls it out. That'll stop it sticking to the rolling pin too.'

Chapter Ten

As everyone had predicted, Gino did not prove to be a success in the pub. He did try to do what he was told, but he kept getting things wrong, moving beer kegs that needed to settle, or failing to chalk up new deliveries, so that nobody could tell which was the next barrel to use.

Katy tried to instruct him in the mechanics of the beer pumps and the fining process, but in the end she gave up, because he simply wasn't able to understand what she was saying, and the risk of him spoiling large quantities of beer was too great. He seemed incapable of using his own initiative, and she found herself having to supervise him so much she might as well have done the work herself. But she persevered, mainly because, as she gradually got to know him, she realised he was desperately homesick.

Prior to the war, Gino had barely left his hilltop village in Lazio. But Mussolini's dreams of extending his fascist empire had eventually sent him to North Africa. Listening to his stumbling account of the horror and brutality he had witnessed in the desert war, Katy wasn't surprised that the Italian forces had ultimately surrendered in such numbers.

But Gino didn't like England very much either. He hated the cold. He hated the rain. He hated the food. And he hated the bombing. The only thing in his life that gave him any joy was Angie.

Until, one morning, a parcel arrived from Molly in Tunisia. Katy and Jen unpacked it in excitement. Molly had sent a pair of leather slippers with orange tassels for Katy, a brightly coloured camel on wheels for Malcolm, a soft woollen blanket for baby Caroline and an exotic silk scarf with a white fringe for Jen. She had also enclosed a wooden yo-yo for George Nelson, a box of sugared almonds for Pam and Alan, and a crocheted doll in traditional dress for little Nellie.

But her largesse didn't stop there. Unaware that Ward had gone away, and knowing his predilection for exotic food, she had put in several jars of spices, half a dozen enormous onions and a large plait of garlic bulbs.

It was these that caught Gino's attention as he ambled past carrying a broom. Stopping with a gasp of delight, he put his hand on his heart and gave a deep sigh of longing.

'Mamma mia,' he said in a kind of ecstatic, high-pitched whimper. '*Aglio.*' Reaching over impulsively, he lifted the plait of garlic and held it to his nose, closing his eyes and breathing deeply, an expression of sublime rapture on his face.

'I think he's died and gone to heaven,' Jen murmured, and Katy had to clamp her hand over her mouth to prevent herself laughing.

Joyce had told them about poor Gino's abortive pasta-making experiment. Now, seeing the sudden animation on his face, Katy felt obliged to offer him the garlic and the spices. She wasn't likely to use them. She wasn't keen on foreign food. And nor was Jen. In fact when Katy had asked Jen if she'd eaten pasta while she'd been in Italy, she had shuddered and said she never wanted to see a plate of the hideous stuff ever again.

'My mother will kill you,' Jen murmured now, as Gino carried the plait away reverently. 'As well as being encrusted with dried dough, the kitchen will stink of garlic too.'

'Oh dear,' Katy giggled. 'I hadn't thought of that. Maybe I'll give her a couple of onions to make up for it.'

But two large onions, although welcome in these spartan times, weren't enough to compensate Joyce for the shock that greeted her a few days later when she got home from the café. It wasn't just the kitchen that stank of garlic, it was the whole house. As soon as she opened the front door, it hit her in the face like a pungent cloud.

'Oh my goodness,' she said, turning to Mr Lorenz, who had escorted her home. 'What's the idiot gone and done now? I was going to offer you a cup of tea, but I can't let you come in with the house smelling like this. We'll need our respirators.'

Mr Lorenz gave a courteous sniff. 'I don't find it unpleasant,' he said. 'But I am happy to go to the pub if you would prefer.'

Joyce hesitated. She didn't really want to go to the pub. She had been looking forward to spending a bit of time with Albert on her own, without any prying eyes. She had expected Angie and Gino to be out. But no, they were sitting with Paul at the kitchen table, empty plates in front of them. And once again the kitchen was in complete disarray.

'Oh dear,' Angie said guiltily. This time she had pasta dough in her hair as well as all over her hands. 'I didn't think you'd be home so soon. Oh, hello, Mr Lorenz, have you come to try some of Gino's cooking?' She waved a sticky hand at a bubbling saucepan on the stove. 'There's still plenty if you'd like to try some.'

As Mr Lorenz turned to glance at her, Joyce saw the mild alarm in his eyes and felt unreasonably gratified. She couldn't help feeling that it was disloyal of Angie and Paul to scoff down Gino's Italian muck with apparent relish when they were so used to her own good English cooking. But then of course both of them had the appetite of a crocodile with tapeworms.

'No,' she said. 'Absolutely not. I'm not having Mr Lorenz poisoned. But you can make us both a nice cup of tea. And then you can tidy things up in here.'

'Oh, but we're all going to the pictures in a minute …'

'Not until you have tidied up,' Joyce said firmly. 'If this kitchen is not spick and span next time I come in, I'll be very cross.'

But when Angie brought the tea tray through a few minutes later, even the milk smelt of garlic. Joyce put her hand to her head. 'I can't cope with much more of this,' she said.

Mr Lorenz chuckled. 'I must admit it does have a rather unusual taste,' he said, putting his cup delicately back on its saucer. 'I still have one bottle of wine at home. Shall I go and fetch it?'

Joyce suddenly felt apprehensive. A cup of tea was one thing, but sharing a bottle of wine, alone in the house together, was quite another. But before she could demur, Angie's face popped round the door again.

'Oh that's a lovely idea, Mr Lorenz,' she said. 'Mum would love that, wouldn't you?' She gave Joyce a big wink. 'And I promise we won't come home too early. Not unless there's a raid.'

At that moment Joyce could have easily killed her. And Gino. And indeed Paul, who was standing behind them grinning like a great dodo.

But Albert took it in his stride. 'That's right,' he said. 'We need a bit of peace and quiet. We have very serious things to discuss.' And that made Joyce feel even more alarmed.

By the time he reappeared with the bottle of wine, two elegant glasses and a corkscrew, she was close to panic.

He smiled when he saw her expression, and having efficiently opened the bottle, carefully poured the wine.

'I decided to take the bull by the horns,' he said as he sat down. 'So I had a word with Mrs Rutherford earlier today, and she suggested that we take our little holiday over the Easter weekend. She is quite happy to cover the café while we're away. With Angie's help, of course.'

Joyce stiffened. What he meant, of course, was that he had somehow persuaded Mrs Rutherford to give her some time off.

He was looking at her expectantly, and although she didn't quite feel capable of speech, he seemed satisfied with what he saw. 'I was wondering about Brighton,' he went on calmly. 'I have never been there myself, but I am told it is a pleasant place to spend a few days, even in wartime.'

'Oh Albert,' Joyce said nervously. 'But what about Angie and Gino? I can't leave them here on their own.'

Mr Lorenz looked as though he had been expecting the objection. 'If you really think it is necessary, we can ask Jen if she would come and sleep here while we are away,' he said. 'But I personally feel that sooner or later you will have to bow to the inevitable and let them get married.'

'Oh no,' Joyce said at once. 'I can't let her marry him. He's got nothing to offer. He's a dead loss.'

Mr Lorenz smiled. 'I'm sure he will find his feet eventually.'

'Well he shows no sign of finding them,' Joyce said crossly. 'I don't suppose he even knows the English word for feet. He's only earning a pittance at the pub. And what if Angie falls pregnant? I certainly can't afford to support them all. And there's Paul to think of too.'

Mr Lorenz fingered his glass. 'If you'd let me, I'd help you. If you and I were married …'

'Oh Albert,' Joyce said again. Her hand shook as she lifted the glass to her lips. 'I can't talk about that now.'

He looked at her with fond frustration. 'Then we'll talk about something else,' he said. He leaned over to top up her wine. 'I wanted to ask if you'd seen in the paper that the King and Queen had taken a meal with the miners in South Wales. Apparently the Queen told a reporter afterwards that she had rarely had a better meal. It makes you wonder what they eat at Buckingham Palace, doesn't it?'

Joyce was grateful for the change of subject, but she had barely formulated an answer when in the distance the sirens started up.

And suddenly she was faced with a dilemma. Should she invite Albert into her dingy Anderson shelter? But she hadn't replenished the gas bottle, and if the children came back, she couldn't imagine him enjoying being huddled in a moth-eaten old blanket, wedged between Paul and Gino and Angie. It was all right for people like the Rutherfords who had a proper cellar, she reflected crossly.

Not for the first time, she wondered what that tarty madam Mrs James over the road did if the sirens went off while she was entertaining one of her customers. Did she risk it, or did she invite them into her Anderson shelter in mid-stride, as it were? Either way, it would surely take the thrill out of it for her clients. Serve them right, she thought sourly.

But Albert was already getting to his feet. 'I'd better go back across the road. What a shame.'

He seemed to want to leave, but as she opened the front door, the siren up on the common seemed somehow louder than usual. And the ARP alarms on Lavender Hill were blaring too. Numerous searchlights were criss-crossing the sky, casting eerie moving shadows over the street. It looked like they might be in for a bad one. Suddenly she didn't like the thought of him being all alone in his shelter.

'You can stay here if you want,' she said gruffly. 'Our shelter's not very warm, mind. And I expect the children will be back soon. But …'

'But until then it would be just you and me.' Mr Lorenz smiled. 'I can't think of anything nicer.'

He was on the brink of stepping back inside when a glimmer of light flashed on the other side of the road as the door of Gillian James's house opened.

Was that the answer? Did Mrs James eject her lovers as soon as the siren sounded? But the figure that emerged wasn't a man; it was Bella, huddled in a thick overcoat.

'Good God,' Joyce muttered, and peremptorily brushing past Mr Lorenz, she called the girl's name.

'Hello, Mrs Carter,' Bella called back in her shy voice. 'Oh, and hello, Mr Lorenz,' she added politely, as the beam of a passing searchlight momentarily illuminated his face.

'Where on earth are you going?' Joyce shouted across. 'Can't you hear the siren?'

Bella hesitated, then crossed the road. 'I'm going to the public shelter up on the common,' she said. She glanced awkwardly at Mr Lorenz and lowered her voice. 'Mummy doesn't like me using our shelter if she's entertaining. In case her friend wants to use it. Sometimes they don't bother, but …'

So that was the answer. Joyce was disgusted. She knew Mrs James was a selfish madam, in more ways than one, but to send her own daughter out to the unsavoury, overcrowded public shelter on her own really took the biscuit.

'Well you'd best come in here with me,' she said.

'Oh, can I?' Bella said. Her voice was eager. 'Are you sure? To tell you the truth, I'm not very keen on the public shelter. It smells, and people look at me.'

At that moment Joyce would happily have driven a stake through Mrs James's heart. She took Bella's arm and steered her into the house. 'Go on through,' she said. 'I'll be with you in just a moment.'

She glanced apologetically back to Mr Lorenz, who was still standing by the gate. 'I'm sorry, Albert,' she said. 'But really … that girl is only fourteen years old.' She hesitated, realising that he was looking at her with an odd smile in his dark eyes. 'But of course you can still come in if you want, although it might get a bit crowded if the others do come home.'

'You are a good woman,' Mr Lorenz said. 'That's one of the many things I admire about you.' He put a gentle hand on her shoulder. She felt the stiff brow of his homburg touch her forehead, and then the brief brush of his lips on her cheek. 'Goodnight,' he said. 'Be safe.'

And then he was gone, his black coat melting into the darkness as he crossed the road.

Once again that night Lavender Road was spared. But in other areas of London there was significant damage. The windows of number 10 Downing Street were blown in. The Great Western Hotel in Paddington went up in flames. Wandsworth Prison was damaged and a barrage balloon fell into the exercise yard, causing fears that inmates might escape by climbing the trailing wires. Twenty thousand books were destroyed by an incendiary at the London Library.

Over the following weekend, the bombers caused even more devastation in South London. The tram lines were damaged at the Clapham Junction end of Falcon Road, several houses were gutted in Putney and fire swept through a block of flats, causing an untold number of deaths.

Louise, incarcerated in her parents' cellar, had spent much of the weekend thinking about Henry Keller. He had been younger than she had expected, probably not much more than thirty, and much more sophisticated. Certainly far too sophisticated for the likes of Jen Carter. She had admired his air of languid self-confidence, and there was no doubt he had handled the incident in the pub with considerable panache.

But then something happened that, temporarily at least, put Henry Keller out of her mind. Because of the bomb damage, she had to go a different way to work on Monday morning, and her new route led her right past the local school. As she approached, she saw George Nelson standing miserably outside the entrance gate. His school jacket was torn, his nose was bleeding and there were damp streaks on his grubby face that looked as though they might have been caused by tears.

'George?' Louise eyed the pitiful figure with alarm. 'What's happened? Are you all right?'

'I'm fine,' he said gruffly. He hadn't noticed her approach and was clearly put out to be found in such disarray.

'You don't look fine,' Louise said. Taking his arm, she drew him out of the way of a gaggle of other children arriving at the school. 'You're covered in blood.'

As she searched in her handbag for a handkerchief, she was relieved to see that he was already scrubbing his face with his sleeve. But she resisted the temptation to walk on. George Nelson certainly wasn't her responsibility, but she felt obliged to at least try to find out what had happened to him.

But he wouldn't tell her. He just licked the blood off his lips and threw her a sullen glance.

Louise glared back at him. 'Then I'd better go and talk to one of your schoolmasters,' she said. She had no intention of doing any such thing, but she had a feeling that it might be a course of action he wouldn't relish. She was right.

'No,' he said. 'Please don't.' He looked at her in sudden anguish. 'That's the problem,' he blurted out. 'My dad talked to Mr Grandison. And the others found out and said I told tales, and I didn't, but they beat me up anyway to teach me a lesson.'

'Good God,' Louise said. 'But that's monstrous. You can't let them get away with it.'

She looked at him standing there pitifully. What could he do? What could anyone do against bullies? She remembered how helpless she herself had felt in the face of Don Wellington's taunting remarks, and suddenly felt sympathy for the boy. Don Wellington might have needled her, but he had never punched her on the nose.

'You have to try to stand up to them,' she said. 'That's the only thing to do with bullies.'

'I do try,' he said. He aimed an angry kick at the wall. 'But they're bigger than me and they always steal my salvage if they catch me bringing it in.'

Louise stared at him in concern. She wished she could help him, but she felt powerless. She was also very conscious of the time. The stream of children entering the school gates had already slowed to a trickle. 'So what are you going to do?' she asked. 'Go home?'

For a brief moment he looked sorely tempted, but then his chin came up. 'I can't,' he said. 'Because if I go home, they win.'

It seemed to Louise that they had won anyway. But she was grudgingly impressed by his gritty courage. In his position she would have run straight home and told her mother what had happened.

'Do you want me to talk to your parents?' she offered. She didn't know Mr and Mrs Nelson well, and couldn't imagine that they would welcome her interference. On the other hand ...

But George was looking appalled. 'No,' he said in extreme agitation. 'You mustn't tell anyone. You must promise not to. It would only make things much worse.'

Louise shrugged. 'In that case I think you'd better go in,' she said. 'Otherwise we are both going to get into trouble for being late.'

He put on his mulish look. 'You haven't promised,' he said. 'I want you to promise.'

'All right, all right,' she said with a resigned sigh. She simply didn't have time to persuade him otherwise. 'I promise.'

'Cross your heart and hope to die,' he insisted.

'Oh for goodness' sake,' she said irritably. 'I promise I won't tell anyone.'

But as she watched him brace his thin little shoulders and walk through the gate, she no longer felt irritable, she felt angry. She hated the injustice of it, that just because they were physically bigger and more ruthless, these bullies could deprive George of his chance of winning the rabbit.

It wasn't surprising, she thought, as she hurried on down the hill towards the factory. Boys after all were only younger version of men. And men were always trying to dominate one another. That was how the stupid war had started. Nobody had been prepared to stand up to the biggest bully of them all until it was too late.

As she turned the last corner, she could hear the factory start-up bell, and she broke into a painful run. But at the gates, to her dismay, she found her access blocked by a large truck parked right across the entrance.

'It's the wreckage lorry,' the man on the gate told her. 'We had a bit of damage overnight, nothing major, but Mr Gregg wants it all tidied up before that American colonel arrives.' He turned away and yelled to the driver. ''Ere, mate,' he shouted. 'You might as well take them sacks of swarf and offcuts while you're at it. Make a bit more space in the yard.'

But the driver wasn't inclined to rush, and Louise waited impatiently while he slowly heaved the first few sacks up onto the lorry. 'Can't you hurry him up a bit?' she said to the gateman.

Unfortunately the lorry driver heard her. 'Keep yer hair on, love,' he shouted. 'A couple of minutes won't hurt you. There is a bloody war on, you know.'

'I know there's a war on,' Louise shouted back angrily. 'That's why I need to get in.' But then a sudden thought occurred to her, and she turned to the gateman. 'What normally happens to the swarf? Where does it go?'

'It gets collected with the rubbish,' he said. 'I don't know what happens to it after that.'

'So nobody pays Mr Gregg for it or anything?'

He looked at her as though she was mad. ''Ere, Donnie,' he shouted. 'She thinks you should pay for the sacks of offcuts and all.'

The driver responded with a rude remark, but Louise wasn't listening any more. Swarf was still metal, even if it did consist of millions of tiny pieces. If her mother's old chicken-feeding saucepan counted as salvage, then surely swarf would too.

'Can you ask him to leave a few sacks?' she asked. 'I've got a young friend who's collecting salvage for a prize.'

The gateman relayed her request, but by this time the driver had finally finished loading the sacks and he made it clear that he wasn't prepared to expend another iota of effort. And certainly not at the request of a 'la-di-da little madam'. 'If she wants them, she can get them her bleedin' self,' he said.

For Louise, it was the last straw. Little missy had been bad enough. But being called a la-di-da little madam was going too far. She surprised the gate guard by thrusting her handbag and gas mask box into his hands, then shrugged off her coat and made him hold that too. 'All right,' she said grimly. 'I will.'

Luckily she was wearing slacks, so her modesty was more or less preserved. But climbing up onto the rubbish lorry turned out to be more difficult than it looked. Spread-eagled halfway up the side, with one hand grasping the top of the side panel, one foot on the wheel arch and the other on a bolt jutting out from the axle, she was beginning to realise she had bitten off more than she could chew when she heard a vehicle draw up behind her.

'Do we have some kind of problem here?'

Louise couldn't look round, but she didn't need to. She recognised the American accent at once and knew it belonged to Colonel Westwood. She wondered wildly if he would recognise her protruding bottom and desperately hoped not.

'No, sir,' the gateman responded quickly. 'I'll get this truck moved right away, sir. Eh, Donnie,' he shouted. 'Didn't you hear? Get this truck out of the colonel's way.'

'That won't be so easy,' the driver retorted, unimpressed by his former ally's peremptory tone. 'Not with Miss La-di-da clinging to the side like a bleedin' limpet.'

There was a moment's silence, during which Louise closed her eyes and rested her hot face against the cold metal side of the truck.

'I reckon as she's stuck,' the gateman said. He raised his voice as though she was deaf as well as physically incompetent. 'Are you stuck, love?'

'Yes,' Louise snapped. 'Of course I'm stuck. I would have thought that was pretty obvious by now.'

There was another pause, and she imagined them all chortling silently.

But Colonel Westwood didn't sound amused. 'Well help her down, man,' he said impatiently. 'What is she doing up there anyway?'

'She was trying to get at the swarf, sir,' the gateman said. Reluctantly he reached up to offer Louise a hand. But Louise knew that if she let go long enough to take it, she would lose what balance she had left.

With a murmur of annoyance, Colonel Westwood pushed the man out of the way. 'Listen to me,' he said. 'I am going to put my hand on your back to steady you. When I give you the command, I want you to put your left hand on my shoulder. Then I'll be able to lift you down.'

And that was what happened. And it was as she put her hand on his shoulder and he looked up into her face that he finally recognised her. She wasn't sure if it was surprise, amusement or possibly even attraction that made his dark, deep-set eyes flicker, but for her part she was very conscious

115

of the reassuringly firm grip on her hand and his calm strength as he lowered her efficiently to the ground.

He was wearing uniform today, and she could feel the metal pip and crown on his shoulder epaulette under her clutching fingers. While she regained her balance, he kept her other hand in his. Then he released her, pushing her gently away.

He eyed the smirking gateman with disfavour. 'The truck?' he asked. There was a note in his voice that caused the grin to fade rapidly from the man's face.

'Yes, sir, at once, sir,' he said. And eventually, with a grinding of gears and a great belch of smoke from the exhaust, the lorry began to manoeuvre out of the gate.

Colonel Westwood glanced at Louise. 'Do you need me to stop him, or shall I let him go?'

'Let him go,' Louise said weakly. The thought of any more embarrassment was more than she could bear. 'But thank you,' she shouted over the roaring of the engine. 'And I'm so sorry. You must think I'm a complete idiot.'

He didn't react to that, merely waiting for the noisy vehicle to leave before waving the staff car through into the yard.

When it was quiet again, he turned back to her. 'So what *were* you doing?' he asked.

'I was only trying to save back some sacks of swarf,' she said crossly. 'I know this boy who's trying to collect metal salvage to win a white rabbit, but the bigger boys are pinching it off him, and it's not fair, and I thought …'

She caught the slight narrowing of Colonel Westwood's eyes and stopped, belatedly remembering who she was talking to. Oh God, she groaned inwardly, lowering her own eyes in some confusion. This wasn't just some benevolent stranger that she had inadvertently bumped into at the gate. This was a senior American army officer, in charge of a top-secret project. Not only that, he was her future boss. What on earth was she doing burbling on about white rabbits and stupid children? This was hardly the way to impress him.

'You thought you could help him out?' he prompted.

'Yes,' she said, discomfited by his unnervingly steady gaze. 'But those stupid men wouldn't help me.'

'So you decided to take matters into your own hands.'

Was that amusement in his voice? Or disapproval? Either way, Louise felt heat creeping into her cheeks. 'Yes. But as you saw, I wasn't very successful.'

He inclined his head but didn't return her awkward smile. 'No,' he agreed. 'But you have at least shown me that I am going to have to tighten up on security before we start production here. In the meantime, I reckon your best

116

bet would be to discuss it with the factory foreman. See if he can help you.' He glanced at his watch and lifted his hands in a polite gesture of regret. 'I have to go. I'm already late for Mr Gregg. I won't have time to talk with you today. But I'll try to catch up with you before you head off to the ATS.' He frowned. 'That's early next month, right?'

Louise nodded, feeling oddly gratified that he knew. She gave him a shy glance. 'Yes, the sixth of March. To be honest, I'm a bit scared about it.'

'You'll do fine,' he said. Then for the first time he gave the faintest flicker of a smile. 'I sure hope so, because I'm kind of looking forward to having you under my command.' And with that he walked briskly away towards Mr Gregg's office, leaving Louise standing at the factory gate, feeling extremely flustered.

Chapter Eleven

Jen had also had a difficult journey into town that morning. But the Theatre Royal had not been affected by the heavy bombing, and the high-pillared portico over the entrance remained as imposing as ever.

Jen was concerned that the ENSA staff might wonder why Henry had asked her to work in the offices instead of giving her a part in one of his shows, but in the event nobody batted an eyelid, perhaps because they were too busy. 'There are so many shows going out,' Henry's secretary, Beryl, said as she escorted Jen into the auditorium to find him, 'and so many performers wanting to be in them, we are all rushed off our feet with auditions and administration.'

It didn't take Jen long to realise that what she said was true. And it wasn't just the admin staff who were busy. Apart from when he introduced her to a brisk lady called Maggie, who was in charge of the audition process, Jen barely saw Henry that first day. She assumed he was deliberately avoiding her, but a surreptitious glance at the appointment book Beryl kept for him showed that he was up to his ears in meetings with various ENSA grandees and big-name stars.

But Jen didn't have time to feel neglected. Apparently determined to throw her straight in at the deep end, Maggie gave her a list of all the people coming in for auditions that day, and told her that her job was to make sure they arrived on stage at the right time.

It wasn't an easy task. By the end of the day, Jen had decided that herding performers was somewhat like herding fish. They always seemed to be sliding off to greet friends they'd spotted in another part of the theatre, or disappearing at the crucial moment to practise their acts or warm up their voices in the privacy of the lavatory.

The following morning proceeded in much the same way. After a prolonged hunt backstage, she found one man, a juggler, sitting on the front steps of the theatre calmly eating his sandwiches.

'What on earth are you doing?' she asked him irritably. 'You were due on stage five minutes ago.'

'I can't perform on an empty stomach,' he said indignantly. 'I have a condition called hyperinsulinism, which means I need to eat regularly.'

'You'll have a condition called no-job-with-ENSA if you don't come and perform your routine right now,' Jen said.

As she stalked back up the steps, she heard a low laugh behind her. 'It sounds as if you're getting into the swing of things.' And turning round, she found Henry standing behind her.

'Well really,' she said. 'I've been hunting high and low for him. And he's just sitting there, cool as a cucumber, stuffing his face. Although I must say,' she added. 'Those sandwiches did look rather tasty.'

Henry laughed as he pushed open the heavily sandbagged door. 'Are you hungry?' he asked. 'I would offer to take you to lunch, but I've got a backlog of paperwork to get through after being away last week. But I have some sandwiches in my office I would be happy to share, if Maggie will give you a few minutes off.'

Of course Maggie was more than willing to oblige Henry Keller. She worshipped the ground he stood on. Which meant that half an hour later, Jen found herself tucking into a succulent cheese sandwich in Henry's office, trying not to think about the awkward interview she had endured last time she had been in there.

For his part, despite the piles of paperwork waiting on his desk, Henry seemed relaxed and at his ease.

'How are you settling in?' he asked as he handed her a cup of tea from the tray Beryl had brought to his office.

'All right, I think,' Jen said. 'If you can call it settling in when all I've been doing is running about after these so-called entertainers.'

He heard the disparaging tone in her voice. 'You're not impressed?'

She felt suddenly embarrassed. It was hardly her place to criticise the ENSA modus operandi. Nor, she realised, had she yet managed to thank Henry for arranging the job for her, or to apologise for her churlish behaviour in the pub the previous weekend.

'Well,' she prevaricated. 'Some of them do have talent. But there are one or two idiots calling themselves comedians who'd honestly get more laughs cleaning out the hyena cage at the zoo.'

Henry looked amused. 'In our defence,' he said, 'not everyone gets taken on.' He looked at her contemplatively as he sipped his tea. 'How are you getting on with Maggie? She can be a bit of a tartar, but she knows the business inside out.'

'I like her,' Jen said. 'She's been very kind.' She hesitated. 'Henry, look, I'm really sorry I was grumpy about coming to work here and everything the other weekend. I'd had a bad day and it was kind of you to set it up.'

He smiled. 'You don't need to apologise. I probably wasn't at my most tactful myself. There had been a bit of an ugly scene in the pub ...'

'Yes, Katy told me,' Jen said. 'I gather you were incredibly heroic.' Actually

119

she had laughed when Katy had told her the details of Henry's gallant intervention; it had sounded most out of character for the blasé, well-modulated man that she knew. She was aware that he could be a tough and decisive theatrical producer, but she couldn't imagine him willingly facing down a drunken thug.

Henry gave a self-deprecating laugh. 'Hardly that,' he said. 'But I must admit it left a bad taste in my mouth. I hate that kind of intolerance. We expect it from the Nazis, but somehow not from the Americans.' He shook his head. 'I was impressed with your friend, Louise. She certainly wasn't going to back off from a fight.'

Jen looked at him in astonishment. 'Louise isn't a friend of mine.'

He seemed surprised. 'I got the impression you knew each other quite well.'

'Yes, of course I know her,' Jen said irritably. 'I've known her for years. But she thinks she's a cut above the rest of us because she lives in the big house at the end of our road. Her mother owns the café where my mother works, and Mr Rutherford owns the local brewery. There's a ghastly brother, too. He's an officer in one of the Guards regiments. He thinks he's the bee's knees, but actually he's a prat.'

She saw Henry's lips twitch, and lifted her chin. 'No, he really is,' she insisted. 'He once tried to touch up Angie in the back yard of the pub. But he hasn't seen a moment's military action,' she went on scornfully. 'And now he's languishing in hospital in Tunisia pretending he's been heroically injured quelling some native uprising when what really happened was that he got kicked in the face while taunting some poor, unsuspecting camel.'

Henry had been watching her thoughtfully, but that made him laugh.

'So what does Louise do?' he asked. 'I notice her fingers were stained. I assumed she must work in an armaments factory somewhere.'

Jen took an impatient bite of her sandwich. She wished he would stop talking about Louise. It was getting on her nerves.

'She does at the moment,' she said. 'But she's joining the ATS soon.' And hopefully her training camp would be a long way from London, she added silently to herself, well out of Henry's orbit.

Needless to say, Henry looked impressed. 'Really? Good for her.'

Jen lifted her shoulders dismissively. 'Oh, I don't think she's going to be doing any actual soldiering,' she said. 'It's only a formality so she can get a better-paid job at her factory.' She laughed sourly. 'That's what a posh accent and a nice little finishing school does for you.'

Hearing the chippy tone in her own voice, she stood up quickly. 'I'd better go,' she said. She gave a self-conscious laugh. 'And now that I've spent the whole time running down the Rutherfords, you'll think I'm mean and nasty

120

along with everything else you already think about me.'

Henry looked up at her for a long second, then stood up too. 'I don't think you are mean or nasty,' he said. 'As for what else I think about you, I seem to remember promising not to express it. Suffice to say that I continue to think you are charming.' He paused. 'And maybe working here will prove to you that background and upbringing are less important than you think. They certainly don't matter to me.'

That was all very well for him to say, Jen thought as she walked back through the warren of dark subterranean passages to the auditorium. But you only needed to look at all the pleased-with-themselves little actresses who came swanning out of RADA straight into solo roles in ENSA shows to know that wealth and privilege could take you a lot further than mere hard work and ambition.

However, she didn't have time to dwell on what Henry had said, because she was far too busy. By the end of the week, she was exhausted. And when she fell onto her makeshift bed in the pub cellar on Friday night, despite dreaming of risqué comedians, troupes of contortionists and one particular hideously off-key soubrette, for the first time since she had got back to England, she slept right through until morning.

Louise's encounter with Colonel Westwood had strengthened her determination to help George Nelson, but before attempting to sweet-talk the somewhat irascible factory foreman into handing over some sacks of swarf, she decided to ask Katy if she knew anyone locally by the name of Garrow.

Katy's face had darkened at once. 'Yes, of course I have,' she said. 'Garrow was the name of the man who kept stealing my beer glasses last year. He was in cahoots with that awful child-molester, Barry Fish. Thanks to George Nelson, Mr Fish is dead, and Mr Garrow's in jail. Or at least I certainly hope he is.' She had looked at Louise with alarm. 'Why do you ask?'

Louise would have liked to tell her, but her promise to George was ringing in her ears. Katy was after all a close friend of his mother. So she just said that she'd heard someone mention the name at work and left it at that.

But she no longer felt uncomfortable about her intentions. Young Garrow, George's tormentor, was obviously a chip off the old block, and deserved to be thwarted. She certainly wasn't going to let him get his nasty little hands on an innocent rabbit.

She decided that the best way to ensure victory for George was to make sure that the sacks of metal arrived at school on the final day of the competition. Any earlier and there would be a risk that the Garrow boy might somehow trump George's success with extra input of his own at the last minute. For the same reason she decided to keep George in the dark about her plan, in case he blabbed and let the cat out of the bag too soon.

The factory foreman, when she waylaid him in the canteen the next day, was understandably astonished by her request, but when she explained that the offcuts would be donated to a WVS salvage initiative, he grudgingly agreed that she could have as much as she could carry.

'Which won't be much,' he added. 'Because those sacks weigh a good half-hundredweight each.' And indeed, when she tried to pick one up, she could hardly get it off the ground. Which was good as far as George's tally in the competition was concerned, but left her with the dilemma of how on earth to transport the metal from the factory to the school.

But then fate, or more specifically, Colonel Westwood's concerns about security at the factory, played into her hands.

Arriving at Gregg Bros one morning, Louise discovered that the irritating gateman, who for the last week had insisted on making stupid jokes about mountaineering ropes and crampons, was nowhere to be seen.

In his place were a couple of American soldiers, carefully checking everyone's ID. And not only were the two black GIs, Moses and Ben, part of the detail, but parked in the factory yard was a large US Army jeep.

Louise couldn't believe her luck. And Moses and Ben, once they had got over their amazement that she worked at the factory, were only too happy to offer their services to ferry the swarf up to the school.

'Hey, it's the least we can do, ma'am,' Ben said. 'It's all thanks to you that we didn't get beat up that night in the Flag and Garter.'

Katy was delighted to see the improvement in Jen's morale. Who would have thought that a boring old admin job, a job that Jen had very definitely not wanted, would have such a beneficial effect on her? But something about it had lightened her spirit, and even her occasional mentions of Henry seemed fractionally warmer than before.

And that pleased Katy too. The more she thought about it, the more she realised that Henry Keller would be the perfect partner for Jen. It wasn't just that he was handsome and successful; he was clearly kind as well. Like her, he had clearly understood that Jen wasn't yet in a fit state to pick up her former career.

Another benefit of her new job was that Jen was sleeping better. Katy no longer heard her prowling around in the middle of the night. And for the last week there had been no sign of her uncharacteristic tearfulness.

But nor had there been any sign that she was about to fall back into Henry's arms.

Katy couldn't help wondering what Henry felt about working in such proximity with Jen. If he was still in love with her, it couldn't be easy for him. But maybe he was playing a clever game. Whatever he was doing, even though she missed Jen's company during the day, Katy was grateful for his intervention. As she had been for his intervention over the two black GIs.

She had been worried that letting the black Americans have free run of the pub might turn out to be bad for business. But actually the opposite was true. Word had spread quickly about Moses' prowess on the piano, and although, thankfully, the unpleasant Corporal Crowe and his cronies never reappeared, most evenings now the bar was teeming with other American servicemen, who didn't seem to care two hoots about the lack of segregation. And they of course attracted local girls on the sniff for perfume, nylons and bright red Elizabeth Arden lipstick.

It was exhausting, but it was good for trade, and Katy certainly wasn't going to complain about extra washing-up when her till was full of cash at the end of each evening.

She knew it wouldn't last forever, because the unprecedented influx of servicemen meant only one thing. An invasion force was being built up, ready for an assault on Nazi-occupied Europe. And when that happened, all the GIs would disappear, as they had prior to the invasion of Italy last year, and of North Africa before that.

But for now, thanks to Moses, business was good. What was more, he was perfectly happy to play all night if necessary. He knew all the popular tunes, but his speciality was 'As Time Goes By' from the film *Casablanca*.

And every time she heard the moody lyrics, Katy felt tears prickling her eyes. Because they made her think of Ward. It was indeed the same old story. Ward was far too prepared to do or die. And it was a long time since she had last heard from him, which presumably meant he was already involved in some dangerous activity behind enemy lines, probably in France.

But she couldn't make too much of a fuss about it, because she wasn't the only one feeling bereft. Nearly every family in the area had a son or a husband away in the forces.

And it was clearly going to get worse. There was much speculation about the so-called Second Front and when it might happen. But although people were impatient for it to start, they also knew it wasn't going to be an easy ride, because inevitably it would involve casualties, even more than the current battle in Italy. Already in the press there were worrying reports of deserters, especially among some of the foreign troops now stationed in Britain.

And then there was Gino. Not a deserter precisely, but certainly reluctant to fight. And fairly reluctant to work either.

Jen had no patience with him at all, and kept telling Katy to sack him. But he was at least an extra pair of hands, and finding staff in the current climate was impossible. Everyone was either in the forces or doing National Service in some way or other. It was a shame, Katy thought, that despite their morale-boosting quality, pubs weren't considered part of the war effort.

She was missing Jen's help too. Not that Jen was much cop as a barmaid – she hated getting her hands dirty and she was hopeless at remembering the prices – but she had been willing to take the children out to do the shopping, even though Katy suspected that Malcolm's constant chit-chat got on her nerves.

Gino, on the other hand, adored both Malcolm and baby Caroline. Katy was constantly finding him shirking his tasks in order to play with them. He called Caroline *ma bellissima*, and was thrilled when she started to smile each time he said it.

Malcolm, for his part, was intrigued by Gino's inability to speak English. Malcolm was nearly two and a half now, and he soaked up new words like a sponge. Katy had hoped that his constant repetition of his favourite phrases might help Gino to get a handle on the English language, but unfortunately it quickly became clear that it was working the other way round. Malcolm was picking up far more from Gino than Gino was from Malcolm.

Katy was polishing glasses one morning, humming 'As Time Goes By' and trying not to think of Ward, when she heard a rumpus in the cellar.

Over the noise of Lucky's frantic barking, she could hear Gino shouting something about *un topo*. And Malcolm's shrill little voice in response: '*È dietro il barile di birra. Prendilo, Lucky, prendilo!*' She had no idea what he was saying, but the horrendous squealing noise that followed made her blood run cold. Almost throwing herself headlong down the cellar steps in her haste to protect Malcolm from Lucky's aggression, she could hardly believe the tableau that greeted her at the bottom.

White-faced and trembling, Gino was crouching on top of a beer barrel, while Malcolm was dancing around clapping his hands with glee. Lucky, for his part, was standing proudly by Caroline's playpen with an enormous rat, dead but still twitching, dangling from his mouth.

'Oh my God,' Katy said, putting her hand over her racing heart.

'Gino was frightened of the *topo*,' Malcolm shouted at her in delight. 'But Lucky caught it. Lucky killed it! Clever Lucky.'

Clever Lucky indeed, Katy thought. In two whole months, it was the first useful thing the dog had done.

Doris finally came back to work at the factory at the end of February. She had been discharged from hospital two weeks before, and Louise had dutifully visited her at her home in Battersea. It hadn't been a pleasant experience. Doris and her invalid husband, Sid, who had lost one of his legs to gangrene during the Great War and was now suffering from some unspecified lung disease as well, occupied a small flat on the third floor of a huge tenement block.

Louise had never in her life set foot in such a hideous place. Admittedly, Doris and Sid's flat was clean and tidy, but Louise wondered how they could put up with the foul smell of urine and cooking that seemed to permeate the rest of the building. As far as living conditions went, it was a hundred times worse than the squalid little houses on Lavender Road.

Looking at poor incapacitated Sid, who could hardly raise a smile of welcome without coughing, Louise had thought it a miracle that Doris was so relentlessly good-humoured. She very much enjoyed Louise's story about the swarf lorry, especially the bit about the lorry driver calling her Miss La-di-da.

'Mrs Gibbons popped in yesterday,' Doris said when she had stopped laughing. She lowered her voice, perhaps to spare Sid the effort of trying to listen, and cast a sly glance at Louise. 'She says he's a bit of all right, that colonel. No wonder you want to join his unit. Is he married?'

Louise gave a nonchalant chuckle. 'I have no idea,' she said. She had in fact asked Moses and Ben if they happened to know Colonel Westwood's marital status, but unfortunately they didn't know anything about him, except that they had been put on guard duty at the factory because of his top-secret project.

Doris had only been back at work a day when Mr Gregg told her that Colonel Westwood wanted her to take charge of the production line for the equipment for his new secret project, which was due to go into operation the following week.

'And I'm getting a pay rise too,' she confided to Louise when she came out of Mr Gregg's office. 'Not as much as you, I don't suppose. But it's better than a kick in the teeth.'

'Or a bit of swarf in the eye,' Louise said.

Doris thought that was hilarious. 'So if you do end up being the liaison person,' she chortled, 'it's me you'll be liaising with. And I hope it is you, because I don't fancy liaising with Don Wellington.'

Louise was shocked. It hadn't occurred to her that she might be in direct competition with Don Wellington. But she had more important things to worry about. Time was running on, and she decided the moment had now come when she needed to brief George Nelson about what she had planned.

The following morning, she got up extra early and lay in wait in the freezing cold at the corner of Lavender Road until she saw him leave the Nelsons' house. He looked somewhat down in the mouth as he slammed the door behind him and trundled off down the road with a small bundle under his arm. He looked even more disgruntled when she caught him up.

'Hello, George,' she said brightly. 'Do you mind if I walk with you?'

He stared at her suspiciously. 'Why?' he asked.

Louise wondered why she had decided to help the little brat.

'How's your salvage collection going?' she said.

He kicked the ground. 'I'm still trying.' He proffered the bundle disconsolately. 'Dad got me some bottle tops from the brewery, but it won't make up for what I've lost.'

'Is Garrow still making your life difficult?

He stopped abruptly. 'How do you know his name?' he asked accusatorily. 'I never told it you.'

'You did.'

'I didn't.'

Louise felt like shaking him. 'You did,' she insisted. 'Not last time we met, but the time before.'

But he seemed determined to hold on to his attitude of mistrustful hostility. 'I don't want you telling anyone his name. I don't want people thinking I've told tales.'

'Oh for goodness' sake,' Louise snapped in exasperation. 'I'm not going to tell anyone his name. Don't you realise I'm trying to help you?'

'What do you mean?'

'I mean that I have access to lots of metal salvage at the factory. And if you want, I can bring it to the school to help you win the rabbit.'

She was expecting him to be pleased, but the stupid child just looked at her even more warily, as though fearing a trap.

'Why?'

'What do you mean, why?'

'Why do you want to help me?'

Louise groaned, but it was a perfectly reasonable question and one that she had from time to time asked herself. 'Because what's happening to you isn't fair,' she said. 'And when people bully other people, especially people smaller than themselves, you have to do something about it. It's like us standing up to Hitler when he started invading all those weaker countries like Poland and Belgium.'

She looked at him, but he didn't seem impressed by the analogy. He just stood there looking sulky. 'Anyway,' she went on irritably, 'I'm going to get it delivered to your school on Saturday morning.'

He didn't respond. She felt like punching him herself. 'Do you understand?'

He nodded, but he still looked unconvinced.

'That's when the final tally is being calculated,' she said. 'Which is lucky, because I'm leaving the following day to join the army.'

That got his attention. His eyes widened. 'You're joining the army?'

'Yes. Well, the ATS anyway.'

'Are you going to kill people?'

'No, of course not.'

He seemed disappointed. 'I thought that was what people did in the army,' he said.

'Well, yes,' Louise agreed reluctantly. 'But not women.'

'What do women soldiers do then?'

'Goodness, I don't know,' Louise said. She was losing patience with him now. 'They deal with barrage balloons and searchlights and that sort of thing.' She looked at her watch. She was going to be late for work again if she wasn't careful. 'But I'm not doing any of that. I'm going to be working on a military project back at the factory.'

George looked unimpressed. He obviously thought that sounded extremely tame compared to killing people.

But he didn't look remotely unimpressed when the American army jeep drew up at the school gates on Saturday morning.

'Hey, little feller.' Moses hailed him in his strange sing-song voice. 'I guess you must be the guy we have to deliver to. So where do you want it?'

George looked completely astounded, as did his schoolfellows when they saw him marching across the playground a few minutes later, followed by Louise and two black GIs laden with bulging sacks of metal.

At the crucial moment, however they hit an unexpected obstacle. Mr Grandison, the master in charge of logging the salvage, seemed inclined to think that George was contravening the rules by bringing in metal he hadn't collected himself.

But Louise wasn't a Rutherford for nothing. And she was damned if she was going to have all her good work ruined by some pompous nit-picking schoolmaster. 'Nonsense,' she said. 'It is perfectly legitimate.'

Mr Grandison had been busy lighting a pipe when they arrived, but now he withdrew it from his mouth and pointed the stem at her like a gun. 'And who, may I ask, are you?' he asked.

Louise was about to tell him exactly who she was, but then suddenly thought better of it. 'It doesn't matter who I am,' she said briskly. 'The whole point of this competition was to collect as much salvage as possible. And that is what this child has done. It would be a travesty if he was penalised for showing initiative. There is a war on, you know.'

'Well I can't weigh all these sacks,' Mr Grandison said petulantly. 'Our scales aren't big enough.'

'I can tell you exactly what they weigh,' Louise responded. 'They weigh half a hundredweight each.' And you can put that in your pipe and smoke it, she thought. 'So eight sacks represents four hundredweight of salvage.'

'I can do the calculation,' he snapped.

'Good,' she said. 'Then that's what needs to be added to George Nelson's tally.'

The schoolmaster glanced irritably at George, who was standing tensely at Louise's side. 'This is most irregular.'

As far as Louise was concerned, the only irregularity was how shockingly dilatory and unperceptive Mr Grandison had been in his supervision of the children under his care. But she could feel George's nervous, watchful eyes on her, so she reluctantly refrained from saying so and smiled sweetly instead. 'Think of how delighted the WVS will be with the additional salvage,' she said. 'It will show the school in a very good light. And I'm sure you know that Mrs Rutherford is very friendly with the headmaster.'

And with that she turned on her heel and swept out.

'Well you sure told him, ma'am,' said Moses with a dry laugh as he swung himself back into the jeep. 'I figure you'll do well in the army. If you talk like that, you'll soon have them girl soldiers all runnin' around like lemmings.'

Chapter Twelve

Jen had thought that working behind the scenes would be dull compared with being on stage, but actually she found she was rather enjoying it. Over the last couple of weeks an extraordinary range of performers had trooped through the theatre: fire-eaters, jugglers, accordionists, comics, crooners, ventriloquists, acrobats, ballet dancers, hoofers and goodness knows what else, all keen to do their bit to entertain the troops.

Occasionally she bumped into people she knew from earlier in her career. At first she had braced herself for unwelcome questions, or snarky comments about how the mighty were fallen. But in fact most of them were very friendly, perhaps hoping that she might put in a word for them with one of the entertainments officers.

It was also an eye-opener to see the effort that went into the ENSA programme. The number of pins stuck in the world map in the overseas section pretty much said it all. And that was on top of all the groups and shows touring munitions factories and military establishments in the UK.

It was an organisational nightmare. Performers, scenery, lights, props, costumes, musical instruments, even pianos, had to be transported and accommodated on tours sometimes lasting as long as six months. The wardrobe department alone was currently turning out about four hundred costumes a week.

Jen also gained a new insight into the production process, and in particularly into Henry Keller. She already knew how well respected he was. Before the war, he had produced several smash-hit shows. That was, after all, why Basil Dean, the autocratic head of ENSA, had brought him into the organisation. And she knew how much he demanded of his performers. But now she was able to see the extraordinary amount of work he himself put in, and the skill he employed to coax the very best out of his casts and crews. Some of the other entertainment officers were much less adept. But even with the short turn-around time, the shows that Henry put out were slick, professional and highly entertaining.

Much of the rest of his time was spent recruiting and cosseting the big-name stars. Janette Pymm was one of his regular visitors, and Jen was gratified to discover that the pin-up girl wasn't popular with the rest of the staff.

'She's too much of a prima donna for my taste,' Maggie said. 'If you want to know how a star should behave, take your lead from Vivien Leigh. For all her fame, she's friendly to a fault.'

'I once had a boyfriend who said I looked like Vivien Leigh,' Jen said. She gave a self-deprecating laugh, but she remembered how thrilled she had been when Sean Byrne had said it all those years ago. It had given her a much-needed boost at the beginning of her career. 'But I get the impression Henry thinks Janette Pymm is prettier than Vivien Leigh.'

Maggie sniffed. 'Prettiness isn't everything,' she said. 'Henry Keller could have his pick of pretty faces. But he's not like that. Not like our lord and master, Basil Dean, who's already on his third pretty wife. I'd certainly advise you to keep clear of him.'

Jen looked at her suspiciously. Did Maggie know more about her chequered relationship with Henry than she let on? But the other woman was already consulting her clipboard, and a moment later she strode off briskly down the corridor.

But whether Maggie's remark had been deliberate or not, as she made her way back to the auditorium, Jen realised she felt warmer towards Henry than she had in a long while. In any case, there simply wasn't time to be constantly worrying about what he might think, or what she shouldn't or shouldn't say to him. And give him his due, he hadn't tried to make her feel guilty for turning him down. He hadn't really done anything, except share an occasional giggle about some of the ENSA hopefuls.

One of these was a Russian soprano called Oda Slobodskaya. Her warbling rendition of 'Now Sleeps the Crimson Petal' was the funniest thing Jen had seen so far. Armed with an enormous gold chiffon hanky, Miss Slobodskaya adjured the three solemn entertainments officers sitting the stalls to 'sleeep into my booosom and be lost in me'. Even from her eyrie in the wings, Jen could hear one of them weeping with laughter, and wished she had time to fetch Henry from his office to share the joke.

Another time she found Henry standing behind her as she watched a pianist thump his way through some unidentifiable classical piece. 'He plays like he's in jail,' he had remarked drily. 'Behind bars and can't find the key.'

But as well as giving her a few unexpected laughs, working at ENSA also had the effect of putting her ordeal in Italy into perspective. It wasn't just would-be performers who filled the corridors of the Theatre Royal; there were also plenty of artistes returning from overseas tours. And some of their hair-raising adventures made Jen's experiences pale into insignificance.

One morning she met a girl who had just come back from a long tour in East Africa. On arrival at Accra docks her troupe had been given yellow fever vaccinations that immediately went septic, everyone in the party got malaria, their only form of transport was a clapped-out ambulance that kept breaking down in the bush, and at one point she was nearly raped by a South African mercenary who hadn't seen a white woman for over two years. 'But overall I enjoyed it,' the girl said. 'Not the near-miss rape and that, but we did have a laugh.'

Another girl told her how her concert party had been given digs in a former brothel in Cairo, and every night they were woken up by randy Egyptians trying to get in the door. 'I slept with my high heels under the pillow in case one broke in and I had to sock him one.'

Jen had laughed with the others, but a couple of days later, when she was browsing through the newspaper in the secretaries' office on a short break, she read an article suggesting that the Nazis were forcing female prisoners of war to work in brothels, and she felt the blood drain from her face.

'Jen?' Dimly she heard one of the girls call her name. 'Are you all right?'

'Yes,' she said. 'Yes, I'm fine.' But she wasn't. She suddenly felt ice cold and shaky, and for a nasty moment she thought she was going to faint.

'I'm going to fetch Maggie,' the girl said.

But it was Henry who appeared first. Striding into the room, he shooed everyone else out and shut the door. Desperately Jen tried to pull herself together. But she couldn't respond to his anxious questions. She couldn't do anything except sit there completely rigid, yet somehow trembling at the same time.

'Breathe,' he said. 'Try to breathe. It's just a panic attack. It will pass.'

A minute or two later, he gently eased open her fingers and put a cup of tea into her hand.

'It could have been me,' she whispered, pointing to the newspaper article. 'That's where they were taking us when we managed to escape.'

She saw him glance at the paper and heard his sharp intake of breath. 'My God,' he said.

She looked at him, startled by the suppressed fury in his tone.

He was right, though. The panic had passed, almost as suddenly as it had come.

'But it didn't happen,' she said. 'We got away.'

And now she felt weak and stupid.

Henry perched on the secretary's desk. He picked up a pencil and twiddled it in his long fingers. 'In your mind it has probably happened a hundred times,' he said. 'And our thoughts often have more effect on us than reality.'

'But I haven't been thinking about it,' Jen protested. 'I've been specifically trying *not* to think about it.'

'You've been blocking it out,' Henry said evenly. 'But it was there. In your subconscious. Waiting to pounce.'

Jen looked at him accusingly. She felt even more of an idiot now. 'You knew, didn't you? You knew something like this might happen. And you didn't want it to happen on stage.'

'I didn't want it to happen anywhere,' Henry said with a hint of asperity. He shook his head. 'It was obvious that there was something wrong.' He put the pencil down on the desk and stood up. 'And yes, that's why I wanted to give you time.' He smiled gently. 'Time to get back to your former glory.'

To her horror, Jen felt her eyes watering. Oh no, she thought. Not now. Not when I already feel such a fool.

'I'm sorry,' she said. 'I hate being like this. You must think I'm pathetic.'

He took the cup out of her hand and drew her to her feet. 'That's the last thing I think,' he said. Unhurriedly he pulled her to him and closed his arms gently round her.

Jen could feel the steady beat of his heart against her cheekbone. She closed her eyes and let herself relax against him. He didn't move, and gradually her rapid breathing subsided. She felt calmer, and slightly less crazy.

'Are you OK?' he asked after a while.

'I think so,' she said.

'Good,' he said. 'Because I've just remembered that I've left Ivor Novello sitting in my office. He's in a terrible state because he's just been given an eight-week sentence in Wormwood Scrubs for obtaining illegal petrol coupons for his Rolls-Royce.'

Roused from her lethargy, Jen pulled back in astonishment. 'You're joking?'

'No, I'm not,' Henry said. 'One of his fans stole them for him.' He gave a wry grimace. 'He thinks he might have got away with it if he hadn't tried to bribe the arresting officer.'

He released her and peered at her closely. 'You still look rather pale. Do you want to go home?'

Jen shook her head. 'No, I'm feeling better now.' She glanced nervously at the door. 'But what will I say? To the others, I mean?'

'You don't have to say anything. Good God, they know you spent time in a Nazi POW camp. You're bound to have some bad memories. It's nothing to be ashamed of.'

Jen looked up at him gratefully. Suddenly she didn't want him to go. 'Henry, I'm so sorry. You've been so kind, and I feel so—'

'Jen, I told you,' he interrupted. 'You don't have to apologise.'

'I didn't mean about this.' She waved her hand around the secretaries' office. 'I meant about you and me. I've been so stupid. And now ...'

He took her hand, and slowly lifting it to his mouth, he kissed it.

'Give it time,' he said. 'There's no rush. Let's just take it easy and see how we go on.'

Pam was waiting for George to come home from school so she could take him down to Arding and Hobbs to see if she could find him a new school cap. It was annoying, because it would require a clothing coupon she could ill afford. Yesterday at school he had somehow managed to lose not only his cap, but also the yo-yo that Molly had sent him from Tunisia. And that was sad, because he adored Molly. It was she who had taught him to do magic tricks when they were both incarcerated with chickenpox last year. But when Pam tried to berate him for his carelessness, he had once again become sulky and uncommunicative.

If only Mr Grandison had been more helpful when Alan went to see him, Pam thought now. But according to Alan, Mr Grandison had blamed *her* for George's unruly behaviour. 'Boys like George need a firm hand,' he had said. 'I suspect your wife is too soft on him. Boys are always getting cuts and bruises. A bit of rough and tumble in the playground is good for them. Teaches them self-reliance. I'm sure you don't want him to turn into a mummy's boy.'

Pam had been furious. As far as she was concerned, George was about as far from a mummy's boy as it was possible to be. The day after Alan had seen Mr Grandison, he had come home from school with a bloody nose and a torn jacket and adamantly refused to tell her how he had come by either.

Hearing the front door open, she stood up and braced herself for the inevitable confrontation.

But today it seemed as though a completely different child had come home from school. Instead of tramping sullenly up to his bedroom as he usually did, George came running in like a whirlwind, flinging his satchel and gas mask box off in the hallway and speeding straight through the kitchen and out of the back door.

'What are you going?' Pam called after him.

'I need to see if the yard is safe,' he said.

'What do you mean, safe?' Pam asked in alarm.

'Safe so the rabbit can't escape,' he shouted.

'But you haven't won the rabbit yet. Mrs Rutherford said the winners aren't being announced until tomorrow after church.'

George reappeared briefly at the back door. 'I know,' he said. He wrinkled his nose pensively, then gave her a bright smile. 'But if I do win, I need to be sure the yard is safe.'

Through the kitchen window Pam watched him carefully inspecting the bottom of the fence panels and her heart twisted. Even though he was a handful, even though he wouldn't talk to her properly, wouldn't tell her about

133

his friends, or what he got up to at school, she loved him, and she didn't want him to be disappointed.

'If he doesn't win this damned rabbit,' she said to Alan later, 'I think we should try to get him one anyway. It might do him good to have a pet to look after.'

Alan looked up from his paper. 'I agree. But I'm not sure how easy it is to get hold of rabbits nowadays. I have a nasty feeling most of them have been eaten.'

Louise's sense of achievement at having successfully got the swarf to the school was tempered by the imminence of her departure to the ATS. She was due to leave early the following morning, and although she managed to gather together most of the things she thought she might need, she still hadn't found time to pack. She had splurged most of her hard-earned factory pay and coupons on two rather flattering dresses at Arding and Hobbs. By pleading with Mr Gregg to let her off early one afternoon, she had even managed to race up to Harrods before closing time, just in time to get hold of some silk stockings.

In all the rush to get ready, she had barely had time to think about Henry Keller, or indeed about Colonel Westwood, who disappointingly had failed to keep his promise of coming to see her in the factory before she left.

She had, however, been visited by a rather nondescript man from Military Intelligence, who came to get her to sign the Official Secrets Act. She had to do it in Mr Gregg's office and felt terribly important. But when she had asked him when Colonel Westwood would next be coming in, he had frowned slightly. 'Ivo Westwood?' he said. 'I think he's gone back to America.'

Louise stared at him. Ivo? Was that Colonel's Westwood's Christian name? What a brilliant name. But much more importantly ... 'America?' she queried, aghast.

'Yes, I believe so. There was some delay over components that he needed to sort out.'

'But is he coming back?'

The man gave a short laugh. 'Well I certainly hope so. We'll all have gone to a lot of unnecessary trouble if he doesn't.'

Louise had hoped so too. But he hadn't come, and all she could do now was pack her suitcases and say her goodbyes.

Doris had organised a nice little send-off from the factory on Saturday afternoon, and everyone had signed a card wishing her good luck, which was touching.

In the evening, she went to the pub, but she didn't stay long, partly because she wanted to set her hair ready for the morning, and partly because

Jen Carter was there, making everyone laugh with some ridiculous story about Ivor Novello.

Perhaps Ivo was short for Ivor, Louise thought as she sipped the farewell drink that Mr Lorenz had kindly bought her. Moses and Ben weren't there, but Angie gave her a suffocating hug, and Gino shook her by the hand and solemnly wished her *buona fortuna*.

And then Katy clapped for silence and made a little toast saying that she was certain that Louise would be prove to be a huge success in the ATS, and everyone, except Jen Carter, clapped appreciatively.

If she had thought of it, Louise would have asked Ben and Moses to give her a lift to the station in their jeep the following morning, but she hadn't thought of it, and having realised that she couldn't possibly carry three suitcases herself, she had instead splashed out, and ordered a taxi. It was due to arrive at almost the same moment her parents set off for church. In the hallway, her mother was busy running over her speech for her little salvage cogs prize-giving, which was to follow the service.

'So who's won?' Louise asked. 'Who is going to get the rabbit?'

Her mother shook her head. 'We're keeping that a secret until the prize-giving,' she said. 'We don't want word getting out before the church service, or half the children won't come.'

'Oh for goodness' sake, Mummy,' Louise said irritably. 'It's not exactly a state secret. I'm hardly likely to spill the beans on my way to the station, am I?'

'Louise!' Greville Rutherford said sharply, striding into the hall. 'How dare you speak to your mother in that tone of voice?' He observed the pile of suitcases waiting by the door. 'Good Lord, what's all this?'

'My luggage,' Louise said sulkily. 'You knew I was leaving today.'

'I knew you were leaving,' he said. 'But I didn't know you were taking your entire wardrobe with you. You're joining the army, young lady, not setting up home.'

'Well it's too late to do anything about it now,' her mother intervened hastily. She stepped forward and gave Louise an awkward hug. 'So we'll wish you all the best, darling. We'll see you when you get back at Easter. Oh, and if you know of any soldiers who are based nearby, or who might be home on leave on the twenty-fifth of March, Daddy is looking for one to lead his Salute the Soldier parade, aren't you, Greville?'

Louise turned to her father. 'Perhaps you could use me,' she said. 'I'm only going to be at Bracknell. That's not far.'

He looked at her incredulously. 'Good Lord,' he said. 'It's a fine, upstanding man I want. A proper soldier. Someone who knows how to march. Not just some pretty girl in uniform.' He eyed Louise thoughtfully.

'Although I am looking for some kind of mascot as well. Something to interest the children.'

'Why don't you use one of Mrs Trewgarth's rabbits?' Louise snapped. 'You could get your fine, upstanding soldier to lead it along on a leash.'

For a nasty moment it looked as though her father might explode with fury. But then, fortuitously, they heard the taxi turning into the driveway, and in the kerfuffle of getting her bags loaded, her facetious remark was forgotten.

And then she was on her way to the station, and suddenly she realised she felt rather sick.

'I have found a hotel,' Mr Lorenz murmured. 'It sounds very nice. It's called the Old Ship. It's right on the seafront at Brighton.'

Joyce caught her breath. They were sitting in the saloon bar at the Flag and Garter on Sunday evening, and she suddenly felt as though she needed something stronger than the small sherry that stood on the table in front of her. A whisky would be more like it. Or a tumbler of brandy.

'Oh my word,' she said.

He looked concerned. 'I can always cancel the booking,' he said. 'If you don't like the sound of it.'

Joyce felt the ground shaking beneath her feet. Stupid old fool, she thought. It wasn't the hotel she was worried about. It was …

But then she felt his fingers touch her hand. He was looking at her with a compassionate smile in his eyes. 'You don't need to worry,' he said. 'I've booked two rooms. All I want is to give you a break. A little treat.'

'Oh Albert,' she whispered, and reached over to squeeze his hand, only to jerk away a second later as Angie loomed into view.

Joyce looked up irritably, but for once there was no giggle. On the contrary, Angie was white-faced and shaking. In her hand she was clutching a note.

Oh no, Joyce thought, not one of the boys. Not Mick. Or Pete. Or Bob. If it has to be someone, please let it be Gino, fallen under a bus.

'It's Paul,' Angie said. 'I just popped back home to get some more money, and I found this.' She thrust the note into Joyce's hand and burst into tears. 'He's run off to join the army. And he won't tell us where, in case you try and get him back.'

Jen was upstairs when Angie brought the note into the pub. She had heard Caroline crying and knowing that Katy was busy had gone up to see what was wrong.

Malcolm thankfully was fast asleep, and keen not to wake him, Jen decided

136

to carry the restless baby back downstairs. That was when she heard the news about Paul.

Shocked by her brother's decision, she eased the baby up onto her shoulder and sat down heavily in one of the armchairs by the fire. Paul was only fifteen. How could he be so brave and so stupid? In the background, unaware of the crisis, Moses was moving effortlessly into his trademark tune, 'As Time Goes By'.

As the baby wriggled slightly, Jen tried to soothe her. 'I think she's hungry,' she murmured to Katy, who was standing nearby with a tray of dirty glasses. 'Do you want me to do those while you feed her?'

But oddly Katy didn't respond, and looking up, Jen saw that she was staring, apparently transfixed by something, or someone, over by the door. Or was she just listening to the song?

Moses was well into his stride now. Even the noisiest drinkers had fallen silent. '*And when two lovers meet* ...' His crooning, melodic voice held everyone in its thrall.

Jen knew that this particular song got to Katy. It got to her sometimes too. She, like everyone else, had wept buckets when Rick sacrificed his own happiness to let Ilsa go with Victor Laszlo.

But surely Katy hadn't lost all the colour in her face because of *Casablanca*. It must be something else that had caused ... Sure enough, Katy was leaning in towards her now.

'Jen,' she whispered urgently. 'Don't look now, but, oh my God. Isn't that ...?'

And turning her head the other way, Jen found herself staring across the bar straight into the blue eyes of her former lover, Sean Byrne.

Chapter Thirteen

He was walking towards her now. And to Jen it seemed as though he was walking in slow motion.

Sean Byrne.

She had thought she would never see him again. He was older, of course, but none the less attractive for that. Time had treated him well, although he still had that same slightly shifty look she remembered, as though he constantly wanted to check over his shoulder to see who was standing behind him.

But he wasn't looking over his shoulder now. He was looking right at her. And as he stopped in front of her, there was a look in his eyes that she had never seen before. A look of dread.

'Please tell me that baby isn't yours,' he said.

Beside her, Jen heard Katy give a muffled gasp of consternation. And then, without even thinking about it, as though she was in a trance, Jen was standing up, handing Caroline to Katy and holding out her hands to Sean.

'Sean,' she said. 'I can't believe it. Is it really you?'

'Well I think so,' he said as he took her hands. He leaned back slightly and looked her over. 'But now I see you standing there looking at me with those tawny eyes, just as beautiful as ever you were, I'm wondering have I somehow slipped back a couple of years without noticing it.'

His hands were cold and rough to the touch. That was different. Jen remembered them being smooth as silk, just like the seductive smile that was already forming on his lips as he realised there was no wedding ring on her finger.

'So no baby, and no husband?'

Jen shook her head, and saw the last remnant of dread leave his eyes. He caressed her hands and circled his thumbs seductively into her palms.

'Then let me take you somewhere where I can kiss you,' he said.

But just as Jen felt a shiver of anticipation run up her body, Angie came barging forward. 'What about Paul?' she said. 'You can't go running off kissing people when Mum needs you. And what about Henry?'

'Go away, Angie,' Jen snapped. 'Give me some privacy.'

Sean gave an approving laugh. 'Well said.' He glanced around the crowded bar. 'But there's not much privacy we'll be getting in here.' He lowered his voice. 'Will you not come outside with me, Jen Carter Leigh? I just want you to myself for a minute.'

But Angie's intervention had brought Jen to her senses. What was she doing? She couldn't just fall back into Sean Byrne's arms as though nothing had happened. And what about Henry indeed? Henry, who had been so kind to her yesterday. Sean might be the man who'd said she looked like Vivien Leigh, but he was also the man who had run off and left her utterly heartbroken. She jerked her hands from his and tried to ignore the flicker of disappointment in his eyes.

But she did move with him to the fireplace, out of Angie's earshot. 'You've come at a bad time,' she said. 'We've just heard that my youngest brother has run away to join the army.'

Sean looked at her for a long moment. 'Well, to be sure, I am sorry to hear that,' he said. He reached for her hand again. 'But even so ...'

'No,' Jen said. 'I'm not coming outside with you.'

He began to unbutton his coat. 'Then dance with me. That way I can at least hold you in my arms.'

'No.'

'Come on, Jen,' he pleaded. 'You owe me that.'

'I don't owe you anything,' Jen snapped at him. 'You ran off and left me looking like an idiot.'

He looked aggrieved. 'I wrote. I wanted you to come to Ireland. I even sent you money for the journey.'

'I sent it back,' Jen said. 'I saw a picture of you with a girl in the Irish paper. Aisling O'Donnel. She said she was going on a hunger strike if the man she loved wasn't released from jail.'

He held her angry gaze for a long moment, then looked away. 'Yes,' he said. 'Aisling is a lovely girl. Very beautiful. Very loyal.' He paused and lifted his eyes back to Jen's. His face was unreadable. 'But she is not my girl, and never has been.'

Jen swallowed. 'So who ...?'

'Ah, well. That would be my friend and comrade Jerry Gallagher. He was falsely accused too. He and Aisling are married now, with two little ones already.'

As Jen tried to take it in, her mistake, all that unnecessary anguish, Sean smiled slowly. 'There has only ever been one girl who found her way into my heart.' When she didn't respond, the smile faded. 'But perhaps I'm too late after all? Perhaps I'd better leave you to your family crisis.'

And Jen remembered that too. The emotional blackmail. And her ridiculous compulsion to give him his own way. But he was so attractive. So skin-tinglingly desirable. And those come-to-bed eyes ...

His voice was low, warm. 'You're remembering, are you not?'

'No,' Jen said.

'You are so.'

'I'm not.'

His smile was complacent. 'Do you want me to remind you?' he murmured.

'No,' she said. 'Well, not now, anyway.' She needed time. Time to adjust. Time to recover.

'Tomorrow?'

She knew she should say no. But she just couldn't bring herself to do it. 'All right,' she said.

'Will I meet you here?' His lips curved in a suggestive smile. 'We could take a little walk on the common, in the dark, like old times.'

'No, not here,' she said. She remembered those walks too, and she didn't want to set tongues wagging any more than they already were. 'I'll meet you at Piccadilly Circus. At five thirty.'

His eyes narrowed slightly, but he nodded. 'All right then,' he said. 'I'll be there.' He buttoned up his coat and turned to leave. Then he paused. 'Glory to God, Jen,' he said. 'I swear that when I saw you nursing that damned baby like the Virgin Mary herself, I thought I had missed my chance.' He gave a low laugh. 'Not that I'd have much of a chance with the Virgin Mary, of course. But it was a nasty moment right enough.'

But you have lost your chance, Jen wanted to shout after him. How dare he come swaggering in after all this time as though nothing had happened? All those months of torment. All that despair.

Aisling O'Donnel or not, Sean had run away and left her. Left her feeling like a fool.

But she still couldn't resist him. She still couldn't say no. Not as though she meant it. Not when he looked at her with those smiling eyes. And her heart ached. Dear God, she prayed. Please don't make me go through all that again.

Once she had found the right train, and had managed to get a porter to help her with her cases, Louise's journey to Bracknell had passed comfortably enough. The train was crowded, but the porter secured her a nice position by the window, and even though the glass was covered with blackout paper, there was a small torn section through which she could see the passing countryside. In the bright March sunshine it all looked exceptionally lush and green. Even the air seemed cleaner and fresher. It certainly made a nice change from grey, dirty, bomb-damaged London, and Louise began to think that, if nothing else, it would be a pleasant change to spend a few weeks in

140

the country.

It was only when the train reached Bracknell that things started to go downhill.

At the beginning of the war, all the signs had been taken down at railway stations in order to make things difficult for foreign spies, but it made it difficult for passengers too. And by the time Louise had ascertained that this was indeed Bracknell, she was almost too late to get off. Struggling her cases off in such a hurry was a nightmare. She couldn't see any porters on the platform, and nobody else seemed inclined to help.

Eventually she managed it, and stood panting on the platform wondering what to do next. As the smoke of the departing train cleared, at the other end of the station she saw a queue of young women standing in front of a soldier with a clipboard. Leaving her luggage where it was, Louise went along to see if he was anything to do with the ATS. He was, but she was last in the queue, and by the time she got to the front, all the other girls had disappeared outside.

'You must be Rutherford,' he said. 'You're the last one.'

'Yes, that's me,' Louise said. She smiled and nodded along the platform. 'I wonder if you could give me a hand with my luggage?'

He glanced at the distant suitcases. 'Sorry, love,' he said. 'I'm a soldier, not a porter. If you want them, you'll have to fetch them yourself. But you'd better get a move on, because the transport is leaving pretty pronto.'

It wasn't a good start, but luckily the stationmaster took pity on her, and not only carried two of her cases outside for her but also heaved them over the tailgate of the canvas-sided lorry, and courteously helped Louise climb up after them.

Astonishingly, there were no seats, and the assembled girls were all holding on to straps hanging from the roof. There was some nervous giggling as the lorry pulled away and everyone lost balance and trod on each other's feet, but after that, they travelled in grim silence, putting all their concentration into clinging on for dear life as the driver swirled round corners as though wolves were after them.

By the time they arrived at the camp, Louise's arm was aching. But the discomfort didn't stop there.

An ATS corporal with a mighty bust straining the highly polished buttons on her khaki uniform was yelling at them to line up in silence at the guardroom with their call-up papers in their hand. For some reason, none of the other girls seemed to have any luggage, and by the time Louise had dragged her cases off the lorry, she was once again last in the queue.

By this time she was not only tired but hungry. But her mild request to the buxom corporal, asking if there was somewhere she could get a cup of tea while she waited for her turn, was greeted with incredulity.

'A cup of tea?' The woman turned to bellow across to the ATS sergeant behind the desk. 'We've got a right one here. Did you hear that, Sarge? One of our new recruits wants a cup of tea.'

And there was no less incredulity when Louise finally reached the desk.

'What the hell is all this?' the sergeant asked, peering over the table at Louise's luggage. 'Didn't you receive your Instructions on Embodiment leaflet with your joining documents?'

Louise nodded. 'Yes, of course. And I've brought everything on the list. Dressing gown, towel, hairbrush, toothbrush, polishing brush, face cloth, mending cottons, khaki handkerchief, soap, gas mask ...' She ticked them off on her fingers. It had taken her ages to find some of the more obscure items.

'And it didn't occur to you that these were the *only* items you were expected to bring?'

Louise frowned. 'No, of course not. Otherwise what would I wear?'

'Uniform,' the sergeant said bluntly.

'But not all the time, surely?' Louise was aghast. 'What about in the evenings and weekends?' What about the pretty dresses she had bought specially in Arding and Hobbs?

The sergeant looked as though she could hardly believe what she was hearing. 'This isn't a holiday camp. This is the ATS. This is the army. And that means uniform. *At all times.*'

Louise recoiled at the loudness of the final three words. 'How was I to know?'

The sergeant looked at her in mounting irritation. 'Common sense, I'd have thought,' she snapped. 'Or don't they teach that at finishing school?'

'You clearly didn't notice the "what not to bring" section either,' the busty corporal suddenly chipped in, pointing at Louise's bracelet and earrings. 'Handbag, jewellery, umbrella. Didn't they teach you to read, either?'

Having poked about with gleeful disbelief in her suitcases, they eventually allowed her to keep her sponge bag, her new lacy dressing gown and the other meagre items on the embodiment list. Everything else was confiscated and consigned to a secure locker room, for which she was not given a key.

By this time Louise was seething. But there were more horrors in store.

The corporal led her across the parade ground to a dormitory in a bleak wooden hut. All the other girls had already claimed their bunks, leaving her one right by the door, which was clearly going to be both noisy and draughty. In the centre of the hut was an unlit stove.

Louise had barely had time to dump her things on the bed and visit the toilet block next door when a roar came from the doorway behind her. It was the same ghastly corporal.

'Hut Six,' she shouted. 'On the parade ground in five minutes.'

Struggling back outside, the new recruits were shuffled around until they were roughly in height order. Then they had to line up in rows of four. 'Look to your left and right, in front and behind,' the corporal yelled at them when she was finally satisfied. 'This is the order I expect you in at all times when in a squad.'

They were then ordered to march to the quartermaster's stores. It wasn't a success. As she tried to get her feet to keep in step with the girl next to her, while not bumping into the incompetent girl in front, Louise was very glad her father couldn't see her.

As she was in the second row of the squad, Louise was expecting to be one of the first in the queue, only to discover that this time they were to line up in alphabetical order. And now she regretted reverting to her maiden name. If she had stuck with Jack's surname, Delmaine, she would have been done and dusted a good hour earlier. As it was, there was only one girl further down the alphabet than Rutherford, a small, mousy girl called, rather appropriately, Voles. But when, bored to distraction by the interminable wait, Louise tried to elicit Voles's Christian name, she was shouted at by the corporal.

'No talking at the back of the queue!'

'My name's Susan,' Voles whispered when the corporal had moved away. She had a strong Yorkshire accent. 'But we aren't allowed to use first names. Didn't you hear her say?'

'No,' Louise said. 'I didn't.' She wondered what else she might have missed. She also wondered how much of this she was going to be able to put up with. She hadn't eaten or drunk anything since breakfast, and her earlier anger was beginning to give way to a distinct sense of self-pity. What on earth was she doing here among these ghastly common women? What had any of this to do with Colonel Westwood's secret manufacturing unit?

And then finally she was at the counter. The first thing she was given was a small brown book. This was Army Book 64, her service and pay book, which she was told to keep on her person at all times. Then her measurements were being estimated by a huge ATS quartermaster sergeant, whose own uniform would have comfortably fitted a barrage balloon.

'Five foot six,' the sergeant shouted to someone in the storeroom behind her. 'Waist twenty-four to twenty-six, bust thirty-six, hips forty.'

It obviously hadn't occurred to them to use a tape measure, Louise thought sourly. Or indeed to ask. She knew her waist was only twenty-three. And her hips were nowhere near forty. But she was too weary to argue the point. In any case, a tape measure would probably have been thought too

143

sissy for these mannish old harridans.

A cap and two pairs of heavy shoes followed, and a few minutes later, once it had all been carefully noted down in her AB64, Louise was struggling back to Hut 6 with her kit: a khaki jacket and skirt, a greatcoat, shirts, bras, suspenders, bloomers, thick vomit-coloured stockings, a groundsheet, and two pairs of blue flannelette pyjamas, all of which had to be stored away neatly in a grey metal box by her bed.

The shoes, however, were to be tried on straight away. Hard brown leather, with studs in the soles, they were the most unfashionable and uncomfortable shoes Louise had ever seen. Worn with civilian clothes they looked unbelievably frumpy. Some of the girls thought it was funny. Louise didn't think it was funny at all. Especially when, still wearing them, they had to form up in their squad outside the hut, and march in a discordant, shambling rattle of hobnails on tarmac over to the canteen.

There she discovered that the tea was served from two enormous metal buckets. One purportedly with sugar, one without. They both tasted exactly the same, of curdled, lukewarm powdered milk and water. For Louise it was the last straw. And when later, after a plateful of grey stew and boiled potatoes, they were marched back to Hut 6, she put the flannelette pyjamas on over her underwear, climbed straight into bed, pulled the cardboard sheet and rough blanket up to her chin, and turned her face to the wall.

But it still wasn't over. Ten minutes later, the door crashed open again, bringing a gust of cold night air into the already freezing cold hut. Of course it was the ubiquitous corporal.

'Tomorrow,' she yelled. 'Reveille six a.m. Breakfast parade six thirty a.m. In full uniform. Hair will be tied up off the collar. No nail varnish. No make-up. No lipstick. You are in the army now, ladies. And we're not going to let you forget it. '

Louise closed her eyes and hoped nobody heard her sudden despairing sob. There was little chance of her forgetting. She was pretty confident she would remember this loathsome day for the rest of her life.

Jen was not feeling her bright and sparkling best either, as she walked up to the theatre on Monday morning. As soon as Sean had left the pub last night, she had got it in the neck from her mother. In fact Joyce had seemed almost more upset about Sean's arrival than she was about Paul's departure.

'What's that good-for-nothing doing back here?' she had hissed. 'I thought we'd seen the back of him.'

Angie was up in arms too. 'Who is this Sean Byrne person?' she had asked mistrustfully. 'What's he doing here?'

'He's just an old friend,' Jen said. 'That's all.'

But despite her attempts to make light of Sean's visit, she was rattled.

She had been mad about Sean when he had been in London before. And mad was the word. She had known he was a scoundrel. She had known that he had the gift of the gab and used it indiscriminately to get what he wanted. But she had been young and impressionable, and she had fallen for him hook, line and sinker.

But now it was different. She was different.

And there was Henry to consider. She still didn't really know how she felt about Henry, but she certainly didn't want to spoil their fragile new rapport by letting him find out about Sean. That really would be madness.

When she arrived at the theatre, she discovered that Henry had gone to Manchester to sort out some problem with one of his big shows. If Maggie noticed her relief, she didn't show it. Nor, somewhat surprisingly, did she complain about the multitude of mistakes Jen made that day. Perhaps Henry had warned her to be extra tolerant after Jen's nervous collapse on Saturday.

But Jen's nerves on Saturday were nothing compared with how she felt as she hurried over to Piccadilly Circus at five thirty on Monday afternoon.

Of course, Sean was late. He had always been late in the old days, and Jen had sometimes suspected that it was a deliberate technique to keep her in a state of anxiety about the level of his ardour.

But there was no doubt about his ardour now. She was in his arms almost before she had said hello. According to Sean, he had been working tirelessly to raise the money to get back to England ever since he had left four years before. And over the next hour or so in the hot and noisy Queen's Head pub in Piccadilly, he tried to convince her of his undying affection.

The pub was crowded with after-work drinkers, and Jen had to lean in close to hear what he was saying. She could feel the casual familiarity of his thigh against hers, see the warmth in his blue eyes. But more than anything, she was aware of the scent of him, that indefinable mixture of tobacco, beer, soap and sweat that made her want to bury her face in his neck.

But even though she was affected by his physical proximity, she wasn't going to let him get away with his baloney, flattering though it was.

'So why didn't you write to tell me you were coming?' she asked. 'What if I had been happily married? I could have had two or three children by now for all you knew.'

But he wasn't put out. 'That's one of the things I remember about you,' he said mournfully. 'However much I tried, I could never pull the wool over your eyes.' He leaned one elbow closer to her on the bar. 'The truth is that I didn't have time to write. A man I know needed to get some urgent medical supplies over to his ailing old mother in London and he paid me to do it.'

'So you didn't come specially to see me at all?' Jen said indignantly. 'You probably haven't given me a moment's thought for four years.'

'Of course I have,' he protested. 'But when you didn't reply to my letter …' He ran a hand over his face, smoothing back the lock of hair that fell appealingly over his forehead. 'The truth is that I wanted to forget you. But I couldn't, and when I had the chance to come to London, I had to come looking for you. And when I caught sight of you with that damned baby, well, I knew then that I was still smitten.'

The sincerity in his tone caused the fine hairs to rise on Jen's skin.

'How long are you staying?' she asked nervously.

'I have a ticket for the Sunday ship from Fishguard to Rosslare,' he said. He smiled and leaned in very close. 'So that gives me five days to persuade you to come with me.'

Jen shivered. The touch of his lips on her ear was almost too much for her. If there had been a bed handy, she would have ripped off her clothes there and then and jumped in, dragging him after her. But luckily the Queen's Head didn't provide beds for their patrons.

'I'm not going to come with you,' she said.

He put his finger up to caress her lips. 'Are you quite sure about that?'

She turned her head away. 'Yes,' she said.

He didn't seem to mind unduly. But he lowered his arm. 'Well, to be sure, it would have been my lucky day if you had agreed on day one,' he said. He drained his glass and put it down on the counter. 'So while you're making your mind up, why don't we have a bit of fun?'

'What sort of fun?' Jen asked suspiciously.

Laughter danced in his eyes. 'Any kind you want, my darling,' he said promptly. 'But myself, I was thinking of starting off with a bite to eat, if we can find anything half decent in this wretched town. It's too noisy in here and I want to hear if you've made your name on the stage yet. Or has the bloody war put paid to that?' He looped his arm round her to steer her through the chattering throng of people towards the door. 'I also want to know why a beautiful, sexy girl like you hasn't been snatched up by a rich, handsome husband. Or was it that you were waiting for me?'

'Well, well.' Mrs Rutherford looked up from counting the money in the till. 'The takings are up again, Mrs Carter. You've obviously had a busy few days.'

Joyce was conscious of a stab of irritation. All Mrs Rutherford seemed to do these days was come in to collect the takings. If only she had helped out more over the last few weeks, Joyce would have had more time to spend with Paul. And then she might have cottoned on to what he was about to do, and had a chance to stop him.

But she prudently didn't express her thoughts. She just grunted noncommittally, and started to beat her cake mixture rather more violently than usual. She knew she was taking her guilt and frustration out on it. But it didn't matter. With no baking powder in the shops, the only way to get it to rise was to beat some air into it.

As she worked, she thought about Albert. At lunchtime today he had started telling her some story about his young relative being bullied in the Polish unit up in Scotland. And all she had wanted to do was scream at him to leave her alone. She had enough on her plate with Paul without worrying about some young foreigner she had never met.

She had gone down to the local recruiting office first thing that morning to see what could be done about Paul, but there seemed little likelihood of getting him back. 'He didn't come through here,' the recruiting sergeant had said. 'Not unless he used a false name. That's what they do, these lads, you know, and they pretend their birth certificates have been lost in a bombing raid.' He saw Joyce's expression and gave a sympathetic smile. 'I'll put the word out, of course, but other than that, there's not much we can do about it.'

'How are the cakes coming on, Mrs Carter?' Mrs Rutherford called through the hatch. 'I need to get to the bank before it closes.'

Joyce gritted her teeth. 'Nearly there,' she called back. It wasn't just Paul. What had added to her bad mood was, of course, the unexpected reappearance of that Irish blighter Sean Byrne. Even so, she shouldn't have been short with poor Albert when he kindly offered to postpone their little holiday.

But it seemed wrong to be thinking about her own happiness when her children were in such disarray.

She was still beating the mixture, but suddenly, arrested by her own thought, she stopped, the wooden spoon trembling in her hand.

Happiness? That was the first time she had associated happiness with Albert Lorenz. Financial security, yes. Comfort. Companionship. Even perhaps contentment. But *happiness*?

Was such a thing possible? Life with Stanley had been a constant battle. And since he had died, she had been struggling so hard to keep food on the family table that happiness hadn't even come into the picture. But now, suddenly, there it was. An elusive glimmer, in a distant corner of her mind. But definitely there.

Mrs Rutherford came bustling in with a bundle of clinking money bags. 'Right then,' she said. 'I'll pop these down to the bank on my way.' She paused. 'Are you feeling quite all right, Mrs Carter? You look rather flushed.'

Joyce cleaned the wooden spoon with her finger and then dropped it in the sink. 'I'm fine,' she said. 'I just wanted to get some rise into the cakes.'

She smiled to herself as she licked the succulent mixture off her finger. She had her worries. Of course she did. Everyone did, especially in wartime. But just for now, they didn't seem quite so overpowering. Yes, there were unknown dangers ahead. But they had all survived so far. And the war wouldn't last for ever.

Whether it was the warm afternoon light streaming in through the kitchen window, or some shift in her thinking, either way Joyce felt suddenly as though she had woken from a long sleep. Rather like Monty, her precious tortoise, who that very morning had emerged from hibernation and poked his head out of his box with a look of vague anticipation in his eyes. It had been a long winter, but now he was clearly looking forward to dandelions, sunshine and better things ahead.

She hadn't got time now, not with Mrs Rutherford breathing down her neck, but later in the week she would make a nice little Victoria sponge for Albert and drop it off at his house one evening as a surprise. He deserved a treat.

Chapter Fourteen

Louise's expectation that things at the ATS camp couldn't get any worse quickly proved to be wide of the mark.

The first indignity was the inspection of their new uniforms. They had to parade in front of the quartermaster sergeant and a steely-eyed ATS junior commander. This was the first female officer Louise had seen, the equivalent of a captain in the men's army, and it didn't take her long to realise that she was even more of a tartar than the non-commissioned officers she had met.

Louise had often had clothes made by her mother's dressmaker and was well used to having them pinned and adjusted. But the dressmaker always solicited her opinion on shape and comfort, whereas these women treated her as if she was a tailor's dummy. And when she did venture to speak, she was immediately shouted down. 'Silence,' the sergeant snapped. 'If Junior Commander Harris wants your opinion, she will ask for it.'

And the junior commander clearly didn't want her opinion, because she ignored her completely, merely telling the quartermaster sergeant that the waistband on Rutherford's skirt needed taking in, and to make sure that something was done about her hair.

As Louise had gone to considerable effort that morning, in the five minutes she had available at 6.25 a.m., to style her hair in an elegant chignon at the neck, this was extremely galling. Incensed, she opened her mouth, but the glare she received from the QM sergeant made her close it again. And when the parade was finally over, the beastly corporal in charge of their hut told her that if in future she didn't tie her hair up properly in a bun or a stocking roll well above the collar, it would be cut off.

For the rest of that day, Louise had to wear her civilian skirt with the rest of her uniform, which made her look even more ridiculous. When her khaki skirt was returned the following day, even this minor incident had to be noted in the ever-present Army Book 64, which was carried at all times in the right-hand breast pocket of her jacket.

Over the next few days, her bosom flattening AB64 gradually filled up with other annotations. There was an unpleasantly intimate medical inspection. A dental inspection. An eye test. A hearing test. And on Wednesday morning, after yet another long wait at the back of the queue, Louise found herself in the humiliating position of having her hair inspected.

To her horror, although her hair was, of course, declared clear of parasites, half the girls in the intake were found to have either lice or nits.

And then, just when she thought there couldn't possibly be anything else left to queue for, came a round of vaccinations. This was made considerable worse by the fact that the medical officer only felt it necessary to change the needle when it became too blunt to pierce the skin. Louise tried to argue that she had already had every inoculation possible, but as she had no certificates to prove it, nobody took any notice.

The first two injections weren't too painful, but the final one, smallpox, involved a bifurcated needle, which the medical officer had to stab into the arm several times to release the vaccine. Several girls screamed, and one struggled so much she had to be held down by two medical orderlies.

By the time Louise's turn came, she was so petrified she could hardly move, but when she burst into tears of pain afterwards, nobody paid any attention, because Susan Voles, the girl waiting behind her in the queue, had in the meantime collapsed in a dead faint and cracked her head on the floor. It didn't get her out of having the jab, though, and Louise was briskly told to pull herself together so she could take her back to the accommodation block to lie down for five minutes.

'I'm sorry,' Susan Voles whimpered as they limped back to Hut 6. 'I'm so sorry.'

'It's not your fault,' Louise said. Although actually she thought Voles had been rather pathetic. 'It's those sadistic women. Anyone would think we were in Nazi Germany the way they go on.'

That made Voles laugh. 'They are teaching us how to salute later on,' she said. 'We'll have to be careful not to do the Heil Hitler.'

Louise looked at her with mild surprise. Maybe she wasn't such a drip after all. But there wasn't time to pursue the joke, because they had barely had time to rest their painful arms for two seconds before the corporal was summoning them back to the parade ground.

And now the constant round of queuing gave way to endless gruelling sessions of drill.

Such was the stress of getting it right that when they were eventually stood down that evening, some of the girls insisted on marching up and down the central aisle of the hut in their dressing gowns. This caused much merriment for those involved, and much irritation for Louise, who was lying on her bed, huddled under her blanket, nursing her swollen arm.

'Come on, Rutherford, we need to practise,' they shouted. But Louise couldn't face standing up again, and anyway, it wasn't her who was always out of step on the parade ground.

By Friday she had had enough. She had woken up aching all over, partly in reaction to the jabs, and partly from the undue strain on her bad hip of the endless marching. Not only that, she was fed up to the back teeth with all the shouting and barked commands. Even at the factory she had been treated better than this. She found herself missing Doris's kindly camaraderie and Mrs Gibbons's acerbic humour. All the girls here were either unbearably keen and hearty, or unbelievably dim and stupid.

The keen ones took delight in adopting the military terminology, and their inane prattle at mealtimes was suddenly full of acronyms and abbreviations: DS for directing staff, CO for the commanding officer, 2IC for second-in-command, QM for the quartermaster, NCO for the non-commissioned officers. And there was other popular jargon as well. AWOL meant absent without leave, jankers were punishments meted out for misdemeanours, and POM was the term for a recruit considered to be potential officer material.

There was one particular girl in Hut 6 to whom Louise had taken an instant dislike. Her surname was Buller; Louise hadn't bothered to find out her Christian name. Buller thought she knew absolutely everything about the army, and was constantly reminding her hut mates not to forget their AB46s, or officiously telling them that Bluebell metal polish gave the best shine on brass buttons, or demonstrating how best to execute the 'about turn' command on the parade ground.

'You know the DS are ranking our performance?' she announced one evening. 'Well, I think we should all try to make Hut 6 the best hut in this intake. So some of you, like Voles and Rutherford, for example, need to pull your socks up.'

Louise was conscious of a sudden urge to thrust her socks down Buller's throat.

But the directing staff clearly liked Buller's enthusiasm, and as a result, some of the girls thought she was potential officer material, and hung on her every word.

POM or not, it soon transpired that Louise should indeed have taken more notice of Buller. Because it was forgetting to take her AB64 onto the parade ground on Friday morning that caused her the most misery of that whole excruciating first week.

As usual before a drill session there was an inspection, and the ATS sergeant noticed at once that Louise's bust was its normal rounded shape.

'Where is your AB64, Rutherford?' she asked.

'I must have left it in the hut,' Louise said.

'I mutht have left it in the hut,' the sergeant mimicked in a fake posh voice, far removed from her own ugly Midlands accent. 'Do you remember me telling you to keep it with you at all times?'

'Yes, but—' Louise began.

The sergeant stopped her with a sharp bark, and to Louise's dismay, she was told to march back to the hut to fetch it. She felt so conscious of everyone's eyes on her back as she marched away over the parade ground that for the first time, her arms and legs got out of sync.

Behind her she heard the sergeant's taunting voice. 'You see how Rutherford marches? Like a penguin. Right arm and leg going forward at the same time?'

There was a pause, then Buller's sycophantic voice. 'Yes, Sarge.'

'Well, don't do it like that.'

When Louise came marching back with the AB64 in her hand, on the right foot this time, but aware that everyone in the squad was avoiding her eyes, the sergeant told her to go back and do it all over again.

'That's not fair ...' Louise protested.

'Are you querying my order, Rutherford?' the sergeant asked dangerously.

'No,' Louise said. 'But—'

The 'but' was a bridge too far for the sergeant. 'Not only will you march over to Hut Six and back twice more, Rutherford, but I am also placing you on a charge for insubordination.'

There was a shocked intake of breath from the entire squad. They had been warned about charges, but as yet nobody had been put on one.

'You will report to the commanding officer at eight a.m. on Monday morning. She will mete out appropriate punishment for your insolence.'

'Will you not come back to my lodgings tonight,' Sean whispered to Jen. It was Friday night, and they were at the pictures. He put his hand on her thigh and rubbed it gently, gradually drawing up the hem of her skirt so he could slip his hand underneath.

It was clearly a well-practised technique, but even while she idly wondered how many girls he had practised it on, Jen could feel herself going weak at the knees. Rigidly she stared straight ahead at the screen. Ingrid Bergman was staring in glorious Technicolor into Gary Cooper's eyes. They were in Spain, but apart from that, she had no idea what was going on.

'I'm not allowed to bring women back,' Sean added as his cool fingers found the top of her stocking. 'But I'm sure I could smuggle you in somehow.'

Jen was tempted. He knew so well how to arouse her. Two nights ago, as they'd said goodbye at the entrance to Leicester Square tube station, he had kissed her. Brazenly. Deeply. Right there, where anybody could see. And desire had shot through her like a bullet.

But she had managed to pull back. To tell him off. To cover up her confusion. And she had gone home alone.

So far she had resisted him.

But now, as his fingers brushed over her panties, she wondered how long she could hold out. She wanted to do it. It was like a mad craving. Every day, all day, this week she had been thinking about it. She couldn't help it. Wondering if she should give in as she had before. Just once, for old times' sake. Nobody need know. And, after all, would it be so wrong?

And now Sean's other hand was on her chin, turning her face towards him. But he didn't kiss her. He just brushed his lips tauntingly over her skin. Meanwhile, his fingers were sliding back down her thigh. She could hardly bear it. It took all the willpower she possessed not to grab his hand and move it back up again. But she knew that was what he wanted her to do. He had always been a tease. It was all part of his modus operandi. He knew his deliberate withholding would drive her wild. He wanted the ultimate request to come from her. He wanted to make her plead.

But whether she did it or not, he would still go back to Ireland, leaving her alone again. And she didn't want to go to Ireland, despite all the meat and other luxuries he promised her there.

Sean had spent the entire week grumbling about the food in London. How small the portions were, and the lack of variety. Once, at a restaurant in Tottenham Court Road, he had spotted a dish called Moby Dick pie on the menu and asked the waitress what it was.

'Whale meat,' she had replied. Seeing his reaction, she leaned forward and lowered her voice. 'If I was you, I'd have the Patriotic Chop.'

Sean looked up at her with his bright blue eyes. 'And what makes the chop so patriotic?' he asked

The girl blushed rosily. 'Because a single chop bone weighing two ounces can supply the explosive charge for two rounds of ammunition,' she said promptly.

'Good God,' Sean said to Jen. 'No wonder your gallant troops haven't made much progress in Italy if they're fighting with bones.'

Needless to say, he rejected the Patriotic Chop in favour of the shepherd's pie. 'Praise the Lord,' he said to the waitress when she came to clear the plates. 'That's the first decent meal I've had since I got here. You should see what we have in Ireland. But that's the benefit of being neutral.'

'It's all very well being neutral when you've got us between you and the Germans,' Jen said. 'Anyway, I'm not sure how neutral you really are. Mr Churchill thinks your government is deliberately undermining our efforts.'

Right through the war there had been rumours of Irish double dealing. Now, as the invasion approached and total secrecy was becoming so important, it had been widely reported that Winston Churchill had asked the Irish prime minister to expel the German and Japanese ambassadors, and was outraged when he refused.

'Winston Churchill has never liked us Irish,' Sean said. 'None of the British do. Look at your family. None of them liked me, did they? Your mother certainly didn't.' He laughed suddenly. 'But I tell you who did, and that's my old landlady, Mrs Nelson. She definitely had a soft spot for me.' He gave a provocative smirk. 'Not as soft as the one you had for me, though. In fact I remember discovering that spot while we were rolling about on the carpet in front of her sitting room fire.'

'Shut up,' Jen said, flushing. 'I must have been mad.'

'No, you were gorgeous.'

That was the night he had kissed her at the tube station.

And now, in the cinema, as he nuzzled her ear lobe, Jen couldn't help wondering why, if there were so many luxuries in Eire, he hadn't brought her a gift.

She thought of her mother scraping the fat off tinned corned beef so she could use it to make pastry. That was how bad it had got in England. Sean must have known that. And yet he hadn't even bothered to bring over a bar of chocolate, or some cigarettes.

'No,' she said, pushing him away. 'Stop it. I'm not going to bed with you, and that's that.'

On the screen, a love scene was taking place. Jen looked away.

'Then come back to Ireland,' Sean said. 'We'll get married.'

Jen felt sweat prickling her armpits. It was the first time he had mentioned marriage. She looked at him askance. Did he mean it?

'No,' she said. 'I'm not coming. Because you would get bored of me in five minutes and run off with someone else. And then I'd be really stuck.'

He shook his head. 'Never,' he whispered. 'I'd never get bored of you, Jennifer Carter Leigh.'

As though to prove it, he delayed his departure from London until the very last minute. And when he finally kissed her goodbye at Paddington station on Sunday morning, his regret that she wasn't going with him really did seem sincere.

Jen was sorry to see him go, but she knew she had made the right decision. It had been hard, but she was glad she hadn't succumbed to his seductive charm. She had held her nerve. But it had been a close call. One more day, one more kiss, and she might have given in.

Katy had barely seen Jen all week. Despite her friend's protestations to the contrary, Katy had been terrified she might once again fall under Sean's spell. So when Jen got back from Paddington on Sunday morning, she was relieved to hear that he had finally set off back to Ireland, alone.

'Are you all right?' she asked tentatively.

Jen didn't reply at once. 'I think so,' she said.

'You weren't tempted to go with him?' Katy asked.

Jen gave a slight grimace. 'I was tempted all right. But the thought of explaining to Henry that I was running off to Ireland to marry my former lover was more than I could bear.'

'So Henry doesn't know?' Katy asked. 'That Sean was here, I mean?'

Jen looked appalled. 'Good God, no,' she said. 'Thankfully he's been away all this week.' She picked up a newspaper lying on one of the bar tables and began flicking through the pages. 'It couldn't have been better timing.'

And what did that mean? Katy wondered. That Jen was keener on Henry than she was letting on? Or that she just wanted to hang on to her job? Sometimes she wondered if Jen even knew herself.

'I think we need something to cheer us up,' Katy said suddenly. 'I'm thinking of organising a pub outing. We could have a collection and hire a coach and take everyone out for the day. Maybe at Easter. What do you think?'

'Frankly I think you've got enough on your plate already,' Jen said. 'But if you are set on the idea, then why don't you take everyone to the Windsor races?' She held up the newspaper. 'It says here the Derby favourite is running on Easter Monday, and they're expecting a huge crowd.'

Katy felt her spirits lift. It was a good idea. Just the thing to appeal to her regulars. She would mention it to Mr Lorenz when he came in later for his Sunday pint. He was a great one for the horses.

But Mr Lorenz wasn't quite as enthusiastic as she had hoped. 'Oh yes, it is certain to be a good event,' he said. 'Orestes is a marvellous horse. I'd very much like to see him run myself.'

There was a slightly wistful note in his voice, and Katy looked at him in surprise. 'But surely you'd come with us, Mr Lorenz?' she said with an encouraging smile. 'We'd need you to give us all some betting tips.'

He smiled politely at her quip, but shook his head. 'I'm afraid I shall be away over the Easter weekend,' he said. And with that he took his beer off to his usual chair by the fireplace.

'Goodness,' Katy whispered to Jen. 'Where on earth do you think he's going? I've never known him go away before.'

'I can't imagine,' Jen said. 'Although Mum did mention that he had recently discovered some long-lost relative in Scotland. Perhaps he's going to visit him.' She gave a sudden laugh. 'Or perhaps he's taking Mum away for a romantic weekend.'

Katy blinked. That really would be a turn-up for the books. But she was pleased to see Jen laugh. Perhaps now that Sean had gone, her spirits would finally improve.

The ATS HQ sergeant eyed Louise with censorious disdain. 'When I give you the command, you will march in, halt in front of the commanding officer's desk, salute, and stand to attention. Only when she gives you the nod – *if* she gives you the nod – will you stand at ease. Do you understand?'

'Yes, Sergeant,' Louise muttered. All her former bravado had deserted her. She could feel her knees shaking. Even though she told herself it was ridiculous to feel so nervous, there was something very serious about all this strict military procedure. Much as she wanted to laugh it off, to mock the stupid rules and regulations, it was impossible, and she couldn't help feeling alarmed at her predicament.

Her fellow recruits hadn't made it easy for her either. The delightful Buller had even suggested that Louise should be sent to Coventry for bringing disrepute on Hut 6. Luckily the idea hadn't taken. Susan Voles had bravely pointed out that it was up to the directing staff to discipline her, not the members of the hut. And although Louise didn't particularly care whether anyone spoke to her or not, she was grateful to Voles for coming to her defence.

Nevertheless, she had passed a miserable weekend. On Saturday they had suffered their first hut inspection, which meant they had had to spend the morning scrubbing and polishing. That was followed by a kit inspection, which involved yet more scrubbing and polishing, albeit on a smaller scale. As Louise had failed to lay out the required items in exactly the prescribed order, she was reprimanded for sloppiness and had to spend the whole evening refolding and re-presenting her kit, until it eventually passed muster.

Then on Sunday, after a long march to a nearby church for an equally long and boring service, a physical fitness test had suddenly appeared on the agenda. The recruits were instructed to put on the unbelievably unattractive elastic-legged khaki bloomers and gym skirts and parade outside the hut.

Louise's feet were already blistered from the heavy shoes, and her hip ached from all the marching. The thought of running even a yard was more than she could bear, let alone five times round the barracks.

'I'm afraid I will have to be excused,' she said. 'I have a bad hip.'

The PT instructor was a thin, wiry woman of uncertain age. 'Bad hip or not,' she said, 'successfully completing a one-mile run is one of the requirements for service in the ATS.'

'But I'm not going to be serving in the ATS,' Louise explained patiently. 'I think there has been some kind of misunderstanding. I'm only here as a formality. I need to be in the army to do a special job at the factory where I work, but I don't—'

'Nobody has said anything to me about a formality,' the PTI snapped, her hands on her hips. 'If you are unable to fulfil the physical requirements of this training course, you will be discharged. It is as simple as that.'

Louise opened her mouth to say she was happy to leave right there and then. But something held her back.

If she walked out now, she would have failed. Even if it was her choice. Nobody would believe that. Least of all her father. She could already imagine the I-told-you-so expression on his face.

And then she thought of Colonel Westwood. She didn't think he was quite as lovely as she once had, since it was him who had doomed her to her current torment, but his project, with its higher pay, still represented her best chance of escaping from her parents' home longer term.

So in the end she did the run. It was agony, but she was damned if she was going to give anyone the satisfaction of saying that she didn't have what it took to be in the stupid ATS. And when she hobbled in at the end, last of the whole intake, apart from one lump of a girl from Hut 2 who barely got out of a walk the whole way round, she felt a strange sense of achievement.

'Well done,' Voles whispered as they marched back to the hut. 'That was brave.'

Louise was almost too tired to respond. All she could manage was a weary nod of gratitude. But brave or not, it hadn't saved her from her appointment with the commanding officer.

Once again, she nervously fingered her tie and checked the shine on her shoes. Nobody had so far set eyes on the CO, as she had been away for the first week of their training, but she was rumoured to be one of the most strict and stringent camp commandants in the ATS.

'Atten-shun!' the HQ sergeant suddenly yelled. 'By the left, quick march. Left, right, left, right, left, right. Halt!' She glared at Louise, then turned to the ATS officer seated behind the desk. 'Recruit Rutherford, ma'am. Reported on a charge of insubordination.'

Unaccountably, Louise suddenly felt as if she was going to cry. Blinking desperately, she managed a rather meagre salute, and then couldn't remember what to do next. Beside her, the sergeant gave her own salute, did a brisk about-turn, and marched out of the room. Absurdly, Louise felt sorry to see her go.

'Please stand at ease,' Senior Commander Cunningham said in a light, pleasant voice.

Louise almost jumped. Nobody had spoken so nicely to her in the whole time she had been at the camp. And now that she dared look at the commanding officer, she saw that she was an attractive woman of perhaps thirty. She wasn't wearing a cap, and her blond hair was styled in short, elegant curls. Her officer's uniform had clearly been professionally tailored to fit her slender figure. Senior Commander Cunningham obviously wasn't going to allow an AB64 to spoil the line of *her* jacket. And the gold crowns on her shoulder epaulettes gleamed as though they had only been polished two moments before.

But despite her glamorous appearance and cultured voice, her eyes were cool.

'Do you understand why you have been brought to see me?' she asked.

Louise nodded. 'Yes, er, ma'am.' The sergeant had given her strict instructions not to say any more than absolutely necessary.

'Then perhaps you would like to explain yourself?'

Louise had been longing for the chance to explain herself ever since arriving in this godforsaken place. But now that she was given the opportunity, she had no idea what to say. Standing there in her frumpy, ill-fitting uniform, she felt gauche and stupid.

'I didn't realise it would be like this,' she muttered. 'So strict and everything. I thought it … well, for me at least, I thought …'

'You thought it was going to be a formality?'

Louise was taken by surprise.

Commander Cunningham nodded. 'Yes,' she said. 'I have been told what you said. But I am afraid you are labouring under a misapprehension. My job is to turn my recruits into disciplined, useful member of the ATS. And that means everybody. Whatever their reason for joining us. Or whatever they are going to do afterwards. Do you understand?'

'Well, yes, but—'

'I have two aims,' Commander Cunningham went on calmly. 'The first is to make sure that my girls are trained in such a way as to enable them to take on whatever military role awaits them. The second is to ensure that they are a credit the ATS.'

Her mouth tightened slightly. 'We are a very young service,' she said. 'There are some who would still prefer that we didn't exist. But we do exist, and in order to continue to exist we have to prove that we are capable of taking our place alongside our male counterparts.' Her eyes were steady and direct. 'I would have thought that with your experience of working in a factory, you would understand that.'

Louise was finding it hard to meet that clear gaze. 'Yes, ma'am,' she said. 'But—'

'We aren't men,' Commander Cunningham went on blithely. 'We don't have their physical strength. But in every other way I believe we are their equal. Or we can be if we try.' She continued to regard Louise calmly. 'You clearly come from a privileged background, Rutherford. And I can see that the rigour of military life has come as a shock to you. Nevertheless, I would expect a girl of your upbringing and education to understand the need for self-restraint. Ill discipline and uncontrolled emotion have no place in a fighting army.' She flicked an invisible speck off her desk. 'I would also expect you to give a lead to those who have been brought up in less fortunate circumstances.'

She paused and tapped one neatly manicured nail thoughtfully on her pad before continuing. 'There are girls here from every conceivable background. I am disappointed to find that it is you, Rutherford, who have been sent to me, rather than one of them.'

All this had been delivered in the same pleasant tone, but by the time she reached the end, Louise was feeling very small. If she could have squirmed, she would have done so. As it was, she had to stand there in the at-ease position, with her hands clasped behind her back, and take it. From having grudgingly admired the look and style of the commanding officer, she now loathed her. How dare she criticise her like that?

'And now you are angry,' Commander Cunningham said implacably. 'It is never nice to be shown the error of one's ways. But I need you to understand that this is not a formality. Whatever your role is to be after this period of basic training, it will certainly require strength of mind. In the physical fitness test this afternoon you showed some grit and determination. It is now up to you to prove to us that you are capable of taking your place in the ATS with efficiency, dignity and self-control.'

She must have pressed a buzzer or made some invisible signal, because at that moment the door opened and the sergeant came marching back in with another round of snappy halting and saluting.

Commander Cunningham accepted the salute with a courteous nod, then turned her attention back to Louise.

'As this is your first infringement, Rutherford, I am not going to charge you formally under King's Regulations. This incident will therefore not be noted on your conduct sheet. But I do feel that you need a lesson in self-discipline and humility. So for the next three evenings, you will be given extra fatigue duties.' She glanced at the sergeant. 'Can I leave that to you, Sergeant?'

'Oh yes, ma'am,' the sergeant responded gleefully.

Louise had to use all the self-discipline she possessed not to turn and punch the blasted woman in the face. But aware that Commander Cunningham's eyes were on her once again, she refrained. There was something in that cool scrutiny that made her square her shoulders instead.

'Do you understand, Rutherford?'

Louise nodded. 'Yes, ma'am.'

'And you will think over what we discussed earlier?'

'Yes, ma'am.' Although it had hardly been a discussion; more like a lecture. A diatribe. Whatever it was, it had been a most unpalatable experience. One she bitterly resented.

'Do you have any questions?'

Louise lowered her eyes submissively. 'No, ma'am.'

The sergeant bellowed the instructions for Louise to come to attention, salute, about-turn and march out. Once outside, she instructed her to report to the guardroom after supper that evening. She gave a sharp laugh. 'And wear your fatigues. You will be scrubbing all the potatoes for tomorrow. And you won't want to get mud on your service dress.'

Louise turned her head away to hide her flush of angry mortification. Scrubbing potatoes? That was one of the tasks her mother had occasionally asked her to do, and of all household chores it was the one she hated most.

As she walked back to Hut 6, she felt utterly humiliated. The punishment was going to be bad enough. But the interview had been worse. With her quiet, oh-so-reasonable voice and air of genteel disappointment, Senior Commander Cunningham had made her feel like a chastised child sent to the corner in a dunce's hat.

Knowing that the morning's army procedures lecture would already have begun, Louise was looking forward to giving in to her misery in the privacy of her bunk. But then she remembered that her bed would still be barracked. Each morning they had to assemble their sheets, pillows, blanket and mattress into a neat, rigorously prescribed roll that to Louise's eyes resembled a very large liquorice allsort. It seemed the final insult that she couldn't lie down and have a comfortable cry.

But as she sat despondently on the bare slats of her bunk, she saw two letters waiting for her on her kit box.

The first was from George Nelson.

Dear Louise,

Thank you for helping me win the rabbit. I have called him Bunny and am teaching him to do magic tricks. Katy has given me an old beer barrel for him to live in. We've cut out the front and put wire there so he can see out. I hope you are having a nice time in the army and that they are teaching you how to kill people after all.

Yours sincerely,

George Nelson

PS I know I already thanked you, but Mum found out about it and said I had to write as well.

PPS I saw those two American soldiers going into the pub so I thanked them again too.

160

Unaccountably, that made her want to cry even more.

The second letter was from Doris. Louise picked it up. Surely a letter from good old Doris would be bound to cheer her up.

Dear Louise,

How are you getting on? I expect they are delighted to have such a well-educated, posh recruit like you. Everything is much the same here, except I have finally met your lovely Colonel Westwood. And I must say, if I didn't have dear old Sid, I'd have had a shot at him myself! Ha ha — as though a man like that would look at a great whale of a thing like me. But I reckon as Mrs Gibbons thinks she's in with a chance. I swear she was wearing lipstick when she came in this morning!

The other news is that Don Wellington is back with us. According to himself, he passed out top of his intake. And can you believe it? He answered an advertisement in the Wandsworth Gazette for a 'fine, upstanding specimen of a British soldier' (cocky bugger that he is) and has now been selected to lead the Clapham Common Salute the Soldier parade on 25 March. He's cock-a-hoop, as you can imagine. Let me know how you are when you get a moment.

With best regards,
Doris

Chapter Fifteen

'Mr Keller wants to see you,' Maggie said as soon as Jen came in on Monday.

'Oh no,' Jen said, taking off her coat. 'Now he'll know I'm late in. But it wasn't my fault. There was a tube breakdown at Kennington.'

But it wasn't her tardiness that Henry wanted to talk about.

He was standing by the window, smoking a cigarette. With the light behind him, Jen couldn't quite make out his expression. But his voice sounded reassuringly calm.

'How are you?' he asked.

'I'm well,' Jen said.

'And what about last week?' he asked. 'While I was away?'

For a fleeting moment Jen was puzzled by the question, but then she recalled that the last time Henry had seen her, she had been in a state of emotional collapse. 'Thank you for helping me that day,' she said. 'I've been perfectly fine since then.'

'Really?' he said. 'That's not quite what I've heard.' He came away from the window and tapped the cigarette into the ashtray on his desk. 'I gather Walter Lowther was summoned to the auditorium to hear some rather famous classical violinists, only to discover he was watching a couple of comedians playing concertinas with cymbals strapped to their knees. He was not very happy. And nor apparently were the violinists, who were kept waiting in the wings for the whole charade.'

Jen glanced at him, taken aback by the seriousness of his tone. She knew he thought that Mr Lowther, the classical music entertainments officer, was fussy and pedantic, and under normal circumstances that was the kind of thing he might have found funny. But he didn't look amused today.

'I know,' she said penitently. 'I'm really sorry about that. I got the timetable mixed up. I don't know how it happened.'

He studied the tip of his cigarette for a moment, then looked up at her with raised eyebrows. 'Too many late nights, perhaps?'

Jen felt a jolt of alarm. 'What do you mean?'

He held her eyes for a long moment. 'That wasn't the only thing that went wrong, was it?' His gaze dropped to the desk. 'I gather Thursday's auditions were a disaster too.' He lifted a piece of paper and began to read. '*Everything ran late and several of the acts I was expecting to see never appeared at all. I wouldn't have minded if I hadn't known that Jen Carter was making a spectacle of herself cavorting about town with a young man at all hours of the night.'*

Jen felt her heart accelerate. 'That's complete nonsense,' she said.

'Really?' Henry sounded unconvinced. 'I'm afraid that's not the only person who mentioned your out-of-hours activities last week. I have also been told about an "intimate embrace" at Leicester Square tube station.' He drew on his cigarette. 'Word gets around, Jen. It's a small world. Looking as you do, nobody is going to miss you. If you don't mind my saying, it would have been wiser to entertain your lover in a less popular area.' He hesitated. 'Unless of course your intention was for people to see you.'

'Of course it wasn't,' Jen snapped. In her efforts to keep Sean away from Clapham, she had completely overlooked the fact that someone from the theatre might see her in the West End. How could she have been so imprudent? And how could she have got so carried away that she hadn't realised that people might be looking at her? Now Henry apparently thought she had done it on purpose as a cowardly way of letting him know that she had found someone else.

'He isn't my lover,' she said

'Well, of course, I am glad to hear that.'

The dry tone in his voice made her cringe. Before she knew it, she was trying to lie her way out. 'He's called Sean Byrne,' she said. 'He's an old friend of my brother Bob. The one who's a POW in Germany.' It was only a little white lie, after all, to spare Henry's feelings.

But Henry just looked at her.

She had to make him believe her. It would be a disaster if he found out who Sean really was. 'He was in London for a few days and didn't know anyone. He's Irish. And yes, he is a bit of a flirt, but there was nothing in it.' She took a breath, trying to sound righteously aggrieved. 'We were hardly *cavorting*. Anyway, he's gone back to Ireland now. So you can tell whoever has been telling tales to mind their own business.'

Henry held her gaze for a moment. She wasn't sure he entirely believed her, but he seemed to be prepared to give her the benefit of the doubt. 'I'm sorry I had to mention it,' he said. 'But I think you can understand why people felt I ought to know. I had to go out on a bit of a limb to get you this job, so any problems are bound to come straight back to me.'

Jen suddenly felt overcome with remorse. 'I'm so sorry, Henry, I really am,' she said. 'I'm grateful for everything you have done for me. The last thing I want is to cause you any embarrassment.'

Henry gave her a faintly quizzical look. 'I thought it might be a case of when the cat's away ...'

'Well it wasn't,' Jen said indignantly. Although of course that was almost exactly what it had been. 'I don't think of you as a cat, and I very much hope you don't think of me as a mouse.'

He gave a slight laugh. 'No, I don't. Although I do think of you as as a menace to mankind. You are almost certainly going to be the death of me. Now for goodness' sake go and do some work before I start getting more complaints.'

As soon as she got back to the admin office, Jen turned on Maggie. 'You knew, didn't you?' she said accusingly. 'You knew someone had been bitching to Henry about me. Why didn't you warn me?'

'It wasn't my business,' Maggie said. 'I didn't know what was going on.'

'Nothing was going on,' Jen said crossly. 'Well, nothing much, anyway. I know Mr Lowther was annoyed about the scheduling mix-up, but who on earth told Henry what I was up to in the evenings?'

Maggie sniffed. 'I suspect it was Janette Pymm,' she said. 'She certainly saw you at the pictures one day last week. And I know she and Mr Keller were due to meet up at the weekend.'

Were they indeed? Jen thought sourly. She might have known that beastly Janette Pymm would take the first opportunity to stick a knife in her back.

Irritably she swung away. And that was when she noticed the newspaper lying on Maggie's desk.

The headline read: BRITAIN BLOCKADES EIRE AS INVASION FEVER INTENSIFIES!

Picking up the paper with trembling fingers, she scanned the leader column.

As of midnight last night, 12 March, all travel between Britain and Ireland has been banned. According to the Home Office, the restriction has been implemented for paramount military reasons, to prevent Allied invasion plans reaching Dublin, where spies could pass word to Berlin. There is no doubt that this will cause a period of isolation for Ireland and will bring discomfort to her people. But as the IRA recently vowed to do anything it can to retard Britain's war effort, the risk of betrayal is too great.

She stared at the paper, trying to remember what Sean had said about his journey. He had a ticket booked on the Sunday-night ferry from Fishguard to Rosslare. What did that mean? Would he have got away before midnight?

She was on tenterhooks for the whole of that day. And the next. But then she relaxed. He must have got away just in the nick of time.

Katy had been trying terribly hard not to worry about Ward, and to a large extent she had been successful. But when on Wednesday morning a letter arrived from Helen de Burrel in Tunisia saying that although Ward was currently 'away on operational duty', she had heard on the grapevine that he was alive and well, the relief was such that Katy treated herself to a small celebratory brandy.

It was while she was sitting at one of the bar tables drinking it that Gino asked if he could have a word.

'Of course,' she said.

'I like very much to work here,' he said. 'But now is possibility for me to work with the Americani.'

'The Americans?' Katy stared at him blankly, wondering if she had understood correctly. What on earth would the Americans want Gino for? Her mind was still on Ward, and for a moment she even wondered if they might be considering using Gino as a secret agent to insert into Italy ahead of the Allied advance. But then she took another glug of brandy and shook her head. It seemed highly unlikely. Surely even the gung-ho Americans wouldn't be as crazy as that.

And it turned out they weren't. All they had actually offered him was a job in the barracks kitchen.

'Is good for me,' Gino said earnestly, as Katy struggled not to laugh. 'I like to learn more a little bit the cooking, no?'

Katy didn't know if it was good or not. But as the brandy seemed to have gone straight to her head, she was unable to do anything but giggle weakly. Ward was OK, and at the moment that was all that mattered.

'I think it's good riddance,' Jen said that night. 'But I pity the poor old Americans. Goodness knows what they'll end up eating with Gino in the kitchen. And you'll soon find someone better to help you here.'

Katy wasn't so sure. Gino hadn't been much use behind the bar, but he had at least provided an extra pair of hands.

The following morning, aware that she was already running badly behind with the chores, the last person Katy wanted to see walking into the pub was Louise's father, Greville Rutherford.

He arrived at a particularly awkward time, when she had just hitched her skirt up into her knickers in order to wash the floor. The bar couldn't have been looking worse. The chairs were tipped up on the tables. The whole place stank of beer and sweat. Damp sawdust littered the entrance. And now here was the owner of the brewery, her ultimate boss, standing just inside the door, looking around with a sneer of distaste on his pompous face.

'Oh, Mr Rutherford,' she said, hastily straightening her skirt. 'What can I do for you?' He had never called out of the blue before, and Katy had a sudden panic that she might have inadvertently committed some terrible infringement of her lease.

He frowned. 'I gather you have a dog.'

'Yes,' Katy said. 'I do.' Were dogs not allowed in leased pubs? She had never thought to check.

His frown deepened. 'And is the animal here?'

'He's out in the back yard,' Katy stammered. Or he had been last time she'd looked. For all she knew, he might have escaped since then and was even now savaging Mrs Rutherford's chickens.

'May I see him?'

Oh no, Katy thought. What on earth had Lucky done?

Reluctantly she went to open the back door. To her relief, Lucky came bounding in at once, wagging his tail ingratiatingly. But as soon as he spotted her visitor, he stopped and bared his teeth with a low, menacing growl.

Mr Rutherford took a step back in alarm. 'Goodness me, I didn't realise he'd be so fierce.'

'He's not,' Katy said, hastily grabbing Lucky's collar. 'He's actually very friendly. Just rather protective. He doesn't like strange men. Not that you are strange. I mean ...' She stopped in confusion.

But Mr Rutherford didn't seem to be listening. He was in fact eyeing Lucky with considerable approval. 'The reason I am here, Mrs Frazer, is that I am looking for a mascot for the Salute the Soldier parade next weekend, and I wanted to see if your dog would be suitable. And I must say, he is quite a fine-looking animal.'

Katy felt her mouth fall open. Fine-looking or not, she could hardly imagine an animal less suitable. Lucky was entirely disobedient, hated walking on a leash, and if he got wind of a bitch on heat somewhere in the vicinity ... well, the thought didn't bear thinking about.

'Oh no,' she began quickly. 'I don't think—'

'You should consider it an honour,' Greville Rutherford said sharply. 'He will lead the entire parade.'

Of course she couldn't say no. She couldn't afford to alienate the man who held her livelihood in his hands. After he had gone, Katy leaned weakly against the door. Hearing a whine, she turned round to find Lucky watching her anxiously with his head on one side. She shook her head in humorous despair, wishing she could somehow let Ward know of the honour about to be conferred on his confounded dog.

Shocked by how much she had minded incurring Henry's displeasure, Jen had been looking for an opportunity to get back in his good books.

On Thursday, she found it. She was glancing idly through the day's schedule when her eye alighted on an act called the Canine Comics. 'Oh my goodness,' she said. 'It can't be.'

But it was. It was the same man dressed in the same shiny green suit, and armed with four performing poodles. One of which was the infamous Pookie.

Hoping against hope that he wouldn't recognise her, Jen told the dog trainer he would have to wait for a few minutes before going on.

'I can't wait,' he grumbled. 'The poodles are primed to perform right now.'

'Well you'll have to keep them primed for another few minutes,' Jen said, and sprinted off down through the warren of corridors to Henry's office.

'You must come and see,' she gasped when he answered her knock on the door. 'Pookie the poodle is here. The one Katy's dog Lucky was after that night in Clapham. I thought you might like to watch him perform.'

Henry, in shirtsleeves, had been looking over a pile of papers. But obedient to her command, he stood up, shrugged on his jacket and followed her back out of the door.

'I was under the impression that Pookie was female,' he remarked.

That made Jen laugh. 'Yes, I suppose she must be,' she said. As they approached the auditorium, she paused. 'Where do you want to watch from? The stalls? Or the wings?'

'The wings,' Henry said.

When she joined him there a few minutes later, after ushering the Canine Comics onto the stage, she found him leaning against a piece of spare scenery, watching the antics of the poodles and their ridiculous ringmaster with distinct amusement.

'Pookie is a very attractive animal,' he murmured, as Jen squeezed in beside him. 'I'm not surprised Lucky was so smitten.'

Jen giggled, and felt a responsive chuckle course through his body.

And then she was suddenly aware of his proximity in a different way. She could feel the hard wall of his chest behind her shoulders. At first he kept very still, then after a moment or two he reached up to smooth a strand of her hair away from his face. As the backs of his fingers brushed her cheek, she held her breath, and was conscious of her heartbeat accelerating sharply.

But nothing happened.

Lowering his hand abruptly, Henry took a casual step away from her, and turned to greet Maggie, who had suddenly appeared through the curtain beside them.

Maggie looked startled. 'Oh, I'm sorry, Mr Keller,' she muttered, backing away. 'I didn't know you were here.'

Henry waved a casual hand towards the stage. 'I was keen to see the Canine Comics,' he said. 'But I didn't want to disturb the entertainments officers in the auditorium, so I thought I'd watch discreetly from here. Marvellous act, don't you think? Pookie is a particularly fine performer.'

Maggie tried manfully to hide her astonishment. 'Well,' she said doubtfully. 'I don't know about that. But I expect the soldiers will like it.'

'Oh, I'm sure they will,' Henry agreed heartily.

When Maggie had gone, he glanced at Jen with a comical look on his face. 'You have completely ruined my credibility,' he said. 'Maggie will never trust my judgement again.'

'Well it's your own fault for going on about Pookie,' Jen said indignantly.

Henry glanced back at the stage, where Pookie and her three canine colleagues were now pirouetting on top of four small red and white boxes. 'You have to hand it to her. Her timing is excellent.' He turned back to Jen. 'Unlike mine,' he said wryly. 'Although it could have been worse. Another minute and Maggie might have caught me kissing you. And that would have been a disaster.'

Jen held his eyes for a shocked second, then looked away, flushing. What had he meant? In what way would it have been a disaster?

But she couldn't ask, because the poodles were already taking their bows. Then, one by one, they leapt into their trainer's arms to leave the stage.

Henry moved hastily out of the way. 'I'd better leave you to it,' he murmured. 'But thank you. And do let me know if you think there are any other acts I should see. I'd forgotten how pleasurable it can be to watch from the wings.'

Jen watched him go in considerable confusion, but she didn't have time to think about what had just happened, because other acts were already queuing up. She stored it up like a scene from a favourite film, and promised herself that she would replay every second of it on her way home that evening.

But that was not to be.

Because when she left the theatre at half past five, the first thing she saw was Sean Byrne, leaning against the lamp post on the corner of Catherine Street.

Oh no, Jen thought. Oh no, oh no, oh no.

Lazily he straightened up and came towards her. For once he wasn't smiling. 'They cancelled all travel to Ireland.'

'I know,' she said. 'I saw it in the paper. But I thought you might have got away in time.' Keen to get him out of sight of the theatre, she steered him in the direction of Leicester Square.

'I would have done, but the train was slow and I missed the ferry,' he said as he fell into step beside her. 'By the time the next one was due, they wouldn't let it sail.'

'Oh Sean,' she said. 'I knew you should have left earlier.'

He heard the irritation in her voice and bridled. 'How was I to know they were about to blockade us? It's not my fault. It's the bloody British government and their bloody war. I tried everything. I even went up to Holyhead to see if I could get into the north. But it was like bloody Fort Knox. There were hundreds of people trying to find some way of getting over the water, and police everywhere blocking access to the docks. In the end there was nothing I could do but come back to London.'

'So what are you going to do?'

'I don't know. I suppose I'm relying on you to help me.'

Jen stopped abruptly and turned to stare at him. 'What do you mean?'

'Jen, for the love of God,' he said. 'I've spent all my money. I've nothing left and nowhere to stay.'

'But I ...'

'Surely you can at least find me a bed for a night or two while I work out what to do.' He pulled her to him. 'Or will I share yours? That would be the best solution.'

Jen wrenched away. 'No,' she said. 'That would not be the best solution.' She felt like screaming. This was all her fault. If only she had been stronger last week, he would have gone straight back to Ireland and none of this would have happened. But no, she had been weak-willed and irresolute, and now she really was in the soup.

'What is it?' he asked. 'You were happy enough to kiss and cuddle last week. Maybe this is just what we needed. A chance to spend a bit more time together.'

Jen groaned. If she had any money on her, she would have given it to him to find a room somewhere. But she didn't.

She clearly couldn't just abandon him. But she had no idea how long this travel ban would last. It could be weeks, or even months for all she knew. 'What about your friend's mother?' she asked. 'Wouldn't she give you a bed? After all, you did bring her the medicine.'

Sean shook his head. 'The poor old biddy was living all alone in a single room.'

They were outside Leicester Square Underground station now. Jen didn't want to stand there arguing. It was far too public a place. 'OK. You'll have to come back to the pub,' she said. 'I expect Katy will let you sleep in the cellar tonight at least.'

'That's my girl,' he said, as she hustled him down into the tube station and bought him a ticket. 'I knew I could rely on you.'

'I'm not your girl,' Jen said. 'I know we fooled around a bit last week, but that was last week. It's different now.'

He laughed and leaned over to kiss her. 'The only thing that's different as far as I'm concerned is that you have your prudy face on. But I don't think it

169

will take me too long to get rid of that.'

Louise's hands had been red and raw by the time she had finished her three nights of potato scrubbing. And it wasn't just her hands that were sore, but also her pride. Commander Cunningham's cutting comments rankled more and more each time Louise thought about them. Despite her pique, though, there was one thing that kept coming back to her. In all the ghastliness of her initiation into the ATS, she had completely forgotten her resolution to be nice.

But it was hard to be nice when one was constantly being picked up for the tiniest mistakes. One day her bed roll wasn't quite aligned properly, the next a tiny strand of her hair was touching her collar. Or her salute was sloppy. Her shoelace was loose. Her cap was too far forward. There was a piece of grass under her bunk. She was looking out of the window during the lecture about personal hygiene. She didn't know the words to the ATS song. She spent too long in the washroom. She was incapable of climbing a rope. After all that, it was no wonder she was grumpy. And no wonder that nobody liked her.

Oddly enough, her first chance to demonstrate a better side to her nature came on a visit to a gas chamber in Aldershot on Friday.

They were taken there in a coach, and it made a pleasant change to be driving out of the camp rather than constantly marching round the parade square, listening to excruciatingly dull lectures or trying unsuccessfully to vault over a horse in the gym.

Louise was one of the first to get on the coach and had a nasty few moments of worry that nobody was going to choose to sit next to her. But luckily Voles obliged, preventing her from feeling any more of a pariah than she already did.

They weren't allowed to talk on the journey, but they were allowed to sing, and it was under cover of a rousing chorus of 'Greensleeves' that Voles confided to Louise that she had a terrible fear of gas.

Louise glanced at her in surprise. 'It's only to make sure we know how to use the army respirators,' she said reassuringly. 'They're hardly going to poison us.'

But as the first hour of the visit was taken up with a gruesome lecture on the various types of gas and their effects on the skin, lungs and nervous system, by the time they were taken to the specially designed chamber, even Louise was feeling somewhat daunted.

When the moment came, they were inserted into the sealed chamber in groups of six. Louise and Voles went in with Buller and three girls from another hut who they didn't know by name but who Louise recognised as some of the ones who had had nits.

The six of them had only been in there a moment before Louise felt Voles clutch at her arm. Even through her slightly fogged mask, she could see that the other girl was white as a sheet and trembling like a jelly. She looked as though she was holding her breath.

It was impossible to give her any encouragement from inside the respirator, but Louise waved her hand urgently, trying to imitate the motion of breathing. She was too late. Voles was already swaying alarmingly. Grabbing her arms to stop her crashing to the floor, Louise tried to indicate to Buller and the other girls that she needed help. But they all seemed oblivious to what was going on, and when she kicked Buller's leg to attract her attention, the girl moved irritably out of the way.

In desperation, still holding the comatose Voles, Louise struggled to the sealed door and banged on it.

There was no response. In the protective gloves, it was impossible to knock hard enough to make any real noise. So without thinking, she ripped off her mask and started shouting to be let out.

Thankfully, almost at once, the heavy metal door swung open. Two members of the directing staff were standing there. They looked astounded at the scene that confronted them. Quickly they turned off the gas and hauled the unconscious Voles outside into the fresh air. Louise, her eyes streaming, was sent off to a washroom and told to rinse her face in plenty of cold water.

But when she eventually emerged, red-eyed, instead of the praise she was expecting, she got a severe telling-off.

'What on earth were you doing?' the instructor shouted at her. 'You were told to keep your gas mask on at all times.'

'I had to take it off to make you hear,' Louise said indignantly. 'I banged on the door but you didn't take any notice. I couldn't just leave her lying on the floor. She was dying for all I knew.'

But of course, even though it was stupid Voles who was in the wrong for panicking and failing to breathe, it was Louise who was once again put on a charge, for breaching gas chamber etiquette.

This time Louise was brought up in front of the po-faced 2IC and told that, as punishment for illegally removing her gas mask, she would be put on restriction of privileges for three days and would therefore not be allowed to attend the NAAFI entertainment on Sunday evening.

It wasn't as bad as cleaning potatoes, but it was still clearly unfair, and for the first time Louise was aware of a touch of sympathy from some of the other girls. Voles, in particular, mortified that it was her weakness that had caused Louise to get into trouble, felt she should have been rewarded rather than penalised for her heroic action.

But despite feeling aggrieved, Louise took it on the chin. She didn't much care about missing the entertainment. She had heard about these ENSA variety shows, and the thought of listening to some second-rate soprano like Jen Carter singing so-called popular songs, or an appalling comedian making off-colour jokes, left her feeling pretty cold.

She would be perfectly happy to lie on her bunk and read a magazine instead. It would in fact be a relief to have some time to herself. She might finally get round to writing some letters. She would treat herself to a cup of tea and a slice of Madeira cake from the NAAFI. And if she had the energy, she might even try and light the hut stove to keep herself warm.

One of the most annoying things about Sean Byrne, Katy decided, was that both Malcolm and Lucky did exactly what he said. Whereas for her, they both did the absolute opposite. Right now she was trying to fit the pump to a new barrel, and Malcolm and Lucky were annoying her by ragging around under her feet. She had twice asked Malcolm to take Lucky out to the back yard, and was shooing him away for the third time when Sean came up from the cellar.

'Will you not listen to your mother,' he said sternly to Malcolm. 'Take Lucky outside right now.' And at once boy and dog scurried off down the passage towards the back door.

'They never do that for me,' Katy said, straightening up. 'Why do they take notice of you?'

Sean smiled. 'Well, to be sure,' he said, 'I use the same technique on children and animals as I do on women. Once they know who's boss, they're happy to eat out of your hand.'

And Katy had been forced to laugh. Thankfully she at least was immune to his blarney.

She had been horrified when Jen had brought Sean back to the pub on Thursday evening. But having reluctantly agreed to let him sleep in the cellar for a couple of nights, she had found that she rather liked him. Not in a romantic way, thankfully, but then he didn't turn the full force of his charm on her. He reserved that for Jen, or indeed any other pretty girl that happened to come into the bar.

Even Elsa, madly in love with Aaref, flushed when Sean smiled at her. And Angie Carter, predisposed to resent his presence in Jen's life because of her affection for Henry, only held on to her antagonism for one night. Once Sean had told her that Gino was the luckiest man on earth to have won the affections of such an accomplished dancer, she too was won over.

But Sean Byrne had other attributes as well as his undoubted sex appeal, and one of those was that he was turning out to be surprisingly helpful. As a result, Katy told him he could stay on in return for lending a hand in the pub.

That had not gone down at all well with Jen.

'No,' she said, almost dropping baby Caroline in horror. 'He's got to go. I don't want him here.'

'But he is awfully useful,' Katy said. 'And he's great with the children, and with Lucky. I don't mean for ever. But just until he can get back to Ireland. After all, what else is he going to do? He's got no money and no means of earning any as far as I can see.'

Jen looked stricken. 'Katy, please,' she said. 'Can't you see what he does to me? I really don't want to get involved with him again, but it's so hard when we're living under the same roof. It's bad enough already. Goodness knows what everyone is thinking.'

Katy knew exactly what most people were thinking, but prudently didn't say so. Jen's mother in particular had been vocal in her disapproval, and although Katy had tried to reassure her that Sean was banished to the cellar at night, she doubted Joyce believed her.

It wasn't hard to guess what Jen's real problem was. 'You're worried that Henry will find out, aren't you?' Katy asked.

'Well, yes,' Jen admitted. 'Although I don't see why he should care, when he spends all his time away visiting the touring shows, or dining out with that little snitch Janette Pymm.'

Katy smiled sympathetically. 'Well,' she said, 'if that's what you're worried about, maybe the best thing would be for you to move back into your mother's house.'

Jen's pretty face flushed up at once. 'Oh, I see,' she hissed. 'I'm getting booted out, am I? I've got to go back and suffer Angie's snoring just so that you can have my former boyfriend to help you in the bar.'

Katy bit her lip. 'Jen, it's not like that,' she said. 'You know it's not. I'm only trying to think of a way to suit everybody.'

'Well it doesn't suit me,' Jen said. And dumping Caroline on the bed, she turned on her heel and went downstairs to the bar.

Chapter Sixteen

Louise lay on her bunk and watched the other girls getting ready for the Sunday-night NAAFI entertainment. With only the very minimum of make-up allowed, there was a limit to what they could do, but they all seemed determined to look as pretty as possible for the ENSA concert. As though the entertainers would care, Louise thought sourly. She doubted they would even notice. But there was a rumour that there were one or two male performers in the show, and as they'd barely set eyes on a man for two weeks now, there was a definite frisson of excitement. Even Buller was attempting to pin up her hair in a slightly more feminine style.

Louise was wishing they would all just go and leave her in peace when Susan Voles appeared at the foot of her bunk. 'Are you sure you don't want me to stay here with you?' she asked.

'Goodness, no,' Louise said, appalled at the thought of spending an evening alone with the pitiful Voles. 'You go and enjoy yourself. You deserve it.'

But her sarcasm passed straight over the other girl's head.

'No, it's you that deserves it,' Voles said earnestly. 'But I'll make it up to you, I promise.'

And then eventually, thankfully, with a final trill of goodbyes, they were gone.

Now that the moment had come, Louise couldn't be bothered to light the stove. She wrapped herself in her blanket, picked up her pen and the lettercards she had bought at the NAAFI, and began to think about what to write.

It wasn't easy. She could hardly pretend things were going well. But nor did she want to let on how badly she was doing. Especially not when Doris had already told her that Don Wellington had passed out top of his intake. How galling was that? Almost as galling as the thought of him leading her father's Salute the Soldier parade on Clapham Common next weekend. And it sounded from Katy's letter as though he would be leading Ward Frazer's dog into the bargain.

For some reason Louise found that even more annoying. She didn't want Don Wellington getting all cosy with Katy. The last thing she wanted to find when she eventually got home was him propping up the bar in the Flag and

Garter. Jen Carter living there was bad enough.

To make it even more difficult, she had to be careful what she put because she knew all military mail was censored. She decided to tell Katy how horrid Don Wellington had been to her at the factory. She didn't think the censors would worry about that, it wasn't exactly a military secret; nor did she think they'd be interested in her eager questions about Jen Carter's former boyfriend, Sean Byrne. Katy had mentioned in her letter that he had come to stay at the pub, and Louise was agog to know how that had come about.

Having finished her letter to Katy and scrawled another to Doris, she decided to go over to the NAAFI to get a cup of tea and a snack.

The ENSA entertainment was taking place in the gym, and as Louise crossed the dark parade ground, she could hear distant clapping and laughing.

Because of the show, there was hardly anyone in the NAAFI, just a couple of girls playing cards over by the window, and two of the duty DS chatting in front of the noticeboard.

Reluctant to sit at a table all on her own, Louise was just carrying her slice of Madeira cake and cup of tea across towards the exit when the door opened and a man came in.

It was odd enough to see a man at all in the ATS NAAFI. But to see one in a smart pinstriped suit was even odder. And as Louise paused to take in this extraordinary phenomenon, she belatedly realised that it was Henry Keller.

He didn't recognise her in her uniform, but he held the door politely, and looked somewhat taken aback when she didn't move.

'You're Henry Keller, aren't you?' Louise said. 'We met at the pub in Lavender Road a few weeks ago. You rescued me from that horrible American corporal.'

'Good Lord,' he said. 'That's right. It's Louise, isn't it? Come to think of it, Jen told me you were joining the ATS. But I had no idea I'd bump into you here.' He was still holding the door; now he took a polite step back. 'I'm sorry, I'm delaying you. I assume you are on your way back to the show?'

'I'm not allowed to go to the show,' she said. She gave what she hoped was a comical pout. 'I was naughty and my punishment was not to go to it.'

He looked startled. 'I'm sorry to hear that. Dare I ask what you did wrong?'

'Someone passed out in the gas chamber and I illegally took off my gas mask to help her.'

'Good God,' he said. Letting the door swing shut, he drew her back into the canteen. 'And apart from demonstrating such valour in the gas chamber, how are you enjoying military life?'

Louise didn't know what to say. It was so nice to see a friendly face after all this time, she suddenly felt rather choked. She swallowed bravely, but something in her face must have given her away, because he gave her a compassionate look and pulled out a chair for her at one of the tables. 'You look as though you could do with something a little stronger than tea,' he said. 'After seeing the opening section of that show, I certainly could. I was on my way in for a stiff brandy.'

But unfortunately the NAAFI didn't serve brandy. Or any alcohol at all, come to that.

'Apparently they have some in the officers' mess,' Henry said, coming back to the table. 'If you don't mind waiting, I'll go and get us a couple of glasses from there.'

Louise didn't mind waiting at all. She couldn't think of anything nicer than sitting in the NAAFI sipping brandy with Henry Keller.

And what was even better, they were still there when everyone poured out of the show for the interval. Louise could feel her kudos rising as her ATS cohort caught sight of her handsome companion. She graciously beckoned Voles and one or two others over to be introduced, and Henry was charm personified, as he had been the entire evening.

He had listened with sympathy to her account of the horrors of the first week, and congratulated her on sticking it out. 'It sounds much worse than my first experience of the army,' he said. 'I certainly don't remember being put in a gas chamber.'

'I didn't know you'd been in the army,' Louise said. 'I assumed you'd always been in the theatre.'

He shook his head. 'When war was declared, I volunteered for the Rifle Brigade. They sent me to one of the officer corps training units, and when I was commissioned I served briefly in Belgium. But after Dunkirk, I was summoned to ENSA, and that's where I've been ever since.' He offered Louise a cigarette, and when she refused, he lit one himself.

'Goodness,' Louise said. 'That was a lucky break.'

He lifted his shoulders slightly. 'In some ways, but not in others. I know ENSA counts as National Service, but I would much prefer to be fighting, especially with the invasion coming up.'

'You sound like my brother Douglas,' Louise said. 'He's dying to get into action. He's an officer in the Coldstream Guards. Daddy is terribly proud of him.'

Henry raised his eyebrows. 'I'm sure he's proud of you too.'

Louise almost laughed. 'Daddy? No, he's not. Not at all. He's always raving on about Douglas, how marvellous he is, how patriotic and brave and everything. But when I said I was joining up, he just laughed. And neither he nor Mummy are bothering to come to my passing-out parade on Easter

Saturday. Apparently they're too busy.' She stopped, aware that she sounded sulky and childish. And she realised that she very much didn't want Henry Keller to think she was childish.

But he seemed more interested in Douglas. 'Where is your brother stationed?' he asked.

'In Tunisia,' Louise said. 'He should have been in Italy by now, but he was injured recently while quelling a native uprising.' She rolled her eyes. 'Daddy, of course, was terribly impressed.'

'Was he?' Henry's brows rose slightly. 'I'm not sure he should have been.'

Louise frowned. 'What do you mean? Do you know my brother?'

Henry drew on his cigarette. 'I don't know him, but I do know of him, and I have reason to believe that he might have been pulling the wool over your father's eyes.'

'Really?' Louise was intrigued. 'What, you mean there wasn't an uprising? Then how did he get injured?'

Henry smiled faintly. 'I probably shouldn't tell you this,' he said, 'but it might make you feel better. The story I heard is that your brother was teasing a camel and it took umbrage and kicked him in the face.'

Louise stared at him incredulously, then put her hand to her mouth and started to laugh. Poor old Douglas. How humiliating to be laid low by a camel! She wasn't surprised he had tried to bluff his way out of it. That was completely typical of him. And her parents had fallen for it hook, line and sinker.

And that was when the ENSA audience came in.

When they had gone again for the second half of the show, Henry went back to the officers' mess to fetch two more brandies.

'Shouldn't you be watching the show?' Louise asked when he returned. Not that she wanted him to leave; far from it. She hadn't had such an enjoyable evening in a long time. And the brandies were making her feel pleasantly mellow.

Henry glanced at the clock. 'Yes, I suppose I ought to go back in,' he said. 'I missed seeing one of the sopranos when she auditioned at Drury Lane, and I want to hear her sing in case I need her for one of my own shows.'

Louise was disappointed. The pleasant interlude was clearly coming to an end. And sure enough, a few minutes later he picked up his glass and drained the rest of his brandy. When he put the empty glass back on the table, she thought he would stand up. But instead he paused for a moment, then lit another cigarette.

'Tell me,' he said. 'Do you know someone called Sean Byrne?'

Startled by the question, Louise shook her head. 'No,' she said. 'But I know who he is.'

Henry inclined his head politely. 'And who is he exactly?'

Louise suddenly felt uncomfortable. 'Well, he's an old boyfriend of Jen's,' she said awkwardly. 'From ages ago. Right back at the beginning of the war.'

She glanced at Henry anxiously, but his face was impassive. He nodded. 'But originally he was a friend of one of her brothers?'

Louise tried to remember. She hadn't really known Jen in those days. Not to talk to. 'I don't think so,' she said. 'I don't think any of Jen's family liked him. Nobody liked him very much. People suspected him of being IRA. I think in the end he left because the police were after him.'

'I see.' Henry drew on his cigarette. 'Nevertheless, whatever he was suspected of doing presumably wasn't serious enough to stop him coming back to London occasionally?'

'No,' Louise said. 'Presumably not. Because he's here now. I just had a letter from Katy. He's staying at the pub in Lavender Road.'

As soon as she said the words, she regretted them. She saw his whole body tense up. His hand froze with the cigarette halfway to his mouth. Then he leaned over and very carefully tapped the ash into the metal ashtray on the table.

Louise was dismayed. She had forgotten that Jen was staying in the pub too. She didn't particularly mind dropping Jen in it, but she liked Henry and hadn't meant to cause him distress. What was more, she was grateful to him for sitting here with her when really he should have been watching the ENSA show. For the first time in two weeks, perhaps more, she'd felt like a normal human being rather than a slightly defective khaki robot.

'I'm sure there's nothing in it,' she said.

'Are you?' His voice was hard.

Louise lowered her eyes. 'I'm sorry,' she said. 'I shouldn't have said anything. I think I must be a bit tipsy. But I assumed you knew ...'

'I knew he'd been in London,' Henry said. 'I didn't know he was still here.'

'Well according to Katy, he did leave, but then the government banned all travel to Ireland,' she said. 'So he came back again.'

'And took up residence in the pub?'

'I suppose he hadn't anywhere else to go,' Louise said.

Henry raised his eyebrows.

'You should ask Jen,' Louise said rather desperately. 'I'm sure she'll explain.'

'Oh, I'm sure she will,' he said. But then, perhaps hearing the bitterness in his tone, he raised his hands apologetically. 'I'm sorry,' he said. 'It's not your fault.'

He stubbed out his cigarette and sat back in his chair. 'So,' he said with an easy smile, as though nothing had happened. 'When do you finish here? We'll have to meet up in London sometime so you can tell me how the rest of your training passed off.'

But much as Louise was thrilled at the idea of meeting Henry in London, it wasn't quite the same after that, and it wasn't long before he got up to go.

'Thank you for the brandies,' she said. 'And thank you for rescuing me again. I would have had a sad, lonely evening on my bunk if you hadn't turned up.'

'It was a pleasure,' he said. At the door, he smiled as he leaned over to kiss her on the cheek. 'Chin up,' he murmured. 'I'm sure things will improve. It sounds to me as though you'll be a fine soldier. I think they're lucky to have you.'

Oh dear, Louise thought as she stumbled rather drunkenly across the parade ground to Hut 6. I think I might have just fallen in love with Henry Keller.

Joyce was in her front room. On the mantelpiece the wireless was burbling on about the latest Allied assault on Monte Cassino. There was also a report about Allied gliders landing behind Japanese enemy lines in Burma, but as Joyce had no idea where Burma was, or indeed what was happening there, she didn't bother to listen to that, nor to the report that the war was costing thirteen and a half million pounds every day. Such a figure was completely beyond her comprehension; ten bob seemed a lot to her. In any case, she had more important things on her mind.

That morning she had finally received a note from Paul. He didn't tell her where he was, but he did tell her that he was hoping to join the 3rd Infantry Division as soon as his initial training was over. He was clearly excited about that. He sent his love to Jen, Angie and Gino, and said he missed her cooking.

So even though she didn't like it, at least she knew he was safe, for now. She had been scared they might have sent him straight off to act as cannon fodder in Italy. And as far as she knew, his brothers were safely out of harm's way too. Pete was at his REME training camp. Bob was of course still in the POW camp in Germany. She had no idea where Mick in the merchant marine might be, but until she heard otherwise, she would assume he was safe too.

But now she was worried about Jen again. Even though Katy had assured her that there was no funny business going on, Joyce wasn't sure she believed her. Jen had let her hair down with Sean Byrne once before. What was to stop her doing it again? Especially as they were living under the same roof.

Even more worrying than that, though, was that for the last two days Albert had been behaving very oddly. On Friday he had looked pale and distracted. And on Saturday he hadn't come into the café at all. Concerned that he might be ill, she had knocked at his door, but even though she was certain he was there, he hadn't answered.

And now she really was worried. Usually on a Sunday evening he took her to the pub for a drink, but tonight he hadn't appeared.

Suddenly she got to her feet. In the kitchen was a small cake. She had smuggled it out of the café with the intention of offering him a slice when they got back from the pub. But instead she would take it across the road to him now. She wouldn't embarrass him by mentioning the pub; she would just tell him the cake was a little thank-you for all the wine and drinks he had bought her recently, and leave it at that.

But as she went through his front gate, she heard voices inside. Raised voices. Talking a foreign language. Startled, she took a step back. No wonder he hadn't come over if he had visitors. Who could it be? In all the time she had known him, she had never seen anyone else set foot in his house.

She hesitated. She didn't want to intrude. But nor did she want to leave without knowing what was going on.

Taking a breath, she stepped forward and knocked on the door.

At once there was silence. Then, after a moment, the hall light went off. The door opened a crack and Albert's face peered out.

'Oh, Mrs Carter,' he said.

She heard relief in his voice. 'Is everything all right?' she asked.

'Oh yes, yes, everything is quite all right. But I'm feeling a little under the weather this evening, so I think I'd better give the pub a miss.'

Joyce peered at him through the darkness. He seemed unusually nervous, and she suddenly had a vision of some murderous foreigner holding a gun to his head behind the door.

'I know there's somebody there,' she whispered. 'Do you want me to call the police?'

Mr Lorenz's eyes widened in horror. 'No, goodness me, no. Oh dear,' he said. 'I wanted to keep you out of this, Mrs Carter. But perhaps you had better come in.'

Perplexed, still carrying the cake, Joyce followed him into the house.

In Albert's very formal front room, sitting awkwardly on a chair with his hands between his knees, was a young man wearing an unfamiliar military uniform. When Joyce came in, he stood up at once. He had a thin, angular face, and his eyes flicked nervously from her to Albert.

'This is my friend Mrs Carter,' Mr Lorenz said. The young man bowed his head slightly, clicking his heels in a strange foreign courtesy. 'And this is Lech Zemniak, the son of my cousin. His friends call him Leszek.'

Joyce regarded the visitor with considerable relief. 'Oh yes,' she said. 'This is the boy you mentioned. The one who's serving in the Polish armoured regiment in Scotland?'

There was an awkward pause.

'Well he was,' Mr Lorenz said at last. 'But I am sorry to say that he has absented himself and come to London.'

'Oh my goodness,' Joyce said. *A deserter?* She had read in the paper that this was happening a lot, especially among some of the foreign troops, in the run-up to the invasion. No wonder Albert was keeping the boy well under wraps.

'He is not the only one,' Mr Lorenz hastened to say. 'He has come to London with twenty other Jewish boys. They are not deserting; they just want to transfer to an English regiment.'

He pulled a chair forward for Joyce, and once he had settled her to his satisfaction, he explained that the young Jews had been suffering considerable abuse in the Polish regiment they had been allocated to. It seemed that many of the ethnic Poles, both officers and men, were just as anti-Semitic as the Nazis. 'My cousin and his friends were beginning to fear for their lives,' Albert said. 'It is shocking, the stories that he tells.'

Joyce nodded. Shocking though it was, she knew that the Germans weren't the only people in the world who disliked Jews. She had read a letter of complaint in the newspaper only last week from a London man who had been refused membership of a local golf club simply because he was Jewish. And that was despite the fact that one of his sons had died fighting for the Allies in Algeria, and the other was currently serving in Italy.

But she also knew that unless these young Polish Jews could make a good case for their absence, they would certainly be treated as deserters. And goodness only knew what happened to deserters nowadays. Nothing good, that was for sure. They might even be shot.

'I had hoped to keep you out of all this,' Albert said quietly. 'But now you've found out, perhaps you might be able to help.'

Joyce blinked at him in bewilderment. 'Me?' she said. 'What on earth could I do?' She remembered she was still holding the cake. Abruptly she thrust it into his hands. 'Here,' she said. Give the poor boy a slice of that. He looks as though he could do with something to eat.'

Albert took the cake gratefully, but his smile was anxious. 'We need to find someone to listen to their side of the story. A sympathetic lawyer or a journalist. I wondered if you might ask Mr Keller?'

'Mr Keller?' Joyce repeated blankly. But even as she said the name, she realised he was right. A well-connected man like Henry Keller was exactly the kind of person they needed. He might even be Jewish himself, for all she knew. A lot of these theatrical people were. And even if he wasn't, he would surely know someone in a position to help.

But she didn't really feel she knew him well enough to approach him herself. 'I'll get Jen to ask him,' she said.

She stood up with the intention of going to the pub there and then, but before she could move towards the door, the sirens started up outside. It was the first time in several weeks, and Joyce felt a rush of furious anger.

'Bloody Hitler,' she cried. 'Can't he leave us alone for five minutes? Doesn't it occur to him that we have enough to worry about without his damned bombs?'

Mr Lorenz put his hand gently on her arm. 'You are very welcome to stay with us in the shelter. It is quite comfortable. I have a paraffin lamp and a small heater.'

'No, I'm all right,' Joyce said. 'I'd best get back over the road. Angie will be worried if she comes home and finds I'm not there.'

The thing about air raids, Pam thought, was that you never imagined the bombs would get you. But sometimes they did. George's mother had been killed by a Luftwaffe bomb. And so had Katy Frazer's father.

Then there was the other side of the equation. If two bombs had already landed in one street, surely the chances of another were statistically slimmer.

Nevertheless, she disliked being alone in the Anderson shelter with the children. And this raid sounded particularly heavy. Earlier she had heard the guns up on the common blasting away as planes passed overhead. She had heard the clatter and crash of flak, and the distant crump of an explosion.

She wished Alan was in there with them, but he was away overnight on some Home Guard training exercise in Surrey. Normally he enjoyed playing soldiers, especially as his job at the brewery prevented him from being part of Mr Rutherford's ack-ack squadron, but on this occasion he hadn't wanted to go. Nothing had been said, but Pam suspected that part of the reason for that was the reappearance of Sean Byrne. Not that Pam had set eyes on the Irishman yet. But she knew he was there, in the pub, and sooner or later she was going to bump into him.

'Do you think we'll win the war?' George asked when the guns had stopped firing and they were sitting waiting for the all-clear.

He had been reading his Magic-Beano annual by the meagre light of their small paraffin lamp. Pam was sure it was bad for his eyes, but apart from sleeping, which he was reluctant to do, there wasn't much else to occupy him in the shelter. Thankfully, tonight the violent antics of the ostrich, Big Eggo, and Koko the Pup had kept him amused for the last hour or so. Next to him on the bench, swathed in blankets, Nellie was sleeping peacefully in the carrycot, which was rapidly getting too small for her. And under their feet, Bunny was snuggled up in a small box of straw that Alan had brought back from the brewery stable.

'Of course we'll win,' Pam said stoutly.

'What I don't understand,' George said, 'is why the RAF don't drop a bomb right on Hitler's head.'

'I suppose they don't know exactly where he is,' Pam said.

'Then someone should put one under his bed and time the fuse to go off in the middle of the night and blow him to smithereens.'

Perhaps luckily, before George's suggestions for Hitler's demise became even more gruesome, the all-clear sounded. Pam sighed with relief. 'Put Bunny back in his barrel,' she said. 'And make sure the wire meshing is secure. And then go straight upstairs to bed. I'll just change Nellie's nappy, then I'll come up and tuck you in.'

She barely had time to carry the baby into the kitchen and get her nappy off before she heard George coming back downstairs.

'Mummy,' he said. 'I think there's a bomb in my bed.'

'What?' Pam looked up impatiently. But then she saw his face. George often played pranks, but even he couldn't fake that staring, wide-eyed expression of shock. And now, behind him in the passage, against the subdued light of the hall lamp, she could see motes of dust floating in the air.

Her whole body went cold. A bomb?

'I could see the sky through my bedroom ceiling,' he said. 'And a huge metal thing with fins lying on the bed.'

Inadvertently Pam looked up. George's room was right above the kitchen. Thank God he'd had the sense not to shout. She'd read in the newspaper that the smallest vibration could set off an unexploded bomb.

She swallowed convulsively. 'Quick,' she whispered urgently. 'Go and unlock the front door, then run and see if you can find Mr Broome at the ARP post. Tell him what's happened. And stay well away from the house. Don't come back in.'

Oh my God, she thought as she bundled the naked baby back into the carrycot. Her limbs felt absurdly sluggish. Her fingers were numb. A bomb? She couldn't think straight. If it went off, it would be the end of her house. Her home.

If it went off, it would be the end of her and Nellie if she didn't get a move on.

Then somehow she was out in the street, and in the thin moonlight she could see Mr Broome and one of his ARP colleagues running towards her with shrouded torches.

'Clear the area,' he shouted at some people further up the street. 'No, don't come this way. We may have an unexploded bomb. We need to cordon it off. And we need to evacuate everyone from the immediate area.'

*

183

The first Jen knew of the bomb was when an ARP warden came bursting into the pub shouting that they needed to evacuate immediately. She and Katy were in the process of carrying the children back upstairs. They had spent most of the evening in the cellar. When the all-clear had sounded a few minutes ago, all the customers had left, and now Jen was looking forward to her bed.

Since Sean's arrival, there had hardly been any raids, and she and Katy no longer slept in the cellar. But now Sean grasped her arm. 'Let Katy and the children go,' he murmured. 'Then you and I can snuggle down together in the cellar. We'd be safe enough there.'

'No way,' Jen said. 'I've told you. I'm not doing any snuggling anywhere with you.'

'Oh come on, Jen,' he pleaded. 'It's so hard for me having you so close but not being allowed to touch you.'

'Well that's your lookout,' Jen said. 'I didn't ask you to come back.'

But it was hard for her too. Four long years had elapsed since she had last been to bed with him, but even after all that time she could remember clearly what it had been like to feel his hands on her bare skin. The shocking intimacy. The spiralling passion. 'Anyway,' she said curtly. 'Katy can't manage both children on her own.'

By the time they got outside, Katy holding the sleeping baby, Sean carrying Malcolm on his shoulders, and Jen with Lucky on a leash, the top end of the street was already cordoned off and the people who had been told to leave their houses were milling about nervously. Quite a few were in dressing gowns and bedroom slippers; several were clutching blankets round their shoulders. Others wore coats over nightdresses and pyjamas.

'Move along, move along,' Mr Broome was shouting. 'There's nothing to see. The bomb disposal team are on their way.'

On the other side of the small crowd, Jen heard Mrs Rutherford offering accommodation in the St Aldate's church hall. 'Everyone is welcome,' she was calling out in her imperious, well-to-do voice. She was clearly in her element, enjoying every moment. 'We have hot soup and plenty of blankets.'

But nobody seemed inclined to take her up on the invitation. They seemed more interested in gawping up the empty street towards the Nelsons' house and speculating about what might happen next.

And then there was Pam Nelson, hurrying along with Nellie in the carrycot. Beside her was George, looking unusually pale. He brightened slightly when he saw the little party from the pub, especially Lucky, who he greeted with a fond pat on the head.

'Are you all right?' Katy asked Pam. 'What happened? How did you—'

But she was interrupted by George. 'What about Bunny?' he said. 'I'll have to go back.'

Pam caught his arm. 'No,' she said urgently. 'You can't go back.'

'But he might get blown up if I leave him there,' George objected. He was looking back at the house with terror in his eyes.

'Perhaps you could ask Mr Broome,' Katy suggested.

But Mr Broome seemed disinclined to risk his life for the sake of a rabbit. 'He'll be all right, sonny,' he said. 'With any luck the bomb disposal boys will be able to defuse the bomb.'

'But what if they can't?' George wailed. 'It might be booby-trapped. And even if they do a controlled explosion, he's right there in the yard. He's bound to be killed.'

And of course he was right. He hadn't lived in London for the last four years for nothing. He knew about death and destruction. He knew that the Nazis often fitted anti-tampering devices on their bombs to catch unwary Royal Engineer bomb disposal teams. He also knew that controlled explosions often weren't as painless as they sounded.

Sean stepped forward. He swung Malcolm off his shoulders and into Jen's arms. 'I'll go,' he said.

'No, you can't,' Jen said. 'The bomb might go off at any moment.'

'The boy's right,' Sean said. 'It's much more likely to go off once the bomb disposal boys start fiddling with it.'

'But …' Jen began in horror.

He leant in towards her and kissed her hard on the mouth. 'What have I got to lose?' he murmured. 'If you won't let me near you, I might as well die.'

He swung round to Pam. 'Where exactly is this rabbit?' he asked.

But for some reason Pam seemed incapable of speech. It was George who told him that Bunny lived in an old beer barrel in the back yard. 'You go straight along the passage to the kitchen,' he said earnestly. 'The back door is next to the sink …'

'I know the way,' Sean said. He grinned and ruffled George's hair. 'You're probably too young to remember, but I used to live in your house at one time.' His blue eyes glinted in the moonlight. 'Isn't that right, Mrs Nelson? And a very agreeable time I had there too.'

And then he was gone, ducking under the tape and walking purposefully up the dark, empty street, completely ignoring Mr Broome's angry protestations.

'Oh my God,' Jen whispered. Clutching Malcolm to her shoulder with one hand, she felt Katy grasp the other, and they stood together, hand in hand, watching in silent dread as Sean turned in at Pam's gate and calmly pushed open the front door.

Chapter Seventeen

The bomb didn't go off. The Royal Engineers defused it successfully and it was eventually carried away on a truck at four in the morning. By that time Jen, Katy and the children were installed in Jen's mother's house, while Pam, George, Nellie and the rabbit had been whisked off by Mrs Rutherford to her WVS emergency accommodation in the church hall.

It was a long night. It took all Katy's powers of persuasion to get Malcolm to settle down after all the excitement. Joyce hadn't wanted Sean to stay, but in the end he had bunked in with Gino for a couple of hours before going back to guard the pub from looters. Katy and the children had bedded down in Angie's room. And Jen had slept in her mother's bed.

Jen had never once in her whole life shared a bed with her mother. It was nearly one o'clock in the morning when they eventually went upstairs, and she felt awkward stripping down to her underwear and climbing into the bed. It smelt of washing powder and the lavender eau de toilette that Mr Lorenz had given her mother for Christmas. She made sure to keep very close to her side, and hoped Joyce would want to go straight to sleep.

But no, her mother had wanted to chat. Or not chat precisely, but to ask for her help. Jen had been forced to stay awake to hear the pitiful tale Mr Lorenz's Polish cousin.

Even though she was dying to go to sleep, she felt sorry for the oddly named Leszek Zemniak. But she baulked at the idea of asking for Henry's help.

'Mum, I can't,' she said. 'He's done so much for me already.'

'You must,' Joyce said. 'I'm sure he'd know who to ask, and he'd do anything for you.' She gave a slight snort in the darkness. 'Although I can't imagine why, the way you've treated him.'

Jen thought of Henry's light embrace in the wings of the theatre on Thursday. She hadn't seen him since then because he had left London for a couple of days to visit some ENSA shows. But she knew he was due back at the theatre tomorrow.

She moved restlessly under the lumpy eiderdown. If only Henry wasn't so important and well connected, things would be much easier. She liked him. She might even be a bit in love with him. But she was also in awe of him. And she couldn't in a million years imagine being married to him. She'd have

186

to entertain people like Ivor Novello and Laurence Olivier, for goodness' sake. She wouldn't know where to begin.

Sean's presence on the scene didn't help. It wasn't his fault he couldn't get back to Ireland, but Jen was still cross with Katy for letting him to stay on at the pub, even though she understood her reasons. For Katy, Sean was a godsend. Even the locals, initially suspicious of having a non-combatant Irishman in their midst, were beginning to warm to him. Once word got round about his courageous rabbit rescue, he would be even more popular.

Especially with Pam Nelson. It was only when Sean had come strolling casually back down the road with the rabbit tucked into the front of his jacket that Jen remembered him saying that Pam Nelson had fancied him when he was in London before.

Certainly Pam had seemed unduly tongue-tied this evening. Poor old Pam. Jen knew how she felt. That was exactly the effect Sean had had on her in the old days. It wasn't quite so bad now, but when he brushed past her in the bar, or looked at her in a certain way, she could still feel her knees going weak. And unfortunately, despite her protestations to the contrary, he knew it.

'All right,' she said suddenly to Joyce. 'I'll talk to Henry about Mr Lorenz's cousin. But I have a favour to ask in return.'

Her mother jumped; she had obviously just been dropping off. 'What sort of favour?' she asked groggily.

'Can I come back and live here again?'

'Good God.' Joyce said. 'I thought with that smarmy Irishman tucked into the pub, that would be the last thing you wanted.'

'Well you're wrong,' Jen said. 'It's not like that between me and Sean. Not any more. But it is a bit awkward us both being there. And I don't want people to talk.' She certainly didn't want anyone talking to Henry. She was walking a tightrope as it was.

Joyce gave a grunt of surprise. 'Since when have you cared what people thought?'

Jen ignored that. 'Can I come back? I'm earning now so I can pay my way.'

There was a moment's pause, then Joyce turned over to face her, causing a cold draught to blow down the bed between them. 'Of course you can come back,' she said. 'I never wanted you to go in the first place. And if nothing else, you can keep an eye on Angie and Gino over Easter.'

'Why?' Jen asked. 'What's happening over Easter?'

'Nothing,' Joyce said. She fiddled with the eiderdown. 'I'm going away for a few days, that's all.'

'Oh really?' Jen said. She raised herself on her elbow. 'And that wouldn't have anything to do with the fact that Mr Lorenz is unexpectedly going away over Easter too, would it?'

She waited for her mother to deny it, and when she didn't, Jen slumped back onto the pillow. 'Well, well,' she murmured. 'You're a fine one to cast aspersions about me and Sean.'

'It's not like that,' Joyce said.

'Isn't it?' Jen asked.

'Certainly not,' Joyce said.

Jen was amused by her unequivocal tone. 'How can you be so sure?'

'Because he's booked single rooms.'

Suddenly, unexpectedly, they were both laughing, and Angie was banging on the wall, trying to hush them. 'We're trying to sleep in here,' she hissed. 'Malcolm has only just gone off. For goodness' sake don't wake him up.'

'Good God,' Joyce said. 'What a cheek. To think of the sleepless nights that little madam has caused me with her gallivanting.'

'And me with her snoring,' Jen said. And that made them laugh even more.

Now it was Monday morning, and Jen was exhausted. She was late for work as usual.

And Henry said he didn't want to see her.

His secretary was embarrassed. 'He is awfully busy today,' she whispered apologetically, putting her hand over the receiver. 'Can it wait until later in the week?'

'No,' Jen said. 'It can't.'

Ten minutes later, she was once again standing in Henry's office. He stood up politely as she came in, but he didn't look very welcoming.

'I'm sorry,' she said, as he waved her to the chair in front of his desk. She smiled uncertainly. 'I know you're busy, but I promised my mother I'd talk to you today.'

His brows rose slightly, but he didn't return her smile. After a moment, he resumed his seat and inclined his head. 'OK,' he said, rather tightly. 'Go ahead.'

His expression didn't invite small talk, so she launched instead into a somewhat garbled story of Mr Lorenz's cousin and the maltreatment he and his friends had suffered at the hands of his Jew-hating compatriots in the Polish regiment in Scotland.

'It's not that they're trying to avoid doing their duty,' she said. 'They aren't shirkers like stupid old Gino and some of the ENSA boys. But they want to join a British regiment instead. They're scared that once the invasion starts, these horrid Nazi Poles will shoot them instead of the Germans.' She looked at him, hoping for a favourable reaction, but his face remained unnervingly impassive, almost rigid. 'I know it's an imposition,' she persevered manfully. 'But would you mind at least talking to Mr Lorenz?'

There was a long pause. Henry was looking at her rather strangely, almost as though he didn't want to meet her eyes. Indeed, as Jen smiled hopefully, he dropped his gaze and took a slow breath. 'That wasn't what I was expecting you to say,' he said.

Jen frowned. 'What were you expecting me to say?'

It seemed for an instant as though Henry was going to tell her, but then he looked up at the clock. 'It doesn't matter,' he said. 'Let's just deal with one thing at a time. Yes, of course I'll talk to Mr Lorenz. I may even know someone who could help him.' He picked up a pen and made a note on his pad. 'I'll see what I can do.'

It was better than Jen had expected. But she had no idea why Henry was being so cold and businesslike. Was he already regretting the embrace they had shared in the wings?

Whatever the reason, she found it extremely disconcerting. Worse than that, she felt snubbed.

'Thank you,' she said stiffly. 'I really appreciate it.'

And that was that.

Later that day, his secretary brought her a short note saying that the MP Tom Driberg would be prepared to meet Mr Lorenz's nephew and his comrades at the weekend. If they were interested, could they please suggest a place and time?

'What's the matter with Henry?' Jen asked Maggie. 'He seems awfully grumpy today.'

Maggie looked up from her work. 'I'm sure he's not,' she said. 'Mr Keller is never grumpy. But I know he's putting together a new show, so maybe there's been some problem with that.'

A new show? Jen pricked up her ears. Was that why Henry had been so odd that morning? Perhaps he was about to offer her a part, and hadn't wanted to jump the gun. Was this going to be her chance to make a big comeback?

But no. The following day, the cast was announced for a new touring drama show, and Jen's name wasn't on the list. There, right at the top, however, was Janette Pymm's name, as the leading lady.

Jen was outraged. 'I can't believe it,' she exploded to Maggie. 'He didn't even ask me if I wanted to be in it.'

'Maybe there isn't a suitable part for you,' Maggie said mildly.

'There's Janette Pymm's part,' Jen said sourly.

'Come on, Jen, be reasonable,' Maggie said. 'You haven't been on stage for over a year. Nobody is going to put you straight in at the top of the bill.'

'Nobody is ever going to put me in at the top of the bill,' Jen said. She put on a theatrical sneer and mimicked Janette Pymm's patronisingly sing-song voice. 'Because I haven't been to RADA.'

But Maggie was getting bored with her histrionics. 'Well why don't you apply, then,' she said impatiently, 'if it means so much to you?'

Jen glowered at her. 'Because I haven't got any money. I'm not some posh little public school girl who takes a fancy to be on the stage and can get Daddy to pay,' she snapped. 'Anyway, they'd never let me in because I don't have the right sort of plummy accent.'

The main outcome of the unexploded bomb in George's bed was that, to Pam's considerable dismay, he and Sean became firm friends. Sean had risked his own life to rescue Bunny, and in George's eyes that made him a hero. Sean was also brilliant with Lucky. George loved watching him teaching the dog to sit, stay, and lie down. He especially enjoyed the game where they hid behind a tree and Sean whistled Lucky to come and find them.

And then, when it turned out that there were no builders available to mend the hole in the roof, who should offer to help patch it up but Sean.

'To be sure, it's the least I can do,' he said to Pam when he bumped into her one afternoon on his way back from the common with Lucky and Malcolm.

It was the third week of March, the evenings were finally getting lighter, and Pam and George had come to check on Bunny, who had been reinstalled in his barrel in the back yard of their damaged house, even though the rest of the family were still camping out in the church hall, courtesy of the WVS.

'After all,' Sean went on smoothly, 'you were very kind to me last time I was in London. Indeed, I seem to recall that you were most tolerant of my naughty ways.'

Pam was stunned by his gall. Naughty ways was putting it mildly. They both knew that he had several times had sex with Jen Carter on Pam's sitting room carpet.

But here he was, smiling that old smile, looking at her in that irresistible way he had, expecting her to share the joke. 'I can't quite remember, Mrs Nelson,' he murmured, 'but didn't we once share a little bit of fun ourselves?'

'No we did not,' Pam gasped as the colour flew to her cheeks. She glanced round quickly to make sure George hadn't heard.

Sean looked disappointed. 'Is that right? I could have sworn ...' He stopped and laughed at her expression. 'Don't worry, Mrs Nelson. Your secret is safe with me.'

There was nothing she could say. They may not have had sex on the rug, but she certainly remembered a stolen kiss at the kitchen sink.

Sean smiled and nodded towards George, who had run off down the street with Malcolm clinging to his back like a little monkey, Lucky in hot pursuit. 'It's a great thing that you were able to give that young feller a nice home,' he said. 'I remember him from before, when he lived over the road. Considering all he's been through, he's come out well, has he not?'

Pam made a face. 'I'm not sure,' she said. 'I do worry about him. He can be very wild, and goodness knows what he gets up to at school. He's always covered in cuts and bruises when he comes home.'

She expected Sean to shrug off her worry as Alan so often did, but instead he frowned. 'What sort of bruises?' he asked.

And now Pam wished she hadn't said anything. She didn't want Sean to concern himself with George. Or indeed her. She wanted him to help Alan repair the roof and then to go away and mind his own business. But despite herself, she found herself telling him.

'Well, for example, today he has a horrid abrasion round his wrist. He says he got it caught in a door, but I don't know.'

'It sounds like a Chinese burn to me,' Sean said.

Seeing her blank expression, he reached out and took her hand. Pushing back her sleeve, he circled her wrist with the thumb and first finger of each hand and started to turn them in opposite directions. At once Pam felt the burning sensation as her skin twisted between them. 'Stop it,' she said, snatching her hand away. 'What are you doing?'

'That's a Chinese burn,' he said. 'It's the kind of thing boys inflict on each other in the school yard.'

Pam frowned as she rubbed her tingling wrist. 'But why would they do that?'

He shook his head forgivingly. 'It's an innocent you are to be sure, Mrs Nelson. Why do boys do anything? They do it to see how tough they are. To gain supremacy.' His eyes slid thoughtfully up the road towards the children. 'Or to taunt a weaker boy.'

'George isn't weak,' Pam said. 'I know he looks angelic, but I can assure you he's not.' If anything, she worried that he was too aggressive. Certainly too bloodthirsty.

But Sean was already smiling again. 'It's a dangerous world we live in, Mrs Nelson,' he said. 'We all need to learn how to defend ourselves from pain, don't you think?' He glanced at her wrist. 'I hope I didn't hurt you. Would you like me to kiss it better?'

Pam felt herself colouring again, but George was already running back towards them, Lucky barking at his heels. 'No,' she said quickly. 'And I don't want you teaching George anything like that. I don't want you to teach him

191

anything at all. I'll tell Alan that you offered to help with the roof, but that's all.'

But Sean just laughed. 'Now don't be getting all hoity-toity Mrs Nelson,' he murmured as George came running up, panting with the effort of carrying Malcolm. 'You know very well it doesn't work on me.'

Ignoring Malcolm's squealing protest, he plucked him off George's back and swung him onto his own shoulders. 'But you're right, we must get that roof covered as soon as possible. You don't want to be dossing down in the church hall for ever.' Amusement sparkled suddenly in his blue eyes. 'You can tell your husband I'm ready and willing to serve you whenever you want. As always, Mrs Nelson, I await your command.'

He whistled Lucky to heel, and walked off back towards the pub.

Louise's third week at the ATS was proving to be marginally less ghastly than the previous two. Henry Keller's visit had helped. The sight of her casually chatting to the handsome impresario in the NAAFI had impressed her cohort to such an extent that some of them had become quite friendly towards her. Even the DS seemed to be treating her with slightly more respect. As a result, Louise had found it easier to cope with the rigid routine of drill, sport, lectures, eating, ironing, polishing and cleaning, although she was hard pressed not to draw the line when her turn came to sluicing out the lavatory block.

Although she wasn't enjoying army life, unlike Buller and her acolytes, who seemed to take patriotic delight in every task, even latrine duty, she managed to suffer it without complaining. In fact now that her squad had finally learned to march in time, she was even able to tolerate the endless hours of drill. In an odd way it reminded her of her long days in the factory turning out bolts. It was that same focus on a repetitive task that somehow liberated the mind. There was even some pleasure to be gained from getting it right, the arms all swinging to exactly the right height, the feet absolutely in sync.

And when they heard that Commander Cunningham was going to inspect them on Saturday morning, the first time they had had that privilege, Louise resolved to try to impress her. Up until now, she had always been pulled up for something: a dull patch on her shoe, a crease in her shirt, a slight kink in her tie. Or she wasn't sufficiently upright, her feet weren't square, her eyes were wandering, her demeanour was too aggressive, or too apathetic. Whatever she did, it was wrong. And it had begun to drive her mad.

But this time, absolutely determined not to be chastised again by the oh so cool and immaculate Commander Cunningham, she made an enormous effort to get every aspect of her deportment right. She even asked Voles to check her over before the parade.

Voles was flattered by the request, but pointed out that she wasn't the best person to ask because she too was constantly being told off too. It was true. Susan Voles suffered even more at the hands of the DS than Louise did. But Louise drew the line at asking the officious Buller.

Despite her doubts, however, Voles did a good job. She found a speck of dust on Louise's cap, and pointed out that the bows on her shoelaces weren't quite perfectly aligned.

When the parade was brought to attention and the crucial moment of inspection came, Louise could feel her knees trembling. But in the end, it was all right. Commander Cunningham looked her over appraisingly, but didn't make any adverse comments. In fact, Louise was convinced that she gave the tiniest nod of approval as she moved on to the next girl. And thanks to the fact that Louise had retied Voles's tie, and tacked up a section of her drooping skirt lining, she passed muster too.

Now it was over, thank the Lord, and there were only two weeks to go. Their passing-out parade was scheduled for Easter Saturday morning. Some of the girls were planning to go and stay at the YWCA in London for the bank holiday prior to joining their new units. Quite a few of them had never set foot in the city and were longing to see Buckingham Palace and Piccadilly Circus.

Louise had no desire to spend her weekend tramping around sights she had known all her life, but it had occurred to her that she could invite one or two of the girls to stay, and she had written to ask her mother if she'd mind. She'd got a note back saying no, it wouldn't be convenient; her mother was relying on her to help in the café over the Easter weekend as Mrs Carter was going to be away.

Louise was furious. Especially when she thought of how many times Douglas had brought pals home, both from school and from the army. But of course they had been posh little public schoolboys, or young cavalry officers with upper-class voices and double-barrelled names. Not Susan Voles from Barnsley with an accent so thick you could butter bread with it.

And so Louise was in a bit of a fix. She certainly didn't want to go home if it meant taking Mrs Carter's place in the café. How infra dig was that? She'd had quite enough of drudgery and humiliation in the ATS.

Then out of the blue, a letter arrived from one of her old finishing school friends, Lucinda Veale. *As the government are urging us all to have a stay-at-home Easter*, Lucinda wrote in her beautiful Cheltenham Ladies' College handwriting, *I'm getting up a little house party in Henley and wondered if you would care to join us?*

Delighted that her problem had been solved so easily, and excited at the thought of a glam weekend in Henley, Louise was just about to scribble off a grateful acceptance when Susan Voles appeared at the end of her bunk.

'You know you said you didn't want to go home for Easter,' Voles said diffidently. 'Well, you've probably got other plans, but I'm going to stay at my uncle and aunt's house in Slough. And they've written to ask if I wanted to bring a friend.'

Louise stared at her in astonishment. Slough? Why on earth would anyone want to spend a weekend in Slough? She couldn't begin to imagine what Voles's uncle's house would be like. Let alone the uncle and aunt. Knowing that Susan's family originated from Yorkshire, she had a sudden vision of flat caps, whippets and an outside toilet, possibly even racing pigeons. One thing she knew for certain was that it would be a million miles away from Lucinda's swanky little gathering.

Relieved that she had a ready-made excuse handy, she held up Lucinda's letter. 'Oh what a shame,' she said. 'I've just been invited to join a house party in Henley.'

Voles's face fell. 'Oh well, never mind,' she said. 'Maybe another time.'

As she turned away, Louise noticed with exasperation that her hem had come down again. Susan Voles really was quite hopeless, but she was a nice girl, and suddenly Louise felt touched that she had wanted to spend the weekend with her. And how kind of the unknown uncle and aunt to invite her, when her own parents had been so stand-offish.

Almost before she knew what she was doing, she was calling Voles back. After all, what had she got to lose but a weekend of gossip about society people she didn't know, excruciating games of charades and hearty walks along the river? 'I don't have to accept the Henley invitation,' she said. 'If you really want me to come to your uncle's, I will.'

Susan's thin face lit up with pleasure. 'That would be grand. My uncle will be so pleased. I told them about you rescuing me from the gas chamber. They can't wait to meet you.'

And Louise realised she was smiling too. It was amazing what the army could do for you, she thought. Not so long ago, she would have been appalled at the prospect of a weekend in Slough with a girl she barely knew. Now, after three weeks of hell, it almost seemed like something to look forward to.

Sean and Alan finally covered up the hole in the Nelsons' roof on the morning of the Salute the Soldier parade. Aaref Hoch had produced a huge tarpaulin and some rope from one of his nefarious sources, and Mr Rutherford had lent Alan a ladder and grudgingly given him the morning off.

Alan hadn't wanted Sean's help. 'I'm damned if I'm going to have that smarmy Irish bastard helping me,' he said. But in the end he'd had no choice. There was nobody else fit enough and brave enough to scramble about on a rooftop.

It took them two hours. Pam watched anxiously from below, more concerned that they might come to blows than that they would fall off the roof.

She was pleased when it was done. The novelty of living in the church hall had begun to pall, even for George. Now all they had to do was clear out the debris that had come down with the bomb, mend the wiring, patch up the hole in George's bedroom ceiling and hope that Mr Poole, the builder, would have time to do a more comprehensive repair before the next gale. Over the past few years three thousand houses had been destroyed locally, with nearly forty thousand damaged. It was no wonder builders were busy.

'I think you should take the children away somewhere until it's habitable again,' Alan said as he and Pam surveyed the dust-filled rooms. 'It's good enough for me, but I can't expect you to live in this mess.'

'I don't want to go away,' Pam said at once. Anyway, where would she go? She had no relatives who could put them up. And they certainly couldn't afford to pay for lodgings. 'No, I want to stay here. I'm sure it won't take us long to get the house back in order.' But instead of being grateful for her stoicism, Alan was looking uneasy, almost upset, and Pam shook her head in despair. She knew what this was about. It was about Sean Byrne. 'Alan, for goodness' sake ...' she began.

Alan was already shaking his head. 'I'm not blind, Pam. I can see the way he looks at you.'

'Alan, we've been through this before ...'

But he wouldn't listen. 'I know we have,' he said tightly. 'And I don't think I can bear to go through it again. He's a very good-looking man, Pam. And we both know he could charm the birds out of the trees.'

'Well I'm not a bird,' Pam said. 'And I'm not in a tree. For goodness' sake, listen to me. Yes, he is attractive. And yes, last time he was here in London I was flattered by his attentions. But things were different then. You and I weren't getting on, and I was lonely and stupid. But now I have George and Nellie. I have you.' She stepped forward and put her arms round his neck. 'I don't need Sean Byrne.'

'Oh Pam,' Alan said, and his voice was husky as he hugged her to him. Then suddenly he gave a choked laugh. 'Oh my God,' he said. 'I'd forgotten about old man Rutherford's parade. I'd better go and get ready.'

The bands and the various units involved in the Clapham Salute the Soldier parade were due to assemble in Battersea Park by 1 p.m. At 2 p.m. they would

195

set off on a long and circuitous march up to Speakers' Corner on Clapham Common, where the mayor of Wandsworth would take the salute.

Sean had been training Lucky for his starring role. By lunchtime, he and Malcolm had the dog all neatly brushed and ready. George had even raced back from Saturday-morning school to see him go off.

But to everyone's disappointment, Don Wellington, the soldier due to lead him in the parade, put a dampener on proceedings from the start.

'Blimey,' he had said when he arrived at the pub. 'I thought at least it would be a wolfhound or a Dalmatian. I'll look a right Charlie leading a mongrel.'

'He's not a mongrel,' George said crossly. 'He came all the way from Corsica.'

'He might have come all the way from Timbuktoo, for all I care,' Wellington said. 'He still looks like a bloody mongrel to me.'

Unfortunately, Lucky was not impressed by this slur on his pedigree. As soon as Wellington picked up the leash, the dog hunkered down on the floor and refused to budge.

'I thought you said you'd trained him,' Wellington said accusingly to Sean.

'I have trained him,' Sean said. 'And he'll come right enough if you don't yank at him.'

'I know how to handle dogs,' Wellington said and gave Lucky a boot up the backside. Lucky yelped and bared his teeth.

'Hey,' Katy admonished the soldier angrily. 'Don't do that.' She didn't get on with Lucky all that well herself, but she didn't approve of anyone being rough with him. Despite his fierce appearance, Lucky was a friendly animal, and she didn't want that spoilt.

In the end, to keep the peace, Sean agreed to walk up the road with them until Lucky settled down.

George and Malcolm wanted to go too, but Katy held them back, pacifying them with a glass of lemonade each.

'I think Louise was right about that man,' Elsa murmured to Katy as she squeezed past to the kitchen with a tray of empties. 'I didn't like him much either.'

'Nor did I,' Katy said. 'I can just imagine him giving her a rough ride in the factory. But then she can be a bit of a prima donna herself.'

George looked up. 'Louise is my friend,' he said stoutly. 'And if that man was nasty to her, then he deserves to die.'

'George,' Katy admonished him. 'You mustn't say things like that. I'm sure he's perfectly nice really.'

'He wasn't very nice to Lucky,' George said darkly.

*

196

An hour or so later, Katy was standing with Sean and Malcolm up on the common, waiting for the parade to arrive. They could already hear the band approaching up the hill behind them, and the rhythmical thudding of marching feet.

And then Malcolm started squealing with excitement. 'I can see Lucky,' he shouted from his vantage point on Sean's shoulders. 'Lucky's coming! Lucky's coming!'

And indeed Lucky was coming. But unfortunately he was coming at a tremendously high speed, with Don Wellington clinging to his leash for dear life. The rest of the parade was almost having to run to keep up with them. They rounded the corner onto the common at a rate of knots.

'What's the matter with Lucky?' Katy murmured to Sean, as people began to laugh. 'Why is he straining at the leash like that?'

But even as she spoke, over the sound of the breathless band she heard a shrill whistle coming from the direction of the common. Lucky's ears pricked up, and he veered off across the road towards the bandstand, almost causing Wellington to trip over his own feet.

Beside her, Sean was craning up over everyone's heads, looking towards the trees. 'Oh no,' he murmured.

'What is it?' Katy asked.

'It's that little blighter George Nelson,' he said. 'He's hiding in the trees over by the bandstand there and he's copying my whistle.'

'Well for goodness' sake stop him,' Katy said.

'How can I do that?'

'I don't know. Do another whistle or something.'

'If I whistle from here, Lucky will come rushing over in this direction and your friend Mr Wellington will be dragged into the crowd. I'm no great fan of the British forces, but I don't think that would be a good idea.'

The people in the crowd who could see what was going on were almost hysterical now, but it was clear that the majority of the marchers had no idea why they were racing along so fast. Katy watched as a platoon of Americans flashed by almost at a trot, followed by a contingent of Free French and some panting firemen. It was a warm day and it had already been quite a pull up the hill, and the less fit of the marchers were sweating profusely. When the WVS contingent rounded the corner, Katy had never seen Mrs Rutherford so red in the face, and Mrs Trewgarth looked as though she was about to expire.

'Do something,' she hissed at Sean. 'Or he's going to spoil the whole thing. Mr Rutherford is my boss. I don't want him taking it out on me.'

And give Sean his due, he did. He thrust Malcolm into her arms and, pushing through the crowds, set off at a run across the road, weaving between a troop of horrified Girl Guides and a po-faced group of ATS.

That was the last Katy saw of him for a few minutes, but gradually the pace of the parade slowed, and on the second circuit, as they approached the podium for the final salute, Lucky was once again walking quite normally. If anyone thought it was odd that over the noise of the bands and the parade sergeant major's stentorian commands, an Irishman in civilian clothes was shouting completely different orders from the sidelines, nobody mentioned it. Nor that at the same time he had a firm grip on the collar of an angelic-looking ten-year-old boy.

When the parade was finally brought to a halt for the mayor to make his speech urging everyone to buy National Savings in support of 'our gallant soldiers', Lucky sat down as good as gold at Don Wellington's feet, panting slightly and looking very pleased with himself.

Wellington, on the other hand, as neat as a pin when he'd come to the pub, now looked distinctly dishevelled. And extremely angry.

'Bloody dog,' he snarled as he handed Lucky back to Katy afterwards. It turned out that he had received a flea in the ear from the sergeant major for going too fast, and when he had tried to blame Lucky, Mr Rutherford had called him an incompetent nincompoop.

'Wait until I get my hands on that child who was whistling him,' Wellington said grimly. 'He'll soon be laughing on the other side of his face.'

'Well you won't be getting your hands on him, because I've sent him home,' Katy said. She smiled benignly at Lucky, who was busy licking Malcolm's face. 'And frankly, the only person to blame is yourself. Lucky was only obeying George's whistle. And if you hadn't kicked him and yanked him, George would never have interfered.'

As Henry had been so off with her earlier in the week, it hadn't occurred to Jen that he would expect her to go with him to the meeting with the Jewish deserters. After that awkward interview, she had barely seen him all week. But he caught her crossing the foyer on Saturday afternoon.

'I think Mr Lorenz would like you to come,' he said. 'Or have you other plans for this evening?'

As it happened, Jen had been intending to move her things back to her mother's house. But alarmed by Henry's sardonic tone, she had shaken her head. 'No,' she said. 'I'd like to come.'

In the taxi, Henry was uncharacteristically quiet, and in her desperation to break the uneasy silence, Jen heard herself asking what he thought about the idea of her applying to drama school.

'I think it would be a waste of your time and money,' he said. 'But you know that. I've told you before.'

'I know you think that,' she said. 'But if I did decide to apply, would you be prepared to put in a good word for me? I don't think I'd ever get in otherwise. Certainly not into RADA. But with a recommendation from the celebrated Henry Keller …'

Glancing over at him hopefully, Jen was startled when he reached forward suddenly and snapped shut the screen between them and the driver. Then he leaned back in his seat and ran a hand over his face as if he was suddenly tired.

'So,' he said. 'Another favour. And what do I get in return for all these favours?'

It was dark in the taxi and Jen couldn't see his expression, but she was unnerved by his hard tone. 'Well, I don't know,' she said uncertainly. 'I thought …' She stopped awkwardly and started again. 'You've always said you wanted to help me with my career.'

'I did,' he said.

Jen flinched at the past tense. 'I didn't know you expected anything in return,' she stammered. 'I …'

He moved impatiently. 'At the very least I expected some honesty.'

'But I have been honest,' Jen said indignantly. 'You knew I was feeling upset after Italy. I thought you were giving me time to make up my mind.'

'Time to make up your mind, yes,' he agreed. 'Not time to rekindle an old romance.'

Jen felt a terrible heat creep into her face.

'There's no point in denying it,' Henry said wearily. 'I know he's staying at the pub with you. I don't care about that.' He gave a low, bitter laugh. 'Well, obviously I do. But I am prepared to accept that it is a prior attachment. What I care about is that you lied to me. Sean Byrne is no more a friend of your brother's than I am.'

Jen's mind was in turmoil. How did he know? How had he found out? And how could she have been so stupid as to lie to him? 'I said it to spare your feelings,' she muttered.

'Spare my feelings?' Henry's voice was incredulous. 'Good God. You have trampled so heavily over my feelings, I'm not sure I have any left.' He took a sharp breath. 'I loved you, Jen. Can't you understand that? I asked you to marry me.' He paused abruptly, and when he spoke again, his voice was reasonable, calm. 'And I have tried to be patient. To help you recover from your ordeal. But you make it very difficult.'

'Well you make it difficult too,' Jen said sulkily. 'I never know what you feel either. What with Janette Pymm always hanging around. Running to you and telling tales. How do I know there's nothing going on between you and her?'

199

Henry turned his head sharply. 'Janette Pymm is one of our most popular stars,' he said. 'Of course I have to look after her.'

'What about looking after me? I'm better now, but you didn't even offer me a part in your new show. And you gave Janette the lead.'

'Yes,' Henry said drily. 'I did. And I can hardly think you'd want to be in the same show as Janette. Let's face it, you've made it pretty clear what you feel about her.'

'What about another show?' Jen asked crossly. 'I can't hang about in the offices forever.'

There was another short silence. 'OK,' Henry said eventually. 'If you really think you're ready, then I will find you a part in a show. But with another director.'

It sounded very final. And scary. Jen didn't want to work for another director. She wanted to work for him.

'But Henry, I promise there isn't anything between me and Sean any more.'

'You expect me to believe that?'

'Yes, I do.'

She stared at him angrily in the darkness. His eyes held hers for a long, tense moment. Then he shook his head. 'I can't, Jen. I'd like to, but I can't. I think it's best if we agree that whatever we had is over.'

'But Henry ...'

There was no time for any more. The taxi had turned into a dingy side street and was pulling up outside a dark church hall.

Chapter Eighteen

The hall in East End Lane was dimly lit. There must have been nearly a hundred men inside. A strange aroma hung over them like a dark cloud, vying with the pall of cigarette smoke and the fug of unwashed bodies. Jen recognised that smell from the POW camp in Italy. It was the smell of fear. These young Jews knew they were sitting on a knife edge. At any moment the police might arrive to arrest them. They had no idea who they could trust.

In the darkened hall, Jen couldn't see their faces properly, and their hushed, accented voices came eerily out of a smoke-filled gloom. Some spoke no English, and others, more fluent, interpreted.

First they talked of how they came to be there, stories of horrors in Russian labour camps, starvation, abuse, disease. It quickly became apparent that these men were the lucky ones. Many of their former comrades had perished at the hands of the Germans and Russians; hundreds more had fallen by the wayside on endless marches from one brutal camp to another.

Then they told of their current persecution at the hands of the Poles.

'The Polish soldiers tell us that when we land in France, it will be one bullet for a German, and one for you, you bloody Yid,' one of the spokesmen said. 'And they speak the truth. They hate us. Like vermin.'

Sitting on a hard bench at the side of the hall next to Mr Lorenz, Jen barely heard the terrible stories. All she could think about was that she had lost Henry, and she couldn't see any way to get him back.

Eventually Henry's friend Tom Driberg stood up. He was a Member of Parliament and clearly well used to public speaking. His languid voice was confident and sympathetic. He understood their concerns, he felt they had a genuine case, and he promised to raise the issue of reassignment in Parliament and with the Polish government in exile.

The leader of the deserters gave a short but emotional speech thanking Henry and Mr Driberg for their help. Everyone clapped. There was a lot of hand-shaking, and then suddenly it was all over.

The men left in silence, melting nervously into the night in small groups. They knew that the police, both civilian and military, were searching for them, and none of them wanted to get caught and returned to their regiments before an agreement for clemency had been reached.

And then Jen was outside and Henry was at her side. 'I'm sorry,' he said quietly. 'I shouldn't have put you through that.'

Jen thought at first he was apologising for his anger on the way over in the taxi and felt a surge of hope. But then she realised he meant the meeting.

'Mr Lorenz will take you home,' he said. 'I need to go and talk to Tom.'

Jen nodded. She understood. He didn't want to share a taxi back with her.

He frowned, perhaps misreading her expression. 'I shall be away quite a bit over the next couple of weeks,' he said. 'But I'll talk to the other entertainments officers before I go and see if we can come up with something for you.'

And then he was gone, climbing into a taxi with Tom Driberg. Mr Lorenz ushered Jen courteously towards another. His cousin, Leszek, was already inside.

'I can't thank you sufficiently, Miss Carter,' the boy said. '*Mój Boże*. I am so grateful to you for bringing this man, Mr Driberg. It is more than we could hope. If there is any service I can ever do for you, please let me know.'

Jen didn't know if it was the tension of the meeting, or Henry's snub, but she took one look at Leszek Zemniak's grateful face and burst into tears. 'There's nothing anyone can do for me,' she sobbed.

As the taxi drew away, Mr Lorenz patted her hand. 'I'm sure we are all feeling a little overwrought,' he said. 'It is distressing to hear about such suffering. But then life is never easy. And I'm sure we will win through in our various ways.'

And then Jen felt guilty for thinking about herself instead of the poor persecuted Jews.

'I hope Mr Driberg will find a good solution,' she mumbled.

'I'm sure he will,' Mr Lorenz said. He paused. 'And so will you. You have the same strong independent spirit as your mother.'

Jen blew her nose crossly. She didn't like being compared to her mother. But perhaps he was right; perhaps that was why neither of them were able to make a decent relationship. 'You'd have an independent spirit if you'd lived all your life with my father,' she said.

She saw the glint of Mr Lorenz's glasses as he turned to look at her. 'We are all products of our past,' he said. 'In one way or another. The trick is not to let it get in the way of our future happiness.'

Jen felt her eyes watering again. Her future didn't look very happy at the moment. She knew Henry would be true to his word. He would find her a role in an ENSA show. But after that she would be on her own.

Lost in her bleak thoughts, she was barely conscious of the journey back to Clapham. The two men chatted quietly in Polish, their voices almost lulling her to sleep. When the taxi finally pulled into Lavender Road, she roused herself and turned to Mr Lorenz.

'You won't tell anyone, will you?' she said. 'That I cried, I mean.' The last thing she wanted was for her mother to start ranting on about Henry all over again. Telling her how stupid she had been.

'Of course I won't,' he said. Behind his glasses his eyes were kind. 'But you should never be ashamed of tears. It shows that you care.'

Suddenly it was the end of March, and it felt as though spring had finally arrived. Crocuses and daffodils were in bloom under the charred trees on the common. The London buses had been painted red again, and fresh vegetables were appearing in the shops. Elsa and Aaref had decided on the third weekend of May for their wedding. Altogether there was a sense of optimism in the air.

Even Winston Churchill's sonorous warning that 'The hour of our greatest effort is approaching' was greeted with a sense of satisfaction. People knew he was talking about an invasion of Nazi-occupied France. It might be bloody, but nobody doubted the ultimate outcome. They had been told it would be the beginning of the end. And everyone wanted the war to end.

But nobody knew when the invasion would be. Not for another couple of months at least, people thought. Sean couldn't believe that he would be stuck in England all that time.

'For the love of God,' he said to Katy. 'Can you keep me that long?'

Katy said she could. She had got an emergency ration book for him now, which helped. And there was no doubt that he was extremely useful around the pub. He was even prepared to take the children out to do the shopping. He said he was only doing it to keep them out of her hair, but she suspected that he actually enjoyed flirting with the women in the endless queues. And he was good at persuading the butcher to give him bits of offal and tripe for Lucky.

Molly Coogan had written that she would definitely be back by the summer, and Katy had heaved a sigh of relief. If Sean could help her out until Molly came home, then she would be all right.

The other news was that, despite Lucky's errant behaviour, the Salute the Soldier parade had been deemed a great success. A huge amount of money had been raised and Mr Rutherford had sent a polite note thanking her for the loan of Lucky.

All in all, Katy was feeling more relaxed than she had for some time. Even her plans for the trip to Windsor on Easter Monday were progressing well. The money in her collecting box had grown steadily. Most of her regulars had signed up for the outing, she had booked a coach, and Elsa and Aaref had agreed to hold the fort in the pub so she could go too.

Even better, for nearly a week there had been no bombing. Nobody knew why it had suddenly stopped again, but as night after night passed peacefully, everyone began to look less tired.

Everyone except Jen.

She had hardly said a word when she got back on Saturday night, and Katy had felt somewhat aggrieved when, first thing the following morning, she had packed up her few possessions and moved back across the road to her mother's house.

But when, later in the week, Jen called at the pub one evening just before opening time, she looked so brought down that Katy immediately forgot her irritation.

'Are you all right?' she asked. 'You look terrible.'

Momentarily it seemed as though Jen was going to put on a brave face, but then she gave a small groan. 'Henry found out about Sean still being here,' she said. 'And he's furious.'

She suddenly looked almost tearful, and Katy poured her a tot of brandy. 'I can't imagine Henry being furious,' she said. 'He's always so civilised and cool.'

Jen took a grateful sip. 'He's still civilised and cool,' she said. 'But underneath I know he's furious. What I don't understand is who could possibly have told him?'

Katy felt a creeping sense of unease come over her. Suddenly her throat felt dry. 'Louise has seen him,' she said.

Jen looked up sharply 'Louise has seen Henry? When?'

'Last weekend, I think,' Katy said nervously. 'He went to see a show at her camp.'

As Jen picked up the brandy again, for an awful moment Katy thought she was going to throw the glass across the room.

'It's not her fault,' Katy said quickly. 'I told her that Sean was staying here. She wasn't to know it was a secret.'

'Maybe not,' Jen snapped. She banged the glass back on the counter and pushed it away angrily. 'But I'm quite sure she relished the opportunity to drop me in it with Henry.'

Katy quailed at the biting fury in her voice. She had occasionally seen Jen in a temper before, but never like this. She didn't know what to say. 'I'm so sorry,' she said. 'It's entirely my fault. But she sounded so homesick, and she wanted me to tell her all the news.'

Jen had heard enough. With an angry look, she swung on her heel and stormed out of the bar, slamming the door so hard that the bottles shook on the racks.

Katy was left feeling utterly dreadful.

'Well, well,' Sean said, emerging from the kitchen. 'So we're both in trouble now.'

Katy gaped at him in dismay. 'I didn't know you were there.' Her hand flew to her mouth. 'Oh no. And now you know about Henry.'

Sean shrugged. 'I've known all along there was someone else,' he said. 'Why else would Jen have turned me down?' He grinned and knocked back the remains of the brandy in Jen's glass. 'But if finding out about me has put the fellow off, it sounds as though you might have done me a favour.'

'No, Sean,' Katy said urgently. 'Don't. Just leave her alone. It's not fair to take advantage of her distress.'

He laughed. 'You're too soft on her, Katy. What Jen needs is a firm hand, and she clearly hasn't had it from this damned Henry.'

Oh no, Katy thought as she picked up a cloth and started wiping the counter with a shaking hand. This was turning into a nightmare.

'Rutherford, are you listening to me?'

Louise jumped as Buller's irate voice pierced her thoughts. It was 1 April, the final Saturday before the end of the course. For the last few days, instead of lectures, they had been put through a raft of classroom tests: English, maths, comprehension, memory, visual recognition and co-ordination. The results, they were told, together with their individual assessment of proficiency, would determine what kind of unit they would be sent to after basic training.

As Louise knew she was going back to the factory, she hadn't bothered much with the tests. But some of the other girls were very keen to impress in the hope of making the grade for the more prestigious units like the REME and ack-ack.

Today they had a leadership and initiative test. The members of each hut comprised a team, and each team was lined up in front of a pile of camping equipment. The task was to get it as quickly as possible to a field at the top of the hill and put up a tent. The team who erected the neatest tent in the fastest time would win.

One sniff of the word 'leadership' and Buller had immediately taken control.

'Come on, everyone,' she shouted to the members of the Hut 6 team. 'We'll carry everything up the hill first, then put it together. If we all make several journeys, we'll have it up there in no time. Come on, Rutherford, chop chop, don't just stand there. We'll take all the bits and pieces then come back for the canvas. Rutherford, are you listening to me?'

'Yes, I am listening,' Louise said irritably. 'But I don't think you're going about this the right way.'

To her surprise, some of the girls stopped what they were doing and looked at her expectantly. She was suddenly conscious of a couple of the directing staff hovering nearby, well within earshot, and her heart sank. Was this going to lead to another black mark against her name?

'I think we ought to work out who is good at doing what before we start,' she said. 'There's no point in expecting people like me and Voles to run backwards and forwards up the hill; we are both hopeless at sport. You ought to get the strongest, fittest girls to do that while Voles and I work out how to put everything together. That way we can make sure we get the pieces up there in the right order. Otherwise we might start building the stupid tent only to find that there's some crucial bit, like the canvas, still down here.'

'She's right,' Voles said staunchly.

'No she's not,' Buller said. 'We don't want to waste time faffing about. The quicker we get everything up there, the better.'

'OK,' Louise said. 'Do it your way. I don't care.'

'That's your problem, Rutherford,' Buller snapped. 'You don't care about anything. You're always letting the side down with your lazy ways and bad attitude.'

A moment's silence followed this outburst. Several of the girls had already picked up a few bits and pieces of equipment, but they didn't move off up the hill. They just stood there looking uneasy.

On the other side of the parade ground, the other teams were already setting off, armed with a motley selection of poles and ropes.

'Well I care,' Voles said at last. 'And I think we should do it Rutherford's way. It makes sense to work things out first. It might save time in the long run. What do you say, everyone? Let's have a vote.'

And to Louise's secret glee, more hands went up for her than for Buller. This is Henry Keller's fault, she thought. Nevertheless, she hoped the DS observers had noticed.

As the die was cast, she had to carry through. And by and large, once they had got over the shock of Buller being voted down, everyone pretty much did as she suggested.

Even though Louise had never put up a tent in her life, it was obvious that the canvas was going to be the first thing they would need. Once they got it to the top of the hill, they would be able to spread it out on the ground and work out how the central poles fitted into it. Then presumably they would somehow have to pull it up and secure one side with the other poles and guy ropes, before stretching out the other.

Louise took considerable delight in selecting Buller to be one of the six girls to carry the enormously heavy pile of canvas up the hill.

'Chop chop,' she said, as they lurched off, staggering under the weight of it. 'The quicker we get it up there, the better.'

Voles laughed so much she nearly dropped the tent poles she was holding. But as she turned to follow the others up the hill, the laugh froze on her lips. 'Oh my goodness,' she whispered. 'It's Commander Cunningham. She's got an American army officer with her. Blimey, he's got red in his hat; he must be a colonel. And they're coming this way.'

An American colonel? Louise swung round. Surely it couldn't be …?

But it was.

Strolling slowly across the parade ground towards them, chatting like old friends, were Commander Cunningham and Lieutenant Colonel Ivo Westwood.

They stopped to consult the DS who had been observing the Hut 6 team, and then casually came on.

Louise suddenly felt quite peculiar. She hadn't seen Colonel Westwood since he had lifted her off the lorry outside the factory. It seemed an age ago. But now, out of the blue, here he was. And looking as attractive as ever in his smart, well-cut uniform. Even the immaculate Commander Cunningham looked pleasantly flustered.

Louise couldn't believe it. It was like her old life and her new life had suddenly collided. Beside her, Voles dropped the poles she was carrying and, gasping in pain as one of them fell on her foot, saluted sharply. 'Good afternoon, ma'am, sir,' she stammered.

Self-consciously, Louise and the other remaining girls in the team followed suit. Colonel Westwood returned their salutes in the rather negligent American way, just touching his fingers to the brim of his forage cap.

'I'm sorry to disturb you,' he said. 'But I need to have a quick word with Recruit Rutherford here. I'll try not to keep her too long.'

You can keep me as long as you like, Louise thought. In fact, the longer the better. Although it would be a shame if it meant she wouldn't see the culmination of her efforts on the tent front. Surprising herself with the thought, she took a moment to respond, and Commander Cunningham gave her a quick reproving look before turning to address Colonel Westwood. 'You are welcome to use my office,' she said with a smile. 'I'll stay here and watch the end of the exercise.'

'You'll have to take over,' Louise murmured to Voles.

Voles looked astonished. 'Nobody will take any notice of me.'

'Tell them I've appointed you my 2IC,' Louise said with a giggle. 'Buller will love that.'

And then she was walking across the parade ground with Colonel Westwood. Her status must be rising by the minute, she reflected. First Henry Keller, and now Colonel Westwood.

But the smile was wiped off her face when she found out the purpose of the colonel's visit.

'Things have moved on since we last met,' he said. 'And now I'm thinking it might be kind of useful if we got you gunnery trained. How do you feel about that?'

Louise gaped at him. Gunnery? That meant more army. More hardship. More drill. And presumably more ghastly ATS.

'I think I feel a bit horrified,' she said. 'What happens if I say no?'

He shrugged. 'Well, I guess we just put you back in the factory and I'll use your colleague Don Wellington as my liaison person instead.'

Louise frowned. 'Has Don Wellington agreed to do gunnery training?'

'Sure he has. He's starting soon after Easter.'

Colonel Westwood paused, and his dark, rather deep-set eyes rested on Louise's face. 'Even if you agree, we still have a couple of problems to overcome. Some of the directing staff here feel that you are not giving your best, and your math is currently not up to the required standard for gunnery.' His eyes narrowed slightly. 'Nevertheless, Commander Cunningham seems to believe that if I can somehow manage to engage your interest, you might have the potential to be a useful member of my team.'

Louise felt herself flushing again. He had certainly managed to engage her interest. But she was astonished to hear that Commander Cunningham thought she might be a useful member of anyone's team.

'What is the team?' she asked. 'What exactly would I have to do?'

Colonel Westwood stood up. 'Walk with me to my vehicle,' he said.

Once they were outside, he glanced around and lowered his voice. 'What I am going to tell you is top secret.'

The parade ground was empty now. In the distance Louise could see some khaki canvas flapping out on the hill. He looked at her as though to make sure she was concentrating, and she quickly brought her attention back to him.

'Bullets and artillery shells generally only detonate when they make direct impact with something solid,' he said. 'It means that to bring down an aircraft, gunners have to make a direct hit, which is very difficult on a moving target.'

Louise nodded. 'That's what my father said when I asked why the ack-ack guns up on Clapham Common never seem to bring down any planes.'

'Exactly.' They had reached his car now. The driver was over by the guardroom, smoking and chatting to the ATS sentries. As soon as he saw them, he stubbed out his cigarette and started towards them, but Colonel Westwood waved him away, and stood with one foot on the running board.

He wasn't classically handsome, Louise thought. Not like Ward Frazer, or

208

Henry. He wasn't even particularly charming. He rarely smiled. But there was something about him. He was clearly fearfully intelligent, and there was an intensity in his dark eyes that made shivers run up her spine.

'What we are developing is a fuse designed to detonate when it gets within a certain distance of the target,' he said. 'It fits on the front of a shell. When that shell comes in proximity of a target, a radio transmitter in the nose locates the target and receives back a signal to detonate at the appropriate moment.'

He leaned back against the side of the car. 'But it's not easy, because all the components have to be so small. Up until now, no electronic circuits have ever been made that can withstand the g-force of a spinning shell or missile.'

Even though she didn't fully understand what he was talking about, Louise was impressed. Instead of actually having to make a direct hit on an enemy plane to bring it down, you'd just have to aim the shell somewhere in its proximity. Even to her unschooled ears it sounded like a good idea. It would certainly make her father's life easier on the anti-aircraft guns. 'So that's what you're making at the factory?' she said.

'Not making so much as refining,' he said. 'We have had success with these fuses in the navy, but now we need to perfect them for land use. And that's where you come in. I figure that involving the production team in the development will speed things up. That's why I want you to do the gunnery training.'

Louise suddenly thought about the tent. And about Voles and Buller and all the other girls who wanted so desperately to go on to ack-ack training. And now here she was being handed it on a plate. Not only that, the plate was being offered to her by the lovely Colonel Westwood. The thought of working in close proximity to him was extremely appealing. She just hoped she wouldn't explode with the excitement of it.

'OK,' she said. 'If you and Commander Cunningham think I'm up to it, I'm happy to have a go.'

'Good,' he said briskly. He beckoned the driver over. 'Commander Cunningham will make all the arrangements. But now I've got to go. As always, I'm running late. I'll catch up with you again soon.' He got into the car and rolled down the window. 'Don't forget. Not a word to anyone. And work on your math. You may need it.'

Louise flushed, and caught a flash of humour in his eyes as the driver pulled away. She stood watching as the barrier swung up to let them out. She saw the ATS guard come to attention and give a smart salute. Then, belatedly, she saluted too. It was the best salute she had ever given. She didn't know if he saw. But she hoped he did.

I must remember to ask Doris to find out if he's married, she said to herself as she hurried off towards the hill.

She wanted to see how the Hut 6 team was doing. Suddenly it seemed very important that they should win.

Joyce was making soup when Angie came into the café kitchen looking portentous with news. 'Mum,' she said. 'A terrible thing has happened.'

She's pregnant, Joyce thought. I knew it. I just knew that would happen. 'What?' she said. 'What is it?'

'They've just announced a ban on anyone going within ten miles of the coast,' Angie said. 'It's in the paper this morning.'

For a blank moment Joyce couldn't think what she was talking about. What had that got to do with anything? But then she realised. Her holiday with Albert. He had booked a hotel in Brighton, right on the seafront.

Then she remembered what day it was. 'Is this an April fool?' she asked suspiciously.

Angie shook her head earnestly. 'No, it's true,' she said. She sounded as disappointed as Joyce suddenly felt. And Joyce immediately suspected that she had been looking forward to a few days alone with Gino without her mother's repressing presence in the house.

Joyce would rather have kept her trip a secret from Angie, but with all the arrangements she'd had to make, it had proved impossible. She had tried to impress upon her that it was going to be very correct and demure. Just two old friends taking a little platonic break together. But Angie was having none of that. 'How romantic,' she had breathed, clutching her heart, and then spoiled it completely by adding, 'I wish Gino and me could have a few days in Brighton.'

When he came in later, Albert was looking distraught too. But it turned out that the government's coastal access ban was the least of his worries. 'Some of the Jewish boys have been taken into custody,' he murmured. 'They had arranged to meet in a café, but word must have got out and it was raided by the police. All I am thankful for is that Leszek wasn't there.'

'Oh no,' Joyce said. 'But surely Mr Driberg will help them?'

'I hope so,' Mr Lorenz said. 'He has been informed, and he has already raised the issue in Parliament and in the press.' He looked at her apologetically. 'But this has nothing to do with our little holiday. Shall I try to find somewhere else?'

Joyce shook her head. 'No,' she said. 'I don't think you should leave Leszek on his own. It's too dangerous. He could be picked up at any time. At the moment, if the police come he can escape out the back and come over to me. But if we were away, goodness only knows what might happen. Let's

210

leave it until things are quieter again.'

He looked at her gratefully. 'It's not the same,' he said, 'but perhaps we could treat ourselves to a nice day out instead. Why don't we book ourselves on the Flag and Garter trip to the Windsor races?'

The last week of Louise's ATS basic training passed in a blur of activity. On the final day they were given their results, and Voles was thrilled to discover that, despite failing in other areas, a perfect score in the maths exams had put her in with a chance of selection for ack-ack training. Somewhat to her surprise, Louise had achieved quite a good mark as well. Perhaps her maths wasn't so bad after all. Buller, inevitably, had passed everything with flying colours.

Before the passing-out parade, there was a short prize-giving ceremony. And although, despite Buller's exhortations, Hut 6 had been pipped at the post by Hut 3 for the overall prize, they did win various other prizes, including that for the tent-building exercise.

After that, they formed up on the parade ground for the last time. As she listened to Commander Cunningham's speech congratulating them for making the grade, and encouraging them to wear the ATS cap badge with courage, pride and dignity, Louise was finally able to appreciate how extraordinary it was that the motley and diverse group of girls who had arrived at the camp five weeks ago had been transformed by a rigid process of drill and discipline into a smart, alert, obedient unit.

It made her even more disappointed that her parents hadn't come to see her march off the parade ground with her new cap badge and white lanyard.

But the enthusiasm of Voles's uncle and aunt more than made up for it.

'How smart you both look,' Mrs Voles said. 'Goodness me, Susan, is all this your luggage?'

Voles giggled. 'No, it's Louise's. She brought all her fancy clothes to the camp. She didn't realise we'd be wearing uniform all the time.'

'Well, it's no problem,' Mrs Voles said comfortably as Louise started to apologise. 'I'm sure we'll fit it into the taxi somehow. How lovely to meet you, Louise. Susan has told us all about you. We are so grateful to you for saving her life in the gas chamber.'

Louise laughed. 'I hardly saved her life,' she said. 'She only fainted for a minute or two.'

But Mrs Voles was adamant in her admiration. 'You looked out for her and that's what matters,' she said firmly as Mr Voles helped the taxi driver tie Louise's suitcases and their newly issued canvas kitbags onto the roof of the cab. 'And we are going to give you both a lovely weekend. Tomorrow we're going to have a picnic on the river. Gerry has borrowed a friend's boat.

But if there's anything else you'd like to do, Louise, anything at all, you only have to ask.'

And it was a lovely weekend. The Voleses' house was larger than Louise had expected. Mr Voles had clearly made quite a bit of money at some stage in his life, but you would never have known it from his broad Yorkshire accent, his bluff easy-going good humour and the way he ate copious amounts of bread and margarine with every meal. And Mrs Voles was the friendliest person Louise had ever met. Nothing was too much trouble. When Louise compared their eager desire to please with her own parents' constant nit-picking, she came to the conclusion that perhaps class didn't count for so much after all.

She and Susan spent the first evening regaling the sympathetic Mr and Mrs Voles with all the gory details of their five weeks of torment. On Easter Day, after a lie-in with decorated boiled eggs served in bed by Mrs Voles, they spent the day cruising up the river on the elegant boat Mr Voles had borrowed from his friend.

On Monday morning, Mr Voles suggested they all go to the race meeting at Windsor. 'I gather the world and his wife is going,' he said. 'So we don't want to miss out on the fun.' He winked at Louise. 'We'll take a bit of cash with us too, and see if we can't win you girls a nice little nest egg to see you through your artillery training. What do you say to that?'

'I can't possibly allow you to pay for my bets,' Louise responded. 'But otherwise it sounds lovely. Some friends from my local pub are going to be there too; perhaps we'll bump into them.'

Mr Voles was right. The crowds were unbelievable. It seemed that half of London had decided to take advantage of the bank holiday to treat themselves to a day at the races. The lack of petrol hadn't deterred them. People had come by foot, bicycle, boat, and even by horse and cart. Thankfully Mr Voles had somehow secured a special pass that allowed them to bypass the main queue, which stretched back for nearly a mile. But when they finally pushed through the turnstiles, it wasn't the contingent from the Flag and Garter they bumped into, it was someone else entirely.

'Goodness, Louise, look,' Susan said as they followed her uncle towards the stands. She grabbed Louise's arm and pointed to a small group of people standing at the entrance to the owners' enclosure. 'Isn't that Mr Keller?'

It was indeed. What's more, Henry was looking very smart in a well-cut navy sports jacket and grey flannels. Beckoning them over in response to Louise's tentative wave, he glanced appreciatively at her pretty summer frock and elegant jacket. 'I'm glad to see that you've managed to escape the ATS dragons.'

A round of introductions followed, and Henry's frightfully grand friend, introduced as Lord Freddy, genially invited them all to join him for a drink in his box. 'I've got a runner in the next race,' he said. 'But there's plenty of time for a quick snifter first.'

'No, no,' Mr Voles said at once, backing away. 'You girls go and have fun. We'll meet up with you later.'

'So which horse are we going to put our money on?' Angie shouted eagerly as she pushed through the turnstiles. The first race was already in progress, and the roar of the crowds was deafening.

'If I had any money I'd put it on Orestes in the Upper Sixpenny Stakes,' Sean said. 'He's the Derby favourite and they say he's a dead cert. But I haven't, of course, since your government has apparently trapped me here in exile till the end of my living days.'

Angie giggled. 'Mum will lend you some, won't you, Mum?'

'No I will not,' Joyce said.

The loudspeaker was suddenly blaring and there was a tumultuous cheer.

'Where are the horses?' Malcolm screamed in consternation. 'I want to see horses!'

'I'm not so sure about Orestes,' Mr Lorenz murmured to Angie. 'I rather fancy the Solicitor might have a good run today. He's an outsider so you would get better odds. But we should go and look at the runners in the earlier races first. That will help you get your eye in.'

'I don't know one end of a horse from another,' Angie said. 'But Gino knows all about them. His grandfather used to have one in his village in Italy.'

Everyone laughed uproariously at that. But Jen groaned. She was beginning to wish she hadn't come. There were far too many people, and she wasn't in the mood for a lot of pushing and shoving. But Katy had persuaded her. 'Oh go on, Jen,' she had said. 'You can't be angry with me for ever. And after all, it was your idea in the first place. You never know, you might win some money. If nothing else, I could do with some help with the children.'

At first they tried to stay as one big group, but inevitably people started to want to go in different directions, and since all Malcolm wanted was to see a horse, Jen, Sean and Katy set off for the paddock to look at the runners parading before the next race.

But there were so many people at the ringside that even on Sean's shoulders Malcolm couldn't see, and Katy asked Sean and Jen to try and get him a position at the front. 'I'll stay here with the pram,' she said.

Sean proved to be a dab hand at worming through the crowd. 'I've got a little 'un here, desperate to see the runners,' he would murmur, and to Jen's amazement, people would smile and step to the side to let them through.

When they got to the front, it turned out that Malcolm wasn't content just to see the horses; he wanted to stroke them too. And ideally ride them. He started kicking at Sean in excitement, wanting to be let down so he could get into the ring. 'Good God,' Sean muttered, putting his spare arm round Jen's shoulders to steady himself. 'Hang on to his legs, Jen, or I'll be entering the bloody race myself.'

The owners were strolling into the ring now to inspect their horses and brief the jockeys. Laughing, Jen was trying to catch Malcolm's flailing feet when he suddenly stopped kicking and instead pointed at the group clustering round a particularly fine-looking grey.

'It's Louise,' he screamed. 'Look, Jen, it's Louise.'

Oh no, Jen thought. That's all I need. But when she awkwardly turned her head to look, it was worse than that.

It wasn't just Louise. It was Henry too, with his hand on Louise's back, courteously ushering her forward to pat one of the horses.

Jen couldn't believe it. She simply couldn't believe it.

But before she could move, before she could even think of disentangling herself from Sean's embrace, attracted by Malcolm's continuing rumpus, Louise and Henry had both swung round.

And even over the enthusiastic excitement of the crowd, Jen quite clearly heard Louise's insufferably posh little voice. 'Look, Henry,' she exclaimed. 'It's Katy's little boy, Malcolm, and Jen Carter. And, oh my goodness, I think that must be Sean Byrne.'

Chapter Nineteen

For an instant it was as though all the noise of the crowds, the owners and the jockeys had been turned off. The only thing Louise heard was Henry's sharp intake of breath as he stared across the paddock at Jen Carter. Perhaps aware of the sudden tension in the air, the grey horse pirouetted fretfully, and immediately the spell was broken. The racecourse noise came rushing back and Louise felt Henry's hand on her arm, drawing her out of the way. Belatedly she gave Malcolm a friendly wave. It wasn't his fault he was with Jen Carter, after all.

'Are those friends of yours, Louise?' Susan asked brightly. 'What an attractive family. Isn't it nice to see people looking so happy?'

Louise couldn't believe it. Susan had barely uttered a single word all the time they had been up in the box. She had clearly been overawed by Henry and the jovial upper-class Lord Freddy. And now when she finally decided to speak, it was ironic that she would put her foot in it so comprehensively.

She was right, though: for that split second, Jen and Sean and Malcolm had indeed looked like a happy little family.

But Jen wasn't looking happy any more. Louise couldn't tell if it was anger or embarrassment that reddened her face as she yanked Malcolm off Sean's shoulders and dragged him away kicking and screaming through the ringside crowd.

By that time, Henry was no longer watching. Even as Louise muttered some response to Susan to shut her up, she saw him turn back to Lord Freddy with a polite comment about the horse. And then the jockey was being thrown up into the saddle, and they were all standing back admiringly as the horse frisked about, showing satisfactory signs of vim and vigour.

That was the last they had seen of Jen and Sean, but back in the box as they waited for the race to start, Louise was conscious of Henry discreetly scanning the crowd. His courteous good humour had barely wavered at the sight of Jen embracing the Irishman – he had continued to smile and was as attentive as ever – but it was as though a shutter had come down behind his eyes.

Louise felt sorry for him and wondered what it was about Sean Byrne that had caused Jen to throw Henry over. She had only managed to have a quick look at the Irishman but although he was obviously an attractive man, as

Susan had so helpfully pointed out, he didn't seem to be anything special. Not compared to Henry, anyway.

Perhaps aware of her watching him, Henry turned and asked if she would like to borrow his binoculars to watch the race. But as neither she nor Voles had used binoculars before, it took a lot of coaching from Henry and the affable Lord Freddy before they got the hang of it.

'Oh, I can see now,' Susan suddenly squeaked.

'Me too,' Louise said. 'And it's amazing.' Lifting her eyes, she smiled gratefully at Lord Freddy, who had been explaining how to bring the double image into focus. 'I can even see the horses' eyelashes.'

Both Henry and Lord Freddy laughed. 'I don't know about eyelashes,' Henry said. 'But it should stand you in good stead for identifying aircraft. You're bound to be using binoculars during your ack-ack training. Now you'll be one step ahead of the others.'

To everyone's disappointment, Lord Freddy's horse only came third. 'Bloody animal,' he said. 'Might have known it would let me down in front of you lovely ladies. Still, we might as well open another bottle. If we can't celebrate, we might as well commiserate, don't you think?'

But they didn't commiserate for very long, because the big race of the day, the Upper Sixpenny Stakes, was already being called. And although it would have been fun to watch it from Freddy's box, Louise and Susan had promised to meet Mr and Mrs Voles. Susan was concerned that if they missed the rendezvous, they would never find them again among all the crowds.

Some other of Lord Freddy's friends arrived in his box just then, so after regretful goodbyes, Henry escorted the girls back down to the paddock.

Mrs Voles was clearly delighted that her niece was moving in such exalted circles. 'My word, Susan, when we caught sight of you up in that box with Lord Freddy, you looked like royalty.'

Henry laughed. 'Freddy would be flattered. Most people think he looks more like an overgrown Labrador puppy.'

Then suddenly the loudspeakers were blaring, and the runners in the Sixpenny Stakes were in the paddock.

'By the way,' Henry said as he took his leave, 'I've got a new show opening soon at the Saville Theatre, starring Janette Pymm. If either of you are in London on the twenty-fourth of April, do come along.'

'Coo,' Susan said in awe. 'I love Janette Pymm. But what a shame, we'll have started gunnery training by then, so we won't be in—'

'Of course we'll come,' Louise interrupted, glaring her down. 'We can certainly try to, anyway.'

Henry looked amused. 'I'll leave tickets at the box office in your names just in case.'

'He's such a gentleman,' Susan whispered as he walked away. 'I think he really likes you. Free tickets to one of his shows. That must mean something.'

Louise was watching Henry's retreating back. 'He asked you too.'

'Yes, but only out of courtesy.'

Louise wondered if she was right. Or was it just wishful thinking? Henry certainly liked her. She was sure of that. But there was nothing in his manner to suggest anything more amorous. But if Jen Carter had cooked her goose, and it certainly looked today as though she had, then maybe …

'But what about Colonel Westwood?' Susan asked. 'He's gorgeous too, in a completely different way.'

Louise wrinkled her nose thoughtfully. The two men couldn't actually be more dissimilar. Henry Keller, the artistic impresario, with his classic good looks, immaculate manners and dry English sense of humour. And dark-haired, narrow-faced Colonel Westwood, with his American accent, deep-set eyes and scientific intensity.

'I know,' she said. 'They are both rather nice.' More than nice, in fact. But what she didn't yet know was whether she had a chance with either of them.

Joyce had to admit that she was enjoying the day at the races, and Albert was in his element. It was well known on Lavender Road that he was a betting man, and now everyone wanted his advice. And being a kind man too, he was willing to help. He tried to explain about odds, weights and form. He also warned them not to put too much money on, or at least to puts bets on each way. 'There's less chance of making a fortune, but also less chance of losing your shirt.'

Joyce listened to him with a mixture of pride and disapproval. Stanley had been a gambler, and there had been many occasions when he had lost the entire week's housekeeping on the horses or dogs. She certainly wasn't going to do any betting herself.

'I haven't got money to burn,' she said when Angie pressed her.

'You can't go to the races without having a flutter,' Angie said.

Mr Lorenz smiled. 'She's got more sense than the rest of us,' he said. 'You never see a poor bookie.'

'But it's more exciting if you put a bit on,' Angie insisted. She had already won five bob and was thrilled with her success. 'I'm going to put everything I've got on the Solicitor in the last race,' she announced. 'And I'm putting it on to win.'

'No, no,' Mr Lorenz said with concern. 'You mustn't do that. Just use a small proportion of your winnings. That's the way to do it.'

'No, I'm going all out,' Angie said adamantly. 'It's my only chance of a wedding.'

Joyce groaned inwardly, but before she could protest, she caught sight of Jen and Sean approaching. Behind them Katy was pushing the pram, with Malcolm hanging on her hand. But although Malcolm was chattering excitedly about everything they had seen, Jen was looking distinctly tight-lipped.

'What's the matter with you?' Joyce asked her. 'Lost all your money?'

'No,' Jen said.

Catching Joyce's curious glance, Katy made a despairing face. 'Henry Keller's here,' she murmured. 'With Louise Rutherford.'

'Henry?' Angie looked round eagerly. 'Where?'

'Don't you go smarming up to him,' Jen said.

'I must say, Louise is a remarkably fine-looking girl,' Sean remarked, and Jen's eyes flashed daggers.

Mr Lorenz came to the rescue. 'We need to get our bets on,' he said, 'or we will be too late.'

'Oh Jen, will you not lend me a pound to put on Orestes?' Sean asked.

'No,' Jen snapped.

'I would if I could,' Angie said. 'But I can't because I'm putting all mine on the Solicitor.'

'If she wins, I'll kill you,' Joyce whispered to Albert.

'You never told me your little sister was a madwoman,' Sean said to Jen.

And for a while it did indeed look as if Angie was going to lose all her money.

When the wire went up, Orestes, the 4/1 favourite, moved straight to the front of the pack. The Solicitor was right at the back. The spectators were already in full voice, delighted to see the Derby hopeful take the lead. Orestes was carrying a lot of their cash on his back.

When the horses went out of sight round the bend, they had to rely on the loudspeaker, but the commentator rattled the names off so fast, it was hard to make out what was happening, and the noise of the crowd died away a fraction. But when eventually the horses came back in sight and Orestes was still in the lead, the cheering and shouting urging him on must have been heard almost in London.

'Which one is the Solicitor?' Angie yelled anxiously.

Mr Lorenz was the only member of the party with binoculars. 'He's coming up,' he said. And even his voice, normally so measured, sounded excited. He offered her the binoculars, but she was trembling too much to see out of them.

Then the horses were thundering towards them up the straight, and like everyone else, Joyce was craning to see. Suddenly everyone was screaming. It was clear that the Solicitor was indeed inching up on the outside.

And now he was suddenly challenging the leaders, and Orestes was putting on a final spurt of effort.

'Come on, Solicitor!' Angie screamed.

The crowd was roaring too, but the twelve horses thundered past so fast, in such a close bunch, that it was impossible to tell which was which. The jockeys were a blur of flashing colour. A few seconds later, they were past the post.

'What happened?' Angie yelled in desperation. 'What happened? Who won?'

There was a long pause, and then the loudspeaker was rattling off the result.

A deep groan of disappointment echoed round the racecourse. Orestes, the favourite, had been beaten into second place, and that meant a lot of money had been lost.

But Mr Lorenz was smiling. 'The Solicitor won,' he said to Angie. 'How much did you put on in the end?'

'Five bob,' Angie said eagerly. 'How much will I win?'

'The odds were a hundred and seven to one,' he said. 'You should collect about twenty-five pounds, give or take.'

Joyce almost fell over. 'Twenty-five pounds?' she gasped. She could hardly believe her ears. Twenty-five pounds would pay her rent for six months.

But her shock was nothing to Angie's. The girl's face was a picture. Her mouth fell open and her cheeks went white, then suddenly red. It was the first time Joyce had ever seen her completely lost for words.

Joyce glanced at Albert. He looked as calm and collected as normal now. But he must have made a killing too. She hadn't seen exactly how much he had put on the Solicitor, but she was pretty sure it was more than five bob.

'I can get married,' Angie whispered at last. 'Gino and I can get married.' And then she was dancing about kissing everyone, and laughing and screaming, and everyone was clapping her. Everyone except Jen, who was looking as though someone had slapped her in the face with a dead fish.

Joyce turned to Albert and found him looking at her.

'I'm sorry,' he murmured penitently. But his eyes were twinkling behind his glasses. He handed her a betting slip. 'But I took the liberty of putting a little bit on the Solicitor on your behalf too. So perhaps one day in the not-too-distant future, we might be able to get married too.'

Louise didn't get back to London until late that evening. Mr Voles had insisted on escorting her and her suitcases to Slough railway station in a taxi. But the train was already packed to the gunnels with returning racegoers, many rather the worse for wear, and in the end she had to travel in the crowded guard's van all the way to Paddington. Then she had to heave her cases and kitbag onto a bus to Victoria, and then to Clapham Junction, where she waited an eternity for a taxi to take her up to Lavender Road.

By the time she struggled in through the front door, she was ratty and exhausted, and the welcome she received from her parents didn't help.

'Oh there you are at last,' her mother said, barely looking up from her knitting. 'I thought I'd made it clear I needed your help in the café today. As it was, I had to do the whole thing almost single-handed.'

Her father was even less effusive. 'Well, well,' he said. 'Not in uniform, then? Why's that? Didn't you pass the course?'

'Of course I did,' Louise said. 'In fact they want me to do gunnery training next.'

As he had done ack-ack training with the Home Guard, she assumed he might at least be impressed by that. But no, he just chuckled benevolently.

'Gunnery training?' he said. 'Is that what they call it? Well, I suppose they might teach you some of the backroom jobs. But they're hardly going to let you loose on the actual guns themselves, are they?'

Louise had no idea, but it annoyed her that he was so quick to dismiss the ATS. 'I don't see why not,' she said crossly.

'You don't see why not?' He turned to her mother. 'Did you hear that, my dear? One month at an ATS training camp and she thinks she's a soldier. I can assure you, young lady, that being a soldier is more than doing a bit of drill and learning to salute. Winston Churchill himself has said that women should be kept out of direct combat. It's nothing to be ashamed of. Girls just aren't up to that kind of thing, and that's all there is to it.'

'That's not all there is to it,' Louise snapped. She grabbed one of her suitcases and started heaving it up the stairs. 'We may not have the physical strength of men, but otherwise there is nothing to stop us doing the same jobs they do. Why can't you be proud of me for once, instead of always running me down?'

'Well, you have just proved my point,' he called after her. 'There is no place on a gun position for histrionics. I had hoped the army would have taught you some self-discipline, but clearly I was mistaken.'

It was almost as bad the next morning at the factory. Don Wellington had come to work in his army uniform. It hadn't occurred to Louise to do that.

Now that it was over, she felt a sense of achievement that she had successfully passed out from the ATS training programme, but she still didn't want people laughing at how frumpy she looked in her uniform.

'Oh dear,' Don Wellington said when he caught sight of her in her civvies. 'Did they throw you out? Or couldn't you hack getting your hands dirty?'

Louise suddenly thought of how much she had hated scrubbing all those filthy potatoes and couldn't stop a flush heating her cheeks. He saw it and chuckled. 'I thought it would be too roughy-toughy for a posh girl like you.'

But Doris stood up for her. 'She did really well, if you must know,' she said. 'And her team won the leadership and initiative test. So you'd better look to your laurels and not get too big for your Wellington boots.'

Everyone in earshot laughed at that. And it gave Louise a chance to recover.

'Taken any dogs for a march recently?' she asked sweetly when the merriment died down. And that caused an even bigger laugh. Word had clearly got out about Lucky's antics at the parade.

But Don Wellington was not amused. 'That was the dog's fault,' he said. 'Not mine.'

'A bad workman always blames his tools,' Louise murmured, and his face darkened alarmingly. But luckily the start-up bell sounded then and prevented the badinage from getting too vitriolic.

Things had changed at Gregg Brothers since she had been away. The special project team, as they were called, now occupied a small section at the back of the main workshop, screened off from the rest of the factory. The entrance was guarded by a white-capped American military policeman.

'They are allowed to search us,' Doris whispered. 'So don't get on the wrong side of them or they'll be patting you down morning, noon and night.'

Louise followed Doris over to the new special project area. 'Look.' Doris picked up a small conical metal casing. 'This is what we're making now, but it's very fiddly. Every ring and thread has to be exactly to specification.'

Louise examined it. She knew from what Colonel Westwood had told her that this must be the housing for his prototype fuse.

It was indeed tiny, fitting neatly into the palm of her hand. There was no sign of any other components, fuse boards or batteries. Presumably they would be inserted later. No wonder it had to be so precise. Louise couldn't for the life of her see how so many technical elements could possibly be fitted into such a small space. But she could now understand why he had been looking for technicians with nimble fingers.

The bad news was that, having been away for so long, her hands had become unused to the delicate work. She was clumsy, and the parting tool kept slipping in her fingers. When Doris rejected her first two attempts, she began to panic that she had lost her knack.

She could see Don Wellington smirking at his own lathe, but Doris was sanguine. 'Take it steady,' she said. 'It took us all a couple of weeks to get the hang of it.'

But Louise didn't get a couple of weeks. When she returned home that evening, she found a posting order waiting for her. She was to report to the Arborfield Royal Artillery Barracks in Surrey at 1 p.m. on Sunday 16 April, exactly a week away.

Jen wished she had stuck by her original decision and not gone to the races. She had hardly been able to bear the riotous journey back to Clapham on the coach. But worse than Angie's ridiculous glee at her amazing win was the haunting memory of that scene in the paddock.

Talk about cavorting! It clearly hadn't taken Henry long to find solace for his so-called heartache. And as for trampling over his feelings, it hadn't done much for *her* feelings to see him with his hand so familiarly on Louise's back.

What was Louise doing there anyway, looking so smart and at ease among all the toffs in her stupid little summer frock and pretty hat? She was meant to be in the army, having a miserable time. She certainly hadn't been having a miserable time in the owners' enclosure at Windsor. Far from it.

Jen could hardly bring herself to go to work on Tuesday morning. As soon as she arrived, she was summoned to Henry's office and discovered that he had found her a job in a touring troupe.

'They call themselves the Violets,' he said briskly. 'It's a husband-and-wife team. Veronica Violet is a singer and accordionist, Roger is a pianist. There are a couple of other performers as well; I think six of them altogether. Or there were. One of them was killed recently during the bombing, which is why they need a new soprano.' He glanced at her coolly. 'I hope you don't mind stepping into a dead girl's shoes?'

Jen shook her head. A job was a job, however she came by it. She knew she should feel pleased. Henry had done as she had requested. But it had happened so quickly, she wondered if really he just wanted to get her out of the way.

'I think it will suit you,' he said. 'Roger and Veronica are both talented musicians. And I think you'll be familiar with most of the songs in their repertoire.'

Jen studied his face, wondering what he was really thinking. Was he, like her, still mulling over their unfortunate encounter at Windsor yesterday? It was impossible to tell. He seemed as relaxed and composed as usual. If he had been annoyed about seeing her there with Sean, it didn't show.

'They obviously want to meet you first,' he said. 'But if that goes well, you'll spend the next few evenings rehearsing. After that, you will be doing shows in and around London for a week or two, before touring RAF bases in East Anglia.'

It sounded all right. Well-known songs. Relatively local shows. It wasn't going to make her famous, but it was good enough.

'Thank you,' she said.

He inclined his head as he stood up to open the door. 'I hope you'll like them. They are good people. Honest, reliable and extremely trustworthy.'

Jen flinched. Was that a dig at her? 'I'll try not to let you down,' she said.

But his expression was bland, unemotional. 'Good,' he said. 'I'd appreciate that.'

Overall Katy thought the pub outing to Windsor had gone off well. Everyone, except Jen, had had a good time. Malcolm had certainly thoroughly enjoyed it. To his utter delight, one of the winning jockeys had lifted him up onto his sweaty horse as it was led away after a race. And he had loved all the jolly singing on the coach on the way home. Thankfully, by the time the songs got rather blue, he had fallen asleep in her lap, and had been so deeply asleep when they arrived back in Lavender Road that Sean was able to carry him upstairs and put him to bed without waking him.

But although the outing itself had gone off without too many hitches, the repercussions were less positive. Angie Carter was determined to use her winnings to marry Gino, and Joyce was equally determined to stop her. Jen was furious that Louise had apparently got her hooks into Henry. And Sean seemed intent on rubbing it in by saying what a very attractive girl Louise was, and how he couldn't wait to meet her.

'Don't take any notice of him,' Katy said to Jen. 'He's only trying to make you jealous. It's all part of his plan to get you back.'

Jen had grunted irritably. 'Well you can tell him from me that it's not working.'

Katy of course had told him no such thing. But knowing that Louise was back in London, and dreading an encounter between her and Jen, she was relieved to discover that Jen's new job required her to rehearse each evening that week.

As it turned out, when Louise called in on Wednesday night, it wasn't Jen that Katy was worried about her meeting; it was Sean.

He was standing beside her at the bar when Louise came through the door. 'Aha,' he murmured with satisfaction. 'I was right. She is a looker.'

'Sean, for goodness' sake,' Katy whispered. 'Leave her alone. You'll only make more trouble.'

But her words fell on deaf ears. Sean was already turning on his seductive smile and smoothing his hair. And when Louise approached the bar, it was him she was looking at.

'Well hello there,' he said. 'You must be Louise I've heard a lot about you.'

'Really?' Louise cast a nervous glance around the room. 'Who from? Not Jen Carter, I hope?'

'No.' Sean smiled blithely. 'From George Nelson.' He leaned over the bar confidingly, giving her the full force of his bright blue eyes. 'I know he's only a youngster but he's clearly more than half in love with you. And now I've met you for myself, I can see he's got good taste. What can I get you to drink?'

As Louise laughed delightedly and ordered a gin and tonic, Katy felt her heart sinking like a stone.

Jen's first meeting with the Violets had been in one of the rehearsal rooms backstage at Drury Lane. Henry had effected the introductions, suggesting that they run through a couple of pieces together before making the final decision. In the past he would surely have stayed to make sure everything went OK, but apparently those days were over, because on this occasion, with some excuse about pressure of work, he had ruthlessly abandoned her to her fate.

It was a long time since Jen had sung in public, and she felt quite nervous. It was an odd set-up, not quite an audition, but certainly an assessment of her suitability. The Violets had been working together for over a year. It wasn't going to be easy for them to accept a new face.

Jen didn't know how much Henry had told them about her, but, anxious to make a good impression, she had spent the last twenty-four hours carefully warming up her voice, and by the time they had run through 'He Wears a Pair of Silver Wings', 'Bye Bye Blackbird' and 'A Nightingale Sang in Berkeley Square', it was clear Roger and Veronica Violet were pleased with her.

'Well, Mr Keller said you had a lovely voice, and he certainly wasn't lying,' Roger had said. He turned to his colleagues. 'What do you think, my dears? I know we can never replace poor Sally, but I think Jen would make a wonderful addition to our group.'

'Yes indeed,' his wife agreed. 'We'll have to pick out some nice solo sections for you too. Mr Keller was very insistent about that.'

As well as Roger and Veronica Violet, there was an older man, a competent tenor called Philip, and two other women, a plump middle-aged trouper called Betty, who belted out the old favourites as though her life depended on them, and a young soubrette who masqueraded under the stage name of Adele Bellaire.

Perhaps concerned that she was going to be upstaged, in terms of both talent and glamour, Adele was the only one who had greeted Jen with misgiving. Although as soon as Jen clapped eyes on the costumes the following night, she realised that Adele needn't worry on that score. The men were in perfectly reasonable dark suits and violet-coloured ties. But the ladies wore sleeveless, high-waisted evening dresses, more mauve than violet, with an elasticated bust that emphasised the hips and made even Jen, slender as she was, feel distinctly matronly.

Friday was her last day working in the ENSA offices. By then, despite her reservations about her costume, she was feeling quite excited about joining the Violets. It was hardly the Old Vic, but it was a lot better than she had expected. Despite his disenchantment with her, Henry had been true to his word, and when he turned up at the little farewell gathering of admin staff that Maggie had organised for her, she was able to thank him with genuine gratitude.

He inclined his head. 'I'm glad you like them,' he said. 'And the repertoire's not too challenging. You can sing most of those songs standing on your head.'

'I don't think Veronica Violet would approve of that,' Jen said drily. 'Not in that purple dress.'

For a moment, a smile flickered in Henry's eyes. 'When's the first performance?' he asked.

'On Monday,' Jen said. 'At the Hans Crescent Club near Victoria.' She hesitated. 'Will you be coming?'

He returned her hopeful gaze dispassionately. 'I'm sure you'll have plenty of other admirers,' he said. 'You won't need me.'

Jen set her teeth at the hint of cynicism in his tone. So that was it, was it?

She glanced around to make sure nobody was listening. 'It wasn't what you thought, at Windsor,' she said. 'Sean and I aren't—'

'Oh for goodness' sake, Jen,' he interrupted wearily. He ran a hand over his face. 'We've already been through this.'

But we haven't, Jen thought in frustration. Not really. Henry had jumped to conclusions and she had never had a chance to put the record straight. But there wasn't a chance just then either, because suddenly his secretary was at his side murmuring that Mr Gielgud was on the telephone wanting to talk to him.

He nodded and turned briefly back to Jen. 'I already have another commitment that night,' he said. 'But I'll come if I can.'

Chapter Twenty

'Oh go on, Mum,' Angie pleaded for perhaps the hundredth time as they prepared the vegetables on Saturday morning. 'I'm not asking you to pay. Not now I've got my winnings. And nothing would really change. I'd still work here in the café.' She giggled. 'The only difference would be that you'd have to let me and Gino sleep in the same room.'

Avoiding her daughter's heartfelt look, Joyce guiltily picked up one of the winter cabbages Mrs Rutherford had brought in that morning, and started cutting the leaves off it, discreetly reserving the tenderest ones for Monty the tortoise.

She hadn't told anyone that she had also won at the races the previous weekend. In all the excitement of Angie's twenty-five pounds, she had managed to conceal her own luck at winning forty. Not that you could call it luck exactly, more Albert's kindness. Whatever it was – and she had only accepted it because he absolutely insisted – it was more money than she had ever had in her entire life. It made her feel quite pink to think about it. She had hidden it under her mattress and had secretly counted it several times. It still didn't seem real.

But the money didn't help her to know what to do about Angie and Gino. The only thing stopping them getting married was the fact that Angie was underage and needed Joyce's permission to tie the knot. But if Angie and Gino were married, there would no longer be anything stopping her and Albert getting married either. And that was a rather nerve-racking thought.

'Mum, watch out,' Angie squealed. 'Look, you've cut your finger. You're dripping blood.'

Joyce gasped and turned quickly to hold her finger under the tap, watching the blood drip onto the white Belfast sink.

Angie was watching too. 'Look,' she whispered in awe. 'It must be an omen.'

Following her rapt gaze, Joyce could indeed see that the water had swirled the blood into the shape of a heart. She couldn't help laughing. 'Oh go on then,' she said despairingly. 'You can get married if you want to. But don't come running to me if it goes wrong.'

But Angie wasn't listening to the caveat. The only person she wanted to run to at that moment was Gino. With an ear-splitting shriek of excitement, she flung the potatoes back into the sack, ripped off her apron and dashed for the door.

'Hey,' Joyce called after her. 'What about my finger?'

Angie only paused long enough to poke her head back through the hatch. 'Mr Lorenz has just come in,' she said with an ear-to-ear grin. 'I think you should ask him to kiss it better.'

Joyce didn't go that far, but she did ask him, somewhat self-consciously in the light of Angie's loud suggestion, to help her put a dressing on it, and rather liked the feel of his gentle fingers on hers as he fixed the tape. Not that she said so, of course. In any case, he was already talking about Angie.

'I'm sure you've done the right thing,' he said. 'She was going to wear you down sooner or later. And I have no doubt that she is in love with him.'

'In lust more like,' Joyce said. 'Though I can't see why. He's not exactly Clark Gable, is he?'

Albert gave a wry smile. 'There's no accounting for taste,' he said.

Joyce flushed. Albert wasn't exactly a pin-up either. And she herself was hardly Janette Pymm. 'No,' she said awkwardly. 'I suppose not. Talking of taste, what do you want for your lunch today? We've got a mutton hotpot. There's not much mutton in it, to be honest, but I'll try to fish you out a bit if I can.'

In order to be able to muster sufficient rations to feed his cousin, Albert had been taking most of his own meals at the café. Joyce tried to slip him a bit extra for the boy when she could: a piece of cheese, or a rasher of bacon. But she had to be careful. Mrs Rutherford watched the store cupboard like a hawk and wouldn't be happy to discover that her precious provisions were being used to feed a Jewish deserter.

'I'll certainly take the hotpot if you recommend it,' Albert said.

Joyce lowered her voice. 'Would you mind taking this bag of veg scraps as well? I'll collect them off you later. They're for Monty, and I promised a few to young George Nelson too, for his rabbit, in exchange for some dandelions. But I don't want Mrs Rutherford to know I'm taking them, because technically it's illegal to use human food for pets.'

'Hm,' he murmured thoughtfully as she handed him a bulging brown paper bag. 'So you are happy to ask me to be your partner in crime. But not in wedlock?'

Joyce flinched, but then saw that his eyes were twinkling. She thought of that blood-red heart in the sink. And the money under her mattress. 'Well,' she mumbled. 'Once Angie is off my hands, maybe we can see …'

He reached over the counter and lifted her bandaged hand to his lips. 'Is that a promise?'

Joyce could feel herself colouring again. 'Only if you don't let Mrs

Rutherford catch you stealing all that veg,' she said gruffly.

He released her hand. 'I will guard it with my life,' he said solemnly.

Louise hadn't expected to like Sean Byrne, but it was hard not to be flattered by his blatant admiration. It wasn't so much what he said, although he certainly wasn't short on charm; it was more the seductive way he looked at her, and the way he held the glass a fraction too long when he passed her drinks across the bar. In the old days, she would almost certainly have been swept of her feet, literally, but she had bigger and better fish to fry than Sean Byrne at the moment, and although she was happy to pass the time of day with him when she popped into the pub each evening after work, she made it clear that she wasn't going to go any further than that.

That didn't stop him trying it on, of course. And on Saturday night, when she announced that she had to go home early in order to get ready for her departure the following morning for Arborfield, she wasn't all that surprised when he followed her out of the pub.

'I'll walk you home,' he said. Louise looked at him beadily. She knew exactly what he had in mind. And although the idea of a quick kiss and a cuddle on the moonlit common with Sean Byrne was not unappealing, especially after four gin and tonics, she knew it would be a mistake. Especially if Jen Carter ever found out. Or, God forbid, her father.

'Well you can walk me home,' she said as he fell into step beside her. 'But that's all. Nothing else.'

'What makes you think I'm after anything else?'

'Because it hasn't escaped my notice that you've been plying me with drinks all evening,' she said. 'I couldn't help putting two and two together.'

He laughed. 'You're smarter than you look.'

'Thank you,' Louise said. 'And you're not as smart as you look, because you should have realised by now that your Irish flattery isn't going to work on me.'

Give him his due, he took the rebuff in good part. 'Oh well,' he said. 'It was worth a try. Especially with a girl as pretty as you.'

They were at the corner now, at the end of her parents' driveway. She stopped and held out her hand. She wasn't going to let him come right up to the house.

'Thank you for walking me home,' she said demurely.

Ignoring her hand, he leaned forward and kissed her briefly on the lips. 'Goodbye,' he murmured against her ear. 'I'll miss you.' And then, letting her go, he turned away across the road towards the common.

Wondering if he was as drunk as she suddenly felt, Louise felt obliged to point out that he was going the wrong way. 'Aren't you going back to the pub?'

He stopped in the middle of the road and turned round to face her. 'No,' he said. 'I'm going to take a brisk walk to work off my ardour.'

Louise giggled. 'Well, good luck with that,' she said.

'And good luck to you with your soldiering,' he replied. 'I'll look forward to seeing you when you get back. Maybe by then you'll have come to your senses.'

Despite feeling somewhat the worse for wear, Louise was delighted to find Susan Voles at the Royal Artillery barracks at Arborfield when she arrived at lunchtime the following day. What was more, Susan had saved her the bunk underneath her own, right at the back of the ATS accommodation hut. They hadn't been sure that they would be posted to the same ack-ack training depot, but it was a huge relief that they had been. The only downside was that Buller was there as well, and as full of herself as ever.

She pounced on them as soon as she saw them. 'For goodness' sake, Voles,' she said officiously. 'Your hem is hanging down already. Why can't you just sew it up properly for once?' And then, turning to Louise, 'Goodness, I didn't expect to see you here. I sincerely hope you've pulled your socks up since Bracknell.'

'I'll pull her socks up if she's not careful,' Louise muttered grimly as Buller went off to get ready for their first parade.

'Yes indeed,' Susan said. 'I'd like to sew up her hem and all.'

Despite her headache, that made Louise laugh, and she was still laughing as they trooped out onto the parade ground. Her good humour didn't last long. A couple of corporals were already barking out orders. The new intake were initially to form up in two squads: one comprising the ATS contingent, and the other, soldiers of the Royal Artillery.

Although she had knew that Arborfield was a mixed camp, it hadn't occurred to Louise that they would be actually training with men. And it certainly hadn't occurred to her that one of those men would be Don Wellington. He had left the factory at the beginning of the week, and she had assumed he had started his gunnery training already.

But no, he must have taken a few days' leave, and now here he was, larger than life, swaggering about in his full battle dress and heavy boots.

As she and Voles hurried across to join the ATS contingent, he spotted her at once. 'Watch out, lads,' he called out in his over-loud, cocksure voice. 'See that girl there, the one with the limp? I know her, and she's trouble. Posh as you like, but with a tongue like a viper.'

Louise longed to come up with some snappy retort, but she felt self-conscious enough as it was without people laughing at her accent. In any case, a sergeant was already reading out lists of names to create four mixed sections.

It was Louise and Voles's bad luck to get allocated to the same troop as Buller and Don Wellington. While other sections marched off to collect stores, or for medical examinations, their troop was marched to a lecture hut, where they were ordered to halt and fall out.

Louise and Voles had barely sat down when a scream came from the doorway, 'Section, atten-shun!' and they were all jumping to their feet again, the men's nailed boots clattering on the bare wooden floor.

A young male second lieutenant came into the room accompanied by the troop sergeant, who immediately gave the order to stand at ease, followed by stand easy, and for some reason unknown to Louise, everyone sat down again.

The officer introduced himself as Lieutenant Masterson. He then began to address his troop. 'It wasn't my choice to be here, nor to be in charge of a mixed section,' he said. 'I would much rather be fighting in Italy. But I have to get used to it, and so will you. As of now, you are B section of 563 (mixed) Heavy Anti-Aircraft Battery of the Royal Artillery.'

He explained that the two key weapons in the British air defence arsenal were the anti-aircraft artillery batteries, commonly known as ack-ack, and RAF Fighter Command. 'Our job is quite simply to defend Britain from attacks from the air, and that means from the Luftwaffe. And to do that, we have to work as a team. It is not just about the guns. The command post instruments are equally important. Without correct range-finding calculations, the guns would never hit anything.

'Every single person in the section will have an important job to do, regardless of sex,' Lieutenant Masterson went on, tapping his swagger stick on the floor to emphasise the point. 'You male gunners will therefore treat the ATS as equals. Winning the war is all that matters.'

He cleared his throat and squared his shoulders as he reached the conclusion of his speech. 'With that one aim always in mind, we must be prepared to live and work together,' he said. 'And quite possibly die together.'

At his final words, Louise felt goose bumps break out on her skin. She wasn't the only one affected. She was conscious of a frisson of nervous expectation running around the room.

Oh my, she thought, standing up sharply with the others as Lieutenant Masterson left the room. What on earth have I let myself in for now?

For Katy, 16 April was a day of mixed emotions, because as well as being her birthday, it was the anniversary of her father's death three years ago during the Blitz. That awful day had also been the day she had heard that Ward had been captured by the Nazis in France. He had eventually escaped, of course, and made his perilous way back to England ready to fight again. Nevertheless, that birthday three years ago had gone down in the annals as being the worst day of Katy's life.

This year, Ward was absent once again. Katy hadn't heard anything for weeks, and she was getting increasingly frightened for his safety. She had secretly been hoping for a reassuring birthday letter from Helen de Burrel, who was sometimes able to glean news of him via the clandestine SOE networks. But so far there was nothing.

The only birthday mail she had received was a greetings card from Ward's aunts enclosing an anxious letter from her mother complaining about Sean staying at the pub. Mary Parsons clearly remembered Sean from his previous visit to London at the beginning of the war, and the effect he'd had on Jen. *Is it quite wise?* she had written in her painstaking hand. *I'm not suggesting that anything untoward is going on. But what will people think? What will Ward think?* If only she had left it at that. But she hadn't. *Now that the bombing seems to have stopped, I'm thinking of coming back to London. I don't like the thought of you being alone in the pub with a man like that. Anything could happen.*

Katy had closed her eyes. She didn't want her mother to come back, but she could understand her concerns even though they were unfounded. Sean might be perfectly well behaved with her, but she wouldn't trust him an inch with anyone else. It hadn't escaped her notice that he had left the pub with Louise last night. And she was pretty sure it hadn't escaped anyone else's notice either. The only good thing was that, because she was busy with her rehearsals, Jen hadn't been there to witness his defection.

Katy's relief was short-lived. When Jen came in at lunchtime to wish her a happy birthday, it quickly became clear that someone had been gossiping.

At first Jen didn't seem too bothered. 'I hear you and Louise have been seeing a lot of each other this week,' she remarked to Sean as he poured her out a tonic water.

Sean looked momentarily puzzled. 'Louise? Oh, the pretty soldier girl from the top of the road, you mean? The one that your Henry seems to like? Well, to be sure, she has been in here once or twice this week, has she not, Katy? But I don't think you're justified in saying I've seen a lot of her.'

'Well I think I'm justified in saying that you're a brazen, bare-faced liar,' Jen retorted. 'And not just bare-*faced*, from what I hear.'

Oh my goodness, Katy thought. This was worse than she'd feared.

But Sean was looking amused. 'And what is it you have been hearing?' he asked.

'That not content with flirting all week, the two of you disappeared off together last night and were never seen again.'

231

Sean opened his hands with a complacent smile. 'You're seeing me now, are you not?'

'Yes, I am,' Jen said. 'And I wish I wasn't.' She suddenly swung back to Katy. 'I can't think why you've let him stay,' she snapped. 'I told you he'd cause trouble.'

'Oh come on now, Jen,' Sean said. 'Don't take it out on Katy. It's not her fault. I only did it to make you jealous.'

'You haven't made me jealous,' Jen flashed back. 'You've made me cross.'

Sean winked at Katy. 'She looks beautiful when she's cross, doesn't she? With those glittering eyes and … Well, you can see why I love her.'

Katy saw Jen's expression and groaned. This was going from bad to worse. It's my birthday, she wanted to shout at them. I'm meant to be trying to have a happy day.

But she didn't say it, because there was a commotion at the door and she swung round to see Pam, George, Malcolm, Angie and Bella trooping in with great excitement, bearing a small birthday cake. And suddenly everyone in the bar was singing a rousing chorus of 'Happy Birthday to You'. Everyone except Jen, that was, who had taken one look at the jolly little candles burning on the cake and disappeared out of the door, almost knocking over a post girl who had just come in.

Jen didn't seem to notice the post girl. But Katy did. And seeing a yellow telegram envelope in her hand, she gave a gasp of dismay.

At once the noise died away, replaced by an awful silence. Only baby Caroline continued to gurgle happily to herself as she tried to catch her toes. Unnoticed, Malcolm gave a furtive puff and the candles on the cake flickered and died.

Katy suddenly felt as though a cold hand was encircling her heart. She was aware of the faint sulphurous smell of the extinguished candles, of Lucky's warning growl, of the pub door shutting hastily behind the post girl.

Somehow the flimsy envelope was in her hand, and somehow she was slitting it open.

She saw the unevenly typed words, but for a second she couldn't take them in.

From Frazer Ajaccio Corsica. Happy birthday sweetheart stop home soon stop love to kids stop Ward stop.

As she read it, tears filled her eyes. Ward was safe after all. And he was coming home.

232

Chapter Twenty One

'Jen! Wake up!'

Jen could hear the voice, but she was so deep in her dream, it didn't make sense. When someone jiggled her shoulder, she flinched away in terror.

'Jen, it's me,' Angie said. 'You're making these awful wailing noises in your sleep. Are you all right?'

Jen didn't know if she was all right or not. She certainly didn't feel all right; her heart was hammering and she was dripping with sweat. On the other hand, she was awake, the dream hadn't been real after all, and the relief of that far outweighed her physical discomfort.

'I was having this awful dream,' she muttered.

Angie giggled. 'Yes, even I could tell that. Was someone after you with a meat cleaver or something?'

Jen sat up and flapped the covers to let some air into the bed. It felt icy cold on her burning skin. She didn't want to think about the dream. She didn't want to think about the horrible moment in it when she had stood naked on a stage in front of a huge audience of Nazi SS officers. She could still see their hated black uniforms with the red swastika armbands and tight silver-rimmed caps, still feel the mortification as they booed and jeered at the sight of her bare breasts and freckled skin. She had a nasty feeling that one of them might have been Sean.

'No,' she said. 'There weren't any meat cleavers.' She wished there had been. It would have given her immense satisfaction to run riot with a meat cleaver among that audience. In a dream it might have been possible. In reality it would never have been. She shuddered. She wasn't going to mention it to Angie, but she knew the dream had been triggered by a real-life moment in Italy when she had been forced to strip naked in front of a Gestapo doctor to be assessed for her suitability to work in a Nazi brothel. That incident had clearly got muddled up in her mind with the debut performance she was due to give tonight with the Violets in front of a crowd of servicemen at the Hans Crescent Club.

Her eyes were accustoming themselves to the darkness now. The sight of Angie, wild-haired and goggle-eyed in her voluminous white nightdress, was enough to give anyone a bad dream. Goodness only knew what Gino saw in her.

'Sorry,' Jen said. 'I didn't mean to wake you up. I'm probably just a bit nervous about tonight.'

'You don't need to be nervous,' Angie said, climbing back into her own bed. 'You'll be brilliant.'

I hope so, Jen thought. She was about to lie down again when she heard a tap on the door. It was Gino, peering owlishly into the room in his pyjamas.

'Angie,' he whispered. 'Is all OK? I hear noises.'

'It was Jen,' Angie said. 'She was squealing in her sleep.'

'What is this squeeayling?' Gino asked. 'I do not understand.'

Angie giggled. 'It's like frightened shouting,' she said. 'Jen was frightened of something in her dream.'

'Oh for goodness' sake,' Jen said. 'It's the middle of the night. We don't need to have a language lesson.'

And now she could hear her mother's door opening too.

'What are you doing?' Joyce asked Gino. 'You aren't married yet, you know.'

'It's all right, Mum,' Jen called. 'It's my fault. I was having a bad dream and woke everyone up.'

'Jen was squeeayling,' Gino added helpfully.

'What?' Joyce sounded muzzy with sleep. 'What is he trying to say?'

'Oh please, everyone, just go back to sleep,' Jen wailed.

But of course, although everyone else went back to sleep, she stayed awake. And at six thirty, when Angie started snoring, she gave up, and, shrugging on her dressing gown and slippers, tiptoed down to the sitting room to look at her music for the millionth time.

It was already getting light, and as she pulled back the blackout curtains, she looked across at Mr Lorenz's house opposite and wondered how well Leszek Zemniak slept. She was well aware from her own experience in Italy that it wasn't easy getting a good night's sleep when you knew that one false step, or a bad word from a neighbour, could lead to capture.

There was no sign of movement in Mr Lorenz's house, the curtains all tightly drawn as usual, but just as Jen was about to turn away from the window, she caught sight of a man leaving the house next door to Mr Lorenz's. Gillian James's house.

Jen was quite used to seeing men coming and going from Gillian James's house – you couldn't live in Lavender Road without knowing how the glamorous widow earned her living – but it was unusual for her customers to stay the whole night. Normally they were in and out, as it were, in a couple of hours.

Rubbing the condensation off the window pane, Jen peered more closely. Her mouth fell open. She recognised that hand brushing through the tousled hair, the quick glance over the shoulder. Sean Byrne. She could hardly believe her eyes. It was only the night before last that he had been with Louise, for goodness' sake.

Jen had always known Sean was keen on sex, but this was getting beyond a joke. She wondered if Gillian James made him pay. Or did he charm favours out of her like he did with everyone else?

For a second she toyed with the idea of going out and confronting him, but he was already letting himself back into the pub. And what could she say to him after all? He would only think she was jealous.

And the truth was that she *was* jealous. Not of Louise or Mrs James precisely, but that he had moved on to other pastures so quickly. As had Henry, of course. It wasn't exactly flattering. She would have hoped that they might both have held out a bit longer. She wondered if Henry was the sort of man who would visit a prostitute. It seemed highly unlikely, but perhaps all men did sooner or later. Certainly SS Hauptsturmführer Wessel had seemed to feel that selecting suitably attractive girls to satisfy the sexual needs of Nazi officers was a justifiable use of his time.

Crossly she tried to put thoughts of men out of her head and picked up her sheet music. She needed to be word perfect by this evening. But she found it hard to concentrate.

And suddenly she felt angry. Damn Henry. Damn Sean Byrne. Damn Gino with his hopeless English and stupid floppy pyjamas. Damn them all. She was fed up with men. She would belt out the songs to the servicemen at the club tonight and wouldn't give a damn if they didn't enjoy it.

Her angry determination kept her nerves at bay all day, but at seven o'clock that evening, as she put on the long lilac frock for the first time, her confidence deserted her. And suddenly, as the gorge rose in her throat, she knew that she wasn't going to be able to perform.

Veronica Violet had already changed and done her hair and was calmly sitting on a box of props in the dressing room, knitting. Veronica spent every spare moment knitting for the Red Cross. It was clearly a virtuous pastime, but Jen couldn't help wondering what British prisoners of war would think of receiving socks in baby blue and pink. She didn't think her brother Bob would be very impressed. All he ever seemed to want in his POW stalag in Bavaria was cigarettes and chocolate.

'Jen, are you all right?' Veronica asked, glancing up suddenly. 'You look very pale.'

'No, I feel terribly sick,' Jen said. And barging across the room, she made a dash down the short corridor to the toilet.

When she emerged ten minutes later, Veronica and Roger were standing outside the door looking worried.

'I'm really sorry,' Jen said. 'But I'm not going to be able to go on.'

'Is it just nerves?' Roger enquired tentatively. 'Or are you ill?'

Jen was shaking so hard her teeth were rattling. 'I don't know,' she said.

'Perhaps it's something you ate?' Veronica suggested.

Jen cast her mind back to the surprisingly delicious French toast that Gino had knocked up that morning out of bread and dried egg and milk powder, and the mutton soup that her mother had given her in the café at lunchtime. Maybe something had been off. Maybe it was more than just nerves.

But the Violets were looking at each other. 'Mr Keller warned us that something like this might happen,' Veronica said.

Jen turned her eyes on her incredulously. Henry had told them she might falter? That when it came to it she might chicken out? She could hardly believe her ears. How dare he undermine her like that? No wonder the Violets had been so kind to her, constantly reassuring her that she was doing well, glossing over her mistakes, treating her like some kind of flighty, unstable prima donna. It all made sense now. They didn't really think she was brilliant; they just didn't want her to let them down at the crucial moment.

'Did he indeed?' she snapped.

And now her earlier anger was back again. For all his weasel words, deep down Henry clearly didn't believe she was up to it. No wonder he didn't think she ought to try for RADA; he probably thought she would be wasting not only her money, but the teaching staff's time as well.

Well, she might never be a RADA actress, but she was a concert party pro. And she would damn well make them all eat their words. She would show them. Sick or not.

She glared at the Violets, suddenly infuriated by their concern. 'OK,' she said grittily. 'If you can find me a brandy somewhere, I'll try to go on.' She swung away from them as her stomach heaved once more, and put a hand to her mouth. 'But I need to be sick again first.'

And she did go on. It wasn't a large venue, and over the footlights the rows of servicemen all seemed very close. They were packed in like sardines under a fug of cigarette smoke, beer and sweat.

As she battled through the first number, Jen wondered what would happen if she actually threw up on stage. But she didn't. The brandy had its effect. And gradually she relaxed. They liked her. She wasn't naked. They weren't SS. They weren't jeering or booing. On the contrary, the applause was enthusiastic. Even though she was looking about as bad as she had ever looked on stage. One glance in the mirror in the dressing room had told her that. Her reddish hair clashed with the hideous lilac dress, and the lipstick she had put on made her mouth look like a gash in her clammy, almost green face.

As she clung for dear life to the microphone during one of her solo pieces, to her ears her voice sounded tight and strained. But the audience loved her. They laughed at her little humorous asides in the comic songs, and when the nausea came on her again during 'Land of Hope and Glory' and her voice cracked, they thought it was emotion, and clapped wildly at the end.

Jen had forgotten how much she liked the sound of applause.

I can do this, she thought. Even in this condition, I can do it. And everyone else, including Henry Keller, can take a running jump.

When it was over, the soldiers queued up for autographs.

Jen was just signing a young marine's bare arm when she became aware that the skin on the back of her neck was tingling, and knew that Henry was standing behind her.

'Are you all right?' he asked quietly.

For a second she ignored him, then she swung round. 'Oh, yes,' she said. 'Apart from vomiting up everything I've eaten today, and half my stomach lining as well, I'm absolutely fine.' She saw his eyes narrow sharply at her biting sarcasm. 'And I'd appreciate it in future if you would refrain from warning everyone that I might bottle out.'

'I didn't say that,' he said.

'Well you certainly said something,' she hissed. 'And I don't like being talked about behind my back.'

She thought she saw anger flash in his eyes, but then he held up his hands and took a slow breath. 'I was going to ask if you wanted to come out for a drink to celebrate your debut,' he said. 'But I can see you aren't in the mood.'

'Not only am I not in the mood,' Jen said, 'but whether you believe it or not, I am still feeling sick. So once I have finished signing these autographs, I'm going to go home. On my own.'

'In that case, I'll just say congratulations on getting through the show,' he said. 'I'm sure you'll be able to refine your performance once you're feeling better.'

And with that he was gone. Leaving Jen feeling almost incandescent with fury. And very close to tears.

Blindly she handed back the pen to the nearest soldier. 'I'm sorry,' she said. 'I can't sign any more. I'm not feeling very well.'

Life at Arborfield was similar to life at Bracknell, but considerably more taxing. When Lieutenant Masterson had said that the men and women would be treated equally in everything, he had meant it.

They still had to suffer kit inspections, parades and endless drill. And this time they had to differentiate the barked commands of their instructor from others drilling their squads at the same time. At first this caused mix-ups, as when half the ATS contingent wheeled left on the command of the wrong drill sergeant and collided with his male squad, causing complete disarray.

'It's not their fault, Sarge,' Don Wellington called out as the men broke ranks in an effort to disentangle themselves. 'They're girls. You can't expect them to have a sense of direction.'

'I reckon it's our magnetic personalities,' another squaddie chipped in. 'They just can't keep their hands off of us.'

The instructors, however, had not been amused. The result of this fiasco was that the ATS squad was kept on the parade square for an extra hour. After that, the girls began to listen much more attentively to the not-so-dulcet voice of their own drill sergeant. Nobody, least of all Louise, wanted to give Don Wellington and his chauvinistic comrades any more opportunities to gloat.

But the real challenge came in the gun park. Close up, the 3.7 inch guns were much larger and more intimidating than Louise had expected. As was the command post machinery used to locate the target. It was all painted the same dark olive green, surprisingly cold to the touch and dauntingly technical.

There was a height- and range-finder machine, a radar unit, an automated anti-aircraft fire-control system called the Kerry, and a kine-theodolite, which recorded the location of the shell burst.

Male gunners and ATS trained together in teams, the men operating the guns and the girls on the instruments. Everyone was allocated a specific job number in range-finder, predictor or gun ops. On the gun site everyone was referred to the number linked to their role. Spotters located the target with binoculars. Height-finders adjusted the image on the double-vision screen, and predictors, armed with a huge adjustable metal telescope, would calculate where the target would be when the guns fired.

The whole procedure was supremely complicated. Wind speed, bearing and range all had to be taken into account, and the various dials had to be adjusted and accurately matched up before the information was fed to the gunners manning the gun. That first week, nobody, least of all Louise, could imagine how they would ever get the hang of it. It was lucky that none of the training guns actually fired. Otherwise half of Berkshire would probably have been obliterated.

'I'm never going to get it right,' Voles wailed one day as once again the system broke down and she sent the wrong co-ordinates to the gun.

'You'd better start getting it right,' the instructor responded curtly. 'And pretty damn soon. The defence of Great Britain depends on it.' He scowled at them. 'OK, everyone, change over. Let's see if the other team can do any better.'

The teams trained in turns, and those not actively manning the instruments or guns sat on nearby benches to observe. Louise was the first to learn that their section instructor had eyes in the back of his head. One morning when she was meant to be studying the actions of her counterpart predictor operator in the other team, her eyes had wandered over to the gun position, where the men were practising manhandling the huge replica high-explosive shells into position. She was idly wondering how Colonel Westwood would incorporate his new proximity fuses into the rigorous procedure when Voles nudged her hard in the ribs.

'Number three,' their instructor was shouting. 'Are you with us?'

Louise's head jerked back. 'Yes,' she said.

'Then tell me, how do you calculate wind speed?'

Louise glanced at Voles helplessly, but although her friend was mouthing the answer, Louise couldn't read her lips.

'I don't know,' she admitted.

'With a slide rule,' the instructor bellowed. 'Do you know how to use a slide rule?'

She shook her head helplessly.

'Well you'd better find out pretty damn pronto, or you'll be off the course.'

He strode up to her and ordered her to stand up. 'The Royal Artillery has no use for dimwits or slackers. We all know a woman's place is in the home. So if you would rather go and work in the kitchens, just let me know.'

Louise gritted her teeth. She could feel the spray of his spittle landing on her face, and forced herself not to wipe it off. He was watching her like a snake, waiting to pounce on any sign of weakness or retaliation. She could sense Voles beside her holding her breath, and hoped she wouldn't faint again.

'No, I don't want to work in the kitchens,' Louise said steadily.

Thwarted, he glowered at her. 'Then concentrate,' he snarled. 'Or that's where you'll end up.'

'Yes, Sarge,' Louise muttered meekly as she went to sit down again.

'Oh no you don't,' he said. 'As you don't seem to be able to concentrate when you are sitting down, you can stay on your feet for the rest of the session.'

After that humiliation, Louise made sure she kept her eyes focused rigidly on the appropriate instrument.

Voles was deeply sympathetic. 'You poor thing,' she whispered when she got a chance. 'But you were awfully brave. I'd have died if he'd shouted at me like that. I nearly fainted as it was.'

Voles might be nervy, but she was very good at maths, and that evening

239

Louise asked her to show her how to use a slide rule.

Colonel Westwood had advised her to brush up on her maths. Or math, as he called it. And she was paying the price for not heeding his warning. But her success in the exam at Bracknell had given her a false sense of security. Now she realised that if she didn't quickly get to grips with how to work out wind speed and other variables, she would get thrown off the course.

Buller, of course, delighted in her misfortune. 'It serves you right, Rutherford,' she said, leaning over the table in the NAAFI where Voles, pencil in hand, was attempting to explain to her the concept of triangulation. 'I always knew you would bring the ATS into disrepute. You'll make a laughing stock of us all if you aren't careful.'

And Don Wellington had to put in his halfpenny's worth as well. 'Oh dear,' he murmured, passing by on his way to the counter. 'Poor old Rutherford, actually having to put in some effort. I hope your dopey little sidekick there can bring you up to speed. If not, maybe you should try blackmailing the DS?'

'What was that about?' Voles asked as Wellington continued on his way to the counter.

'Nothing,' Louise said irritably. 'I was always better than him at the factory and he can't resist an opportunity to get back at me, that's all.'

But it wasn't only in the gun park that Louise had problems. Alongside the practical training were daily lectures on security, defence, operating procedure, gun control and, most important of all, aircraft recognition. Learning the difference between Allied planes and German ones was clearly crucial. Nobody wanted to shoot down a Spitfire or a Wellington instead of a Junker or a Messerschmitt. But telling them apart was a total nightmare.

Indeed, on the night of 24 April, when Louise and Susan managed, to their mutual delight, to secure an evening pass to enable them to go up to London to the premiere of Henry's play, they took their aircraft recognition handbook with them and, much to the amusement of the other passengers in the carriage, spent the entire journey testing each other by holding up the pictures and silhouettes with their hands over the names.

'You two are a credit to the ATS,' one old gentleman said as he got off at Richmond. 'I'll feel safer sleeping in my bed tonight now I know how seriously you girls take your air defence duties.' And they both glowed with pride. Although he might not have been quite so confident if he had seen them in the ladies' room at Waterloo station half an hour later, putting on lipstick, eyeshadow and kohl that they had smuggled out of camp in their respirator bags.

It was a shame they hadn't been able to wear evening dresses too, but although Louise had toyed with racing home to Clapham to get changed

240

before the show, there simply wasn't time, so in the end they had to make do with uniform.

Apart from their own lack of glamour, the evening was everything they had hoped for. Certainly everything Susan had hoped for. She had rarely been to London and goggled at all the people, the variety of uniforms, and the bomb-scarred buildings. She sat transfixed throughout the show, and clapped so hard when Janette Pymm led Henry out to take a bow that she bruised the palms of her hands. And when Louise was cheeky enough to send their names backstage after the show, Susan nearly passed out in excitement when Henry took them along to Janette Pymm's dressing room to introduce them to the star.

Afterwards he invited them to join him for a drink with some of the cast in a nearby pub. Everyone was very friendly, and at one rather delicious point Louise found herself wedged so close to Henry round a crowded table that he was forced to put his arm round the back of her chair to give himself space to breathe.

'I'm sorry,' he murmured to her with a smile as he lit a cigarette with his gold lighter. 'I hadn't realised that the entire cast would come.'

'You must be thrilled it was such a success,' Louise said. She was very close to him and noticed for the first time that he had tiny laughter lines at the edges of his eyes. She glanced across the table and nearly burst out laughing herself at Susan's excitedly encouraging expression.

'Yes,' Henry said. 'I'm glad it went down so well. That's the aim of these shows after all, to boost morale.'

'It's certainly boosted my morale,' Louise said. She nodded across the table. 'And I don't think Susan will ever be the same again.'

He laughed. 'It's nice to see her enjoying herself.'

'She loved the Windsor races too,' Louise said. 'We both did. It was so kind of you to ask us up to your friend's box. It was the highlight of our day.' Then, as Henry stiffened slightly, she belatedly remembered that for him the Windsor races had not been entirely pleasurable. Jen Carter and Sean Byrne had seen to that.

Still, he nodded politely. 'It was my pleasure,' he said. Then he looked away and drew on his cigarette, and Louise kicked herself for spoiling the convivial atmosphere.

She was wondering what she could say to take his mind off Jen Carter when Henry suddenly clicked his fingers. 'That reminds me,' he said. 'Freddy wants your address and I promised to ask you for it if I saw you again.'

'Really?' Louise couldn't for the life of her imagine why Henry's aristocratic friend might want her address. She cast her mind back, wondering if perhaps she had left something in his box that he wanted to return. 'Well,

241

I'm at Arborfield now for the next few weeks,' she said. 'After that I'll be back in London. But why on earth does he want to contact me?'

Henry smiled through the smoke of his cigarette. 'I may be wrong,' he said. 'But I think he had some idea of asking you to marry him.'

'*Marry* him!' If Henry hadn't been wedged so close, Louise probably would have fallen off her chair. 'But I can hardly even remember what he looks like.'

'Oh dear,' Henry said. 'That doesn't bode well. You made a big hit with him, you know.'

She gaped at him. No, she didn't know. Surely he was joking? She really didn't remember much about Lord Freddy. That, of course, was because she had only had eyes for Henry. But she could hardly tell him that, especially as he was clearly still holding a candle for Jen Carter.

'I only spoke to him for about five minutes,' she objected. 'Just while he was showing me how to use the binoculars.'

Henry leaned past her to tap his cigarette in the ashtray. 'That didn't seem to worry him,' he said. 'He told me he had fallen for you lock, stock and barrel.' He laughed again, and held up his hands as she began to protest. 'I know, I know. He's got a bit of a reputation for being impulsive. But if you *were* looking for a husband, you could do worse. He's a very nice man, and fabulously wealthy, of course.'

I *am* looking for a husband, Louise thought. And urgently. The thought of returning to her parents' house at the end of her training was not at all appealing. But then nor was staying in the army. It was just about bearable for a month at a time, but any longer than that would be out of the question.

But she didn't want Lord Freddy. No, she decided, as she and Susan journeyed back to Bracknell later in the darkness of a blacked-out train, the man she really wanted was Henry.

But unfortunately, whether he intended to or not, Henry had made it clear that he wasn't, as yet at least, thinking of her in those terms.

All was not lost, however. Henry liked her. Surely that was a good start. He might even fancy her a little bit. He didn't seem to have been averse to touching her, although admittedly that might have been due to the lack of space in the pub. If only she could wean him off blasted Jen Carter, she might be in with a chance.

After much deliberation, Angie chose Saturday 27 May as the date for her wedding. It seemed to her to be the perfect date. The weekend after Aaref and Elsa's. Not quite a month away. And she was going to need all that time to organise it. Because, despite the restrictions and the government's call for restraint on celebrations, she was absolutely determined to go the whole hog.

Joyce had been amused one day to hear Mrs Rutherford advising Angie that the sensible and patriotic thing to do with her race winnings was to buy National Savings Certificates. 'We all need to save up for a rainy day,' she said.

But Angie wasn't having any of that. 'Oh no,' she said. 'I don't want to use it on a rainy day. I want to spend it all on my wedding and give the biggest party I can afford.'

Concerned that her military friends might get called away before her big day, she had even considered writing to Mr Churchill asking him to delay the invasion plans until later in the summer. Because it had become clear even to Angie that an assault on the European mainland was coming ever closer. At the end of April, the government had extended its travel ban on Ireland to anywhere abroad. Britain had now essentially become one huge gated army camp.

In the meantime, a new push was underway at the apparently impregnable Nazi stronghold of Monte Cassino in Italy. Surely this time the Allies would get through. Even the stubborn Germans couldn't hold out for ever.

But the Germans apparently weren't the only stubborn ones. The Poles seemed just as bad. A court-martial date had now been set by the Polish military for the trial of the captured Jewish deserters. And that meant that Leszek Zemniak had to continue hiding in Albert's house. It was far too risky for him to show his face in case someone reported him to the authorities.

The only good piece of news was that in April, for the first time in four years, there had been no deaths from air raids in the UK. Perhaps, Joyce thought hopefully, the relentless bombing of Germany was finally weakening Hitler's military muscle.

But then Celia Rutherford let slip that the WVS had been asked to help prepare decontamination centres in various parts of London. The authorities apparently feared that, in their desperation to thwart an invasion, the Nazis might resort to using poison gas. What was more, she had added, if Hitler's much vaunted, but as yet unseen, secret weapon turned out to be bombs filled with nerve gas, then the civilian population would be at risk too.

'Lady Reading says we have to be ready for anything,' she said briskly when Joyce looked at her askance. 'Didn't you hear her speech on the wireless last night? She said that the Second Front army will be dependent on our efforts at home. The final battle for freedom will require courage and self-sacrifice, both here and abroad.'

Joyce didn't like the sound of self-sacrifice and was suddenly glad that Angie's grandiose wedding plans involved sending invitations to all her brothers.

Bob wouldn't be able to come, of course. Hitler was hardly going to let him out of his POW camp to attend his sister's wedding. And since the last time she had heard from Mick he'd been heading down to Africa on his merchant ship, it was unlikely that he would make it either. But Pete was definitely coming, and if Angie's invitation, sent to the 3rd Infantry Division, found its way to Paul, then surely he would feel it was safe to come home, especially as Angie wanted him to be Gino's best man.

Aware of a slight constriction in her throat, Joyce turned back to her cooking. It would be nice to see Paul and Pete once more. Before they were sent off to France.

It only took Jen twenty-four hours to recover from her sickness, but she still felt angry with Henry. The fact that he had been right about the quality of her performance at the Hans Crescent Club hadn't made his cutting words any easier to swallow.

But she and the rest of the Violets had done plenty of shows since then. They met at the Drury Lane theatre at lunchtime each day and travelled out of London in an old workmen's van with the ENSA logo stencilled in white paint on the side. They played mostly in military canteens and clubs. So many, in fact, that they had already begun to blur together. Jen had indeed refined her performance, and now, despite herself, she wished that Henry would come again and see the improvement.

But he didn't.

As private revenge, she decided not to go to the opening night of his new play. She couldn't have gone anyway, as it happened, even if he had invited her, which he hadn't, because the Violets were performing in Croydon that night, and she couldn't have got back to London in time.

But she saw the rave reviews in the papers the next day and felt unreasonably jealous at the accolades Janette Pymm received for her outstanding performance. If only she had played her cards right with Henry, Jen thought, it might have been her. He had often said he was going to help her become a star. After the incident at the Hans Cresent Club, that seemed increasingly unlikely.

Jen had apologised to the Violets for the anxiety she had caused them that night. And they had apologised for doubting her. They were kind people, and she guessed Henry had chosen to put her in their troupe because he knew they would look after her. And they had. Getting back on stage, resuming her career, would have been much harder with less sympathetic companions.

Roger Violet always drove the van. Beside him in the passenger seat sat Philip. His job was to find the way, which wasn't easy, because most of the country's signposts had been removed at the beginning of the war in case of invasion. He took his self-appointed role very seriously. Armed with a compass and a huge map spread across his lap, he spent most journeys muttering place names and distances with such nervous intensity that anyone would think he was guiding the advance party of the invasion force rather than a small, insignificant concert party.

In the back of the van were four canvas fold-up chairs. These provided a modicum of comfort for the girls, but had a tendency to slide about on sharp corners. At their feet were two large ENSA wicker hampers. One held Roger's piano stool, Veronica's accordion, Philip's violin and copious amounts of sheet music. The other was the wardrobe box containing Roger and Philip's suits and the girls' hideous purple frocks. It had often occurred to Jen to leave the back door of the van ajar in the hope that the second hamper might fly out on a sharp bend and end up in a deep ditch, or preferably a river.

So far she hadn't dared. Instead she had got used to the endless clack of Veronica and Betty's knitting needles, and the homely chit-chat about shortages, recipes, and news of their various friends and relatives serving in the forces in various parts of the world. Adele, as far as Jen could see, was entirely brainless and spent most of their travelling time perusing various popular magazines looking for pictures of good-looking men. When she found one she liked, she would make them all inspect him and give him marks out of ten, which always caused great hilarity.

As this was all interspersed with plenty of entirely unfunny have-you-heard-the-one-about jokes from Roger in the front, all in all, Jen thought, it was rather like travelling round with a selection of people chosen at random from the WI, the Clapham Junction hairdresser's, and Katy's pub.

But as soon as, thanks to Philip's impeccable map-reading, they arrived at a venue, they all immediately clicked into work mode, and on stage she couldn't fault their professionalism. It was a competent, neat little show and Jen had already begun to enjoy being part of it.

As she didn't really care where they were going, she didn't normally take much notice of Philip's musings about road numbers and villages they were passing through. But when one afternoon she heard him mention a familiar name, she leaned forward quickly.

'Did you say Arborfield?' she asked.

'Yes, we're looking for the Royal Artillery barracks,' Philip said, swivelling his head to peer at her in the dark interior of the van. 'Did you see a sign?'

'No,' she said. 'But I know someone in the ATS who's stationed here.'

'Oh that's nice, dear,' Veronica remarked. 'Do you think she'll come to the show?'

'I sincerely hope not,' Jen said. 'Because if she does, I might be tempted to ram your accordion down her throat.'

245

Chapter Twenty Two

It had been a long day in the gun park, and Louise wasn't going to bother with the ENSA entertainments taking place that night. But Susan Voles persuaded her. 'Oh go on, Louise, you missed the one at Bracknell, and we all deserve a treat.'

'I don't think it will be much of a treat,' Louise said. 'More likely a nightmare, judging from what Henry said about the other one.'

But in the end she gave in. And her worst fears were realised, although not quite in the way she had expected.

As the concert party filed onto the makeshift stage in the barracks gymnasium, Louise's eyes were drawn to the singer on the left. Unused to seeing Jen dressed in such unflattering garb, it took her a moment to realise who it was. And then she hastily sank down in her seat in the hope that the other girl wouldn't be able to see her over the bright footlights.

But as the show progressed, Louise reluctantly began to understand why Henry Keller was so smitten with Jen. As she took the microphone to sing her first solo number, the emotive 'Stormy Weather', her voice was pure and true, and even in the unbelievably hideous long lilac dress, with the lights on her wild reddish hair she looked startlingly beautiful. It went against the grain to say it, but Louise had to admit that she was very good.

It was in the comic numbers, 'Oh! Mr Porter', and 'Burlington Bertie', that Jen really came into her own. She had a way of laughing with her eyes, inviting the audience to laugh with her even as she sang the lyrics quite seriously. And the Arborfield gunners lapped it up, reacting just as she intended them to, guffawing at all the right moments and cheering wildly at the end when she came back on for her 'Burlington Bertie' encore wearing a top hat.

When the show eventually came to an end, Louise calculated that if she delayed her exit from the gymnasium long enough, she would avoid bumping into Jen in the lobby, so she kept Susan chatting in their seats as long as she could.

But she hadn't accounted for the number of soldiers wanting autographs.

When she and Susan eventually got up and went out, Jen was still there with a queue of admirers in front of her.

As though by some sixth sense, she looked up from her signing at once.

There was no way of avoiding her.

'Hello, Jen,' Louise said.

'I thought I saw you in the audience.' Jen's tone suggested clearly that it hadn't been a pleasure.

Susan, of course, didn't seem to notice. 'I loved the show,' she said gushingly. 'You were really good.'

Jen ignored her. She let her eyes wander over Louise. 'Nice uniform,' she said sardonically.

Louise clenched her jaw. She didn't particularly mind Jen being rude to her, but she felt oddly protective of Voles and didn't like her being snubbed.

'Do tell me,' Jen said, as she signed with an ostentatious flourish the back of an envelope for a young gunner with bad acne. 'Have you by any chance seen Henry recently?'

Her voice sounded indifferent, but Louise hesitated. She knew Jen had been angry about seeing her with Henry at Windsor. Remembering how capable Jen was of making a scene, she was about to deny it when Susan chipped in helpfully.

'Oh yes,' she said. 'Henry invited us to the premiere of his new play. It was amazing. Janette Pymm was absolutely brilliant, wasn't she, Louise?'

Louise could tell at once that this wasn't what Jen had wanted to hear. Her face darkened alarmingly.

'Yes, she was,' Louise said. She smiled kindly. 'But your show was jolly good too.' She saw Jen wince and felt she had scored a hit. Wanting to escape while the going was good, she gestured at the impatient soldiers. 'But I can see you are busy. And I'm quite sure you'll want to change out of that *lovely* frock as soon as possible. So I'll say good-bye.' And turning on her heel, she opened the door and, leaving the others in the lobby, walked briskly away across the dark parade ground.

She thought she had got away with it, but Jen caught her up just before she reached the NAAFI. Her tawny eyes flashed in the moonlight like a wild cat's. She must have been hot on Louise's heels, because she was still holding the spotty soldier's pen. 'I'd appreciate it if you'd keep away from Henry,' she snapped.

'Oh come on, Jen,' Louise said. 'If you're not going to marry him, you hardly have exclusive rights over him. Anyway, you've got Sean. You can't have your cake and eat it.'

But Jen was clearly not in the mood to see reason. 'It's nothing to do with cake. It's to do with you trying to smarm up to Henry behind my back.'

Louise bit back her irritation and gave a light laugh. 'I can't help it if men find me desirable. You treat them so badly, it's not surprising that they—'

'Oh yes?' Jen interrupted. 'You're a fine one to talk. Since when have you treated men so well?'

Louise felt herself bristle. 'What do you mean by that?'

'Well you aren't exactly Miss Perfect, are you?' Jen said. 'You led poor Aaref Hoch right up the garden path, then dumped him flat. And everyone knows you messed around behind Jack's back, and even his death didn't stop you.'

Louise recoiled. The cruel accusation hit her like a punch in the stomach. She knew people had thought it, but nobody had ever actually come out and said it. For a moment or two she was speechless. Then she felt her whole body go rigid with rage. She was hard pushed not to slap Jen's spiteful little face.

'How dare you—' she began furiously.

But catching a slight movement to one side of her, she stopped abruptly. And drew back in horror as Don Wellington stepped out from the shadow of a nearby building.

He had clearly been there for some time.

'Now, now, girlies,' he said with a gleeful smirk. 'Put your claws away or someone will get hurt.'

But he hadn't accounted for Jen, who turned on him like an angry tiger. 'I don't know who you are,' she snarled. 'But if you don't bugger off right now, you're the one who'll be getting hurt. What are you doing skulking around in the shadows anyway?'

If Louise hadn't been so angry, she might have found it funny. Don Wellington, for all his chauvinist bravado, was no match for Jen Carter. Louise saw his eyes flicker nervously to the pen in Jen's hand, and he backed away hastily, perhaps fearing she was about to stab it into his eye.

'I only wanted to get your autograph,' he muttered sulkily.

'I don't give my autograph to eavesdroppers,' Jen snapped. 'If you want to lurk about spying on people, you ought to go to Germany and join the Gestapo.'

He was wise enough not to respond to that, and Louise watched with a certain amount of satisfaction as he scuttled off towards the NAAFI. 'That told him,' she remarked.

Jen shrugged. 'I don't like people poking their nose into my business,' she said.

'Yes, you made that quite clear,' Louse said drily.

Jen gave a slightly self-conscious laugh. 'I hope he's not a friend of yours.'

'No,' Louise said. 'Far from it. But I do know him, and as you rightly pointed out, he's a nosy git.'

She waited until Don Wellington was out of earshot, then turned back to Jen. 'If you must know, I was devastated by Jack's death,' she said.

But despite their brief moment of rapport over the routing of Don Wellington, Jen's underlying resentment clearly hadn't abated.

'Well you'd never think it from the way you've been carrying on these last few months,' she said. 'And not just with Henry. With Sean, too.' She caught Louise's start of surprise. 'Yes, I know what you were up to with him the other week. And for your information, you can't be quite as *desirable* as you think you are, because he spent the very next night with Gillian James.'

'And for *your* information, I didn't spend any nights with Sean Byrne,' Louise retorted angrily. 'I may have flirted with him a bit, but I would never go that far. He is hardly the kind of man one would want to have a relationship with, let alone marry.'

Jen's eyes flashed. 'What about Henry?' she asked. 'How *far* have you gone with him?'

Louise was on the point of hotly denying any physical involvement with Henry at all when she realised this was a chance to pay Jen back.

'Oh, Henry,' she murmured. She lowered her eyes with a coy little smirk. 'Well, that's a completely different matter.'

And she was just in time, because at that moment the door of the NAAFI opened and a crowd of soldiers came pouring out, laughing and joking.

Louise heard Jen's low grunt of annoyance as she swung away, disappearing across the dark parade ground like a lilac wraith. The last Louise saw of her was in the brief flash of light as she let herself back into the lobby of the gymnasium.

Katy had been trying to persuade her mother not to return to London.

'I really hope she won't come,' she confided to Pam, who had dropped in with George and Nellie for a cup of tea. She watched Pam lean down to steady Nellie as she tried to stand up with the aid of the table leg, and remembered how excited she had been when Malcolm took his first steps. He was so grown-up and agile now; he could outrun her, and often did. She glanced at him fondly. For once he was standing still, painstakingly inspecting a small bag of marbles that George had brought over to show him.

Lucky, meanwhile, was sniffing at Pam's shopping bag. 'I feel bad to say it,' Katy went on, shooing him away. 'But she isn't really up to looking after the children. And having her here made more work for me, not less.'

'Well let's hope Ward will be home soon, and he'll be able to convince her that you haven't fallen victim to Sean Byrne's irresistible charm,' Pam said, and then suddenly went very pink as Sean himself emerged from the pantry.

'What's this?' he said with one of his disingenuous grins. 'Is someone casting aspersions on my good name?'

Katy almost laughed. What good name? she wondered. She knew

perfectly well that Sean had taken to secretly slipping out at night to visit Gillian James. 'My mother is labouring under the impression that you and I are …' she began instead. And then stopped, abruptly realising that George was watching them with interest from across the room.

'Are what?' Sean asked. He saw her confusion and chuckled. 'Chance would be a fine thing,' he murmured. He shook his head. 'But you know, if you ladies had any sense, you'd be taking advantage of my masculine charms right now.' And Katy couldn't help noticing that although his teasing smile embraced them both, it lingered on Pam. 'Because as soon as this ill-fated invasion happens, I'll be gone. And then you'll be wondering what fun you've missed.'

Abandoning the marbles, George stood up and came over. 'Why do you say the invasion is ill-fated?' he asked. 'I thought we were going to thrash the Germans.'

'Of course we will,' Pam said.

'Well let's hope so, of course,' Sean said. 'But it's worth remembering that you didn't last time.'

'What do you mean?' George looked puzzled. 'What last time?'

'Did you never hear about Dunkirk?' Sean asked him. 'When all your fine British soldiers turned tail and ran away?'

'Stop it, Sean,' Katy admonished him angrily. 'That's not true. It wasn't like that.'

George looked uncertainly at Pam. 'Is it true? I always thought Dunkirk was a success.'

Katy glanced at Pam and caught her anguished look. George can only have been six years old when the Dunkirk evacuation had taken place in May 1940. And his real father had died in the debacle.

'It *was* a success,' Pam said firmly. 'It was a miracle that so many soldiers were saved by people like Alan going over in their little boats. Brave men like your father held the Germans back as long as they could so that the rest could escape.' She threw Sean an angry look. 'But yes, Sean is partly right. It was a retreat. The German forces were too strong. There weren't enough of our soldiers to overpower them.'

But Pam's reassurance wasn't enough for George. He turned anxiously to Sean. 'We will overpower them this time, won't we?'

Sean punched him gently on the shoulder. 'Of course you will,' he said. 'To be sure, I was only teasing your mother. I like it when she gets all patriotic like that. She's right, of course. You can't win every battle. There's no point in fighting a lost cause. Especially if there's a chance of getting hurt.'

Malcolm came running over then. 'Who got hurt?' he cried. 'Not Daddy?'

Katy winced. 'No,' she said quickly. 'Not Daddy.'

'Then who?' Malcolm insisted.

'Nobody has got hurt,' Sean said, grabbing him and sweeping him up into the air. 'And nobody is going to get hurt. Not unless I drop you.'

Katy's heart lurched as he pretended to do just that. Malcolm of course just screamed with delight.

Pam stood up abruptly. 'I'd better go,' she said.

'You haven't finished your cup of tea,' Katy said. But Pam was adamant. Briskly she gathered Nellie up off the floor and settled her back in the pram.

Malcolm didn't want them to go, and started to make a fuss. He adored George. It was as Katy tried to pacify him that she heard Sean murmur to Pam, 'Now who's running away?'

Pam didn't respond, but Katy sensed she was gritting her teeth as she trundled the pram out of the door.

'She's a fine, spirited woman, is she not?' Sean murmured as the door closed behind them.

'Leave her alone, Sean. She's happily married,' Katy snapped angrily. 'And if I ever, ever hear you use that defeatist talk in front of the children again, teasing or not, you'll be out on the street.'

The Royal Academy of Dramatic Art was accommodated in an imposing building in Gower Street. Jen stood outside, bracing herself for several minutes, before stepping under the engraved marble plaque flanked by the two masked actors, one male one female, one comedy one tragedy, that stood over the entrance.

She was fully expecting to be turned away, or somehow ridiculed for her pretension in entering the hallowed interior. But in fact all that happened was that a pleasant elderly woman offered her a prospectus booklet and told her that a non-returnable fee of one guinea had to be submitted with the application form. Fees for the drama diploma were fifteen guineas a term, seventeen if she wished to take French acting classes. The selection criteria were stringent, the woman warned her; competition for places, and especially for scholarships, was very tough. If invited to audition, she would need two contrasting monologues, one Shakespearean or Jacobean and one modern, and must be prepared to answer questions from a selection panel.

Fifteen guineas? Jen stared at the receptionist in dismay. Even if she got an audition, even if by some miracle she got in, she couldn't possibly afford fifteen guineas. She was happy to forgo French acting classes, whatever they were, but the one guinea entrance fee was bad enough. No wonder all the RADA graduates were so posh and well spoken. They were the only people who could afford to go there.

Two minutes later, she was back in Gower Street. As she crossed the road and walked along Chenies Street to Goodge Street underground station, she suddenly felt very hard done by. It was all very well for Henry to say she didn't need to go to drama school. He didn't know how difficult it was for a girl brought up on the back streets of Clapham to be taken seriously in the elitist theatrical world. If she'd been born into money, like Louise Rutherford, for example, she would already have the posh voice, the confidence and self-assurance that came with private schools, class and cash.

And the irony was that fifteen guineas would be nothing to blasted Louise.

Jen glowered at the ticket officer at Goodge Street station. She was glad now that she had laid into Louise the other night. It had been a release to get rid of some of her anger, although she felt slightly guilty for mentioning Jack. But discovering that Henry had invited Louise and her drippy little ATS friend to his opening night had tipped her over the edge.

She was cross about Louise and Sean too, of course, but oddly not quite so much. Since catching sight of Sean slinking out of Gillian James's house, her resolve had strengthened. Sean Byrne was an attractive man. But as Louise had so snootily pointed out, he wasn't the kind of man one wanted to marry.

Emerging from the underground at Clapham Common, Jen walked slowly back along the edge of the common towards Lavender Road. Tomorrow she would be heading off with the Violets on a tour of RAF bases in East Anglia. But for now she had the rest of the day free. The sun was out, and it was nice, for once, not to be spending the afternoon bumping along in the back of the ENSA van.

Today, as for much of the past month, Mr Rutherford's ack-ack guns were lying still and silent. Jen peered at them through the chain-link fence. They were huge great things. Was Louise really learning to operate guns like this? It seemed an odd thing for her to want to do.

Turning the corner into Lavender Road, she was diverted from her thoughts by the sight of her mother emerging from Mr Lorenz's house looking distinctly hot and flustered.

'O-ho,' Jen called out gleefully. 'And what have you been up to in there at three o'clock in the afternoon?'

But instead of looking embarrassed, her mother came running up the street towards her. 'Where've you been?' she panted. 'Henry was here looking for you.'

Jen felt her heart leap. 'Henry? Why? What's happened?'

'He came to tell us about the court martial yesterday. Of the Jewish deserters. They were sentenced to death and—'

'What?' Jen exclaimed in horror. Her blood ran cold. She suddenly felt mortified. In all her agitation about RADA, she had completely forgotten about the fate of the young Jewish men.

'No, but listen,' Joyce said. 'Thanks to Henry and Mr Driberg, the government have put pressure on the Polish authorities, and the deserters are now going to be pardoned. So Leszek will be able to join a British regiment. I've just been in to tell him. He's absolutely thrilled.'

Jen wasn't sure quite how thrilled she would be in Leszek's shoes. Although taking his chances against German machine guns on a French beach was probably a better option than being summarily shot by a firing squad.

She frowned. 'Did you say Henry was looking for me?'

Joyce nodded. 'He came to tell us as soon as he heard the news from Mr Driberg. He thought you were on a day off. But when you weren't at the house, he came to the café. It was so kind of—'

'So where is he now?' Jen interrupted sharply.

'He's gone down to Northcote Road to tell Albert. If you hurry, you might catch him there.'

Jen did hurry. But she didn't catch him. When she burst into Mr Lorenz's dark little shop on Northcote Road ten minutes later, she discovered that Henry had already left.

'I'm sorry,' Mr Lorenz said as Jen leant on the counter to catch her breath after her mad dash down the hill. 'But he said he had to get back to town.'

Jen tried to hide her disappointment. 'It doesn't matter,' she said. Although, given her luck, it did seem somehow inevitable that she would have chosen to go to RADA on the one day when Henry had come looking for her. 'I'm glad it was good news for Leszek, anyway.'

'Oh yes,' Mr Lorenz agreed. 'This is wonderful news. Wonderful.' But even though he was smiling, his eyes were concerned. 'I'm sure if Mr Keller had known you wanted to see him, he would have waited.'

Would he? Jen wasn't so sure about that. She shrugged and looked away.

'I am very grateful to you, Jen,' Mr Lorenz went on after a moment. 'If you hadn't got Mr Keller involved, the outcome might have been very different.'

Jen glanced round his grim little shop with its racks of sad, unredeemed trinkets. She had been one of Mr Lorenz's customers in the past, trying to pawn some stolen jewellery to pay for acting lessons as she started out on her career at the beginning of the war. All of a sudden she felt a terrible sense of dejection. At the high hopes she had had in those days. And at the cruel twist of fate that had brought her back here again, four years later, her ambition unrealised, and still needing money for acting lessons.

She was about to turn away, but then she hesitated. 'I may need to raise

253

some money,' she said. 'I haven't really got anything valuable I could sell, but if I brought in some of my better clothes and shoes, would you give me something for them?'

She looked at him, hoping for a nod, but he just regarded her steadily through his wire-rimmed glasses. 'May I ask what you would be raising the money for?' he asked.

She stiffened, daring him to laugh. 'I want to apply to RADA,' she said. 'The acting school. I may not get in. But even if I did, I can't afford it.'

He didn't laugh. 'How much is it?' he asked after a moment.

Jen took a breath. 'Fifteen guineas a term.'

He didn't even flinch. He just continued to look at her. 'I'm happy to give you the money,' he said. 'You don't need to pawn anything.'

Jen hadn't always been very kind to Mr Lorenz. She had often joked about his patient, long-suffering pursuit of her mother. But now she felt a surge of affection for him. And a surge of regret.

'I can't,' she said. 'I can't let you. You've already given me an awful lot. You paid for my throat operation last year. I can't possibly ask you for anything else.' The truth was that if Mr Lorenz hadn't paid for Dr Goodacre to remove the polyp from her larynx, she would never have been able to continue her career at all.

There was a long pause, during which Mr Lorenz laid his hands flat on the counter. 'I think you know that I am hoping to marry your mother,' he said at last. 'In which case I would become your stepfather.'

Jen nodded. She hadn't thought of it like that before. 'Even so,' she muttered awkwardly. 'Mum would kill me if she thought I'd come asking you for money.'

'You didn't ask,' he said. 'I offered.' He gave one of his faint smiles, and behind the glasses she saw his dark eyes twinkle. 'I don't think we need to tell your mother. Not yet at least. But if you get a place, then I can assure you it would give me great pleasure to fund it.'

It soon transpired that Louise wasn't the only person struggling with the range-finding calculations. Susan Voles now had quite a few ATS girls gathered round her in the NAAFI each evening for extra tuition in geometry, equations and trigonometry.

'Why weren't we taught all this at school?' one of them complained as she grappled with her slide rule.

'I suppose the powers-that-be felt girls didn't need maths,' someone else replied. 'In my school they only taught us enough to tot up a few groceries or weigh out cooking ingredients.'

'And the powers-that-be are always men, of course,' Louise muttered grumpily. 'Not teaching women proper maths is probably a deliberate ruse to hold us back.'

As she spoke, she heard a noise behind her, and recognised it as one of Don Wellington's snarky chuckles. 'Judging from what that friend of yours said the other night, you need holding back,' he said. 'And not just in maths.'

Louise looked round sharply. 'Eavesdropping again?' she asked. And then regretted it. She saw the vengeful look in his eyes, and for a horrible moment she thought he was going to tell her new friends exactly what Jen had said.

Jen's accusations had upset her, but they had also hit home. She had behaved badly towards Aaref and Jack. Neither of them had deserved it. Aaref had always been kind and supportive. And Jack had been so nice, and so very much in love with her. The only good thing about it was that he had never found out about her infidelity with the smooth-talking Charlie Hawkridge.

'I may have made the odd mistake in the past,' she said. 'But at least I'm not frightened of a girl with a pen.'

She thought Don Wellington would be annoyed, but actually he laughed. 'Bloody hell,' he said. 'Damn right I was frightened. I thought she was going to stab it into my eye.'

He saw the startled expressions of the other girls at the table. 'We're talking about that singer in the ENSA show,' he said. 'Jennifer Carter. She was all sweetness and light on stage, but afterwards she turned into a wildcat. She had a right go at Rutherford here, and then she turned on me. There I was leaning against the wall in a bit of shadow, having a quiet smoke, and she more or less accused me of acting like the Gestapo.' He glanced back at Louise. 'What was all that about? What can she possibly know about the Gestapo?'

'Quite a lot, probably,' Louise said. 'Her ship was torpedoed on the way to North Africa last year and she ended up in a POW camp in Italy run by the Nazis.' She shrugged. 'She may have come up against the Gestapo there for all I know. But in the end she and another girl managed to escape, and somehow she made her way back to England.'

She stopped, realising that the others were all gazing at her in astonished silence. Susan was staring at her open-mouthed. 'Goodness,' she whispered. 'You never told me that.'

Even Don Wellington looked impressed. 'Good God. No wonder she's a bit oversensitive.'

'Blimey,' one of the other girls said. 'And we thought we were having a tough time here.'

That made everyone laugh, but as Don Wellington wandered off and the others turned their attention back to their logarithm tables, Louise was conscious of feeling a grudging respect for Jen. Instead of bragging about her experiences in Italy, she had been unusually reticent. And as a result, Louise hadn't taken much notice. But it couldn't have been fun for her and Molly in Italy. And maybe, as Don Wellington had said, it explained why Jen had been so bad-tempered since she got back.

Louise wondered if Molly had reacted in the same way. But she was unlikely to find out, because Molly disliked her even more than Jen did. Molly had been keen on Aaref at one time, and Louise had stolen him off her.

She grimaced to herself. And now, of course, Elsa had stolen him from them both.

That morning she had received a hand-written note from Aaref inviting her to their wedding party on Sunday 21 May. And almost as though fate wanted to rub salt into the wound, in the afternoon post another wedding invitation had arrived, this one printed in swirly embossed writing on a smart little card with a gold border.

Mrs Joyce Carter requests your presence at the marriage of her daughter
Angela to Gino Moretti
at St Aldate's Church, Clapham Common, on 27 May 1944
RSVP

'Coo, how posh,' Susan exclaimed when Louise showed it to her after the maths session.

Louise couldn't help laughing. 'You wouldn't say that if you knew Angie Carter,' she said. 'And the fat little Italian she's marrying is even worse.'

But Susan had a dreamy look in her eye. 'You must admit it's very romantic,' she said. 'You lucky thing. Two weddings in a row.'

And neither of them mine, Louise thought dismally.

She didn't want to go to either of them. Especially not Aaref's. But it was generous of him and Elsa to invite her. As Jen had so kindly pointed out, she had probably caused Aaref considerable heartache in the past. And she hadn't been very nice to Elsa either.

'Of course you must go,' Susan said bracingly. 'All you have to do is pretend you're delighted for them and give them a nice wedding present.'

But finding nice wedding presents was easier said than done. Something for the bottom drawer was traditional, but there was nothing in the shops, let alone the NAAFI. Sheets, towels, tea services, saucepans and cutlery were all impossible to find. And in any case, the chances of either couple being able to set up their own home any time soon was most unlikely.

It seemed a much better idea to think of something they could enjoy now. Louise racked her brains, but the only thing she herself enjoyed at the moment was a mild sense of achievement when no one made a mistake on the gun drill, and Lieutenant Masterson gave one of his rare smiles and stood them down for five minutes' rest. How her world had changed.

And then she thought of theatre tickets. It would be fun for Elsa and Aaref to have a night out together. And even better, it would be an excuse to write to Henry.

Theatre tickets wouldn't be any good for Angie Carter, though. She would giggle at the wrong moment, and Gino would never understand the words. But then Louise remembered that Angie and Gino both had a sweet tooth. And the one thing you could get in the NAAFI was chocolate. As long as you had coupons.

She stuck a note on the NAAFI noticeboard offering to swap her cigarette coupons and her daily ration of dessert for other people's sweet coupons. By the end of that week she had given up two portions of spotted dick, a Bakewell tart and a jam roly-poly in exchange for five bars of Cadbury's Ration Chocolate. And there was still another week to go.

Her letter to Henry, written with Susan's assistance, took almost as long to compose. It combined an innocent request for information about good West End shows with a subtle hint that it would be rather nice to meet up to discuss it.

And when she received a letter in an unknown hand two days later, she opened it eagerly.

But it wasn't from Henry, it was from Lord Freddy.

'Oh my goodness,' she said. And burst out laughing.

'What is it?' Susan asked, leaning down from her bunk. 'What's happened?'

'It's a letter from Lord Freddy.'

'Blimey,' Susan said, leaning down even further. Despite having no pretensions to romance herself, she was highly enthusiastic about Louise's chances.

With a giggle, Louise read out the letter.

Dear Louise,

Please forgive me for the delay in writing to you, but it has taken me some time to winkle your current whereabouts out of Henry Keller. I've been wanting to tell you how much I enjoyed meeting you at Windsor. My only regret, apart of course from the shocking performance of my horse, which you will be glad to know has since been shot (joke!), is that I wasn't able to spend more time with you. Because I can sincerely say that you are exactly the sort of beautiful, dutiful, patriotic girl I have been waiting for all my life.

I'm quite sure that none of these things will influence you one way or the other, because you probably think I am a complete idiot, and ugly to boot, but I'd like you to know that

I have a very pleasant house in Berkshire and a flat in Belgravia, I am a serving officer in the navy (commander), currently working in the Admiralty, and I am also, for my sins, a peer of the realm, albeit holding the rather meagre title of baron.

If, in the unlikely event that any of this is remotely of interest to you, I would be delighted to offer you my hand in marriage. Obviously it would be nice to get to know each other a little better first, but I can assure you that my mind is made up and there is very little you could do (apart from perhaps murdering me) that would sway me from my intention of making you my wife.

With love and hope,

Frederick Manson

By the time she got to the end, Susan was laughing so much Louise thought she might fall off her bunk.

'He's completely bonkers,' Louise said.

'No, I don't think so,' Susan objected. 'He sounds sweet. Quick wedding are all the rage after all. Winston Churchill's son, Randolph, proposed to that Pamela Digby after one blind date. And they were married a month later.'

'At least they had had one date!' Louise said. 'I don't know this Freddy at all.'

'You do. He gave you champagne and showed you how to use the binoculars.'

'But I wasn't looking at him, I was looking at Henry!'

'I know,' Susan agreed. 'But if Henry doesn't come up to scratch, then maybe Lord Freddy is the one. You said you wanted a wealthy husband. And you'd make a lovely lady, with your posh voice and all.' She gave a sudden gurgle of laughter as she settled herself back on her bunk. 'I hope you'll ask me to the wedding!'

'Of course I will,' Louise said. 'You can be my maid of honour.'

But she couldn't take it seriously. A few months ago she would have been absolutely thrilled by the prospect of a wealthy, titled admirer, but now she just thought it was funny. What had changed? she wondered. Was it the army? Or was it just that she wasn't at home? Maybe she would feel more inclined to think kindly of Lord Freddy if she had to spend her evenings with her parents instead of giggling about slide rules and logarithm tables with Susan and the other mathematically challenged ATS girls in the NAAFI.

'So how are you going to respond?' Susan asked, leaning down again over the edge of the bunk. 'You could meet up with him when you're back in London at the end of the course?'

'Goodness, I don't know,' Louise said. 'I don't even know if I want to go back to London.' She folded the letter and slid it back into the envelope. 'I'm thinking of asking if I can go on to live firing camp with the rest of you. After suffering all this beastly training, it would be nice to know if we can actually hit anything.'

And now finally Susan did fall off her bunk. 'Are you telling me you'd prefer to go to firing camp than back to your comfy life in London?' she said incredulously as she picked herself up off the floor. 'I think it's you that's gone mad, not Lord Freddy!'

'Have you seen this?' Katy asked Sean. She was sitting at one of the bar tables reading a newspaper someone had left behind. 'It says here that in March this year some poor American flight sergeant fell three and a half miles from a burning bomber on the way back from a raid over Berlin, landed in a snowdrift somewhere in Germany and survived. And after all that, the poor fellow's now a prisoner of war.'

Sean didn't respond, and she looked up at him, surprised. Normally he was so chatty. And that was just the kind of military bad-luck story he enjoyed.

But he wasn't looking at her. Instead he seemed to be staring at something over her shoulder.

Had someone come in? Katy frowned and swung round on her chair. Had she been so engrossed in the story that she hadn't heard the door open? It seemed unlikely. She was normally so alert. Always hoping against hope that the next time someone came in it would be Ward.

And to her utter astonishment, this time it was.

He was standing there just inside the blackout curtain, with his kitbag over his shoulder. But he wasn't looking at her. He was looking at Sean.

Katy dropped the newspaper and put her hand to her chest. 'Oh Ward,' she said. And then louder, 'Oh Ward.'

She could hardly believe it. She wanted to stand up, but her legs suddenly felt numb.

And now he was looking at her. With a slightly questioning smile on his face. And then somehow she was in his arms, kissing him, hugging him and almost weeping with relief at seeing him safe and sound.

She heard Sean clear his throat behind her. He was still standing slightly awkwardly behind the bar.

'Oh Ward,' Katy said, pulling back. 'I must introduce you to Sean Byrne.'

Ward stepped over to the bar and extended his hand. 'Hi,' he said. 'I'm sure glad to meet you at last. Especially as I hear you've been having an affair with my wife.'

Chapter Twenty Three

Katy had never seen Sean so discomfited. He looked as if he thought Ward was going to leap over the counter and break his neck.

'No, to be sure ... There's been nothing like that,' he stammered. 'Honest to God, Mr Frazer, I swear ...'

But Ward was already laughing. 'I know,' he said. He reached over the counter, offering Sean his hand. 'I could tell right away from Katy's expression.'

'Who told you that?' Katy asked as they shook hands.

Ward leaned over the pram and smiled at Caroline, who obligingly smiled back. 'Your mother wrote me,' he said. 'Her letter was waiting at the SOE.'

'I'll kill her,' Katy said.

'No, I don't think you should do that.' He lifted Caroline up on his shoulder and blew gentle puffs of air into her neck, which made her gurgle with delight. 'She seemed very upset about it.'

But Katy wasn't mollified. 'If I had been having an affair with Sean, it would have been her fault for leaving me in the lurch,' she said.

Ward put Caroline back in her pram and drew Katy into his arms. 'No,' he said. 'It would have been my fault for leaving my beautiful wife all on her own.'

As she rested her face against his chest, Katy wished she could stay in his embrace forever, but at that point the yard door flew open, and Lucky came hurtling up the passage. He must have heard Ward's voice, because without pausing to take stock, he launched himself right at him. It was as much as Ward could do to keep his balance. Desperate to lick his face, Lucky started jumping up and down in front of him as though his legs were on springs. It took Ward a minute to calm him, and it was only then that he noticed Malcolm standing wide-eyed by the bar.

'Hey, is that my son?' he asked. And fending Lucky off once again, he crouched down in front of Malcolm. Katy's heart twisted. The two of them seemed so alike, with their dark hair and grey eyes. Malcolm was looking at his father in wonderment, which increased when Ward put his hand in his pocket and drew out something concealed in his fist. 'I've got a present for you.'

'What is it?' Malcolm squeaked excitedly. 'I want to see.'

Ward turned his hand over and let Malcolm prise open his fingers. Lying on his palm was the largest, most colourful marble Katy had ever seen. She felt tears sting her eyes. He couldn't have chosen a better present if he had tried.

Malcolm lifted it up in awe. 'It's bigger than all of George's,' he said. Then, completely ignoring his long-absent father, he swung round eagerly to address Sean. 'Can we go and show it to him?'

Katy looked at Ward in dismay. These homecomings were never easy. It was impossible to predict how Malcolm would react. There was so much she wanted to say, to explain, but it was awkward with Sean standing there watching.

Sean obviously thought so too. 'I think that's a good idea,' he said to Malcolm. 'And why don't we take Lucky and Caroline too? I expect your parents would like a little bit of peace and quiet together after all this time apart.' He gave Katy a mischievous, meaningful wink. 'But we'll be back for opening time.'

Ward watched in silence as Sean flicked the brake off the pram with practised ease, swung George up onto his shoulders, whistled Lucky to heel and headed for the door.

As soon as they had gone, Katy glanced uneasily at him. She knew he had seen that suggestive wink. 'He's a bit of a rogue,' she said. 'But he's been a godsend. I couldn't have managed without him.'

Ward turned slowly and studied her face. 'Even so,' he said, 'you look tired. You look like you need a vacation.'

If only, she thought, but she smiled at the Canadianism; nobody called holidays vacations in England. 'Of course I'm tired,' she said. 'Everyone in London is tired.'

She realised he looked tired too. There were shadows under his eyes, and signs of strain around his mouth. Goodness only knew what he had been up to.

She knew he would never tell her, and in any case he was reaching out now to take her hands.

'Why don't we all go away for a couple of days?' he said. He grinned. 'Just you, me and the kids, I mean. Not Sean Byrne.'

Katy stared up into his handsome face. Had he gone mad?

'But we can't,' she said, aghast. 'What about the pub? We can't just ...'

He pulled her to him and tipped her face up with a finger. Then he lowered his lips to hers. 'Sure we can,' he whispered against her mouth. 'I'll think of a way. But not right now. Because right now I want to kiss you. Then I want to hold you so tight, I may never let you go. My God, Katy. When I read that damn letter from your mother, I felt as though someone had ripped

261

out my heart.'

Just like the ATS basic training course at Bracknell, the Arborfield anti-
aircraft defence course ended with a series of assessment exercises. But this
time, as well as the candidates having to prove their competence on
command post drill and fire discipline, each gun team had to undertake an
assault course in full combat uniform. Anyone failing to get round would fail
the course and would either be back-squadded, having to do the entire course
again, or possibly even dispatched to retrain for a less demanding, less
prestigious trade.

Full combat uniform meant not only battledress – jacket and trousers –
socks, gaiters and boots, but also a steel helmet, a camouflaged gas cape,
which was carried rolled up into an enormous sausage-shaped bundle at the
back of the neck, and a respirator fastened across the chest.

'Oh no,' Susan whispered, and Louise knew how she felt. Susan might be
a whizz at maths, but she was even more hopeless at sport than Louise. The
assault course had caused them both problems before; dressed like that, it
was going to be nigh on impossible to complete it in the allocated time.

Buller and her two cronies, on the other hand, were almost rubbing their
hands in glee. They loved the roughy-toughy stuff and couldn't wait to show
off their physical prowess.

There were twelve of them in their gun team: the five ATS girls, and seven
men, including Don Wellington.

By the time Susan and Louise had teetered along the first obstacle, a
balance beam, the rest of the team were already forging ahead. The assault
course was laid out in a figure of eight, with some obstacles having to be
completed twice. Having just managed to struggle across the overhead
ladder, Louise was spread-eagled halfway up the cargo net when Buller and a
couple of the young gunners came powering up behind her for their second
pass.

Struggling to get out of their way, Louise heard a strangled scream behind
her and glanced over her shoulder just in time to see Voles fall off the
overhead ladder into the mud below.

She grabbed Buller's arm as she came up alongside her on the net. 'Hey,'
she said. 'Wait a minute. I think you should go back and give Voles a hand.'

But Buller was determined to keep her lead. 'She'll be all right,' she panted,
standing painfully on Louise's hand in her effort to scramble past her. 'I
haven't got time to stop; I'm in line to win the physical excellence trophy. It
would be the first time an ATS has ever won it.'

'You can be in line to win the Victoria Cross for all I care,' Louise
muttered grimly. 'But if Voles doesn't get round the course, she'll be back-

squadded.'

But Buller was already climbing down the other side of the net. 'Get out of the way, Rutherford,' she hissed. 'You're causing a traffic jam.'

Snatching her hand away before Buller's boot came down on it for a second time, Louise seized the elbow of one of the young soldiers as he started to climb past her. 'Listen,' she gasped. 'Surely this is meant to be a team effort? There's no point any of us winning if we leave someone behind.'

The boy hesitated, then nodded. Louise didn't know him well, but he was a nice lad, and obligingly he dropped back to the ground and ran back to steady Voles as she tried once again to struggle across the slippery overhead ladder.

After that, he stayed with them, helping them both over the scaling wall and waiting to grab their hands as they jumped over the open ditches. And he wasn't the only one. By the time they reached the end of the second loop, two of the other gunners were helping them too, and the rest of the team, having already finished, were urging them on from the sidelines. Even Don Wellington was there, laughing as Louise, impaled on top of the wall, leaned back over to pull Susan up before falling down the other side herself.

'Come on, Rutherford,' he shouted. 'Show a leg. Don't forget you're doing it for King and country.'

'I'll show you more than a leg if you aren't careful,' Louise muttered, wiping mud off her face.

'O-ho,' Don Wellington chortled. 'Now you're talking.'

As Louise limped across the finishing line and collapsed to her knees, half on top of Voles, everyone started clapping.

'Get up, both of you,' Buller hissed. 'Lieutenant Masterson is coming over.'

'I can't,' Louise wailed. 'I don't think I'll ever be able to stand up again.'

Indeed, much to everyone's amusement, as she tried to struggle to her feet, the top-heavy weight of her gas cape and respirator caused her to topple over backwards again.

'You'll get us all into trouble if you don't watch out,' Buller said.

'Oh shut up, Buller,' Louise said. 'If there was any justice in the world, it's you who'd be getting into trouble for not stopping to help us.'

'You aren't worth helping,' Buller snapped. 'You and Voles seem determined to bring the ATS into disrepute.'

To Louise's irritation, Buller did ultimately win the prize for physical excellence. But as he announced the award, Lieutenant Masterson also made a point of congratulating the teams who had managed to get all their members across the line.

'Individual competence is important,' he said. 'But nobody can fire a field gun on their own. As I said at the beginning, it's necessary to work together as a team. A team is only as strong as its weakest member.'

'Quite right,' Don Wellington murmured. 'And our weakest member is weaker than most. I can't think why she wasn't booted out a long time ago. Hey, Voles,' he yelled across, 'ever thought of choosing a different career?'

'It's not her fault,' Louise snapped. 'We can't all be good at everything.'

'Yeah, but Voles is a complete disaster. She isn't good at anything.'

'She is,' Louise said indignantly. 'She's brilliant at maths.'

Don Wellington gave a sneering laugh. 'What are you? Her fan club?'

'No,' Louise said. 'I'm her friend.'

Later that day, a list was put up on the noticeboard of where everyone would be sent when the course ended the following day. Although the rest of her gun team, including Don Wellington, were all down as going straight on to live firing camp, Louise's name wasn't on the list at all. When she went to the admin office to ask why, Lieutenant Masterson told her that she had been summoned back to London.

'It seems you are needed in your former job,' he said. He smiled briefly. 'I will be sorry to lose you, Rutherford. I've enjoyed working with you. And in case I don't see you again, I'll wish you the very best of luck.'

'Thank you, sir,' Louise said gruffly. She liked Lieutenant Masterson. He had been strict but fair in his dealings with her. But she didn't want to go back to London. Back to the dull, repetitive grind at the factory. Even the thought of seeing Colonel Westwood again wasn't enough to assuage her sense of disappointment. After all the effort she had put into the gunnery course, it seemed like an anticlimax.

What made it all the more galling was that everyone assumed that she hadn't made the grade.

'Hard luck, Rutherford,' Buller crowed in the NAAFI later. 'But then it was obvious you were never quite up to it.'

Louise was so tempted to tell her about Colonel Westwood's top-secret proximity fuse. So tempted to tell her that she had more important things to do than manning an ack-ack gun. But she had given her word to keep every aspect of his project secret, and so with some difficulty she held her tongue, and received a grin from Don Wellington for her pains.

'Well done,' he said. 'I was all set to throttle you if you started spilling the beans.' He gave one of his irritating smirks. 'Not that you are up to it, of course, which is presumably why I'm going on and you're going back.'

Louise wished she could think of a good retort, but failed. Buller and Wellington's low opinion of her was more than made up for by Voles, however, who was distraught at the thought of their imminent separation.

'I can't believe you aren't coming with us,' she wailed. 'How am I going to cope? I would never have got through all this without you.'

'And I wouldn't have got through it without you,' Louise said. And she meant it. Voles had been a staunch ally from the first. Louise knew she would miss her. And some of the other girls too. Over the last few weeks they had built a grim kind of camaraderie, and it was galling to think of them going on to pastures new without her.

'Of course you would,' Voles said stoutly. 'Whatever anyone else says, I've always thought you were POM.'

It took Louise a second to recall what POM was, then she remembered it was the acronym for potential officer material, and laughed. 'Good God,' she said. 'I'm about as un-POM as you can get. Surely you're mixing me up with Buller?'

Susan shook her head. 'No, Buller's far too bossy and full of herself. It's made everyone hate her. But you're nice, and they like you because even though you're clever and posh, you're happy to have a laugh.'

Louise felt touched. And when the following evening she helped Voles and the others lift their kitbags onto the trucks that were to take them off to a live firing camp somewhere in South Wales, she felt quite emotional. She had no idea when she would see any of them again.

Then the final goodbyes were over, and the trucks were pulling away, leaving Louise alone at the guardroom, waiting for her transport to the station.

At first, spurred on by Mrs Rutherford's patriotic frugality, Joyce had tried to curb the excesses of Angie's wedding plans. But her efforts were in vain. Angie had set her heart on a white wedding with all the trimmings – including pretty dresses for her two bridesmaids, Jen and Bella James, and a fancy reception for her multitude of guests – and that was that.

Even with the money Angie had won at Windsor, Joyce couldn't imagine how she was going to manage it. Money or no money, there was no wedding paraphernalia in the shops, and even if there was, it would take huge amounts of coupons to lay hands on it.

But Joyce hadn't taken into account Angie's ingenuity. Somehow she had got wind of a wedding dress sent over from America for the use of war brides. Unfortunately, when it actually arrived, it was far too small for her, but nothing daunted, she asked Bella's mother to sew in an extra panel cut out of an old sheet.

'Mrs James makes all her own clothes,' Angie explained when Joyce expressed consternation at her choice of seamstress. 'And she always looks so glamorous herself, I thought she'd be just the person to do it for me.'

But Joyce disapproved of Gillian James, whose disgraceful nocturnal activities gave the street a bad name. It was bad enough that Angie had asked Bella to be a bridesmaid. 'For goodness' sake, Angie,' she protested. 'You can't ask a woman like that to—'

Angie brushed aside her objections. 'She's awfully nice when you get to know her,' she said. In any case, it was too late. The alterations were already under way.

Angie had also spotted two pink satin nightgowns with puff sleeves in Arding and Hobbs that with some embellishment she felt would be perfect for the bridesmaids. Having persuaded various friends to lend her enough clothing coupons to buy the two nightdresses, she then tracked down ten yards of butter muslin and some off-ration satin ribbon, which she attempted to dye pink. The special Fairy colouring agent she used had looked highly effective in the newspaper advertisement, but was unfortunately not at all easy to use, and not only did she end up ruining two of Joyce's precious saucepans, she also managed to leave a great red stain on the kitchen lino, as though someone had been stabbed to death on the floor.

But Gillian James once again worked some needlework magic, and Angie, at least, was delighted with the result.

She was also delighted to learn from *Woman's Weekly* that catering establishments were allowed additional rations for weddings. Joyce duly filled out the forms and eventually received coupons for a small extra quota of dried egg, margarine and cheese. Together she and Angie made a fruit cake using prunes instead of sultanas, and semolina instead of flour. They couldn't ice it, of course, because icing sugar was currently banned for use on cakes. Mrs Rutherford suggested using decorated white paper instead, but Angie wasn't going to tolerate anything as prosaic as that.

She persuaded Gino's colleagues in the kitchens at the American barracks to donate half a pound of caster sugar and a recipe for what they called cake frosting. It wouldn't be the kind of hard, smooth wedding cake icing people were used to, but it would at least be both edible and pretty, especially as, to Angie's delight, Albert had produced a small plastic model of a bride and groom to sit on top.

'Wherever did you find that?' Joyce asked him.

'I saw it in Arding and Hobbs when I was looking for a wedding gift,' he said.

Joyce frowned. 'I hope you aren't intending to get her anything too expensive?'

'I was trying to find her some saucepans,' he said. 'I thought you might feel that would be a useful present, in the circumstances. Unfortunately, however, there were none to be had.'

266

Joyce looked at him with affection. He really was a most thoughtful man.

And Leszek Zemniak was a nice boy too. Joyce had felt quite touched when he'd come in to say goodbye the previous day, before leaving for his new British regiment.

'Thank you so much, Mrs Carter,' he had said. 'I will forever be grateful to you, and to your daughter. If I have the honour to fight in Europe, I will be fighting not only for the liberation of my own people, but also for you.'

Unexpected tears had come to Joyce's eyes. 'You look after yourself,' she said gruffly. She glanced through the hatch into the kitchen to make sure Celia Rutherford wasn't looking, and thrust a couple of scones into his hand. 'Here, take these,' she said. 'In case you get peckish on the train.'

Unfortunately Celia had emerged from the kitchen just as he was going out of the door. 'Who was that?' she asked in her brisk way. 'He sounded foreign. I hope he wasn't one of those deserters I've read about in the paper?'

'Oh no,' Joyce said quickly. 'Not at all. That was Mr Lorenz's cousin. He's just passing through London on his way to a new unit.'

Celia gave her a dry look. 'Then Mr Lorenz should have brought him in for a decent meal while he was here,' she said. 'The poor boy was all skin and bone.'

Louise was delighted to find Ward Frazer back at the pub when she called in on her first evening back in London. It had just been announced on the six o'clock news on the wireless that Monte Cassino had finally been captured after six months of fighting. Now, even though there was an outcry that the historic monastery had been utterly destroyed by shelling and bombing, the way was finally clear for the Allies to battle on to Rome.

Ward was standing behind the bar talking to Elsa. But when he caught sight of Louise, he came round at once to embrace her.

'Hey, Louise,' he said. 'It's good to see you. I hear that you're an expert gunner these days. I guess they could have done with you at Monte Cassino.'

Louise laughed. It was good to see him too. She had no idea what he got up to on his long absences from London, but she knew it was dangerous and she knew that Katy would be relieved to have him back in one piece.

And Katy was indeed looking pleased, although it seemed his return had brought her a new anxiety. 'He wants to take me away,' she confided to Louise. 'And he's persuaded Elsa and Aaref to move in here after their wedding to look after the place. As a kind of busman's honeymoon. But I'm nervous something awful will happen while I'm not here.'

'I'm sure everything will be fine,' Louise said. 'You deserve a break. And I'm back in London now, so I can always keep an eye on things …' Seeing Katy's eyes flicker, she stopped abruptly, remembering what had happened last time she had tried to help out during Katy's absence.

'Well, I don't think—' Katy began awkwardly.

Louise quickly cut in. 'I know what you're going to say,' she said. 'And I know I was bossy and stupid at Christmas and everyone hated me. But I've changed.' She made a rueful face. 'Or maybe the army has changed me. Anyway, I promise not to upset anyone this time.'

Katy still looked uneasy. 'Thank you,' she said. 'That's very kind. But I honestly think they'd rather be on their own. And Sean will be around to help.'

'Oh well,' Louise said, trying not to feel hurt all over again. 'The offer's there if you need me.'

And somewhat to her relief, before Katy could rub her nose in it any more, Angie came rushing over to regale her with all the plans for her wedding.

Angie was clearly pulling out all the stops, but Aaref and Elsa's wedding, which took place on Louise's first Sunday back in London, was a very discreet affair. And in the end, Louise was glad that she wasn't marrying Aaref after all, because it was all very odd and foreign.

The ceremony itself was reserved for the two families and Mrs D'Arcy Billière, the rather eccentric woman who had taken Aaref and his brothers in at the beginning of the war. Afterwards they came back to the pub, where the rest of the twenty or so guests were gathered.

Somewhat to Louise's relief, Jen wasn't there. She was away in Norfolk on a tour of RAF bases. Lucky the dog was also absent. Katy had tied him up in the back yard in fear of him helping himself to the various plates of traditional Jewish wedding food that Elsa and her mother had prepared for the occasion.

The first item was a plaited loaf of bread called a challah, which was solemnly blessed by Elsa's father, and then cut up and offered round by the happy couple so that everyone present could share in their joy.

'This is a really nice idea,' Angie enthused, tucking in eagerly. She turned to her mother, who was eyeing it with professional interest. 'Could you make Gino and me a loaf to hand round next weekend, Mum?'

'No,' Joyce said. 'For one thing you aren't Jewish, and for another I've used every last spare grain of flour to make your blasted cake.'

Once everyone had eaten, one of Aaref's friends started playing the piano, and Elsa and Aaref were lifted up on chairs and paraded precariously round the bar holding hands while everyone else danced and clapped around them.

'I hope young Angie won't want to be doing that next weekend,' Sean remarked to Louise. 'If she does, I reckon half the guests will end up in hospital with broken backs.'

Louise had to smile. He was right. Carrying sylph-like Elsa round the room was one thing; heaving buxom Angie up into the air would be quite another.

'I think it must be all the pasta Gino cooks for her these days,' Sean said. Louise giggled, and he glanced at her with a speculative smile. 'You know, I missed you while you were away. What do you say we carry on where we left off?'

'Oh, I don't think so,' Louise said. 'It sounds to me as though you're already doing quite enough carrying-on with Mrs James.'

It was the first time she had ever seen Sean look embarrassed. 'How did you know about that?'

'Jen told me,' Louise said.

He swore softly under his breath. 'And how did she find out?'

'I don't know,' Louise said. She took a sip of her drink. 'But she didn't seem very pleased about it. I hope you weren't expecting to win her back, because as they say in the army, I think you might have shot yourself in the foot.'

The wedding party ended with Elsa's father carefully mixing two glasses of wine together as a cup of blessing, and inviting the newlyweds to drink from it. As most of the ceremonial was in Hebrew, nobody had much idea of what was going on. But it was clearly very sincere and traditional and actually rather touching. Louise noticed Ward discreetly take Katy's hand as the final blessing was said, and felt a stab of envy. She wondered if she would ever find someone who wanted to hold hands with her at someone else's wedding. Or indeed at her own.

The following morning, Elsa thanked her for the theatre tickets. Henry had responded promptly to her letter with a couple of recommendations, and although they hadn't managed to meet up yet, she had plumped for *Meet Me Victoria* with the celebrated Lupino Lane and Dorothy Ward.

'It is so kind,' Elsa said. 'I have never been to the theatre in London. In Paris my family used to go quite often and I loved it so much.'

'It's a pleasure,' Louise said awkwardly 'I just wanted to give you and Aaref a fun night out.'

As she slid the tickets into her purse for safe keeping, a slight flush crept up Elsa's face. 'Katy tell me that you offered to help with us in the pub while she is away,' she said shyly. 'I would like this very much. It would be much easier for me when it becomes busy in the evening.'

Ward and Katy's holiday didn't get off to a very good start. Ward had booked a taxi to take them all to Paddington station, and there was a slight altercation with the taxi driver about Lucky's presence in the party. Eventually that was sorted out, but the clamour and bustle of the station terrified baby Caroline and made her cry. Malcolm, on the other hand, was wild with excitement. But once they were installed on the Taunton train, everyone settled down.

The journey took three hours, and they eventually alighted at a small station a couple of stops on from Bristol. Somehow Ward had managed to find rooms on a farm in the village where his aunts and Katy's mother lived, and to Malcolm's intense joy, the farmer was waiting at the station with a horse and cart. From then on the holiday was everything Katy had hoped for.

The May weather was perfect. The sun was shining. The beds were comfortable. The food was fresh and plentiful. And the farmer was friendly as could be. Malcolm was allowed to pet the animals and help with the milking. Lucky thoroughly enjoyed himself chasing rabbits in the fields. And when Ward's aunts and Katy's mother came to call, the farmer's wife served them with glasses of fresh milk and home-made biscuits as they sat in deckchairs in the shade of a tree.

Katy couldn't believe how wonderful it was not to have to wake up every morning with a list of things that needed doing in the pub. Instead she woke in Ward's arms, knowing that another delightful day stretched lazily ahead of her. Ward seemed happy too. Happy to be spending precious time with his little family.

And the time was precious, because he had warned her that he would probably be leaving again soon. He hadn't said where he was going. But it wasn't hard to guess that this time it would be something to do with the forthcoming invasion. Katy tried hard not to think about it. Tried not to think of him parachuting in behind enemy lines. Or creeping up a heavily mined beach from a submarine. She didn't want to spoil what little time they had by worrying about a perilous future.

In the daytime, she could sometimes forget. But at night, when she felt his strong, hard body against hers, the caress of his hand, the touch of his lips, she clung to him, trying to store up the wonderful feel of him, the scent of him, even the taste of him, agonised by the thought that this could so easily be the last time they would ever be together.

'It's good to have you back,' Colonel Westwood said. They were in Mr Gregg's office, Louise perched on an upright chair, the colonel leaning back in Larry Gregg's more comfortable chair on the other side of the desk. He was in uniform and looked just as gorgeous as she remembered.

'It's nice to be back,' Louise said. And at that moment, looking across the desk into his intense dark eyes, it really was.

'Good,' he said. The brief formalities over, he leaned forward and rested his forearms on the desk. 'But now we need to get to work. It's taken longer than I'd hoped, but I believe we finally have some usable fuses. So now I want you to start thinking how we can speed up the production process. Then next week I'll get you to come down to Wiltshire to watch the trials. Is that OK with you?'

It was more than OK. Louise felt a shiver of excitement run up her spine. Who cared about missing firing camp if the reward was a day out in Wiltshire with Colonel Westwood?

'Yes, of course,' she said. Sensing the interview was over, she stood up. It seemed odd not to have to salute, but as she wasn't in uniform, it would have looked idiotic.

He stood up too and walked over to open the door for her. 'Well done for completing the gunnery training,' he said. 'I know it didn't come easy. But in the end you got quite a good report.' His lips curved into one of his rare smiles. 'I gather you even managed to complete the assault course.'

She certainly wouldn't have been able to complete an assault course at that moment. Her knees felt far too weak. It was as much as she could do to stagger back past the American guards to the secure screened-off area where the new fuses were being made.

'I think I'm in love,' she whispered to Doris as she came up behind her.

Doris gave a snort of mirth. 'Really? I reckon that will wear off once you realise just how fiddly and frustrating these little bastards are to get right.' She nodded to the small, conical piece of metal in her hand. 'I bet you a pound to a penny that you'll soon wish you were back in the army.'

Chapter Twenty Four

The following Saturday was Angie and Gino's wedding, and in order to get Jen back to London in time, the Violets had set off after their Friday-evening show at an RAF base near Norwich. But now it seemed as though every military unit in the whole of East Anglia was on the move as well; at some junctions they had to wait nearly an hour as long lines of armoured vehicles trundled past. What was worse was that the convoys all seemed to be heading south, the same direction as them.

'I suppose they're moving under cover of darkness so the Jerry planes can't see where they're going,' Roger Violet remarked as the ENSA van crawled along in the wake of ten canvas-sided troop carriers.

Betty looked up from her knitting. 'I wonder where they *are* going,' she said.

'I reckon they're headed for the south coast,' Roger said. 'And we all know what that means.'

'But I thought the invasion was going to kick off from Essex,' Adele said.

Philip shot a sharp look over his shoulder. 'Maybe that's what the War Office wants the Germans to think too,' he said. 'So don't you tell anyone what we've seen tonight. Walls have ears, you know.'

Jen groaned. If Roger was right, they were going to get back to London much later than she had hoped. And she was dying to get home. She hadn't enjoyed the last week at all. The RAF guys had been appreciative enough, but the morbid silence that fell whenever a squadron of planes returned from a bombing mission over Germany gave her the creeps. Everything stopped while camp personnel gathered at the windows to count them in. If there were planes missing, which there invariably were, it threw a dampener on the whole evening. The troupe often found themselves having to adjust the running order of the show, tactfully holding the comedy numbers back until the second half, or in some cases cutting them out altogether.

They finally shook off the convoys on the outskirts of London, but even when they had reached Leytonstone, where Veronica and Roger lived, Jen still had a long haul back to Clapham on the tube. And when she eventually got back to Lavender Road, she discovered she was going to have to sleep in the pub, because not only had all three of her younger brothers come home, but Angie had failed to tell anyone that she had invited her former evacuee hosts Mr and Mrs Baxter to the wedding.

'Blasted girl,' Joyce muttered to Jen. 'It never occurred to her that the poor souls would need somewhere to sleep having traipsed all the way up from Devon. I've had to give them your room. Angie will have to come in with me.'

As someone had pointed out that it was bad luck for the groom to sleep under the same roof the night before the wedding, Gino and his best man, young Paul, were also sleeping in the pub, but Katy had put them in the cellar.

Sean, it transpired, had gallantly offered to spend the night with Gillian James to free up the space.

'Has he indeed?' Jen said sourly.

'There wouldn't have been enough room for the boys otherwise,' Katy said. 'I hope you don't mind.'

'No,' Jen said. 'I don't mind.' But she did. She felt that it reflected badly on her somehow that her former boyfriend would take up so brazenly with the local prostitute.

And to make things even worse, the next morning she discovered that she had to visit Gillian James herself in order for the self-styled seamstress to make adjustments to the hideous nightgown Jen was expected to wear as a bridesmaid's dress.

Jen's stony silence didn't go unnoticed.

'He's still in love with you, you know,' Gillian James murmured through a mouthful of pins as she turned up the hem. 'He's only come to me because he's upset about you.'

Jen glared down at her bowed head. 'He told you to say that, didn't he?'

Gillian stood up. 'No, he didn't actually,' she said. 'I just thought you ought to know.'

As Mrs James threaded a needle, Jen studied her covertly. She could quite see why Sean would have been attracted to her. There was no doubt that she was a very attractive woman. Close up you could see from the faint lines around her eyes and mouth that she was older than she seemed, but the signs of ageing were skilfully concealed with careful make-up.

She crouched down again and began to sew up the hem with quick, neat stitches. 'You shouldn't blame him for seeking a bit of pleasure,' she said in her soft, lilting voice. 'He's a man after all. And a nice man, I think, underneath all that blarney. It's not been easy for him being stuck in England all this time. Not when all he really wants is you.'

Jen gritted her teeth. She didn't want to listen to Gillian James making excuses for Sean. And when she ran into him in the street as she carried the dress back over to her mother's house a few minutes later, she eyed him beadily.

'Hi, Sean,' she said. 'You're looking very smart.'

He smiled self-consciously and ran his hands down the dark jacket he was wearing. 'Ward was kind enough to lend me this suit, though it's a bit loose on me, do you not think?'

'That's because he's a bigger man than you,' Jen said. She glanced back across the road to the house she had just left. 'I'm sure Mrs James knows her way round a man's suit. Why don't you ask her to give you a few nips and tucks?' She was gratified to see colour creep into his cheeks.

Pleased with her little jibe, Jen was smiling as she let herself into the house. But an hour later, just as they were preparing to leave for the church, Angie let slip that she had invited Henry to the wedding.

'What?' Jen turned on her angrily. 'Angie, how could you? Henry is my friend, not yours.'

'He's not just your friend,' Angie objected. 'He's my friend too.' She was standing in front of the mirror, squirming around, trying to see the full glory of her wedding dress. She glanced coyly at Jen and fiddled with her veil. 'Anyway, I thought it would be romantic if you got back together at my wedding.'

Jen had been about to step out of the front door, but instead she swung round dangerously. 'I hope to God you haven't said anything like that to Henry.'

Angie looked distressed. 'No, I haven't said anything. I just sent him an invitation, that's all.'

'But he's definitely coming?'

'Yes. He sent back a very formal note saying it would give him great pleasure to accept.' She looked at Jen pleadingly. 'But I'm sure he's only coming because he wants to see you.'

'Oh yes,' Jen said grimly. 'And I wonder what he'll think when he sees me wearing an ill-fitting, badly dyed nightdress?'

'For goodness' sake, Jen,' Joyce intervened quickly. 'It's her wedding day. She only meant it for the best. And you look lovely. You all do.'

Jen closed her eyes. She didn't feel lovely. Her bridesmaid's dress was even less flattering than her Violets dress, and the colour made her look pallid and tired. She glanced out of the door at Bella James, who was waiting eagerly by the front gate. She, of course, looked like an angel in hers.

Jen felt slightly sick as she stood beside the taxi Mr Lorenz had provided for them. If she was going to have to see Henry, she would have preferred it to be on her terms, not looking like an overdressed frump covered in pink ribbons.

As Joyce hurried off on foot to make sure Gino was ready and waiting at the church, Jen, Bella and Mr Lorenz tried to get Angie into the taxi without creasing her dress. Jen had been amused to find that Angie had asked Mr Lorenz to give her away. Instead of his usual dark suit, today he was today wearing traditional wedding attire of black tailcoat and grey trousers. As always, he looked very neat and dapper.

'Are you ready?' he asked Angie solicitously.

Behind her veil, Angie nodded nervously. 'I think so,' she said. 'But I do feel a bit of a flutter, so can we drive once round the common first?'

Oh for goodness' sake, Jen wanted to say. It's only Gino who's waiting at the church, not Clark Gable. But then she wondered how she would feel if she was in Angie's shoes and it was Henry waiting in the church. Absolutely petrified, most likely. It was bad enough knowing he was going to be there when she wasn't the bride.

As the taxi pulled away, she felt Angie touch her arm. 'I'm sorry about inviting Henry without asking you,' she whispered. 'I didn't realise it would upset you.'

Jen squeezed her hand reassuringly. 'I'm not upset,' she lied. 'It's just that we aren't on very good terms at the moment. But I'm sure it will be fine. We're both grown-ups, after all.'

As she got ready for Angie and Gino's wedding, Louise found herself wishing she had had the forethought to invite some suitable man to go with her as her partner.

Lord Freddy would probably have jumped at the chance, she thought wryly, but unfortunately she had already written back to him saying that although she was flattered by his interest in her, her military duties prevented her from meeting up at the moment.

She sighed. Being single at Aaref's wedding had been bad enough, but it seemed very infra dig to be going to Angie Carter's wedding in the company of her parents.

Her father felt it was infra dig to be going to the wedding at all. And he was even more reluctant to wear morning dress.

'I've never heard anything so absurd,' he had grumbled at breakfast. 'I don't suppose that fat Carter girl even knows what morning dress is.'

But unusually, her mother had put her foot down. 'Angie is a hard worker and a loyal member of my staff,' she said. 'The least we can do is attend her wedding properly clad.'

'That Italian fellow shouldn't be loafing about in London in the first place,' Greville responded irritably. 'He should have been packed off to Italy to fight.'

'Like Douglas, you mean?' Louise chipped in. 'Is he fighting yet? I was fully expecting to hear that it was his contribution that finally overcame

Monte Cassino.'

'Don't be sarcastic, Louise,' her father snapped. 'It's unbecoming. Douglas is longing to participate in the liberation of Italy. It's just unfortunate that he was injured in that dangerous incident earlier in the year. He's still not been declared fit to fight.'

Louise swallowed her last mouthful of toast. She had been waiting a long time for an opportunity to put her father right about Douglas. And here it was. 'There was no incident,' she said. 'At least not a dangerous one.' She saw her father's eyes widen, and shrugged negligently. 'Oh, I know he gave you a lot of guff about local insurgents and so on. But he made all that up. The reason he was injured was because he was taunting a camel and it got annoyed and kicked him in the face.'

'What nonsense,' her father said at once. He glanced at his wife, and then angrily back at Louise. 'Who on earth told you that?'

Louise put down her napkin. 'A very reliable source,' she said. 'And if you don't believe me, then I suggest you write to Douglas to ask him about it.' She lifted her shoulders dismissively. 'Anyway, I suppose he'll get to see some action eventually. Although if he's still malingering in Tunisia, presumably he won't be taking part in the liberation of France either.' She smiled sweetly as she stood up. 'Now if you'll excuse me, I'll go and get changed. As Mummy said, it's important to be properly clad.'

St Aldate's Church was only a minute's walk along the side of the common from her parents' house. It was where she and Jack had got married, and despite her mild sense of satisfaction at undermining her father's opinion of Douglas, Louise felt a terrible sense of loss as they approached. Her wedding day had been the happiest day of her life.

As she followed her parents under the lychgate, a taxi drew up behind her, and to her delight she saw Henry Keller paying off the driver. Like her father, he was wearing morning dress, and he looked very smart and handsome.

As she introduced him to her parents, she could tell that her father was impressed. Even he had heard of Henry Keller, and he shook hands readily.

'It's good to see you,' Henry said to Louise. 'I thought you might still be away learning about guns.'

Louise shook her head. 'No,' she said. 'I've been summoned back to the factory to oversee a new manufacturing project.'

'That's her story,' her father said. 'I think it's more likely that the authorities realised the error of their ways. Female gunners?' He gave a jovial man-to-man laugh. 'I've never heard such nonsense.'

Henry's brows rose in faint surprise. 'Really? All the ATS servicewomen I know are highly professional and well up to the task.'

A group of noisy GIs came up behind them then, and as her father moved hastily forward into the church, he missed his chance to respond.

'I didn't know you knew any other ATS,' Louise whispered to Henry as they followed her parents into the hushed darkness inside.

'I don't,' he said. 'You're actually the only one. But I'm quite sure you are up to the task.'

As Louise stifled a giggle, he gave her a quick complicit wink, and she remembered telling him how disparaging her father had been about her soldiering.

Despite Henry's mild snub, her father invited him to sit with them. Henry accepted civilly, and a moment later Louise found herself walking down the aisle with him side by side.

It felt rather agreeable. And she clearly wasn't the only one who was indulging in a bit of wishful thinking.

'He's very nice, darling,' her mother whispered to her as they slid into the pew. 'I can tell Daddy likes him.'

Her parents knelt in prayer, but after a token bow of his head, Henry seemed more interested in studying the congregation. Louise guessed he was trying to locate Jen.

'She won't be here yet,' she said drily. 'She's one of the bridesmaids.' She slanted him a coy smile. 'And according to Angie, she's wearing a nightgown.'

Aware that he had been caught out, Henry returned her smile with a wry grimace. 'I've waited a long time to see Jen in a nightgown,' he murmured.

'When's it going to start?' Malcolm asked loudly, and to Katy's dismay, a low rumble of amusement ran round the adjacent pews.

'Any minute now,' she said. And indeed, she now saw Mrs Carter hurrying down the aisle. At the front, Gino and Paul Carter glanced at each other nervously. A moment later, the vicar raised his hands to indicate that everyone should stand up.

'Old Henry seems very thick with the Rutherfords,' Ward observed quietly, watching Mrs Rutherford leaning round Louise to offer Henry a hymn book a few rows in front of them. 'I knew things weren't going too well between him and Jen, but you didn't tell me Louise had stepped into the breach.'

'I didn't know,' Katy said. 'And I'm not sure Jen does either.'

'I've got nothing against Louise,' Ward said. 'But I was kind of hoping Henry and Jen would make a go of it. Maybe I should have a quiet word with him.'

Katy looked at him in alarm. 'No, you mustn't say anything,' she said. 'If Jen found out you'd interfered, she'd be furious. And it would be me that

277

would suffer, because the chances are you wouldn't be around to take the blame.'

Even as she spoke the warning words, she saw his grey eyes flicker away from hers, and knew at once there was something wrong. 'What is it?' she whispered urgently as the organist struck up the wedding march. 'What's the matter?'

After a moment's hesitation, Ward leaned in towards her. 'I wasn't going to tell you until later,' he said. 'But my orders have come through. I'm going to have to leave tomorrow.'

Katy felt her blood run cold, then hot. 'And you are telling me now, here, in church, because you know I can't make a fuss?'

He took her hand and raised it to his lips. 'I'm telling you now because I can't lie to you,' he said. 'I can't go the whole day pretending everything is OK. I want to treasure these last hours we have together, and I—'

'Someone's coming!' Malcolm shouted. He was standing up on the pew now, craning to see the back of the church. 'Is it Angie? I can't see, 'cos she's got a white cloth on her head.'

The thing about weddings, Joyce thought, was that they took forever to arrange, and then were over in a flash. She had barely got used to sitting in the front row of the church, sandwiched between Pete and Mick, before the vicar had started up about fidelity and sanctity. The next thing, he was asking if anyone had just cause or impediment, then Angie and Gino were making their vows. Before she knew it, the veil had been thrown back, and they were all surging into the vestry to sign the register. And then it was over, Angie and Gino were posing for photographs in the churchyard, and Joyce was slipping away, hobbling back down Lavender Road in the slightly too tight shoes that she'd found in Arding and Hobbs, to make sure that everything was ready in the café when everyone arrived.

When they did arrive, in a great crowd of chatter and excitement, it was even worse. With sixty guests crushed into such a small space, there was no time to blink. Certainly no time to wonder why Katy Frazer was looking so pale, or why Jen was avoiding Henry Keller, even though his eyes followed her as she moved round the room with a tray of sandwiches. Nor why she felt the need to offer them so flirtily to Sean Byrne and the American GIs.

Nor was there time to worry about the boys. Mick seemed to be happy enough in the merchant navy. But Paul and Pete would presumably soon be heading off across the English Channel, in the full knowledge that the mighty German army was waiting for them on the other side. She hated the very thought of it. She'd tried to remonstrate with Paul last night, but it had had no effect. He was a fully paid-up soldier now, and eager for action, and short of hitting him over the head and locking him in the attic, there wasn't anything she could do about it.

Angie was enjoying herself, and that was the main thing. Dancing around with a huge smile on her face, introducing Gino to all the people he didn't know, she seemed blissfully unaware of the underlying tensions in the room. She had achieved her dream, and she was determined to make the most of it. When it was time for the speeches, she nearly cried with joy when Mr Lorenz said that she was the most beautiful, radiant bride he had ever seen. And she laughed uproariously with everyone else when Paul, looking ridiculously young to be a best man, gave a surprisingly witty speech about Gino. He finished off by saying that if the American military could survive having Gino working in their kitchens, he was sure they could put up with anything that Hitler threw at them, which caused much merriment among the GIs.

And then it was Gino's turn. Despite having spent the last week learning his speech by heart, he forgot his words after the first stumbling sentence, and everyone had to wait ages while he fumbled around in his pockets searching for his notes.

'I am the luckiest man in the earth,' he began again in his slow, nervous English, the crumpled piece of paper shaking in his hand. 'When I first met Angie in Devon at the farm of Mr and Mrs Baxter, I thought I had seen an angel. And in this I was correct. Angela is my angel. She has a heart like the size of an elephant and the beauty of a perfect rose.'

'I think he might have got that the wrong way round,' Jen murmured, and glancing sharply across, Joyce saw her and Sean suddenly convulse with silent laughter.

'I became enamoured with her from this moment,' Gino went on solemnly, unaware of the merriment going on behind him. 'I will always treasure her. And I know with certainment that when eventually this terrible war is over and I can introduce her to my family in Italy, they will treasure her also. My only sorrow is that they cannot be here with me today, and I pray for their safety. Instead I now have my English family, who have been so kind with me, even though they knew I was wishing to steal their beloved Angie. And now it pleases me to make toast, yes, to the two beautiful bridesmaids, Jen and Bella, but also to my new mother, Joyce. All I can say is thank you.'

As everyone dabbed their eyes, and clapped, and raised their glasses, even Joyce felt a little bit emotional. Discreetly she took out her handkerchief and blew her nose, and saw Albert smiling affectionately at her from across the room. She returned his smile. Perhaps he was right. Perhaps Gino wasn't such a bad boy after all.

*

279

The GIs left at five o'clock; they had to be back at their barracks by six, so they missed seeing the bride and groom go away in a taxi half an hour later, followed by a clatter of old tin cans that her brothers had tied to the bumpers.

With the last of her winnings, Angie had booked a hotel in the West End for two nights as a mini honeymoon. Jen was just wondering what the staff at the Grosvenor would make of her and Gino turning up in all their wedding finery when she found Henry standing at her elbow.

'You've been avoiding me,' he said.

'I haven't,' she lied. 'I've been doing my duty as a bridesmaid. Anyway, you seemed so busy chatting to Louise that—'

She stopped as his brows rose sharply. 'I think I've chatted to almost everyone in the room,' he said. 'Not least your delightful brothers. I even had an invigorating discussion with a young man called George Nelson, who apparently wants to be a magician when he grows up. It took some considerable powers of persuasion to prevent him from going home to fetch his white rabbit to show me.'

Jen laughed and relaxed slightly. 'George Nelson is a brat,' she said. 'But he is good at magic. He and Molly, who I was with in Italy, taught themselves some tricks when they were convalescing from chickenpox last year. It was one of those tricks that helped Molly and me escape. She spirited a pair of scissors out of a Gestapo doctor's bag and hid them up her sleeve.'

'Good God,' Henry said. 'He didn't tell me that.'

'I don't think he knows,' Jen said. 'I haven't told him.'

He looked at her curiously. 'Why not?'

'I don't know,' Jen said. 'I suppose I was trying not to think about it.' She shrugged. 'Molly can tell him if she wants to. She's been in Tunisia ever since then, teaching people about this new medicine, penicillin.'

Henry looked impressed. And why wouldn't he? thought Jen. Their stint in Italy obviously hadn't affected Molly the way it had affected her. On the contrary, Molly seemed to be having such a good time in Tunisia that she clearly didn't feel any desire to come home.

She was conscious of Henry watching her meditatively, and felt the faint tingling on her skin that so often happened when he was close to her. Suddenly she wished she could turn the clock back and start all over again. She hated this awkward, impersonal coldness that had sprung up between them. And she hated the fact that he didn't seem remotely impersonal or cold with Louise ...

'It was a lovely wedding,' he said. 'I know you don't approve of Gino, but I think they'll be happy together, don't you?'

Jen gazed up into his handsome face. It could have been me, she told herself. This could have been my wedding. It could have been me and Henry going off to the Grosvenor for a couple of nights of honeymoon bliss.

She felt herself flushing and jumped in alarm as he reached out to touch her bare arm. He withdrew his hand abruptly. 'For goodness' sake, Jen,' he said. 'What's the matter?' But then, noticing that Sean Byrne had emerged from the café, he stiffened.

Jen had seen him too. But it wasn't just Sean standing on the pavement outside the café; her brothers were there too, politely shaking hands with the departing guests. Jen suddenly felt proud of them, and smiled affectionately in their direction. They might not necessarily be the sharpest tacks in the box, but today they had looked smart and gutsy in their various uniforms, and she had appreciated how fond of them she was.

She turned back to Henry and realised he was watching her.

'Henry, I'm sorry,' she said. 'Everyone's leaving and I ought to go and …'

But something in his rather rigid expression made her pause. She didn't know if it was regret, resignation, irritation or pain. Henry's face was always hard to read. But this time he looked as though he had made up his mind about something. Something very final, very absolute.

And she couldn't imagine why. Surely he didn't think it was Sean she had been smiling at. Whether he did or not, at that moment Jen knew for certain that she didn't want to let him go. She didn't want this to be the end of the road. Her mind spun helplessly. If only she and Henry could have a bit of time together. A chance to talk without always being in a rush. Maybe she should ask him to come for a drink at the pub, or even a walk up on the common, or …

But she was too late. Before she could do anything at all, Mrs Rutherford loomed into view.

'Ah, there you are, Henry,' she said. 'Greville and I are just leaving, and we wondered if you would care to come home with us for a bit of supper. It's only pot roast, I'm afraid, but I think we can stretch it to four.'

It wasn't the most appealing of invitations, but Henry barely hesitated. 'Thank you,' he said. 'I'd like that.'

Jen had an almost overwhelming urge to scream. But she bit it back and dug her nails into her palms instead. By the time Celia Rutherford had moved off, she had managed to force a careless smile onto her lips. 'Goodness,' she said sarcastically. 'Pot roast with Greville Rutherford. What a treat.'

Henry looked at her. 'I had such high hopes for us, Jen. Where did we go wrong?'

He spoke very quietly, and so indifferently that Jen felt as though he had slapped her in the face. She could feel heat surging to her cheeks.

'I don't know,' she stammered. There were so many reasons. So many mistakes. She half hoped he would pursue it. But he didn't.

'I gather from Roger Violet that the audiences are loving your performances,' he said. 'It sounds as though you are well and truly back on your feet again.'

But I'm not, Jen wanted to shout. If anything, I'm feeling worse. I feel sick with nerves. I'm still not sleeping well. I haven't heard back from RADA. And above all, I don't want you to go to supper at the Rutherfords'.

But she didn't say any of it. How could she?

In any case, Henry was already saying goodbye and turning away.

And there was Louise tripping down the street towards him, looking like the cat that had got the cream.

As it turned out, Angie had only just got her wedding done and dusted in the nick of time. If she had left it a moment longer, half her guests would have been unable to come, because on 31 May, all military leave was cancelled.

From one day to the next, London lost virtually all of its service personnel. They simply vanished overnight. Theatre seats were left unoccupied, restaurants were empty, pubs deserted. The American servicemen's clubs closed completely.

It seemed that after all the talk and speculation, the long-awaited invasion of German-occupied France was finally about to be launched and the troops were being mustered in readiness.

But everything hung on the weather. The Allied generals had learnt their lesson from the invasion of Italy, when so many glider crews and disembarking troops had been lost or drowned due to poor meteorological conditions. This time General Eisenhower wanted calm seas and good visibility. But the British weather wasn't co-operating. After a brief spell of sunshine over the weekend of Angie's wedding, it had become blustery and overcast. And so everyone hunkered down to wait.

It was a strange feeling. Even in the factory, Louise was aware of a kind of hushed expectancy.

In Lavender Road, things were even more subdued. Ward Frazer had unobtrusively departed the day after Angie's wedding. The Carter boys had left too, Pete and Paul back to their units, Mick back to his ship. Even Jen had gone, back to Norfolk with the Violets to continue their tour of RAF bases.

The only people unaffected by the sudden tension in the air were Angie and Gino. Back from their short sojourn at the Grosvenor Hotel, they hardly seemed to notice that in their absence Gino had lost his job, Moses and Ben and all their GI friends had been transferred to a holding camp near the coast, and the barracks was already being turned into a temporary hospital. They were married, that was all that mattered. And judging from Angie's jubilant demeanour, and Gino's look of total exhaustion, the honeymoon had been a success.

Louise was still secretly revelling in Henry's unexpected appearance at Angie's wedding. His presence had made the whole event a hundred times more enjoyable, and having him back for supper afterwards had been the icing on the cake. The downside was that she hadn't heard a squeak from him since, apart from a polite thank-you note addressed to her mother.

Nor had there been any word from Colonel Westwood about the proposed trip to Wiltshire. All Louise could do in the meantime was try to perfect her technique for making and assembling the fuses.

As Doris had warned her, it was fiddly, frustrating work, made worse by the fact that the tiny components seemed to have a life of their own and were constantly slipping out of their fingers.

'We ought to use tweezers,' Louise muttered irritably. 'That would make it easier.'

'What are these blasted things for?' Doris grumbled as once again a microscopic electric detonator pinged onto the floor. 'What's so special about them?'

Louise had to shake her head. 'I can't tell you,' she said. 'I'm sworn to secrecy.'

'Well it's obvious they're fuses,' Doris said. 'And presumably that means they make things explode. So what I'm wondering is why someone doesn't take one over to Germany and stuff it up Hitler's arse.'

Louise giggled. 'If only,' she said.

In the absence of any volunteers for that task, or of any sign of the invasion actually commencing, one by one the days ticked nervously by. The military commanders might feel confident about the outcome of an assault on occupied Europe, but the civilian population was preparing for the worst. Despite being told not to, people tried to stock up on provisions. Gas masks were hung back on pegs by front doors. Anderson shelters were cleaned out. Buckets were filled with sand, and stirrup water pumps on street corners were tested. In some of the London squares, makeshift huts were erected as temporary living accommodation for the huge numbers of people expected to be displaced by the advancing Allied army or Nazi gas attacks.

In all the speculation about when the invasion might kick off, people had almost forgotten about the Italian campaign. But on Monday 5 June, the BBC wireless news announced that Rome had been liberated by the Allies.

After the months of bitter fighting at Monte Cassino, it was an enormous triumph. That evening in the pub, Gino was almost weeping with excitement. It was the most animated Louise had ever seen him. 'My village is not many distance from Roma,' he said. 'Soon my family will be liberate.' He even went so far as to buy everyone a drink with the last of his wages.

Rome was the first European capital to be freed from Nazi control, and in all the jubilation, now it was the impending invasion that was forgotten. Anyway, the weather was still playing up. A grey, windy drizzle had plagued the south-east for the last few days, and nobody had any expectation of anything happening until it cleared.

But at five o'clock on the morning of 6 June, Louise jerked awake to the sound of planes overhead.

At first she thought it must be an air raid and she was going to have to decamp to the cellar, but there were no sirens blaring, and in any case, German bombers invariably came in from the east or south-east. These planes sounded as though they were travelling in the opposite direction.

And then she heard her mother's footstep outside her door.

'Louise, are you awake?'

Louise got out of bed and opened the door. 'What is it?' she said. 'What's happening?'

'I think it's started,' her mother said. She sounded breathless. Turning off the landing light, she went straight to the window and opened the blackout curtains. 'Yes,' she whispered in awe. 'Look.'

Louise joined her at the window. It was still dark, but for the first time in nearly a week, the sky was clear, and as her eyes acclimatised, she saw a mass of shapes slowly moving overhead. West to east. Towards the coast. Towards France.

'Oh my God,' she said. She put a hand to her mouth. The planes were almost wingtip to wingtip, many towing gliders. They were all painted in black and white stripes, presumably to aid recognition among inexperienced Allied troops, and to prevent incidents of so-called friendly fire.

As she watched them in amazement, she couldn't help thinking of the thousands of young men on board. And of the ones presumably even now heading out across the Channel, or perhaps already struggling off landing craft on dark French beaches. Young men like Moses and Ben, and the Carter boys. What were they thinking now?

Suddenly it all seemed terribly real. The campaigns in North Africa and Italy had been so far away. This was here. This was now. And nobody knew how strong the German resistance would be, what carnage would ensue, how many lives would be cut short. Today. Tomorrow. However long it took.

She felt tears springing to her eyes and saw that her mother was similarly affected. Suddenly they were holding hands. Then somehow Louise was in her arms. As she clung to her mother, feeling the bony shape of her shoulder, smelling the perm in her hair, she realised it was probably the first time they had embraced since she was a child.

'What do we do now?' she whispered tearfully.

Celia drew in a long, shuddering breath. 'I think the best thing we can do,' she said, 'is to go downstairs and make a cup of tea.'

Chapter Twenty Five

Joyce had been woken up early too, not by the noise of aircraft engines, but by Angie and Gino's vigorous lovemaking in the adjacent room. She knew from her experience over the last week, since they had come back from their brief honeymoon, that the bumping, squealing and giggling wouldn't be over any time soon, so giving up on sleep, she had gone downstairs.

Glancing out of the kitchen window and seeing that, for once, it wasn't raining, she decided to do all the laundry that had been waiting since Angie's wedding weekend. It was only as she carried the first batch of washing outside, to put it through the mangle before hanging it up on the line, that she noticed the zebra-striped planes passing overhead.

She took one look, swallowed hard, and went back indoors. 'Hey, Angie,' she shouted urgently up the stairs. 'You need to get up. I think the café's going to be busy this morning.'

The café was indeed very busy, with everyone conjecturing wildly about what might or might not be happening. At half past eight, another wave of planes roared overhead, and people who had missed the earlier ones ran outside to watch and cheer.

At nine o'clock, just as Joyce and Angie were getting over the breakfast rush, Mrs Rutherford bustled in carrying her wireless. 'We don't want to miss the news,' she said.

And just after nine thirty, sure enough, there was a special BBC Home Service broadcast. Everyone fell silent. Even the tea urn stopped bubbling.

'This is the BBC Home Service. And here is a special bulletin, read by John Snagge.' There was a moment's pause, then the clipped, unemotional voice: 'D-Day has come. Early this morning, the Allies began the assault on the north-western face of Hitler's European fortress ...'

The rest was drowned out by a spontaneous cheer. But although she smiled and clapped with the rest, Joyce didn't really feel like cheering. She felt as if a large stone had wedged itself in her gut. And it was obvious that she wasn't the only person who felt like that. Nobody said anything, nobody wanted to spoil the general sense of optimism, but the jubilation of those people who knew that their sons or husbands were part of the invasion forces was definitely more restrained than that of those who had no friends or family at risk. A lot of wood was touched and a lot of fingers were surreptitiously crossed that morning.

It didn't take long for people to start wondering what form Hitler's retaliation would take. Because there was little doubt that there would be some kind of retaliation. Hitler was hardly going to take an invasion of his conquered lands lying down.

'I wish he *would* lie down,' Joyce remarked sourly to Albert at lunchtime. 'So our boys could roll a damn great tank over him.'

Earlier in the year, the Germans had boasted about a miracle weapon, but it had never materialised. What everyone feared most was gas. According to Mrs Rutherford, twenty tons of bleach powder had been delivered to the new decontamination centre in Wandsworth. No one knew whether it was earmarked for Londoners, or for poisoned soldiers coming back from France.

What everyone did know was that today was probably going to be one of the most critical days of their lives.

Fleets of plane continued to pass across the London skies all day. It seemed incredible that there could be so many. By the afternoon, the euphoric mood had changed to a kind of fearful silence.

Long queues formed at newsstands. As Joyce waited in line, she saw that people had hung Union Jack flags out of their windows on Lavender Hill. And the gypsy flower seller on the corner by Arding and Hobbs was peddling patriotic red and white buttonholes.

When the paper van arrived, there was another cheer. The headlines said it all: *THE GREAT INVASION; CHURCHILL ANNOUNCES SUCCESSFUL MASSED LANDINGS; 11,000 PLANES. 4,000 SHIPS. 640 GUNS; WE HOLD BEACHHEAD.*

The newspaper vendor was euphoric. 'It's looking good,' he said as he thrust the *Evening Standard* into Joyce's hand. 'Victory is certain now.'

Let's hope so, Joyce thought as she walked away. We don't want to have gone through all this for nothing.

What was certain was that General Eisenhower had chosen exactly the right moment for his invasion. By the time Joyce got home, the wind was rising again and there was rain in the air. Remembering that she had left her washing out on the line to dry, she hurried out to fetch it in, only to find that everything was splattered with flecks of black grease. She looked at it in dismay. The 11,000 planes had left their mark. And now the whole lot would have to be done again.

Louise was beginning to think that she would never see Colonel Westwood again, but three days after D-Day, he appeared in the factory.

'We had to put the testing on hold in the run-up to the invasion,' he said.

287

'But now that it's under way, we can get going. Thankfully not every artillery unit has gone to France. Not yet, at least.' He glanced at the neatly stacked crates in the corner. 'How are we doing at this end?'

They were doing well. Louise had asked all the girls in the factory to bring in their tweezers, and as a result the assembly had speeded up considerably.

He seemed impressed. 'Good work,' he said, and Louise glowed with pleasure. But he was already turning to Doris. 'Right,' he said briskly. 'I'd like you and your team to crate up all the finished product you have available and load it onto the vehicle outside.'

'What about me?' Louise asked anxiously.

'You're going to come with me,' he said. He frowned slightly. 'But you're going to need to be in uniform.'

Louise was dismayed. 'Oh dear,' she said. 'My uniform's at home. I don't like wearing it in the factory. It's much easier to work in overalls.'

'How far away do you live?'

'Not far, just up on Clapham Common. About ten minutes' walk.'

'OK,' he said. 'In that case, I guess you should go home and change while we get loaded up here. We'll pick you up on the way through.'

'What sort of uniform do you want me in?' Louise asked. He himself was looking very smart in his well-tailored service dress.

He looked at her blankly. 'I don't know,' he said. 'What do you have? Fatigues? Combat uniform? Something you don't mind getting dirty. And decent boots, because we'll be out with the guns and it may be kind of muddy.'

'Battledress,' Louise said. Her heart sank. She looked bad enough in her ATS skirt and jacket; she looked even worse in bulky battledress.

But when he arrived at her parents' house half an hour later, she was too astonished to worry about how she looked. There wasn't just one vehicle rolling up the driveway; there were three: a closed truck, a large olive-green staff car, and a jeep with armed soldiers on board as escort.

More than anything, Louise wished her parents were at home to witness her spectacular departure. But sadly they were both out, and she had to be content with the fact that not only had she managed to keep Colonel Westwood waiting, but she was going to be travelling in his staff car, albeit in the back.

As she emerged from the house and saluted smartly, the corporal who was driving the car leapt out and opened the door for her. Louise felt frightfully grand climbing in, thanking him graciously.

They pulled out, and Colonel Westwood turned round from his seat in the front and nodded over at the common. 'I see you have a gun emplacement up there.'

'It's operated by the Home Guard,' Louise said. 'My father is the unit commander.'

'Really?' He looked thoughtful. 'That's good to know. Maybe he'd be prepared to loan us his guns for our trials. The unit I'm using now could be sent over to France any day. And if that happens, we're going to be kind of stuck.'

Louise laughed. 'Goodness, Daddy wouldn't allow that in a million years.'

The colonel's brows rose in surprise. 'Why not?'

'He's very old-school,' she said. 'He would rather die than let a mere woman get anywhere near one of his precious guns, let alone an American. He's convinced British soldiers are the only ones with any competence or discipline.'

Colonel Westwood gave a short laugh. 'Is that right?' he said. 'Well, I guess we're just going to have to prove him wrong.' And with that, he turned back to the front and unfolded a map.

He was obviously a skilled map-reader; the lack of signposts didn't seem to worry him, and each time he told the driver which way to go, the man responded with a crisp and immediate 'Yes, sir!' which Louise found amusing.

But it didn't make for a chatty journey. The presence of the monosyllabic corporal was inhibiting, and in any case, when he wasn't map-reading, Colonel Westwood spent the time studying some technical documents he had brought with him. Once or twice he did turn slightly in his seat to engage Louise in brief conversation, first about the route they were taking – which he pronounced 'rout' – and then about the invasion. He seemed concerned that the Allies were not making the progress they had hoped for. He was particularly worried about the US 5th Corps, who had apparently taken massive casualties at Omaha Beach in Normandy.

Louise shuddered. She knew that her mother was busy with her WVS ladies today, trying to persuade everyone to give blood, specifically for the wounded coming back from France.

'But you do think we will win through in the end, don't you?' she asked nervously.

Colonel Westwood had been talking half over his shoulder, but now he put his arm over the back of his seat and levered himself round to face her. 'Sure I do,' he said. He didn't smile precisely, but his eyes crinkled slightly at the corners. 'Despite what your father might think, with us Americans on side, there's no way that bastard Hitler is going to win.' He glanced at the driver as he turned back to face the front. 'Isn't that right, Corporal?'

'Yes, sir,' the driver responded, and Louise had to bite her lip to stop herself laughing.

Later the colonel pointed out that they were passing quite close to Arborfield, and that led to some mild chit-chat about her ack-ack course. But then he went back to his papers and Louise had to be satisfied with staring at the back of his head for the rest of the journey, trying not to think about what it would feel like to run her fingers through his closely cut, thick dark hair.

But as soon as they arrived at the test site on Salisbury Plain, he swung immediately into action, and that was the end of her peace and quiet.

The first time the guns fired, she thought her head was going to explode. The shock wave nearly knocked her off her feet. It was her first experience of live firing. She had heard the guns on Clapham Common, of course, but only from the comparative safety of her parents' cellar. She had had no idea that close up it would be so incredibly loud and bruising. But somehow she managed to conceal her discomposure. It was bad enough being the only woman present, and the only English person. She didn't want any of these smart, energetic Americans to think she was a complete drip as well, even though she was sure her eardrums were bleeding.

The firing routine was much the same as she had learned. But the American gunners carried it out with incredible speed and efficiency. They were clearly highly trained and extremely well practised, and put the shambling efforts of her section at Arborfield to shame.

'OK.' Colonel Westwood suddenly loomed into view through the cordite-scented smoke. 'You see what we are doing? The new fuses are fitted with batteries and screwed on to the nose of the fragmentation shell.'

Louise nodded. She could barely hear what he was saying because her ears were still ringing. But she had learned about fragmentation shells at Arborfield. They carried simple fuses, and like pretty much all bombs and shells, it was the impact with a physical target that made them explode.

The main difference between them and Colonel Westwood's new proximity fuses was that the new fuses sensed when they were in damaging distance of a target. Each one carried a miniature wireless sending and receiving set. Once in flight, it sent out radio waves like feelers. When the shell came within range of something solid, like a plane, a tank, or even just the ground, the radio waves were reflected back to the fuse, which then triggered the firing system and exploded the charge, sending fragments of metal flying out in all directions. How the business with the radio waves actually worked was a mystery to Louise, but that was the gist of it, and that was what they were trying to test.

The gunners were aiming at a ground target about half a mile down the range. The idea was to get the fuse to detonate just before making physical contact, so that the fragments were dispersed over a much wider area than they would be if the explosion occurred on impact like a traditional shell.

'Because the explosion occurs in the air,' Colonel Westwood explained, imitating the explosion with his flared hands, 'it will be much more effective against enemy soldiers or vehicles hidden in trenches or behind defensive walls, which previously would only be destroyed by a direct hit.'

Louise tried to look as if she understood. But really she was studying his lovely hands.

'If we can get this to work, it will give us one hell of an advantage in a ground battle,' he added, with grim satisfaction. 'And against enemy aircraft too.'

As the 'On target!' and 'Fire!' commands rang out again, Louise surreptitiously covered her ears. She wondered how her former ATS comrades were coping with all this at live firing camp. Not very well by the sound of Susan's last letter. If nothing else, they would probably all be stone deaf next time she saw them.

What particularly interested Colonel Westwood, of course, was the performance of the fuse. And that was what he wanted her to observe. Each time the gun was fired, a forensic team was sent down the range to inspect the fragments and to mark the point of explosion. He also wanted her to learn how the complete fuse unit was assembled. As well as the casing and the bits and pieces made in the factory, there was a switch, a fuel section and a battery. The various elements were very carefully and precisely attached together, primed and then screwed onto the nose of the shell.

Each battery was tested on a special machine before use. The fuses were so expensive to make that Colonel Westwood didn't want to waste any because of a defective battery.

'It's a shame they weren't ready for D-Day,' Louise said as they waited for the latest report to be radioed up from the range.

'Yeah, sounds like they sure could have done with them on Omaha Beach,' he said. He lifted his shoulders slightly. 'But even if we had been ready, they wouldn't have been used. The generals figured there was too much of a risk that our artillery could get captured. And nobody wants the Germans to get their hands on this technology.' He lifted one of the fuses out of the crate and cradled it gently in his palm. 'These little guys are set to revolutionise warfare. The last thing we need just now is to find them being used against us.'

Louise shuddered at the thought. She could already see how lethally effective the new fuses might be. And by the end of the day, she was watching as eagerly as Colonel Westwood to see if they were performing as they should. Mostly they were, though inevitably there were some minor adjustments to be made, mainly in the way the various components fitted together.

Back in London the next day, she was able to implement a rather neat change in the way they drilled the base of the tiny conical unit, to improve the connection.

'So what do you think of the lovely colonel now?' Doris asked.

Louise smiled. It wasn't a difficult question. She had thought about very little else since saluting him goodbye at the British artillery barracks at Larkhill, just below Salisbury Plain. He had stayed down there for further trials, but Louise had returned to London in the escort jeep, which had been significantly less comfortable than her journey down.

'I really like him,' she said. 'Mainly because he treats me like a normal human being rather than a brainless ATS private, fit only to be shouted at and bullied into submission.'

'I wouldn't mind him bullying me into submission,' Doris remarked. 'Although you'd best not tell my husband that.'

Louise laughed. She felt the same. But Colonel Westwood didn't need to bully her. There was already something about him that made her want to impress him, both personally and professionally. To that end, she put a lot of effort into ensuring that the next batch of fuses were made exactly to his new specification.

For Jen, the invasion meant a sudden cessation of work. The Violets had exhausted the Norfolk RAF bases, perhaps in more ways than one, and other military camps were either closed to non-military for security reasons, or the soldiers had already left. After a couple of abortive attempts to find new venues, in the end they were summoned back to London to await further instructions.

Jen was delighted. Now that Angie and Gino were married, she would finally get a room to herself, and she was looking forward to some revitalising sleep after weeks sharing with fidgety Adele.

But she hadn't accounted for Angie and Gino's vigorous night-time activities. Angie's snoring had been bad enough; this was a hundred times worse. Eventually, in desperation, she banged on the thin wall that divided the two rooms, but that just resulted in uncontrolled giggling from Angie, and a few minutes later they started up again. Blimey, Jen thought with weary fury, Gino must have the stamina of an ox.

As soon as it got light, she pulled on her dressing gown and went downstairs, where she found her mother getting ready to go to the café.

'You're up early,' Joyce said.

'I couldn't sleep,' Jen replied. She glanced up at the ceiling. 'Is it like this every night?'

Joyce nodded. 'Yes,' she said sourly. She shrugged on her coat and was just about to head off down the hallway when she paused and slid an envelope out from behind Angie's gas mask box on the hall table. 'By the way,' she said. 'This came for you last week.'

Jen almost snatched it out of her hand. Her fingers were trembling as she ripped it open. It was from RADA, inviting her for an audition on 20 June, less than a week away.

Joyce was already opening the front door.

'Why didn't you give me this yesterday when I got home?' Jen said angrily. 'More to the point, why didn't you forward it to me via ENSA?'

Joyce swung round. 'Because I've had more important things to worry about,' she snapped. She picked up her shopping basket. 'You may not have noticed, but we invaded France last week. And for all I know, your brothers might even now be lying dead on a beach in Normandy. Is it surprising I forgot about your letter?'

As the door slammed, Jen put her head in her hands. She was worried about the boys. Of course she was. But this letter was important too. As far as she was concerned, it could hardly have been more important. Or more scary. Even touching the flimsy paper it was written on made her feel queasy. What was more, thanks to her mother's inefficiency, she was only just in time to confirm that she was able to attend.

As soon as she was dressed, she ran down to the telephone box on Lavender Hill, only to discover it was out of order. She had to go all the way to Clapham Junction to find one that worked. And then there was a snooty voice on the other end that didn't seem to care one way or another whether she could make the audition or not.

All in all, Jen was not in a good mood when she called at the pub on her way home. She had hoped to find Katy, but the only person there was Sean, busy heaving a barrel up the cellar steps.

'I thought you'd have gone back to Ireland,' Jen said. 'Now that the invasion has happened, surely the borders are open again?'

Sean straightened up. 'They should be, but they're not,' he said. 'I reckon your bloody government is taking it out on us Irish for having the sense to keep out of their stupid, ill-judged war.'

But he had chosen the wrong morning to tangle with Jen. 'Ill-judged?' she said. 'How dare you say that when so many men are even now risking their lives to rid Europe of that brutal tyrant in Germany? Not you, of course,' she added sarcastically. 'But people like Ward Frazer, and my brothers.'

Sean shrugged. 'I can say what I like,' he retorted. 'It's not my war.' He saw her lips tighten, and held up his hand. 'And don't start getting at me, Jen. Your damned Henry isn't risking his life, is he?'

He stared challengingly at her and gave a slight snort of derision when her eyes wavered. 'Or is that the problem? Not just that he's a cold fish.'

'Of course it's not,' Jen snapped. 'And he's not a cold fish.'

'Then why didn't you marry him when you had the chance?'

Jen tensed and quickly lowered her eyes from his sharp gaze. 'That's none of your business,' she said.

'Oh yes it is,' Sean responded. 'Because something about him has turned you away from me.' He shoved the barrel under the counter. 'But we both know he's not right for you. He's much more suited to Louise.' He saw her wince, and made a dismissive gesture. 'Oh come on, Jen, you can see it just by looking at them. They've both got that same superior attitude. It's not surprising. That's the way they've been brought up. These rich, privileged types always think they're a cut above. But that's not you. That's not what you need.'

'No?' Jen said dangerously. 'And what in your humble opinion *do* I need?'

He shrugged off her anger with a smile. 'You need a man like me. Someone who knows what it's like to fight their corner.' He came round the counter and took her hand. 'We fancy each other, Jen,' he murmured. He lifted her hand to his mouth and his eyes glinted over her knuckles. 'You know we do. And I know you won't admit it, but I believe deep down that we love each other too.'

Jen stared at him in amazement.

'I want you to marry me,' he said. 'I want you to come back to Ireland with me. There's nothing for you here. London is finished. England is finished. Look how run-down everything is already. Another year of war and the whole country will be bankrupt.' He smiled into her eyes. 'Come to Dublin. You won't believe what a life we could have there. There are theatres and concert halls galore. You'd be a star in no time. Maybe even in the films, like your lookalike Vivien Leigh.'

Jen shut her eyes, feeling the seductive rub of his thumb on the palm of her hand. When she opened them again, he was still looking at her, his blue gaze so sincere.

'What about Gillian James?' she asked.

He gave an impatient laugh. 'Oh come on, Jen,' he said. 'You know that's nothing. Don't hold that against me. It's you I want. It's always been you.' He caught her gesture of disbelief, and his eyes flashed angrily. 'For the love of God, Jen, you know it's true. I could have found a job somewhere else. Maybe I could even have got back to Ireland somehow. But I wanted to stay here for you.'

Jen knew only too well what it was like to be rejected. But however much she felt for him, for his pain, it was too late.

'I do still fancy you,' she said. 'Maybe I still love you a little bit too. But it's not enough. I need more than that.'

He stared at her incredulously. 'What more could you possibly need?'

She shrugged impatiently. 'I don't know. But whatever it is, you don't have it.'

Sean's face darkened. 'It's money, isn't it?' he said. 'You want to find someone with money. Someone who will give you the high life. Like your oh-so-wonderful Henry.'

Jen heard the scorn in his voice and was suddenly aware of something cracking. For a moment she thought it might be her teeth. Then she realised it was her temper. 'No, it's not money,' she said. 'If you must know, it's integrity. Honesty. Honour. Reliability. Dependability. Trustworthiness. Genuine kindness. Generosity of spirit. All the things you don't seem to have.'

Sean's eyes flashed. 'And Henry does, I suppose?'

'Yes, he does,' she said.

Sean looked away. He was silent. Jen could see the emotion in the clench of his jaw. Oddly, she felt slightly choked herself and cleared her throat impatiently. After a moment, he turned back to her. 'OK,' he said. 'If that's how you really feel.'

He was genuinely upset. She could see it. Hear it in his voice. His dream was in ruins. His hopes shattered. She had it in her heart to feel sorry for him.

He put a hand behind her head and kissed her hard on the lips.

A second later, he had disappeared back down into the cellar.

Jen stood in the empty bar. Her emotion had gone now, but she was left feeling shaky and rather mean. She was tempted to go after him – she was sure that was what he intended her to do – but then she took a long breath and walked out of the pub into the street.

Later that morning she went up to ENSA, only to discover that Henry was away. By the time she got back, Sean had packed his few possessions into a bag and left.

Katy came over to the house to tell her. She was clearly upset.

'But he said Ireland was still barred,' Jen said. 'How's he going to get home?'

'I don't know,' Katy said. 'He said he'd take his chances.' She bit her lip. 'God, Jen, why couldn't you have waited a few weeks? Just until Molly got home.'

'I'm sorry,' Jen said. There was nothing else she could say. She could hardly agree to marry Sean just to please Katy, after all. She was glad when later that afternoon she received a note from Roger Violet to say that ENSA had secured them some engagements on the south coast, and that they would pick her up at Clapham Junction as they passed by the following morning.

Katy felt mean snapping at Jen, but even though Sean's departure had left her feeling bereft, she understood why he had gone. Under that casual exterior, he had a fierce Irish pride. And once he had realised that Jen wasn't ever coming back to him, that was it. He had no choice but to cut his losses and go.

But it was hard on little Malcolm, and George was upset too. 'He promised to take me to the circus,' he said. When Pam offered to take him instead, he shrugged glumly. 'It won't be the same without Sean.'

Lucky was even worse.

The evening after Sean left, the dog wouldn't settle. He roamed around restlessly, sniffing at the door and whining morosely. Every time someone came into the pub, his ears pricked, then dropped back again when he saw it wasn't Sean. Katy could hardly bear it. Lucky's unhappiness seemed to amplify her own. She had got so used to Sean's help. Now she was going to have to ask Bella James to start coming in after school again to help with the children.

When it was time to go to bed, Lucky tried to follow Katy upstairs. Normally he slept in the cellar with Sean, but tonight he stubbornly refused to go down there. In the end, in desperation, Katy left him in the bar, telling him firmly that that was where he had to stay.

She glared at him as he lay down mournfully at the bottom of the stairs. It wasn't as though she didn't have enough to worry about. Tonight in the pub there had been talk of unexplained local explosions. Someone had been told they had been caused by a faulty gas main. Someone else said it was a Nazi plane that had crashed. Whatever it was, it had clearly been hushed up by the authorities, because there was nothing about it in the evening paper.

Instead there were reports of yet more troops being sent over the Channel. And as more soldiers were sent over, more injured came back. A porter at the Wilhelmina who drank at the pub had told her that a trainload of badly wounded Americans had been admitted to the hospital that very afternoon.

'Right bust up, they are,' he had said. 'And these are some of the lucky ones. I dread to think what happened to the rest.'

But there was still no doubt in anyone's mind that Hitler needed stopping.

The newspapers had recently reported that forty-seven Allied airmen had been shot dead while trying to escape from a POW camp in Silesia. For a horrible minute Katy had wondered if Ward might have been among them, but then she realised the timing was wrong. He couldn't possibly have gone to Europe, been captured, sent to an oflag in Silesia and escaped, all in a period of a couple of weeks. But even so. Those poor, brave young men.

And today on the wireless she had heard that the Nazis had massacred an entire village near Limoges in revenge for the alleged murder of an SS officer. The men had been taken into a barn and shot and the women and children had been locked in a church, drenched with paraffin and burnt. Only seven people out of more than seven hundred had survived.

As she got ready for bed, Katy couldn't stop thinking about the women and children in that church, and felt an almost physical pain as she checked on her own children, sleeping peacefully in the other room.

It took her a long time to go to sleep, and she was having a nightmare about Ward fighting off a group of SS officers bearing burning crosses when she felt a movement next to her on the bed. A depression of the mattress. A weight.

She woke in confusion, her heart jumping.

Was it Ward? Had he miraculously come home?

Then she heard a snuffling noise, and felt the rasp of a wet tongue on her arm.

'No,' she mumbled. 'You can't come up here.'

She turned on the bedside lamp. Lucky was sitting bolt upright on the bed, watching her anxiously, his big, liquid, pleading eyes blinking nervously in the sudden light.

She groaned in dismay. But she didn't have the energy, or the heart, to shoo him off. Instead she let him curl up against the back of her legs. He settled with a contented sigh. And to her surprise, his heavy warmth gave her some comfort.

'Louise? It's Henry on the phone for you,' her mother shouted. 'Are you coming?'

'Of course I'm coming,' Louise muttered. It was Saturday morning, and she was rushing to get ready for work. But now she dropped the hairclip she was trying to position and ran downstairs.

'Louise?' Henry's voice sounded warm, and she felt her heart accelerate. 'I'm glad I caught you. I'm meeting up with a few friends in Chelsea this evening, and I wondered if you would like to come along. We thought we'd eat at the Draycott in Cadogan Gardens and then go on to the Embassy Club.'

'Gosh! That sounds lovely,' Louise said, hoping he wouldn't hear the childish excitement in her voice.

Whether he did or not, he gave a slight laugh. 'I should perhaps mention that Freddy will be there,' he added. 'It was he who suggested inviting you.'

Louise's heartbeat slowed down again. She would have much preferred it to have been Henry's idea. Nevertheless, it all sounded frightfully grand. And she deserved a treat. She had been down to Wiltshire again this week. Her ears were still buzzing from the firing exercises, and she had strained her eyes trying to follow the trajectory of the test shells.

She still hadn't managed to find out if Colonel Westwood was married, but she had got a lot more interested in the development of the proximity fuse. It had become a matter of pride now that the factory should produce the perfect model, the one that worked every time, that fitted neatly into its casing and exploded at exactly the right moment.

But all of that faded into the background at the thought of going to the Embassy Club with Henry.

'I'd love to come,' she said.

'Excellent,' Henry replied. 'Will you be able to make your own way? Or shall I ask Freddy to come and collect you?'

'Oh no,' she said hastily. 'That won't be necessary. I'm in the army, don't forget. I can find my way to the Draycott Hotel.'

Henry laughed. 'We'll see you there then. Freddy will be thrilled.'

Will he indeed? Louise thought. Nevertheless, she took a lot of trouble getting ready. She didn't want Henry, or Lord Freddy come to that, thinking she was out of her league.

Her mother was in the hallway when she left. She eyed Louise approvingly, perhaps hopeful of her chances with Henry. 'You look lovely, darling,' she said. 'Very elegant. But do be careful. I think there's some kind of scare on this evening. The barrage balloons are up. And Daddy's spending the evening on the guns.'

Indeed, as Louise set off, she could see activity at the gun emplacement on the common, and paused to watch for a moment, wishing her father was more accommodating, as she would have been interested to know what kind of range-finding equipment the Home Guard were using. But there was no likelihood of her finding out. When she had ventured to enquire at dinner one night, Greville had given her a resounding snub. 'Didn't they teach you anything in the army? Surely you must know that kind of information is highly confidential.'

Turning the corner onto Lavender Road, she saw Mr Lorenz emerge from the pub on the other side of the street. She gave him a little wave and he raised his hat politely. She was about to cross over to say hello when she spotted George Nelson coming up the road towards her and her heart sank slightly. Ever since the salvage episode, George had treated her as though she was his best friend, jabbering away about the blasted rabbit and all sorts of other nonsense every time he saw her.

And today was no different. This time he launched straight into a description of the circus he had been to the previous week. According to him, one of the best acts had been a real live man being fired out of a cannon.

He was halfway through a vivid description of this phenomenon when he stopped suddenly and frowned.

'What's that noise?' he said. And then Louise heard it too, somewhere above and behind her, a kind of rattling buzz like an old motorbike.

She swung round and looked up at the sky. She couldn't see anything. But then George pointed. 'Look,' he said. 'It's a plane.'

Louise strained her eyes, and caught a faint flash of silver high up, approaching fast towards the common.

But it wasn't a plane. Certainly not one that featured in her aircraft recognition handbook. It was far smaller than any plane she had ever seen; she doubted there was even room for a pilot.

As she tried to keep track of it among the light clouds, wondering why the sirens hadn't started up, one of the AA guns opened fire. She felt the juddering vibration and saw the tracer stream off into the sky. It was followed by another. But they were way off target. She imagined her father frantically shouting at his crew to recalibrate the aim.

She caught the glint of silver once more. It seemed to be flying straight towards them from the south-east. And it kept on coming. As the first volley from the guns died away, she and George could hear the dull grinding noise again.

It must be some kind of missile, she thought wildly. But it had wings. A rocket?

'What is it?' George asked.

'I don't know,' she said.

And then suddenly the sinister, relentless noise stopped.

For a second, she was reassured. Perhaps the Home Guard had hit it after all? But then her mind went into overdrive. If they had, there would have been an explosion, and she hadn't spent hour after hour at the range on Salisbury Plain without being able to spot a mid-air explosion when she saw one. But if the engine had stopped, then whatever it was would be falling …

Instinctively she began working out the trajectory. She had to guess at height and speed. But she had already worked out the direction, and it didn't look good.

Abruptly she grabbed George's arm and dragged him through the gate into Mrs Carter's front garden. She was conscious of Mr Lorenz turning to look at her curiously from the other side of the road.

'Take cover,' she shouted at him. But her voice didn't come out properly. She tried again. 'Take cover!'

She could hear Colonel Westwood's voice in her head. 'With traditional fuses, it is harder to make any impact on a target concealed behind a defensive wall.'

Mrs Carter's front garden wall was only two and a half feet high. It was hardly very defensive. But it was better than nothing.

In any case, there was no time to think. She screamed at George to lie down, and scrambled down on top of him, pressing them both as close as she could to the base of the wall, holding her hands over his ears.

I'm going to look like a complete idiot if nothing happens, she thought.

And that was the last thing she thought for a long time.

Because an instant later, there was a rending, screaming, deafening explosion, followed by a shock wave of such magnitude that it punched all the air out of her lungs.

Chapter Twenty Six

Katy couldn't believe it. There had been no warning. Nothing. The pub was noisy and they hadn't even heard the guns opening fire. One minute she had been pulling a pint; the next there was a piercing, earth-shattering crash and all the windows in the pub blew out into the street. And it wasn't just the windows. It was the glasses too. Her precious glasses, which she had been preserving so carefully. They exploded off the shelves and tables as though detonated by a fuse. The rest shattered in people's hands. For an odd frozen moment, that was the only thing Katy noticed, her customers' blank expressions as they realised that all they were holding was a few shards of glass.

And then reality kicked in.

As everyone charged towards the door, Katy swung round wildly to Bella, who was standing at the bottom of the stairs, silhouetted against a cloud of dust billowing down from above.

'The children?' she shouted. Ridiculously, she couldn't remember where they were. But nor apparently could Bella. The girl just stood there, rigid, ashen-faced, her eyes wide and staring, as though she had seen a ghost.

Out of the corner of her eye, Katy caught a movement on the cellar steps. It was Malcolm, clinging to Lucky's collar. 'I heard a bang,' he said. And then Katy remembered that he'd been playing with the sand buckets in the cellar. Thank God he had been safe down there.

But Caroline was upstairs. Bella had been putting her to bed and had just come downstairs to fetch Malcolm.

'Stay there,' Katy shouted at Malcolm as she ran, panic-stricken, towards the stairs. 'And don't move.'

Bella didn't move either. Katy had to physically push the girl out of the way to get up the narrow staircase. By the time she reached the top, she could hardly see for swirling dust. She bumped hard into a chair and screamed. She thought she was going mad. All the furniture appeared to be in the wrong place. The wall between the sitting room and her bedroom didn't seem to be there at all. 'Please,' she whispered, as she stumbled blindly across to the children's room. 'Please God, let it be all right …'

But it wasn't all right. The cot was there. Close to the shattered window. But Caroline wasn't in it.

Katy didn't know what to do. Her mind was completely blank. Somewhere in the recesses of her brain she knew she was in shock. But that didn't help. She still didn't know what to do.

She heard a faint noise behind her and screamed as two small white shapes materialised in the doorway. It took her a second to identify them as Malcolm and Lucky. She stared at them in horror, heart hammering, only belatedly realising that the reason for their ghostly appearance was that they were both liberally coated in fine dust.

'What's wrong with Bella?' Malcolm asked. 'She won't talk to me.'

'I told you to stay downstairs,' Katy said weakly.

'Lucky wanted to come up,' Malcolm said. He ran over and peered through the bars into the empty cot. 'Where's Caroline?'

Katy put her hand to her mouth. She could hardly bring herself to say the words. She suddenly felt icy cold. 'I don't know.'

And now, to make it worse, Lucky started whining. The sound echoed eerily around the ravaged room. It sounded horribly woeful, and Katy wished she had the energy to shout at him to stop. Because she knew what had happened. Caroline had been sucked out of the broken window by the shock wave of the blast. And no baby could survive a fall like that. She would have—

'Look, Mummy,' Malcolm squeaked suddenly. He pointed to the floor at the side of the bed. 'Clever Lucky find Caroline.'

And he was right. There she was. Tiny and snug and completely alive, beaming happily in the middle of a jumble of blankets and pillows.

Katy stared at her in disbelief. Gradually her muddled thoughts settled back into some kind of order. Bella must have left Caroline lying on the bed while she came downstairs to fetch Malcolm, and the blast had blown the bedding off onto the floor, and the baby with it.

She thought she was going to faint with relief. As she bent to pick Caroline up, her knees gave way and she slumped down on the corner of the bare mattress. Reaching out, she pulled Malcolm to her and sat there hugging them both to her, tears dripping down her face.

But Malcolm didn't want to be hugged. He was far too excited. He wriggled away and began looking eagerly around the ruined dust-filled room. 'Was it a bomb?' he asked.

'Yes, I think so,' Katy said weakly. She sniffed and wiped her eyes. I ought to go out, she thought. I ought to go and see what's happened. And if I can give any help.

But she didn't move. She didn't want to go outside. She didn't want to see what had happened. She didn't want to see the destruction. The devastation. She didn't want to know which of her neighbour's houses had been

302

destroyed. Who was dead or injured. All she wanted to do was stay here in peace. In safety. With her little family.

It had been a busy day at the café. There had been a sale of old stock at Arding and Hobbs, and, having spent their carefully preserved coupons on previously unaffordable silk vests and lisle hose, quite a few ladies had come in for refreshment. Joyce and Angie had stayed on later than usual, partly to clear up and partly because they were intending to call in at the pictures on the way home. The King was in France visiting the troops, and apparently there was footage of it on the Pathé news.

'You never know,' Joyce said, as she put away the clean knives and forks. 'We might catch a glimpse of one of the boys.' She knew Angie was as worried about Pete and Paul as she was. Some of her customers had received brief, reassuring missives from their sons and husbands in France, but as yet she hadn't heard anything from either of her boys. Her only consolation was that neither of them were much cop at writing letters.

But Angie wasn't listening. She was staring out of the window. 'Something's happened,' she said. 'There's people running up the road.'

Joyce closed the cutlery drawer and went over to the door. She saw one of the ARP wardens lumbering up the hill on the other side of the road, carrying a stirrup pump and coiled hose in one hand and a gas rattle in the other. 'What's happened?' she shouted at him.

The man was already out of breath, but he didn't even break stride. 'I'm not sure,' he gasped as he struggled past. 'All I know is that Lavender Road has copped it.'

Dazedly, Joyce stood there staring at his receding back. But Angie wasn't dazed. 'Gino!' she shrieked, and took off up the hill like a rocket.

And then Joyce too leapt into action. Pausing only to grab their gas masks off the peg and lock the door, she set off in hot pursuit, only to meet Angie coming back again.

'You can't get through,' Angie gasped. 'The road's completely blocked. We'll have to go round the other way.'

'Could you see what had happened?' Joyce panted as they ran up one of the adjacent roads towards the common. Angie was fitter than her. It must be all that sex, Joyce thought. And then, as she pounded on in her daughter's wake, she wondered why she was thinking about sex at a time like this. But she couldn't bear to think about anything else. About her house. About her tortoise. Or worst of all, about Albert. He had called at the café earlier, on his way home.

'No,' Angie shouted back. 'There was too much smoke. But the ARP man said half the street had gone.'

'Gone?' Joyce was struggling for breath. 'What do you mean, gone?'

But Angie didn't reply. Her pace slowed suddenly, and Joyce could see from her heaving shoulders that she was crying.

Catching her up at the top of the road, she put her arm round her, but when they turned into Lavender Road a minute later, they could see that the ARP man wasn't far off.

It wasn't smoke that had obscured the view from the other end of the street; it was dust, billowing down the road on the breeze from the common like the aftermath of an earthquake.

From their vantage point at the corner, Joyce and Angie could see that the houses at the top end of the street down as far as the pub were still intact. But beyond the pub, there was total devastation. At least five or six houses on the left-hand side of the road had been blasted out of all recognition.

Joyce could hardly take it in. The road itself was covered almost shoulder high in mangled debris, and the houses on the right-hand side, her side, were half buried in great piles of rubble. Through the hazy cloud of dust she recognised the tattered shreds of curtains hanging at her own shattered bedroom window.

Most of the bombing during the Blitz had been at night. You knew what had happened, but you couldn't really see it. This time you could see it all too well. The dust was beginning to settle, and the survivors were milling about, looking grey and shocked in the soft evening light, staring in horror as the full extent of the damage was gradually revealed. Some were already speculating about what had caused the explosion, or grumbling that there had been no air-raid warning. Others were trying to identify who was safe and who was missing. Somewhere behind her, Joyce heard Pam Nelson's desperate voice asking if anyone had seen George. And now the wardens were trying to cordon off the site, bellowing at everyone to move back.

As Joyce searched the crowd for Albert, she heard a shriek from Angie behind her. 'Oh Gino! My darling, thank God you're safe!'

And there indeed was Gino, looking even more bemused than usual. His face was smeared with blood, and when he brought one of his hands up to push back his lank, dusty hair, Joyce noticed that his fingers were bleeding. But other than that he seemed unharmed, and Angie had already launched herself into his arms, sobbing uncontrollably.

Joyce caught sight of Katy stumbling out of the pub with the baby in her arms. Malcolm and the dog were close behind. They looked like a family of ghosts, all covered in white dust.

Joyce hurried over to them. 'Have you seen Albert?' she asked. 'He told me earlier that he was going to the pub.'

But Katy was staring in horror down the ravaged street. 'Oh my God,' she said. 'Oh my God.' Slowly she turned back to Joyce. 'What am I going to tell Bella? I left her in the pub, just standing there like a zombie.'

But Joyce didn't have time to worry about Bella James. If she was standing in the pub, at least she was alive. What more did she want? Joyce was much more concerned about Albert.

'Katy, listen to me,' she said urgently. 'Was Albert in the pub when all this happened?'

'Who?' Katy looked perplexed.

'Albert,' Joyce said irritably. 'Mr Lorenz?'

Katy stared at her and paled even more. She put a hand to her head. 'I don't know,' she said helplessly. 'I can't remember.'

Joyce felt like shaking her. She was the landlady of the blasted pub. Surely she must know who had been in there. But she was acting like some kind of zombie herself.

Joyce turned away from her impatiently and saw Angie walking unsteadily towards her.

'Oh Mum.' Angie's eyes were huge in her tear-stained face. 'Gino says Mr Lorenz was in the pub, but he left a minute or two before the explosion.'

Joyce looked at her. And then at the ARP warden, Mr Poole.

'Why aren't you doing something?' she screamed at him. 'Why are you just standing there?'

'Give us a chance,' he said. 'The emergency services are on their way.'

She waved her hand frantically in the direction of the blast. 'But there might still be people alive in those houses,' she said.

He turned his head to glance briefly down the road. 'I doubt it,' he said grimly.

Joyce felt a sudden sensation of being icy cold. And then slowly, very slowly, she followed his gaze and for the first time allowed her eyes to rest on what used to be Albert's house. This morning it had been a neat little two-up two-down. All that remained now, and all that remained of Mrs James's house next door, and the houses beyond, were some jagged segments of wall and a tangle of contorted metalwork. Everything else had been blown out into the street, a great avalanched mound of bricks, beams, pipes, joists, slates, girders, wires and fragments of broken furniture.

Much of the glass and some smaller items had been flung even further afield. Joyce saw something lying by Angie's foot and bent over to pick it up. It was an ivory hairbrush, a man's hairbrush, with a few short dark hairs caught in the bristles.

Joyce looked at it, then clasped it to her chest. Oh no, she thought. Please no. Not Albert.

There was a sound of engines, and everyone swung round. A light rescue truck and a military van turned into the road. People looked at each other in relief. Help had finally arrived. The vehicles stopped a little way up the street, just beyond the door of the pub, where Katy was still standing.

Three men got out and started briskly down the road. But they didn't get very far.

Lucky had been sniffing around the edges of the debris, but suddenly spotting three uniformed strangers advancing purposefully on his mistress, he leapt into action. Hackles up menacingly, he bounded back up the road towards them, barking ferociously. The men took one look at him and retreated hastily to their vehicles.

Joyce felt a surge of fury so strong she almost thought she would explode and burst into a thousand fragments herself. 'Katy, for goodness' sake,' she yelled. 'Get that damned animal under control.'

Deep under the rubble, Louise could hear someone calling her name, but she couldn't do anything about it. In any case, the voice was faint. It was clearly coming from a long way away.

And now something was poking painfully at her stomach. The distant voice came again. 'Louise? Are you alive? If you are, please can you move, because you're squashing me?'

Louise wondered if she was alive. It seemed unlikely. She couldn't see and she couldn't hear. And she couldn't move. But she could still feel the uncomfortable prodding sensation underneath her.

'Stop it,' she said.

'But I can't breathe.'

And dimly she realised that nor could she. Belatedly she recognised the voice as belonging to George Nelson. But he wasn't far away at all; on the contrary, he seemed to be right underneath her.

Unfortunately, as clarity returned, so did her senses, and the first thing she felt was a pain in her hip so intense that she thought she was going to black out again.

But she didn't. Somehow she managed to draw a meagre breath.

'Are you all right?' she whispered.

'Yes, I think so,' he said. 'Are you?'

'No,' she said. Something very heavy was pressing down hard on the small of her back. Excruciatingly hard. 'Not really.'

'I'm glad you're alive, at least,' he said.

And suddenly she had a ridiculous urge to laugh. But it was far too painful.

'I'm glad you are too,' she said. How British we are, she thought. Polite to the bitter end.

There was a pause, during which she heard George trying to spit something out of his mouth and realised it was probably her hair. Or perhaps it was dust. She could taste it in her own mouth and feel it clogging her nose. She opened her eyes again, and felt a horrid grittiness in those as well.

It was pitch black. She tried to work out what that meant. Had she gone blind? Or had she been unconscious for a long time and night had already fallen? Or were they buried too deep? Too deep for daylight to penetrate?

'Do you think anyone will find us?' George asked.

Louise closed her eyes again. 'Of course they will,' she said.

But would they? It occurred to her that the only person who had seen them in the road was Mr Lorenz. And if he had been caught in the blast as well, which he almost certainly had been, then it might take quite a while for their friends or family to think of searching for them. If indeed any of their friends or family were still alive. She had no way of knowing how wide an area had been affected.

George's thoughts were obviously running on similar lines. 'Daddy was at the brewery,' he whispered. 'But I hope Mummy and Nellie are all right. And Bunny.'

Louise didn't trust herself to speak.

'Can you hear anything?' George asked after a moment.

She tried to listen, but all she could hear was something creaking ominously above her. A shudder of fear coursed through her. They were alive. But how long would that last?

She shook her head, then regretted it as a sharp pain shot up her neck. 'No,' she said.

George spat some more. 'Should we shout?' he asked.

'I can't,' she muttered grimly. 'But you could try.'

He did try, but she was pressing down on him too heavily. He couldn't get enough air in his lungs to make more than a faint croak.

'I'm getting wet,' he said after a moment.

'I'm afraid it's blood,' Louise said. 'My blood.' She could feel it, a warm trickle running down her cheek and into her ear. At first she had thought it was water, but she could taste it now, tacky with dust on her tongue.

'Do you think we're going to die?' George whispered.

'No,' she replied. And wished her voice sounded firmer. But by any standard things weren't looking good. I don't want to die, she thought. I really don't want to die. And she didn't want George to die either. But there wasn't much she could do about it. They were both completely jammed, and one shift of the mass of wreckage above them would almost certainly be the end of them.

They were silent again for another minute. She felt George's fingers twitching under her stomach. Heard his increasingly shallow breaths. His chest was barely moving now. She wished she could lift herself up off him, to give him more room, but she couldn't. She couldn't do anything. Half her body was numb, the other half was in agony. And she was losing blood. She could feel an unpleasant pumping sensation behind her ear.

She was just wondering how long it took for someone to bleed to death when she felt George's body tense underneath her. 'I think I can hear something,' he whispered. 'It sounds like barking.'

Louise couldn't hear anything. She could barely even hear his voice.

'Do you think it's Lucky?' he asked.

'I don't know,' she mumbled. Suddenly all she wanted to do was close her eyes and sleep.

But it seemed George had a plan. 'I might be able to whistle,' he said. 'Do you think he might hear me?'

Louise tried to concentrate, but she was struggling even to stay conscious. 'I don't know,' she said again.

'It's a special whistle,' he said. 'The one Sean used. But I need to use my fingers. Can you move your arm so I can get my hand up to my mouth?'

'No,' Louise said. She knew that if she moved one inch, her hip was going to break. She recognised the pain. She had experienced it before, in the bomb attack on the tube station in Balham. How can I be so unlucky? she wondered. One bomb blast was surely enough for anyone.

'Are you frightened?' George asked suddenly.

And then she remembered that this wasn't the first time George had been caught in an explosion either. He had been rescued from the ruins of his parents' house during the Blitz. His mother had died that night, crushed to death under the wreckage.

Yes, she wanted to shout. I am completely, utterly terrified. But it wasn't death she feared so much; that would almost be a relief at this precise moment. No, what she really feared was being crippled for life. Or facially disfigured. Or both.

But she didn't say it. Instead she forced herself to think about him. He was only ten years old. He was alive. And apparently uninjured. Her future was clearly bleak. But she had to try to help him. At least to give him a chance.

'Listen,' she whispered. 'I'm going to try to lever myself up so you can get your arm out. But I'm warning you, I might scream, or I might pass out. So whatever happens to me, just do the whistle if you can. And if someone answers, tell them to hurry.'

She didn't want to do it. It was the last thing in the world she wanted to do. It was probably the last thing she would ever do, come to that. But she knew she had to try. It was their only hope.

She took two slow breaths and pressed down tentatively on her elbow, trying to take some of her own weight. 'One, two, three,' she murmured. And pushed her shoulder up as hard as she could against the heavy, unyielding object that was pinning her down.

As George wriggled frantically beneath her, she was conscious of searing agony in her hip. A final sharp crack of pain. And then, mercifully, oblivion.

In the end, it was Malcolm who caught Lucky. Katy had tried, and failed, as had one or two other brave souls, Joyce included. But Malcolm just marched blithely up to him, apparently oblivious to the fact the blasted animal was apparently intent on savaging anyone who came within biting distance of his enormous teeth.

Before they could drag him back inside the pub, however, the dog's ears pricked up. Nearly knocking Malcolm off his feet, he swung round sharply. A second later he had jerked out of his grasp and was off, bounding blithely through the crowd of onlookers. And then he was under the cordon and scrabbling his way up and over the pile of wreckage like a shaggy mountain goat.

'He must have heard something,' someone shouted. And at once everyone fell silent. All eyes were on the dog. And when he stopped, poised high on some broken timbers right in front of her house, and started pawing at the rubble beneath him, Joyce felt a moment of hope.

It was then that they heard the whistle. Very faint, but quite distinct.

'That's Sean's whistle,' Katy said. 'But he's not here any … Oh my goodness.' She put her hand to her mouth. 'It must be George.' And as Pam Nelson let out a scream and ran to the cordon, Joyce was hard pushed not to feel disappointed. She had so hoped it would be Albert.

And then it turned out it wasn't just George trapped under there, but Louise Rutherford as well. Although according to George, she was either dead or unconscious.

'We need the heavy lifting gear,' the ARP warden had muttered when this information was relayed back to him from one of the light rescue team who had climbed tentatively up onto the rubble to try to talk to George. 'At the very least we need a bulldozer.'

But there wasn't time to wait for a bulldozer, or a crane.

Nor was there time to look for a middle-aged pawnbroker who had almost certainly perished in the blast. Not when a ten-year-old boy was definitely still alive, trapped under the dead or dying daughter of local bigwigs like the Rutherfords. Already everyone was galvanising themselves for action. Under instruction from the rescue team, they formed a human chain to clear away the chunks of rubble that were blocking the route to where George and Louise lay.

It was an agonisingly slow, painstaking task. Everyone knew that one false step could cause a fatal slippage.

It took two hours. And for Joyce it was the longest, most frustrating two hours of her life.

It was dark when the victims were finally revealed in all their gruesome glory. Apart from some bruises and being soaked to the skin with Louise's blood, George seemed miraculously unharmed. But anyone could see that Louise was in a bad way. Even Mrs Rutherford looked daunted by the sight of her unconscious daughter lying like a battered corpse on the ambulance stretcher.

Her whimper of horrified dismay was a far cry from the resilience she had shown when she had arrived on the scene earlier. Having learned of the precarious position Louise and George were in, and the fact that Mr Lorenz and several others were unaccounted for, she had clamped back any emotion she felt and immediately swept into action. The first thing she had done was to summon Mrs Trewgarth and the WVS canteen van.

'Right then, ladies,' she had called out bracingly. 'Chin up. Worrying won't help. As Lady Reading always says, doing is more useful than talking, so let's make everyone a nice strong cup of tea to keep them going.'

Joyce would have preferred something a bit stronger than tea. Something to stop her thinking about what might be happening to Albert while everyone concentrated on liberating George and Louise.

Thankfully, in due course, Katy produced a bottle of whisky from the ravaged pub, and Joyce was already on her third tot when Louise was finally lifted into a waiting ambulance.

Mrs Trewgarth had soup on the go now too, and as the ambulance roared away, the rescuers queued up at the WVS van, desperate for some sustenance after their labours.

'I reckon it must have been a gas main explosion,' someone was saying. 'Or maybe a rogue bomber.'

But before anyone could respond, they heard George's surprisingly chirpy voice emanating from the second ambulance. 'No it wasn't,' he called out. 'It was a rocket. Me and Louise saw it coming over. And when the engine cut out, she said we had to take cover, and she threw me down behind Mrs Carter's wall and lay on top of me and put her hands over my ears.'

'Good God,' someone muttered. 'Sounds like she saved the little blighter's life.'

Joyce peered into the dimly lit ambulance, where a Red Cross nurse was trying to clean George up. Pam was in there too, looking white as a sheet. Joyce didn't blame her; the sight of the bucket of bloody water and the soiled rags made her feel quite queasy herself.

Surreptitiously she clicked her fingers to attract George's attention. 'Do you remember seeing anyone else?' she asked him. 'Like Mr Lorenz? Or Mrs James? Before it happened, I mean?'

But Alan Nelson was already trying to draw her away. 'Mrs Carter, really,' he objected. 'He's had a terrible ordeal ...'

But George was staring at her over the rim of his cup of soup. 'Mr Lorenz was just outside his house,' he said. 'Louise shouted at him to take cover. But we were already lying under the wall when the explosion came, so I didn't see what happened to him.'

One of the medical orderlies came up to close the doors of the ambulance then, and Joyce reluctantly stepped out of the way.

Once both ambulances had gone, it was very quiet. No one was talking now. They were all exhausted. Some were slumped on the ground; others were leaning wearily against the side of the canteen van.

Joyce picked up a discarded torch and shone it over the cordon. She listened carefully, but there was no noise from the left-hand side of the street, from Albert's side, Gillian James's side. None at all.

'They might be lying there unconscious,' she said. 'Like Louise.'

She kept saying it. And everyone looked at her kindly.

But when they had finished their soup, they started again. Gino, Aaref Hoch and his two brothers, four of Katy's regulars, the soldiers from the light rescue team, two ARP wardens, Alan Nelson, three men who had also just come off duty from the Home Guard, Elsa and her family, and Angie.

And even though their fingers were bleeding; even though it was now dark and beginning to rain, they kept going.

Katy brought out some old sheets, and they tore them into strips and bound up their hands. And finally, by the light of the rescue team's shrouded torches and the gun emplacement searchlights, which were criss-crossing the night sky behind them, piece by awkward piece, person to person, hand to bandaged hand, the masonry and rubble was lifted out and carried away. Gradually they crept forward until they reached the spot on the pavement where Pam Nelson had painted the number of Albert's house right back at the beginning of the year.

It was then that a mortuary van turned into the road and drew to a discreet halt by the pub.

Ten minutes later, they found him. Somebody saw his shoe poking out from under a section of broken wardrobe, and a low murmur ran through the line. Carefully they heaved away the lump of masonry that had fallen on top of him, a huge, hard chunk of brick and mortar, in comparison with which a body, even a lean, sinewy middle-aged man's body, seemed soft and fragile.

He was lying close up against the low wall that ran in front of his house. Almost the mirror image of where Louise and George had taken shelter on the other side of the road.

They tried to keep Joyce away. They didn't want her to see him.

But she wanted to see him. She wanted to know how he had died. And when she stumbled forward and found him lying there, so completely still, his right leg twisted at such a horrible angle, the back of his head black and crusted with blood, she felt a surge of emotion. Of love. Of regret. She had never told him she loved him. Now she had left it too late.

He was so obviously dead, so obviously not breathing, that nobody bothered to check his vital signs. It was only as they rolled his broken body onto the mortuary van's stretcher that Gino noticed the faint flicker of a pulse still beating in his neck.

Chapter Twenty Seven

When Louise came round, she was in a private room in the Wilhelmina Hospital at Clapham Junction. At first she was glad to be alive, but then the pain kicked in and she wished she had died.

After the bomb at Balham station, she had languished in the Wilhelmina for weeks on end. She hadn't enjoyed it then, and she had a feeling she was going to enjoy it even less now. She hated the brisk, unemotional nurses, and the patronising Dr Mallet, who spent all his time toadying to her father, who was on the hospital committee, and hardly any time at all doing anything about the agony she was in.

'You're suffering a little bit of concussion,' he said. 'And you have a nasty cut on your head which will need to heal. But the X-ray of your lower back doesn't show up any broken bones. I am therefore expecting you to be back on your feet in no time.' He turned confidingly to her father. 'Of course, young women tend to have a very low pain threshold,' he murmured. 'They like to make the most of the slightest injury.'

Louise felt like screaming. But she knew that Mr Lorenz was even now lying unconscious on one of the men's wards with a fractured skull and numerous broken bones, and that Gillian James, Bella's infamous mother, had eventually been found dead in the ruins of her house with her head almost completely severed from her body. Two other people had perished at the scene, and two more, dragged alive from the rubble at the other end of the road, had since died from their wounds. All in all Louise knew she was lucky, and as a result, she was determined to try and remain stoical.

But the excruciating pain in her lower back didn't show any sign of wearing off, and it was only when Katy came to visit her on Monday afternoon that anyone really started to take her complaints seriously.

Katy had been a nurse at the Wilhelmina before she married Ward Frazer and knew Dr Mallet of old. 'You shouldn't still be in this much pain,' she said. 'Why don't you get your parents to ask Dr Goodacre to come and have a look at you? He's a much better doctor than old Mallet.'

It took some persuasion, as her father was reluctant to put Dr Mallet's nose out of joint, but eventually her mother stepped in and insisted on a second opinion. And it was worth it. Dr Goodacre was a completely different kettle of fish. Louise had noticed him at Angie Carter's wedding enthusing about the cake Mrs Carter had made. He was equally enthusiastic about her painful pelvis.

'Ah yes,' he said. 'Of course the cause of lower back pain is notoriously hard to pinpoint. But I suspect our culprit is either the acetabulofemoral joint or the sacroiliac. And a previous injury left you with a slight limp, I understand?' He rubbed his hands together with relish, then gave a sly wink. 'I think we might risk Dr Mallet's disfavour by taking another X-ray from a slightly different angle.'

When he reappeared later on, he was beaming even more. 'Well, well,' he said. 'It's just as I thought. A subluxation of the sacroiliac joint.'

'What's a subluxation?' Louise asked nervously.

'A dislocation,' he said happily. 'The bones are displaced, which stresses the ligaments that holds the joint together and puts strain on the surrounding structures. I suspect you have been suffering with it for some time, but it has clearly been exacerbated by the trauma of the explosion.' He eyed her thoughtfully. 'Dr Mallet has a poor opinion of women,' he said. 'But my belief is that you are just as brave as men, if not braver.'

Louise returned his look suspiciously. 'That sounds ominous,' she said.

He laughed delightedly. 'All I am saying is that with just a little twist and a bit of sharp pressure, we should be able to put it right.'

Louise was aware of her palms starting to sweat. She didn't like the sound of sharp pressure. She had already had enough pressure on her hip to last her a lifetime.

But swayed by his eager confidence, she allowed herself to be persuaded, and soon found herself in the most extraordinary position, balanced lengthways on the edge of the bed, with her arms round Dr Goodacre's neck.

'Perfect,' he said. 'Take a breath.' He waited for her to do it. 'Now relax and let it go,' and as she began to exhale, he jerked her first towards him and then hard down on the side of the bed.

Louise's shriek of pain brought the nurse running into the room. But Dr Goodacre was already rolling her back onto the mattress. 'Did you feel that click?' he asked. 'Yes. I'm afraid it will be a bit sore for a few hours, but then I hope we will begin to see some improvement.'

So did Louise. 'A bit sore' was the understatement of the year. She glared at him through watering eyes, wishing she could give him a sharp click somewhere where it hurt.

But his prognosis was correct. By that night, she felt considerably more comfortable. And by the following day, she was able to sit up without screaming in agony.

Which was lucky, because Henry Keller was coming to see her that afternoon. Concerned that Louise had failed to materialise at his dinner, he had rung the house several times before finally reaching her mother and discovering what had happened.

'He asked if there was anything he could do,' Celia said. She smiled conspiratorially. 'So I told him that I thought a visit from him would do you a power of good.' She had even been obliging enough to bring in a hairbrush and some face powder so Louise could tidy herself up, as she put it, before his arrival.

Joyce was just starting to prepare her vegetables for the café lunch when she heard a sharp crash from the other side of the wall, followed by a muffled Italian exclamation, '*Merda!*'

Running through, she saw white shards scattered all over the floor by the counter.

Since the rocket attack on Saturday, Angie had refused to let Gino leave her side, and Joyce had been forced to let him come and help out at the café. But his clumsiness was driving her nuts. This was the second plate he had broken in two days.

'For goodness' sake,' she shouted at him. 'What's the matter with you? We're short enough of crockery as it is.'

As Gino hung his head and floundered for the words to apologise, Angie leapt to his defence.

'It's not his fault,' she said. 'His fingers are still sore from Saturday.'

And Joyce knew there was nothing she could say to that. If it hadn't been for Gino, Albert might even now be lying in the morgue with Gillian James and the other unlucky victims of the explosion, rather than merely unconscious in the Wilhelmina.

Leaving Angie and Gino to clear up the mess, she went back into the kitchen. She picked up her knife, then put it down again and, leaning over the sideboard, closed her eyes.

Once, some years ago, she had seen a film about an Arctic explorer. She remembered vividly the flickering black and white pictures of the wide expanses of polar ice, and the terrible moment when the husky sleigh had suddenly plunged through a crack into the sub-zero water below. She had hardly been able to watch as the dogs and their drivers thrashed about trying desperately to clamber back onto safe ground.

That was rather how she felt now. From one moment to the next her whole life had plunged into disarray, and she was struggling to regain her equilibrium. Not only was Albert at death's door, but her house had been declared unsafe for habitation. According to an officious man from the council, it had been undermined by the blast.

So now, courtesy of the WVS, she and Angie and Gino were sleeping in the church hall. Not that you could call it sleeping; what with the uncomfortable military-issue camp beds and all the snoring and restless murmuring of the other bombed-out occupants, it was hard to get more than forty winks at a time. The only saving grace was that Angie and Gino had, so far at least, managed to refrain from having sex.

Though unlike the unfortunate Mrs James, at least Angie and Gino were alive. As was poor little orphaned Bella.

But Joyce didn't have the energy to worry about Bella just now. All her concern was focused on Albert. He was alive too. But only just. Nobody was saying anything yet, but she could tell from the compassionate glances of the nurses on his ward that the chances of him coming round, let alone recovering, were diminishing daily.

And on top of all that, there was the ever-present likelihood of another diving bomb coming down and finishing the rest of them off. The government was clearly trying to keep the details out of the press, presumably to frustrate the Nazis' attempts to perfect their aim, but by now too many had exploded for people not to know that London was once again under attack. The damn things had already garnered various nicknames: divers, crashers, flying bombs, buzz bombs, doodlebugs.

Shortly after Lavender Road had been devastated, another of the bombs had fallen on St John's Hill, hitting a trolley bus and killing everyone inside. Since then, two more had exploded in Clapham, one in Webb's Road and the other in Tennyson Street.

And it wasn't just south London that was suffering. On Sunday, one of the beastly things had hit the Guards Chapel in Birdcage Walk during the matins service, causing the roof to collapse on top of the congregation. A hundred and nineteen of the guardsmen and their families had died in that one incident, with a hundred and forty injured. Another rocket had plunged down on the Air Ministry at Bush House, where a number of off-duty secretaries and airwomen were sunbathing on the roof terrace. Casualty figures for that attack had not yet been published, but rumour had it that the rescue services had to spend an entire day picking human remains out of the trees on the Aldwych.

'Greville says they are impossible to bring down because they are so small and so fast,' Mrs Rutherford said. 'So unless the invasion forces can push forward and destroy the launch sites, we are going to be suffering the damned things for some time yet.'

Joyce pressed her hands to her temples. And that was another worry. The invasion forces weren't making the progress everyone had hoped. Montgomery was slowly advancing on Caen, but the German resistance was strong, and the casualty figures were mounting. On Albert's ward at the

Wilhelmina there were at least a dozen soldiers who had been brought back from France and were now fighting for their lives in hospital, instead of on the battlefield. Goodness only knew how many more there were elsewhere. Or lying dead in France. She just prayed Paul and Pete weren't among them.

'Are you all right, Mum?' Angie asked from the door. 'You've been standing there like that for ages.'

Reluctantly Joyce straightened up and opened her eyes. 'Yes, I'm all right,' she said. 'A bit tired, that's all.'

Glancing at the clock, she picked up the knife again and turned back to her chopping. Only three hours to go before visiting time at the Wilhelmina. Perhaps today there would be finally be some good news about Albert.

Joyce wasn't the only person who was tired. At that moment, Jen was standing on Gower Street, looking across at the RADA building once again, and she didn't know which was causing her more concern, her gritty-eyed tiredness, or her absolute terror of what lay ahead.

She hadn't known that a rocket had hit Lavender Road until she had arrived back in London the previous evening. In all the trauma and disarray, nobody had thought to write to tell her. But she did know about Hitler's new weapons of revenge, because it wasn't just London that had suffered the recent spate of attacks; the south-east had had their fair share too. Jen had even heard one of the damn things droning past overhead during a concert, although thankfully its engine hadn't cut out, which everyone now knew to be the danger sign. But it had been shocking to come home and find half the street destroyed and Mr Lorenz in hospital. It was also somewhat shocking to discover that everyone was talking about Louise Rutherford as though she was some kind of heroine for purportedly saving George Nelson's life.

Unwilling to sleep with Joyce, Angie and Gino in the church hall, Jen had persuaded Katy to let her spend the night in the pub cellar. But that wasn't much better. Without Sean's authoritative presence, Malcolm was noisy and overexcited, and Katy was clearly under considerable strain. She had at least managed to get the pub windows boarded up so that it couldn't be looted, but she hadn't yet managed to do anything about the damage upstairs. Nor did she know what to do about Bella, who had refused to speak one single word since her mother died.

'I think she's suffering from some kind of shock,' Katy said. 'But the odd thing is that she stopped talking the moment the blast went off. It was almost as though she knew.'

'Perhaps she did,' Jen said. 'Don't they call it second sight? I can remember teasing Molly once because she told me she'd met someone with second sight. But maybe she was right.'

Katy gave a slight moan. 'Oh I do wish Molly would come home,' she said. 'I could really do with her just now.'

But Molly hadn't come home. And the only prediction that Jen could make about her own immediate future was that it was going to take all the courage she possessed to walk up those steps into the RADA entrance hall.

Suddenly she remembered her abortive Old Vic audition at the New Theatre all those months ago, and hoped she wasn't tempting fate by having chosen the same speech from *Romeo and Juliet* for today. For her contemporary piece, she had picked Mabel Chiltern's proposal speech from Oscar Wilde's *An Ideal Husband*. She had practised them both endlessly. One tragic, one comic. But she didn't know if she was any good. She hadn't wanted to tell the Violets what she was doing, otherwise she could have asked them to hear her. And if she hadn't messed things up with Henry, she could have tried them out on him. But she had messed things up with Henry. And now she was paying the price.

As it turned out, losing the chance of Henry's help wasn't the only price she was going to pay that afternoon. She was also going to pay for losing her temper at the Old Vic audition. Because there, sitting on the selection panel, was the same ghastly man she had met in the foyer of the New Theatre. She recognised him immediately she stepped into the room. How could she ever forget that ridiculous yellow bow tie, the absurd cigarette holder, the air of foppish arrogance? And he knew her too. She could see that at once from the curl of his lip as he disdainfully tapped out his cigarette.

She tried not to let it affect her, but she couldn't help recalling Henry's caustic comment: 'Jason Cavell may be a bit of an arse, but he's very influential.'

And now here the blasted man was, with the perfect opportunity to influence his fellow selectors against her.

Of course that was exactly what happened. They heard her pieces. They asked her a few questions about her career to date, and her aspirations, then they made her wait, right there on the stage, while they discussed her performance. She couldn't hear exactly what they were saying, but she could tell by the tone of their voices that they weren't impressed. And to be honest, she didn't blame them. She knew her pieces had been lacklustre, and her answers to their questions had sounded defensive even to her ears. And when she heard Jason Cavell making some sotto voce remark about overambitious variety soubrettes, she knew that she might as well have thrown her one guinea non-returnable entrance fee in the river.

Eventually one of the women on the panel leaned forward to address her. 'Thank you, Miss Carter,' she said in a husky grande dame kind of voice. 'As

I am sure you are aware, places here at RADA are very limited. We have to be sure we are selecting the most promising of our applicants. I'm afraid you haven't quite made the grade today, but we wish you the very best for your future career.'

There were plenty of things Jen would have liked to say in response, not least that it seemed completely unfair that she should be auditioned by someone who was already prejudiced against her. But she didn't. She just clamped her jaw shut, nodded and left.

So that was the end of her dream, she thought, as she walked blindly away down Gower Street.

The only saving grace was that she'd had the sense not to tell anyone where she was going or what she was doing. At least she wasn't going to have to put up with any well-meant commiserations or sympathy.

The person she ought to tell was Mr Lorenz, as he had been kind enough to offer to pay for the RADA course, but she couldn't even tell him. Suddenly Jen felt guilty. It seemed wrong to be bemoaning her fate when poor old Mr Lorenz was lying in a coma in the Wilhelmina. Well, she wasn't going to need his money now. And what about Mrs James? Even if she had been a prostitute, she hadn't deserved to die. Only three weeks ago she had been pinning up Jen's bridesmaid's dress. No, in the scheme of things, failing to get into RADA was hardly an earth-shattering disaster, despite how devastating it felt to her at the moment.

And it did feel devastating. However much she tried to put it in context, it felt as if the bottom had fallen out of her world. She had been pinning her hopes on RADA ever since she had thought of it. And now she was back at square one.

She was also, rather surprisingly, back at Victoria station. She had been walking for over an hour, and now she was running late. She needed to get back to Woking, where the Violets were performing that evening. But first she had to pick up her overnight bag from the pub. And maybe, just maybe, she would confide in Katy. Perhaps it would be nice to get some sympathy after all.

But when she arrived back at the pub, Katy was standing by the bar looking worried. She had just had a visit from Mrs Rutherford. 'They're making plans to evacuate all the local children, and she thinks I ought to let Malcolm go.' She looked at Jen piteously. 'He's so young to be sent away, but I don't know if I can keep him safe here. I can't keep him in the cellar the whole time. It wasn't so bad when the bombing was just at night. But these beastly doodlebugs seem to be coming over all the time now.'

And Jen knew immediately that she couldn't burden Katy with her own problems. As far as Katy was concerned, she had been up to town for a fitting for a new ENSA costume. The last thing she needed was to know that Jen's future was in tatters.

'What about sending him to your mother and Ward's aunts?' she suggested.

Katy shook her head. 'I can't,' she said. 'I wish I could, but they would never be able to manage him. My mother is too frail and Ward's aunts are too old.'

'Well, can't he go with someone he knows?' Jen said. 'What about George Nelson? I know he's a bit of a menace, but he likes Malcolm and surely he'd keep an eye on him?' She hesitated. 'You've got a lot on your plate at the moment, Katy. What with being lumbered with Bella, and all the damage upstairs to sort out, let alone looking after Caroline and the pub. Maybe you'd find it all easier to cope with if at least you knew Malcolm was safe. After all, it may not be for very long.'

Katy looked harrowed. 'Perhaps you're right,' she said. 'But is anyone really safe these days?'

Jen knew she wasn't just thinking about Malcolm. She was thinking about Ward too. And maybe all the young men battling away in France and Italy as well.

This bloody war, Jen thought, as she hugged her goodbye. It's going to be the death of us all if we aren't careful.

Even more depressed, she headed off to Clapham Junction. Hoping she wasn't going to miss her train, she was just hurrying up St John's Road when a taxi pulled up ahead of her at the entrance to the Wilhelmina, and to her utter astonishment, she saw Henry Keller getting out of it.

For an extraordinary moment, Jen thought she must be hallucinating. But she wasn't. It was Henry all right. Looking fit and unusually tanned, as though he had been enjoying the summer weather.

He was too busy paying off the driver to notice her. She saw him wave away the change with an easy smile, and was aware of her heart giving a little kick of pleasure. For all his faults, Henry had always been one of the most generous people she knew. He was also the one person in the world just now who might be able to cheer her up.

Unthinkingly, instinctively, she took a step towards him, and was just about to call his name when the taxi driver said something to him, and with a slight laugh Henry reached back into the cab and withdrew a bunch of red roses.

It was a huge bunch. One might even say extravagant, especially in this austere day and age. There must have been two dozen blooms. The eager greeting died on Jen's lips, and hastily, unobtrusively, she stepped sideways into a doorway. And now, belatedly, she remembered that Mr Lorenz wasn't the only person languishing in the Wilhelmina.

Louise blasted Rutherford was in there too, recovering from her heroic wounds.

Jen stood in that doorway for a long time. Then she blew her nose, took a long, shaky breath and walked on to the station.

Louise had been looking forward to Henry's visit, but in the event, she was dozing when he arrived.

Hearing a tap on the door, she opened her eyes with a start to see him standing in the doorway.

'I'm sorry,' he said as she struggled up into a more becoming position. 'I didn't mean to disturb you.'

He had disturbed her. Just seeing him looking at her with such concern disturbed her. But what made her eyes really widen was the sight of the huge bouquet of roses he was carrying. Before she could jump to any conclusions, however, he made an apologetic gesture.

'These are from Freddy,' he said. 'He wanted to bring them himself, but I felt that might be too much for you in your weakened condition. So I brought them down instead.'

Louise was aware of a stab of disappointment. But she smiled obligingly. 'You're quite right,' she said. 'An ardent suitor is the last thing I need just now.' Although even as she said it, she knew it wasn't true. She would have been perfectly happy for Henry to show a little ardour.

But he didn't get a chance, because just then one of the nurses came in and started clucking with delight over the flowers.

'Shall I put them in a vase for you, Miss Rutherford?' she asked.

'Thank you,' Louise replied, although she knew the nurse had only come in to have a look at Henry. Judging from the way she fluttered her eyelashes at him as she left the room with the roses, she was impressed with what she saw.

Henry was looking amused. 'You seem to get very good service here,' he said.

Louise rolled her eyes. 'Daddy's on the board of governors,' she said, and that made him laugh.

Sadly, he didn't stay long.

'I'm on my way to Winchester,' he said as he stood up regretfully. 'To meet my old colonel in the Rifle Brigade. I want to rejoin the regiment. I feel bad sitting around in London listening to news reports of the fighting in France. I have to do my bit.'

Louise put her hand to her chest. 'Goodness,' she said. 'And are they going to let you?'

He smiled. 'Yes, I think so. It's more a matter of persuading ENSA to let me go.' He came up to the side of the bed and leaned over to give her a light kiss on the cheek. 'It's not public knowledge yet,' he added as he straightened up. 'So please don't tell anyone. It might make things awkward if word got out too soon.'

Louise looked up at him demurely. 'My lips are sealed,' she said. Although she couldn't help thinking that they certainly wouldn't stay sealed for long if he ever got round to kissing her properly.

'Take care,' she said quickly, hoping he wouldn't notice her sudden flush. 'And let me know what happens.'

'Of course I will,' he said. 'And you take care too. Don't get in the way of any more missiles.'

Almost as soon as he had gone, the nurse came back into the room.

'Coo,' she murmured as she placed the vase of roses reverently on the windowsill. 'I wouldn't mind having an admirer like him. He made me feel quite flustered.'

But if the nurse had been flustered by Henry, she was made even more so a few minutes later by the sight of Colonel Westwood in his crisp American officer's uniform adorned with the impressive silver oak leaf on his epaulette.

Louise didn't blame her. She felt rather flustered herself. She'd had no idea he was going to visit, and wished she'd had time to hide the roses. She didn't want him to get the impression she was already spoken for.

But it was too late. He was already in the room, averting his gaze politely as Louise once again heaved herself awkwardly up in the bed.

'How are you doing?' he asked. 'That was a real bad thing. Sounds like you're lucky to be alive.'

Louise smiled at him. 'It's actually thanks to you that I *am* still alive,' she said. 'I remembered what you said about explosions and defensive barriers, so when I saw the rocket heading in my direction, I lay down behind a neighbour's wall. And it seemed to work.' She rubbed her hip through the blanket and gave a rueful grimace. 'More or less.'

'Good God,' he said. But his professional interest was aroused. His gaze only flickered briefly to her hip and then quickly away again. 'So you actually saw it coming?'

Louise nodded. 'Yes, I saw it quite clearly. It must have been travelling at between two and three thousand feet before the engine cut out. I assume it's designed to dive down and explode wherever it lands.'

His eyes narrowed. 'The Germans are calling them *Vergeltungswaffen*,' he said. 'Reprisal weapons. Any idea of speed?'

'Fast, that's all I know,' Louise said. She grimaced. 'My father was on the guns that night. They were firing at it like mad. But they didn't get near it.

Even if they had managed to shoot it down, it would presumably still have exploded and caused damage.'

Colonel Westwood nodded. 'I gather the War Office is intending to shift all the ack-ack to the south coast,' he said. 'Try to stop the missiles before they reach urbanised areas.'

'That's not going to be easy,' Louise said. 'Judging from the one I saw, they're too small and too fast for traditional artillery.' She glanced at the door and lowered her voice. 'But I think we could have hit it with the new fuse.'

'If only,' he said.

Louise frowned. 'What do you mean?'

He was silent for a moment, then stood up and pushed the door closed.

'I've lost most of my unit,' he said. 'They've been sent over to France to bolster the artillery units over there.'

'Then why don't you use British gunners?'

'The situation is much the same.' He shrugged. 'I thought about trying to borrow some Home Guard units like your father's, but like I said, they're all being reassigned to the south coast.'

Louise looked at his face. She could see how frustrating it was for him.

'Well, why don't you use girls?' she said suddenly.

'Girls?'

'Yes,' Louise said. 'Why not? They're presumably not going to get sent to France.' She looked at him eagerly. 'I know they aren't allowed to actually fire the guns, but they can do pretty much everything else. All the technical work, the spotting and tracking, and the range-finding calculations.'

He had been pacing the room, but now he stopped and leaned back against the windowsill next to the roses. 'You know, that's not a bad idea,' he said slowly. 'But how would I get hold of them?'

Louise had to bite her lip to prevent herself giggling. Wasn't that what all the boys wanted to know? She thought how discombobulated Susan Voles would be if Colonel Westwood got hold of her.

'I can't see the ATS being willing to risk their resources on a technology they've never heard of,' he said. 'Plus the British War Office doesn't like anything unorthodox. It was hard enough persuading anyone to agree to train you and Don Wellington on our behalf.'

Louise could believe it. She knew to her cost that everything in the army was done exactly by the rulebook. Especially in the ATS.

'Why don't you ask Commander Cunningham?' she suggested. 'You met her when you came to see me at Bracknell. She might know how to cut a few corners.'

But then she remembered the way the glamorous Commander Cunningham had looked at him as they strolled convivially across the parade ground. 'Or if you haven't got time, maybe I could go and talk to her?' she said. 'On your behalf.'

For a brief moment he looked enthusiastic, but then his brows drew together. 'But what about your injuries? I got the impression from Mr Gregg that you'd be staying in hospital for quite a while.'

Louise looked at him and felt a tingle of excitement. She liked the way his eyes seemed even deeper and darker when he frowned. She lifted her shoulders dismissively. 'I haven't got time to linger about in hospital,' she said. She put on a brave smile. 'There is a war on, you know.'

Joyce knew something was wrong as soon as she pushed open the door of the men's surgical ward, because her old friend Sister Morris was there, waiting for her. And it wasn't even her ward.

Her eyes flew to the bed three along from the door, and she felt momentarily reassured. Albert was still there, in exactly the same position she had left him in yesterday. Flat on his back, arms at his sides, his eyes closed, his chest barely moving, the well-starched hospital sheets tucked tightly over him.

But before she could go to him, Sister Morris put her hand on her arm and drew her to one side.

'The doctors are concerned that Mr Lorenz may have had a bleed on the brain,' she said in her crisp, no-nonsense way. 'I'm afraid he could pass away at any moment.' She paused. 'The longer we go on, the less likelihood there is of a happy outcome. Even if he does regain consciousness, which seems increasingly unlikely, he may not be the same person he was before the accident.'

Once again Joyce felt as though she was standing on that ice floe. All the warmth of the sunny June day seemed to drain out of her body. She could almost feel the ice cracking beneath her feet, and she put out a hand to steady herself against the wall.

The whole ward suddenly seemed very quiet. She didn't know if it was because everyone was watching her, or whether it was just that the sudden pounding sensation in her ears was blocking out all other sound. She didn't care. All she could think about was Albert as he had been, his eyes watching her with unswerving warmth and affection from behind his spectacles; his shy, twinkling smile.

'Are you all right, Mrs Carter?' Sister Morris's brisk voice broke into her thoughts. She nodded to a nearby chair. 'Perhaps you should sit down?'

Joyce shook her head. 'No,' she said. 'I'd rather sit with Albert.'

Sister Morris led her across the ward to his bed and settled her down beside him. She hesitated, then reached under the starched sheet and carefully

324

drew out his one undamaged hand, laying it on the cover next to Joyce.

Then she wheeled over two canvas screens and positioned them carefully round the bed.

'It will give you a little privacy,' she said. 'In case you want to say your goodbyes.'

Chapter Twenty Eight

Joyce sat there staring at Albert's hand lying lifelessly on the white sheet. It took her a long time to muster the courage to reach out and take it in her own. It felt oddly heavy, awkward, unnatural. She could feel the bones inside. The skin felt dry. But it was warm. The blood was clearly still moving round him, even if the rest of him was closing down.

It was a hard thought. One she could not bring herself to accept. It was too soon. They hadn't had time to get to know each other properly. Let alone time to love.

It seemed cruelly unfair. They might have had fun together. Albert had deserved a bit of fun. And she could have been the one to give it to him. He had always liked her sense of humour. Always smiled at her little jokes. Never took offence if she was ratty, or if her language was a bit blue. He was kind and tolerant. They would probably have rubbed along together quite well. He had always been there when she needed him, and deep down she had been relying on him to support her in the future too, if anything happened to the boys, or to Jen or Angie, or if Mrs Rutherford suddenly decided to pull the plug on the café. He would have stood by her whatever happened. And now some beastly hand of fate was pulling the plug on *him*.

Slowly she lifted his hand and kissed his grazed fingers. They smelt clean and pleasantly antiseptic. She noticed through a blur of tears that his nails were neatly trimmed. She had a sudden vision of him standing in his bathroom painstakingly clipping them, making sure they were regular, with no sharp edges.

'I never told you before,' she whispered. 'It's been creeping up on me for a long time. But it's time now. Time for you to know ...' But she couldn't say any more. The words choked up in her throat.

It was as she lowered his hand back to the bed that she felt the faint responsive pressure on her fingers. At first she couldn't believe it. But then it came again. And then to her astonishment, his lips moved.

His voice was very faint. She had to bend her head to hear. But the words were quite clear. 'Time for me to know what?'

She stared at him. Had she imagined it? But now his eyes were open and he was looking at her, albeit rather blankly. Fleetingly she was alarmed, but then she realised that perhaps he couldn't see her properly without his glasses.

And suddenly she wanted him to know. Even if this turned out to be his last lucid moment, she wanted him to know how she felt.

'I love you,' she said.

There was a long pause, and she watched him anxiously. His lips curved slightly. 'I love you too,' he said. Then he gave a contented sigh, closed his eyes and slept.

But it wasn't his last lucid moment. The next time he woke up, he asked for a drink. By that evening the hospital doctors thought the danger had passed. Although he had no recollection of what had happened, in every other way his brain seemed to be operating normally. It would take time for his other wounds and broken bones to heal, but there was no reason why he shouldn't make a full recovery.

Louise heard the news from her mother. 'So now perhaps they will be able to get married after all,' Celia said. 'Wouldn't that be wonderful?'

Louise nodded, but actually the thought of Mrs Carter entering into a conjugal relationship with Mr Lorenz was more extraordinary than wonderful, and she was hard pushed not to laugh.

Perhaps misinterpreting her lack of enthusiasm for jealousy, Celia's eyes flickered to the red roses that still adorned the windowsill. 'Well, you never know,' she said bracingly. 'It might be you next.'

Ever since Angie's wedding, her mother had been hoping that Henry might be 'the one'. But discovering that the roses had come from an even more eligible admirer, her aspirations had changed abruptly. 'A lord? Goodness, Louise,' she had said. 'That would be something, wouldn't it? Marrying into the aristocracy. Daddy would be awfully pleased.'

Louise had rolled her eyes. 'I'm not going to marry someone just to please Daddy,' she said. 'Nor am I going to marry someone just because he's rich.' Although, of course, that was exactly what she had wanted to do at the beginning of the year. But somehow things were different now. *She* was different. She certainly didn't want to end up like her mother, tied for better or worse to a man she didn't love.

Looking at Celia now, standing at the end of her bed in her tweed coat with the WVS armband sewn neatly on her sleeve, Louise realised that the war had probably been her mother's salvation. Setting up the café and embracing her WVS duties so eagerly had probably been her way of escaping her husband's patriarchal tyranny. It had also given her a chance to use her indisputable organisational abilities. She was already trying to decide where to accommodate Mr Lorenz when he eventually came out of hospital.

'Mrs Carter's house is still out of bounds,' she said. 'And I can't possibly put him in the church hall. The poor man is going to need a proper bed and someone to see to his needs. If we're not careful, the hospital will transfer him to a convalescent home miles away.'

'Then why don't you invite him and Mrs Carter to stay in our house?' Louise said. It was a deliberate taunt. It still rankled that her parents had refused to accommodate any of her ATS friends for the Easter weekend. Now she would see if her mother was more generous towards her own friends.

Celia looked considerably taken aback. 'Oh, I don't think Daddy would agree to that,' she said at once. 'Mrs Carter is an employee, after all. And as for Mr Lorenz, well ...' She stopped uncomfortably.

Louise looked at her. 'He's Jewish,' she said.

Her mother coloured. 'I don't mind that,' she said. 'But I don't think Daddy would like it.'

'Then why doesn't Daddy go and live in Germany?' Louise said angrily. 'He would feel quite at home there. He's got more prejudices than Adolf Hitler.'

'That's enough, Louise,' her mother snapped. 'Daddy may be old-fashioned in his views, but he is your father. If it wasn't for him, you wouldn't be lying comfortably here in an expensive private room; you'd be taking your chances on one of the general wards.'

Louise eyed her with resentful hostility. Comfortable indeed. She had never spent a less comfortable few days in all her life. 'Well, he won't have to pay for it much longer,' she said. 'I'm hoping to be discharged in a day or two, and then I'm going straight back to work.'

'Don't be silly,' her mother said. 'You're not nearly well enough to go back to work. Dr Mallet told me that you'd have to rest up for several weeks. I thought you could go and stay with Granny in the country.'

Louise shook her head. 'I don't want to go and stay with Granny,' she said. 'Nor do I want to rest up. I'm not a malingerer like Douglas. I've got a job to do, and I intend to do it, whatever it takes.'

In the event, it wasn't until the following Tuesday that she found herself sitting in an American army jeep on her way to see Senior Commander Cunningham.

Even the optimistic Dr Goodacre had been reluctant to discharge her too soon. 'The pelvis might feel more comfortable,' he said. 'But we mustn't overlook the fact that you have suffered a serious concussion. We need to keep an eye on you until we are sure there aren't going to be any unexpected consequences.'

But eventually they had let her go. And now, as the jeep rattled its way through the ravaged south London streets, Louise had to admit that she felt extremely shaky, although she wasn't sure if that was caused by unexpected consequences, or by the thought of seeing Commander Cunningham again.

When they arrived at the ATS barracks at Bracknell, she asked the driver if she could use the driving mirror to check herself over. She was already wearing her best uniform, but she wanted to make sure there wasn't a hair out of place.

The frosty-faced HQ company sergeant looked astonished to see her. As well she might. It probably wasn't every day of the week that a former recruit came calling on the camp commandant. She was also probably remembering that the last time Louise had marched into Commander Cunningham's office was in order to receive a severe reprimand for insubordination.

Louise couldn't help remembering it too. But this time was different. This time she had a letter in her pocket from Colonel Westwood authorising her to speak on his behalf.

When she gained access to the commandant's office and explained her errand, however, Commander Cunningham looked puzzled. 'But there are well-known procedures for staffing requests.'

'I know, ma'am,' Louise said. 'But Colonel Westwood's project is shrouded in secrecy, which slows everything down. We thought you might be able to help us get round some of the red tape.'

Commander Cunningham's neatly plucked eyebrows rose sharply. 'Did you indeed?' she said. 'And what, may I ask, made you think that?'

Louise shuffled uncomfortably on her seat. 'Well, you always seemed more … um … open-minded than some of the other officers I've met.' She saw the other woman's eyes narrow and hurried on. 'And you told me once that in your opinion women are equal to men in everything but physical strength. That made a big impression on me. You also said you wanted the ATS to take their position alongside men. And this is an opportunity for them to do that.'

Commander Cunningham was regarding her steadily. 'But you can't tell me exactly what this secret weapon is?'

Louise shook her head reluctantly. 'No. All I can say is that if we can make it work, it could make a huge difference to the defence of London.'

'And would the work put ATS girls in danger?'

'No, I don't think so. No more than they would be on any ack-ack gun position.'

There was a long pause. Then Commander Cunningham tapped a shapely fingernail on her desk. 'How many girls would you need?'

'I think six would be enough,' Louise said. 'But …'

'But what?'

She hesitated, knowing that she was about to step outside her brief. 'The thing is, we only want good people.'

Once again the commandant's brows rose sharply. 'And what do you mean by that?'

Louise dropped her gaze. 'We need people who are flexible and adaptable. We don't want people like Private Buller who think they know it all already.' She glanced up apologetically. 'I know the DS here and at Arborfield thought a lot of her, but ...' She tailed off uneasily.

Commander Cunningham held her gaze for a moment, then bent her head to consult a printed list on her desk. 'In that case,' she said, 'I am sure you will be glad to learn that Private Buller has already been posted to an ack-ack unit.'

Louise was extremely glad to learn that. And relieved. 'The person I'd really like is Susan Voles,' she said.

But Commander Cunningham shook her head. 'Private Voles failed the live firing course,' she said. 'She is in a holding unit at the moment, waiting for reallocation.'

Louise blinked in dismay. This was news to her. She had been pinning her hopes on getting Voles. 'How on earth did she manage to fail? Surely not on her technical ability?'

'I gather she wasn't considered to be sufficiently robust,' Commander Cunningham said. 'Physically or emotionally.'

Louise frowned. She knew from Susan's letters that she hadn't been enjoying live firing camp, but she didn't know why. 'I expect the others bullied her,' she said. 'But if she's happy to come, then I know Colonel Westwood would be pleased with her. She'll be all right with me.'

Commander Cunningham raised her eyes from the list. 'You seem very certain about that.'

'I am,' she said. 'Voles is a good soldier. She's just lacking in self-confidence, that's all.'

Commander Cunningham sat back in her chair and studied her thoughtfully. 'One of the most satisfying things in life is to be proved right,' she murmured. She caught Louise's bewildered look and inclined her head slightly. 'I had high hopes of you, Private Rutherford, and it seems as though I am not going to be disappointed.'

Louise felt herself flushing. 'Thank you, ma'am,' she stammered. 'But I'm only doing what I can to help Colonel Westwood.'

'You are doing what you can to help win this war,' Commander Cunningham said. 'And if a few corners have to be cut, then so be it.' She stood up. 'Leave it with me. I'll see what I can do to help you.'

'Thank you,' Louise said. She stood up too, and saluted smartly.

Commander Cunningham smiled. 'I wish you well with your efforts,' she said. 'I look forward to hearing great things of you in the future.'

Louise laughed. 'I don't know about that,' she said. 'You'll probably hear that I've been court-martialled for stepping out of line.'

George was appalled when he heard that he was going to be evacuated with his school to some safe part of the country.

'I don't want to go,' he said at once. He stared in horror at Celia Rutherford, who was standing on the doorstep in her dark green WVS uniform with a clipboard in her hand. Then he swung round to Pam. 'Is Nellie going?'

Pam shook her head, wishing she had had the chance to tell him herself in private, but unfortunately Mrs Rutherford had jumped the gun. 'Nellie is too young to be evacuated,' she said. 'But Malcolm is going with you. Mrs Rutherford has arranged it with the school. You will be billeted together. With a nice family in the country.'

'I don't want a nice family in the country. I don't like the country.'

Pam knew that mulish tone of old and her heart sank. But Mrs Rutherford looked shocked. She was already somewhat disenchanted with George because of his refusal to continue collecting salvage after winning the rabbit. This new recalcitrance was not likely to raise him in her estimation.

'Goodness,' she said. 'I never heard such nonsense.' She focused her stern gaze on George. 'If you were older, you would be joining the armed forces. You wouldn't make a fuss about that, would you?'

She waited while he shook his head reluctantly. 'Well, this is no different,' she said. 'You won't be fighting, but you will be doing your duty by saving your parents some worry, and by looking after Malcolm Frazer, from whom, I may say, I haven't heard one word of reluctance, even though he is significantly younger than you.'

Pam caught George's agonised look and her heart twisted. She knew how he felt. She didn't want him to go away either. Not at all. But the rocket attacks were intensifying. One had come over yesterday while she was in Northcote Road, and everyone had paused and guiltily willed it to continue on its way, even though they knew that meant it would fall on someone else. The very sound of it, that horrible grating buzz of the engines, had sent shivers up her spine, reminding her of the gut-wrenching fear she had experienced while George had been trapped under the wreckage of Mr Lorenz's house.

She had thought he would relish the idea of going away with his classmates. But it seemed not. She was oddly touched that he would apparently prefer to stay in London with her and Alan. Or perhaps it was the thought of leaving Bunny that was making him look so apprehensive.

She glanced at Mrs Rutherford. 'Is there any chance he could take his rabbit with him?' she asked. Perhaps Bunny's presence would make the separation less painful.

But Mrs Rutherford looked aghast. 'Good Lord,' she said. 'That's quite out of the question.'

'But surely, in the circumstances, you could make an exception …?'

'Certainly not. Imagine the mayhem that would ensue if I allowed every child to bring a pet.'

'I don't want to take Bunny anyway,' George said suddenly. 'He wouldn't like it.'

Pam frowned, disconcerted by the resolute tone in his voice, but all Mrs Rutherford heard was the capitulation. 'That's the spirit,' she said bracingly. 'He'll be much safer here.'

Pam glanced uneasily at George. She thought he was bound to question the logic of Mrs Rutherford's remark. But after a moment's hesitation, he just clamped his lips, turned on his heel and walked away down the passage.

'Well, I'm glad he has come to his senses,' Mrs Rutherford said. 'I hadn't realised he was quite so headstrong. I know it's not easy when you are dealing with adopted children, but I think all he needs is a firm hand.'

Pam felt like giving her a firm hand. She wanted to run after George to see if he was all right, but it wasn't just the evacuation arrangements Mrs Rutherford had come about; she wanted to talk about WVS business too. What with all the damage from the V-1 rockets, there was suddenly an awful lot of extra work to be done. Getting all the displaced persons housed and fed was a major task. Then there were the injured to be visited in hospital, blood donors to be found, families of the deceased to be written to, even some burials or cremations to be arranged where bodies remained unclaimed by next of kin.

By the time she had left, George had completely disappeared. Pam hunted for him everywhere. In the end, she guessed that he must have climbed over the back wall and escaped via the Rutherfords' garden.

She scanned the sky nervously. But although she was concerned about him, she didn't grudge him his moment of freedom. Children shouldn't have to be sent away, separated from their families and their pets just in order to keep them safe. They ought to be able to play and explore wherever they wanted without the risk of being blown up.

By the time he eventually got back, it was already dark and Pam was getting extremely worried. But George was not only unrepentant about his prolonged absence, he was also hopeful of a reprieve.

'The ack-ack guns are being taken away,' he said. 'I just saw them being loaded up on trailers. Mr Rutherford was there and everything. I asked one of the soldiers, and he told me they are going to the south coast so they can shoot down all the rockets before they get to London. So now Malcolm and I won't have to go to the country after all.'

Jen was pleased to get a note from her mother saying that Mr Lorenz had come round from his coma and was now making a good recovery. But the news didn't do much to cheer her. She had felt low and out of sorts ever since the RADA fiasco.

On 1 July, the Violets arrived at Salisbury to do a few days' worth of concerts at the Guildhall. As Jen dismounted stiffly from the van, her eye caught a poster advertising an upcoming ENSA production of *Romeo and Juliet* at another venue in Salisbury, the Garrison Theatre. And who should be in the lead role but Janette Pymm. It seemed to Jen as though fate was determined not only to put a knife in her, but to give it a good twist at the same time.

Although it went against the grain, later that day she walked round to the Garrison Theatre and discovered from a man at the box office that the producer of *Romeo and Juliet* was Walter Lowther, the very same self-important man who had complained to Henry about her so-called cavorting with Sean all those weeks ago.

Jen had never liked Walter Lowther very much, and she had liked him even less after that. As far as she was concerned, he and Janette Pymm deserved each other, and she hoped the show would be a resounding flop.

So she was astonished when the following morning she was summoned to Roger Violet's dressing room and found Walter Lowther himself sitting on one of the costume crates.

She was even more astonished to hear what he had to say. It seemed his *Romeo and Juliet* production had been struck by disaster before rehearsals had even begun. Like many other big venues in London, the theatre where it had been due to go on had been closed due to the V-1 threat, so he had moved the production to Salisbury instead. Then Janette Pymm's understudy had been killed in a car accident in the blackout, and now Janette herself had been struck down with influenza and was not likely to be fit enough to perform at the much-advertised opening night the following week.

Jen, relishing the fact that for once her wish had come true, was wondering why Walter Lowther was telling her all this when he stopped and cleared his throat. 'So that's why I'm here,' he said. 'I know you and I haven't always seen eye to eye, but Janette saw your name on the Violets' poster and thought you might be able to help us out. Apparently Henry Keller once told her that you were a good actress.'

333

Jen had been perching on Roger Violet's dressing table, but at that she nearly fell off. 'Good God,' she said. 'Are you telling me that Janette Pymm suggested I take over her part as Juliet?'

He nodded. 'Well yes,' he said. 'Although only in rehearsal, and perhaps for one or two shows, until she is well enough to perform again.'

Jen opened her mouth and tried to speak, but no words came out, so she closed it again. The only time she had performed the part of Juliet had been in a school production five years ago, before the war had even begun.

Walter Lowther turned his gaze to Roger. 'But only if she can be spared, of course?'

'Goodness.' Roger almost fell off his own chair in his eagerness to please. 'Of course she can be spared. It would be an honour to spare her for something like this.'

'So what do you say?' Walter Lowther eyed Jen speculatively. 'I hardly need to tell you that it would be hard work. We are already well into rehearsals. But the cast will help you. And we have a good prompt.'

Jen was conscious of a shiver of anticipation. Was this the chance she had been waiting for? Or was it a potential fiasco? Juliet was a huge role. With such a short time to rehearse, she might so very easily mess it up. Maybe that was exactly what that minx Janette Pymm was secretly hoping. Jen wouldn't put it past her.

'Can you give me a few minutes to think about it?' she asked.

Walter Lowther frowned, but consented grudgingly. He didn't have much choice. He was clearly desperate. He certainly wouldn't have asked her otherwise. 'I need to be back at the theatre in half an hour,' he said, taking out his pocket watch and glancing at it pedantically.

Jen scurried back to the girls' dressing room to collect her purse, then ran out to the telephone box on the corner outside the theatre. Lifting the receiver, she asked the operator for the Theatre Royal, Drury Lane, in London. There was a long delay and then finally she was instructed to put her money in.

One of the secretaries answered, and Jen asked her to put her through to Henry. She glanced nervously at the coins in her hand. It was a long-distance call, so it was going to be expensive.

But in the end it was quite cheap. Henry wasn't there, and nobody was able to tell her when he might be back.

Jen put the receiver down and pushed through the heavy door back into the street. Right in front of her, stuck to the wall, was a brightly coloured bill advertising a forthcoming circus. Incongruously, right next to it was the rather more discreet *Romeo and Juliet* poster. The opening night was scheduled for the 8th of July. Just over a week away. Was it even possible to learn such

334

a major role in a week?

Numbly Jen stared at the poster. Then she ran back to the Guildhall. Outside Roger Violet's dressing room door she took a long breath and crossed her fingers.

Walter Lowther seemed startled to see her back so soon.

'OK,' she said. 'I'll do it.'

George's hopes of a reprieve were unfounded. The ack-ack guns had indeed gone, leaving Clapham feeling oddly unprotected. It was the first time for several years that there had been no guns up on the common. But although the government talked confidently about the air defence batteries forming a protective shield on the south coast, there was very little evidence of it working. It certainly wasn't stopping the rockets appearing over London at regular intervals.

Sirens seemed to ring constantly, or not at all. It became obvious that the doodlebugs were too small or too fast to be picked up by the early-warning systems. Businesses therefore began to instigate their own lookouts, only allowing their staff to take cover if a rocket was coming right in their direction. It was hardly the protection people had been hoping for, and soon the fateful day arrived when Pam and Katy had to take George and Malcolm down to the WVS evacuee muster point at Clapham Junction station.

As the mothers were under strict instructions not to cry for fear of distressing the children, Katy had discreetly taken a slug of brandy before setting off to give herself some Dutch courage. Not that Malcolm seemed remotely distressed. He was thoroughly looking forward to the adventure. George, on the other hand, was unusually silent, but his face was set. He was clearly determined not to let himself down.

The station was crowded with carefully labelled children. Stern-looking teachers and a number of Mrs Rutherford's WVS cronies were attempting to get them lined up in some kind of order. Katy stared in dismay. Although there were a few younger siblings, most of the schoolboys were at least twice the size of Malcolm. Not only that, some of them seemed distinctly rough. Two or three looked positively dangerous, and glared at George and Malcolm if it was somehow their fault that they were being sent away.

'You'll look after Malcolm, won't you?' Katy said anxiously to George 'He's only little.'

George nodded and rather grimly took Malcolm's hand.

Katy was glad of the brandy. As it was, she could hardly speak as she hugged them both goodbye. Malcolm didn't really know what was happening, but he loved trains and he was happy to be going away with George. Katy prayed that the reality of the situation wouldn't come as a nasty shock.

'Here comes Mr Grandison,' Pam said suddenly. 'He's George's teacher.'

Katy straightened up and saw a cross-looking man approaching armed with a clipboard and a list.

Pam effected the introductions. 'This is Mrs Frazer,' she said. 'I think Mrs Rutherford told you that her son Malcolm was to be billeted with George?'

'It's very kind of you to take him ...' Katy began.

But the schoolmaster barely glanced at her, or indeed Malcolm; he was much more interested in his list. 'Yes,' he said. 'I have him down here.' He ticked off the names, then curtly instructed George and Malcolm to pin on their labels and wait with the other boys. He saw Katy instinctively reach out to Malcolm, and gave her a disapproving look. 'Best not to spin out the goodbyes,' he said. 'We're trying to avoid any unnecessary emotional scenes.'

Katy felt as though he had punched her in the stomach, but Pam bravely tried to hold him back as he went to move away 'You'll let me know at once if there are any problems?' she said. 'And an address where we can write to them?'

'Yes, yes,' he said impatiently. 'But it will take a day or two until we have everything sorted out, so don't expect to hear too soon.' Then he was gone, marshalling his young troops onto the train.

That was the last they saw of them. The train windows were blacked out, so Pam and Katy couldn't see what was going on inside. They didn't even get to wave goodbye. They waited in silence until the train eventually pulled out, then walked slowly out of the station.

Katy held herself together until they were back on St John's Hill. Then she stopped abruptly and put a hand on the wall to steady herself. 'Oh God,' she said. She glanced at Pam and saw the tears brimming in her eyes too. 'I don't know if I can bear it.'

'I know I can't,' Pam said. And as one, they leant against the wall and cried.

Exhausted by her visit to Bracknell, Louise had spent the next day reclining on the sofa in her parents' sitting room, gulping painkillers. Then she went back to work at the factory. It was a nerve-racking few days. There was a spotter on the roof, and if a rocket came into sight, a bell was rung and they had to down tools and crouch under the workbenches until the danger was past.

It was a relief when Colonel Westwood came into the factory with the news that Commander Cunningham had lived up to her word and produced some girls. He had also got his hands on two ack-ack guns.

'I figure I just about have sufficient crew to operate them,' he said. 'So we'll leave Mrs Smith in charge here while we head down to Salisbury Plain. We have range time allocated to us this week, and we're going to need it to get our motley crew into some kind of shape.'

Motley crew was the word. The remaining American gunners had been joined by four British soldiers, including Don Wellington. And thanks to Commander Cunningham, there was also an ATS corporal and six ATS privates, one of whom was Private Voles.

'You are a star,' Susan whispered as she and Louise stood by their bunks in the barrack room they had been allocated. 'I couldn't believe it when I got the posting order.' She eyed Louise with concern. 'But how are you feeling? The last I heard, you were flat on your back in hospital.'

Louise was surprised at how pleased she was to see her. 'I'm not a hundred per cent,' she said. 'But as long as I keep taking the painkillers I seem to be able to keep going. I'm just grateful not to be dead.'

'Well I'm grateful that you're not dead too,' Susan said. 'If it hadn't been for you, I'd probably have ended up in some horrible NAAFI canteen, washing dishes.' She looked anxious. 'I didn't pass the gunnery course, you know.'

Louise nodded. 'I know,' she said. 'Commander Cunningham told me. But it doesn't matter. I know you'll be able to do it.'

'I hope so,' Susan said nervously. 'I don't want to let you and lovely Colonel Westwood down.'

Louise smiled. 'You won't let us down,' she said.

The other girls were busy making up their beds and unpacking their things and generally making themselves at home. Louise only recognised two of them, both from Arborfield. Private McEvoy and Private Wilson. They were both range-finders. Of the others, one was a kine-theodolite operator, one a spotter and one a radar operator, while the sixth girl, Private Rees, was a large, good-natured creature who didn't seem to be trained as anything much, but whom Louise could see being useful for lumping equipment around, possibly even shells.

Louise initially treated the ATS corporal with some wariness. Commander Cunningham had obviously sent her to keep an eye on them all. But Corporal Clifton turned out to be perfectly nice, and although she was firm about dress and discipline, she clearly wasn't going to be constantly finding fault. And actually, Louise was glad to have her there, because she didn't have the energy to deal with petty problems about wobbly bunks and missing pay dockets. It was as much as she could do to get through the next day on the range.

As they weren't yet using the fuses, Colonel Westwood had allocated her the relatively easy job of ensuring that information passed smoothly between the command post and the guns. But even that was surprisingly taxing.

Luckily she was aided by the unexpected arrival of Lieutenant Masterson, her former section commander from Arborfield. 'I was intrigued by your secret project,' he said. 'So when my battery commander asked if anyone would be interested in helping to run some gunnery experiments, I volunteered.'

It couldn't have been better. Lieutenant Masterson hit it off with Colonel Westwood straight away. But getting everyone else to work together effectively was a different matter. The modern American range-finding equipment was sufficiently different to cause problems. And it wasn't just the equipment. The terminology was different too. Where the British gunners spoke of 'switches', 'witness points' and 'range tables', the Americans said 'deflection', 'check points' and 'firing tables'. It all led to considerable confusion, and as well as her other duties, Louise found herself acting as unofficial interpreter between the two nationalities.

'Rome wasn't built in a day,' Lieutenant Masterson said when she got frustrated at yet another mix-up.

'It won't get built at all at this rate,' Louise said irritably.

In the event, it took several days before the diverse group was able to operate as a recognisable gun crew. And all that time, the V-1 rockets were landing in London and the south-east, causing more and more death and destruction.

On the fourth day, they managed to get the gun drill into some kind of order. Both guns hit the prescribed ground target in the prescribed time. It was a considerable breakthrough, and it was just in time, because on the fifth day Colonel Westwood had arranged for a plane to come in towing a target to simulate a V-1 rocket. Louise was terrified that they would bring down the plane by mistake. And it seemed from his increasingly acerbic comments over the radio that the pilot was pretty terrified too.

'Calm and careful,' Lieutenant Masterson said admonishingly to his team. 'Listen to each other, remember your fire drill and make the adjustments calmly and carefully. OK, Private Voles, are you listening? Let's run again. Here he comes now. Target acquired ... Fire by order ... Fire!'

On the sixth attempt they got it right and one of the guns scored a direct hit.

It was their first real success. and even Colonel Westwood and the solemn Lieutenant Masterson smiled as the girls supporting that gun jumped about hugging each other, while the better-disciplined Americans watched in disapproval.

'We did it!' Susan Voles squealed in triumph.

'You did it *once*,' Don Wellington called across from the other gun team. 'With no danger of getting hit yourself. Wait until a V-1 comes buzzing overhead and see how calm and careful you are then.'

Louise saw Voles flinch apprehensively. 'Ignore him,' she whispered. 'He's only jealous. Just do your job. Don't take any notice of him.' She grimaced wryly to herself, remembering Doris giving her almost the exact same advice in the factory all those months ago.

She glanced over at Don Wellington. She still didn't like him – he was snarky and full of himself – but she had to admit he was a good gunner. He was quick on the uptake and rarely made a mistake. And when his team hit the trailed target on the next attempt, she found herself clapping enthusiastically along with the others.

Colonel Westwood looked pleased. When he smiled at her and winked, Louise would have liked to hug him too, but she managed to confine herself to a reciprocal smile of triumph.

But their successes were short-lived. The next two attempts went astray, and the third did indeed nearly bring down the plane. If they had been using the proximity fuse, it would certainly have been destroyed. The pilot's invective over the radio as he flew away was unrepeatable.

But Colonel Westwood didn't seem too dismayed. 'OK,' he said. 'I figure we're ready to test the fuses. If that goes OK, then another couple of days and we should be ready to take on the V-1s.'

And then disaster struck.

Word came from Mr Gregg that the block of flats where Doris Smith lived had been hit by a V-1 and Doris's husband had been killed. As a result, she was not in work, and production of fuses had stopped.

Colonel Westwood called Louise off the gun position. 'I need you to go back to London,' he said. 'If you can't get Mrs Smith back to work, then you will have to take her place on the production line. Whatever happens, we're going to need more fuses.'

Louise was aggrieved. 'But that's not fair,' she said. 'Why can't Don Wellington go?'

Colonel Westwood's brows rose sharply. She had never talked to him like that before. His reply was very firm. 'Because I need him on the guns. I need *you* to get things going again at the factory.'

Louise flinched. She knew she had spoken out of turn, but she couldn't hide her disappointment. After everything she had done for him, he was going to send her away.

'I'm sorry, sir,' she muttered, lowering her gaze. 'It's just that I don't want to miss anything here.'

He relented a fraction and drew her to one side. 'Listen. I know it's kind of disappointing to leave just when we are making progress. But I need you to do this for me. This is a big problem. And right now you are pretty much the only person who can fix it.'

Chapter Twenty Nine

It was on the following morning, 5 July, that Gillian James was cremated. The short ceremony had been organised by Katy and Mrs Rutherford on Bella's behalf and paid for by the Local Council Welfare Fund. All Mrs James's personal effects had been destroyed in the blast, and as she had failed to register any next of kin other than Bella, they had no idea of who else to contact. But due to the continued V-1 attacks, there was a shortage of space in the morgue, so in the end they had to make the decision.

Bella still hadn't spoken a single word. Nor would she write anything down. When they asked her if her mother had had any other relatives, she just looked blank and shook her head. But in every other way she was fine. She did what Katy told her with no demur, she was happy to tend to little Caroline, walk Lucky on the common, and carry out countless other helpful tasks. It was just that she was either unable or unwilling to communicate, leaving Katy wishing for the hundredth time that Ward was there. Or Molly. It was so hard dealing with the girl on her own.

She had taken Bella to the local GP, but he had been hopeless. With all that was going on, he clearly didn't feel inclined to waste his time on a girl who had nothing discernibly wrong with her. 'I expect she'll get over it,' he said. 'Shock does odd things.'

Katy knew that was true. She still felt very peculiar herself. As though she was there and not there all at the same time. The more she thought about that sour-faced teacher Mr Grandison, the more she wished she hadn't sent Malcolm away. He was far too young to be on his own. And what madness had made her think that George would take care of him? He would probably forget all about him in the excitement of being with his own school friends.

Mrs Rutherford had offered to arrange for Bella to be handed over to the authorities, but Katy couldn't bring herself to let her go. She couldn't bear to think what might happen to Bella if she was declared a war orphan. There were already stories of such children being shipped off to Australia for a so-called better life. God only knew what happened to them when they got there. The combination of Bella's startling beauty and her unsavoury upbringing would make her especially vulnerable.

A busy drinking man's pub wasn't a particularly suitable environment for her either, but Katy felt obliged to look after her, at least until a better solution could be found.

She kept a careful eye on the girl during the cremation service. She had a clean handkerchief ready in her pocket just in case. But Bella didn't cry. Nor did she pray. She just sat there, straight and silent and very pale, and Katy's heart ached for her. It was impossible to know what was going through her mind. For all Katy knew, she was thinking that if she hadn't been helping out in the pub that night, she would almost certainly have been killed too.

There were very few people in the congregation. Normally more men than women attended funerals, but not many men wanted to be seen at the funeral of the local prostitute. Gillian had never set foot in St Aldate's Church, and at first the vicar had been reluctant to even hold a service for her. But Mrs Rutherford had twisted his arm, and in the end he had taken pity on Bella's plight. No mention was made of Gillian James's occupation during the short service. Only that she had been an accomplished seamstress, a good mother and a helpful member of the community.

'Good mother?' Joyce Carter murmured to Katy as they all walked back to the bus stop. 'I can hardly think how she could have been a worse one. I reckon that poor child will be better off without her.'

Katy frowned. That was easy for Joyce to say, she thought irritably. She wasn't having to look after her. But then she felt guilty. Mrs Carter had enough problems of her own at the moment. Not least that there was no sign of the council sending anyone to repair her house.

Katy knew how difficult it was to get hold of workmen. Thanks to Aaref Hoch, the hole in the corner of her own bedroom was now covered by a sheet of tarpaulin. Because of the doodlebugs, she and Caroline and Bella were sleeping in the cellar, so it didn't matter that the tarp flapped and hissed like a trapped eagle whenever it was windy. But she would have to get it properly seen to before Malcolm came home.

Malcolm. Even though the July day was warm and sunny, Katy felt a guilty shiver run down her spine. She had been so concerned about Bella and the cremation that she had briefly forgotten to worry about Malcolm. Let alone about Ward.

Pam was missing George, too. Every time she fed Bunny, she wept. She couldn't help it. She found herself picking him up and dripping tears into his warm fur. And the thought of how much George must be missing him made her feel even worse.

Mrs Rutherford had told her that George and Malcolm had arrived safely in the village of Winterbourne, near Salisbury and had been allocated to a nice family. But since the WVS escorts had returned home, nothing more had been heard. And now three whole days had elapsed.

342

Alan was trying to be reassuring. 'I'm sure they're both fine. I expect the teachers are just busy sorting everything out. But if the worst comes to the worst, I could take the train down there at the weekend and find out what's going on,' he said.

But Pam knew that was easier said than done. With Mr Rutherford away on the south coast with his ack-ack battery, Alan was in charge of the brewery. If he did a good job, Mr Rutherford would be grateful – you might even say indebted – and that could mean advancement, or at the very least a little bonus on his return. Either of which would be very welcome. But it was not an easy time to be in charge, because of the beastly V-1s. Mr Rutherford certainly wouldn't approve of Alan abandoning his post to go and check on George.

And Pam was busy too. Mrs Rutherford had taken advantage of George being away to ask her to take on the job of finding accommodation for people bombed out of their own homes.

'We have far too many in the church hall,' she said. 'I need you to persuade people in undamaged houses to offer their spare rooms. You might want to think about it yourself, Mrs Nelson. With young George away, you must have at least one spare bed, after all?'

Pam looked at her. 'Yes, we do,' she said. 'Though I'm afraid we're keeping it for Molly Coogan, who is due back from North Africa any day now.' She smiled sweetly. 'But now you have given me the task, I suppose I ought to ask how many people you might be able to take in at Cedars House?'

A line of colour appeared across Mrs Rutherford's high cheekbones. 'Well, that's an entirely different matter,' she said. She pulled on her gloves and fiddled with the catch on her leather handbag. 'I will need to talk to my husband about that. Unfortunately, as you know, he is away at the moment with the ack-ack.'

'Well, do let me know as soon as possible,' Pam said. 'I'd obviously try to find you some reasonably respectable people. And in the meantime, if you hear any news of the evacuees, I'd be very grateful if you would pass it on, because I am getting rather concerned.'

Having travelled up to London that morning, it took Louise all afternoon to track Doris down. Eventually she found her in a hot, busy WVS emergency accommodation unit at a now evacuated school in Battersea. It was a different WVS catchment area to Lavender Road, so she didn't recognise any of the ladies in attendance, but they were exactly the same type as her mother: brisk, tweedy and somewhat impersonal.

'I'm afraid Mrs Smith is in a rather bad way,' one of them said as she led Louise across the crowded assembly hall. 'The rocket attack was very severe;

the whole tenement block collapsed. I believe it was complete carnage. The rescue services are finding it hard to piece together the body parts.'

Louise was already trying to breathe through her mouth, nauseated by the smell of boiled cabbage and unwashed bodies. Now she felt even worse.

But when she saw Doris, she immediately forgot her own discomfort. The older woman was slumped on a small classroom chair, staring into the middle distance, her normally jovial face sagging with anguish.

'I know he was sick,' she said, when Louise crouched awkwardly beside her to express her sympathy. 'I know he was often cross and grumpy. But he was mine. He was my Sid and I loved him.'

Louise didn't know what to say. In some desperation she looked around for another chair, and, spotting an empty one on the other side of the room, carried it across so she could sit down next to Doris. She found Doris's unobtrusive grief oddly humbling. She couldn't help remembering the terrible fuss she herself had made when Jack had died. It embarrassed her now to think of all the weeping and wailing she had inflicted on her friends and her parents. She had had weeks off work and had only gone back in the end because Mr Gregg had threatened her with the sack. It had seemed harsh at the time, but it had made her pull herself together. And now somehow she needed to get Doris back to work too.

She leaned forward and poked her friend gently in the arm. 'We need you to come back to the factory,' she said quietly. 'We are almost ready to start shooting down the rockets.' She saw Doris's uncaring shrug and made a sympathetic face. 'I know it won't help Sid, but it might help someone else.' She waved her hand round the crowded room. 'Every one of the beastly things we bring down will stop other people dying.'

Doris shook her head dully. 'Everyone says the ack-ack barrage hardly touches them.'

'But that's the point,' Louise said. 'You know it's hush-hush, but with Colonel Westwood's special fuses, we *will* be able to touch them. Not only touch them, but blast them to kingdom come.'

Doris's eyes flickered. 'Is that true?'

Louise smiled encouragingly. 'Colonel Westwood certainly thinks so. But to make it happen, we're all going to have to work our socks off. Both at the factory and down on Salisbury Plain. Me, you, Don Wellington, everybody.'

For some reason the mention of Don Wellington diverted Doris from her gloomy thoughts. 'I didn't know you'd got him down there with you,' she said. 'How are you coping with that?'

Louise rolled her eyes. 'He's all right. Give him his due, he's a hard worker. I've even laughed at his stupid jokes once or twice.'

Doris gave a watery smile. 'I never thought I'd hear you say that.'

'I can hardly believe I'm saying it myself,' Louise said. 'But I've learnt a few things over the last few months, and one of them is how to deal with bullies.'

'What about the lovely colonel?' Doris asked.

Louise risked a wink. 'He sends his love.'

Doris gave a small chortle. 'You may have learnt how to deal with bullies, but you obviously haven't learnt to tell the truth,' she said.

'Well, his sympathy then,' Louise said. 'He was very concerned to hear what had happened. He's definitely got a soft spot for you.'

'Have you found out if he's married yet?'

'No. And I'm not going to tell you if I do. I don't want you snatching him out from under my nose.'

Doris let out another chortle of laughter, then sobered abruptly as though it was wrong to laugh. 'I couldn't snatch a handkerchief from under your nose,' she said. 'Let alone a handsome man like that.' Her face worked, and for an awful moment Louise thought she was going to start crying. But then she shook her head. 'It's nice of you to try to cheer me up,' she said. 'But you don't need me. Not really.'

'We do need you,' Louise said. 'Something has gone wrong with the production line, and we need you to get it back on track. If we're going to bring down these damned V-1s, we need a new batch of fuses. And we need them ASAP.'

'Surely one of the chaps at the factory can sort that out? Or ask Larry Gregg.'

'But they can't,' Louise insisted. 'They're a bunch of morons. And Larry Gregg isn't much better.'

Doris gave a sour chuckle. 'Did you know he's installed a Morrison shelter in his office to hide under if a V-1 falls on the factory? While the rest of us have to cower under our benches.' She looked away, perhaps wondering if Sid might have been saved by a Morrison shelter. After a moment she turned back to Louise. 'And you really think these fuses are going to make a difference?'

Louise nodded. 'They're going to make all the difference.' She crossed her fingers behind her back. She didn't need to tell Doris about the problems. The difficulties in terminology. Susan Voles almost jumping out of her skin every time the guns fired. Don Wellington's caustic remarks. Let alone the rest of the motley, scrambled-together gun crew that would be trying to make Colonel Westwood's new technology work.

There was a long pause. Then Doris took a breath. 'All right,' she said. 'I'll do it. I'll do it for you, and I'll do it for Sid.'

*

345

It didn't take long for Jen to realise that stepping into the shoes of a renowned star was not an easy thing to do. Nor was it easy to work for someone who didn't particularly like her. Before he had been brought into ENSA, Walter Lowther had been a record producer. He knew everything there was to know about classical music, but not, it seemed, very much about theatrical productions. It wasn't clear why the *Romeo and Juliet* production had fallen into his remit, but luckily there was an assistant producer too, and he at least seemed to know what he was doing. Though that didn't stop the rest of the cast constantly saying, 'Janette did it like this,' or 'Janette didn't do it like that.'

'Well I'm not blasted Janette,' Jen raged on the second day. 'She's welcome to do it any way she wants, but if it doesn't work for me, then you'll have to put up with me doing it a different way.'

She had learned the main speeches reasonably quickly. The Violets had helped her with that. But remembering the cues and stage directions was much more difficult. The other actors were a mixed bunch. Some were professional old hands. One or two had come out of retirement in a desire to aid the ENSA war effort, or to earn a bit of cash. Others were not much more than amateurs, and it was these who caused the most problems, as, having doggedly learned their moves, they seemed entirely unable to adapt to her different style. She wished Henry was there. He would know how to make them pull together, a feat well beyond the competence of Walter Lowther.

Nevertheless, she was determined to do her best. This was a real chance to prove to everyone that she was up to it. And when she said everyone, she meant Henry. To that end, she had taken the brave step of writing to him at Drury Lane, inviting him to the opening night.

But now she was regretting it, because the rehearsals weren't going very well and everything seemed laboured and unconvincing.

The main problem was that Romeo was an idiot. He was a public school boy from a theatrical family who had by some judicious string-pulling become a child star in a West End show. Now he was seventeen and keen to make his name in adult theatre. He was nice-looking, Jen had to hand him that; certainly any young women in the audience would drool over him. But despite his well-bred panache, he kept on fluffing his lines, and in the love scenes he was absurdly stiff and unresponsive.

'Look, I know I'm way too old for you,' Jen snapped at him one day in the wings. 'But I'm not as old as Janette Pymm. You could at least try to look interested in me.'

He flushed. 'Actually I am interested in you.' He pushed a lock of hair out of his eyes and gave a boyish smile. 'I was all right with Janette. I didn't fancy her. But I think you're really sexy. And it's making me feel all self-conscious the way you look at me on stage.'

It was Jen's turn to colour up. She was mildly gratified that at least one person in the world found her more attractive than Janette Pymm, but it was no help in making their stage relationship work.

'Well,' she said. 'The first time I performed Juliet, Romeo was played by a girl in my class at school, so you can imagine I felt pretty self-conscious then. But I was pretending with her and I'm pretending with you. It's called acting. So don't go getting any ideas. You're far too young for me. And in any case, my interest lies elsewhere.'

'Oh really?' he said. He glanced at her jealously. 'So who is the lucky man?'

Jen lifted her chin. 'That's none of your business,' she said. 'But for goodness' sake try to show a bit of romantic sparkle in the next scene. It's the dress rehearsal tomorrow and it's going to be extremely embarrassing if the audience falls asleep.'

Joyce was standing by the cordon in Lavender Road. It was a sorry sight. Most of the masonry had been cleared away, but there was still a lot of rubble in the street; sharp fragments of roof tiles, splinters of wood. And the tarmac was pitted and dented from the force of the blast and the crushing weight of the debris. Even the numbers Pam Nelson had laboriously painted on the pavement all those months ago were scratched and peeling.

Averting her eyes from the gaping breach in the terrace on the other side of the road, Joyce glanced quickly around to check that nobody was watching her, then ducked under the tape and let herself into her house.

It felt cold and bleak, as though all the life had gone out of it. Which it had, of course. Apart from a brief visit from Aaref Hoch and Alan Nelson to rehang her front door and board up her downstairs windows, and her own quick, illegal visits to feed poor old Monty the tortoise, who was still residing in the back yard, nobody had set foot in the place for ages.

Walking through the narrow corridor to the kitchen, Joyce opened the back door and went outside to see if Monty had eaten yesterday's dinner. She had been so preoccupied with Albert for the last couple of weeks that she hadn't noticed immediately, but now, once again, she saw that the tortoise had pushed to one side all the vegetable scraps she had given him over the last few days.

Monty had always been a faddy eater, but this was completely out of character. Could he be ill?

She looked at him in concern as he lay in a patch of sunlight next to the air-raid shelter. He definitely looked morose. He was never a bundle of laughs, of course – he was a tortoise, after all, and they weren't known for their humour – but he was usually more animated than this. Joyce suddenly wondered if he was lonely. Perhaps he was missing having the family around.

Like her. She missed the boys. She missed Jen. And she missed sitting with her feet up in the front room listening to the wireless while Angie and Gino giggled over their attempts to cook Italian food in the kitchen.

It wasn't the same in the church hall. There was no wireless there. No comfortable chairs. No peace and quiet. It was hot and smelly, and Angie and Gino were hardly ever there anyway. Or only to sleep. Goodness knew where they were the rest of the time – out dancing, according to Angie, or in the pub.

Joyce gave a wry laugh. It came to something when she found herself feeling nostalgic for Gino making a mess in the kitchen.

She picked up Monty, holding him close to her face while she gently stroked the back of his leathery head.

'Don't worry,' she said. 'We'll be back as soon as I can get the house seen to.'

It was as she walked back through to the front door that she heard the noise. A strange, rhythmical creaking coming from upstairs. She felt a moment's panic. She didn't want the house to fall down. Not on top of her. Not at all. Things were quite bad enough as it was.

But then the noise came again, and this time it was accompanied by a hastily stifled giggle.

And suddenly it all fell into place.

'Angie?' she called. 'Is that you? What on earth are you doing up there?' Although she knew perfectly well. No wonder Angie and Gino spent so little time in the church hall.

Sure enough, a moment later Angie appeared at the top of the stairs, looking distinctly dishevelled. 'Hello, Mum.'

'Good God,' Joyce said. 'Are you mad? According to the council, the house might collapse at any minute.'

Angie jiggled the banister experimentally. 'Well it hasn't fallen down yet,' she said. 'And Gino and me have given it plenty of chances.'

Joyce stared up at her blankly. Then suddenly, unexpectedly, she saw the funny side.

'I bet you have,' she gasped. She took out her handkerchief and wiped her eyes. 'But I can hardly tell that to the council surveyor, can I?'

'It's Gino's fault,' Angie said. 'He's just so gorgeous, I can't resist him.'

And that set Joyce off again. 'Well, you'll just have to resist him,' she said. 'At least until the house is repaired.'

'But we've got nowhere else to go,' Angie grumbled. 'Not where we can be private. It's all right for you to laugh. It may not matter to you, what with

Mr Lorenz being in hospital and that, but we—'

'Angie!' Joyce expostulated. 'I'll have you know that Mr Lorenz and I have never …' She stopped, unsure just how to phrase what she and Mr Lorenz had never done.

'Haven't you?' Angie looked astonished. Then she rallied. 'But you surely will when you're married, and—'

'And nothing,' Joyce said hastily. 'What Mr Lorenz and I decide to do or not to do is none of your business. And if I catch you in here again, I'll be very cross.'

Louise was just running out of the house when the telephone started ringing. It was Friday afternoon. She had spent the last three days working like stink with Doris and her little team in the factory to get as many fuses as possible ready.

And despite having to take shelter at least half a dozen times while V-1s whined past overhead, they had done brilliantly. Even the militant, clock-watching Mrs Gibbons had stayed late to help. And despite her bereavement, Doris had risen magnificently to the occasion. So much so that Louise now felt able to leave her in charge so that she could return to Salisbury Plain.

An hour ago, Colonel Westwood's transport had arrived at the factory to fetch the latest batch of fuses. It was the same detail as before, with the same drivers, and when they said they would be happy to take her with them, Louise had once again scurried back to her parents' house to collect her things. Already she could hear the small convoy turning into the driveway to pick her up.

But there was something compelling about a ringing telephone, and signalling to the escort corporal that she wanted him to wait, she darted back into the hallway just as her mother picked up the receiver.

'Yes, this is Mrs Rutherford,' she said, and then her eyes lit up in excitement. 'Oh, I see. Yes, of course you can. She's right here. I'll put her on.'

'Who is it?' Louise said, puzzled by her mother's sycophantic tone.

'It's someone called Freddy,' Celia whispered as she handed the receiver to Louise. 'I think that's your lord, isn't it?'

Louise couldn't help giggling. It was indeed Lord Freddy. She recognised his humorous, upper-class voice at once.

'Aha,' he said. 'I've finally managed to track you down. And now that I've found you, I want to invite you out to dinner tonight, to make up for last time. I do hope you are well enough to make the trip to town.'

Louise gave a slightly nervous laugh. 'Yes, I'm fine now,' she said. 'I've actually been back at work for two weeks. But I'm afraid I can't come out tonight.'

'Damn and blast,' he said. 'If I'd known you were back on your feet, I'd have got on the blower sooner, but that bounder Henry Keller told me you'd be out of action for weeks.'

Louise smothered another giggle. 'You mustn't blame Henry,' she said. 'When he came to see me, I was still in quite a bad way.' She hesitated. 'I hope he passed on my thanks for the lovely roses.'

'Yes, he did, and I'm delighted that you liked them. I was horrified to hear what had happened. I believe that's partly why Henry decided to go back into the forces. Did he tell you he's been asked to join some special unit charged with finding and destroying the missile launch sites?'

'Goodness,' Louise said. 'He didn't tell me that.'

Lord Freddy gave a cheery laugh. 'No, I don't suppose he would. He's always been a bit of a dark horse. But you know what Henry's like. Always up for a challenge.'

No, I didn't know that, Louise thought. 'So where is he now?'

'Still in Winchester, as far as I know. But I imagine he'll be leaving for Europe any day now. They're not going to hang about. Not with these damn things coming over every few minutes. And the ack-ack units seem quite hopeless at bringing them down.'

Louise glanced out of the front door. 'Talking of which,' she said, 'I really do have to go. I'm involved in air defence myself, and even as we speak, there's a convoy of army trucks sitting outside in our driveway waiting to take me back to my unit.'

'Oh Lord,' Freddy said jovially. 'And now I've put my big foot in it, haven't I? I'd forgotten you were going into the ack-ack. Well in that case, I feel much more confident about our chances. I might have known it would end up being women who would save the world from this damned mess we're in.' He chuckled benignly. 'Oh, and the next time you're back in town with some time on your hands, we really must meet up so that I can try to convince you to become my wife.'

Louise shook her head in despair as she put down the receiver. He really was too absurd. She couldn't take him seriously. But nor did she want to hurt his feelings. She had done enough of that in the past. In any case, under all that enthusiastic bluster, Lord Freddy sounded rather sweet.

She caught sight of her mother hovering by the dining room door. 'What did he say?' she asked.

Louise shrugged. 'He asked me to marry him.' She picked up her kitbag. 'But I haven't got time to think about that now. I've got to go and save the world.'

And with that she ran down the steps and climbed into the leading jeep, leaving her mother standing in the doorway with her mouth open.

But before she started saving the world, she wanted to know if Katy had heard any news of Malcolm and George, so she asked the MT corporal if he'd mind stopping the convoy outside the pub in Lavender Road for a minute.

Katy still hadn't heard a bleep. 'I'm sure George is all right,' she said. 'He's got all his schoolmates there with him. But I thought at least that horrid Mr Grandison might have let me know how Malcolm was getting on.'

'I'm sure he's all right as well,' Louise said. Then she faltered. How on earth could she be sure? She knew absolutely nothing about it. She suddenly began to feel uneasy too. She thought back to the problems George had had with his so-called schoolmates earlier in the year. And she remembered Mr Grandison. She certainly wouldn't want to rely on him to look after a child of hers.

'Where are they?' she asked. 'Maybe you could go and visit them just to make sure?'

Katy gave her a wild look and waved a hand round the empty bar. 'How can I?' she said. 'They're right down in Wiltshire, somewhere near Salisbury. It would take me all day to get there and back.'

'Salisbury?' Louise said. 'That's where I'm going now.' And then she saw her friend's expression and wished she had held her tongue.

Sudden hope had filled Katy's eyes. 'Could you go and check on them?' she asked.

'Katy, I can't,' Louise said. She nodded out of the open door towards the waiting vehicles. 'We won't get back until late tonight, and tomorrow I imagine we'll be moving across to the south coast.'

Katy stared at her pleadingly. 'Oh please, Louise,' she said. 'It wouldn't take long and it would be such a relief to know they're OK.'

Louise quailed at the thought of what Lieutenant Masterson would say if she told him she wanted to leave her post to check up on a friend's child. Let alone Colonel Westwood. But she also knew she was going to have to do it. Even if she did get into trouble for it. Katy was her friend. She owed it to her. And she owed it to George Nelson. If he hadn't thought of whistling to Lucky when they were stuck under that beastly rubble, she almost certainly would have died.

'Pam would be so grateful,' Katy said, inadvertently rubbing in her obligation.

Louise didn't have time to delay any longer. Outside in the road she could see the corporal stubbing out his cigarette with his shoe and glancing impatiently at his watch.

351

She sighed. 'All right,' she said. 'I'll see what I can do.'

Chapter Thirty

The easiest thing would have been to ask the escort corporal if he would mind deviating via Winterbourne on the way back to camp. He was a nice guy and Louise was pretty confident he would oblige, but it was late in the evening by the time the little convoy reached Salisbury Plain, and she didn't feel she could go marching into the village demanding to see the children at that hour.

Instead, when they turned in to the barracks, she asked the guardroom sentry to send a message to Colonel Westwood in the officers' mess. To her disappointment, it was Lieutenant Masterson who emerged. By the time he had arranged for the fuses to be secured in the armoury, it was even later, and Louise was beginning to wilt. It had been an exhausting week, and the long, rattling journey in the open jeep had nearly finished her off. But there was one more thing she had to do.

'Is there any chance I could have a little bit of time off tomorrow morning, sir?' she asked tentatively.

Lieutenant Masterson looked astonished.' Good God, no. We're moving out tomorrow night. We heard this morning that we've been allocated a firing position somewhere near Rye. Colonel Westwood's over at US HQ trying to rustle up some extra equipment. So it's going to be all hands to the pumps here tomorrow getting everything packed up and ready.'

Louise looked at him in consternation. 'But I've promised my friend,' she said when she had explained the situation. 'And I can't let her down.' She saw him start to frown, but before he could protest, she lowered her eyes demurely and glanced at him through her lashes. 'After all, I did work like stink all this week to get these extra fuses ready. I've looked at the map, and the village where the boys are staying isn't far away. It would only take me an hour or so there and back.'

It was the eyelashes that did it. She had always known that Lieutenant Masterson liked her, but now she saw that it was perhaps even more than that. Faint colour tinged his cheeks. 'It's most unorthodox,' he said. 'But I suppose I can spare you for an hour tomorrow morning.' He looked at her sternly. 'But no more than that.'

Louise could have kissed him. 'Thank you, sir,' she said, and saluted sharply. But as she lowered her arm, she hesitated. 'There is one other thing.'

She gave him a pleading smile. 'I'm going to need some transport.'

Lieutenant Masterson gave a despairing laugh. 'I'll see what I can arrange. But you'll have to persuade the other girls to cover for you.'

The ATS girls didn't take much persuading. They knew that it was only due to her that they had been plucked from obscurity and placed in this unconventional and excitingly secret unit. 'Of course we don't mind,' Susan Voles said at once. 'Goodness, it was bad enough for me leaving home to join the ATS. I dread to think what it must be like for children. Poor little mites, I hope they're not too homesick.'

Louise hid a smile; she couldn't quite think of George Nelson as a mite. But the other girls were nodding in agreement, and she was grateful for their support. 'I'll be as quick as I can,' she said. 'I promise to make it up to you.'

Needless to say, Don Wellington wasn't so compassionate the following morning when he spotted her climbing into the military utility vehicle Lieutenant Masterson had provided. 'Skiving off again?' he asked.

'I'm on an important mission,' Louise said stiffly.

'Really?' He raised his eyebrows. 'I heard that you were going to visit some evacuee children. Doesn't sound very important to me. What are you going to do? Ask them to come and help out on the guns?' He gave a mocking laugh and slapped the roof of the Tilly car as he moved away. 'They'd certainly be more use than you ATS girls.'

The driver of the car glanced at her suspiciously. 'Children?' he said. 'Nobody told me nothing about children.'

Louise groaned. Tilly cars were civilian vehicles converted for military use by opening up the back to make a kind of flat bed for equipment. This one had clearly seen better days. As had the Motor Corps driver. He was a surly barrel of a man with a big scar across his cheekbone, and an equally big chip on his shoulder. He clearly felt he had better things to do than act as chauffeur to a mere ATS private.

Louise didn't care. All she needed him to do was take her to Winterbourne so she could make sure that George and Malcolm were OK, and then drive her to Salisbury so that she could send a reassuring telegram to Katy. With any luck the whole thing should be done and dusted well within the hour Lieutenant Masterson had allocated.

But unfortunately that morning luck was conspicuously absent.

They found Winterbourne with no difficulty, but it took much longer than expected to locate Mr Grandison. She eventually ran him to earth in the village hall, which had been turned into a makeshift classroom. The schoolmaster didn't seem at all pleased to see her. 'We don't encourage visits from friends and relatives,' he said, when she introduced herself and explained her mission. 'It unsettles the children.'

Some kind of history lesson was in progress. Louise could see *Great War 1914–1918* written on an easel blackboard. An elderly teacher was pointing to it with a cane. Two or three boys were diligently copying the dates into their exercise books. The rest were staring over towards the door.

'I don't care what it does to them,' Louise said. 'I want to see them, and I haven't got time to waste arguing about it. So please tell me where they are.' She squared her shoulders and looked at him expectantly.

There was a short pause during which he glared back, a muscle twitching in his jaw. 'I don't know exactly where they are,' he admitted at last.

Louise felt a flicker of unease. 'What do you mean?'

He made an impatient gesture. 'They appear to be missing,' he said. 'But they're bound to be here somewhere. They can't have gone far.'

'Have you spoken to the other boys?' Louise asked. 'And the family they're staying with?'

'Of course I have,' he said irritably. 'But nobody has seen them since breakfast time.'

Louise took a breath. 'And have you told the police?'

'The police?' Mr Grandison looked astonished. 'This isn't a matter for the police. Between ourselves, George Nelson has been a nuisance ever since we got here. Fighting with the other boys and so on. Knowing him as I do, I suspect this is just one more of his pranks.'

Louise could feel her body shaking with anger. Or perhaps with fear. 'You clearly don't know him at all,' she said sharply. 'But I do. And it sounds to me as though he's being bullied again. I suspect he's run away and taken Malcolm with him.'

But Mr Grandison wasn't prepared to consider that eventuality. 'What nonsense,' he said. 'You are just being hysterical, young lady. And in any case, where could they have gone? They've got no money. No transport. No, no, I'm sure they are just hiding out somewhere to avoid lessons.'

Louise tried to think about it rationally. She wouldn't put it past George to hide out. If the lesson being taught behind her was anything to go by, she'd probably have hidden out herself if she had been in his shoes. But it wouldn't be easy to hide with Malcolm in tow. He was such a noisy little blighter, and he would get bored in no time; surely in such a small village someone would notice him.

She looked around helplessly, wondering what to do. 'Where's the nearest police station?' she asked.

Mr Grandison frowned. 'Salisbury, I imagine,' he said. 'But—'

'Then I'm going to Salisbury,' she said. 'I'm going to report them missing. And I'm going to send a telegram to that effect to their parents.'

Mr Grandison paled. He put out his hand. 'No, please, Miss Rutherford, really, that would be most unwise. There's no reason for them to know.'

Louise shook him off. 'They have every right to know,' she said. 'And I'm going to tell my mother, too. She will be appalled to hear of such shocking negligence. So if I was you, I would stop pretending that nothing's happened, and start making some serious efforts to find them.'

Jen had woken up that morning in her digs with a sense of impending doom. The dress rehearsal the previous evening had been a complete fiasco. Almost everything that could have gone wrong had gone wrong, including a scenery disaster when the rail of the balcony broke and Jen plummeted down on top of Romeo right in the middle of his soliloquy, scratching her hand on the fake rose trellis as she passed.

Once she had disentangled herself and applied some TCP to the graze, they had manfully carried on, but the mood had been spoilt, and when she briefly forgot her lines a few minutes later, she thought she heard someone chortling with laughter at the back of the auditorium. As the show limped to its conclusion, the final lines seemed entirely appropriate: *Never was a story of more woe than this of Juliet and her Romeo.* The whole thing had been woeful indeed.

Afterwards she guessed that it had been Janette Pymm who had laughed, because as soon as the curtain came down, the ailing star appeared backstage with Walter Lowther, looking winsomely weak and pale.

'What a shame about the balcony scene,' she said with gushing insincerity. 'But apart from that, you all did awfully well.'

Jen felt her temper rising. 'Oh for goodness' sake, Janette,' she said. 'Why don't you just come out and say it? It was terrible. Probably the worst *Romeo and Juliet* anyone has ever seen.'

Janette Pymm gave her trilling laugh. 'Well, it wasn't perfect,' she said. 'But don't be too hard on yourself. That's what dress rehearsals are for. To show up the problems before it's too late.'

It is too late, Jen thought sourly. And it was obvious the producers thought so too. Walter Lowther's post-performance notes had been very lacklustre. He was probably just hoping the show could limp along for a day or two until Janette felt well enough to resume her role and give it some sparkle. Jen couldn't help thinking how much more hands-on and encouraging Henry would have been. But Henry would probably never have chosen her to play Juliet in the first place. She had wanted Henry to come to the first night so she could prove to him that she was up to it, but now she was praying that he wouldn't.

The assistant producer had been the only one who had shown any faith in Jen, but even he had looked at her with disquiet as she left the theatre. 'You've been working very hard,' he said. 'Make sure you take a bit of time to relax tomorrow before the show.'

But Jen couldn't relax. She couldn't settle. And in any case, her landlady didn't like her guests hanging round the place when she was trying to clean.

Deciding she needed some fresh air, Jen was checking her appearance in the hall mirror when the landlady came lumbering down the stairs with an old fashioned carpet sweeper. 'Cheer up, lovey,' she said. 'It'll be all right on the night.'

Jen felt a sinking feeling in her stomach. She suddenly felt terribly alone. She wished the Violets were still around to give her some moral support. But they had been summoned back to London to perform to injured invasion troops in various hospitals and convalescent homes. If only there was someone around to remind her how good she was, she thought. Someone on her side. That was all she needed.

She closed her eyes, fighting a sudden sense of despondency. Then, squaring her shoulders bravely, she opened the front door and stepped out into the street.

And bumped smack into Louise Rutherford.

'Oh yes,' Mr Lorenz said. 'That's much better.' His eyes twinkled behind the new spectacles Joyce had managed to procure for him from the optician in Northcote Road. 'Now I can see your lovely face again.'

'Albert, really.' Joyce hushed him reprovingly. But actually she was pleased to see him looking so perky. It had been nice to find something she could do for him. She had brought him books, too, borrowed from Katy's collection at the pub. And at his request, she had stuck a sign on the door of his shop on Northcote Road saying: *Closed due to indisposition of owner. All payments deferred and loans extended until further notice.*

She had also managed to salvage what she could from the wreckage of his house. Most of his personal items and furniture had been blown to smithereens, but a few things had survived in his heavy oak wardrobe: a couple of pairs of shoes, and two suits, which she had sent to the cleaner's.

In the meantime, she had found him a nice pair of striped pyjamas and a paisley silk dressing gown in the WVS emergency clothing store. The nurses had had to cut one of the sleeves to get it over the plaster cast on his arm, but at least he looked tidy and respectable, more like his old self.

And gradually he was returning to his old self too. The bruising on his face was healing well, and he was already able to move about a bit on crutches. Which meant that the Wilhelmina wanted to discharge him.

Joyce understood. She really did. You only had to look at the parlous state

357

of the young soldiers waiting on stretchers in the lobby to know that the need for beds was great. But she didn't want Albert to be sent away. And in the absence of any suitable accommodation locally, the hospital authorities were now talking about a convalescent home in Watford, which would be much too far for her to visit regularly. Or at all, come to that.

If only she could get her house repaired, she could look after him in there. But there was a shortage of both builders and building materials. It had been in the paper last week that nine million square feet of glass was currently needed to repair broken windows in Battersea and Wandsworth alone. That would be enough to cover the entire area of Clapham Common. No wonder Katy Frazer had a sign hanging outside the pub saying: *A penny off every drink if you bring your own glass.*

Back at the café, Joyce found Mrs Rutherford totting up that day's till takings.

'Ah, Mrs Carter,' she said. 'I wanted to have a word with you.'

Her voice sounded unusually serious, and Joyce's mind leapt to what terrible misdemeanour she might inadvertently have committed. Or was it something Angie had done? Or Gino? She could hear them both clattering about in the kitchen, and prayed that neither of them had done something awful, like borrow money from the till while she was at the hospital.

Realising that Mrs Rutherford was looking at her rather oddly, she tried to force an unconcerned smile onto her lips. 'Oh yes?' she said.

'Well, the thing is,' Mrs Rutherford began awkwardly, 'you've been in the church hall for rather a long time now. And it's getting very crowded.'

Joyce stared at her in trepidation. She's going to ask me to make alternative arrangements, she thought. But where on earth else can we go?

'So.' Mrs Rutherford took a breath. 'I was wondering if you would like to come and stay at Cedars House.' She gave a slightly strained smile. 'And Mr Lorenz too, if you felt that would be appropriate. We could put a bed in Greville's study for him so he wouldn't have to use the stairs.'

Joyce felt her mouth fall open and had to make a conscious effort to close it. Had her posh, proud employer just offered to put her up? She could hardly believe it. She knew the Rutherfords' house, of course, from when she'd worked there as a cleaner at the beginning of the war. But she had never thought she would be invited to stay. However, it seemed she had heard correctly, because Mrs Rutherford was watching her expectantly, clearly waiting for a reply.

'Oh my,' Joyce mumbled. 'I don't know what to say. That would be wonderful, but surely it would be a terrible imposition ...' She stopped. There was another consideration too. 'What about your husband? I don't think he ...'

'My husband is away with the guns on the south coast at the moment,' Celia said.

Joyce blinked. 'But his study? Surely …'

Celia Rutherford lifted her chin. 'There is a war on, you know. We all have to make our little sacrifices.'

Joyce stared at her incredulously. She was fairly certain that finding out that the local Jewish pawnbroker was using his office as a convalescent bedroom might be considerably more of a sacrifice than that pompous old fool Greville Rutherford was prepared to make. But it was hardly her place to say so.

In any case, she didn't get the chance, because at that moment Angie's face loomed through the hatch. 'Coo,' she said. 'That's kind of you, Mrs R. Mr Lorenz will be delighted, won't he, Mum? But what about me and Gino? Can we come and all?'

'Angie!' Joyce exclaimed. 'That's quite out of the question.' Turning hastily back to Mrs Rutherford to apologise for her daughter's temerity, she was startled to see that she was laughing.

'Well, why not?' Celia said, ignoring Joyce's frantically shaking head. 'You are a respectable married couple now after all.'

Oh no! Joyce stared at her in horror. Had the woman gone mad? Angie and Gino? Respectable?

She had a sudden terrible vision of them going at it like knives in one of Mrs Rutherford's elegant spare bedrooms, and her heart quailed.

'What?' Jen's brows rose incredulously. 'Are you crazy? You've sent a telegram to Katy saying that the boys have gone missing? My God. She'll have a fit.'

Louise gritted her teeth. She might have known that Jen Carter would put a spanner in the works.

Oddly, when she'd caught sight of Jen emerging from the guest house, Louise had felt relieved that she had someone to share the problem with. But that relief had quickly turned to irritation. 'What else could I do?' she snapped. 'I promised to let her know. And I had to tell the police.'

Not that the police had been remotely helpful. There had only been one elderly bobby on duty, and it had taken him an age to write down all the details.

She glared at Jen, taking in her pretty summer dress and fancy hairdo. In comparison, she knew she looked an overheated frump in her thick khaki uniform and cap. 'Why?' she asked. 'What would you have done?'

'I'd have made more effort to find them, for a start,' Jen retorted. 'Why don't you go back to the village and track them from there?'

'I can't,' Louise said. 'I need to get back to camp. My unit is moving to a new location tonight and I've got to help get everything ready.' She grimaced. 'Anyway, I've got this horrid driver. I'd never be able to persuade him to go all the way back to Winterbourne. I'm only a private. I've got no authority over him.'

'Who needs authority?' Jen said grimly. 'Let me talk to him.'

Sure enough, to Louise's intense irritation, the driver seemed impressed by Jen. 'I saw you sing a couple of weeks ago,' he said. 'You did "Burlington Bertie", and you was in a top hat. I got your autograph and all.'

Two minutes later, they were on their way back to Winterbourne in the Tilly, with Jen sitting up next to the driver like Lady Muck, and Louise perched uncomfortably on the metal bench seat in the back.

But tracking the boys' movements was easier said than done. The kindly lady where they had been staying clearly had no idea where they had gone. But she did give them a clue as to the reason for their disappearance. 'The older lad, George, had this big bruise on his leg,' she said. 'He wouldn't tell me where he got it, so I reported it to Mr Grandison, but he just said George had a reputation for getting into scraps. But I know boys, and young George doesn't look like a fighter to me.' She hesitated. 'Between you and me, I'm not sure about that Mr Grandison. It seems hard on the boys, not allowing them to write letters home and that. They are only children, after all. It's bound to take a while for them to settle in.'

'Of course it is,' Jen said grimly. She glanced at Louise. 'I think we need another word with Mr Grandison.'

Jen was never one to pull her punches, and in other circumstances Louise would have been amused to witness the way the schoolmaster backed down in the face of her biting sarcasm and flashing eyes.

'Miss Rutherford here knows that George Nelson was being tormented by one of his classmates earlier in the year,' Jen said. 'And we suspect it has been happening again. You apparently don't care about that. But we do, and we want to see the boy in question.' She turned to Louise. 'What was the bully's name?'

'Garrow,' Louse responded meekly. 'I can't remember his first name.'

When a thuggish boy with bold, piggy eyes was finally produced, Jen insisted that she and Louise interview him alone.

She fixed the boy with a steely glare. 'What have you done with George Nelson and Malcolm Frazer?' she asked.

'I ain't done nothing with them,' he responded.

Louise noticed the slight smirk that accompanied his words. 'You're lying,' she said. 'I can see it in your eyes. Where are they?'

'I don't know.'

He was nearly as tall as her, and the impudent, almost mocking look in his eyes made her want to slap him. 'Well you know something,' she said. 'And you are going to tell us.'

The boy almost laughed. 'You can't make me tell you nothing,' he said. 'I'm not frightened of you.'

'You should be,' Jen snapped. 'You think because we're women we can't hurt you. Well I can't tell you how wrong you are. And when you grow up – if you ever grow up, which seems unlikely – you'll learn that women can hurt you much more than you think.' She waved her hand in Louise's direction. 'Take Miss Rutherford here,' she said grittily. 'She's a past master of the art of hurting men.'

The boy looked uneasily at Louise. And whether it was Jen's vicious words or the sudden responsive rage in Louise's eyes, something made him suddenly capitulate.

'All right. All right. I'll admit it,' he said. 'We may've teased the nipper a bit.'

Louise was still too angry to speak, but Jen was straight on to him. 'What do you mean?' she asked dangerously. 'What sort of teasing?'

The boy shrugged. 'We hung him out of the window of the train on the way down here. And once we got here, we caught him and left him tied up in a tree. And Nelson got all antsy and we had a bit of a scrap. But there was no harm done. We never hurt them. Not really. Just a few bruises. It was only paying them back for what they did to my dad.'

Louise could feel herself gaping at him in horror, but Jen's voice was steady as a rock. 'What did they do to your dad?'

The boy scowled. 'It's because of them that my dad got put inside. And his friend Mr Fish got killed.'

It was Jen's turn to look startled, and Louise felt it was time for her to re-enter the fray. 'Your dad was caught red-handed stealing glasses from the pub,' she said. 'He deserved to be put away. And his friend Mr Fish was even worse.' She was on the point of adding that Mr Fish and his cronies had been molesting underage girls as well, but thought better of it. This Garrow was a nasty piece of work, but he was only a boy after all, albeit an obnoxious one.

He was already smirking again. 'So what are you going to do about it?' he sneered. 'Hit me with your handbags?'

Louise was tempted to do just that, but Jen gave a mirthless laugh. 'You think you're clever, don't you?' she asked, and her voice was like flint. 'But I'd like you to think about this. If she wasn't having to waste her time here talking to you, Miss Rutherford would even now be on the ack-ack guns shooting down V-1 rockets. Or don't you care if people in London are dying while you're spending your time tying toddlers to trees?'

He flushed slightly, but before he could respond, Jen went on. 'Even as we speak, soldiers are dying to protect the people of this country. And frankly, when I look at people like you, and your father, sometimes I wonder why they bother.'

'Yes,' Louise agreed. 'Why indeed? Perhaps you would rather have lived in Germany? Perhaps you'd have liked to join the Hitler Youth? A thug like you would have felt quite at home.'

He looked daunted, and she pressed home her advantage. 'I'm going to give you one last chance. Where are George and Malcolm?'

He shook his head. 'I swear I don't know where they are.'

Louise glanced at Jen and saw her slight nod.

'OK, I believe you,' she said. 'But if I find out that you've been lying, or if I ever, ever hear that you've been bullying anyone ever again, you'll have me and Miss Carter to answer to. Not only that, you'll be sent to borstal.' She stared into his piggy eyes. 'My father is a Justice of the Peace, and I'll make sure that he sees to it. Do you understand me, Garrow?'

He nodded. 'Yes,' he mumbled. 'I understand.'

As he slunk out of the room, Louise rounded on Jen. 'I told you they had run away,' she said. She was still seething about Jen's comment about hurting men, but there wasn't time to take issue with her about that now. 'But how?'

'Maybe they got on a bus,' Jen said.

'Mr Grandison said they hadn't got any money. And anyway, someone would surely have seen them at the bus stop.'

Jen shook her head. 'I don't think so,' she said. 'George is a slippery little devil. He knows about things like that. About being inconspicuous. He learnt it from Ward Frazer. And he taught it to Molly. Half the reason we managed to escape from Italy was because of what Molly had learnt from George.' She lowered her head and swore under her breath. 'I hope to God he and Malcolm are all right. I don't like to think of them roaming about the countryside on their own.'

Louise saw the flicker of pain cross Jen's pretty face and suddenly felt guilty for feeling so angry towards her. 'Was it bad?' she asked. 'In Italy, I mean? I never asked before.'

Jen gave her an odd look. 'It could have been worse,' she said. 'To be honest, thinking about what might have happened has been worse than what actually happened. It's taken me a while to get over that.' She shook her head as though she didn't want to talk about it any more. 'They must be heading for London,' she said. 'We should go back to Salisbury to see if anyone has seen them at the station.'

Louise nodded. 'After that, we'll have to leave it to the police, because if I don't get back to camp soon, I'll be court-martialled.'

'And I need to get back to the theatre,' Jen said. 'Otherwise they'll start thinking I've done a runner. Especially after the disastrous dress rehearsal we had last night.'

But there was no sign of the runaways at the railway station. And the stationmaster said he was sure he would have noticed two unaccompanied children.

'So they aren't heading back to London,' Louise said.

'But how can two children just disappear? Where on earth else would they have gone?'

'I don't know,' Louise said. But as she stared in despair up the platform, her eye was caught by a gaudy poster stuck to the wall.

She ran forward to inspect it more closely. 'Oh my goodness,' she said. 'Ginnett's Circus. The last time I spoke to George, just before we got hit by the V-1, he was telling me all about a man being fired from a gun at the circus. And look, there's a picture of exactly that on this poster.'

They looked at each other.

Then, as one, they ran back to the car.

The driver folded his paper and looked up resignedly. 'Where to now?'

'The circus,' Jen said.

'You've got to be joking me.'

'I'm not,' Jen said grimly. 'I've never been more serious in my whole life.'

Katy and Pam were frantic. When Louise's telegram had arrived, Katy thought she was going to be sick. The only thing she could do was run across the road to tell Pam.

Pam had fetched Alan back from the brewery. He had been to the local police and they were now in contact with the constable in Salisbury. A bobby was dispatched to Winterbourne, and at lunchtime news came back that two girls had been to the village in search of the missing children.

'Two girls?' Pam asked.

The Clapham policeman who had come to the pub to relay the news referred to his notes. 'It was a Miss Rutherford and a Miss Carter,' he said.

Pam glanced at Katy. 'Jen? What on earth is she doing there?'

But Katy was far too worried about Malcolm to bother wondering how Jen had hooked up with Louise. 'It doesn't matter,' she said irritably. 'All that matters is that they are obviously trying to find the boys. Which is more than the police seem to be doing.'

But according to the Clapham policeman, the Wiltshire bobby was convinced that the pair were already on their way back to London. He put the blame squarely in the lap of Mr Grandison. 'A couple of ladies in the village told him they had seen your boys in difficulties more than once and had reported it to Mr Grandison,' the Clapham policeman said disapprovingly. 'And he did nothing about it.'

'I knew that Mr Grandison was a bastard,' Pam burst out. She swung round furiously to Alan. 'I told you I didn't like him. We should never have trusted him.'

But shivers of alarm were running down Katy's spine. 'What sort of difficulties?' she asked.

The policeman looked uncomfortable. 'He didn't go into detail,' he said. 'But it seems your little lad was getting picked on by some bigger boys, and Mrs Nelson's son was trying to protect him.' He pursed his lips. 'I know boys will be boys, but even so …'

'Oh my God,' Katy whispered. She suddenly felt faint. She glanced at Pam and saw the angry colour drain from her face too. It sounded awful. More than awful. But all they could do was wait. And hope.

Ginnett's Circus was set up on a playing field just outside the town. After a little argy-bargy with a villainous-looking man in the kiosk, who was initially disinclined to allow them access to the site outside of show time, Louise and Jen were escorted to a dirty caravan behind the colourful big top.

And there they discovered the truants, seemingly completely at their ease, chatting happily to a giant of a man with very bad teeth, a lithe young woman of Oriental extraction, and a small, rotund man whose face still bore the remnants of a clown's make-up.

It was an extraordinary scene. The five of them, almost invisible in the malodorous cloud of cigarette smoke that filled the caravan, were sitting on two fixed benches, crammed round a very small table on which stood three cups of tea in fancy china, several ashtrays and two glasses of orange squash. The three adults were smoking pungent roll-up cigarettes, and the children were busily making inroads into two large toffee apples.

George looked up in amazement as Louise and Jen climbed into the caravan, but Malcolm was the first to speak. 'Look, George,' he squealed excitedly. 'It's Louise. And Jen.'

'It is indeed,' Jen said grimly.

George clearly felt obliged to make the rest of the introductions. 'This is Mr Rolf,' he said. 'He's a clown. And this is Miss Helga Highwire, and this is Ronaldo the lion tamer.'

Jen and Louise found themselves solemnly shaking hands all round.

'And now, if you don't mind, Master George,' Jen said when the courtesies had been done and two small stacking stools had been procured for the newcomers, 'we'd like to know what you are doing here.'

George swallowed a large lump of toffee apple. 'We ran away,' he said.

'We gathered that,' Jen said drily.

George looked aggrieved. 'We had to. It was like Dunkirk. The enemy was too strong. I could protect myself, but I couldn't protect Malcolm.' He nodded towards Louise. 'She told me it was our duty to look out for people smaller than ourselves. She said it was like the war. England couldn't stand by and watch Hitler smashing up smaller countries.'

'Ah,' Jen murmured. 'So it's your fault. I might have known.'

Louise lifted her chin. 'He's right,' she said. 'I did say that. And I'm proud of him for trying to protect Malcolm.' She shot Jen an angry glance, then turned back to George. 'But how did you get away?'

George had just taken another bite of toffee apple, but he obligingly wedged it into his cheek so he could talk. 'We hid for a while in the garden,' he mumbled. 'Then when no one was looking, we climbed over the back wall and went across the field to the next village. Then we got on the bus. I was aiming for the railway station at Salisbury, but at the bus stop we saw a sign for the circus, and I knew it was the same one that had been up on the common at home, so we came here first. I wanted to show Malcolm the man being fired out of the cannon.'

Malcolm nodded eagerly. 'Want to see man in the cannon.'

'That's our colleague Gary Gunpowder,' the clown explained helpfully.

Louise caught Jen's eye and bit her lip.

'But we missed the early show,' George added. 'So now we're waiting for the evening performance.'

'And may I ask how you paid for all this?' Louise asked sternly.

George hesitated. 'I took it out of Mr Grandison's pocket,' he said.

The lion tamer suddenly slapped a huge scarred hand on the table, making them all jump. 'Well that was naughty,' he growled. 'You didn't tell us that.'

George looked at him indignantly. 'I didn't see why I shouldn't take it. It was my money in the first place. He stole it off us when we arrived in the village.' He swung back to Louise anxiously. 'You aren't going to send us back there, are you?'

'No,' Louise said. 'We are going to take you straight home.'

Jen raised her eyebrows. 'I hope that's the royal we,' she said. 'Because there's no way I can take them home. I've got a show to perform.'

After his previous rather disconcerting interruption, the lion tamer had lapsed into silence, but at this he pricked up his ears. 'What show's that then?' he asked.

Jen gave a slight wince. 'I'm playing Juliet in a new production of *Romeo and Juliet* at the Garrison Theatre,' she said. 'It's the opening night tonight. I'm standing in for Janette Pymm, who's ill.'

Louise was impressed, but everyone else looked completely blank.

'What's that then?' the clown asked kindly. 'Some kind of ballet?'

Jen's face was a picture, and once again Louise had to bite back a laugh. But actually the situation wasn't that funny. She looked at her watch. She had already been gone far too long. She dreaded to think what Lieutenant Masterson was going to say. Let alone Colonel Westwood.

'So what are we going to do?' she murmured to Jen. 'I can't take them to London either. I'm probably going to get court-martialled as it is.'

George looked from her to Jen and back again. 'We could stay here,' he ventured hopefully.

To her consternation, Louise saw the lion tamer starting to nod. 'No, no, you can't stay here,' she said hastily. She racked her brains for a solution. Then she glanced at Jen. 'If I take them back to barracks with me now, will you call off the police and telegram Katy? Then if I can somehow get them to you after your show, could you keep them overnight and take them back up to London first thing tomorrow morning?'

Jen groaned. 'I suppose so.'

George put on his mulish face. 'But that means we'll miss the man in the cannon.'

'I want to see the cannon,' Malcolm shouted. 'I want to see the cannon.'

Louise looked at him in concern, but Jen wasn't having any of that. 'One more word from either of you and I'll fire you both from a bloody cannon,' she said.

This time Louise was unable to hold back her laughter. And then suddenly she couldn't stop. She could feel the circus folk looking at her in concern. But she didn't care. The boys were safe. And for now that was all that mattered.

Chapter Thirty One

Louise arriving back at the barracks with two angelic-looking boys in tow took the wind out of Lieutenant Masterson's sails.

'I see you found them,' he said. Then, remembering that she had been gone much longer than her allocated hour, he tried to frown. But before he could chastise her, Voles came running up with a couple of the other girls.

'Oh, I'm so glad they're safe,' she said. 'We've all been so worried.'

Don Wellington seemed to be the only person not entirely pleased to see the runaways.

'I know you,' he said, pointing at George. 'You're the boy that caused me so much trouble on the parade with your damned dog.'

'Lucky not his dog,' Malcolm said. 'Lucky is my dog.'

But George was eyeing Don Wellington defiantly. 'I only did it because you'd been horrid to Louise,' he said. 'And you kicked Lucky too. So it served you right.'

To Louise's delight, everyone laughed, and Don Wellington looked aggrieved.

'George is right,' she said. 'You had been horrid to me. Come to think of it, you're still horrid to me. And to Voles.'

'Then I'd do it again,' George said stoutly. 'You shouldn't be horrid to people smaller than yourself.'

And that made everyone laugh even more. But Don Wellington's discomfiture didn't last as long as Louise would have liked.

'Watch out,' Voles whispered suddenly. 'Here comes the colonel.'

At once everyone fell silent, came to attention and saluted.

Unlike the others, who were dressed in workaday fatigues, Colonel Westwood was looking very crisp and smart in his service dress. The silver oak leaves on his epaulettes glinted in the afternoon sun as he touched his hat in acknowledgement of their salutes.

'What's the rumpus?' he asked,

Lieutenant Masterson braced himself slightly. 'Private Rutherford has finally returned, sir,' he said. 'But she has brought the two children with her.'

'So I see.' Colonel Westwood's dark eyes narrowed as he glanced at the two boys, who were both regarding him with undisguised awe. Then his gaze came to rest on Louise.

Louise swallowed. 'I'm sorry, sir,' she said. 'But I didn't know what else to do with them, so I decided to bring them back here.'

'And how long do we have the pleasure of their company?'

'I've arranged for someone to take them home tomorrow,' Louise said. 'A friend from London. She's an actress called Jen Carter. She couldn't do it tonight because she's performing in *Romeo and Juliet* in Salisbury. It's her opening night, you see, and ...' She stopped abruptly, aware that she was gabbling. But she was nervous. She didn't want to be told off by Colonel Westwood. Not in front of everyone. Not at all.

'It's my fault, sir,' George said suddenly. He was almost standing to attention too. 'But they tied Malcolm to a tree. And I was scared about what they might do to him next, so we ran away. And I'm glad Louise found us at the circus, because I don't think I had enough money to get to London. But I don't want her to get into trouble.'

Louise wanted to hug him. She suddenly felt terribly proud of him. She heard Voles sniff and, casting a quick glance, saw that she wasn't the only one holding back tears.

'She's not going to get into trouble,' Colonel Westwood said. 'But we are moving out of here tonight.' He glanced at Lieutenant Masterson. 'How much have you still got left to do, Lieutenant?'

'Everyone has worked really hard, sir,' Lieutenant Masterson responded promptly. 'Maybe another two hours and we'll be all packed up and ready to go.'

'Is that right?' Colonel Westwood looked thoughtful. 'In that case, once it's done, I guess we can all take the evening off. Get some rest. This may well be the last chance we have for a while.'

Voles shuffled her feet. 'Would we be allowed off camp, sir?'

Louise's head swung round in astonishment. It wasn't like Voles to speak up. Colonel Westwood looked considerably taken aback too. 'What were you thinking, Private?'

Voles flushed. 'I wondered if we could go to see *Romeo and Juliet*. I've seen Jen Carter perform before and she's really something.'

Don Wellington rolled his eyes and made a disparaging comment under his breath. It didn't escape Colonel Westwood's ears. 'Is Shakespeare not to your taste, Wellington?'

He flushed. 'Jen Carter's not to my taste, sir.'

'Jen Carter is nice,' George said reprovingly. 'And I'd like to see her play too. But I'd rather see the guns.'

'Want to see guns too,' Malcolm piped up eagerly. He turned his eyes to Louise. 'You promised.'

Louise almost let out a moan. Oh no, she thought. Precocious brats.

368

Whatever happened to children being seen and not heard?

Once again Colonel Westwood's eyes were on her. 'What exactly did you promise, Private Rutherford?'

'I said I would show them our guns,' she muttered. 'To make up for not seeing the man at the circus being fired from a cannon.'

His lips twitched slightly. 'I see.' He held her gaze for a moment, then glanced at Lieutenant Masterson. 'Our artillery is already loaded up, right? But I can hear firing on the ranges. So how about I take the boys up there for an hour or so. And then when you're all done here, those that wish to can go to the play.'

Lieutenant Masterson looked dumbfounded. As well he might. It was hardly the colonel's job to entertain a couple of uninvited children. But he nodded and began to order everyone back to work.

Louise glanced doubtfully at George and Malcolm. They'd been through a lot over the last few days. Malcolm was so young, not even three yet. He seemed unscathed by his ordeal, but would he be happy going off with a man he had never met? And more to the point, would Colonel Westwood be able to cope with them? They looked as though butter wouldn't melt in their mouths right now, but she knew all too well how naughty George could be, and how overexcited Malcolm could get.

Colonel Westwood saw her hesitation. 'They'll be fine.'

'I'm more worried about you,' Louise said helplessly. She fixed the boys with a steely gaze. 'Now listen,' she said sternly. 'You're to do exactly what the colonel says. And don't be a nuisance.'

'Of course we won't be a nuisance,' George said indignantly. His eyes were gleaming with excitement. He looked shyly at Colonel Westwood. 'Although I do have quite a lot of questions to ask.'

'So do I,' Malcolm said.

Colonel Westwood looked amused. 'Have you indeed?' With a reassuring wink at Louise, he turned and led his charges off towards the headquarters building. 'In that case, let's go find ourselves a driver and some field glasses,' she heard him say as they walked away. 'And then you can both fire away …'

'Coo, you've got a nice place here, Mrs R,' Angie enthused. 'I knew it was big from the outside, but I didn't know it would be as grand as this. With all this ancient old furniture and that.'

Joyce tried to frown her down, but she knew it was a lost cause. Angie was incapable of restraint. In any case, Mrs Rutherford was already leading the way up the wide staircase. When Angie saw the large double bed in the room she and Gino were to be allocated, her eyes lit up even more. 'Oh, I say,' she said. 'It will be just like our honeymoon all over again.'

Give him his due, even Gino seemed mildly discomfited by that, and Mrs Rutherford looked positively pink around the gills. Hastily she led the way out of the room again. 'I think the next thing we should do is carry the spare bed from your mother's room down into my husband's study for Mr Lorenz.' She turned to Joyce. 'You may remember that there's a convenient water closet next to the study.' She shuffled her feet uncomfortably. 'I am assuming that Gino will help Mr Lorenz with his ablutions? Because it wouldn't be quite the thing for you to do it, or at least not until you are married.'

Joyce swallowed. Married? Ablutions?

But Mrs Rutherford was already pressing on. 'As you see, the cellar has nice wide steps. It's well lit and warm. Mr Lorenz will be quite safe down there while you are at work.'

Joyce was still thinking about the disturbing prospect of helping Albert with his ablutions, but when she saw Mrs Rutherford looking at her expectantly, she tried to pull herself together. 'You've thought of everything,' she said.

Mrs Rutherford nodded complacently. 'Covering all eventualities is one of the maxims of the WVS.'

Joyce hesitated. 'There is just one more thing,' she said. 'Would you mind terribly if Monty the tortoise came to stay as well?'

Mrs Rutherford looked at her with misgiving. 'In the house?'

'No, no,' Joyce said hastily. 'In the garden. I could get Gino to make a run for him. It's just that I'm worried he's a bit lonely without us at home.'

Mrs Rutherford gave a bark of laughter. 'I hadn't thought of that. But certainly he can. And perhaps Gino would check the fence round the vegetable patch while he's at it. The hens got in there the other week and scratched up all my seedlings. Quite a few of my carrots were missing too. I can't imagine how that happened.'

Joyce glanced out of the window. It wasn't hard to imagine how it had happened. Even from here she could see scuff marks on the wall that adjoined the Nelsons' garden. She had occasionally caught sight from her own back window of George in the Rutherfords' garden, and had suspected that he had been stealing vegetables to feed his rabbit.

She had wondered about blackmailing him into giving her a few for Monty, but it would have been awkward if word had got out. Instead she had relied on Bella James to bring her dandelions or stinging nettles in return for a bun or a piece of cake. The girl always looked so undernourished, and it had been a tactful way of getting a bit of food into her. Of course the poor child looked even worse now.

Yesterday Joyce had bumped into Dr Goodacre at the hospital and ventured to ask him if he knew anything about people who suddenly refused to speak.

'Ah yes,' he had said at once. '*Aphasia voluntaria*. It's a kind of instinctive mutism. It often follows trauma or shock. It was a common phenomenon in soldiers returning from the Great War. Sadly it's not uncommon these days either. Especially in sensitive children.'

That sounded about right, Joyce thought. 'Does it eventually wear off?' she asked.

'Oh yes,' he said. 'But it needs very careful handling. Sufferers who find themselves in a happy, relaxed environment generally do better than those who feel insecure or fearful. Why do you ask, Mrs Carter? I hope we aren't talking about a member of your family?'

'No, no,' Joyce said. 'It's the girl who was Angie's bridesmaid, Bella James. Her mother was killed in the same rocket attack that injured Mr Lorenz. And she hasn't uttered a word since.'

Dr Goodacre nodded wisely. 'Classic trauma,' he said. 'Poor child. Pretty little thing, as I recall. Bring her to see me if you like. People are often dismissive of what they see as merely mental conditions. But the brain is part of the body after all.' He smiled suddenly. Take Mr Lorenz, for example.' He saw Joyce's perplexed expression and chuckled delightedly. 'Everyone is surprised by his remarkable recovery, but they don't take his mental state into account. He had something to look forward to, you see. He had *you* to look forward to, Mrs Carter. I'm quite sure it will have made all the difference.'

Joyce had felt gratified, but now, as she followed Mrs Rutherford back into the hallway, she was once again thinking of poor little Bella. She didn't have much to look forward to at the moment.

When Jen eventually got back to the theatre, she found the cast in a state of disarray. Walter Lowther was steaming. 'Where on earth have you been?' he shouted at her. 'We've all been worried to death.'

But not only had Jen had to visit the police station and send a telegram to Katy, she had also had to persuade her landlady to allow her to bring two children back with her after the show. And that hadn't been an easy task.

All in all, she could have wrung those children's necks. But the one good thing about the afternoon was that it had taken her mind off the show.

Now, though, the nerves were back with a vengeance. And she was pitifully grateful when the Violets appeared unexpectedly in her dressing room.

'We're off to Dorset tomorrow,' Veronica said. 'But we decided to come and give you some moral support on our way.'

'I need more than moral support,' Jen said. 'My knees are so weak I might need crutches.'

What she really needed was Henry. She suddenly longed for his calming confidence. But there was no sign of him. No word at all. And it was too late now anyway. The front-of-house manager was encouraging people to take their seats. The show was about to begin.

Jen found Romeo in the wings, peering through a discreet crack in the curtain, shaking with fear.

'It's a huge audience,' he said.

Jen pushed him out of the way and took his place at the crack. Most people had already taken their seats, but people were still coming in at the back.

'Oh no,' Jen gasped. 'Oh no!'

'What?' Romeo sounded alarmed. 'What is it?'

'Oh my God,' Jen said. She pulled him forward and pointed. 'See that man walking down the aisle? In a yellow bow tie? I absolutely loathe and despise him. He's the bane of my life. What the *hell* is he doing here?'

There was a tiny pause. Romeo drew back from the curtain. 'That's Jason Cavell,' he said. 'He's my uncle. I invited him.'

Jen looked at him aghast. She felt the stage tilt slightly under her feet and clutched at a nearby bit of scenery to steady herself. Talk about putting your foot in it. She wished the stage would open up and swallow her. His uncle!

She let go of the flat and took hold of Romeo's arm instead. 'Don't tell him what I said,' she said. 'Please promise you won't tell him. He hates me enough as it is.'

Romeo gave an uncertain laugh. 'Then kiss me,' he said. 'And I won't.'

Jen drew back in horror. But what else could she do? Time was rapidly running out. The chorus and the opening members of the cast would be taking their places on stage any minute. 'OK,' she said. 'Just one kiss.'

'And a hug.'

She rolled her eyes. 'All right. A kiss and a hug.' She looked at him severely. 'But that's all.'

It wasn't so hard. He was a nice boy. Although sadly he had no idea how to kiss. His technique was poor. He needed a few lessons from Sean, Jen thought. Or indeed Henry. She suddenly remembered Henry kissing her once, a long time ago, before she went to Italy, and how nice it had been.

Hearing a noise behind her, she jerked away and glanced nervously over her shoulder. It would be just her luck if Henry suddenly materialised and caught her grappling with Romeo in the wings. But it wasn't Henry. It was Sampson and Gregory, two of the Capulet servants, nervously checking their costumes with the aid of a small hand mirror. Jen glanced again through the curtain.

This time she saw Louise Rutherford hurrying in with George and a number of army people. One of them had Malcolm clinging to his back like a monkey. Jen stared in horror as they filed into the same row as Walter Lowther.

She felt Romeo move awkwardly beside her. 'Tell me it meant something,' he said.

She groaned. She had forgotten all about the kiss. 'Yes, it meant something,' she said. 'But not very much.' She smiled and patted his cheek consolingly. 'However, if you don't forget your words tonight, and if you manage to look as if you are in love with me, you might even get another.'

'I am in love with you,' he said.

Jen shook her head in despair. 'Well then for goodness' sake make it show.'

And he did.

The first couple of scenes were as laboured as they had been the night before, but from the moment Romeo stepped out onto the stage, he sparkled. He spoke the archaic language as fast and fluently as though he conversed in it every day. And his eager energy made the others buck up their ideas too. When he announced, 'In sadness, cousin, I do love a women,' even Jen, watching from the wings, was aware of a prickle of emotion, and the audience was absolutely silent, rapt, hanging on his words as he outlined Juliet's charms.

As her first cue approached, Jen felt terribly afraid. She knew the audience was disappointed that they weren't going to see Janette Pymm. She had heard the groans when the front-of-house manager had announced the change just before the curtain went up. Now she could feel the tension in her throat, and hummed a low chord to loosen up her voice. It was down to her now. It would be her fault if it all went wrong.

In the end, George and Malcolm had spent over two hours with Colonel Westwood, only just getting back in time to eat a hearty meal of sausages and Heinz baked beans in the NAAFI before setting off to the theatre in Salisbury.

Louise would have preferred to skip the play. She had never been much of a one for Shakespeare, and she was sure that George and Malcolm would be bored to death. But they insisted on going, and when she discovered that Colonel Westwood was also intending to join the party, she quickly stifled her objections.

After a couple of hours in the colonel's company, George and Malcolm were both completely in his thrall. 'Colonel Westwood took us right to the gun position and we watched the guns firing,' George said. 'He made us wear headphones and he explained everything. It was brilliant.'

'We went in a jeep,' Malcolm said. 'Really fast.'

Colonel Westwood looked slightly guilty. 'They seemed to kind of like it,' he said.

But Louise was much less certain they would like *Romeo and Juliet*. 'We'll bring a blanket,' Susan said. 'If Malcolm feels sleepy, he can curl up on the floor.'

'I won't feel sleepy,' Malcolm said.

But after the novelty of recognising Jen on stage had worn off, he did. And while everyone else in the audience was gripped by the tragic romance, he spent most of the play fast asleep, sprawled across Louise and Colonel Westwood's laps.

In the short second interval, Susan nudged Louise. 'You look like such loving parents,' she whispered. Louise shushed her urgently, terrified that Colonel Westwood would hear.

'What do you think of Romeo?' Susan asked.

Louise giggled. 'Too young for me,' she said.

'I know,' Susan said regretfully. 'But he's very handsome. And isn't Jen wonderful? Honestly, you can hear a pin drop when she is on.'

And yes, Jen was good. Even Louise had to admit that. The chemistry between her and the youthful Romeo was extraordinary. You really felt for them. For their doomed love. Even George was gripped. And in the death scene, Louise was aware of feeling quite emotional. It was ridiculous. It was only stupid Jen Carter after all. But somehow the play had got to her. And she realised she felt oddly proud to know Jen, and to bask in her reflected glory. The applause was tumultuous. Everyone was on their feet. Colonel Westwood hefted the sleeping Malcolm onto his shoulder so he and Louise could stand up too, to show their support.

George was standing on his chair, clapping and whistling with the others. Next to him a fussy-looking man in a bow tie appeared rather pained.

Louise leaned round George to address him. 'I hope he hasn't been a nuisance,' she said.

The man pursed his lips. 'On the contrary. He's a very engaging young man. We had quite a chat in the interval.'

'Did you enjoy the play?'

The man gave a prissy smile. 'Somewhat to my surprise, I did,' he said. 'Of course I was expecting to see Janette Pymm.'

Suddenly Susan poked her head through from the row behind. 'Oh, I love Janette Pymm too,' she said. 'But Jen Carter was absolutely brilliant, wasn't she? I cried at the end.' She giggled self-consciously and dabbed her eyes with her hanky. 'I'm still crying now.'

*

Jen felt stunned. It had been one of those shows. She had read about them. When something magical happened and it all just clicked. She was almost overwhelmed by the cheers when she took her curtain call.

She had been applauded when she played Juliet all those years ago in her school play. That had been pretty special too. But they were applauding her then because she was one of the few who had managed to remember her lines. This was completely different.

'One more,' Walter Lowther had hissed from the wings. In reply, Jen had graciously waved him forward to take his own bow. Then she and Romeo took his hands, and as she sank into her last curtsey, she felt him squeeze her fingers. 'Well done,' he whispered, and the applause surged once more. Then the curtain swung closed for the last time and the entire cast was hugging and kissing, astonished by their unexpected success.

Back in her dressing room, Jen felt heady and peculiar. She sat on her make-up stool and looked at herself in the mirror. 'I did it,' she whispered. 'I did it.' Somehow she had pulled the rabbit out of the hat. And the sense of jubilation was worth all the angst, the terror and the sickness put together.

At that moment, someone tapped softly on her door.

She swung round. Oh please let it be Henry, she thought. She so wanted him to have witnessed her moment of glory. She didn't want to see anyone else. Not yet. She just wanted some time to herself. Some time to come back to earth.

'Who is it?' she called.

Without bothering to reply, Walter Lowther came swaggering in, accompanied by Jason Cavell. He was clearly exultant that his debut production had been witnessed by such a theatrical celebrity. 'This is Mr Cavell,' he said gushingly to Jen. 'He—'

'Yes,' Jen cut in coldly. 'I know. We've met before.'

She was bracing herself for a cutting response, but instead Jason Cavell stepped forward and held out his hand. 'Congratulations,' he said. 'That was a remarkable performance.'

Jen was completely thrown off balance. Awkwardly she leant forward and took his hand. She knew she really ought to stand up, but she thought that if she did, she would probably pass out in a dead faint on the floor.

'I think it was a bit of a fluke,' she stammered. 'It was all down to your nephew really.'

He made a blasé gesture with his programme. 'And he said it was all down to you. He said you inspired him.'

Jen almost laughed. She knew exactly what had inspired young Romeo, but she was hardly going to tell his influential uncle. Jason Cavell was already looking at her pensively.

'We got off to a bad start,' he said. 'When we first met in London.'

Jen felt herself colouring. 'I know,' she said. 'And I'm sorry. I was very rude. I wasn't in the best shape. I had just got back from Italy, and—'

'Yes,' he cut in. 'So I heard from a young friend of yours in the audience. He told me quite a lot about you.'

Oh no, Jen thought. That must have been George. She dreaded to think what else he might have said.

'I was too quick to dismiss you,' Jason Cavell went on. 'It's a bad trait of mine. But fluke or not, a Juliet who can make half the audience dissolve into tears is not to be sniffed at.' He had rolled up his programme, and now he tapped it lightly on the palm of his other hand. 'I gather you are coming up to London tomorrow morning?'

Jen nodded. George had clearly been very busy with his information.

'Then if possible, I'd like you to come in to RADA,' Jason Cavell said. 'We have another round of auditions tomorrow and I'd like my colleagues to hear you again.' He caught her thunderstruck expression and hesitated. 'I assume you are still interested in taking the diploma?'

Jen knew she was staring at him, but she couldn't help it. She had a sudden nasty feeling that she was dreaming and was going to wake up to find that the last two hours hadn't happened. Or had the applause gone to her head? Either way, she was having a hard time acknowledging her sudden reversal of fortune.

'Oh yes,' she finally managed. 'I'm definitely still interested.'

'Good,' he said. He glanced at Walter Lowther, who was standing by the door, glowing with vicarious pride. 'In that case I'll look forward to seeing you tomorrow. Shall we say eleven o'clock?'

Joyce was luxuriating in the serene comfort of Mrs Rutherford's spare bed when she heard the front door open, and a muffled discussion in the hallway at the bottom of the stairs. Angie and Gino were clearly back from the cinema. She prayed they wouldn't wake their hostess, not on the first night. But to her horror, a moment later she heard the sound of a small herd of elephants rampaging up the stairs.

'Mum! Are you awake?'

'I am now,' Joyce said sourly as the door opened. She sat up. 'Angie, really, shhh, you must try to be more quiet.' And now Gino was in the room too. Joyce hastily pulled the sheet up to her chin, appalled at being caught in the new lacy nightdress she had extravagantly bought that afternoon from Arding and Hobbs.

'No, but Mum,' Angie was clearly brimming with news, 'we had to come and tell you. After the film they had the Pathé news. And guess what?'

'What?' Joyce lifted her eyebrows. 'Don't tell me the war's over.'

Angie let out an ear-splitting giggle. 'No,' she chortled. 'I don't suppose you'll believe me, but we saw Paul and Pete. They showed a clip of General Montgomery celebrating the liberation of some French village, and he had all these troops around him, waiting to shake hands, and there was Paul and Pete, large as life. They were standing there side by side, weren't they, Gino? We saw them ever so clear. Right at the front. Smiling all over their faces.'

Joyce suddenly found she was smiling all over hers. Her boys were alive. Her eyes were watering so much, she didn't see Gino plunging forward to shake her hand. The first she knew of it was when he caught his foot on the Persian bedside mat and only just managed to prevent himself from nose-diving into her bosom.

By now, Mrs Rutherford had emerged from her own bedroom. 'Goodness,' she said, goggling blearily at the sight of Gino sprawling on the bed at Joyce's side. 'What's going on?'

'It's Pete and Paul,' Angie said. 'Me and Gino just saw them with Monty.'

Mrs Rutherford had clearly just been woken from a deep sleep. 'With the tortoise?' she said. 'In the garden?'

'No!' Angie gave a scream of hysterical laughter. 'With General Montgomery. In France. On the Pathé news.'

And now Joyce was laughing too. It was ridiculous. She was aware of a profound sense of relief. The war wasn't over yet. There was probably a long way to go. But at least for now, her sons weren't lying dead in a French field.

Leaving Colonel Westwood and Voles in temporary charge of the boys, Louise went to see if Jen was ready to take possession of them. She found her sitting in her dressing room, staring at herself in the mirror. She swung round as Louise came in and stood up rather shakily. She looked pale and somehow much smaller than she had on stage.

Louise had a sudden urge to hug her, and before she had time to think better of it, she crossed the room and embraced her. Jen looked flabbergasted, but Louise gave her no chance to recoil. 'Everyone thought you were amazing,' she said.

As they disengaged, Jen raised her eyebrows. 'What? Even Malcolm?'

Louise laughed and took a step back. 'Well, no,' she admitted. 'He slept through most of it. But George really enjoyed it.'

There was a slightly awkward pause, then Jen took another step back. 'I'm sorry about what I said this afternoon,' she said. 'About you hurting men. I was out of order.'

It was Louise's turn to feel flabbergasted. 'No, you were right,' she said. 'I have been careless of people's emotions in the past. But I've changed.' She gave a self-conscious laugh. 'I'm trying to be nicer. Kinder.'

Jen looked away. After a moment, she sat down at her dressing table again. But Louise could see her pretty face reflected in the mirror, and was puzzled by the bleakness in her eyes. She would have thought that after her success tonight, Jen would have been exultant, jubilant. Certainly in the past she would have gloated over her triumph. But tonight she seemed almost brought down by it all.

'It's Henry, isn't it?' Jen said suddenly. 'It's Henry who's changed you.' Louise gazed at her dumbfounded. 'And I'm glad you've changed,' Jen went on. 'Because I don't want you to break his heart.'

She sounded almost tearful. Louise could hardly believe it. 'I'm not going to break his heart,' she said. In the past, she might have lied. Just to get back at Jen for all her needling over the years. But now she felt obliged to tell the truth.

'Henry has never been interested in me,' she said. 'Not really.' She caught Jen's incredulous look in the mirror. 'No, it's true. He likes me. We've had a laugh. And he has been kind to me.' She paused. She felt her palms prickle and clenched them. This was the moment. She didn't know if she could do it. But she could see from Jen's reaction that it was important. She was honour bound to say it, even though it would almost certainly mean the end of her dreams.

'It's always been you,' she said. 'All he ever wanted to talk about was you. It's you he loves, not me.'

'But what about those roses?'

Louise was puzzled. What roses? What was she talking about?

'I saw Henry bringing a bunch of red roses into the Wilhelmina,' Jen said.

Light dawned. 'Oh yes, he did,' Louise said. 'But they weren't from him. He was just delivering them to me from someone else. A friend of his.'

Jen held her eyes in the mirror, then swung round to face her. Louise could see that she wanted to believe her, but something was holding her back. 'If that's true, why didn't he come tonight?' Jen said. Her voice shook. 'I sent an invitation to Drury Lane last week, but I haven't heard a word back from him. Not one word. Not even a note of encouragement.'

Louise stared at her. 'You don't know, do you?'

'What?' Jen looked alarmed. 'What don't I know?'

'He's not at Drury Lane any more.'

'What do you mean?'

'I mean he's left ENSA. He's joined up. Some special unit. They're going to try to destroy the V-1 launch sites. It sounds awfully dangerous, but ...'

Louise saw the colour drain from Jen's face. For a horrible second she thought she was going to pass out.

'Oh my God,' Jen whispered. 'Why didn't he tell me?'

Louise grimaced. 'I think he thought it was all over between you.'

Jen put her head in her hands.

Louise had it in her heart to feel sorry for her. She had no idea why Jen had given Henry such a runaround if she felt like this, but there was no doubt she was in love with him.

A sudden commotion outside presaged the arrival of the children.

'He was at the Rifle Brigade barracks in Winchester last time I heard,' Louise said quickly. 'He may not have left yet, but it sounded as though he'd be going quite soon.'

Before Jen could respond, the children had burst into the dressing room like two bullets, wide awake and raring to go.

'We went on a jeep,' Malcolm shouted.

'I loved it when you stabbed yourself to death,' George said. 'But that wasn't very good poison. Why didn't it work?'

Jen met Louise's eyes. 'Do you really have to leave them with me?'

'Yes, she does,' George said. 'Because she's going to somewhere called Rye with Colonel Westwood and Private Voles tonight to shoot down all the V-1s with their new secret weapon.'

Louise laughed. So much for Colonel Westwood's tight security. 'Maybe not all of them,' she said. 'But I'll be disappointed if we don't get at least one.'

She hugged the boys and told them to be good. 'I don't know when I'll be back in London,' she said. 'But give everyone my love.'

She could feel tears in her own eyes now, but as she moved hastily to the door, she heard Jen's voice behind her.

'Are you sure?' she said. 'About … everything. Because …' She stopped and waved her hands helplessly at herself. 'I'm such an idiot.'

Louise turned and smiled. 'I know,' she said. 'But I have it on good authority that Henry likes a challenge.'

Outside, Louise found Colonel Westwood waiting for her at the stage door. The others had already set off back to Larkhill in the truck.

As they walked round to the car park, she thanked him for his help with the boys.

'It was my pleasure,' he said. 'I have boys of my own. I miss them, and it was kind of nice to spend time with your two.'

It was already late and getting dark, but that didn't stop Louise halting in her tracks and staring at him aghast. He had boys of his own? That meant …

'But I thought …' she began. Then she stopped and put her hands to her mouth.

He peered at her through the darkness. 'What did you think?'

Of course he was married. Why wouldn't he be? A lovely man like him.

She could feel her mind flailing for an answer to his question. She couldn't possibly tell him what she'd thought. But nor could she think of anything else to say. And anyway, it was too late. She could see in his eyes that he knew.

She saw the tension in his jaw as he looked away.

He waited in silence while a couple of the actors came up behind them, chattering and laughing, clearly still pumped up with exhilaration.

In contrast, Louise felt as though someone had pulled all her stuffing out.

As the performers passed out of earshot, Colonel Westwood took a slow breath. 'I like you very much, Louise. But I love my wife. And I would never do anything to jeopardise that.'

She heard the concern in his voice. The compassion. She was also aware that perhaps for the first time he had called her by her Christian name.

And she realised then how stupid she had been. He had never given her any reason to think he was interested in her. Not once. He had been supportive. Inspiring. Adaptable. Friendly, yes, but nothing more than that. It had all been in her mind. In her silly schoolgirlish fantasy.

He was looking uncomfortable now, clearly mulling over the implications. 'Is this going to be a problem going forward?' he asked quietly.

'No, of course not,' Louise stammered. 'It's not what you think.' But the crack in her voice belied her words.

It wasn't just the loss of Colonel Ivo Westwood. She had lost Henry too. She had lost them both within the space of five minutes. It had been an exhausting, emotional day and suddenly she was overcome by a sense of her own foolishness. It wasn't Jen that was an idiot. It was her.

'Listen,' he said. His voice was kind, but firm. 'This may sound tough, but we have a long night ahead and a real important day tomorrow. I need to know if you can cope. If not, I guess it's better that I send you back to London.'

Louise looked at him through swimming eyes. 'But surely you need me to prime the fuses?'

'Yes,' he said slowly. 'I do. But you've had a bad time recently, and if you feel it's too much for you ...'

He left the sentence hanging, and she made a valiant effort to pull herself together. He was blaming the accident, giving her a way out. And he was right. It would be easier just to go back to the factory. Away from the inquisitive eyes of her colleagues. Away from the humiliation of having been found out.

'No,' she said. 'I want to come. Please don't send me back to London.'

Chapter Thirty Two

Colonel Westwood had not been wrong. It was a very long night. After an awkwardly silent trip back to camp in his staff car, Louise hardly had a moment to regain her equilibrium before she was being heaved up into a canvas-sided truck with the other girls for the journey to the coast.

The troop carrier, open at the back, was fitted with hard, splintery bench seats and had almost no suspension. It was cold, noisy and uncomfortable, and Louise spent the entire journey longing for the moment when she could crawl into bed and forget the trauma of the day.

But when they finally arrived at their destination at one o'clock in the morning, they discovered that this wasn't the kind of established army camp they were used to. It was a bare field in the middle of nowhere. The advance party had been tasked with getting things ready for their arrival, but although they had prepared the ground for the gun positions, they hadn't had time to organise any sleeping accommodation. So the ATS girls were told to put up tents.

In order to give them some privacy, the pitch they were allocated was quite a way away from everyone else. But that meant they had no one to help them, and exhausted from the jolting of the lorry, they were hardly in any fit shape to carry the equipment, let alone erect the tents.

The only time any of them had ever put up a tent before was in basic training camp, and some of them hadn't even done that. And although Louise and Voles tried to bring their former expertise to bear, it was hopeless. In the thin moonlight they couldn't see what they were doing – which bit of canvas they needed, or which guy rope to tether – and tempers quickly began to fray.

'This is ridiculous,' Louise said. 'It will be light by the time we get the damn things up. Why don't we just bed down in one of the lorries for now and finish them off in the morning?'

Ten minutes later, they had spread out their coats and nestled in among their kitbags, dragging a huge sheet of tarpaulin right over the top. After their earlier rigours, it was surprisingly warm and comfortable. But it wasn't restful.

While they had been grappling with the tent, they had been dimly aware of distant voices, presumably belonging to troops in adjacent units on either side of their position. They knew that the authorities were trying to put together a continuous line of ack-ack units in the hope of catching the V-1s as they crossed the coastline on their way to London, but they hadn't expected them to begin firing in the middle of the night.

The first time the barrage started up, the girls jumped out of their skins. Voles even went so far as to scream, and although Corporal Clifton tutted at her, Louise thought she had just cause. The barrage was unbelievably loud in the still night air. It sounded as though the guns were right on top of them, and as shrapnel started to rain down, they scrambled out of the lorry and crawled underneath it instead. Now they could see why they had been issued with steel helmets, although in fact both the helmets and the shelter were only symbolic. Even as they listened in terror to the grinding buzz of the approaching rocket getting louder and louder, they knew that if it fell anywhere nearby, the lorry would be blown to kingdom come along with the entire unit.

And now as the beastly thing zoomed overhead, they could see the tail of fire from its exhaust. Nobody had seen one at night before, and it sent shivers through them.

'It's so fast,' McEvoy whispered. 'How are we ever going to be able to shoot one down?'

Certainly neither of the neighbouring units was having any success. They must have expended thousands of rounds of ammunition already, Louise thought, and had made no impact on the rocket at all. It was well out of range now, heading blissfully on its way, presumably to wreak devastation on London.

The girls were subdued as they climbed back into the lorry. New fuses or not, suddenly the task ahead of them seemed insurmountable. They also realised that they were in considerable danger. There were no cellars or air-raid shelters here.

As she curled up again against her kitbag, with Voles's dew-soaked boots almost in her face, Louise suddenly remembered Lieutenant Masterson's introductory speech at Arborfield. 'Winning the war is all that matters,' he had said. 'With that one aim always in mind, we must be prepared to live and work together. And quite possibly die together.'

At this precise moment, she thought grimly, a well-aimed V-1 might be the very best thing that could happen. At least it would put her out of her misery.

Jen also had a sleepless night. The excitement of the show and Jason Cavell's unexpected turnaround was partly to blame. But what really kept her awake was what Louise had told her about Henry. Ever since then, her emotions had been in turmoil. As the dark hours ticked by, one thought began to override all the others. The thought of him going off on some hazardous mission to France, without knowing how she felt, caused her to feel an anguish so extreme, she found she could hardly breathe.

As soon as it began to get light, she eased herself out of bed, tensing as a floorboard creaked under her foot. She needn't have worried. Neatly tucked in, one at each end of the other bed, Malcolm and George were both dead to the world. She watched them for a moment, envying their innocent, carefree slumber. It was a long time since she had slept straight through a night.

Shrugging on her overcoat over her nightdress, she slipped on her shoes and tiptoed downstairs. Carefully leaving the front door ajar so she could get back in, she ran down Fisherton Street to the railway station to check the train timetables. But the route she wanted was impossible if she was going to get to RADA by eleven.

Five minutes later, she was tapping on Roger and Veronica Violet's door.

When Roger opened up, wearing a pair of old-fashioned flannelette pyjamas, he looked alarmed to find Jen standing in the passage, panting and wild-haired from her mad dash back from the station.

'Is everything all right?'

'No,' Jen said. 'It's not. I need to try and see Henry Keller before he goes to France. I know you're heading off to Dorset today, and I know it's completely out of your way, but is there any chance you could take me and the boys to Winchester before you go? We can go on to London from there.'

'Wakey wakey!' bellowed a loud voice. Jerking awake, Louise saw Don Wellington peering into the back of the lorry. 'Good God,' he said. 'Talk about sleeping beauties. Or not! What a sight.'

'What do you want?' Louise snapped.

'I've been sent to find out why you girlies aren't up and about,' he said. 'But I can already see why.' His mocking glance drifted towards the canvas, mallets, tent poles and tangled coils of rope lying abandoned by the lorry, and he gave a gleeful chuckle. 'What a shambles. I can't wait to see the colonel's face when he sees this. I don't think fluttering your eyelashes is going to get you off the hook this time.'

He was right. It was a complete shambles. The one tent they had almost managed to erect was still listing over drunkenly to one side; the other had failed to get off the ground at all.

What made it worse was that now that it was getting light, the girls could clearly see the neighbouring camp two hundred or so yards away to their left, where two lines of camouflaged tents were laid out with military precision, taut and neatly pegged, all beautifully aligned, with an identical-sized gap between each one.

'It looks like a mixed squadron,' Voles remarked, squinting across through her binoculars. 'I can definitely see some ATS. I wonder if we'll know any of them.'

She didn't have to wonder long. 'Oh no,' she said suddenly. 'Someone's coming across, and I think it might be Buller.'

It was. Buller had clearly been busy with her binoculars too, and couldn't resist a chance to gloat.

'Well, well,' she called as she came into earshot. 'I might have known. What a disgrace. I thought putting up tents was the one thing you were meant to be good at, Rutherford. You certainly weren't any good at anything else. And yes, I can see you too, Voles, there's no point hiding behind the lorry.'

As Voles sheepishly emerged, Buller looked around with obnoxious relish, taking in their makeshift sleeping accommodation and the piles of unpacked kit. 'What is this?' she asked. 'Some kind of gypsy encampment?'

'Hello, Buller,' Louise said sweetly. 'It's lovely to see you too. After all this time.'

Her sarcasm washed straight over Buller's head. 'No wonder you both failed the course,' she said. 'I'm amazed they let you loose at all.'

'We didn't fail the course,' Louise said. 'We got taken out because we had special skills.'

'Oh yes?' Buller gave a scornful laugh. 'And what special skills are those? They certainly don't include looking like professional soldiers. I'm tempted to report you to the ATS for bringing the service into disrepute.'

Louise waved her arm grandly. 'Feel free,' she said. 'Be my guest. In fact why don't you contact Commander Cunningham at Bracknell? Because it was her who selected us for this special unit.' She saw Buller's smug smile waver and pressed home her advantage. 'It would be lovely to talk some more,' she said. 'For example, I'm sure we'd all love to know how successful you've been in bringing down the V-1s. But I'm afraid we don't really have time for social chit-chat.'

She turned away then, and thwarted, Buller stalked off back to her own lines. Pleased with her small victory, Louise looked around to see if Voles had been impressed, and was disappointed to find that she and all the other girls had mysteriously disappeared.

Hearing a sudden choking noise emanating from behind the lorry, she went to investigate and found them all, including Corporal Clifton, convulsed with laughter.

'That told her,' Voles chortled. But then she sobered. 'But you've thrown down a gauntlet now. We'd better make damn sure we do hit one of those rockets. And if possible, sooner rather than later.'

*

'What's in here?' George asked, fingering the wicker crate.

'Our props,' Jen said.

'Can I see?'

'No,' Jen said. 'You've caused enough trouble as it is.'

'Oh, let him,' Adele said. Her voice was still bleary with sleep. 'It might keep them quiet.'

They were in the back of the Violets' van, heading for Winchester. Perhaps influenced by the tragically mistimed outcome of *Romeo and Juliet*, Roger and Veronica had risen to the occasion. After an anxious discussion with Philip about fuel, they had roused Adele and Betty, and everyone had obligingly bundled themselves into the van for the mercy dash to Winchester.

Unfortunately, as it turned out, it was more of a mercy meander than a dash, as in order to eke out his limited supply of petrol for the unscheduled journey, Roger was forced to freewheel down the hills and crawl up the other side with painful slowness. Jen watched with mounting frustration as the countryside crept past.

'There's a top hat,' George remarked.

'That's mine,' Jen said.

'I need a top hat for tricks with Bunny,' George said enviously. 'Can I try it on?'

'No,' Jen said.

'Course you can, love,' Adele said. 'She's only grumpy because she's nervous of seeing Mr Keller.'

But instead of putting the hat on, George plonked it on Malcolm's head instead. It slipped right down over the toddler's eyes, which made everyone laugh, except Jen.

Jen was too nervous to laugh.

'What will you do if he's already left?' Adele whispered.

'I don't know,' Jen said. 'Throw myself off a cliff, probably.'

'You shouldn't do that,' George said. He took the top hat off Malcolm and stroked it reverently. 'But if you do, can I have your hat?'

Leaving Angie in sole charge of the café for the first time ever, Joyce took Gino with her to collect Albert from the hospital and bring him back to Cedars House.

Albert was ready and waiting in a wheelchair, armed with a pair of crutches. Clean-shaven, his new spectacles sparkling, he was dressed in one of his own suits, his tie neatly tied. Joyce smiled at the sight of him. If you overlooked the unpicked seams on his trouser leg and sleeve, which allowed access for his plaster casts, he was almost his old spick-and-span self again.

Gino was waiting outside with a black cab, and with the aid of some acerbic advice from the driver, they managed to lift Albert inside.

The driver also helped them get him out of the taxi again a few minutes later, and into the sitting room of Cedars House. Gratefully Joyce paid him off and he left. She hoped Gino would go too, but instead he started to fuss around with cushions and footstools, and even offered to make a cup of tea.

'Thank you, Gino,' she said pointedly. 'We'll be all right now.'

But Gino didn't take the hint. After a bit more fidgeting, he came and stood in front of her and held his hands together as if he was about to start praying.

'Eh, Mrs Carter,' he said. 'Not to displease, but I have a requestion for you.'

Joyce stared at him. She had no idea what he was talking about.

But Albert was eying him more kindly. 'What is your request?' he asked.

Gino smiled at him gratefully. 'Is not easy for me, the English,' he said. Joyce wondered rather wildly if he meant the people or the language. Both probably.

'I like very much the cooking,' he continued. 'Angie and I, we are awondering if it is possible to take the café some evening to make the dinners?'

'To make the dinners?' Joyce repeated blankly.

Gino nodded eagerly. '*Sì*, yes, this is possible?'

'But who for?' she said. 'Surely not for paying customers?'

Gino looked puzzled. The word 'customers' seemed to be beyond him. Or perhaps the word 'paying'. 'I think for peoples who like to eat the pasta,' he said nervously.

Joyce couldn't imagine for the life of her who such peoples might be. As far as she was concerned, eating Gino's pasta was like eating soggy worms. But she wanted to get rid of him. This was the first chance she'd had for several weeks to be alone with Albert.

'Yes, yes, all right,' she said, waving her hand dismissively. 'You do whatever you want. But now I think you should go back to the café. Angie's on her own there, and ...'

But Gino showed no sign of going back to the café. Instead, to her astonishment, he lunged forward and kissed her on the cheek. '*Molto grazie*,' he said. '*Sono così grato.*'

Not content with the kiss, he proceeded to shake hands with Albert. '*Dio!* Angie will be so excitable.'

'And that's the truth,' Joyce said sourly when he had finally taken himself off. She saw Albert trying to smother a smile, and grimaced. 'Do you have any idea what I've just agreed to?'

'None at all,' he said promptly. His eyes twinkled. 'But while you are in the agreeing mood, I have a requestion of my own.'

With some difficulty, he put his hand in his pocket. When he withdrew it, there was a little box lying on his palm.

Joyce put her hand to her mouth. 'No,' she whispered.

He opened the box, and there, tucked into a padded silk lining, was a diamond ring.

'Will you marry me?' he said.

Joyce suddenly felt as though her limbs had turned to jelly. 'Oh Albert,' she stammered. 'If you're sure? But how ...?' She gaped at the ring. It was hardly something he could have picked up from the WVS trolley in the hospital. 'Where did that come from?'

'I got Angie to fetch it from my shop,' he said. 'I've had it waiting in the safe there for a very long time.'

He saw her confusion, and gently taking her left hand, he fitted the ring carefully onto her third finger. He hesitated. 'She found something else in the shop too.'

He reached into his pocket again and pulled out an envelope marked *On Active Service*. Inside was a pre-printed card containing four bland sentences. There was a tick against the first sentence, *I am alive and well.* The other three options – *I am wounded. I am at a base hospital. I am a prisoner of war* – were crossed out, and the card was signed *Leszek Zemniak.* Underneath, a short Polish phrase was scrawled in pencil, and then, in English, *Please pass my grateful regards to my friends in Lavender Road.*

Joyce felt her eyes fill with tears. 'Oh Albert,' she said. 'I am so pleased.'

He squeezed her hand. 'So for now, at least, everyone is accounted for,' he said. He looked up at her with a quizzical smile. 'And as Gino and Angie will clearly be spending their evenings serving pasta in the café, perhaps finally we will have a little time to ourselves.'

Joyce nodded, but then she withdrew her hand. 'Well, yes,' she said tentatively. 'Except there is one thing. It's about Bella James. Dr Goodacre told me that he thought she would benefit from a quiet, secure place to live.' She fiddled nervously with the diamond ring. 'And I just wondered, when my house is mended, what you'd think about me asking her to come and ...?'

To her surprise, Albert tipped back his head and laughed. 'My dear Joyce,' he said. He took her hand and lifted it to his lips. 'You are a truly remarkable woman. And I love you with all my heart.'

The Peninsula Barracks in Winchester was an impressive place. Long, formal red-brick buildings with white windows flanked the biggest parade ground Jen had ever seen.

'Good morning, sir,' the young rifleman on the gate said crisply, as Roger rolled down his window. 'I'm afraid you aren't on our list. We aren't expecting any ENSA parties today.'

'No, no,' Roger said hastily. 'We haven't come to perform. We've come to see Mr Henry Keller.'

The soldier straightened up at once and called to an older man who was inside the guardhouse.

"'Ere, Sarge, is that Captain Keller still here? There's a troop of ENSA people to see him.' He leaned forward again to peer over Roger's shoulder into the back, and winked at George and Malcolm. 'And by the looks of it, there's a couple of performing monkeys in here and all.'

George was delighted with this witticism, but Jen frowned. '*Captain* Keller?' she said. 'How on earth can he be a captain already? He's only just joined up.'

'Mr Keller was in the army before,' George said. 'He told me at Angie's wedding. He was fighting in France before Dunkirk. He wouldn't tell me if he'd killed any Germans. But I expect he did.'

There was a short wait while the sergeant talked on the telephone to an undisclosed person, but then the rifleman lifted the barrier. 'Park on the parade ground,' he said crisply. 'Captain Keller will meet you there.'

Jen had seen more than her fair share of military personnel during her time in ENSA, but she had never seen anyone look as dashing as Henry as he came down the wide steps of the imposing white-pillared entrance to meet them. He was wearing service dress, with a red lanyard and a purple and black side cap. He had a polite but puzzled look on his face, but as soon as he caught sight of her standing beside Roger Violet, his expression changed. His step faltered, and for a horrible moment Jen wondered if she had made a terrible mistake. Had Louise deliberately misled her, in some kind of cruel joke?

But even as she felt the blood drain from her face, George was running forward eagerly. 'Hello, Captain Keller,' he said. 'Do you remember me? We met at Angie's wedding.'

Adele called to him. 'George, come back here! I want to show you something in the props basket.' Behind her, Roger and Veronica were already manhandling Malcolm back into the van.

But George ignored Adele's urgent beckoning. He was clearly intent on making his mark with Henry. 'I've already seen everything in the props basket,' he called back airily.

'No you haven't.' Adele's voice was unusually sharp.

George glanced at her suspiciously. Then at Henry. And then at Jen. He gave a comical sigh. 'Oh, I see,' he said disgruntledly. 'It's a romantic thing, isn't it? Like Romeo and Juliet? Oh, all right. I'll come and get back in the van.'

Jen was squirming, but suddenly Henry was looking amused.

He took a step forward and stopped in front of her. '*Is* it a romantic thing?' he asked.

His voice was warm, but his smile was cautious.

Jen was aware of her heart jolting uncomfortably in her chest. This was the moment of truth. Possibly the moment of no return. Was she ready for it?

But she could see the glimmer of hope in his eyes and knew she was doing the right thing. This was what she wanted. This was what she had wanted all along. Standing here now, looking at him, at his handsome face, she wondered how she could have been so unutterably stupid for the last few months. But perhaps his handsome face was to blame. She hadn't been able to see past that. Or past the aura of importance, of ability, of class. She hadn't been able to see through it all to the real man. The man she loved.

'I'd like it to be,' she said. She felt herself colouring up, and added hastily, 'But perhaps it's too late? Perhaps you've changed your mind?'

He closed his eyes for a moment, and then opened them again. She saw a muscle in his jaw tense slightly, and quailed.

'I haven't changed my mind,' he said. 'But it is too late.' He caught her horrified glance, and grimaced. 'Too late to do anything about it, I mean. I'm leaving for France in less than an hour. And I have no idea when I might be back.'

'I know,' Jen said. 'At least, I knew you were leaving soon. Louise told me. That's why I came. I wanted you to know how I felt, before …' She stopped, seeing the emotion in his face. 'But perhaps it's made it worse?'

And then she was in his arms and he was hugging her hard against him. She could feel the strength of him, the desperate urgency of his embrace, his rapidly beating heart against her chest. She could also feel the gold pips on his epaulettes digging into her cheekbone. She smiled to herself. This was a different Henry. She could feel the change in him. A rougher, more elemental Henry. The immaculate pinstriped suits and the languid, jaded air of the impresario were long gone. He was about to go into battle, and this was his last chance to say goodbye.

He kissed her, hard and urgent. 'Oh God, Jen,' he murmured against her lips, and his voice sounded agonised. 'Why the hell didn't you say something sooner?'

'I was frightened,' Jen said. 'I was in such a state when I got back from Italy. I couldn't think straight. And …'

Henry drew back. 'And I put too much pressure on you,' he said. 'I tried to hold back, I really did, but I couldn't help it. I wanted you so badly. And I so badly didn't want you to run off with that bloody Irishman.'

Jen shook her head. 'I was never going to do that,' she said. 'But you're so posh, and you know all the top people, like Laurence Olivier and stupid Janette Pymm, and Ivor Novello, and I felt so hopeless and inadequate in comparison.'

He smiled suddenly, his old perceptive smile. 'But not any more, I suspect?'

'What do you mean?'

'I rang Walter Lowther this morning to ask how it went last night. And I hear it was a triumph.'

Jen gazed at him. 'If you knew it was on, why didn't you come? Didn't you get my invitation?'

'Did you send me an invitation?' He gave a despairing groan. 'I wish I'd known. I wanted to come, I really wanted to come, but I didn't want to rattle you. It was your big night, after all. So I forced myself to stay away.' He paused, and his face contorted as though in pain. 'Or maybe it was because I wasn't sure if I could bear another disappointment.' He shook his head ruefully, and drew her back into his arms. 'Oh my God, Jen, I …'

He was about to kiss her again when they heard a step behind them. And a polite cough. An elderly sergeant was standing there, clearly waiting to speak. 'Excuse me, sir,' he murmured. 'But I thought you ought to know that the colonel is waiting for you in the briefing room, which as you may recall overlooks the parade ground.'

Henry laughed. 'Thank you, Sergeant. Could you tell him I'll be with him in two seconds?' He glanced at Jen, then up at the front of the building. 'I'll probably get drummed out of the regiment for making a spectacle of myself. But I'm going to risk one more kiss. And then I'm going to have to go.'

That final kiss knocked poor Romeo's efforts into a cocked hat. It was tender, loving, arousing, passionate, and finally regretful.

And then it was over and he was striding away, running up the steps back into the building. At the door, he stopped and raised his hand in farewell, both to her and to the others waiting patiently in the van.

'Be safe,' Jen called. And she couldn't keep the shake out of her voice. I love him, she thought. I completely love him.

Henry smiled and touched his fingers to his lips. 'Wait for me,' he called back.

'Oh, I will,' Jen said. 'I will.'

Then he was gone, and she was turning back to the van.

They were all smiling. Even the boys were smiling. They could see that it had been a good outcome. As good as possible in the circumstances. It clearly wasn't ideal that she wasn't going to see him again for months, if ever. But nobody was about to mention that.

'Is it OK if we drop you and the boys at the station?' Roger asked tentatively as they got back into the van. He glanced at his watch. 'It's nearly eleven already and we need to get on the road to Dorset.'

Jen looked at him in utter horror. '*Eleven?*' she gasped. 'Oh my God! I was meant to be at RADA at eleven.' She leaned back against the wall of the van, half crying, half laughing. 'Jason Cavell will be spitting feathers. And do you know? Just now, I simply don't care.'

It took all morning to get the camp into some kind of order. While a REME light aid detachment wired up the radio comms and the range-finding machinery to the mobile generator, the men built a tracker tower out of scaffolding, dug protective slit trenches, heaved the two huge guns into position and bore-sighted them with the antenna beam on the radar van. Having finally managed to get the tents up, the girls began to unpack the crates of equipment and, perhaps more importantly, the various boxes of provisions.

Gradually it all came together. By lunchtime, the battery was just about operational, and Lieutenant Masterson drew everyone together to brief them about rules of engagement. They would be working in close contact with Fighter Command, and to keep the RAF planes safe from friendly fire, the ack-ack guns were restricted to an operational range of 10,000 yards out to sea, 6,000 in height.

Twice during the morning V-1s had come over, and at once the units each side of them had opened fire. But to no avail. The rockets sailed straight through the barrage undeterred. But at least it had given the girls on the range-finding instruments a chance to do a dry run, tracking, aiming and adjusting without actually laying down any fire.

Shortly after the first rocket had gone overhead, to everyone's astonishment a WVS van appeared out of nowhere and proceeded to serve cups of tea and cucumber sandwiches.

'Welcome to the area,' the ladies said. 'We thought you might be in need of a little refreshment.'

Colonel Westwood thanked them with an incredulous laugh. 'Only in England,' he said.

Louise smiled at them warmly. They looked exactly like her mother, tweedy, efficient and with complete disregard for their own safety.

When the next barrage started up, Colonel Westwood frowned. 'We're going to need our neighbours to hold off while we test out our equipment,' he remarked. 'Otherwise we won't be able to figure out who's hit what.'

As soon as the V-1 had passed out of sight, he sent Lieutenant Masterson over to the adjacent units to request that they hold fire next time a rocket was sighted. The mixed artillery unit to their left agreed readily, but the Home Guard unit to the right were less amenable, insisting that the battery commander come to ask them himself.

'The man in charge is called Major Rutherford, sir,' Lieutenant Masterson reported to Colonel Westwood. 'And I should warn you that he doesn't have a very high opinion of Americans.'

'Oh no,' Louise said, appalled. 'That's my father.'

Colonel Westwood's eyes narrowed slightly. 'Then maybe you should come with me to speak with him,' he said.

'Can I come too, sir?' Don Wellington enquired. 'I've met him before. He likes me. Or he did until that damned dog towed me off course,' he added under his breath.

Greville Rutherford's expression when he saw Louise approaching in the wake of Colonel Westwood was priceless. His eyes almost popped out of his head.

'Hello, Daddy,' she said. And as her father very reluctantly saluted Colonel Westwood, she effected the introductions. 'This is Colonel Westwood. And I think you already know Gunner Wellington.'

Her father peered doubtfully at Don Wellington. 'Good God,' he said. 'Wasn't it you who ...?'

But it seemed Colonel Westwood was not in the mood for reminiscences. Or indeed social chit-chat.

'As I'm sure my lieutenant explained,' he said, 'I need you to refrain from opening fire the next couple of times missiles come over. We are testing some new equipment and I want to give my girls an opportunity to calibrate it.'

Greville Rutherford looked flabbergasted. 'Your girls?'

Colonel Westwood nodded briskly. 'Yes. My ATS specialists, like your daughter here, are in charge of range-finding and fuse setting. I had thought of using tracer to differentiate our shots from yours. But in the circumstances, it would be simpler if you would just hold fire.'

His implication that the Home Guard had made no impact on the incoming missiles so far did not go down well with her father. But because Colonel Westwood outranked him, he had no option but to agree.

'Well all right,' he muttered irritably. 'If you insist. But I can assure you that your so-called specialists are soon going to find that bringing these damned things down isn't quite as easy as you might think. We're averaging six to ten thousand rounds for each rocket.'

Colonel Westwood inclined his head. 'Is that right?' he said. 'Well I guess we'll have to see how we get on.' He gave a faint smile. 'Perhaps it just needs a little American expertise. Or maybe a female touch,' he added.

Louise glanced at him in surprise. Had he remembered her saying how down on her her father always was? Or had he just wanted to put him back in his place for being rude about Americans? It was impossible to tell. The colonel's face was coolly impassive. Unlike Don Wellington, who chuckled all the way back to the gun positions.

Katy and Pam had spent the entire day pacing about in the pub like caged lions.

'Why on earth aren't they back?' Pam asked for perhaps the hundredth time. 'What on earth can have happened?'

Katy had no idea, but what she did know was that if they didn't turn up soon, she was going to explode.

Then suddenly there they were. Jen, Malcolm and George. Trundling into the pub, chatting about something or other as though nothing at all untoward had happened.

And far from expressing any delight at seeing her, or relief at being home safely, all Malcolm wanted to do was tell her about some American colonel taking him for a ride in a jeep. 'We went really, really fast,' he said.

'Look,' George said to Pam. 'Jen's given me a top hat.'

Jen, catching her expression, started laughing. 'I'm sorry,' she said. 'We got a bit delayed.'

Katy could have hit her. But then she saw the sparkle in Jen's eyes and peered at her more closely. 'Are you all right?'

'Jen's fallen in love,' George said gleefully. 'Twice, in fact, because she fell in love last night at the theatre as well. But with a different man. That one was called Romeo. She killed herself after that. Luckily she didn't do that today with Captain Keller. But she gave me her top hat anyway.'

'He's going to do a trick with Bunny,' Malcolm explained helpfully.

Katy felt as though the world was spinning. She tried to pick Malcolm up so she could hug him properly, but he wriggled away.

'Where's Lucky?' he shouted. 'I want to see Lucky.'

'And I want to see Bunny,' George said. 'Is he all right, Mummy? Did he miss me?'

Jen caught Katy's eye. 'I need a drink,' she said. 'It's been a long day. Falling in love is very exhausting.'

And suddenly Katy was laughing. It was too much. This wasn't at all what she had expected. She had been worried that Malcolm would arrive back traumatised by his ordeal. But no such thing. He was exactly the same boisterous child he had been before he set off. George seemed equally unaffected.

It was clear, though, that something had changed for Jen. For the first time since she had got back from Italy, she looked fully alive, as though a huge weight had been lifted from her shoulders.

Pam looked different too. Katy could see the love in her eyes as they rested on George. Over the last couple of years, she had struggled with the boy. But now that she had felt the terror of losing him, perhaps it had shown her what he really meant to her.

And now she was laughing too. And they were laughing so much that they didn't hear the door open.

'Goodness,' a voice said. 'What's going on?'

Katy turned round, and there, standing just inside the blackout curtain, with a smart little suitcase in her hand, was Molly. Molly Coogan. Her long-lost friend. Back at last from North Africa.

'Oh Molly,' she cried. 'I'm so glad to see you.'

'And me,' Jen said. 'I should have come with you to Tunisia. I've been a complete disaster without you.'

Then Jen and Molly were hugging. George was dancing around in his top hat. Caroline was gurgling happily in her pram, and the wireless was blaring. Malcolm had let Lucky in, and he was barking. And for the first time since the missile attack, even silent Bella was smiling as she helped Nellie take a few wobbly steps towards George.

Under the cover of the hullabaloo, Molly put her mouth close to Katy's ear. 'I've got a message for you,' she whispered. 'Nobody is allowed to know except you. I don't know how she managed it, but Helen's somehow been in touch with Ward. He's in Paris, waiting for the Allies to arrive. And he's fine. He told her to send you all his love.'

Just then, as tears of relief once again welled in Katy's eyes, Winston Churchill's gravelly voice suddenly boomed out of the wireless. 'London will never be conquered,' he said. 'And will never fail.'

'Quite right,' said Jen. She winked at George. 'From what I hear, Louise Rutherford is going to see to that.'

Chapter Thirty Three

It was an hour before the next missile was spotted on the radar. By then Louise had a dozen fuses ready. She had checked all the batteries, fitted them carefully into the radio units and, with shaking fingers, screwed them onto the noses of the shells and tightened the nuts.

Her job was done, and she watched with a fluttering pulse as one of the American gunners helped Private Rees lift the first shell carefully into the breech of the gun. She saw Don Wellington watching from the other gun. He caught her eye and winked. She smiled nervously; there was no time to do more.

Already Voles was shouting adjustments. One of the gunners was confirming them.

And then Lieutenant Masterson's command: 'Fire!' The gun action crashed forward. A moment later, with a deafening report, the first shell was away, followed immediately by a second in ripple sequence from the other gun.

Louise held her breath. Had she got it right? Had *they* got it right?

The wait seemed interminable. It was too hazy to see the shell with the naked eye, but she imagined the invisible radio antennae probing the air ahead for a target, just waiting for the chance to ignite the fuse.

And then there was a flash, followed a moment later by a booming explosion.

Louise couldn't believe it. Nobody could believe it. Then over the wireless they heard a crackle of congratulations from one of the RAF pilots. 'Good shooting, chaps,' he said.

Louise looked at Colonel Westwood and found he was watching her. But before she had a chance to smile, before she had a chance to do anything, there was more static on the wireless from Fighter Command, followed at once by a sharp cry from the scanning tower: 'Target acquired!'

Louise's heart jumped. Had that first one been a fluke? If so, they would soon know.

She heard Voles correcting the elevation. She heard one of the Americans acknowledge. She heard Private McEvoy call out something about wind speed and Private Wilson respond nervously with an adjustment.

She heard Lieutenant Masterson quietly urging calm. 'Focus,' he said.

'Take it steady. Focus.'

But the girls knew what they were doing. They had practised hard and long. Their fire drill was almost perfect.

Lieutenant Masterson's voice came again. 'Fire by order … fire!'

Louise switched off the battery checker and looked up.

Three seconds later, there was another explosion. And as the flaming sections of the Nazi rocket fell slowly into the sea, this time they did celebrate. It wasn't a fluke. They could never have made a direct hit twice in a row just by chance. Not at that speed. No, the fuses had worked. Their hard work had paid off. Colonel Westwood's hard work had paid off. Two rockets down and only four rounds fired.

As the girls smiled and hugged, they gradually became aware of the stunned silence in the adjacent units. Louise grabbed a pair of binoculars off Voles and scanned the Home Guard position to her right. Even from here she could see the incredulity on her father's face as he stood staring out to sea in the Home Guard conning tower. She swung the binoculars the other way, but sadly she couldn't get a fix on Buller.

Hearing Colonel Westwood calling for her, she hastily handed the binos back to Voles and followed him nervously to the bell tent that was to serve as his office.

He took off his tin helmet and ran a hand through his dark hair. 'I've received a signal from ATS HQ,' he said abruptly. 'There wasn't time to share it with you before.'

Louise stared at him in alarm. All the elation drained out of her. Surely Buller wouldn't really have reported them? She was only a private, after all. Who on earth would take any notice of her? Or had she told tales of their inadequacies to a superior in her squadron? For all Louise knew, one of the ghastly ATS sergeants might be serving next door as well, or even that horrid junior commander from Bracknell.

Or had Colonel Westwood himself complained about her? About her unprofessional conduct last night? She found herself fervently hoping not.

But he was looking very serious, and nervously Louise watched his fingers as he unfolded a flimsy piece of paper. 'Private Rutherford is invited to attend an officer corps training unit,' he read out. 'With a view to being awarded a King's Commission in the Auxiliary Territorial Service.'

Louise almost fell over. A commission? *A commission!* They wanted her to be an officer? It was so far from what she had expected to hear that she could barely take it in.

Colonel Westwood was watching her. 'I'm very pleased for you,' he said. 'I always knew you had potential. You'll make a good officer.'

Louise thought suddenly about what her father would say. It would certainly be one in the eye for him. Would he be proud? She could hardly wait to tell him.

She glanced out of the flap of the tent at her colleagues. To her astonishment, she saw Voles laughing at something Don Wellington was saying. That was a turn-up for the books, too. She saw the glow of satisfaction on both their faces, the triumphant confidence in their gestures, and she felt proud. They were her team. Her unit. Her friends. If she was going to live and die with anyone, she suddenly very much wanted it to be with them.

And then she thought of her friends in London. Katy, the boys, the babies, Mrs Carter, Mr Lorenz, Angie and Gino, Aaref and his brothers, Elsa, Bella, Doris, Mrs Gibbons, Lord Freddy, even Jen. Everything she and Colonel Westwood had done over the last few weeks, they had done for them. To protect them, and people like them. Resilient, patriotic Londoners, trying to go about their daily lives, all longing for this ghastly war to be over.

Abruptly she swung back to Colonel Westwood. 'Do I have to go?' she asked.

That clearly wasn't what he had been expecting to hear either. 'I thought you'd want to go,' he said. He crossed his arms over his chest and cleared his throat. 'I thought you'd be kind of pleased … after last night.'

Louise cringed. Her sudden renewed mortification almost made her agree with him. Then she looked at him again. Colonel Ivo Westwood was undoubtedly gorgeous. She knew she wasn't the only one who thought that, although she was probably the only one who had contrived to express it to him. And that was her fault. Not his. She admired him. Respected him. But she didn't love him. Not really. Her heart wasn't broken, even though it had felt like it last night. Nor had she really been in love with Henry. That had been wishful thinking too.

She looked round again. Her current situation was unsanitary, rough and extremely dangerous. But she knew without doubt that this was where she wanted to be. She didn't need a husband. She had all she needed right here.

'I'm really sorry about last night,' she said. 'I was overwrought. It wasn't what you thought.' She hesitated, then gave a small, self-conscious laugh. 'Well, it was a bit,' she admitted. 'But not enough to matter. Not to me, anyway.'

She saw a flicker of relief in his eyes and rushed on. 'I'd much rather stay with the unit. I'm happy here with you and Lieutenant Masterson and the girls. Even with stupid Don Wellington. I don't need to be an officer.'

He held her gaze for a long, thoughtful moment. 'In that case, I sure would like you to stay,' he said at last. 'Now we know we have a success on our hands, we are going to be real busy equipping and training other units.

I'd like for you to be a part of that. And—'

But before he could go on, there was a shout from the tracker tower.

'Bomber Command reporting new target approaching.'

Louise only waited long enough for Colonel Westwood to nod a dismissal. 'Go to it, Private Rutherford,' he said. He smiled one of his rare smiles. 'Let's see if we can make it three out of three.'

And then she was running back to her post.

'What was that about?' Voles whispered as she sped past.

Louise paused mid-stride. 'The ATS wanted me to be an officer,' she said. 'But I turned them down.'

Voles's eyes widened. 'I always said you were potential officer material,' she said.

'Target acquired,' Lieutenant Masterson shouted. 'Wait for my command.'

'Here we go,' Louise muttered as she ran on.

Voles turned back to her instruments with a satisfied laugh. 'I tell you what,' she called after her. 'I can't wait to tell Buller.'

Author's Note:

At the beginning of the Second World War, Anti-Aircraft (AA) fire was terribly inaccurate. It took thousands of rounds to gain a hit by day, and tens of thousands of rounds at night. In 1940, during the Battle of Britain, approximately 18,500 rounds were expended for each aircraft shot down. This is why it was so hard to protect British cities from German bombers. But by the end of 1944, thanks to the introduction of the proximity fuse, the rate had reduced to 40 rounds per hit, and both the Luftwaffe and the V1s were quickly routed.

Heralded as an achievement 'transcending anything of the time', the development of the top secret proximity fuse was credited by Dwight D. Eisenhower for reducing the duration of the war by at least a year.

By the end of the war over a million people in the UK and the US were working on the production of proximity fuses. Amazingly, there was not one single security breach, and neither German nor Japanese intelligence ever found out about them.

It is impossible to list all the people who have helped me with this novel. Whether it was instructing me about wartime factory production lines, explaining the intricacies of live fire artillery drill, or in Dani O'Connor's case, giving me a twice monthly shoulder massage, their input has been invaluable and I am truly grateful.

Particular thanks have to go to Eirian Short whose amazing memories of her time in the ATS helped me enormously in creating Louise's role in the book (although I should add that Louise's exploits are completely fictional!).

Gillian McGrandles and the staff at Battersea Local History Library have been as helpful as ever. I would like to thank the Imperial War Museum for giving me access to their reading room, and James Thornton at RADA, both for digging up information on the wartime application process, and for his fascinating tour of the academy. I am also very grateful to Michal Benzinski for his advice on the various Polish and Jewish elements in the novel.

Then there are all the people who have helped get THE OTHER SIDE OF THE STREET into print; my agent Anne Williams, my editor Marion Donaldson, and all the staff at Headline and Cambria Publishing who have helped make the process so smooth and easy.

And finally, the biggest thanks of all to my wonderful husband, Marc, and to our two long suffering dogs who have had to wait patiently pretty much all the way through 1944 to get a decent walk.

As always I have set my story against real history and, in this case, a real technological innovation, but while (like the proximity fuse) I make every effort to be accurate, in the end this is a story and the characters, and the things they get up to, are entirely my invention.

I do hope you have enjoyed this novel, if so please do tell your friends or write a review! THE OTHER SIDE OF THE STREET is the fifth novel in my Lavender Road series. VICTORY GIRLS comes next.

Helen Carey
www.helencareybooks.co.uk
Facebook: /helencareybooks
Twitter: @helencareybooks

Next in the Lavender Road series:

HELEN CAREY
Victory Girls

It's August 1944. Allied forces are finally making headway in Europe. But rocket attacks on London are a chilling reminder that the war is not yet won. Victory may be just round the corner, but the fighting is far from over for the women of Lavender Road.

Helen de Burrel knows from bitter experience how dangerous things are in war-torn France, but it's a long time since she heard from André Cabillard, her French fiancé, and nothing is going to stop her going back to track him down. Meanwhile, her friend Molly Coogan has returned to London after a spell of nursing in North Africa, and now it is suddenly important to her to discover the truth about the mother who gave her up for adoption when she was four years old.

Sweeping from London to France and on into Germany as Hitler's army begins to retreat, *Victory Girls* is full of emotion, excitement and suspense, which will hold readers on the edge of their seats.

Praise for Victory Girls:

'Funny, poignant, emotional and unputdownable!' *London Evening Standard*

'An amazing read. It has all the elements of the other books, wonderful characters, a gripping story line and great wartime detail. But it also has something else, a real sense of women rising to the occasion, showing courage and resilience in difficult and dangerous circumstances which I found both exciting and uplifting.' *Maria McCarthy*

'A tale of ordinary people living extraordinary lives.' *Inside Soap*

'It will have you laughing, crying, holding your breath . . . An incredible tale of bravery, love and trust, and is a must read.' *Whispering Stories*

Also by Helen Carey:

Lavender Road
Some Sunny Day
On a Wing and a Prayer
London Calling
The Other Side of the Street
Victory Girls

Slick Deals
The Art of Loving

CPSIA information can be obtained
at www.ICGtesting.com
Printed in the USA
BVHW082016290419
546836BV00002B/324/P

9 781916 453234